WELCOME TO YOUR FIRST COMMAND

"Transit!" shouted Sensor Officer Lubell.

In the tacplot, a single—and very large—red blip had emerged from the warp point.

Lehman at Tactical shouted louder. "It's an SD! *Balu Bay* flushing her racks!"

Wethermere shouted over the others. "Communications, send alert to the Fleet, all sys—"

And then the world turned upside down and wrenched violently sideways. He had a brief impression of Zuniga flung from her chair and straight against the portside bulkhead.

Wethermere almost failed to realize that the world had come to a stop again. He looked around.

Zuniga, Lehman, and Masharraf at Ops were all dead. Zhou had only got his harness half on and was clutching his left arm. Nandita Vikrit, at the combined Communications and Computer Management console, dabbed at the red wash of blood pouring down from her sliced forehead. The other three—Lubell, Anapa at Helm, and Tepple at Weapons—seemed unhurt.

"Anapa, best speed. Heading— [illegible] directly away from that SD." An inele[illegible]rst order as commander [illegible] run Ops through your [illegible]ctical—transfer Weap[illegible]an your post?" Zhou g[illegible]ere decided to interpre[illegible] Lubell, keep one eye on the SD and [illegible] its approximate status—but keep the other eye on the warp point. If there's any change—"

"Got it, sir. Our sensors are in good shape, but *Balu Bay* is—sir, she's gone. Not even flotsam."

ALSO IN THE STARFIRE SERIES

BY DAVID WEBER & STEVE WHITE

Crusade

In Death Ground

The Stars at War

Insurrection

The Shiva Option

The Stars at War II

BY STEVE WHITE & SHIRLEY MEIER

Exodus

BY STEVE WHITE & CHARLES E. GANNON

Extremis

BAEN BOOKS by STEVE WHITE

Blood of the Heroes

The Prometheus Project

Demon's Gate

Forge of the Titans

Eagle Against the Stars

Wolf Among the Stars

Prince of Sunset

The Disinherited

Legacy

Debt of Ages

St. Antony's Fire

Sunset of the Gods (forthcoming)

BAEN BOOKS by CHARLES E. GANNON

1635: The Papal Stakes (with Eric Flint, forthcoming)

To purchase these and all Baen Book titles in e-book format, please go to www.baen.com.

A Starfire Novel

STEVE WHITE &
CHARLES E. GANNON

EXTREMIS

A Baen Book

Baen Publishing Enterprises
P.O. Box 1403
Riverdale, NY 10471
www.baen.com

ISBN: 978-1-4516-3814-1

Cover art by David Seeley
Warpline chart by Randy Asplund

First Baen paperback printing, May 2012

Library of Congress Control Number: 2011002043

Distributed by Simon & Schuster
1230 Avenue of the Americas
New York, NY 10020

Pages by Joy Freeman (www.pagesbyjoy.com)
Printed in the United States of America

EXTREMIS

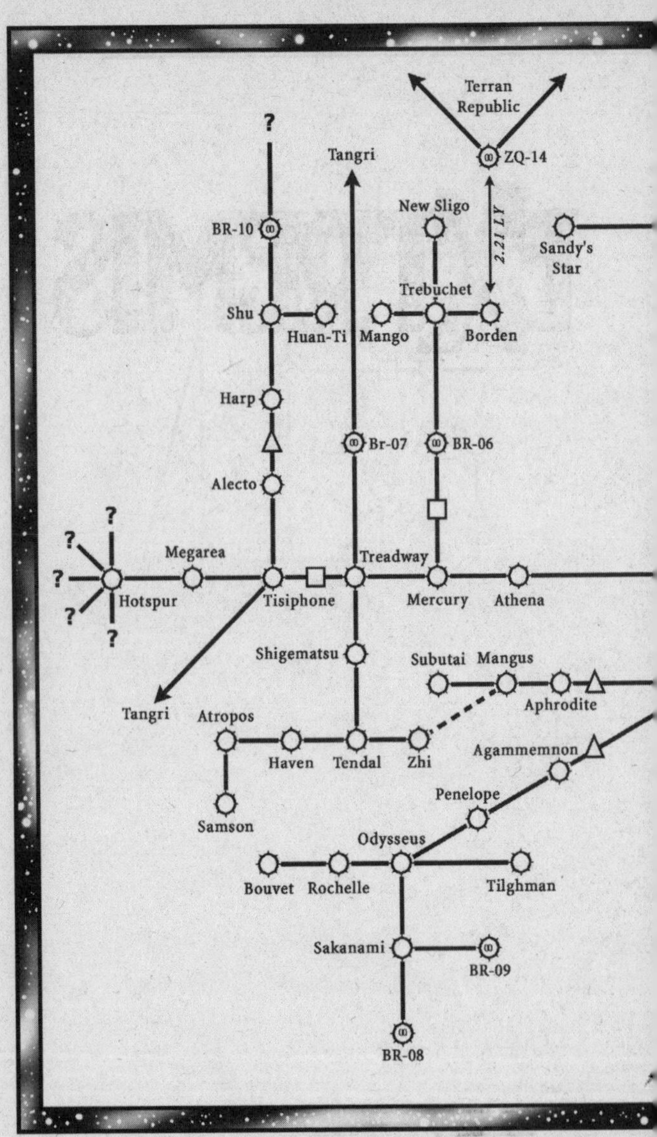
Terran
Republic
?
Tangri
ZQ-14
New Sligo
2.21 LY
BR-10
Sandy's
Star
Trebuchet
Shu
Huan-Ti
Mango
Borden
Harp
Br-07
BR-06
Alecto
?
?
Megarea
Treadway
?
Hotspur
Tisiphone
Mercury
Athena
?
?
Shigematsu
Subutai
Mangus
Tangri
Atropos
Aphrodite
Haven
Tendal
Zhi
Agammemnon
Penelope
Samson
Odysseus
Bouvet
Rochelle
Tilghman
Sakanami
BR-09
BR-08

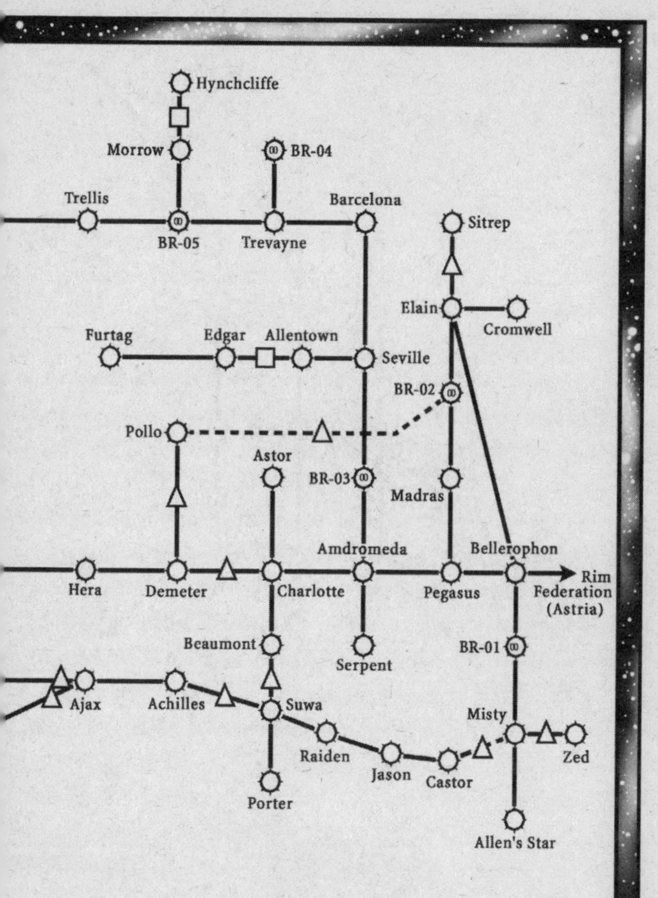
Hynchcliffe
Morrow
BR-04
Trellis
BR-05
Trevayne
Barcelona
Sitrep
Elain
Cromwell
Furtag
Edgar
Allentown
Seville
BR-02
Pollo
Astor
BR-03
Madras
Amdromeda
Bellerophon
Hera
Demeter
Charlotte
Pegasus
Rim Federation (Astria)
Beaumont
Serpent
BR-01
Ajax
Achilles
Suwa
Misty
Raiden
Jason
Castor
Zed
Porter
Allen's Star
Impassible to DT
Impassible to SMT and DT

PROLOGUE

Sandro McGee dove sideways into the dirty alley just as the rooftop defense blister spun and fired a flechette round in his direction. The corner of the alley was immediately and ferociously flayed by a swarm of zipping and spatting high-velocity micro-darts.

"Damn, those alien gizmos are fast," commented Harry "Light Horse" Li.

McGee rolled up into a crouch, readied his assault rifle, prepared to lunge toward the corner for a peek-around. "They're not faster than *me*." He ducked his head around the now-ragged masonry—and flinched away from the blast of automatic gunfire that greeted him.

"Yes, they're faster than you." McGee could hear Harry Li's satisfied smirk.

"No, they're *not*." McGee tugged off his helmet. He rose to his feet and toed it around the corner. That elicited a slightly different greeting: individually fired slugs. McGee smiled at the uneven intervals between impacts. *Ah, now* that's *being fired by meatware.*

McGee swung around the corner—just weapon and eyes—and let the Serrington Arms sight do its work. The "Serrie sight" was the one relatively modern device on

McGee's obsolete battle rifle. Its combined audio-optical "threat-trackback" system instantly assessed the directionality and intensity of sound waves from enemy fire, did a quick laserscan of all objects moving in its front 120 degrees, and threw a targeting solution into the scope. Which McGee followed, elevating the barrel until the crosshairs lay on a partially seen Baldy, hunched low in the cupola of the town hall. The Baldy looked almost human as he profiled himself for a moment—but then McGee registered the absence of ears and nose: he squeezed the trigger. The venerable 8.5 mm battle rifle began hammering against his shoulder—just as the Baldy's smaller, higher-velocity slugs started gouging at the concrete next to McGee's left cheek. For one surreal moment it was more like a personal duel than a firefight: the big human's denser, slower stream of metal punched at the Baldy's armored rooftop cupola; the Baldy's intermittent counterfire stabbed down at the human, fast and vicious. Neither would cede the advantage.

McGee counted through another second, knew his clip was about to burn dry—and then the incoming fire ceased. Shifting down to a clear view over his iron sights, McGee saw a hint of faltering movement. He popped his eye back up to the scope—just in time to see his adversary duck unsteadily down beneath the lip of the cupola.

"Move! Move!" McGee shouted to his rear as he started sprinting toward the front steps of the town hall. "Get tight against the building—under their field of fire!"

Li was right behind McGee, but Varazian, the guy from the Resistance cell out in Lemnos, wasn't. Probably delayed by another snafu with his civvy com-set: the store-bought system occasionally skipped a beat while syncing with the milspec rigs. Whatever the reason, Varazian was the last on his feet and trailed Li by four meters as they charged across the square.

McGee reached the heavy concrete balustrade of the front stairs, looked back to check his team's progress—and saw an antipersonnel rocket rush down and catch Varazian square in the chest. The forty-one-year-old reservist corporal was blown clean off his feet and backward, out of sight.

McGee suppressed a sigh as he put his hand up to his com-rig. He was surprised to feel the wrist flare of his Kevleuron gauntlet graze his ear roughly. *Oh, yeah—I left my helmet behind.* "Varazian, report. Varazian—?"

"Biorelay indicates Varazian is KIA." Captain Falco's voice boomed into the link; there was no mistaking a milspec command set. "Cestus 3, proceed to objective."

"Olympus, Cestus 3 is down to two combat effectives, I repeat, two combat effectives. Request—"

"You're on your own, Cestus 3. Everyone's up to their asses punching through Baldy weapon blisters. No help to send your way. Advise when you have taken objective Alpha to receive new orders. Olympus out."

"Well, ain't that special," McGee grunted as he swapped magazines: only two left. *Damn.* "What's with this shitty load-out, Harry?"

"Old guns and spare ammo is all we've got for local raids." Light Horse Li shifted his AK-74 so that, when he started running again, it would rise directly into an easy assault carry. "Think you've got it bad? Look at this antique."

"You ain't joking. Where'd you get that? Museum?"

Harry shook his head, gathered his legs under him to lead the rush up the stairs. "Nope. From a reenactment group. Here we go."

And Light Horse was off, bounding up the stairs

two at a time. McGee's treelike legs launched his 1.9-meter frame after the smaller man, whose shorter limbs cycled faster and had the advantage over short distances. While Li bounded toward the entry, McGee followed him upward at a fast, crabbed crouch, keeping his Alliant-Rimstar battle rifle sweeping across the upper-story windows. He'd just finished sweeping right when he caught a hint of movement to the far left. *Typical: wait for the sucker to be facing the other way. But I'm no sucker.*

McGee spun down into a tight kneel: two Baldy rifle rounds spat over his head. He sent a matched pair of five-round bursts back at the offending window; the second blast of 8.5 mm discarding sabot rounds chewed through the facade, and a Baldy rifle tumbled down into the street.

"I'm clear!" yelled Harry. "Covering you!"

McGee lurched up and took the remaining steps three at a time. Light Horse had come out a bit from the building's double-doored entry, sweeping the upper-story windows at an impossibly narrow arc but ready to hit them with suppressive fire even so. McGee bounded abreast of Li—who peeled off and joined him in a two-step rush-and-spin that ended with their backs smacking firmly against the wall.

"Well, that was fun," Li observed.

"And I'm sure it gets better."

"Probably so. You take point."

"Me?"

"Of course, Sandro. Age before beauty."

"You little shit—"

"The truth hurts doesn't it, Tank?"

And "Tank" McGee had to admit that Light Horse's

semi-Sino features were smoother and finer than his own, and that the little corporal was three years his junior. But these trivial idiocies had only meant something back in the Real World—which they, and the rest of Bellerophon's human populace, had left behind months ago.

"Laser sensors on," snapped McGee.

"Baldies don't use booby traps," began Light Horse.

"They're sure to start. Maybe today. So—laser sensors on, pip-squeak."

"Yes, Your Immensity. Laser sensor is on."

"Right. Follow me."

And together they rolled around to shoulder open the double doors, going in low and working to either side. The wide, marble-floored hall was empty, apart from a few scattered papers and a forgotten umbrella lying in the center of the floor. Here all activity had stopped the day the Baldies had invaded.

"Looks clear," commented Li.

"Looks can be deceiving—and on battlefields, they usually are." McGee rose to a half crouch, started forward. "We go slow, give the laser sensors time to find any trip wires that the Baldies might have—" That was when his sensor went off.

"I guess I owe you a beer," grumbled Light Horse, who used his sensor to accelerate their triangulation on the laser "trigger beam" that McGee's own sensor had detected. Together they worked toward the signal—and discovered a laser trip wire across the broad, main staircase that was the central feature of the entry hall.

"Hah—Mr. Baldy's locked his cellar door," Li observed, misting the lasers and finding the pattern too tight to wriggle through or under.

"But he didn't use too tricky a lock." McGee pointed

up into the stairwell: a pair of directional mines—human—angled downward.

Li came over to look. "So they're using our old munitions against us now."

"That was only a matter of time."

"So, what's the plan?"

"Any biosigns on this level?"

"My crap-grade civvy scanner reads a definite no. Which means probably not. Which really means maybe." Li put away the bargain-store biosensor.

"Still, that agrees with intel and the prior thermal-imaging sweep. I say we pop the lock and head upstairs fast. Weapons in assault carry, shoot whatever moves."

"Sounds like a plan. But Tank..."

"Yeah?"

"What if they've put in more mines?"

"We keep the laser sensors running, and our own five senses alert. And every second we talk about it gives them one more second to organize a reception. We move."

They fell back, away from the staircase, McGee picking up the umbrella as he took cover behind a bank of chairs. "Ready?"

"Yah."

McGee aimed, flung the umbrella at the base of the stairs, dove for the deck.

Even as he dropped prone, the downward blast from the directional mines gnashed shrapnel teeth against the first five risers and sent marble and metal bits sleeting out into the lobby.

Before the roar had died out, the two Marine Reservists were on their feet, weapons ready. They sprinted through the smoke and the dust, then pounded up the stairs—which split into two narrower flights on either side of an atrium shaft that rose through the remaining two stories of the building. McGee went right; Light Horse left.

Li came to the top of his staircase a moment before McGee, who saw him check his laser sensor and then swing around the corner into the second floor's hallway.

As Li went forward, McGee heard a thin, metallic, almost musical snapping sound—like an impossibly fine piano string breaking. *An old-style, hair-thin trip wire. Damn.*

Because the events that followed were expected—were part of every soldier's waking nightmare—they seemed to unfold with surreal slowness. Li looked down, realized what he'd done, looked back at McGee—maybe for help, maybe to say good-bye. From the hall behind Li, McGee saw a Bouncing Betty—a spring-ejected mine—pop up on a slanting trajectory that would put it waist high when it went off. And from the corner of his right eye, McGee saw its twin clearing the hallway corner he had yet to reach. McGee knew that, being a few meters farther away, he might be lucky enough only to be blinded, his face torn into a hideous shredded oval.

The Bouncing Betty next to Li went off. The blast did not just bisect him: Light Horse Harry Li was completely and utterly blown apart—

blown apart

blown apart

blown apart

And again and again and again and—

"Shit and damn this sim," roared Falco, his voice sharp and furious in McGee's headset. The big Marine opened his eyes, which he hadn't realized he had shut.

The Bouncing Betty on his side of the staircase was suspended in midair, three meters ahead, a bit fuzzy at the edges, as was often the case with VR sim images frozen by a program error.

"What now?" asked McGee.

"Sit tight, McGee," snapped Falco. "We're working on it."

Harry Li had rolled over on his back, hands behind his head. "Hell, I don't have to hold position—I'm dead."

"Lucky you."

"You have no idea. The last time they actually tried to resume a crashed sim, we all had to play 'freeze in place' for twenty minutes."

"Long time to wait to continue a drill."

"Huh. We didn't get to continue. They crashed the program and had to reboot. Game over."

Falco was back on the com-rig. "All right, stand down. The damned computers are well and truly fried for the day. Police your gear and expendables."

"What expendables?" McGee whispered to Li.

"Casings from your blanks; we're actually shooting brass, remember?"

"Oh, yeah. Thanks."

Falco's voice came back. "You can take off your VR rigs now. We're shutting off the feed."

And suddenly the world was gone: just gray static and muffled silence. *Purgatory for computers*, McGee mused, recalling his great-gramama McGee's wondrously Byzantine conviction in the particulars of the afterlife and its convoluted theology. She had been part of an obscure Christian sect—Roman Catholicism, it was called—that had all but died out with her generation.

McGee removed the VR rig—eyepieces, earplugs,

mandibular vibration transducers—and stared around: the interior of the cavernous warehouse yawned back at him in its shabby emptiness. Scattered along its length were other framework sets of prefab walls and staircases, all marked with reflective and transponder-beaded tape. These were the digital guiderails upon which the computer hung and superimposed the detailed images of a virtual world. An odd collection of workers—mostly in hunter's camos—were already folding up the constructs with the brisk efficiency of professional stagehands breaking down a set in a live theater.

Li's voice startled him. "Hey, Sandro, you just gonna stare all day? Let's get going."

"Oh, yeah, right." McGee walked over to join Li, Varazian, and Battisti in policing up their brass—well, not Battisti, since he'd been given the fireteam's one caseless weapon. McGee snagged his helmet, helped scoop up and sort the various, mismatched cartridge casings.

"Sheesh—5.54 mm Russian. Isn't that a . . . a twenty-first century round?"

"Twentieth, Alessandro," corrected Battisti. "When you are done here, not only will you become part of an action team, but a curator of ancient weapons, no?" Battisti's strong Hispa accent marked him as coming from the Kreta Archipelago, where many old Latin-based Terran languages were still spoken at home.

"Damn, acquiring an expertise in obsolete slug-throwers wasn't part of *my* plan," McGee admitted.

"Nor mine." Varazian shrugged as he dug the last of his own 8.5 mm brass out from under the wide-footed base of a modular wall-flat. "I figured we'd spend more time training and less time cleaning the garage."

"The garage needs cleaning every time we use it,

Corporal Varazian." The voice that came from behind them was Falco's. They all stood, turned, and faced the captain. Although the service formalities had been extremely lax since McGee arrived at the secret training camp yesterday, he snapped a salute now: after a combat-training exercise, it seemed to him that they *must* be on duty.

Falco noted the salute with a smile. "Leave it to the new guy to figure out we mean business up here."

Abashed, Li, and then the other two, matched McGee's salute.

"That's better. And Li, since you are already a member of the teams, you should have known better."

"Yes, sir. Sorry, sir."

"That's the last 'sorry' I want to hear from you, Corporal Li. You're active now, and that means you set the pace and the example."

"Yes, sir."

"Then carry on. Debrief in five. Don't hold us up."

Battisti let Falco get out of earshot before asking, "You keep secrets from your friends, Harry? When did you get word you were activated to the teams?"

"Uh... just now, when Falco said it. Damned strange notification protocol."

McGee nodded. "Everything here seems a little strange, if you ask me."

"Yes, it is," agreed Li. "And nobody asked you."

McGee smiled. "True enough. But can't we at least practice with milspec gear? Even if it's the old stuff?"

Li frowned. "There's good reason we don't, Sandro. First, we don't have as much milspec as you might expect. Second, and more importantly, we have to save it."

"Save it? For what?"

"For an operation that really counts. If we start using—and losing—the good gear in day-to-day harrying operations, before you know it the Baldies will have an accurate measure of what we can do and what we do it with. That's two pieces of intel we want to hold back until the last second—so that we get them to underestimate us right when we're ready to spring our nastiest surprise."

"Okay—I get that, but then what's with all the cloak-and-dagger nonsense?"

"Cloak and dagger?"

"You know, the coded invitations for these readiness assessments. The double cut-outs for sending our replies. The fact that none of us Reservists really know who's on the faceless command staff that issues the orders and invitations. And what's with bringing us to Upper Thessalaborea to run through these VR sims? It's cold as hell up here."

"And very remote."

"Yeah—*so* remote that the extra traffic we're putting on these backroads must be attracting the same Baldy attention HQ was trying to avoid."

"Maybe, but the way I hear it, the Baldies don't keep track of much that goes on beyond high population centers—particularly their own."

Varazian nodded. "And even then, they just try to avoid us."

"Not all the time." McGee knew his grim tone would shatter the group's jocular mood like a stone thrown through stained glass, but he just didn't care. Unlike the other Reservists—who did not live next to the Baldies—Alessandro McGee knew that the alien invaders were not always so distant and aloof. It was in McGee's own hometown of Melantho that the aliens had established their own city, had taken schoolchildren hostage, had executed noncompliant humans on the spot, and had ultimately barged unannounced into McGee's own living room. They had snatched his beloved (and very pregnant) Jennifer right out of his arms and, almost as an afterthought, bashed around a thoroughly uncooperative McGee—enough to put him in the hospital for two weeks.

The group had grown quiet: they all knew the story. Quite possibly, it was known to every member of the Resistance by now. Battisti rubbed his hands on his coveralled knees. "We are done policing the practice area. Let us go to the debriefing."

"Yes, let's," said Light Horse, who reached up to put a gentle hand on McGee's very large shoulder. "Ready to go, Tank?"

"Ready to kill some Baldies," McGee amended.

"Ultimately, I think that's the key requisite," Li affirmed with a nod. "Let's go."

Van Felsen stood almost inhumanly straight—possibly because she was almost comically short. "Brothers and sisters in arms, congratulations on your activation, and welcome to the special action teams."

Those who had already earned these honors—seated around the periphery of the small prefab cafeteria/auditorium—applauded long and seriously. No wild enthusiasm, no catcalls: this was a commission to actively and aggressively kill alien invaders, not a fraternity initiation, and the somber tone was a reminder of the mortal resolve that bound them together.

Besides, McGee reflected with a quick glance at the doors leading to the parking lot, a full third of the invitees had been sent their way with thanks, confirmation of their status as alternates, and new orders for their local Resistance cells. But they left without the honor of having been officially reactivated for military service—and without the proud encumbrance of the many duties, risks, and responsibilities attached thereto.

Van Felsen let the applause die before continuing. "So, now down to business, ladies and gentlemen. Most of you are Marines, since that's what our world specializes in producing at Camp Gehenna—our little vacation spot in the Charybdis Islands." A few chuckles, and a few reminiscing groans, were elicited by her reference to the sun-scorched, basalt-fanged, insect-plagued expanse that was the Bellerophon Arm's primary Marine training camp. "However, until such time as Allied fleet elements make a permanent return to this system, all activated personnel are under a joint services command, invoked under the authority of Article Seventeen, paragraph three of the Rim Federation's Code of Military Procedures. No matter your original branch of service, rank structures will follow Marine norms. Accordingly, rank equivalencies will be issued to anyone coming to us from other services before you leave this facility. In all cases, so as to maintain the continuity of our prewar command structure, all reactivated personnel will assume a temporary rank equal to that which they held when they mustered out of active service."

A few surprised noises—including a few grumbles—arose.

Van Felsen snapped into a stiffer, and decidedly fiercer, posture. "Stow that. I know that some of you—particularly those who've been in the Reserves for a long time—are going to lose a lot of rank. Here's my message to you: you're here to serve, not be served. And I can't have a person who's climbed up to major in the Reserves, but who hasn't been qualified on new Marine gear in ten years, commanding folks who were active when the Baldies showed up. It's not practical, and it will get people killed. As it is, we're going to have a lot of Reserve officers who, as staff sergeants, will be issuing orders to twenty-four-year-old corporals. Problem is, those corporals have already forgotten more about the latest milspec gear than any preinvasion weekend warrior ever got the chance to learn." The room was decidedly reserved—particularly when she used the term "weekend warrior."

"And if I've said anything that offends you," she went on, steering straight into the eye of the potential storm of resentment, "then you can do this unit a favor by letting us know, and we will accommodate your wishes—and escort your sorry, ego-bruised asses right off these premises. Is that clear?"

"Yes, sir," came the mollified mumble.

"Either you are mute or I am deaf. I'll ask it one more time. Is that *clear?*"

"Sir, *yes*, *SIR*."

Van Felsen—who could barely see over the top of the lectern—smiled. "That's better. You almost sound like a bunch of leathernecks who are ready to march on hell itself—and whom I might consent to lead down that fiery hole. Is that who you are?"

"Sir, yes, *sir*!"

She's good, McGee admitted, his throat raw with the primal affirmations he'd bellowed along with all the rest.

"Your orders and team rosters will be in packets passed out after this meeting. They are 'read and burn.' No exceptions, no excuses. Read and burn. What did I say, you knobheads?"

The answer was a chorus. "Read and burn."

"Outstanding. I must say that today you have proved yourself to be pretty damned fine Marines—all of you, even the 'honorary Marines' from lesser . . . er, 'other' . . . services." Van Felsen smiled: it was half joke and half serious. "And since you have all been such good boys and girls, we figured we'd give you a treat and let you watch a holo before bedtime—which in your cases means a day-long drive to your scattered homes."

"A holo? What the . . . ?" murmured Li, who looked over at McGee, then Battisti, then seemed ready to look for Varazian as well—but instead dropped his eyes. Varazian had not made the cut and was already driving home.

The murmurs of curiosity and anticipation grew louder when a decidedly archaic holoprojector—the size of a two-ton shipping container—was wheeled ponderously into the room. Van Felsen stepped away from the lectern and stood before them. "Ladies and gentlemen, this war could well be a fight to the finish. Either our efforts to communicate with the invaders are completely flawed, or they are ignoring everything we say. However, we know that they are interested in at least two things: the conquest of our worlds, and the subjugation of our populations. And once they have finished with the former objectives, we cannot know how they might deal with so many populous, captive worlds. They might allow us to live on as their slaves"—

A grim atavistic rumble arose.

—"or they might simply want us out of the way. We can't tell which, but the Baldies do seem both amoral and eminently practical. So unless they have some purpose for us in their vision of a postwar scenario, it is possible that their picture of the endgame is a picture in which humanity no longer appears."

The silence was absolute, tense. McGee looked to either side, saw lips stretched back from teeth, knotted hands, rigid shoulders. He looked down, saw his own immense fists clenched into white weapons of alien annihilation. *Okay, so I guess I look like the rest of my mates right about now. Nothing wrong with that.*

"The holo you are about to see is self-explanatory. For sake of clarity, I will say what I should not need to. Under no circumstances are you to divulge the specific or even general content of this communiqué or its existence. Please give it your full attention."

As if she had to ask for it, thought McGee, who, with dozens of others, craned his neck to see what he knew must be coming: a face and a voice from human space, from beyond the warp points that led out of Bellerophon.

But neither he nor anyone else in the room was prepared for what they saw: the stationary head-and-shoulders figure of a young man—unthinkably young for all the chest-borne fruit salad that bespoke several decades of campaigns, decorations, and ascension through the general ranks. But stranger still was his face—a face so young, and yet so oddly familiar. Viewing it left McGee with the same haunting disorientation he had felt when seeing teenage and college pictures of a friend he had only known as an adult. This was no different: his brain struggled to connect the young, unfamiliar features to the more mature face of a person he knew now. . . .

And McGee suddenly knew who, impossibly, he was looking at—in the same moment that Li and Igor Danilenko hesitantly murmured the corresponding name: "Trevayne?"

Other voices took it up hesitantly. "Trevayne? Ian Trevayne?"

"But he's . . . he's dead. Killed at Zapata, eighty years ago."

"Naw—not dead. They stuck him in suspended animation."

"Like I said, he's *dead*. Those meat-lockers are death traps. Everyone knows it."

"Yeah, well, there he is."

"Nah, can't be. That guy is too young, *way* too young. Wasn't he something like, eh, one hundred forty when he—?"

Van Felsen cleared her throat. "Admiral Ian Trevayne, who fought for and saved the Rim Federation during the—secession—of the Terran Republic, was in fact severely wounded during the war's concluding engagement, the legendary Battle of Zapata. His body was cryogenically preserved against the hope that one day medical science might advance to the point where it could repair his injuries. While we do not have the details on how that has been accomplished, or why he appears so young, we have confirmed that this is indeed Ian Trevayne, not a modified image or holosim representation of him."

"Commander"—it was Major (now First Lieutenant) Peters, who had been the senior Reservist of activation age—"are you at liberty to reveal *how* you got this message?"

"A long story, Tibor, but you asked for it. When the aliens approached Bellerophon on their generation ships, two professors at Philomena University—Doctors Gerard and Duane—detected the exhaust flares of their reaction drives." Van Felsen's voice dropped half a register into a more conspiratorial tone. "However, I have it on good authority that the catch was actually made by our very own Toshi Springer, who was one of the first Reservists we reactivated."

"*Marines lead the way*," solemnized a voice in the front row, invoking the service motto.

"Yes, indeed." Van Felsen smiled. "Although the Baldies then blasted every single one of our orbital arrays, it seems that there was an old ground-based optical telescope that the faculty had built into a roof dome, and that the Astronomy Department also had an old radio-telescope array in storage. So we ordered Lieutenant Springer to return to her duties at the university, teaching a class in the methodological history of astronomy. Using that cover, she surreptitiously organized a small but skilled group to get both instruments operational and to observe our system's warp points on a 24/7 rotation. I'm pleased to report that they've been plenty busy."

"So the amateur astronomers *did* see something," breathed Danilenko.

"Yes, Igor. Since the Baldies occupied Bellerophon, there have been at least two major fleet clashes at the warp point leading into the Astria system. Lieutenant Springer and her team detected multiple antimatter-warhead detonations that blotted out all other radiant energy coming to Bellerophon along those vectors. Both events have been fairly brief—which leads us to conclude that they were either probing or aborted attacks. Had a pitched battle taken place, the energy intensities would have been higher, more saturated, and far longer in duration.

"During both engagements, there were also sustained bursts of coded broadband radio transmissions. The Baldies did their best to jam it, but every single ham operator here on Bellerophon heard and recognized it as a signal of some kind—but whose, and what it meant, were a mystery to them.

"But once we had been alerted by the astrophysical fireworks, and had a full record of the radio emissions, our coding protocols told us how to do the rest. I can't detail how we sifted the necessary data out of the transmissions. I can tell you it was broken into chunks that had to be pieced together like a jigsaw puzzle. Different languages were used, as were variations in transfer rate, prearranged trapdoor codes, and, in some cases, segments of the signals were transmitted in reverse. When we were done extracting, decoding, sorting, and recombining all the pieces, this is what we came up with." Van Felsen nodded at the holo operators.

Ian Trevayne's stationary face became mobile, the pensive expression transforming into a grave smile.

"To all our brothers in arms in the Bellerophon system: our daily thoughts are upon your safety, your health, and your resistance against an invader that came—quite literally—out of the depths of space. And although there is no precedent for a sublight-driven interstellar invasion, I must begin by apologizing to each and every one of you. The collected militaries, commanders, and nations of civilized space failed you. It does not matter that we had no reason to envision interstellar travel that did not rely upon warp points, nor that we lacked the means to detect the invaders' approach. It is a commander's job to think the unthinkable, to foresee the unforeseeable, to imagine the unimaginable. For this, for our failure in foresight and imagination, we offer you our most sincere apologies and confess our bitter shame.

"Because of the passive sensors we left buried in

asteroids before we withdrew, and the automated tight-beam updates they send to any of our ships that enter the Bellerophon system, we know something of your sacrifice and losses.

"We know, for instance, of the widespread dislocation and privation of many urban residents, particularly around the city of Melantho. We learned—with horror—of the pitiless killing of parents who were only trying to control their children's terrified reaction to the invaders, as well as the execution of several who simply attempted to prevent the summary immolation of their child's corpse. But most of all, we were filled with a terrible resolve when we discovered that, in reprisal for a similar incident, the invaders mercilessly and mutely incinerated the entirety of the town in which this act of defiance occurred.

"In consolation of all you have suffered, I can only say: look to the sky, for we are coming. And when the combined forces of the Rim Federation, the Terran Republic, and the Pan-Sentient Union return, be ready to rise up with us and drive the invaders from your land, your seas, your skies."

McGee almost missed Trevayne's next sentence over the glad noises elicited by the news that the Rim's nominal adversary—the one-time "rebels" of the Terran Republic—had joined their cause. The further news that this unprecedented alliance would be buttressed by the enormous (if sadly distant) industrial power of the Pan-Sentient Union was better still.

However, Trevayne's next words engendered frowns of confusion on at least half the faces in the audience. "On a related note, we presume that those of you who were involved in the highly secretive creation of modular hull sections for a classified warcraft have now been compelled to reveal this participation under intensive interrogation or other forms of duress. For any of you who might still be resisting the invaders' attempts to extract details on your activities in that program, or for those of you who may have elected to go into hiding to avoid just such interrogation, I implore you: please do not endanger yourselves by trying to keep this information a secret any longer. We have determined that the enemy has independently deduced that these hull modules were actually designated for our construction of a string of megafortresses of unprecedented size and firepower. Based upon the marked operational caution of the invaders, we must presume that they have learned about the existence of these impregnable battle stations and have adjusted their strategy accordingly."

"What the hell?" muttered Maotulu, a third-generation Marine legacy. "I did space construction in six systems, and I never—"

But Danilenko let out a surprised bark of laughter and evidently slipped back into his family's traditional language. "Maotulu, don't you get it? Is all disinformation—and *bozhemoi*, is *horosho*!"

"You mean . . . ?" whispered Battisti uncertainly.

"All theater for the Baldies," McGee hissed sideways. "Just to make 'em wonder if we've got these megafortresses or not. The Baldies aren't interrogating anyone as far as I've heard, but if they believe Trevayne doesn't know that . . ."

"Then they will believe that his warning is genuine." Battisti finished the thought.

"Or they might still suspect that it's a ruse. But then again, if they guess wrong . . ."

Li nodded. "Head games."

McGee strained to hear again, having missed a few general exhortations. "... which means that our forces are growing daily. So remember. Although you are hundreds of parsecs—and a year's worth of warp transits—away from the planet that gave birth to humanity, Earth has not forgotten you. Earth abides, but she does not abide passively."

"Here we go." Peters folded his arms with a smile. "The stirring wrap-up."

"Eh?" inquired Maotulu.

"Just like De Gaulle to the French. MacArthur to the Filipinos."

"Who the hell is—?"

"Not to worry, Matto. Like me, those stories are ancient history—literally," said Peters.

Holographic Trevayne took no notice of Peters's abortive history lesson. "... meaning that, at this key moment, all the forces of humanity and her allies are united as never before. So look to the skies. All the races of the Pan-Sentient Union—and most particularly, our war brothers the Orions—have demonstrated their solidarity not only by producing needed ships and supplies, but by sending units to the front. We can say nothing more without also furnishing our enemies with strategic intelligence. But you may rest assured of this—just one warp point away, humanity and its many allies wait to both avenge your dead and be rejoined with you.

"And when we arrive, it will be at the head of the greatest armada of ships that has ever been witnessed by any race, in any war, in the long history of the known precincts of this galaxy. Yet that strength in numbers pales beside our strength of purpose, for these many fleets of many races are united in one cause—to liberate you. Brave men and women of Bellerophon, you have our solemn pledge: we are coming. So, each day, every day, remember that pledge . . . and look to the sky."

Trevayne concluded on a smile that was a promise of rescue to humans . . . and death to the Baldies. There was a moment of utter silence—

—and then bedlam. Men and women, having lived for months without any message from beyond the immense prison camp of the Bellerophon system, had heard words of deliverance from one of the greatest heroes of their era—or, more properly, from the era just before their own. Ian Trevayne himself had risen up at their hour of need, like the ancient British myth of the Pendragon, who would ever and again return to save the Green and Pleasant Land in its darkest hour.

McGee watched the happy tumult seethe around him, wanted to join in—but a face rose up and stilled any joy he might have felt: Jennifer. His dear, sweet Jennifer. Who he had pushed away for months before the bastard Baldies had taken her. Pushed her away to save her. Save her from the knowledge that he was conducting unauthorized bombing attacks against the Baldies in Melantho. Save her from the fear that he'd be killed on those missions. Save her from the faintest connection with his activities so that, even if they came for him, they would pass over her. But in some mad reversal of anything vaguely like a sensible unfolding of events, the Baldies had come and taken her for no apparent reason—and left him, bleeding and unconscious, on the doorstep of Melantho General Hospital. Unable to move. Unable to find her. Unable to rescue her. Or to hold her. Jennifer. Jennifer. Jennifer—

Who was suddenly Van Felsen. Who was looking up at him, literally waving in his face. "Hello, McGee? Command to McGee—are you reading me?"

"Uh, yes, ma'am . . . I mean, sir. I heard you loud and clear, sir."

"Sure you did, McGee." Van Felsen quirked the left corner of her mouth at his flustered return to the here and now. "Walk with me."

"Yes, sir."

With Falco in tow, and two others in uniform blacks—signifying they had been on active duty when the invaders had arrived—Van Felsen led him out of the cafeteria and back into the six-acre warehouse. The five of them walked for a while. No one spoke. Grit and sand rasped underfoot.

"Recovered from the aliens' little visit to your house, McGee?"

"Yes, sir. And in fighting shape, sir."

Van Felsen smiled; so did the others—except the thin, reedy one who looked more like a bookkeeper than a Marine.

"Glad to hear it," Van Felsen said with a nod. "I'm sorry about having to send you back to the noncom ranks, McGee, I really am."

"Not any concern to me, sir. I'm ready to—"

"McGee, my regret isn't about any damage done to your delicate ego. It's about sheer practicality. You've got double the logged training time of any Reservist. You've even managed to squeak in a few exercises with the active-duty forces. I can hardly spare you out of the officer cadre—but, damn it, I can't make an exception. Not until you do something that would warrant a promotion. Then I can reinstate your commission."

"Sir, I am fully ready to—"

"Steady, McGee. This is not an encouragement to go off half-cocked on some kind of personal vendetta or renegade bombing spree."

McGee gulped and tried not to look like the kid with his hand caught in the cookie jar: a half-cocked renegade bombing spree was exactly how he had been bringing his private and wholly unauthorized war to the Baldies.

But if Van Felsen knew anything about it, she didn't pin him down or give any other intimation that it was her intent to criticize him. On the other hand, perhaps she *did* know—and this was her way of warning him off further attacks. But why?

"McGee, we're finally getting to the stage where we can think about larger operations, something bigger than the intermittent sniping we use to keep the Baldies off guard. So what I need from every Marine now are disciplined, by-the-book operations, and no lamebrained screwups. You read me?"

"Louder and clearer still, Commander."

Van Felsen looked at him; McGee had the distinct impression that she was trying very hard not to smile. She almost looked like she wanted to pat him on the head. "Glad to hear it," was all she said and then resumed walking, hands folded behind her rather generous posterior.

"You know, McGee, we'd have invited you up here a long time ago if it wasn't for . . . for . . ." Van Felsen trailed off.

"For my personal situation. I know, sir."

Van Felsen sighed, evidently relieved that McGee had made it possible for her to avoid naming his missing, pregnant girlfriend. "Now, because of what's happened to your—family—we have need of your special assistance."

"Anything, sir. Just name it. I'm your man."

Van Felsen stopped and turned to look up—way up—at him. "I know that, Alessandro. More than you can guess. So here's what I need. I need to come for a visit."

"A—a visit, sir?"

"Yes, son, a visit. Me and the rest of the joint forces command. Well, all but two of us. We can't put all the cadre's eggs in one basket, no matter how quiescent the Baldies have been to date. But the rest of us need to get on-site in Melantho, have some specialists look at your house, study where your—where Jennifer worked, socialized, shopped."

"To figure out why they disappeared her, you mean?"

"Well, yes—but *disappearing* often has the context of a permanent disappearance. As in an undisclosed execution."

McGee wouldn't let his head sag. "Yes, sir."

"Well, that's not how we're seeing Jennifer's disappearance. Since you were laid up in the hospital and then came straight up here, there's some news you're probably not aware of. On the day that Jennifer was taken, twenty-two other persons were disappeared in Melantho. Same approach, same methods."

"What?"

"And there's only one connection we've been able to establish among them."

"What's that?"

"They're all artists."

McGee's thoughts chased around purposelessly, like a dog in vigorous pursuit of its own tail. "They're all *artists?*" he echoed.

Van Felsen nodded. "Yes. All twenty-three of the abductees were artists."

"But why—"

Van Felsen stopped and looked at him again, firmly but with a touch of gentleness. "Despite the official line I barked out during the general briefing, our theory is that the Baldies are trying to communicate with us. Art is nonverbal communication—and the whole verbal approach has been a nonstarter for them. And us."

McGee found the theory vaguely intriguing but was unsure where Van Felsen was heading. "I'm sorry, sir, but I don't—"

"Did you *hear* me, Lieut—apologies: I mean, Sergeant? Our theory is that they want to try to *communicate* with us."

McGee heard the broader implication but had spent so long suppressing the uncertainty, the fear, the regret, the self-recriminations, that he didn't dare embrace it all at once. "Communication. They took Jennifer to communicate. So, she might be alive."

"It's only a theory so far. But there *is* something else."

McGee's heart felt like it wanted to soar and plummet, to race and die, all in the same instant. He could only nod and parrot, "Something else?"

"Yes. There has been only one subsequent abduction incident. It happened just recently. The Baldies snatched up two nurses with the OB/GYN unit in Melantho General when they left their overnight shift two days ago. Neither one had any prior contact with the Baldies or the Resistance, and no explanation was given by the abductors."

McGee's heart finally decided on a direction: it leapt up. "You mean . . . ?"

Van Felsen closed her eyes and made a palm-down calming motion. "We have nothing more than that, McGee. But Jennifer was the only one of the twenty-three abducted artists who was pregnant." Then Van Felsen opened her eyes and smiled. "And something tells me the Baldies don't need our help birthing their *own* babies."

Van Felsen had handled a lot of unexpected situations in her years as a pint-sized Marine officer, but she had no experience with, was untrained for, and quite frankly baffled at being snatched up by an immense Marine sergeant into a joyous, smothering bear hug.

1

Undeceived

We are never deceived: we deceive ourselves.
—Goethe

RFNS Gallipoli, *Main Body, Further Rim Fleet, Raiden System*

"Here they come," breathed Vice Admiral Erica Krishmahnta of the Rim Federation. She leaned forward to get a better look as the first enemy ship made its appearance.

Krishmahnta was not looking out a viewport of her flagship, the RFNS *Gallipoli*, but into a hot tub–sized holotank display snugged into a dip at the foot of the captain's chair. There, tiny green arrow points were clustered about a purple circle that floated upright like the hoop of a lion tamer: the green icons depicted her fleet's current deployment around the purple-coded warp point, a hole in space-time that—if entered properly—led to and from the Jason system. As she watched, she felt Captain Yoshi Watanabe leaning over her shoulder for a better look of his own.

The first enemy craft—signified by a bright red mote—blinked into existence, seemingly spat out by the purple ring like a drop of blood. An arterial gush of further enemy contacts was sure to follow.

Krishmahnta leaned sharply forward. "Sensor Ops, what kind of—?"

But before Erica could voice the question, the red icon was gone—and with it went two of the eighty nearly invisible cyan latticeworks that indicated the minefields Krishmahnta had laid down to defend the warp point.

"What the hell?" Watanabe's surprise diminished into an angry hiss.

"It wasn't an anti-mine missile." Helmsman Ensign Witeski's voice cracked, but he sounded sure of himself nonetheless. "It's too big. You could fit ten, maybe twenty of our own into it. So it's not a standard AMBAMM."

"Maybe not," said Captain Velasquez from the Engineering console, where he was hurrying his computer through its analysis of the sensor data, "but the first EM-spectrum results say that some pretty big antimatter warheads went off—bigger than the ones on our HBM ship-killer missiles."

Krishmahnta drummed her fingers. "So what was it?"

"We, uh . . . we don't know, sir. It was gone too quickly for us to get any good data on it."

"Not even images?"

Velasquez shrugged. "Sir, this warp point is pretty big, and from what we can tell, that ship was pretty small. We'd need at least a hundred dedicated imagers running in fast-capture mode if we wanted to get a picture—"

"Then get a hundred imagers aimed at the warp point, running in fast-capture mode, and do it *now*! Captain, if—no, *when*—another of those ships appears, I want to learn as much as we can about it."

"Yes, sir!"

Krishmahnta waited for more enemy arrowheads to

emerge. None did. But then, after a few moments, a swarm of much smaller red motes danced through the purple hole. "Let me guess—recon drones."

"Dead-on, sir," confirmed Commander La Mar at the Tactical station. "Dozens of 'em. We're burning them down."

And Krishmahnta's first line of ships did just that—but two of the bright scarlet gnats seemed to think the better of suicide. They spun about and dove back into the purple circle, which swallowed them.

She leaned back. "Well, they got a look at us, and at the effect of their AMBAMM equivalent. Fine. We were expecting them to probe us before attacking anyhow. La Mar, reconfigure the fleet into intercept formation Myrmidon. Make it a phased redeployment. I don't want to be caught in the air between dance steps if they decide to rush through. Now," she said, changing tone as she looked at Commander Samantha Mackintosh, her chief of operations and resident expert on damned near everything, "how in Vishnu's name does that minesweeper of theirs work, Sam?"

"Uh, sir, as Paulo—er, as Captain Velasquez pointed out, we just don't have any technical specs on—"

"Sam, I know you've got blank data screens right now. I'm talking theoretically. How could they manage an *immediate* discharge—of *any*thing—right after warp transit? Everything we've got—and everything we've seen of theirs—spends at least half a second realigning itself after going through a warp point. But that damn thing's discharge was well-nigh instantaneous."

"To be precise, 0.002 seconds after arrival," supplied Velasquez.

Samantha did not look up from her screens. "Sir—I'm

sorry. I don't have the faintest idea how they're doing that. It shouldn't be possible."

"No," agreed Watanabe, "it shouldn't be. But we just saw it."

"And stood by while it started blasting a path through our mines." Krishmahnta frowned, set an incisor down on her lower lip, then winced away from the swollen blister that had already arisen there in reaction to her habitual biting. "Next time, we'll have to lay the mines back farther from the warp point."

"Which is just what they want, I imagine."

"Then we'll have to find a way to make them wish they'd never wanted it." Krishmahnta rubbed her lip. "Sam, how long—*exactly* how long—does warp-point transit disorient a ship?"

"Well, sir, it depends."

"On what?"

"On a whole lot of variables. Such as the gravitic signature particular to each warp point, the angle of entry, time elapsed since the warp point was last used for a transit, organic systems versus electronic systems, the size of the—"

"Wait a minute. Organics versus electronics—can you detail that?"

"Not much. A little. Back before the Fringe Rebellion, the old Terran Federation did some studies, but they never amounted to much, since you can't—"

"The details, Sam."

"Uh, yes, sir. There are two rules of thumb. First, organics reorient faster than electronics. Second, simple systems reorient faster than complex ones."

"Fastest and slowest rates?"

"Without researching the data, sir, I'm guessing—"

"Then guess, Sam—and hurry it up."

"The simplest organic object, a unicellular organism, would probably reorient in under one-tenth of a second. Conversely, complex electronics like a third-generation quantum computer would take up to two seconds."

Krishmahnta stared at the holotank for a moment. Then: "Lieutenant Lachow, fleet signal direct to Lieutenant Commander Mikopolous, commanding RFNS *Balu Bay*. Have her advance to three light-seconds' distance from the warp point, offset from its center axis by sixty degrees opposite the direction of the ecliptic's rotation, and sixty degrees beneath its zero-reference."

"Sixty trailing by sixty declination. Aye, sir."

"*Balu Bay* is to take up that new position at better than best speed. Once on-site, she is to run all sensors active, full gain."

Lachow looked up from his console. "Sensors *active*, sir?"

"Active, Lieutenant. If we're going to get a look at one of these things, we'll have to have our eyes wide open the instant it transits the warp point."

Watanabe leaned close to Krishmahnta's ear. "Admiral, with sensors active—"

"Your reservations are duly noted, 'Nab—and yes, if the next thing the bastards send through is an SBM-HAWK, *Balu Bay* doesn't have a chance. She's too small, too close to the warp point, and will be too bright a target not to take a contact hit." Which, given the antimatter warheads carried by almost all ship's missiles, meant a certainty of instant vaporization. "But we've got to get a better look at this thing they just used to clear our minefield. And besides, I don't think they're going to switch gears into a full scale attack just now."

"No?"

"No. They tried their new toy, sent RD's through to see how well it worked against our mines. My guess is that right now they're deciding how best to step up the pace of their operations. Which is to say, they're going to clear a path with more of these anti-mine systems and then send their main assault in."

"Or maybe they'll cat-and-mouse us. Keep us on edge with intermittent probes and jabs and wear us down."

"There is always that possibility," agreed Krishmahnta. "Although the Baldies haven't shown much interest in that kind of tactic before."

Witeski looked up, his thin face a mass of confused crinkles. "The 'Baldies,' sir?"

Krishmahnta smiled but kept one eye on the tactical plot in the holotank. "That's what the folks back on Bellerophon are apparently calling the invaders."

Witeski looked around at the unsurprised senior staff. "Eh . . . I thought we were cut off from Bellerophon and its news, sirs. By about four systems."

"We *are* cut off, Wit," Marian Nduku tossed over her shoulder as she crossed the bridge to finish installing new command relays in the engineering console. "But 'Baldies' is what they're called back home."

Witeski, clearly annoyed that even a fellow junior officer should be more in the know than he was, aimed his impatience at her retreating back. "Oh, and how'd you find that out? Did the Baldies tell you themselves?"

"In a manner of speaking, yes, they did, Mr. Witeski." Krishmahnta's answer calmed the ensign, although he might have been made anxious all over again had he seen the soberly assessing look in her jade-green eyes. "While our Intel people were picking through the wrecks they left behind after their first visit to this system"—fierce, satisfied grins sprang up around the bridge—"we found snippets of human com chatter in some of their computers. They must have recorded it when the Home Fleet evidently tried to break into Bellerophon from Astria." The grins gave way to grimly set mouths. "Our best guess is that the aliens kept our chatter in their computers as some kind of reference base for analyzing our signals. And in it, our people were calling them Baldies."

"I can see why," put in Mackintosh. "Did you see the post-action forensic reports on the remains they scooped up after their first attack? Not a hair on their bodies. Three eyes, no nose, tentacles where their fingers ought to be."

Krishmahnta closed her eyes to help her concentrate. "And if I remember correctly, Doc Sadallah made note of how strangely unevolved their vocal apparatus was. Much less neurological complexity than we expected."

Sam studied the backs of her hands as they rested lightly on her reconfigurable touchpad. "I wonder what made Sadallah decide to examine their vocal structures."

Watanabe leaned back from watching a green chevron sidle up to the wormhole in the holotank: RFNS *Balu Bay* was almost in position. "Sadallah told me he saw a note in the technical intel reports about how the Baldy computers had little or no provision for voice input."

Krishmahnta watched the icon of the *Balu Bay* sprout a bright silver stalk: her sensor arrays were active. "So, if they don't talk much, could they be—?"

Mackintosh's face lost its ruddy tone. "Telepathic? A hive mind? Like—"

Krishmahnta shook her head. "They're not like the

Bugs," she heard herself say, while her conscience countered with: *C'mon, Erica, you don't really know that. But you're leader enough to know that you can't afford to have that spectre looming in the Fleet's mind—now or ever.* The Bugs—humanity's most dangerous enemy to date—had initially seemed as unstoppable as they had been inscrutable. No communication had ever been established, and the price of defeating, and ultimately exterminating, them had been horrific. "No, they're not the Bugs. We know the Baldies asked—crudely—for Bellerophon to surrender. And they're not using us as a food source. They just want to push us aside."

"They don't take surrenders in the field," countered Mackintosh. "And they kill our wounded on sight."

"True. But, oddly, they seem to eliminate their own wounded as well, and they ignore disabled ships, or those which pose no threat. No, they are not the Bugs—but they're sure not us, either."

Mackintosh had recovered most of her color. "So, if they don't talk much, how do they communicate?"

"That's just what I was wondering, Sam."

"Light? Pheromone emissions?" offered Witeski.

"Could be, but there's nothing in any of their command-and-control technology that has any interface for those media. But what if—" And Krishmahnta stopped herself, wondering how to proceed without reinvoking the memory of the Bugs. "What if they do have some kind of mind-to-mind contact? *That* could travel at light speed, couldn't it?"

Mackintosh frowned. "For all we know, and given the myriad of ways in which quantum entanglement produces phenomena which seem to exceed the cee limit—"

"Warp point is hot, Admiral," announced Velasquez tightly.

Postures straightened. Eyes became intent on screens, on the holoplot, or both.

A red blip popped out of the purple hoop, edged forward a bit—and was then gone. Another two of the cyan-lattice minefield icons disappeared with it. There were plenty more, but—

"*Balu Bay* is relaying data. A mother lode of it, Admiral."

Krishmahnta leaned back. Fair exchange. Maybe better than that. "Commander La Mar, signal to *Balu Bay*. 'Well done. Choose a new vantage point, this time at four light-seconds' range, your discretion regarding position. Passive sensors only.' "

Thirty seconds later, the green delta of the *Balu Bay* lost her silver mast and began to move.

Ten seconds after that, three red motes—smaller—tore out of the purple hoop, headed toward the *Balu Bay*'s old position—and promptly disappeared from the plot the moment they paused as if pondering the unexpected emptiness before them.

"RFNS *Anzio* reports three Baldy SBMHAWKs destroyed, Admiral."

Of course. And they did just what I would have done—because if I hadn't repositioned Balu Bay... "Where's that data on their minesweeper, Mr. La Mar?"

Velasquez, the head of Engineering, answered. "I'm integrating it, Admiral. First imaging coming through now."

A fragmentary 3-D graphic popped into existence above the holotank's tactical display. The gridwork outline of the Baldy's mystery ship rotated slowly: its main hull was shaped rather like a rugby ball. However, that surface was completely hex-celled, like a beehive. A drive cluster protruded from one end.

Watanabe straightened up. "What the hell is that?"

"A cluster of one-shot missile launchers, hooked up to a rudimentary reactionless drive," declared Samantha Mackintosh as she studied her own console. "A surprisingly simple device, really—an outfacing layer of light, one-shot launch tubes, that apparently discharge short-range HBMs with gigaton-level warheads. The overlapping blasts make a clean sweep of anything close."

"But still no hint as to how they get that damn thing to reorient and trigger so quickly?"

"No, sir. Sorry, sir."

"Not to worry—we'll keep working at it. And when I say 'we,' I of course mean 'you,' Sam."

"Of course, sir."

Krishmahnta leaned back. "But in the meantime, what do we call that thing?"

"It's not an AMBAMM," maintained Witeski.

Erica made a mental note: *Watch Witeski for tunnel vision during a crisis.*

Looking over her shoulder, the unflappable Marian Nduku commented, "Looks like a flying beehive to me."

"A beehive on a stick," amended Velasquez.

Mackintosh looked up with a frown. "The flying beehive on a stick? That sounds a bit . . . cumbersome for a ship classification, don't you think?"

By the time the fifth of the self-immolating minesweepers had come through and blasted deeper into Krishmahnta's minefields, the alien ship had acquired a permanent, sawed-off version of its longer moniker. It was now simply a *stickhive*.

Arduan SDH Shem'pter'ai, *First Fleet of the* Anaht'doh Kainat, *Beaumont System*

Staring at a miniature holographic replica of the planet that the enemy called Beaumont, Admiral Narrok saw that the brown and blue orb swam not only at the center of the tacplot but at the center of a surprisingly wide array of enemy ship icons. *There are too many of the human ships,* he thought, but did not allow this observation to enter the stream of fellow-feeling and telepathy—or *selnarm*—that was the reciprocal communicative medium linking him to the other persons on the bridge. Then he allowed a carefully emended version of his strategic deduction to bleed into the communal mental link. "There are more *griarfeksh* ships than we expected, *Holodah'kri*. Many more."

Urkhot, the visiting high priest—or *holodah'kri*—radiated a *selnarmic* wave of (dismay) at the mention of the size of the enemy fleet. But he also emitted a brief pulse of (satisfaction, relief) when Narrok referred to the humans as *griarfeksh*—a particularly unsavory, hairless carrion eater of their homeworld. However, the last *griarfeksh* had vanished long ago—along with their homeworld, Ardu, and its sun, all destroyed when the nearby blue giant Sekahmant went nova. Narrok felt that the accepted term for humans—*griarfeksh*—was unsuitable and even dangerously misleading, but he had resolved to use it reflexively when he was sharing his *selnarm* with xenophobic militants such as the high priest.

Urkhot—tall and golden-skinned, his third and central eye unblinking—stared at the holographic representation of the clashing fleets as if he could read the whorls of changing icons and data well enough to assess the accuracy of Narrok's strategic deduction. Which he indirectly contested by observing, "*We* seem to outnumber *them*. Vastly."

"And so we do, *Holodah'kri*. But the odds of our success here in Beaumont are not the cause of my concern."

"Ahh . . ." And Urkhot made the wheezing grunt that was the vocal amplification of a modest *selnarmic* (realization). "Now I understand. You are concerned that the *griarfeksh* have not drawn strength from this fleet in order to defend against the simultaneous attack Second Admiral Sarhan is making upon the system they call . . . eh . . ."

"Raiden," supplied Narrok. "No, if anything, the hu—*griarfeksh* commander in Raiden has sent further reinforcements *here*. They are wise."

"They are the whetstone upon which Illudor sharpens our edge." Urkhot projected (resolve, pride).

"Most assuredly." Narrok returned a pulse of (calm agreement).

"So let us attack quickly, before they react."

"*Holodah'kri*, their lack of reaction is not due to surprise. Our immense preparations—with both the *Urret-fah'ah* minesweepers and the SBMHAWK wave attacks—announced our arrival quite clearly. And well beforehand."

"Then why do they not move? Has our preliminary bombardment stunned them, inflicted so many losses that they are paralyzed?"

Narrok kept from coiling his lesser tentacles in dismay. He suppressed his first reaction: *Can you truly be such an imbecile?* Instead, he sent a quick flash of (regret). "It seems unlikely. There is little wreckage, other than that of the mines we destroyed, and of our own *Urret-fah'ah* hulls."

"How could this be? Did you not assure Senior Admiral Torhok and me, and thereby the Council of Twenty, that a massive preliminary bombardment was essential? And that acquiring the capacity to do so by installing the . . . the external-ordnance racks . . . on our older ships would *assure* us of victory?"

"I believe I asserted that it was a prudent if expensive step in the *attempt* to secure victory, *Holodah'kri*. Nothing can *assure* victory. Other than the will of Illudor, of course."

"Which, of course, we are carrying out by expunging these pestilential aliens from the universe."

Narrok sent (calm, agreement). "But as you say, if Illudor sets these *griarfeksh* as our whetstone, then surely we cannot expect an immediate and easy victory. One cannot sharpen a blade without resistance, without friction."

Urkhot's eyes shifted sideways to glance at Narrok. (Agreement, vindication.) "That is well-observed, Admiral. But I still do not understand. Why did our SBMHAWKs not do more damage to them?"

"It may have done more damage than we know. But I suspect a different possibility."

"Which is?"

"That they found a new use for their AMBAMMs—their anti-mine ballistic antimatter missiles."

Urkhot did not even try to feign comprehension. "Please explain what you mean."

"I suspect that the *griarfeksh* used their AMBAMMs to sweep away our SBMHAWKs as they came through the warp point."

Urkhot's larger, central eye blinked. "This would be an effective tactic?"

"Most effective, *Holodah'kri*. If we are to believe their own records and periodicals—"

"Which we may not."

(Soothing.) "Of course—but *if* we were so misguided as to do so, they reveal that the yield of the enemy AMBAMMs is sufficient to completely destroy the largest SBMHAWK salvo we could fire."

"But then what of the smaller flights of missiles we sent through? Surely they did not have enough AMBAMMs to use against them as well."

"I suspect those smaller flights of missiles were eliminated by mines emplaced beyond the range of our *Urret-fah'ah* minesweepers, and by the defensive fire of ships waiting even farther back than that. I believe the *griarfeksh* commander realized that there would be little need for the customary use of AMBAMMs. After all, the enemy is unable to advance against us, and therefore minesweeping devices are of no use to them. Besides, they have surely observed that we are not carrying many static defenses forward with us, since our operations are consistently offensive in nature—"

"As well they should be."

Narrok expressed (accord) but secretly: *if anything defeats us, it will be that "always-attack" reflex.* "So, by this deductive process, the *griarfeksh* would reason their AMBAMMs to be useless, unless—"

"—unless they reconceived of them as massive area-denial and intercept weapons." Narrok's Intelligence Prime and Fleet Second, Mretlak, had joined them from behind, having left his command pod. "Unquestionably, when they detected one of our SBMHAWK surges, they sent one of their AMBAMMs forward. All our missiles would surely be consumed in its conflagration."

The *Holodah'kri* turned slowly toward the Second. (Surprise, disbelief, outrage.) "Are you in the habit of interrupting your admiral, Prime?"

The priest's refusal to address Mretlak by his most senor title—Fleet Second—had clearly stunned Narrok's trusted assistant and protégé. "I-I—"

Narrok intervened. (Reassurance.) "Fleet Second Mretlak and I have worked so closely together these past several months that titles were inefficient. They slowed the speed of our exchange."

Urkhot narrowed his central eye. (Disdain.) "I see. You may continue, *Prime* Mretlak."

Narrok intervened again. "Actually, Fleet Second Mretlak is overdue assembling the report you requested for Senior Admiral Torhok, *Holodah'kri*. He was delayed, seeing to the final details of our attack."

"Very well." And Urkhot turned way in a manner, and with a sudden retraction of his *selnarm* link, that left Mretlak—and anyone else on the bridge—with little doubt that the fleet second had just been dismissed like a truant Firstborn. Mretlak withdrew quietly, his own *selnarm* screened.

When he had departed, Urkhot observed, "Your first blade might learn more deference. He is young for his position. Perhaps you advanced him too quickly."

Narrok projected (open-mindedness) and thought, *not only does this meddling priest question my judgment as an admiral, but he is trying to push us back toward the archaic rank terminology of our barbarous past. He styles Mretlak as my* first blade, *not* fleet second. Not surprising. Torhok—senior admiral and most influential voice in the Council—had been encouraging the resurgence of the primordial forms and ethos of the *Destoshaz*, or warrior caste. He and Urkhot called it "rediscovering the caste's race-duty"; Narrok suspected it was a means of political manipulation as much as it was a genuine outpouring of xenophobic militarism.

Narrok allowed his uncertainty over how to respond to Urkhot to extend into silence: the priest had asked no question, made no request. *Let's see what he does if I do not respond.*

Urkhot simply backtracked . . . and rather awkwardly. "Admiral, while we are on the topic of how the effectiveness of our SBMHAWKs was degraded, I must also express surprise at how few of our regular missiles hit when we drove back the cluster of enemy ships around the warp point. Our missiles are rated for much higher levels of accuracy."

(Appreciation for perspicacity)—even as Narrok wondered if it was also true on human ships that, the less an important visitor knew about naval matters, the more determined the visitor was to criticize and find fault. "This is true, *Holodah'kri*, but the data you cite measure the missiles' accuracy against targets which are not employing a reactionless drive."

"The reactionless drive makes enemy ships too fast to hit?"

"No. A ship traveling under a reactionless drive is a somewhat diaphanous object. It is almost impossible for our sensors to secure an absolutely firm targeting lock. I will point out that the same is true for our adversaries when they fire upon us."

(Puzzlement.) "Then why do our other weapons—force beams, lasers—not suffer this difficulty?"

"Because their targeting is mostly optical. A missile flies home to its target, particularly in its terminal intercept phase, by aiming at the approximate center of that target's most powerful energy emissions. However, the pseudo-velocity field created by the reactionless drive—what engineers call the 'field-effect envelope'—provides some modest protection against missiles. Its alteration of space around the targeted ship also disrupts its various EM emissions. The larger the ship, the greater the distortion, and thus the harder to achieve the lock necessary for a contact hit."

(Bafflement.) "Then how do the missiles destroy the ships at all?"

Narrok sent a mix of (irony, satisfaction). "The antimatter warheads more than compensate for the inability to score a direct hit. They are so powerful that they can severely, even fatally, damage the most heavily armored ships just by getting relatively close."

"How close?"

"Warhead detonation at a range of dozens, even hundreds, of kilometers may be sufficient to not only cripple but vaporize ships."

Urkhot breathed in and out audibly. "Our missiles are so powerful?"

"Yes—and so are theirs, *Holodah'kri*. Actually, a little more powerful than ours."

Urkhot cast a quick worried glance at Narrok, feigning intense interest in the tactical plot, but his *selnarm* and thoughts lingered elsewhere. "At least our anti-cloaking system allows us to see all the enemies that might fire such missiles."

"We can see them—with certainty—only out to this point," amended Narrok, flicking a least tentacle of his left cluster through the hologram: it whipped through the space between the two rough lines of the human fleet.

Urkhot's *selnarm* quickly refocused (concern). "And why no farther than that?"

"Because that is the limit of our anti-cloaking system. Beyond that range, it cannot reach."

"So out there..."

"Out there could be more ships. And we do not know how many, or of what kind." (Patience, serenity, surety.) "Is it still your opinion that we should accelerate the rate of our advance beyond the speed of our fighter screen and reconnaissance drones, *Holodah'kri*?"

Urkhot's *selnarm* shut off with what felt like an almost audible snap. He was long in opening it again. "I trust in your military judgment, Admiral."

Narrok shared (gladness, fellow-feeling). But unshared, thought: *I'm sure you do, you sanctimonious hypocrite.*

RFNS Gallipoli, *Main Body, Further Rim Fleet, Raiden System*

For the fourth time in as many hours, Krishmahnta came bounding out of her bed as soon as the klaxon pealed. She was half into her regulation pants when Mackintosh's voice emerged from the speaker. "Five new SBMHAWKs, Admiral. Could be the prelude to a wave."

"Coming," Krishmahnta grumbled as she buttoned her jacket and stomped her left foot firmly into her shoe. *Yes, it could be an attack wave. Or another Two-o'clock Charlie. Well, I'll soon find out.*

She toggled the door to the bridge. Witeski snapped up from the helm. "Admiral on the bri—"

"Keep your seat, Mr. Witeski, and don't take your

hand off the wheel of this ship. *She's* the grand lady around here. Now: report, Commander La Mar?"

La Mar's grin was very faint and very rueful. "Five SBMHAWKs. And six recon drones were right on their tails. One got back through the warp point. No damage to us, but do we shift to another formation?"

Krishmahnta paused, then rubbed her eyes and nodded. "But sometime soon, it's going to be the real thing. Not just another Two-o'clock Charlie." After a brief silence, she heard Witeski whispering a question toward La Mar. She intervened. "A Two-o'clock Charlie, Mr. Witeski, was a tactic used during the air wars just before the era of space truly began. It was a small, usually nimble aircraft carrying a single bomb. Its purpose—to fly over the enemy positions at night and drop that single bomb into their rear area. Usually between 0100 and 0300 hours."

Witeski frowned. "The target?"

Krishmahnta smiled. "The target was the readiness of the troops in that area. It didn't matter what the bomb hit, Mr. Witeski. What mattered was that none of those soldiers ever got a long, solid block of refreshing sleep. They caught one-hour and, if lucky, two-hour catnaps." She looked around the bridge. "I suspect you can empathize."

From beyond the slouching ring of red-rimmed eyes and gray-fleshed brows and cheeks, a chorus of grunts, and a few annoyed snarls, answered in a bitter affirmative. She stared down into the holotank. "Any sign of follow-up?"

"Not a bit, Admiral," answered La Mar. "All calm."

Calm out there, but not in here, thought Krishmahnta. *With just a little ordnance expenditure, they keep us on edge, keep us shifting our line, keep us on pills. On pills that play havoc with our moods, give us a tendency toward tunnel vision and task fixation in exchange for extended wakefulness.* She rubbed her eyes. *They know what they're doing, all right. They finally read our playbook.*

Well, it wasn't quite "by the book," she conceded, but it achieved the same results. There had been twelve hours of SBMHAWKs. Then a tentative push with a few super-dreadnoughts, probably the last of the class the Baldies had arrived with. Sluggish handling suggested that the ships were largely automated. Those SDs had lasted long enough to send back a flurry of courier drones—which, Krishmahnta had speculated, was all this handful of outmatched dreadnoughts had been meant to achieve: engage and measure the dispersal of her defensive line, confirm the removal of the mines, and send the human fleet a clear message that more hulls—many, many more hulls—would soon be on the way.

Except they didn't come. Instead, a long-range variant of the RFN's own SBMHAWK—an automated ship-killing missile that could transit warp points independently—had made a most unwelcome debut. Hundreds of the missiles had come sleeting through the warp point. Those that survived chased after ships which were, in some cases, as far away as fourteen light-seconds. It was only modestly reassuring that none of those lone wolves survived the concentrated defensive fire to score a hit, because, as Krishmahnta had realized, the Baldies had not intended these weapons to kill ships but merely to send a message: "Even fifteen light-seconds back from the warp point, you are not completely safe. We have SBMHAWKs that can range that far—and what if we launch twenty, two hundred, two thousand? At what point does the density of the attack wave overcome your point-defense systems? At what point do your ships and your people start to die?" And with a question like that hovering overhead, like a ghostly sword of Damocles, sleep came less easily. And the closer to the warp point a ship was stationed, the less easily its off-duty crews found the solace of sleep, listening instead for the klaxons that indicated an inbound enemy weapon.

After that first tsunami of long-reaching Baldy SBM-HAWKs, there was a pause, and then the alien missiles resumed their intrusions, but this time as an irregular trickle. It was the tactical equivalent of Chinese water torture.

And that torture had to stop, decided Krishmahnta. The time had come to counteract her enemy's campaign of psychological warfare via sleep deprivation. "Commander Mackintosh, please pass these orders to the fleet. We are shifting to intercept formation Deep Serry Two. Have all ships confirm their way points and final plots before commencing that evolution. As ships rotate into the second rank, they are to reload all external-ordnance racks from tenders."

Sam raised an eyebrow but only said, "Aye, aye, sir."

Captain Watanabe leaned over as if to inspect the first small repositionings in the tacplot, but it also allowed him to lean close to Krishmahnta's ear, in which he murmured, "If the Baldies were to come through, right now—"

"I know, I know." Erica resisted—sagely—the impulse to bite her now-thoroughly swollen lower lip. Deep Serry Two was a calculated risk: it would ultimately reconfigure the fleet by breaking her engagement forces into two separate lines—which, in the three-dimensional battleground of deep space, would appear as two separate screens. The forward screen would remain on full alert. The rear screen—into which each ship would ultimately be rotated for four hours—would stand down. Instead of running a full watch on full alert, the rear screen would stand down to full bunks and minimal duty shifts—except for double-staffed galleys. In the corridors and the 'tween-deck companionways of the second line, catnaps and hot chow were to be the watchword of the hour. Of course, only the real veterans would actually manage to get real sleep, but the mere ability to close one's eyes, drowse, and recover from watch burnout was rest enough.

"Admiral?"

Erica swayed straight again. "Hmm . . . yes? Yes, Captain?"

There was a wry crinkle at the left corner of Yoshi Watanabe's thin lips. "Are you ready to stand down yourself?"

Krishmahnta breathed in deeply and exhaled through a forcibly bright smile. "Not just yet. I want to watch the evolution. If they stumble on us while we're making the change—"

"—that would be the worst moment," agreed Watanabe "So, you're going to see all your birds safely to their nests?"

Krishmahnta let her smile relax. "Something like that. Just half an hour more, and then I'll catch some sack time myself."

Two and a half hours later, in her bridge-conjoined ready room, lying in full uniform atop her unfolded bunk, Erica Krishmahnta stared at the gray bulkhead above her and attempted to achieve the transcendental state in the fashion her great-grandfather had labored to teach her. But Erica had been a child who, like most of her generation, gave first heed to the culture-leveling call of an increasingly blended humanity. By comparison, her *paradada*'s ways and stories were anachronistic remnants from a time and world that seemed far more distant than Mother Earth.

But there was a greater challenge to Krishmahnta's current serenity than her inexpert efforts at meditation. Lying on her bunk, she was repeatedly haunted by the terrible and growing conviction that—if she stepped wrong now—the combined fleets of the Further Bellerophon Arm, and the many millions of civilians sheltered behind them, might be forfeit.

The losses she had taken in defending Raiden against this renewed attack were minimal: heavy damage to a few of the older, slower monitors was the worst of it. Several of her workhorse picket ships—DD's recently sprung from mothballs—had been unfortunate enough to attract the attention of a few stray force beams and hetlasers during the recon sortie made by the older Baldy SDs: unable to stand up to that kind of ordnance, the small, gutted hulls had been evacuated and scuttled.

But where was the Great Alien Attack that these preliminaries had surely heralded, and which had been the hallmark of the Baldy campaign thus far? A shift in their first, suicidal tactics had been foreseeable, even inevitable—but this mincing, distant fencing match was a complete and utter reversal of their fleet doctrine. Unless . . .

And thus reblossomed the thought that had repeatedly kept Krishmahnta from sinking into the mauve of a delta-wave mental state: What if this was not a doctrine change, but a trap? With an attack looming large at the

Jason warp point here in Raiden, she felt a correspondingly greater temptation to send a courier to Admiral Miharu Yoshikuni in Beaumont and retrieve the capital ships with which she had bolstered that task force's rattled defenses. It was clear—from the unprecedented appearance of the stickhives, the Baldies' meticulous reconnaissance, and their attempts to exhaust her crews—that A Great Attack was coming into Raiden from Jason. Logically, Krishmahnta should meet that force with greater force—as much force as she could muster, in order to smash the invaders back from Raiden yet again.

But the ease with which she came to that conclusion, and the almost primal impulse to respond by taking more forces from Beaumont, was precisely what made Krishmahnta reject that option. As a seasoned flag officer, she had learned—sometimes the hard way—that any action that felt inevitable or compulsory often felt that way because it was a well-laid trap. The Baldies were trying to make her increasingly nervous about her ability to hold Raiden so that she would draw reserves from—and weaken—Yoshikuni's fleet in Beaumont. The Baldies would then smash and roll up Yoshikuni's diminished forces and cut straight through to Suwa. And so they would catch Krishmahnta's swollen fleet in a bottle, plugged at one end by the forces in Jason and sealed at the other by the enemy armada in Suwa.

Of course, the opposite temptation was to fall back on Suwa now and signal Yoshikuni to do the same. But then they'd find themselves in the position of trying to defend two warp points in one system—and as it was, their combined fleets barely had enough strength to permanently secure any one warp point.

So the invaders had to be met in both systems. The

strategy was simply one of attrition: to inflict as much damage upon them as possible as they emerged from the single warp point in each system—rather like intercepting the ships of an old-fashioned water fleet as they passed, one by one, through a narrow strait. And when the time came to fall back, Krishmahnta and Miharu Yoshikuni would have to fall back together. First to Suwa, and then, without delay, farther rearward to Achilles, where, combined, they would dig in behind the single warp point through which the aliens might enter that system.

Such maneuvers all sounded so simple, especially when explained by journalists to lay audiences, Erica thought, smiling as a dim mauve haze rimmed her field of vision. She, the all-powerful and all-seeing Vice Admiral Krishmahnta, need only resist as long as practical. Then both fleets would fall back in good order and at the same time. This would occur with flawless ease, even though the fleets were two systems apart and had no way of communicating except through couriers that took at least half a day each way. What could be simpler? she mused, letting the black irony blend into the rising mauve that was the harbinger of that state of mind in which—

one is none,

none is all, . . .

and . . . all . . . is . . .

". . . One DD inbound, Admiral Krishmahnta. Secure lascom beacon lists her as RFNS *Bucky Sherman*—a courier attached to Admiral Yoshikuni's command. Sorry if we woke you, sir, but you ordered—"

Erica snapped upright, checked the clock. "Yes, fine. Time elapsed since courier was dispatched?"

"Uh . . . beacon code indicates seventeen hours since she left Beaumont, Admiral."

"Tell her to transmit her communiqués and await reply."

"Uh, Admiral...the *Bucky Sherman* is a pretty old DD, mostly converted to automated systems and running low on volatiles and spares. And looking at the rads they're throwing off, a little engine refit wouldn't be out of—"

"Bring her in, then. Her CO is to report to me ASAP—no, belay that. Have Ms. Nduku in Engineering report to their CO with my compliments and a warning that she has to be back aboard *Gallipoli* in two hours. She can help with their refit until then. Is there a flesh-and-blood courier carrying an actual message pouch?"

"Yes, sir, a Lieutenant Wethermere."

"He should be in my ready room five minutes ago."

"Yes, sir."

Captain Yoshi Watanabe stuck his head through the open hatchway into Krishmahnta's ready room. He seemed perplexed. "You paged me, Admiral?"

"Yes, Captain Watanabe. Have a seat."

As he entered, Krishmahnta gestured toward a youngish man—he could have been as little as twenty-five, or as much as forty-five if he was on a reasonable antigerone regimen—who, before Erica could utter a word, stood to attention, giving the captain a well-snapped salute. The gesture was respectful, but not at all nervous. Krishmahnta watched a slightly surprised Captain Watanabe return the salute and wave the lieutenant back down. "At ease, here—*very* at ease, Lieutenant." He turned to Krishmahnta.

She explained. "This is Lieutenant Ossian Wethermere, courier from Admiral Yoshikuni in Beaumont."

Watanabe's eyes flicked back and forth, trying to read hers. "Well, has the balloon gone up there?"

Krishmahnta leaned back with a relieved sigh. "It most

certainly has. Look at this." She spoke to the walls. "Computer: replay Yoshikuni tacplot recording of Beaumont One, 1800-to-1 time compression."

The computer complied, creating a mini holographic tacplot that replayed the Battle of Beaumont as it had progressed up to eighteen hours ago. The fifteen hours of action took only thirty seconds to replay, but the outcome—and future—seemed clear. It was all quite familiar: human minefields were obliterated with stick-hives, then Baldy probes came in, followed by attempts to catch any nearby hulls with SBMHAWKs. Yoshikuni's response had been similar to Krishmahnta's: she slightly altered her deployment after each enemy recon phase so there were no pre-plotted targets for the enemy to strike. But here the invaders had only minced about for a few hours. Then they came in strong and fought a sharp engagement that burned up half a dozen of their old SDs in exchange for an RFN monitor and cruiser. Yoshikuni withdrew in good order into a two-screen position. But in doing so, she also fell back well inside the system's Desai limit. Beaumont itself was suspended like a brownish tennis ball between the heads of two glowing green tennis rackets—the two human screens. Meanwhile, the red motes kept pouring into the system from their entry warp point at six o'clock, spreading out into a single but much larger screen that approached the Desai limit slowly, inexorably. And doubtless would press on toward their ultimate objective: the warp point into Suwa, located at twelve o'clock—directly opposite their entry portal.

"Well, this is new." Captain Watanabe leaned back, rubbing his chin.

"Isn't it? Usually, once the Baldies acquire a toehold in a system, they charge straight in. Here they're coming on slowly, cautiously—probably uncertain what to make of Yoshikuni's ceding the warp point so readily."

"Yeah, about that—why *did* she give it up?" And as soon as he had asked the question, Watanabe called up a replay, which he watched carefully before looking at Krishmahnta. "So, you decided against building warp-point forts in Beaumont?"

Krishmahnta nodded. "It wasn't even a decision, really. We couldn't get them built in time—same as here."

"Well, that's because we lost ours when the Baldies hammered Raiden last time. Beaumont's never been under the gun before."

Krishmahnta shrugged. "True, but Yoshikuni didn't have any extant forts in-system. And given our inevitable withdrawal back to Achilles, it seemed a waste to rush forward fort modules and all the associated construction auxiliaries. Which, it turns out, wouldn't have had the new forts ready in time, anyway."

"So all that gear is—?"

"Still in the rear, back beyond Suwa."

"Added to the defenses in Achilles?"

Krishmahnta nodded. "I mean to hold that line in the sand."

"Erica, we may not be able to—"

"I know. I can count, too, Yoshi. We just may not have the weight of metal to stop them there. But we have to think and play to win. And even if they push us back from Achilles, every extra day we buy for the industrial sites in the Odysseus cluster is a victory. The longer they have to pump out the ships and crews and forts that we need, the more likely that we will be able to hold—really *hold*—the Baldies somewhere farther down the line."

"From your lips to Vishnu's ears." Watanabe smiled.

Krishmahnta looked over her fleet captain's shoulder. "Mr. Wethermere."

He stood immediately. "Sir!"

She smiled, saw his blue eyes—and was suddenly struck by two very different sensations.

Firstly, she had seen those eyes somewhere before. Very light, pure blue. There was even something familiar about their expression: amiable, ready to be amused, but unable to fully mask the ferociously active mind behind them.

But secondly—and more disturbing—was a recollection of her great-grandfather that seemed, at first, completely, even insanely, out of place: it was a tidbit of his old-school Hinduism, which she had largely dismissed as an endearing preoccupation of his dotage. "My child," her *paradada* had said, "you will *know* when you look into the eyes of an Old Soul. You will know what they are, perhaps before they have discovered it themselves. As children and young people, they play and distract themselves with the same sweet frivolities as their peers—but there is in them a way of seeing, and a depth of vision, that comes from having lived many lives. Which you can see looking out through their eyes. I tell you this, little *dhupa*"—for that was his own pet-name for her—"that they will be drawn to your bright karma as surely as flowers turn to the sun. And it may be that the greatest weight of your own karma will be to help them, for before they know what they are, they may be uncertain in their paths. Old Souls are no different from others in how they *begin* their life journey, *dhupa*—only in how they might *end* it. For their path is to Nirvana."

"Admiral? Sir?" Wethermere had taken a solicitous step toward her. "Are you all right?"

Krishmahnta literally felt an impulse to shake the memory—so strong and dislocating—out of her head, but that would hardly set the appropriate command image. She smiled. "My apologies, gentlemen. It seems I haven't quite roused myself from that deeply satisfying twenty-one-minute nap that you interrupted, Mr. Wethermere."

The lieutenant looked both surprised for being so blamed and genuinely repentant. Krishmahnta could hardly keep from smiling as he apologized. "I'm—I'm very sorry, sir."

Watanabe laughed. "Relax, son, the Admiral's just having a laugh. And we can use 'em wherever we find 'em, these days."

"I see, sir."

Krishmahnta resolved to put Wethermere at ease with a smile, and the lieutenant brightened up nicely in response. "So, Mr. Wethermere. I'll have a reply for Admiral Yoshikuni in about five minutes. What are your impressions of the action in Beaumont? Is there anything *not* in the pouch that's worth mentioning?"

"Just this, sir. The rank and file don't understand why Admiral Yoshikuni has split the task force and bracketed Beaumont. Granted, the planet warrants defense, but by moving inside the Desai limit—"

"—she gives up her primary mobility advantage over the Baldies, is that it?"

"Something like that, although it seems that at least half of the Baldy ships now have Desai drives."

"That many? Well, it was sure to come sooner or later." She turned to Watanabe. "This is probably the last time we'll have any drive advantage at all."

"Could be. So we'd better watch ourselves here in Raiden. After we decimated the last Baldy fleet, they'd have had to rebuild it with new ships. And that means new technology."

Krishmahnta nodded, turned back to Wethermere, tried to keep the assessing glint out of her eye. "What about you, Lieutenant? Do you have a guess why Admiral Yoshikuni has pulled back within the Desai limit?"

Wethermere shot a quick glance at the plot. "Well, sir, it extends the engagement."

Captain Watanabe raised an eyebrow. "Really? How?"

"Well, if the engagement stayed out beyond the Desai limit, it would go along at 0.5 c, since large ships with Desai drives double their speeds out there."

"Yes, and barely half the enemy fleet would be able to keep up."

"Well, yes, sir, but the fighting would still collect around the other warp point in a day, maybe two. But this way, if the Baldies come inside the Desai limit and, furthermore, get in close to planets, flank speeds drop to 0.2 or 0.25 c, and fighters become more useful again. All factors taken together, that slows down the resolution of the engagement."

"And where's the tactical advantage in that, Lieutenant?"

"It's a strategic advantage, sir. Slowing them down out here is key to developing our defenses farther on down the line. Out here, we're forced to improvise quite a bit—not enough forts, older hulls, reserve crews, depleted stocks of mines. The way I figure it, our most urgent mission is to delay the Baldies long enough so that our rear area can get enough matériel cranked out and sent up to places with optimally defensible choke points. Like the single warp point at Achilles. Like you and the admiral were discussing earlier."

"You make us sound very expendable, Lieutenant." Krishmahnta allowed herself a faint smile. "Tell me, is your Navy insurance paid up?"

"Sorry if I wasn't clear, sir, but I don't think we're expendable at all. In fact, I suspect the need to preserve every possible unit is the other reason for Admiral Yoshikuni's leisurely pace."

"How do you mean?"

"Admiral, if I read the tea leaves correctly, you are planning to disengage our two fleets from two different enemy forces in two widely separated salients, with the ultimate objective of recombining those two fleets to make a fast, orderly withdrawal back through Suwa to Achilles. Well, sir, if you're to have any chance of getting all your warbirds back to that safe roost, you're going to need all the time and space you can get."

Watanabe tried to scowl dismissively: he was a poor actor. "Lieutenant, do you mind telling us which war college were you were teaching at before you drew courier duty for Admiral Yoshikuni?"

"Uh . . . my courier duty, well, that kind of just . . . happened, sir."

Krishmahnta raised an eyebrow. "Would you care to explain that, Lieutenant?"

"Yes, sir. I was dispatched from the Pan-Sentient Union naval base at Alpha Centauri to take up multi-locus liaison duties among the different militaries of the Rim."

Watanabe closed his eyes. "You're not at HQ anymore, Lieutenant. In English, please."

"Yes, sir, Captain. I was sent out here to help the naval units of different species set up realistic cross-training programs, including field-training in mixed units."

Krishmahnta leaned her chin on her knuckles. "Why

out here? I thought those multispeciate initiatives were mostly the province of the Home Worlds." *And their pie-in-the-sky "all races can work as one" rhetoric. "All races equal?" Yes, absolutely. "All work as one?" Nonsense. It's the triumph of political idealism over irreconcilable physical differences.*

"Yes, sir," Wethermere was answering, "the PSU is certainly the home of multispeciate initiatives. But the real need for them is out here. Against the Tangri."

Captain Watanabe leaned back. "Of course. Everybody's favorite centauroid carnivore pirates."

Wethermere nodded. "Tangri space borders on most of the major interstellar polities, so they are a common problem. But there's been no effort to really arrive at a common solution. Each group—Republic, Federation, Union, Orion, Ophiuchi, Gorm, others—responds in its own space, and in its own fashion. But there's been no coordinated effort or overarching strategy."

"And now there is one?"

"No, sir—not yet."

Krishmahnta heard the beat of hesitation. "Not yet, Lieutenant? Were you expecting to receive a conops folder from Earth just before the Baldies showed up?"

"Er . . . no, sir. I was expecting to start a dialogue with the different leaders who might be interested in formulating one."

Krishmahnta thought she heard an almost evasive tone. "So, you were sent out here with nothing more than a mandate to 'talk' to interested parties about setting up joint training programs. Are you aware that this objective has met with dismal failure during each of its five—no, six—prior attempts? Did someone send you out here as a practical joke, Lieutenant?"

This was the moment where an average lieutenant would possibly have frozen, or shuddered, or stammered, or broken out in a sweat, or evinced some colorful combination of all the preceding. But Wethermere simply looked directly at Krishmahnta and replied, "My mission—a practical joke? Well, yes, sir, sometimes I wonder about that myself."

He doesn't get rattled too easily, Erica thought. And unbidden, she heard her *paradada*'s thickly accented drone: "*You will know, child, when you look into the eyes of an Old Soul.*" And so she did. Wethermere looked back at her—respectful, unassuming—but strangely composed and at home in himself.

Krishmahnta smiled sagely. "Unless you were going to sprout some admiral's shoulder boards upon undertaking those initiatives, Mr. Wethermere, I predict you'd have spent a couple of years chasing your own tail with nothing to show for it. Tell me, who sent you on this assignment?"

"Well, my orders were cut by CINCTER—"

"No, Lieutenant. Who—what *person*—gave you your mission?"

"Erm . . . retired admiral Sanders, sir."

Maybe not a fool's errand after all, thought Krishmahnta as she entertained the hope that Watanabe would shut his hanging jaw sometime within the next minute. "*The* Admiral Sanders? Admiral *Kevin* Sanders? Who was involved in the Bug War? Ultimately ran Naval—and then Federation—Intelligence?" *And God knows what else*. The antediluvian spymaster was rumored to have his sprightly fingers in almost everything.

"Yes, sir. That Admiral Sanders."

And then Krishmahnta looked at Wethermere's blue eyes again and knew. "You're a relative of his, aren't you?"

And the next thing that Wethermere did won Krishmahnta over so completely that it later annoyed her. Ossian Wethermere blushed bright red. "Uh, yes, ma'am—sir. He's a relative. A distant relative."

"How distant?"

Wethermere had to think. "I believe the correct term is a first cousin thrice removed."

Watanabe blinked. "Damn. I don't even know what that means."

Wethermere folded his hands contemplatively. "Well, sir, as I understand it—"

Krishmahnta stood. "That will do nicely, Lieutenant. And thank you for bringing the report. By the way, you're not in PSUN uniform. Have you deserted the Union?" A ready and winning smile flashed in good-natured response to her jest. *If he wasn't so young, I just might—*

"No, sir. I just made it off Bellerophon in time—but my gear didn't. When I reported for duty, they pulled this from spares."

"It suits you, Lieutenant. Dismissed."

Wethermere snapped a salute, smiled, was gone.

Krishmahnta looked at Watanabe—who was already staring at her. "Look what I found in *my* soup," he said, rolling his eyes after the departed lieutenant.

She shook her head. "Just when you think a day can't get any stranger. . . . Well, we've got business to get to—but 'Nab?"

"Yes, sir?"

"Get me a dossier on Mr. Wethermere. Put the request—coded—in the packet back to Miharu. If anyone's got a file on him, it will be her."

"Yes, sir. What next?"

"Send word to Pinnace Group 17. I need them to depart along with the courier he came in on."

"All five pinnaces, sir? Are they just confirming transit of the courier, or—"

"I need confirmation of each step of our signal relay, Yoshi—and separate couriers to Suwa and Achilles to relay them copies of the signal I'm sending to Miharu."

"And what are the couriers transmitting, sir?"

"That we are executing contingency Sierra-Charlie, Captain."

Watanabe released a long, low whistle. "Fast withdrawal from Beaumont? Any operational parameters?"

Krishmahnta nodded to her chief of staff and nominal captain of the *Gallipoli*. "Yoshikuni is to hold eighteen hours from this mark, then an all-haste withdrawal. No taffrails to the enemy, but no dawdling, either. And 'Nab, I need those pinnace jockeys to fly like their lives depend on it—because theirs just might, and ours certainly will. I need proof of message receipt at each system, or our closely timed double withdrawal could turn into a train wreck, with Baldy battlewagons ready to take advantage. So I need to know *exactly* when my order gets through to each system. And if there is *any* failure along the commo chain to Admiral Yoshikuni in Beaumont, I am to be informed immediately. Make it clear to the pinnace crews—this is the most important mission of their careers, and our eyes are upon them."

"Yes, sir. Orders for our fleet, Admiral?"

Krishmahnta shook her head. "No, nothing yet. But in the event of a general attack, COs do not have discretionary release to employ their external ordnance. They keep what's in their racks until they receive a Fleet signal indicating otherwise. Is that clear?"

"Crystal, sir."

"Lastly, send the word that, when it is determined that the enemy from Jason is committed and attacking us in force, we are likely to employ plan Zulu-X-Ray, and the ships designated for that action should be prepared to respond at once."

Yoshi Watanabe stared. "Which plan did you say?"

Krishmahnta could not look him in the eye. "Plan Zulu-X-Ray. We didn't discuss it much."

Watanabe had already found it on his data tablet. He looked up, expressionless. "This is pretty risky. Could be a death sentence."

"For a lot more of them than us, *if* we play it right."

"That's a mighty big if, Admiral."

"It always is, in combat, 'Nab. Send the word to the cruisers first. They should be moving out to a flanking position before the Baldies get here. No reason to—"

The alert klaxon howled. The automated call to battle stations began droning under it.

Krishmahnta was on the bridge by the third peal of the klaxon. She looked down quickly into the holotank. And swallowed the sudden rush of responding bile with utter aplomb: "Here they come again."

In the holotank, red motes swarmed out of the purple hole like angry hornets. And although some were already beginning to flash amber—indicating potentially disabling damage from the combined firepower of the human monitors and supermonitors—the hornets kept coming, swarming, climbing over each other in their mad, burning desire to kill.

To kill Erica Krishmahnta's fleet.

2

Theirs Not to Reason Why

Theirs not to reason why
Theirs but to do and die
—Tennyson

Arduan SDH Shem'pter'ai, *First Fleet of the* Anaht'doh Kainat, *Beaumont System*

Narrok looked over at Urkhot, who was absorbed, *sel-narm* infolded, as he watched the fleets grind against each other. In the bridge's holopod, the titanic struggle appeared to be waged by scintillant gnats that swarmed, tangled, and expired at a very leisurely pace. Theirs was a slow-motion ballet of death—which represented massive ships hurtling through space at twenty percent of the speed of light, intermittently being incinerated or shattered by the scaled-down supernovae of antimatter warheads. At close ranges, the behemoths—here represented as actinic mayflies—actually sliced into each other with matter-annihilating force beams, knife-fighting to the death across light-seconds of open space.

Or, rather, *mostly* open space. The human admiral had kept its second line out of the battle, and wisely so: those rearmost enemy ships were beyond the range of most of Narrok's weapons but were still able to fire long-reaching missiles of great destructive power—HBMs—even while being resupplied by tenders. Narrok had engaged these distant menaces as best he could, but his missiles were of the shorter-ranged CBM and SBM varieties. These smaller missiles launched quickly and were wonderful at overwhelming the humans' defensive fire: the burning, blackened shells of three of their dreadnoughts and two of their monitors were compelling evidence of that capability. But Narrok did not have enough HBMs to overcome the massive and extraordinarily well-coordinated defensive fire of the farther human ships.

The victims of the enemy's steady HBM barrages—fifteen of Narrok's older generation of SDs, and four of his newer ones with the Desai drive—were dull, lifeless *vrel*-colored cinders, motionless in the holopod and dropping rapidly behind the van of his fleet.

"Admiral Narrok," sent his sensor second.

"Yes?"

"We have detected multiple signatures from the Suwa warp point, sir."

Urkhot returned from his absorption in the unfolding battle. "Does this mean they are retreating? At last?"

"No, *Holodah'kri*. I believe the warp activity indicates that the two human fleets are regularly exchanging information by couriers. Which means they have seen through my ruse, as I thought. They are coordinating their responses to our two separate attacks—here and in the Raiden system."

"What will they do?"

(Humor, rue.) "If I knew that, esteemed Urkhot, I would be Illudor's twin. But I may conjecture. Ultimately, they will withdraw. Had they enough force to hold the warp point, they would have done so from the outset."

"So, let us smash them in their weakness and move straight on to Suwa as you suggest."

"I do suggest that, *Holodah'kri*. I also suggest that we make haste slowly. Just because they have insufficient force to defend the warp point does not mean that they have insufficient force to inflict major damage on us here."

"Well, if so, why haven't they used it? And why have they not stayed in the swifter reaches of space beyond this . . . this Desai limit."

"That is what I am pondering, *Holodah'kri*. It may be that, by engaging us within the limit, they wish to keep our newest, fastest ships slowed to half of their maximum speed. This will work to buy more time for their comrades to withdraw from Raiden. Or there may be a trap hidden in the pattern of their current deployment. I am particularly troubled that they have not only put all their forces inside the Desai limit, but have now retreated so far back into it that they are near both the planet and the other side of the limit."

"Is this world—Beaumont—a great military power?"

"No. It has a small population and minimal industry. Our scans confirm this human data as correct. But worlds can be dangerous in other ways."

"How do you mean?"

"The gravitic forces near a planet can further degrade the efficiency of reactionless drives, particularly large ones."

"This is to our advantage. At last we will be able to send forth our flocks of fighters and overwhelm them."

"So it would seem—and this is precisely why I am not quick to take that action."

"What? Why?"

"Because if we can see the tactical implications of the enemy position, the *griarfeksh* commander can certainly see it, too. My question becomes: Given the ground it has chosen, what plans is the *griarfeksh* commander trying to hatch that I do not see?"

Urkhot's lesser tentacle tips switched fitfully. (Impatience.) "Admiral, even in war, things often are simply as they seem. You have said it yourself: the enemy wishes to extend this engagement. Perhaps, in order to do so, they have had to put themselves in a position where they are more vulnerable to our fighters—which they have yet to see us employ in numbers. This could be their oversight . . . or simply the choice they made between two imperfect alternatives."

(Consensus.) "This could, of course, be exactly what we are witnessing, *Holodah'kri*. But so far, caution has—"

"—has made you suspect in the eyes of the Council," interrupted Urkhot with a pulse of (remonstrance). "Decisive action *now* might do much to restore Torhok's opinion of you."

And there it was—a direct threat, indicating how Urkhot's report might influence Narrok's future command of the Fleet. But if Narrok was going to bow to that influence, Urkhot would need to become more insistent—and direct—in his urgings: much more direct.

"*Holodah'kri*, are you saying that you convey Torhok's direct and explicit wishes in this matter?"

Urkhot's *selnarm* retracted for a moment, then flexed forth again with (hauteur): "I know his mind, and his opinions, well enough, Admiral. And it would be his opinion—"

"To attack? Regardless of the uncertainties?"

"Of course to attack! You have assessed the risks

and the advantages as much as you may. Further delay reveals only a lack of resolve, perhaps even an insufficient ardor to ensure the safety and future of our race."

"So Torhok would wish me to attack at this moment?"

"Yes, of course. Have I not made this plain enough?"

(Compliance, calm.) "Plain enough, *Holodah'kri*," affirmed Narrok, who, with a *selnarmic* flick, instructed the computer to make ten recordings of their exchange, make them code-access only, and hide three of them as distributed data-packets throughout the system's active memory, reassemblable only if summoned together by a twenty-digit cipher of his own creation. Then he turned back to his bridge personnel. "Ops Prime."

"Admiral?"

"Summon Fleet Second Mretlak back to the bridge. Fleet orders: target these enemy vessels"—he encircled four older monitors with a quick looping of a lesser tentacle—"with all our fire, including full launch of external ordnance commencing in fifteen seconds. Flight Prime?"

"Sir?"

"Eighty percent of fighters prepare for rapid launch, steady sequence. Mission profile *Tofret-ulz*."

Urkhot wondered. "You will strike at their flank? Not their center, which you will weaken by destroying those four targets?"

"*Tofret-ulz* is a two-pronged attack, *Holodah'kri*. An initial attack to the center, a far-flung sweep by a third of the squadrons to the right—in an attempt to catch their larger ships maneuvering inward to reinforce the center—"

"—and thereby expose their rear blind spots to the approaching fighters."

"That is the theory behind this ploy."

"And are there counters to your ploy?"

(Patience.) "There are always counters, *Holodah'kri*."

RFNS Jellicoe, *Task Force One, Further Rim Fleet, Beaumont System*

"Admiral Yoshikuni, signal from Admiral Krishmahnta."

About damned time. "Give me the short version, Ops."

"She sends 'contingency Sierra-Charlie,' sir."

Miharu Yoshikuni smiled crookedly, and watched the Baldies finally come forward to engage her at close range, right on the heels of a devastating missile barrage. "Well, we'll oblige as soon as we can, but we're in the thick of it now. Pity that signal didn't get here thirty minutes ago."

"Admiral, the *Dawntreader*—she's . . ."

Yoshikuni saw a green delta at the leading edge of her forward screen flicker into amber. "I see it, Tactical. Will she be able to—?"

The amber arrowhead snapped into an inverted gold arch, arms pinched close at the bottom.

"*Dawntreader* is Code Omega, Admiral. Lost with all hands."

Okay, she'd lost two more monitors and two SDs—three, counting *Dawntreader*: that ought to be enough blood for the damn Baldies to believe she was ready to run. "Ops, prepare to send Fleet orders."

"Yes, sir."

"Lead screen fall back, making best speed through our second screen. Lead screen is to reform as the new rear screen, thirty-five light-seconds back, intercept pattern Papa Romeo. Tenders are to come forward to reequip them if there is sufficient range from threat forces. The former second screen is now on point. Hold current formation, but re-center five degrees to trailing of Beaumont. Continue that heading until further orders."

Ops looked up. "Admiral, at that rate our whole screen will be falling behind and to the trailing side of Beaumont."

"I am aware of that, Ops."

"Very good, Admiral."

In the holotank, the two screens of Miharu Yoshikuni's fleet were already showing the first signs of moving through this evolution: the lead screen was breaking apart, its constituent bits picking up speed as they shot rearward through gaps in the second screen, which was now drifting slightly behind Beaumont and its moons. The enemy swarm of red closed in, now equidistant from Yoshikuni's new lead units and the planet.

Yoshikuni shook her head as an orderly brought her sixth cup of tea, and watched the enemy motes track over with the new green screen that faced them. The far edge of the red wave just failed to graze the near side of Beaumont.

Yoshikuni smiled for the first time in an hour. "Tactical, analysis of their line of sight."

"To where, Admi—?"

"You know where."

The Tactical officer cleared this throat; the question had been formally correct, but so specious that it could only have come from a jg. "Enemy units no longer have visual contact with the far side of Beaumont, sir. Or its moons."

"Comm, get me Beaumont Brigade Command."

"Yes, sir. Oh, and Admiral?"

"Yes?"

"Our returning DD courier—RFNS *Bucky Sherman*—has a pouch to convey, sir."

Yoshikuni nodded: probably coded tidbits from Erica, including some special parameters for just how she needed contingency Sierra-Charlie to evolve. "Bring their courier on board, and tell the master of that mouse, Lieutenant Zama—er, Lieutenant Zoma—"

"Lieutenant *Zuniga*, sir."

"Yes—Zuniga. Tell her to stay in our shadow. One good missile hit and she's—"

"Code Omega on the *Yellow Sea*, sir."

Another SD lost. Damn. This was getting expensive. She checked the plot. Almost time, and where the hell was—?

"Beaumont Brigade Command online, sir. Commo's scratchy, though."

Yoshikuni toggled the comm line into her headset. "Beaumont, this is Admiral Miharu Yoshikuni of the Further Rim Fleet, Task Force One. Patch me through to Nathan McCullough, Senior Brigadier."

"On the line and in the flesh," came the bluff reply. "I've been coordinating with your Tactical staff, Admiral. My compliments on them. Commendations, too, if I'd the time."

"Noted and appreciated, Brigadier McCullough. Are your people ready?"

"Aye, Admiral. The Island Brigades are on full alert, although I've little sense what they might do."

Me, either, but—"And the PD Brigade?"

"Planetary Defense Brigade is tubes open, birds hot, Admiral."

She paused. The next answer would tell her if her gamble was going to pan out or not. "And Flight?"

"The Flight Brigade—and its outsystem auxiliaries—is in full readiness. We were a wee bit shy on drop tanks, but we've cannibalized some shuttle emergency fuel pods to function as—"

"Brigadier, you have all our thanks. I've got to sign off, and will hand you back to my Tactical officer. Just assure me of this: when we call for you . . ."

"We'll be there before the echo fades, Admiral. My word as a McCullough."

She exhaled. "Thank you again, Brigadier." She toggled the circuit over to Tactics and leaned back. *Well, maybe this might work, after all.* She luxuriated in that sense of well-being for four seconds, before she heard—

"Admiral, the Baldies are launching fighters. Lots of 'em."

"Give me a count—" she started to order, but then fell silent.

Down in the tacplot, incandescent candy-red pinpricks were bleeding out toward the center of her weakening screen like a deathly, spreading rash.

Arduan SDH Shem'pter'ai, *First Fleet of the* Anaht'doh Kainat, *Beaumont System*

(Exultation, fanatic glee.) "Excellent! Did I not tell you? Action, Narrok, action! This is what shall save the Children of Illudor!"

(Gratification.) But beneath his *selnarm*, Narrok felt anxiety. Yes, they were finally punishing the human fleet; its slower monitors were dying, at last. His immense volleys of missiles had weakened them, shattered at least one of their damnably efficient fire-coordinating datalinks. His many fighters had quickly rushed into that gap in the hyperactive thickets of defensive missiles and force beams. Even now, his small craft were doing executioner's work.

But the shape of his forces troubled him. His fighters had punched a deep bulge into the humans' lead screen. His van of capital ships had tucked in after them, compacting into a dense cone as the more peripheral units had asked—and been given—permission to close range expeditiously with the weakened enemy units. Yes, he had allowed an evolution which brought all his firepower to bear on this weakening spot in the human defenses—

—but the cost had been a contraction of his forces and a loss of responsiveness and theater awareness. He hadn't been comfortable pulling so far away from the planet, behind which he could now no longer see. He had sent some shuttles there, to keep watch, but these had been blasted by a veritable sleetstorm of the planet's short-range defense missiles. Was that part of the enemy's plan, to deny him visibility of the far side of the planet, or just more of the overeager planetary-defense activity mounted by every human world they had conquered so far?

Urkhot actually grasped his shoulder, the main, or clasping, tentacles digging in a bit harder than seemed necessary. "Narrok, will you not celebrate the obvious? Your strategy has succeeded. See how the first enemy screen fell back, and now the second is buckling? And now their losses become as great as ours."

(Calm, objectivity.) "Has it succeeded, Urkhot? The human commander is withdrawing, yes. But too slowly. This is no rout. See how it has reformed its first defensive line behind what had been its second. And as the *griarfeksh* admiral does so, its main body of capital ships comes closer to the other side of the Desai limit, as we grow more distant from any of that disk's edges."

"You are as sour as a *pt'ulul* rind, Narrok. The *gri-arfeksh* commander is falling back. Retreat is retreat, my . . . colleague."

(Mild accord.) "Yes, they are falling back. But in order, and upon the warp point to Suwa—as would I."

(Distaste. Resentment.) Urkhot withdrew his brief wash of fellow feeling. (Petulance) took its place. "'Suwa?' You should not use human names if you can help it, Admiral."

"With respect, *Holodah'kri*, we have only their charts to show us what lies in not just this system, but this whole region of space. In the rush of our advances, we have not had time to devise our own names for stars and planets before distributing navigation charts and accompanying data. This encourages the unfortunate habit of adopting the relevant human labels."

"It is a habit which you all must endeavor to break."

(Soothing agreement.) "It is the first, most crucial business we must attend to, after this combat is resolved."

Urkhot was perhaps not entirely mollified, but at least he was silent. *Would that he were silent someplace other than my bridge.*

Urkhot abandoned his short-lived reticence and pointed into the holopod. "You should push the *gri-arfeksh* harder, Admiral. Push until they break."

RFNS Jellicoe, *Task Force One, Further Rim Fleet, Beaumont System*

"They're going to break us if we don't give up a few more light-seconds, Admiral."

Yoshikuni nodded, studied her data tablet: the external

missile racks of her rearmost screen were eighty-seven percent reloaded. Not ready yet. She checked the relative positions of Beaumont and the two fleets: the bulk of the red swarm was about to move past the planet on the side that was closest to her lead screen. Beaumont would be behind the bulk of the Baldy fleet in the next five, maybe six minutes. She ran the numbers and then called, "Comm."

"Sir?"

"Captain Ludovico on secure channel. Now."

"Yes, sir . . . Captain Ludovico online, sir."

"Patch it to my Line One."

"Yes, Admiral."

Her earplug buzzed a bit, then: "Admiral, is this a social call?"

Damn it, don't get personal now, Roberto. Aloud: "Unfortunately not, Captain. New orders for your carriers."

"Ready."

You think I'm about to ask for the kind of attack you flyboys live for, don't you—particularly with all their fighters swarming around. But we can deal with them . . . "Captain, you are to take *Torrent* and *Buran* on a long, flanking run."

"How long, Admiral?" Ludovico's voice was, thankfully, all business now.

"As far as you can go, Captain. You're to turn hard out of the line, slipping behind Beaumont and—without escort—make for the nearest edge of the Desai limit. Once there, make best speed—plus ten percent—for the warp point back to Charlotte."

"Back to—? Sir, is this some kind of—?"

"I don't have time to joke today, Captain. Yes, I'm sending you right back through the hole they came in.

Our sensors show it's unpatrolled on this side—typical Baldy operations. They figure anything that goes back the way they came will get chewed up on the other side."

"I think they figure right, sir. If we pop out of the warp point in Charlotte, then the only uncertainty is who wins the race to get us first—their laser mines or SDs."

"Captain, I don't think they've had the time—or inclination—to mine the far side. In the course of normal reconnaissance, we got one RD back three days ago. It showed the other six RDs we sent getting torn up by Baldy fighters and shipside batteries—but no static defenses. So you just might get through."

"Well, I guess we're going to find out. And I guess you won't know."

Yoshikuni grinned, doing her best to keep the exchange from getting both personal and poignant. She'd had a surreptitious—would one call it a fling?—with Roberto Ludovico when she was first posted out beyond Bellerophon. She certainly didn't need any hint of that old dalliance worming its way into this conversation—or her resolve—at this moment.

"If you make it through—*when* you make it through—don't try to get back to us. Don't even try to send a report. You might make it to Charlotte, but you won't make it back here again. They'll be right on your tail."

"So, once in Charlotte—what?"

"Steer straight for the Demeter warp point and keep on going. Don't let up until you are sure you've shaken all pursuit. And then, as the Baldies start expanding into where you've come to rest, you hit their supply convoys. No stand-up fights, though. Targets of opportunity, soft ones. When they try hunting you down, you'll probably need to fall back, all the way up the arm to Treadway, eventually. Along the way, link up with the little picket ships we've left out there. On their own, they're not going to do much good, but in conjunction with you—"

Roberto let his voice become the basso croon she had always loved; but right now, she hated hated hated it. "Even so, we're not liable to hurt them much."

"Just making them escort every single convoy will draw off many times the weight of your hulls. That means a corresponding reduction in their frontline strength. Just don't get caught, Captain. Stay light on your feet, and when in doubt, run like hell."

"And when they own all the warp points and I'm out of running room?"

"You know the drill. Find the most junk-strewn, planet-choked, belt-packed system you can and play hide-and-seek in the outer system. You've got the Desai drive. Their rear-echelon security units probably won't have it—meaning that you can strike anything a few light-minutes inside the Desai limit and then get back out to where you can kick in the Desai drive again. And live to fight another day."

"A boring life, playing hide-and-seek at the edge of a system, lying doggo in an Oort cloud, and getting water from ice chunks."

"Poor you. I'll send you postcards from the all-too-radiant front lines. Listen—no time for fond farewells. Just stay alive, okay, Roberto?"

"As per your orders. How can I refuse?"

"That's right, mister—follow my orders. Now Godspeed and on your way."

Arduan SDH Shem'pter'ai, *First Fleet of the* Anaht'doh Kainat, *Beaumont System*

Narrok nodded as two of the smaller human ship icons, which had been hovering between their two screens, broke quickly for the edge of the Desai limit: they trailed a thin screen of fighters as they went.

Urkhot started. (Confusion.) "What are they doing? What can those two ships possibly do?"

"Nothing to our fleet here. But unless I am mistaken, they are heading back for the warp point we came through. To Charlotte."

"Are they mad? If they wish suicide, why not simply rush into our beams?"

Narrok sent (mild rue) and explained, "It is not suicide, *Holodah'kri*—since we left nothing back at the warp point to prevent them from using it."

"Nothing at the warp point? What titanic incompetence is this, Admiral?"

"I find it interesting that you consider Senior Admiral Torhok's express operational instructions to be an example of 'titanic incompetence.' "

"What? What do you mean?"

"I have long wanted to secure all our warp points, from both sides, with both active and static defenses. Senior Admiral Torhok refused on the grounds that all our assets and energies must stay on the attack. 'All claws up front' were his words, I believe."

Urkhot struggled to put himself safely in alignment with Torhok's operational doctrine. "Well—yes, of course, this is prudent. For certainly, our forces back in Charlotte will make quick work of these craft."

"Will they? Note these craft, *Holodah'kri*. They are what the *griarfeksh* label CVLs—light carriers."

"Weak craft—which carry weaker gnats to which our hulls are all but immune."

"Our larger hulls, yes. But consider—carriers, particularly light carriers such as these, are amongst the fastest and most maneuverable of all the *griarfeksh* hulls. I predict that just before they reach the Desai limit, the carriers will reclaim their fighters and then engage their Desai drives. They will arrive swiftly at the warp point—more swiftly than one of our courier drones, even if we sent it now. And once through the warp point in Charlotte, they will again have the immediate advantage of their Desai drive. What is waiting for them there? A few fighters, two transports, and an SD finishing repairs—none of which have Desai drives. The *griarfeksh* will be through the warp point and out of range by the time our forces in Charlotte know to respond."

Urkhot's torso had faintly shifted from its usual iridescent gold to a rather pasty yellow. "But once there, what could these . . . light carriers . . . hope to do against us?"

"Their options are many, *Holodah'kri*. They could attempt to hunt down our supply ships and auxiliaries in that system. They could exit through the Demeter warp point to warn and rally the systems farther along that arm. Or they could hide in the Charlotte system itself and lurk, waiting to strike at small, unsuspecting craft."

"Then you must interdict them. Now."

(Regret.) "To do so, I would have to dispatch several of our heavy superdreadnoughts—they are the only craft fast enough to catch them."

(Impatience.) "And is doing this a problem for our great fleet?"

"Only insofar as it weakens our efforts to secure a prompt victory here, *Holodah'kri*. The SDHs are our best ships, the ones that can keep up with the humans' capital ships and match their firepower. With fewer SDHs here, I cannot press the *griarfeksh* quite so hard. If I cannot press them so hard, they have more time for an orderly, fighting withdrawal through the warp point into Suwa."

Urkhot's grinders rasped against each other. (Indecision.) "I must remain in contact with Torhok, and if the humans cut off our access to Charlotte, and perhaps even Andromeda, then the path of communication back to the Council at New Ardu is severed."

"Yes. Although it would be quite easy to restore it, once we have driven off these—"

(Fear) then (resolution, relief). "My reports and—through me—the wisdom of Illudor must remain accessible to Torhok. At all times."

And Narrok wondered, easing back from his *selnarm* link, *What has happened to my fellow Destoshaz who once held themselves so proudly self-reliant? It almost sounds as though Urkhot needs to know he has an unobstructed means of access to his Supreme Leader. It is as though we are emulating the Pre-Enlightenment warrior cults of—*

"Well?" Urkhot had emitted the *selnarmic* equivalent of a nervous shout. "Have you dispatched the pursuit craft?"

"I was merely considering which SDHs to pull back from the line, *Holodah'kri*. I am issuing the orders now."

And as he issued the orders, Narrok also did the political math of how Urkhot's interference in fleet operations would play in the Council of Twenty. With the Fleet reduced in its ability to exert offensive pressure in Beaumont, the humans would probably extricate more of their ships. A pity, but this was only a marginal setback: the main objective—driving the humans back from Raiden and Beaumont—seemed well under way. The most desirable version of that outcome—the one in which the besieged human commander in Raiden would have obligingly drawn forces from, and thus weakened, the defenders in Beaumont—had not been realized. Well, Narrok had not held much hope for the success of that ruse, anyway. Both human commanders would have had to have been at least marginally stupid to fall for such an obvious trick, and he had seen very few human commanders that could be fairly labeled as "stupid."

On the other hand, complying with Urkhot's request to keep the pathway back to Bellerophon clear at all times would be a useful bargaining chip in Narrok's future dealings with the Council of Twenty. Torhok and his True Destoshaz militants would be sure to find fault with Narrok's handling of the Beaumont assault: nothing ever happened quickly enough for the Senior Admiral and his supporters. However, this delay—and more—could now be ascribed to Urkhot's demand that capital ships be diverted from combat operations to run down the two human carriers. If Torhok was critical that the Battle of Beaumont had been conducted in too slow and cautious a manner, Urkhot's neuroses could now be implicated in that outcome. Meaning Torhok could not seek to undermine Narrok's position without also undermining that of his ally, Urkhot.

The *Holodah'kri's selnarm* tugged at Narrok's. "Will the SDHs catch the carriers?"

Narrok looked at the tactical plot. "Possibly." He felt Urkhot's rising panic. "Probably." The panic subsided. Narrok sent (reassurance), turned away, glanced covertly at the unpromising intercept vectors and concealed his growing (contempt).

RFNS Jellicoe, *Task Force One, Further Rim Fleet, Beaumont System*

"Admiral, they've sent three SDH hounds after our two CVL foxes."

Yoshikuni nodded and glanced at the plot. Roberto might even make it—by the skin of his teeth. "Ops."

"Yes, Admiral?"

"How are our datanets?"

"Took some repatching after we lost the *Jena*, sir, but we've rerouted and they are running strong."

"Damage?"

"We're okay—but we won't be in another thirty minutes."

"The Baldy fighters?"

"I'd say they've lost about half, and they don't seem to have any external ordnance left, just lasers. Not much good against us."

The hatchway to the secondary bridge access tube dilated: a youthful man with a worn black pouch entered. She waved off his salute. "Are you Lieutenant Wethermere, from the *Bucky Sherman*?"

"Yes, sir."

"Take a seat—and start your own recording of the tacplot. This could get interesting."

"Yes, sir."

Yoshikuni stood. "Fleet signal. Front and rear screens, maintain heading and slow advance. Two light-seconds per minute, average rate."

"It's going to get real close, sir."

"It's going to get closer still. Rear screen, ready CBMs to fire in sprint mode—and prepare to flush racks."

"Flush racks, Admir—?"

"Tactics, do you need your hearing checked?"

"Rear screen ready to flush racks, aye, Admiral."

"Now, Comm—put me through to Brigadier McCullough on Beaumont."

"He's already standing by, sir."

Yoshikuni raised her voice so the pickups would catch it. "Brigadier McCullough, is the Flight Brigade ready?"

"Yes, ma'am."

"Then launch all. Stick close in the planet's sensor shadow until you're ready."

"Just as we discussed it, Admiral. Spaceside ETA, seventeen minutes."

"We'll keep them busy until then. And Brigadier—"

"Yes, Admiral?"

"Don't be late."

Arduan SDH Shem'pter'ai, *First Fleet of the* Anaht'doh Kainat, *Beaumont System*

Urkhot was delighted; Narrok was unsettled; Fleet Second Metrak was openly fidgeting.

Urkhot's *selnarm* reeked of (exultation, bloodlust). "At last, they maneuver to engage us. Now our victory is finally at hand."

This time, Narrok did not try to conceal (wariness, misgiving). "Yes—they engage us. And they should not. They have no reason to. Indeed, they have every reason not to."

(Annoyance.) "What do you mean, Admiral?"

Narrok swept a lesser tentacle through the shimmering

silver-white circle that marked the Desai limit: the part of this arc that was closest to the Suwa warp point was also close behind the two human screens. But those screens were now advancing toward the Arduans like a pair of slightly separated but in-line disks. "Look at how close the *griarfeksh* were—and still are—to the Desai limit. They could run from us, and we might not catch them at all. Since they cannot hold this system, such a retreat would be the logical evolution of their battle plan."

"So? Perhaps they reason that they must damage us as much as they can before attempting to flee."

"Perhaps—but with our current advantage in numbers, they cannot hope to destroy many more of our ships than we can of theirs. And that is a much poorer ship-exchange ratio than they have been willing to accept to date. But this is what worries me the most." Narrok moved his cluster over, and then extended all his tentacles into, the compacted mass of Arduan ship icons burgeoning just beyond the holo-image of Beaumont.

(Incredulousness, facetiousness.) "You are worried by our immense advantage in warships?"

"No, I am worried about what the enemy's sudden advance upon us has caused. Yes, more of our ships are in range, but at the expense of our keeping a good formation. First, we reduced the diameter of our screen, which brought more of our hulls into range. Now we are turning into a densely packed mass. With our front slowed by direct engagement with the *griarfeksh*, the rearward units are catching up—but pushing into the very same volume of space."

"Surely you cannot be worried about collisions. You know far better than I that each of those ships is separated by at least fifty thousand kilometers."

"True. I have no fear of collisions. I fear a loss of tactical mobility and data-net optimization."

(Annoyance, incomprehension.) "You fear what?"

"*Holodah'kri*, space is indeed vast—but relative angles and headings still matter and may be compromised when units are too close to deploy a sufficiently wide field of fire. Our ships are too tightly packed here. Their defensive fire systems and their ability to maneuver would be severely limited if they were to be attacked by—"

(Impatience, fury.) "—by what?" seethed Urkhot. "Where are these new, phantom threats that can appear from nowhere and take advantage of this momentary—"

Metlak emitted (URGENCY URGENCY URGENCY). "Admiral!"

(Calm.) "Yes, Fleet Second?"

"Sir, from the planet—fighters!"

"Of course. In fact, they are overdue. We have seen this at every human planet we have approached. How many fighters, Second? A dozen, two dozen?"

"Not dozens, Admiral. Hundreds!"

The phantom threat had appeared. And, having used Beaumont to cover its approach, Nathan McCullough's Flight Brigade had appeared directly on Narrok's rear flank, and at a range of less than fifteen light-seconds.

RFNS Jellicoe, *Task Force One, Further Rim Fleet, Beaumont System*

Ossian Wethermere was hardly conscious that he had stood up and almost failed to notice the strange shuddering quake that marked his first discernible moment in combat: a near miss by a Baldy missile.

"Where did all those fighters come from?" He failed

to add "sir," because his query was not directed at any one individual: it was a general voicing of astonishment.

Yoshikuni cut a sharp glance at him. "From reserve formations and mothballs up and down both mainlines of the Bellerophon Arm. We drained every hangar and holding yard from here up to Samson and Treadway. Now sit down and strap in or you're sure to be the first casualty. It's likely to get a lot rougher, real soon." As if to punctuate the admiral's exhortation, a bone-jarring convulsion rippled through the hull.

Wethermere complied. "But, sir, some of those birds—"

"—date back to before the Insurrection. Their on-board weapons are at least two marks behind current systems, and I'd wager that some of those airframes don't have more than a hundred good hours left in them." Then she smiled like a tiger seeing a steak. "But their *external* ordnance is all brand-new. Now record your recording and let me work."

"Yes, sir."

She smiled before looking away and barking, "Ops: update."

"Shields good, net secure."

"Relay of targeting data?"

"Brigadier McCullough confirms he received it five-by-five. He concurs with Tactical's assessment as to which SDHs are their datalink hubs."

"Let's hope all this mutual admiration on the tactical intel side is warranted. Missile batteries, prepare to cease fire as soon as the fighters have launched their ordnance. Then give me all beams, sustained fire."

"Admiral, that might burn out the capacitors. . . ."

"Then let them burn. After McCullough has shot his bolt, I want the Baldies to focus their defensive fire on him. And yes, I know what that means for the Flight Brigade." There was silence on the bridge. Even Wethermere, new to combat, had an inkling of what the concentrated defensive fire of the Baldy SDs and SDHs would do to fighters with obsolete ECM packages and outdated evasion characteristics.

In the tacplot, the cloud of green gnats that had swarmed out from behind Beaumont now merged into the outermost red membranes of the enemy fleet.

"McCullough's launching."

"How many survived to make the run?"

Tactics checked his board. "Two hundred eighty-three out of four hundred, sir."

In the plot, the blood-red mass of the enemy fleet did not seem to move so much as churn, like a bloated organ bulging and flexing in distress. And in fact, that was what was occurring: the Baldy fleet was trying to wheel about and keep their aft-drive decks—and therefore, defensive blind spot—faced away from a mass attack by fighters. And clearly, not all of the enemy battlewagons were succeeding: omega icons started sprouting inside the organ.

"Admiral, the enemy fighters around us are breaking off en masse. They're heading back to protect their dreadnoughts."

"As expected. All beams: right up their ass."

"All beams on the fighters, aye, sir."

That was when the bulk of McCullough's missiles started hitting—and his fighters started disappearing from the tacplot in swathes. But they were no longer disappearing as fast as Wethermere had expected: several of the Baldy datanets had died along with their SDH master-hubs.

Yoshikuni pulled forward against her shock harness as if she wanted to jump to her feet when she gave the order. "Fleet order to all missile batteries. Best rate of fire. Second screen to flush its racks. Internal magazines launch until they are ten birds away from dry."

The admiral's flagship, the RFNS supermonitor *Jellicoe*, began—and kept—trembling as though a freight train were speeding through its bowels: outbound missiles. Hundreds of them.

With many of their datanets gone, the enemy ships had been forced to concentrate even more of their less-effective defensive fire on the Flight Brigade's fighters. Ironically, most of McCullough's pilots had already launched all their ship-killing weapons. And now, before the van of the Baldy fleet could yet again shift the primary focus of their ill-coordinated defenses back toward Yoshikuni's massive missile salvo, the first of those immense weapons began to strike.

Inside the red mass of the Baldy fleet, the steady trickle of enemy Omega icons suddenly escalated into a flood. Wethermere tried to match the humble death symbols with his imagination of the titanic forces being unleashed upon those enemy ships. A dozen or more light-seconds away, antimatter warheads were violently blossoming into sudden, blue-white spheres of pure, obliterating, noiseless energy. Wave-front halos pulsed out from those micro-stars, tossing, and tearing apart, warships that were almost a kilometer in length. Shields died with rainbow flares; armor buckled, melted, even sublimated wherever the energies actually touched them. And in many cases, the munitions and power plants of the stricken ships joined in the orgy of destruction, consuming themselves with a suddenness that an anthropomorphizing observer might have wrongly labeled as "furious."

Over the course of forty-five seconds, Ossian Wethermere watched almost a quarter of the bulging, diseased sac of red icons deflate, sagging limp where markers of dead enemy ships hung motionless in the plot. The bridge was silent—and then cheering broke out as the sac began retracting, attenuating as its rearmost extents began pulling away from Yoshikuni's fleet.

"Losses?" Yoshikuni's voice was a stern reminder that the stunning victory had not come without a price.

Ops's voice was subdued. "SMT *Hipper*, MTs *Marston Moor*, *Ting-Hsien*, and *Quebec*. SDs *Harrower*, *Resolve*—"

"Just the number lost."

"Six SDs, sir. And a number of pickets. No tenders or auxiliaries."

"And the Flight Brigade?"

"Sir—"

"*And the Flight Brigade?*"

By way of answer, the Communications Officer interrupted by clearing her throat. "Brigadier McCullough on priority channel, sir."

Yoshikuni nodded. "Can you get us his data feed?"

"Trying, sir."

McCullough's voice sounded oddly young, almost cheery. "Quite a ride, out here."

"Brigadier, how are you? How are your—?"

Tac muttered low. "Sir, he has only ninety-eight birds left."

Yoshikuni seemed to swallow back whatever words she had planned on uttering. After a moment, she said, "Well done, Flight Brigade. Time to head back to the barn."

"With the Admiral's pardon, we're not quite done. We are right in amongst them."

"And getting chewed to pieces by their fighters."

If McCullough had heard, he gave no indication of it. "We can get you a second salvo opportunity, can keep them on us a little longer if we—"

"Brigadier, you are disobeying a direct order. You are to—"

Ops interrupted softly. "Admiral?"

"*What?*"

"Sir—his data feed. Look."

Yoshikuni did—and went very pale. "My god. They're running their tuners over the limit."

Ops nodded. "Sir, the rads—"

McCullough had either heard or figured out what the silence meant. "Admiral, you never said it—and nor did I—but we both knew this was a one-way mission. Old hulls, old shielding, old tuners, old pilots: we had to push and spend it all if we were going to get this job done. Now let me talk to the people I have left—"

"Brigadier, I order you to—"

But the priority line snicked off with a buzz; they could still hear McCullough through his data feed, though.

"Flight Brigade, report."

And they did:

"External ordnance gone, Brigadier."

"Racks dry."

"I'm out."

"What now, Skip?"

Instead of answering, McCullough toggled back to Line One, his voice thoughtful. "Admiral, the Baldy sensor arrays are phased, but they get their terminal lock on us with targeting lasers, yeh?"

"Yes, Brigadier, but—"

McCullough cut her off again. "Okay, in we go, boys and girls. Here's the plan: wait until they graze a lock across you. Then dance away quick and give your computers time to get reciprocal telemetry on the source of *their* targeting lasers. Once you've got that, go to continuous fire with your beam weapons. We might not be able to kill these giants—but we can stick our needles straight into their eyes."

And so the last seventy-four fighters of the Flight Brigade rushed in, a flurry of furious gnats attacking a herd of elephants.

And the elephants balked.

None of the behemoths died, but in the tacplot, the red icons shied away from the gnats, possibly believing they still had missiles, or possibly trying to protect against the venomous, gouging bites that were stinging, even momentarily blinding, the eyes that guided and aimed their defensive batteries.

"Admiral, there's further disruption in the Baldy datanet. They're having to reshuffle their sensor coverage in order to— By God, McCullough is doing it, sir."

Yoshikuni strained at her harness. "General order to all units: launch all remaining birds. Sustained fire, all systems, until your capacitors are red lining."

"All fire, aye, sir."

"And McCullough, punch out, damn it—punch out!"

But the sons and daughters of Beaumont, made of the same uncompromising, gritty material that gusted across the deserts and wastes of their rugged homeworld, stayed in their hulls and died—and assured that Yoshikuni's ships sent improbable numbers of the enemy into oblivion. Wethermere watched as the larger green icons of the human fleet lashed out at the roiling enemy mass and another wave of new Omega icons spattered cross it.

Tactics's announcement kept the mood somber. "Flight Brigade down to nineteen, sir."

Yoshikuni slammed back the shoulder bars of her harness and jumped upright. Wethermere saw an evanescent glitter—an incipient tear?—at the edge of the Iron Admiral's left eye. "For God's sake, McCullough, punch out. Don't—"

"Admiral?" It was McCullough.

"Yes?"

"Fight your ship—and remember us."

"McCullough—" But the carrier wave of McCullough's data feed died with a hiss. "God, no," Yoshikuni whispered, and although her voice did not falter and neither her lips nor her brow buckled, a single tear traced a long, glimmering curve down the length of her smooth cheek.

"Admiral?" It was Ops.

"Yes?"

"They—they're gone sir. All of them."

She did not look away, did not even move. Wethermere had the insight—sudden and sure—that she did not dare try to do either. Then she straightened. "Tactical: report."

The Tactical Officer's voice was pitched as if he were delivering a eulogy—which in fact he was. "The final attack of the Flight Brigade broke the Baldies up even more. We took out at least another three SDHs and twelve SDs. Overall, they've lost forty percent of their force since entering the Beaumont system."

But as they watched, the red icons began to not merely move back but away from what had been the axis of their retreat, spreading out radially, evolving back into the screen formation they had compromised upon closing with Yoshikuni's line. They were not withdrawing: they were re-forming.

Yoshikuni sat, and the way she almost fell into her chair left Wethermere with the impression of a person who had just finished running a marathon. "Ops, what's our slowest unit's ETA to the Suwa warp point?"

"Including travel both within and beyond the Desai limit, forty-eight minutes, sir."

"And the fastest Baldy unit's ETA to the same warp point?"

"Fifty-nine minutes, using the same metrics, sir."

Yoshikuni leaned back. "Comm, pass the word: well done." She looked down into the plot, and Wethermere was fairly sure she was staring at the now-receding brown marble that was Beaumont. He unlocked his harness, stopped his recorder, and approached Yoshikuni slowly, carefully. When he was about a meter away, he saw that her lips were moving slightly, and was startled to hear the Iron Admiral of the RFN whispering what sounded like a shred of poetry: "Into the volleys of death flew the four hundred." She looked up slowly. "Mr. Wethermere."

"Sir."

"I want you to carry a message to Suwa. And on to Admiral Krishmahnta. And by drone to Achilles, programmed to broadcast once it gets there. It is a priority message, with instructions for mandatory pass-along and rebroadcast through any and all friendly warp points."

Wethermere felt his left eyebrow rise involuntarily, but all he said was. "Yes, sir. What is the message?"

"Only this: a full recording of the actions—the charge—of the Flight Brigade of Beaumont. You are to append one word to that recording."

Wethermere waited. Yoshikuni, face impassive, finally got the word out in a completely level tone. "The word is: 'Remember.' Send immediately." She looked up at him. "Immediately."

What Ossian Wethermere saw in her eyes—a pain and ferocity and strange, savage longing for which there was no single word—made him start and lean away slightly. What was radiating from her did not bear close approach, and for a moment he couldn't even define it, but then he discerned the dark emotional amalgam: respect for the dead—and guilt for not being with them. "Yes, ma'am—sir," he muttered and quickly moved off.

Arduan SDH Shem'pter'ai, *First Fleet of the* Anaht'doh Kainat, *Beaumont System*

Narrok relaxed his tentacles as Urkhot left the bridge, silent, yellow-pasty from top to bottom, and his *selnarm* infolded so tightly that he seemed to have separated from the Children of Illudor and become his own race.

In the plot, the human forces drew over the Desai limit and sped to the warp point. Pursuit had been pointless: Narrok had too few of his Desai-drive SDHs left to form up a reasonable task force. And his older superdreadnoughts could never hope to catch the enemy fleet. So he had elected to remain closer to Beaumont, retrieve the crews from his drifting hulks, and scuttle what could not be repaired. As the slow, bloody business began, several *murn*-colored pinpricks rose up from the planet itself.

"Sensor Second, identify the contacts."

(Calm, relief.) "Only a few of their interface shuttles, sir."

"And what do they seem to be doing?"

"Given the intermittent nature of their motion, and a few weak radio pulses we detect in the area, I suspect they are attempting to rescue some of their pilots, perhaps retrieve the bodies of the discarnate." (Distaste, revulsion, perplexity.) "We do still have some of our fighters on patrol in that area, and they could easily—"

"Sensor Second, are the enemy shuttles armed?"

"Not apparently, but—"

"Could they, in any conceivable fashion, carry ordnance that would pose a threat to any of our ships at one-light-second range?"

"No, sir."

"Then avoid them and leave them about their business. When they have returned to the planet, transmit our customary message to the local government. First, 'Stop fighting.' Then 'Stop moving.' Is that clear?"

"Yes, Admiral."

Narrok turned away from the plot, stared out the single viewport up into the distant stars, and thought, *What a bitter lesson we learned today.* And then: *I would like to meet the admiral that taught it to us.* Oddly, and somewhat unsettlingly, the thought did not strike him as outré or distasteful.

In fact, it seemed quite normal.

3

Warring in an Unhabitual Way

Genius, in truth, means little more
than the faculty of perceiving
in an unhabitual way.
—William James

RFNS Gallipoli, *Main Body, Further Rim Fleet, Suwa System*

Second Lieutenant Ossian Wethermere had been on the bridge of the RFNS *Gallipoli* for all of thirty seconds when he was handed the flimsy announcing his promotion. It was done without any ceremony; in fact, Wethermere didn't know what the letter contained until he opened it.

Looking after Captain Velasquez, who had handed it to him, Wethermere queried, "Uh, sir?"

"Congratulations." The monotone of Velasquez's response was somewhat muffled: the captain's head and shoulders were already buried inside a console's access panel, which reeked of battle-fried command circuits.

"No—I mean, thanks, but—why? It doesn't say."

"Oh, nothing you've done." Velasquez reemerged from the console. "The admiral apparently got your dossier along with the rest of the data your courier downloaded to us when we popped in-system from Raiden. She noticed you were past review date. We've got casualties, you haven't screwed up, so—congratulations. War is hell. Now I've gotta fix this. Scram." Velasquez wriggled back up into the service niche.

Wethermere stepped away, stared down at the flimsy again—and heard a voice behind him. "I believe congratulations are in order, Lieutenant."

Wethermere turned: Captain Yoshi Watanabe, and he was almost smiling. "Thank you, sir."

"Thank me after you've worn it a while, Lieutenant. Wartime promotions come quickly for a reason—lots of officers die."

"Yes, sir."

"So, we've been keeping you pretty busy, eh?"

"Yes, sir." *This guy is the admiral's chief of staff, and technically CO of this ship. What the hell is he doing spending jaw time with* me*?*

"A pretty pitched battle in Beaumont, from what I've seen of the reports. Is that how it felt to you, Lieutenant?"

How it felt*? He wants to know how I* feel*? I thought CMOs were responsible for psych evaluations*—"Pretty much so, sir. But I was just a bystander. The real heavy action was out in the first screen—and with the local fighters. We had it pretty easy back where we were, I think."

"So did we." Watanabe looked around at the mostly superficial bridge damage.

"Sir, I haven't heard yet. What *did* happen back in Raiden?"

The captain shrugged. "Not many losses for us, a fair amount for them—but nothing like the last time they tried to visit us there. I think their new admiral is suitably cautious. We lost an MT and, unfortunately, most of our cruisers."

"Cruisers? How, sir? Why were they even in the line of battle?"

Watanabe looked Ossian in the eye and spoke with slow precision. "Hear this, Lieutenant. I know that the experts say that nothing under the rating of an SD even qualifies as a ship of the line anymore, but out here we use whatever we've got. Yesterday we used cruisers. But not in the line. They're fast, so the admiral kept them back outside the Desai limit. As we met the Baldies just inside our edge of the limit, the cruisers went around on a flanking maneuver, running under stealth all the time."

"But I thought the Baldies can—well, pull stealth apart, sir."

"They can—at close range. And they're getting pretty fair at long-range detection, as well. But yesterday, just before the Baldies were going to close in, we had our cruisers nose into detection range. The Baldies knew something was out there but couldn't tell how big it was. However, they *did* know it was on their rear flank, so they split into two task forces, one to face us, one to chase the cruisers." Now Watanabe smiled.

"I see, sir—then what did you do?"

His smile broadened. "You tell me."

A test? Watanabe was testing him? Well, okay, that was his prerogative. So, what had they done? Krishmahnta rushes forward, engages the reduced main van of the enemy fleet? No: that would still be too costly. However . . . "Admiral Krishmahnta held position. The Baldy main van didn't have the odds it wanted anymore, so they slowed. Meanwhile, the cruisers reversed bearing, got back over the Desai line, but slowly enough to entice the Baldies to come after them. The enemy gave chase long enough to pull them so far out of position that the admiral was able to back up, get over the Desai line, use that doubled speed to engage the overextended and much smaller Baldy chasing force, and then withdraw to the warp point—just ahead of the main enemy task force. But because you had to use the cruisers both as bait and flypaper, you had disproportionate losses there. Sir."

Captain Watanabe's smile disappeared for a moment. When it came back, it was fainter, but it also seemed very—well, pleased. "Correct, Lieutenant. Now come along."

"Yes, sir." A beat as they walked toward the chart room's hatchway. "Sir, exactly where are we going?"

"The admiral's briefing. She's been working the details with Commanders Mackintosh and La Mar on the withdrawal into Achilles. It's going to be tricky." The hatchway irised open: Watanabe went through.

Wethermere followed—and found himself in a room crowded with both live and holographic people. Most of the CO's in Krishmahnta's fleet were present, along with a few specialists and section chiefs. Yoshikuni wasn't present: she couldn't be, since she was still light-hours away, guarding the warp point back into Beaumont. But it was a certainty that the proceedings were already being beamed to her.

Krishmahnta rose to her feet. The room quieted. "We're here to get every hull of both fleets back to Achilles safely. That is not our optimal outcome. That is our minimum definition of success. Is that clear?"

Murmurs and nods.

"Then let's get down to business. Here are the key facts of this system: the warp-point locations." She waved a stylus at the main plot—an immense circular holotank. "The warp point to Raiden—"

At about the seven o'clock position on the circle, a purple hoop appeared—

"—the warp point to Achilles—"

Another purple hoop. This one was at about eleven o'clock and, like the first, was about halfway between the center of the table and its outer edge.

"—and the warp point to Beaumont."

Which blinked into existence at the two-o'clock position, a little farther out than the other two.

"The key to this operation is making the enemy from Beaumont believe that the warp point to Achilles"—she indicated the one at eleven o'clock—"is actually out *here.*"

With a wave of her stylus, a fourth, almost fuchsia, hoop flashed into existence at the one-o'clock position, but all the way out at the edge of the table. Restless, seat-shifting noises surrounding the mainplot suggested surprise, perhaps confusion.

"Here's why we want the enemy to think that the warp point to Achilles is all the way out here"—and she indicated the far, fuchsia hoop at one o'clock again. "In simplest terms, we have some pretty slow hulls in our formation—particularly the damaged MTs. And the ones coming from our fleet, here at the Raiden warp point, have an awful long journey to make for their exit at Achilles." She drew a line between the seven o'clock warp point and the eleven o'clock warp point. It was a respectable stretch of space. "Bottom line: our ships will not complete that journey in time if they're racing against an enemy that comes through the Beaumont warp point and that knows to head directly to the Achilles exit point." She drew a line from the two o'clock warp point to the eleven o'clock warp point: most decidedly shorter.

"And don't forget that the enemy may elect to only put undamaged ships through from Beaumont. If that's the case, not even the Desai drive is going to help our slowest ships. So we've got to send our opponent on a wild-goose chase that we can set up relatively quickly and will pull them far enough out of position that they won't have enough time to backtrack, once they realize they've been duped.

"So, first things first: how to set up a fake warp point. Three cruisers from Admiral Yoshikuni's fleet will make best speed for the coordinates we've designated as the false warp point. There they will deposit some telltale rubbish consistent with a real warp point—two unexploded mines and a powered-down buoy ostensibly silenced by us to keep our enemies from finding the warp point. One of the cruisers—the *Kris*—will play the part of the door guard. She will be abandoned in place, drives running low. Her stealth will be up but faltering in a manner consistent with modest combat damage. When the Baldies start sweeping for warp points, they should spot these clues pretty quickly, and, we believe, will come sniffing around that area of space. Considering how long a full system sweep takes, and how very close you have to be to an inert warp point to actually detect it, the odds are pretty good that they'll not only take this bait but think themselves extremely lucky."

The hologram of Captain Cicescu stirred. Krishmahnta noticed. "Jaroslav?"

"Admiral, I know we've observed this operational quirk of theirs before—but can we really trust that the enemy will, once again, ignore our system charts, which they must surely have taken from various data sources?"

Krishmahnta nodded slowly. "That's an excellent question. I wish I had an excellent answer. All I can say is that it's been their unexceptioned *modus operandi* thus far to ignore our star charts. I think we can be relatively sure that this has not been an attempt to mislead us so that they can surprise us now—they've taken too many severe beatings already because of this stubborn refusal to believe our maps." Krishmahnta poised her stylus. "At any rate, we have little choice. And if they do make straight for the actual Achilles warp point, then it's a running fight and withdrawal."

"Won't we hold the Beaumont warp point until the last minute?"

Krishmahnta shook her head. "We can't. Firstly, they still have enough weight of metal to push past us. Secondly, Admiral Yoshikuni's fleet is almost entirely out of missiles. That means defending the warp point would have to be a close-range fight—which she'd be sure to lose. Thirdly, we've got a lot of ships to sequence through the Achilles warp point, so they can't arrive there all at once. But finally, Admiral Yoshikuni's fleet is already committed to performing a far more important task."

Captain Everson of the *Actium* raised his patrician chin. "What task is that, Admiral?"

Krishmahnta reactivated her stylus. "They're going to be our stalking horse. They are going to take up positions here"—she indicated the twelve-o'clock position on main plot, half way to the periphery—"and, if the enemy enters, they will commence traveling on a direct heading to the false warp point at best speed. In short, it will look like they're running for home." She drew a line from that spot at twelve o'clock to the *faux* warp point, which was at the extreme edge of the one-o'clock position. "With the evidence we've planted at the false warp point, and with this fleet making best speed directly toward that same warp point, this maximizes the odds that the Baldies will fall for our ruse. At the same time, our ships withdrawing from the Raiden warp point"—she put her stylus on the seven-o'clock hoop—"will also be moving directly for that same point." She drew a line of light reaching from the seven-o'clock point all the way to the fuchsia hoop at the opposite edge of the table.

Everson nodded. "And so, as far as the enemy can tell, all the roads lead to the warp point—which is not there."

"Exactly. Their sensors and all our vectors will tell them the same thing: we are headed to this point." Again she indicated the false warp point at one o'clock. "When they've taken the bait, and our computations show that we can do so safely, all our ships will then turn toward the actual warp point to Achilles. We will have the advantage of position—and of speed. All our vessels will be in Desai space. Conversely, not all of theirs even have that drive—at this point, probably less than forty percent."

Captain Cicescu frowned. "Why wouldn't they try to cut us off this way?" He drew a very short line, that ran directly from the Beaumont warp point at two o'clock to the false line of withdrawal, intercepting it at the twelve-thirty position.

Krishmahnta nodded. "Baldy might try that, and then the race would be very close, and the last of our hulls will be exiting under fire—if they get out at all. But I'm pretty sure our adversary is not going to risk that fast-intercept vector."

"No? Why?"

"Because if the Baldies do that, they'd be horribly vulnerable to any force of ours that might come through from what they will now believe is the Achilles warp point." Krishmahnta tapped it yet again. "No, for Baldy to both intercept us *and* adequately protect his own rear, he's got to mount a proximal defense of the warp point that he believes leads to Achilles. So instead of coming out to get us, he'll sit and wait for us there. And he'll have no reason *not* to do so, because he knows we're too weak to push through his forces guarding the supposed warp point. He also knows that the other Baldy fleet is due in from Raiden. So in the mind of the Baldy admiral coming in from Beaumont, it's just a matter of time before we're caught between his anvil and the hammer swinging in from Raiden."

Everson stared at the seven o'clock warp point. "Yes—and what about the Raiden warp point? What if the enemy fleet there comes through while we're in the middle of this dance of deception?"

Krishmahnta nodded. "That is the wild card in the deck. Did we give them a bloody enough nose in Raiden to make them pause and lick their wounds? We don't know. They've sent a few probes after us just in the last hour, and we've vaporized them all. So they have no precise intel on what's here, but they have to consider that we may be holding this warp point in force. And that means they'll want to bring up almost all of their own forces before they come through. Or they may feel the need to launch a manned recon sortie, if we keep burning off all their recon drones. So for a little while longer, we'll keep a number of our faster SDs here to make this point look as hot and uninviting as possible. But there's going to be about a two-hour period where we've got to have those SDs under way, during which the Baldies could still come through from Raiden and catch us."

"So what's the answer to that problem?"

Krishmahnta looked down. "We will leave two extremely fast ships back there to cover us during that critical interval, ships that can still catch up with us just before the last of our big hulls are projected to make transit to Achilles."

"That sounds like a lousy job."

"No doubt about it, it's the short straw. And the folks who draw it will either have the best or worst day of us all. Either the Baldies in Raiden have decided to take time to regroup and consolidate—in which case our folks watching the warp point will just twiddle their thumbs until it's time to rejoin us. Or the enemy will decide to move swiftly—and our covering force will catch a faceful of Baldies. No middle ground, I'm afraid."

"And who gets this delightful job?"

"Our two fastest ships. One is our speediest mix of muscle and stealth, with enough defensive batteries to burn down up to a dozen RDs all at once. That's the cruiser *Balu Bay*. The other, smaller hull is there for its sensors, enhanced ECM and shielding suites, and a disproportionately large defensive battery: the DD-courier *Bucky Sherman*."

Wethermere was not startled by the choice: he had heard it coming. But he had not considered the onerous detail that Captain Watanabe then whispered as an aside: "Given your promotion, I believe you're now the XO of that courier." Watanabe started scribbling on his data tablet as the briefing began breaking up. "So, how are you liking your first field assignment in a shooting war, Lieutenant Wethermere?"

"Until about thirty seconds ago, it wasn't as bad as I had thought it might be. Now, well, I'll just be happy when it's over, sir."

Fleet Captain Yoshi Watanabe's smile widened. "That's two pieces of basic wisdom learned in one day. Not bad, Lieutenant. We might make a real officer of you yet. Here are the orders for your CO. Carry on."

Ossian Wethermere snapped a salute, started back for the *Bucky Sherman*, and wondered if he'd still be alive come supper time.

The fourteenth time the warp point began to flux after a precise eleven-minute interval, it had become almost a dull routine—except this time it was not a single recon drone. Instead, eight Baldy RDs came through all at once, two of which destroyed each other as they tried to reform in the same volume of space.

Ossian Wethermere watched the tacplot as the *Balu Bay* burned the last six down with lasers and force beams—just as she had thirteen times before.

Zhou, who flew the bridge Engineering console and was a decided wiseass, sneered, "Gee, that time the *Bay*'s gunners actually had to work a bit."

Wethermere felt, as much as saw, the ship's CO—First Lieutenant (senior) Lisette Zuniga—turn slowly: it was the pace at which she did most things. She impaled Zhou with her deep-set, deep brown eyes. Her face—lined despite antigerone treatments—was a wordless reproach: to Ossian, no matter the lighting or her mood, Zuniga always looked like a grieving mother who had wandered out of a Goya canvas. She had been CO of the *Bucky Sherman* for an unprecedented seven years and showed no inclination or ambition to pursue any higher position.

She did not seem to enjoy command—indeed, she did not seem to enjoy people—and now she was having to veer into both of these unwelcome domains at the same time. "Mr. Zhou," she began, "if you cannot constrain your remarks to matters—"

"Transit!" shouted Sensor Officer Lubell.

In the tacplot, a single—and very large—red blip had emerged from the warp point.

Lehman at Tactical shouted louder. "Holy shit—it's an SD! *Balu Bay* flushing her racks!"

Wethermere slammed the shock harness down over his shoulders as Zuniga, eyes wide and staring, started to give an order, then seemed to change her mind—

She's not going to send in time, Wethermere realized in one terrified blink. He shouted over the others. "Communications, send alert to the Fleet, all sys—"

And then the world turned upside down and wrenched violently sideways. He had a brief impression of Zuniga flung from her chair and straight against the portside bulkhead, then propelled headfirst into what momentarily looked and felt like the ceiling-become-the-deck as the gravitic polarizers flip-flopped. A few other bodies tumbled past, glass sleeting straight through one of them as a flatscreen burst outward and the acrid pall of burning wires and insulation seemed to rush into the bridge from all directions.

Wethermere almost failed to realize that the world had come to a stop again. He looked around.

Zuniga, Lehman, and Masharraf at Ops were all dead. Zhou had only got his harness half on and was clutching his left arm. Nandita Vikrit, at the combined Communications and Computer Management console, looked almost bemused as she dabbed at the red wash of blood pouring down from her sliced forehead. The other three—Lubell, Anapa at Helm, and Tepple at Weapons—seemed unhurt.

"Anapa, best speed. Heading—uh, directly away from that SD." An inelegant but effective first order as commander, thought Wethermere. "Ops, status of the *Balu Bay*—" And then he realized he had made a request of a dead man. Time to recrew empty stations. "Nandita, run Ops through your board. Tepple, shift over to Tactical—transfer Weapons there. Zhou, can you still man your post?" Zhou groaned something that Wethermere decided to interpret as an affirmative. "Nandita, send to all ship's sections: report damage and casualties. Lubell, keep one eye on the SD and give me its approximate status—but keep the other eye on the warp point. If there's any change—"

"Got it, sir. Our sensors are in good shape—"

—Zhou tried to agree by saying "yes," but it became "yaaughh" as he winced against the pain in his arm—

"—but *Balu Bay* is—sir, she's gone. Not even flotsam."

"The Baldy SD?"

"She's coming about now, sir. Sluggish. Evidence of internal fires, explosions. A hell of a debris cloud around her."

"Zhou, how are our shields?"

"Fifty percent," the engineer gritted out between clenched teeth. "We've lost our offensive weapon—"

Damn: scratch one force beam . . .

"—and our commo is gone."

"All of it?"

"Take a look, sir." Zhou transferred an external image to the monitor that served the XO's seat: where the complex arrays of the communication mast had been, there were only stars. At the bottom of the screen, a thin protrusion of tortured, twisted metal marked the site of the mast's amputation.

Zhou detailed the consequences. "Long-range lascom and main antennae are history. And internal shorts have burned out the main and backup transmitters."

"Chance of repair?"

"A week—at a Fleet Base."

"It's that bad?"

"It's that bad. Maybe worse."

"I have the ship's status, sir," murmured Vikrit.

Wethermere nodded at her as he started scanning the other engineering data that Zhou had thrown up in the margins of his screen.

"Overall, about thirty percent crew casualties, sir. Two fusion plants off-line. Away boat and bay are wrecked. Engineering deck sections 12 to 16 are flooded with coolants and wastewater."

"Seal the leaks and seal those sections. Evacuate all toxics to vacuum."

"Trying, sir. Not all bulkheads are responding to command circuits."

"Contain as possible." He stared hard at the engine data in the margin of his screen, then turned to face Zhou. "I'm no expert, Mr. Zhou, but do those three red indicators mean what I think they mean?"

"Sir, if you think they mean that we are at about forty percent speed—and losing pseudo-velocity envelope coherence, then yes, sir, your understanding of our situation is quite accurate."

"Time to failure?"

"If we run at half output, maybe a day. At max? She'll shake apart in an hour. And sir—I do mean that she'll shake apart."

"Warning duly noted, Mr. Zhou. How about our escape pods?"

Zhou brightened. "Fifty-five percent show green, twenty-five percent yellow, twenty percent red. So about fifteen percent of us are going to be rolling the dice, sir."

Vikrit leaned in. "Sir, should I instruct the crew to report to evac—?"

"I'll tell you if and when we get to that point, Ensign. And should we find ourselves taking that step, bear this in mind; officers will take compromised pods, starting with the most senior and working on down." *Lucky me.* "No exceptions. Is that understood?"

The noises of assent around the bridge were clear but not enthusiastic.

"Mr. Zhou, about those engines—"

Lubell interrupted. "Sir—missile launch. Closing rapidly."

"Tepple?"

"Range twelve light-seconds and closing. Engaging defense batteries."

Wethermere glanced down in the tacplot; the missile didn't appear there, but the SD did, lumbering after the crippled green speck that was his first command. He waited. Seconds passed. "Mr. Tepple?"

"Sir, I—" Then: "Missile destroyed, sir."

"About time."

"Yes, sir, but—"

"But what, Mr. Tepple?"

"Sir, that missile would never have hit us. It wouldn't have even come close. I had to boost the coverage envelope of the defense battery just to get it to engage."

Wethermere frowned. "Did they ever get a targeting lock on us?"

"Not that I could detect, sir."

Wethermere thought that through for three seconds. Then: "Mr. Tepple, on no condition are you to activate our own targeting arrays."

"Very well, sir—not that we have any reason to. With our force beam out—"

"Never mind that. Take no chances. Take your arrays off-line." He turned to Lubell. "Same goes for sensors—particularly for sensors. We run passive arrays only."

"Passive? Sir, we won't get very precise—"

"Mr. Lubell, would you rather have precise data—or would you rather live to tell your grandchildren that you *didn't* have precise data?"

"Sir, active-array circuitry is off and routed for command override only."

"Very good, Mr. Lubell."

Zhou straightened up. "Skipper—"

"Skipper?" Well, that came fast—but maybe things do, in combat. Or maybe that's just Zhou . . .

"With respect sir, what the hell is going on? What's with the nix on the active arrays? And—an SD? The Baldies sent an *SD*? On a recon run? What the hell were they thinking?"

"They were thinking they might surprise us—which they did pretty well, Mr. Zhou. And I've been inspecting the first few seconds of detailed sensor data we got on the enemy SD. Look at the damage. I'm guessing the Baldies were ready to write her off anyhow, and then figured if she could make transit, last just a few seconds, and get back through the warp point, they'd finally get a look at what was killing all their RDs over here. Or if she didn't get back, they'd reason that we were holding the point in force."

"Okay—seems logical. But then why hasn't she gone back, or at least sent a message?"

"Mr. Lubell, do our sensors give us any answers to that?"

"I think they might, sir." Lubell threw up an old-fashioned 2-D cad-cam approximation of the debris field around the SD, about five seconds after her exchange with the *Balu Bay*. Using a light pencil, Lubell pointed out the remains of half a dozen externally mounted pinnaces. "She may have been equipped to send back messengers—but she lost that in the shootout with *Balu Bay*."

Zhou rubbed his swelling arm. "Okay, but if she carries any internal couriers or fighters..."

Wethermere shook his head. "If she had them, then she'd have launched them already. But look at the emission spikes Lubell got on the passive thermal scans, here—and here."

"What do you figure they are?"

"Internal explosions." Wethermere leaned back, rubbed his chin, felt stubble starting to sprout there. "From what I remember of the technical intelligence on this class of ship, these old SDs were built with only one flight deck. I'll bet those thermal blooms are conventional fuel bunkers cooking off, or the Baldies are venting them to eliminate the possibility of a catastrophic chain of secondary explosions."

Lubell nodded vigorously. "That theory matches up with this sensor reading. At first I thought she was leaking atmosphere, but the pre-dispersal density of the gas is too light. That's pure hydrogen. And there it goes—" A brief thermal spike indicated that the vented fuel had ignited—spectacularly.

Zhou checked his engines again, made a disapproving

clucking sound, and returned to his customary role as devil's advocate. "Okay, so the SD doesn't have any way to send a message back home. So then why doesn't she turn tail and go back herself?"

Ossian Wethermere watched the big red blip overtaking his little green one—slowly but surely—in the tacplot. "Because of us."

"Us? Why us?"

"Because we can report."

"Well, yes—but he can always blow us to pieces first—and *then* go home."

Wethermere smiled at Zhou. "Yes, that would seem like the best plan, wouldn't it?" He thought a moment. Then: "Sensors: bogey's heading?"

Lubell paused, then reported with admirable composure. "Bearing constant, range closing."

Zhou sputtered. "Holy hell, is she—is she trying to *ram* us?"

Wethermere cut him off with a raised hand. "Mr. Lubell, check again. Is her bearing *absolutely* constant?"

"Yes sir, it—no, wait. Bearing has shifted one thousandth of one degree ecliptic declination."

Zhou swallowed, his eyes large but noticeably relieved. "For out here, that's still a damned close pass."

"Yes, it is. Close enough to bring her within a tenth of a light-second, Mr. Lubell?"

"Aye, sir. Close enough to dent our fender—literally."

Wethermere nodded to himself—and didn't realize that a few seconds had passed until Zhou interrupted his thoughts with, "Okay, Skipper, we're all waiting. What's she playing at?"

"I don't know yet. She's obviously having trouble getting a lock on us. Which is consistent with the rest of what we've seen. She hasn't powered up her active arrays once, not even on low power. So I'm thinking they must have been knocked out by *Balu Bay*."

"Okay, but her failure to attack would have to mean that her passive sensors are too imprecise to get a lock on us, also."

"They probably are, but who can know for sure? Passive sensors are—well, passive, so we've got no way of knowing what they're showing her. Hell, they might not be showing her anything. They could be fried along with her active arrays."

"Okay—but if that were the case, why would she stay in-system and chase us? She can't get target lock, so what's she going to do? Space is too big, and we can alter velocity enough that she'll never be able to try visually directed fire. And in her condition, if she encounters anything bigger than a cruiser while she's chasing us, she's a goner."

Wethermere shrugged. "She might be a goner right now, but not in half an hour. She's a big ship—she's got options we don't. Her damage-control parties might be swapping in a brand-new array this very minute—or booting up and calibrating a backup system. And anyhow, she's only coming after us because she needs to silence us."

"Okay, I still don't get that. Why good does it do for her to silence us? Those antimatter missile salvos did a pretty good job of announcing her arrival to everyone in this system."

"They announced *an* arrival—but of what? A ship? A whole fleet? A single SBMHAWK? Our own fire? And the activation of the warp-point doesn't tell our side anything special. Their drones have been triggering warp point transits every ten minutes or so for the last few hours. No, we are the only hull left, the only ones who know that, this time, it was an actual Baldy warship—and that they've taken out the *Balu Bay*. And that, therefore, the door from Raiden into Suwa is wide open. And these Baldies are going to make sure we never get a chance to communicate any of that."

"Too bad they don't know our comms are out."

"They probably do. They've been following right along our vector, which means they've passed what's left of our commo mast. They've encountered our ship class before, so that wreckage tells them which part of us they just amputated. So they know we've got no laser comms. And if we still had a transmitter and juiced it up—"

"They'd get a strong active signal from us, and send a homing missile right up our—nostril."

"Er . . . yes. So even if we had the radio left, we couldn't use it—and they know that."

"Okay, so they've got to kill us. And they're going to. And soon. But how, if they can't get lock? Of course, we can always fight back." Zhou's sarcasm became a sneer. "I say we wait until they're at point-blank range and then use our anti-missile lasers to take some paint off their hull—if we're lucky."

Wethermere visualized the anti-missile lasers—and suddenly stopped hearing Zhou. Instead, he slowly (so it seemed) realized how the SD was going to try to destroy them—and why it needed to get well within a light-second to do so. He turned to Ensign Vikrit. "Nandita, when we returned to Admiral Yoshikuni's fleet in Beaumont, didn't we relay a lot of technical intelligence on the wrecks the Baldies left behind after the First Battle of Raiden?"

"Sure, plenty."

"And did we keep a copy of that in our data banks?"

"Yes. We were slated to escape and retransmit it back in Achilles and beyond if the fleet was defeated."

"Okay. I need you to dig up any data on the targeting range of the Baldy PDF systems."

"Oh, at least ten light-seconds, maybe more like—"

"No, I mean the terminal-targeting arrays."

Vikrit, who had emerged from NOTC just in time to welcome the Baldies to human space, responded with an uncertain echo. "Terminal-targeting arrays?"

Wethermere explained as he looked over her shoulder. "When threat forces come really close to a hull, the main sensors usually hand off the target tracking to a smaller, dedicated point defense fire array. That array is specially designed to maintain lock on targets that, due to their speed and proximity, present the defense batteries with rapid changes in telemetry."

Nandita was poring over her screens. Wethermere turned to Lubell. "Enemy range and rate of closure?"

Lubell had it immediately. "Range: eight light-seconds. Closing at just under one light-second per minute."

Nandita leaned closer to her screens. "Just a moment, just a mo—here. Yes, their PDF batteries are supported by a 'hull-dispersed grid of independent targeting arrays.' Approximate hand-off range of zero point five light-seconds."

Tepple whistled. "That's close."

Wethermere shrugged. "The Baldy systems were designed as much for navigational path clearance as defense, I'm guessing. The SD chasing us was one of their original, multipurpose hulls—only their newest generation of SDH are purpose-built warbirds."

Zhou looked pale now, but tried to sound brave. "So, we have accumulated a wealth of fascinating data that tells us—with great precision—the manner in which the Baldies are going to target and destroy us at point-blank range. Now what?"

Ossian Wethermere looked up and smiled. "Now we're going to use that data to destroy them—and save ourselves."

Because the fumes were not as bad in Engineering's auxiliary control room, Wethermere and Zhou entered there. The two technicians that had been waiting for them saluted. Wethermere returned the salutes. "You're relieved. Report to your pods."

"Yes, sir." They needed no encouragement.

Zhou looked at Wethermere. "You sure you want to do this?"

"You sure you want to live?"

Zhou nodded. "Okay, so what sort of control do you need?"

"A timer would get the job done, but a remote controller will maximize our chances of survival."

"So you need a remote controller. And a backup, too. Fine." And Zhou started changing control settings on the master board. "Care to explain the plan in a little more detail? Blowing up a drive is not going to create a big enough explosion to hurt the Baldies at half a light-second, sir."

"I'm not planning to use our drive failure as a bomb."

"No? Then I'm really in the dark, sir."

"Funny—you were the one who gave me the idea."

"Me, sir?"

"Absolutely. What did you say? When the engines fail, they're going to shake the ship apart—literally shake it apart?"

Zhou frowned. "Yes, sir, I said something like that."

"And why does the ship shake apart instead of explode?"

Zhou actually leaned back and adopted a slightly professorial tone. "Well, you see—"

Wethermere held up his hand. "How long is this lecture going to take?"

"I dunno. About ten minutes?"

"We'll be dead in five. Give me the short version."

"Yes, sir. Look, it's like this—every reactionless-drive field has a stability limit that defines the amount of energy it can handle safely. Combat damage reduces this limit, which is why running a damaged drive at full power is pretty dangerous. When the engines reach their stability limit, the drive, and everything in the ship, begins to experience something that feels and acts a lot like aerodynamic drag. What's happening is that as the drive exceeds its safe limit, the pseudo-velocity envelope—the field that shifts the ship forward through 'bent space'—begins to unravel."

"And so the field's ability to suspend the physics of normal space begins to become less than absolute."

"Yeah—more or less. Most ship systems can't take much of this drag—not more than a four or five gee equivalent, because at that point the phase distortion and interruption is so severe that it compromises the operation of the drive and the power plants. That leads to stresses and loss of coherence, which produces multiple, but not simultaneous, failures. The ship does not explode in a single spasm. It literally shakes apart in a cascade of smaller explosions and a shower of debris."

"Good."

"Uh, yes, sir, but how does that help us?"

"Mr. Zhou, when a ship with a reactionless drive is

destroyed, and its drive field is annihilated, what happens to its wreckage?"

"Well, sir, the wreckage would go from a near-relativistic velocity to a dead stop. Instantly. Pseudo-velocity doesn't involve inertia."

"So I thought. Meaning that, from the perspective of another ship that's still being propelled by a reactionless drive, this wreckage would drop behind in a near-relativistic rush—so fast that you wouldn't have the time to see or scan it. Is that about right?"

"Yes, right." And then the light came on somewhere behind Zhou's eyes. "Oh, I get it."

Wethermere smiled. "Yes, I think you do. And now we've got"—he checked his watch—"about two minutes to get into our pods."

"Yes, sir—and sir?"

"Yes?"

"I think you'd better rethink that business about you taking a compromised pod, sir. Because you're carrying the remote, and if your pod goes pear-shaped—"

"You're right, Zhou. Whoever carries the remote controller has to be in a reliable pod. But I'm not going to be the one carrying the remote."

"No, sir?"

"No. You are."

Zhou looked like he'd swallowed his tongue. "*Me*, sir?"

"Yes, you. You're the engineer, you know the tolerances, and you've got a belly-feel for the ship's drives, even when you're at the other end of her. Or even from inside an escape pod, I'll bet. We'll give the backup unit to Lubell, if you think he's the right officer for it."

Zhou considered. "Absolutely, sir. He'd do fine. Better than me, probably—"

"That's bullshit, Zhou. Don't start getting heroic on me. Now get into your pod, and give me the backup controller. I'll drop it off with Lubell on my way."

Ossian let the escape pod's automated system dog the outer hatch, and then the inner hatch, before he tested the seals. Seemed tight—not that he could tell.

He waited for the automatic harness to snap into place around him: it didn't. Malfunction number one: a bumpy ride at least, hopefully not lethal. He pried a few straps out of the packaging and secured himself as best he could.

His watch chirped. Approximately twenty seconds now.

The small overhead monitor came on. Zhou had linked the screen into a graphical representation of the engine readouts. They were all deeply in the red. A tremor started behind Wethermere and then worked around to the front.

The stability of the drive's pseudo-velocity envelope hovered just below the failure line.

Lubell's voice—tinny and incomplete over the damaged internal comm system—announced. "Range to bogey, 0.7 light-seconds."

Zhou juiced the engines a bit. The pervasive tremor became a violent and irregular quaking.

The envelope gauge hopped above the stability line for the briefest moment, then settled right down on the limit marker.

"Range to bogey, 0.6 light-seconds."

A hiss from behind; Vikrit had remotely primed the pod's thrusters and clearing charges. At least those seemed to be functional.

Zhou pushed the reactionless drives a tiny bit more—and then the shaking became wild, brutal, unpredictable, as if Ossian had fallen into a continental fault line during a tectonic shift. The red indicator hopped over the limit marker—and started flashing black and orange.

"Range to bogey, 0.5 li—"

The pod's ejection charge slammed Ossian forward against the straps: the eight-gee push of the solid boosters double-cracked his head against the pod's monitor even as they kicked him farther away from the *Bucky Sherman*.

And, as his vision blurred and objects seemed to bleed into and across the now-cracked monitor, he saw the flashing engine readouts wrench mightily—and go blank.

Somewhere behind him, in the belly of the crippled courier, a tug of war—waged between real space and folded space—broke the rope that was the containment wall of a fusion reactor, then the coils of a primary drive capacitor, then the drive itself.

The *Bucky Sherman* came apart in a shuddering cascade of flame, star-white fusion plasma, and ferociously tumbling shards of titanium, composites, electro-bonded superdense armors—

Which dropped from 0.11 c pseudo-velocity to the paltry speed imparted by the explosive forces of its destruction, which scattered the pieces wide across space.

The enemy superdreadnought was at 0.51 light-seconds range when the human ship went from being a near-relativistic target to a stationary debris field.

The Arduan ship's passive arrays detected the savagely spinning wreckage 0.51 seconds later. Computers interpreted, assessed, sent a collision warning. At that same instant, the alien ship plowed into the debris field at almost 36,000 kilometers per second.

The behemoth's destruction was instantaneous.

4

Trivial Causes

In war, events of importance
are the result of trivial causes.
—Caesar

Punt City, New Ardu/Bellerophon

Lentsul watched as a large truck turned the corner and approached. It was articulated into three blocky sections, each with an independently powered set of wheels. The lead section—a command cab—was topped by pulsing red, yellow, and *murn* lights: an emergency vehicle. Behind it, Arduans—mostly members of the *Destoshaz* caste—were riding in or atop the other segments of the truck, protective suits on and already half-sealed.

Another, similar vehicle emerged right on its tail, similarly crewed. The boxy vehicle had evidently stood unused since its off-loading on to New Ardu: each wheel hub still had expandable wheel-spikes in place. The remote-deployable spikes had been included to help move bulky loads across the rough surfaces of the uninhabited planet that they—the Star Wanderers—had thought to find.

Instead, the planet they had journeyed many generations to reach, and which they had optimistically labeled

New Ardu, was already inhabited. The world—named Bellerophon by its denizens—was teeming with combative, restive bipeds who called themselves *humans* and styled themselves as sentient, even though they lacked the faintest trace of a *selnarmic* awareness. And here, abutting and partially arrogating one of their harsh, angular, concrete cities, the Children of Illudor had established their own city of Punt.

A dividing line—six of the human "blocks" in width—had been evacuated to create a depopulated zone between the urban complexes of the two races. And today, alarms—and satellite imagery—indicated that two fires were now raging closer to the human side of that zone. The work of local arsonists, no doubt.

Lentsul watched closely as an Enforcer defense sled—hovering about three meters off the ground—followed the second truck into the street, keeping at least ten meters distance, defensive blisters turning restlessly. Then the two of the blisters on the left side of the almost featureless airborne ovoid snapped around and rotated their weapon-sensor clusters skyward, back in the direction of Punt. Two small, vaguely cruciform specks had appeared overhead, their flight having apparently originated in the human precincts that were to the immediate right of the column.

As if they knew they had been detected, the specks began corkscrewing about, doubling back, swooping, climbing and all the while, buzzing like a pair of overgrown *zifrik* worker-drones. The defense sled's left-hand defensive blisters tracked them carefully, watchfully, through their chaotic aerial ballet: in other circumstances, the blisters would simply have brought down what were now obviously remote-controlled toy planes.

However, since the artist roundup three weeks back, orders had changed. Far more provocation was now required before discarnating the *griarfeksh* or discharging weapons in or around their areas of habitation. These little planes pushed the very limit of those new rules of engagement, but the decision was not to fire unless they came within 200 meters. So far, the airborne toys had remained at about 350 meters.

When the planes were spotted, a warning had evidently been passed up the line—by *selnarm* link, since that was fastest. The lead truck obligingly slowed as the Enforcer sled tracked the two specks through their snarling aeronautical display, the second truck thus compelled to stop fully to prevent bumping its leader. A moment passed while, evidently, the defense-sled sensors confirmed that the little planes were nonthreatening—for now. Then the *selnarmic* order to resume driving to the scene of the fires was obviously given: the first truck's immense engines growled, and it heaved forward—

—just as a tiny vehicle, with four wheels that were each almost as big as its body, came whining out of the building to the immediate right of the first truck. Before anyone could react, the little toy car had sped and disappeared under the second segment of the truck, its electric engines screaming. For a moment, there was silence: the truck's immense wheels rolled slowly forward—

Then: a bright, savage flash; a sharp, percussive roar. The center segment of the first truck seemed to jump like startled prey. It twisted as it ripped clear of the head and tail sections, flying upward and sideways against the second story of the building to its left as if it, too, were nothing more than a child's toy. The concussion blasted every window on the block into a spray of glassy sleet, did the same to the windows in the cab of the following truck, which slammed to a halt—just before the rear segment of the lead vehicle, back-flipped by the force that had severed its middle section, cartwheeled into and crushed the cab. *Selnarmic* death spikes—piercing, sudden, wrenching—told the fate of the Arduans there. Similar truncated death jolts came from the other cab a moment later as its fuel lines, ruptured when the middle section tore away, caught fire: a low-pressure wash of flame gushed out the windows of the lead vehicle's cab with a hoarse roar.

That was when the second remote-controlled toy—almost invisible in the smoke and falling debris—skittered out of the doorway of the next farthest building on the right hand side of the street. Bouncing wildly over and through both the stationary and tumbling detritus, it shot under the already-crippled second vehicle.

This time, the explosive-laden toy car must have detonated near a fuel tank; an orange-yellow fireball roiled out from underneath the truck, sending it almost a meter straight up as it broke into its three constituent pieces. The wave of terrified, agonized death surges shocked Lentsul so profoundly that he reflexively pinched down his *selnarm* link—a cowardly act, he knew, but this was not just any discarnation: his brothers and sisters were being incinerated. That manner of passing lasted just long enough to experience the full agony of it. It was a memory that was said to transfer into all later lives with a horribly crisp clarity.

The trailing defense sled—the first in a formation of two—had already lifted quickly up and rearward on its thrusters, thinking to give the second vehicle sufficient space to back away from the flaming wreck at the head of the column. As it turned out, that maneuver fortuitously put the sled just beyond the blast pattern of the largest, flaming chunks of what had been the second vehicle's rear segment.

Then the two cruciform specks doubled back and straight-lined in toward the mortally wounded convoy. As the first Enforcer sled's weapon blisters began firing, and the second sled boosted up over the rooftops to engage them also, a street-level explosion—almost three blocks behind the convoy—sent masonry and old conduits hurtling skyward in a violent, dirty smudge. Then another blast, a block behind that. At the peripheries of the city's jagged skyline, a converging ring of delta shapes—the combat air patrol, inbound to stoop protectively over the stricken vehicles—splintered into different directions, some continuing on their inbound course, but almost half sweeping in the direction of the two explosions.

Almost unnoticed amidst all the destruction and the *selnarmic* waves of horrible pain coming from the wounded, another, smaller toy car appeared out of the smoke. The little truck—covered in an eye-gouging combination of blue, red, and metallic gold—rushed forward with a high-pitched whine, threatening to jump out of the screen at the viewer—

Then the whole scene suddenly seemed to tumble wildly down and away. A brief impression of level flight, a view of the rooftops—

—and then the recording ended.

Heshfet—tall, golden, beautiful, aloof, and, above all, fierce—narrowed her central eye. "That's all?"

Lentsul twitched his smaller cluster tentacles. (Apologetic.) "That's all they sent us from the recon hopper's recording."

(Contempt, disdain.) "Hoppers. A *flixit*-brained idea, those. Instead of a truly useful airborne-observation platform, we get a little aluminum garbage can with some semi-sophisticated electronics and the capability to make rotary-winged hops of a few hundred meters, at best."

Lentsul sent a (reassurance) that was also an appeal to reason. "The hopper was not intended for military reconnaissance, Manip Heshfet. It was originally designed as a drone to survey potential landing sites. They were meant for frontiers, not battlefields."

(Fury.) "Yes, like every other piece of *nerjet*-motleyed equipment we've been given. Everything designed for settlers; nothing for soldiers. If they had given us real military equipment, this would never have happened."

The recording had reset; the first image from the hopper's point of view—of the first truck entering the street—had returned to the playback monitor.

Memreb, Heshfet's first junior manip and fellow *Destoshaz*, stared at the image also. "Why did they not show us these recordings until now? Did they think it would disturb us more than our own memories of the ambush?"

Heshfet switched her tentacles like a flail. "Part of the new post-combat recovery sequestration imposed by the Sleeper Ankaht—that *almgr'sh*."

Lentsul started at the slur. "She is an Elder and a Councilor, Heshfet."

"She is the much-filthed mating pouch I say she is. She stands in the way of our destiny as a race. Taking us off duty for three weeks to 'recuperate' is just a weakening of our forces, of our efforts."

Lentsul projected (calm, counterpoint). "It was her

attempt to ensure that we were protected from further provocation, and so would not thereby discarnate the *gri-arfeksh* by the hundreds, as happened last month at the village they call Bucelas. After we were ambushed"—he gestured at the screen—"we were all furious, desperate to strike back. We would have sought any pretext to discarnate any humans we encountered, however we—"

Heshfet rose to her full height, emitting (suspicion). "You call them 'humans'? And you speak in support of the *almgr'sh* Ankaht? You are indeed no *Destoshaz*, Lentsul"—and she looked down on him from her terrible, and very titillating, height—"but even an *Ixturshaz* such as yourself should be able to see that Ankaht is lethal to our future on this planet. Indeed, I thought such deductive powers were the forte of your caste." The group's collective *selnarm* rippled with derisive sniggers. "So, tell us, little Lentsul"—for he was indeed small and dark, like most of his caste—"what do your deductive powers tell us we should have done after this ambush? Sat about and moaned the loss of our fellows? No. We should have been soldiers and marched to avenge them."

"No. We should have exercised more restraint during the action."

"Restraint? How, and upon what?"

"Restraint when engaging the two aerial toys, and the little one that charged the hopper."

"What madness is this, Second Junior Manip? Has your mind been disordered by all the numbers you count with your other little caste-mates? We were ambushed, we were vulnerable, and so we destroyed all potential remaining threats. And we were angry."

"And we were fools."

"Why? Because we were surprised by the *griarfeksh* trick?"

"No. Because we needlessly destroyed the few remaining pieces of *griarfeksh* equipment that survived the attack."

"And just what would that rubbish have told us?"

Lentsul kept his *selnarm* (patient, clear). "To begin with, the electronics of the toys would have been the basis of reverse-estimating the operator's transmitter range, which has obvious tactical implications. Beyond that, a close examination of the toys might have indicated the place and time of their manufacture, perhaps their distribution."

Heshfet's acquiescence was (grudging). "Agreed. If we had been able to determine the transmitter range, we could have triangulated a controller zone. But what is the use of the production data?"

"Manip Heshfet, the *griarfeksh* manufactured these vehicles as common toys and distributed them as such. This means that, at some point, many of these tiny delivery systems were removed from their place in a legitimate toy-store inventory and became the property of a local Resistance cell. Simply knowing where the toys were last sent as inventory items could have been a clue that allowed us to track down these Resistance fighters. And that would have been a great help to us. This is their fourth, and most devastating, attack, and in each they have depended upon these remote-controlled toys."

Heshfet shook her lesser tentacles in (frustration, stubbornness). "No matter. Now that we are no longer in 'sequestration,' we have been given the honor—and the pleasure—of hunting down the *griarfeksh* who have been mounting these cowardly attacks."

Lentsul raised a lesser tentacle from each cluster. "So you have told us, Manip Heshfet. But you neglected to tell us: from whom do these orders come?"

"It was no less than Second Blade Daihd who so charged us, and in so doing she passes Torhok's direct orders—and encouragement—to us."

Lentsul shifted slightly and projected (tact). "Since the order has to do with the security of Punt, and is therefore primarily a local and domestic matter, should it not come from the Council of Twenty, or one of its officers?"

Heshfet stared down from her height and Lentsul tried to repress—and conceal—the swift mating urge that it excited in him. "It *has* come from the Council, Lentsul. Daihd speaks for Torhok. And is not the senior admiral's voice the greatest in, and first among, the Council of Twenty?"

"Yes, it is the greatest"—and Lentsul elected to skip over the *first among* classification, which was language that leaned toward a military coup—"but my question is this: Should the command not be issued through a Council mandate, passed on to us by—?"

Heshfet actually, physically, smiled. Her *selnarm* was not friendly, however. "Little Lentsul, have you become a prime who specializes in the laws of governance? We are *Destoshaz*—most of us—and we have our orders. They have come to us through a duly recognized chain of command. We need know nothing more than that. We will find the *griarfeksh* who have killed so many of our fellow Wanderers, and we will kill them."

Sandro McGee approached the doors of the store and almost bumped into them when they didn't open on their own. He looked more closely at the entry to the unimaginative, single-level prefab known as *Rashid's Sport and Tool* and saw a note taped on the inside of the right-hand door: "Push." Cocking an eyebrow—and surreptitiously checking the street behind him—McGee entered.

Trained to react swiftly to unexpected noises, McGee almost went prone when he heard a light metallic tinkling as the door swung open—but listening a split-second longer, he discovered that it was but the first in a rapid sequence of tinny musical notes: small copper wind-chimes, bumped when he had opened the door. Evidently, the door's buzzer had been turned off along with the automatic doors. A sign of the times: outages and costs had both increased since the Baldies had come to town.

"Rashid?" McGee's voice was the only sound in the store. Then, a shuffling noise from about two-thirds of the way down the central aisle, and Rashid's head—flecked with more gray than McGee remembered—poked into view around a corner display. "Be there in a minute."

"'Kay." McGee smiled as he said it, then inspected the nearby shelves. A little shabbier than pre-war, but at least Rashid's was still open: the large chains had shut their doors almost immediately after the invasion. Not only did people want to stay close to their homes when shopping, but the big stores had depended upon the big shipments that no longer came. McGee meandered over to the sales registers, saw only one powered up, heard nothing besides the movement of his feet and the hum of the overhead lighting.

"See anything you need?" McGee turned at the sound of Rashid's voice, which had, over the course of the occupation, become as reedy as the rest of him. McGee smiled again and tried not to stare. Always of slight build,

Rashid was starting to look withered, and the onset of a slight stoop told the same story as his graying hair: those persons who were chronologically older felt the loss of the antigerone supplements more profoundly, and more swiftly. Three months ago, Rashid Ketarku had looked about forty; now his chronological age of seventy-eight was rapidly asserting itself. McGee kept his voice casual, cheery, as he said, "Hi, Rashid. Business looks slow today."

The shop's proprietor smiled ruefully. "Yep, hard times," he said, waving at the empty aisles but also following McGee's eyes down toward his own diminished torso. "Now, what can I do for you, Sandro?" His pitch modulated slightly; his smile widened a bit too much. "Your usual supplies?"

"No, Rashid, I need . . . I need to ask you a favor."

"Wouldn't be the first time." The flat tone combined a faint hint of honest irony with Rashid's carefully innocent diction. No Baldy listening in—if they could do so—would detect anything amiss.

McGee put on his best crooked smile. "Look, you know the merchandise I keep here on account?"

"Um . . . let me just check the computer."

He's a pretty good actor, thought McGee. *Hell, I almost believe that he has to check "my account."*

"Yes, I see it. Do you need more, Sandro?"

"Uh, no. Actually, I don't have any immediate need for that merchandise. I was wondering if you could just hold it for me."

Rashid's act broke down for a moment: he looked up sharply. "I can hold on to the toys for as long as you need, Sandro. But the—the construction compounds . . . I can't do it. I—I don't have the right kind of storage space for—special—compounds."

McGee nodded casually for whatever surveillance might be fixed upon the store but felt a needle of dread in his gut. Where else could he stash the explosives he'd ordered through Rashid? He'd drawn away from his friends when he had started his local bombing campaign against the Baldies, because if the invaders ever bothered to mount true counterinsurgency operations, anyone associated with Alessandro McGee, RFN Marine Reserve, would be on the short list for detention and interrogation. Nothing personal, of course: just standard operating procedure.

Rashid interrupted McGee's glum thoughts with a polite cough. "I do, however, have a friend. With a cabin. In the mountains." McGee looked up, filled his lungs with air, thought he might hug the wiry proprietor, who continued with, "But it's a drive—about forty minutes."

"Great, that's great."

Rashid almost smiled. "Okay. So, here's how you get there—"

Jennifer Peitchkov looked down at the small blue bundle in her arms and pushed back a fold of the blanket with a gentle index finger.

Blinking in the light, the even bluer eyes of Alexander McGee looked up. The infant's gaze wandered at first—until he found an object he knew: Jennifer. Or at least her rather long, straight, nose. Two small hands and smaller fingers came up from the folds of the blanket to explore, to confirm the return of that most protuberant and easily grasped part of the face he knew—and a smile suddenly creased the chubby folds of the broad face and high cheekbones that were unmistakable genetic inheritances from his father.

"Zander, Zander," Jennifer whispered to him in a sing-song cadence, ignoring the not-mirrors that lined two walls of her accommodations. Hmm, not really "accommodations": more like "habitat."

At least it was better than the madhouse they had put her in for the first week of her captivity: its appointments were, to put it lightly, eclectic and often eye gouging. The array of personal articles would have been a source of considerable hilarity in a less dire situation: in their obvious ignorance of damned near everything human, the Baldies had thoughtfully furnished her with items both useful and bizarre. As an expectant mother late in her third trimester, she had appreciated the normal toiletries and the immense supply of moisturizers (although she suspected the bounty of emollients was merely a fortunate fluke). However, she was not quite sure what to do with the false eyelashes, the men's aftershave, the pubic depilatory lotion, or the contraceptives—both male and female. What this outré selection of objects underscored to Jennifer was not so much that these beings were alien (for they were far less physiologically dissimilar to homo sapiens than other xenosapients), but that they simply were unable to make any sense of human existence. And somehow, that seemed to fit with what humans had seen as the Baldies' apparent muteness, lack of facial affect, and very limited use of arms and hands—well, snaky limbs and tentacle clusters—as media for self-expression.

The tenor of Jennifer's captivity had changed after the Baldy named Ankaht came in and actually managed to exchange some words with her. Jennifer had a lingering suspicion that Ankaht had been trying another form of communication as well. At the start of each of their four sessions together, Ankaht had sat in a pose that reminded Jennifer of a sphinx, but with an engine idling deep inside. But as the two of them sat motionless, Jennifer had felt tinglings, itchings, and hot flashes ranging from the back of her neck to the top of her head. At first Jennifer had dismissed it as a dermatological reaction to the dry, forced-air heat they used in her room. Then Jennifer attributed the sensations to anxiety, or maybe a rash induced by the presence of this alien invader with whom she had learned to exchange about a dozen words. Then she had dismissed it as one of the myriad symptoms of Her Delicate Condition. About which, the self-help books had not lied; with pregnancy, almost any complaint, ache, or craving was possible.

But at the beginning of her fourth—and last—meeting with Ankaht—she was alarmed when the Baldy pronounced her name very slowly and very clearly—"Jennifer Peitchkov"—and then she'd felt a pulse of that strange, hot tingling just above the base of her skull. It had faded. While Jennifer felt the tingling, Ankaht had changed color faintly, then reattained her black-brown leather appearance as the sensation subsided, all three of her eyes closed. Then her eyes opened again, fixed intently upon Jennifer, and Ankaht again said, "Jennifer Peitchkov"—who felt the itchy heat again. This happened two more times—at which point Jennifer began to think the unthinkable: Was this how the Baldies communicated? Mind to mind, or some species of telepathy? If it was, it would explain a lot.

Very pregnant Jennifer had stood—well, swayed—up, excited, forgetting her tentative resolve to withhold further verbal communication: she had reasoned that it might aid the enemy in their intelligence gathering.

She pointed to Ankaht. "You? Ankaht? You are doing this to me?" She touched the back of her head. "You are trying to send your thoughts to me?"

Which had been just so much futile babble, of course. Ankaht had started back when Jennifer ponderously jumped up. Jennifer's attempts to simplify and then reiterate her question were equally futile. After fifteen minutes more, Ankaht made a diffident gesture with her tentacle clusters—the Baldy equivalent of a shrug, maybe?—and left the room.

And that was the precise moment when Jennifer felt the first twinge that was not simply Alexander repositioning himself to reacquire his favorite sitting position atop her bladder.

She recalled the next eleven hours as a kind of hallucinatory madness. There was the first desperate hour when the Baldies seemed to have no idea what her trouble was. Her response—largely driven by the hormonal impulse and god-given right of all pregnant women to shout at anyone who Does Not Get It—was to let the aliens know what she thought of them and their whole, hideous, town-murdering, planet-stealing species. Then, as they backed away from her using that same slow caution with which sensible people attempt to distance themselves from rabid animals, Jennifer remembered: *Oh, right—they often kill people who start screaming and acting aggressively. Kind of like what I'm doing right now.*

So Jennifer controlled herself—for her baby's sake—and the Baldies eventually reapproached. She finally got the message through to them by digging around in the magazines they had brought her and by pointing—first, to an advertisement for baby formula, depicting an insipidly serene new mother and her gorgeous new infant—and second, to her own distended belly and other relevant regions of her physiology. There was some eye-dancing among the Baldies—some kind of hyperexcited staring match they seemed to engage in right before they changed any established routine—and off they went. Leaving her quite alone.

Her water broke about half an hour before the two hijacked midwives arrived. At whose appearance Jennifer cried like a child—as much for seeing other humans again as for the aid and comfort that their presence ensured. But that presence only lasted seventy-two hours, and Jennifer had neither the clarity of mind, nor training, to think of passing the two women any information useful to the local Resistance—whatever that might be. And the midwives—scared, out of their element, uncertain if the next minute was going to be their last—never brought up, or probably conceived a single thought toward, that topic. When they were removed—almost forcibly—from Jennifer and her infant, their faces fell inward, suddenly seamed and old with the surety of what they presumed would be their imminent execution. Jennifer felt that was a very unlikely outcome. But, unable to reassure them with absolute certainty, and unclear herself exactly *why* she felt so sure of their safety, she spent a critical moment floundering to craft a farewell that was both comforting and true—and in those two seconds, they were gone.

In the days following, things went along rather well—better than Jennifer had expected. The Baldies seemed to have either studied post-natal–care manuals or discovered that in this regard, human needs were not too dissimilar from their own. They were attentive but did not intrude unless something was clearly wanted. Things that were clearly wanted—Jennifer pointed to the items in the various magazines, and then online catalogs—they brought swiftly. Nothing else changed, and that was just fine with Jennifer, who focused on her new son and tried to believe that Sandro was not dead. The Baldies who had abducted her had roughed him up, but the blows had certainly not looked fatal, or even particularly serious.

Two days after the midwives had been removed, Jennifer was led to her new—and very properly appointed—accommodations. Interestingly, the eye-gouging color combinations of her former room were gone: pastels had evidently guided the aesthetic choices made for this environment, with everything being a variation on either blue or white or cream. It was rather dull, but it was also comforting, and she was able to settle into her new routine.

That routine alternated between caring for Zander and reciting lengthy documents for her captors. Once they were able to demonstrate—by rather pathetic pantomime—what they wanted her to do, Jennifer was never without a script in her hand: they had her recite stage plays; they had her recite public addresses dating back to Cicero; they had her read aloud from Aquinas, Aristotle, Sartre, and Seuss. After several days of this, they then encouraged her to share—vocally—her opinions regarding a short film they screened for her, a brief article they had her read, and then an endless array of essays, stories, and more. They asked her to name an insane number of objects—and now, with a baby to care for and a growing sense that the attempt at communication was genuine, she cooperated fully. But still, Ankaht had not returned, and Jennifer actually felt . . . well, not saddened, but disappointed. She had thought that Ankaht was somehow at the center of the efforts to establish communication with her. Jennifer's belief in that conjecture arose not from any message that Ankaht had sent, but from her behavior: specifically, her dogged determination to bridge the gap between them. Likewise, the careful way that Ankaht moved and positioned herself in the room bespoke a studied, meticulous methodology.

Jennifer had also detected an undercurrent of desperation—but *how* had she detected it? Where had that impression come from? Jennifer could not identify its source, but it was strong—almost as though it were an emotion that had been sent to her by Ankaht. And, given what Jennifer had wondered and tried to ask in their last session—whether Ankaht might be trying to link minds with her—perhaps the notion of having been "sent" the impression of desperation was not entirely wrong, after all. But if this were true, and the two of them had been on the verge of making some genuine progress in communication, then why had Ankaht not resumed coming to see—

The door opened—and Ankaht entered. Jennifer took a half step in her direction . . . then stepped back, holding Zander closer to her. She fought the primal defense reflex. No, she would approach the alien—just not while holding her child. Jennifer put up a hand as if giving a traffic signal to wait and paced slowly back to Zander's crib, where she laid him, carefully and gently, among his blankets. After covering him up, she turned and came back toward Ankaht.

The small, dark alien flushed very light—almost olive-drab for a moment—as she lifted her sinuous arms and fanned wide the ten tentacles in each cluster, so that the end of each of her arms suddenly expanded into a pattern very like the spokes of a wagon wheel. However, with each tentacle tapering to a point, it looked more akin to an opening star, or the welcoming gesture of some impossible anemone. And with the gesture came a tingle at the back of Jennifer's skull that mounted, threatened to become almost painful, but then resolved into—

(Celebration.)

Jennifer started: Had she heard, or felt, that sense of . . . "celebration"? And then the not-mirrors to her left revealed that they were not just one-way observation windows: they were projectors of a sort. For across them, in light blue, luminous block letters, words slowly bloomed into existence: "Male child joy congratulations Jennifer Peitchkov."

To which Jennifer Peitchkov responded: "Holy shit." She stared at the words for what seemed like a very long time. They'd been very busy, these Baldies, and they'd come a long way. But she wanted to be sure.

Jennifer went to the beginning of the Baldy "sentence," touched the words "male" and "child" in sequence—noticing that her fingers left a lingering orange glow behind—and then pointed at Zander's crib. She looked back toward Ankaht. "Yes?"

Ankaht's very physical response alarmed Jennifer, who feared that the Baldy was having some kind of fit . . . until she recognized the jerky up-and-down motions of the three-eyed head were not some alien version of an epileptic seizure but her visitor's stiff and awkward attempts to mimic a human nod. Meanwhile, a tingling buzz at the top of Jennifer's spinal column resolved into—

(Affirmative.)

—even as the wall blanked and spelled out: "Yes. Male child. Joy dam Jennifer Peitchkov."

Jennifer smiled but wondered: Had they misspelled "dame" as "dam"? But no, they would be sticking to the dictionary, and come to think of it, the term "dam" did specifically refer to a mother—albeit among species of livestock. So why not simply use "mother"? Unless . . .

Of course. If they're going through our dictionary, they've learned that a "mother" might have adopted *a child, or has many other possible meanings—not all of which are pleasant. But "dam" is a word with only one meaning; it is not susceptible to the same confusions of context—*

And another pulse intruded—gently—upon her thoughts:

"Affirmative. Clarity requirement."

Jennifer looked up: Ankaht was almost tan. She swayed; Jennifer leaped forward, snagging a chair by its backrest and swinging it around and under Ankaht's rather humanlike posterior. The alien sank into the chair, and Jennifer felt—without any tingling in her head whatsoever:

(Gratitude.)

It wasn't a word . . . but it was more than a feeling. And predictably, on the mirror smart-boards of her cage-become-classroom, Jennifer saw the words "Ankaht thank Jennifer Peitchkov."

When Jennifer looked back at Ankaht, she saw the three eyes focused on hers and was suddenly struck by how, studied closely, they were surprisingly like human eyes. She almost imagined they were glad, smiling even. . . .

Jennifer leaned back, set her shoulders, nodded, and

realized she had come to a decision. She was going to learn to communicate with this Baldy. This one felt—right. But before the lessons began, before she started down the path of complete communicative cooperation, there was one thing she had to have, and know, first. And getting this across was not going to be easy....

Ankaht rushed out of the observation cell with her arms in motion, her tentacles writhing. She knew she should calm herself, but at the moment she could not be bothered to conceal her urgency and distress from the members of her human research cluster.

"Ankaht—Elder—what is it? What distresses you so?"

(Insistence, focus.) "When Jennifer Peitchkov was taken from her house, there was a brief altercation. A human male resisted and was subdued. Rendered unconscious. What further information do we have on this?"

Orthezh, the linguistics prime, exchanged glances with Ipshef, the cognitive science prime. "There is no further information, so far as we know."

(Fury.) "Then find the information, and swiftly."

(Shock.) "Yes, at once, Elder—but what is so important about this human male?"

(Composure composure composure.) "This human male is our subject's mate, the father of the human Firstling. And as far as Jennifer Peitchkov knows, he may have died."

Ipshef nodded. "I see, Elder. We shall find if more information was recorded by the Enforcement team that went to collect her from her house. But even if the mate has been discarnated, it is not particularly seri—"

(Patience.) "Ipshef, these beings—the humans—apparently do not believe they incarnate again. They believe they live one life, and that is all. So she fears she has lost her mate to oblivion, to *xenzhet-narmat'ai*. For although my *selnarm* has touched her mind, which makes them people, they nonetheless believe themselves to be *zheteksh*."

Ipshef and Orthezh started at the term *zheteksh*, which had heretofore been a synonym for a nonsentient species. But for a *zheteksh* to be able to think, to anticipate a death without incarnation—*zhet*—was the stuff of Ardu's most fearsome myths. Only the most cursed or tragic of creatures fell forever into the abyss of unlife, torment, and chaos that was called *xenzhet-narmat'ai*—"the place of eternal death beyond order or hope." Ankaht felt Jennifer Peitchkov's distress become very understandable to her two primes.

"We shall search the files," affirmed Ipshef.

Ankaht sent (urgency). "Do more—send an Enforcer unit to her house. I believe she shared it with the male. See if the house is inhabited. If so, determine if the male still lives there, or what his status might be."

"It shall be done as you ask, Elder."

"And call an immediate meeting of the rest of our research cluster. We need to concentrate all our efforts on completing the vocoder."

The two primes looked at each other. "With respect, Ankaht, creating the vocoder is delicate work. To construct a multimedia translation machine is a most difficult and time-consuming project. In order to achieve that goal any faster would require that we take effort away from—"

(Decisiveness, urgency, command.) "Do it. Do whatever you need to do. But complete the vocoder swiftly. Nothing is more important than this. This human, this artist and mother"—she flung all the tentacles of her left cluster so forcefully in Jennifer's direction that they whipped out with a snapping sound—"she is the key—the touchstone and foundation—for the communication we must build with the humans. With her, and the vocoder, we will be able to bridge the gap between our races. But without them both—"

Heshfet toggled the communicator off: she radiated (annoyance). "More make-work." The waves of her *selnarm* were irregular, testy, fierce: again, Lentsul had to temper and conceal his arousal.

"What is required of us?"

Heshfet rose, stretched out her spine with a sinuous and almost violent whipsawing snap and extended her arms and clusters until they quivered, rigid and golden. "The human-research cluster has ordered us to inspect a house near the Zone."

"Suspected terrorists?"

"No such luck for us. We are just being sent to knock on the front door and see if the house is still infested—eh, 'occupied.' Apparently, one of the *griarfeksh* artists being studied by the cluster lived there, and her mate resisted the Enforcers. He was knocked in line and now the pathetic female *griarfeksh* is whining about what might have happened to him. So we have to check and see if he's still in their ugly little warren of foul-patterned rooms." She finished her stretching with a luxurious ripple of her spine.

Lentsul was sure Heshfet knew how provocative her motions were—which made them even more provocative, of course. He watched her remove her machine-pistol from its ready locker, snug the toroid magazine into place beneath it, run a major tentacle through the round aperture made by the juncture between the weapon and the magazine: her *selnarm* radiated a primal (battlelust) that was already spreading to the other members of her group as they donned their torso armor. She seemed to have no consciousness of her own vulnerability, only of her profound certainty as, and eagerness to be, the annihilator of her race's foes. She, like Torhok, took a certain fierce pride that their awareness stopped at the peripheries of their own present lives, which Lentsul could not comprehend. As he carefully slipped into his own armor, he sent a quiet pulse to Heshfet: "Does it not disturb you that you do not remember your past lives, Manip?"

(Amazement, amusement.) "Disturb me? Little *Ixturshaz*, not remembering all that past drivel *liberates* me. My mind is my own—no one has painted upon the canvas of my existence before me. I anoint the points of my *skeerba* with my enemy's blood by my will and my skill alone, not in part-service to memories of times and places long gone, and meaningless to me."

"Then how is it that you *shotan* your soul, your life and incarnations beyond this one? Remembering nothing before this life, does it not feel that this life is your *only* life?"

Heshfet's answer was tossed to him almost as an aside. But it came a little too quickly, and the *selnarm* pulsed a little too stridently, to seem as fully nonchalant a response as Heshfet had apparently intended. "I need not feel a thing myself to know it exists and functions within me. What organ produces our *selnarm*? So far as we can tell, the brain. Have I ever seen my own brain? Has anyone been able to point to one part of it and say, 'Here, here is the source of your *selnarm*?' No and no. Similarly, have

I memories of past lives? No. Do we know how it is that Illudor gathers up our souls and restores us to new bodies? No. Yet I know that both exist and function, and if I have no experience of the latter, I see it in others all around me. Why should I worry? I persist. I am greater than my memories, after all."

I'm not so sure of that, thought Lentsul.

But he kept that thought to himself.

Alessandro McGee steered the old fuel-cell four-wheeler around a bear-sized boulder, then swerved to dodge a tree stump that protruded past the margin of the road. *I know Rashid said the cabin was pretty remote, but hell*!

The forty-minute drive Rashid mentioned had already consumed seventy minutes, and that had only brought McGee to the beginning of the cabin's ungroomed camp-road, off the main highway. And as far as McGee could tell, the only thing that made the last fifteen kilometers of road a "highway" was that it was paved. Or had been, sometime within the last ten years.

McGee checked the chronometer on the dashboard and winced: he was going to be late getting back. In fact, his guests were now sure to arrive at his house before he did: no doubt about it. And Van Felsen would not be happy.

Of course, Van Felsen would have been even less happy if she knew about his private war against the Baldies. On the other hand, given her comments at the training facility in Upper Thessalaborea, McGee suspected that she knew about those activities anyway. But she had also seemed to be sending him a message that, if he stopped, all was forgiven. And maybe, deep down, she understood why he had *had* to carry the war to the Baldies.

And she damn well should *understand,* he thought. *It's easier to wait and watch, now that I'm on a special action team, now that I know we're really going to do something. But before, it had all been just inane training without any action. And that's not my thing. I guess it's just like Harry said when we mustered out: the drill instructors started calling me Tank not because of my size but because of how I deal with obstacles—I plow straight through them.* When Jennifer had arrived in his life, McGee had started to learn how to moderate that headfirst proclivity—but then the Baldies had come, and then the baby, and he couldn't just sit around any longer.

But now I've got to clean up my act, he thought, tapping his pocket communicator. He spoke: "Call home."

The communicator complied. He heard a line open and a faint, rippling hum that meant his call was going through.

Just after the house's comm net stopped toning, Corporal Diane Narejko reached the top of the basement stairs and, upon seeing who had summoned her, snapped her best salute.

"Commander Van Felsen, sir!"

Lieutenant Colonel Elizabeth Van Felsen smiled up at her. "Snap it any harder than that, Corporal, and you'll shake the starch right out of your sleeve. At ease."

Diane stood down into the official at-ease position: legs spread slightly, hands clasped behind her back.

Van Felsen, who had almost turned away, turned back. "Allow me to rephrase, Corporal. Relax—and pull up a chair."

"Sir?"

"Leave your post to Corporal . . . Corporal . . ."

"Corporal Wismer, sir. I can't, sir. He's home with the flu."

"Very well." Van Felsen waved over one of the three burly "hunters"—all Marines—who had accompanied the group to Sandro's house. "Private Dalkilik, please man Corporal Narejko's watchpost down in the basement. A fairly standard comms and concealed-camera monitoring rig—shouldn't be any problem."

"Yes, sir," mumbled the Marine uncertainly. He descended the stairs.

"You know everybody?" asked Van Felsen as she led Narejko to a seat.

Diane shook her head, but then, seeing the ranks clipped on collars, started snapping another set of salutes.

Captain Falco laughed and waved it off, then removed his bars. "You'll wear your arm out, Corporal. Besides, since we're all wearing civvies, we'd better start thinking and acting like civilians, at least insofar as routine gestures and address are concerned. If we're here long enough for anyone to see us, it wouldn't do for them to remember us as saluting each other and standing at attention all the time. Might blow our cover." He grinned at the two remaining, hulking Marines, who would never be mistaken for civilians, regardless of what they wore or did.

Van Felsen nodded. "Captain Falco—er, 'Terrence'—is right. Diane, this is Lieutenant Koyazin—'Vedat,' for now. And that fellow signing off on the comm net is 'Joao,' or just 'Joe,' Adams."

Vedat Koyazin looked up. "Hey, Joe, who was that on the comm?"

Joe slid into a seat at the table next to Diane. "That was McGee. He's going to be back a little later than he expected."

"Is there a problem?" Van Felsen's posture and voice were relaxed, but Diane saw wariness in her eyes.

"No, sir. I mean—'no.'"

Vedat leaned back. "Funny, him being away from his own place when we get here."

Joe smiled. "Really? You think so? Haven't you noticed anything—odd—about this place?"

"Other than that funny soapy smell, no."

"Well, that funny soapy smell is probably connected to why McGee's late."

"Huh?"

Joe pointed at the walls, then into the kitchen. "Look around. Most of this place hasn't been touched in weeks, not since McGee's . . ." Joe trailed off, found a new way to approach the topic without mentioning Jennifer Peitchkov's abduction. "Look, Ved, it's a bachelor apartment now, don't you see? And this bachelor was in mourning until we gave him some real hope just a few days ago. So, until then, he was in hermit mode. No amenities. Just enough food for the next day or two. He's almost out of toilet paper. I'd say half of the rooms haven't been entered since—uh, 'the visit' we've come to investigate."

Ved frowned. "And so you're telling me that McGee is out—?"

"Getting stuff. Some cans of soda, a few rolls of TP. You know—hospitality, Marine-style."

"He told you that?"

"He intimated it."

"Okay." And Ved turned to look at Diane.

She noticed that everyone else had turned to look at her, too . . . except the two big Marines, who were watching the front door and street outside. "What?" she said.

Van Felsen rested her arms on the table and leaned forward. "Diane, does that sound about right to you—what Joe said about Sandro?"

"Yes, si—I mean, yes, ma'am. I mean, he really wasn't around much after the abduction: Jennifer was taken, he got beat up and then was dropped at the hospital by the Baldies. As an afterthought, almost—they only came back to the house after securing her. They picked him up, dumped him curbside at General. After he was released, he was back here a few days, hardly went out, hardly spoke. Then he went off on his trip to Upper Thessalaborea." She looked meaningfully around the table, and they all smiled at her. "He came back just a few days ago. But he's still been pretty distracted."

Van Felsen nodded. "Which is why we're just as happy he's not here, Diane. And why we asked you to join us—and help us find out what happened when the Baldies came for Jennifer."

"Me, si—ma'am? Heck, I'm just an operator. Sandro's an officer, and he—"

"We know that, Diane. But we don't want him in the loop on this. He's not—not the right person to debrief on this situation."

"But why not? Don't you trust him? Sir—ma'am—you can't find a better Marine than Sandro McGee. He's—"

"We know that, too, Diane. If it's any consolation to you, I think I trust Sandro more than I trust myself. But trust is not what this is all about."

"Then what's it about, ma'am?"

Falco leaned forward. "Diane, think it through. He may have a child, who, along with its mother, would be a Baldy captive right now. If the Baldies wake up and smell the coffee on how the intelligence and counterinsurgency game is really played, that means they have leverage."

Diane blinked. "You mean—leverage to turn him? No, sir, not Sandro. Not even with his girl and child under their thumb. He'd never do that."

Van Felsen nodded. "Agreed. I fear he'd do the opposite—that he'd lose control, do anything to get at the monsters who've taken the ones he loves. They don't just call him Tank because he's big, you know. He tends to go straight at a problem—or through it."

"And that's bad?"

Van Felsen sighed. "It is if the Baldies can use his actions to track back to any of us, or our operations, or our organization."

"Yeah," Diane admitted, "I can see how that could happen." She looked up. "So, how can I help you?"

"Diane, I brought most of my command team here because the Baldies' removal of twenty-three of Mel-antho's artists is an act of considerable significance. They've shown little enough interest in assessing—or controlling—our intelligence and insurgency capabilities, which are the lifeblood of any resistance movement. But then they decide to grab a bunch of artists? Diane, the Baldies are not proceeding according to any military or occupation playbook we've ever heard of, so we decided to come have a look for ourselves. In particular, we wanted to conduct a close professional survey of Jen-nifer's art, style, inspirations, surroundings, associates. The Baldies saw something in that demographic matrix that made them believe she was an important piece of some puzzle they're trying to solve. If we can figure out why that piece is important to them, we might be able to infer the shape of the rest of the puzzle and start understanding what they were up to here."

"Do you have a hypothesis on why they're behaving so oddly?" Diane asked.

Van Felsen looked at Joe, and then over to Ved. "We have *more* than one hypothesis. As usual." She smiled.

Joe Adams leaned forward. "I'll take that as a signal to launch."

Van Felsen's smile broadened. "By all means. Fire away, Joe."

He leaned back. "By any military standard we understand, Baldy occupation is outrageously ineffective. Other than our primary data nets and our personal communication services, they left everything else pretty much intact—even the computers at our universities and research centers. They haven't clamped down on businesses and other markets that deal in large-scale provisioning—meaning we have already accumulated immense reserves of most consumables, except high-tech military ordnance and ammunition for advanced weapon systems. And they've left most of this planet unpatrolled. If they've put any widespread monitoring in place, then it's a marvel of unobtrusiveness, because we haven't been able to detect it after months of trying."

Falco shifted. "So, what does that all mean, Joe? That they've got lousy leaders and low skill in military science and counterinsurgency?"

"It could—but we're talking such no-brain factors here that I think it goes beyond military incompetence. I think it means they are not really a military force."

"Uh, Joe, maybe you haven't noticed the immense fleet overhead right now?"

"Oh, I noticed it, Ved—and I also noticed that actually, given its size, it underperformed against our fleet. Massively underperformed. So much so that I'd say the only reason the Baldies could do so poorly is that they're not rigged for combat—not primarily."

Falco frowned. "Meaning what, Joe?"

"Meaning that we've looked at their actions and assumed that reveals their identity. They invaded, so they must be invaders. But what if they're not?"

Ved shook his head. "Joe, judging from their occupation of this planet and their apparent campaign farther into Rim space, I think it's pretty obvious that they *are* invaders."

"Is it? They are willing to fight, yes. But if any of the intelligent races *we* know of decided to assemble a slower-than-light fleet to conquer another star system, they'd think long and hard about the *best* military options for that campaign. Wouldn't we expect their invasion fleet to be tailor-made for such an operation? But we have evidence before us that the Baldy fleet wasn't designed that way. Their ships' firepower-to-weight ratio is piss-poor. Their equipment for ground action is pitiful. Their counterinsurgency measures are either amateurish or nonexistent. So I ask you: Does it make sense that a species capable of building those immense pinhole drives—which each keep a micro–black hole on a leash—would be so lacking in both common sense and practical military experience that they couldn't plan a better invasion than *this*?"

Van Felsen folded her arms. "Okay—but what does that have to do with abducting the artists?"

"Everything—if their intent in taking the artists was to attempt to find a better way to understand us."

Ved tilted his head skeptically. "Joe, I have to say that a group of aliens who demonstrate absolutely no respect for life don't seem like they'd really be interested in sitting down together over coffee for a good heart-to-heart. They slaughter our civilians—kids included—upon detecting the slightest hint of resistance."

Joe nodded. "There's no arguing that they clearly put a different value on life than we do. But let's remember that this is true not only where our lives are concerned, but theirs as well."

"So what?" Ved spread his hands. "Look, maybe their preferred alternative to cutting-edge military technology is a combination of overwhelming us in both material and biological production. Maybe they reproduce as quickly as rats—or faster. And, judging from their corresponding industrial-production efficiency, overwhelming us with sheer, easily produced numbers might be just the right strategy for them."

Joe leaned forward into the debate. "Okay, Ved, so if we presume that they are master strategists—albeit working from a very different set of strengths—then how do you explain their ineptitude in counterinsurgency? If their fleet *is* an invasion fleet, and if its design is the best for their strategy, then it makes their failure as an occupying force all the harder to explain. They excel in all areas *except* counterinsurgency? And they can't fix it or do better?"

"Do they really *need* to do better, Joe? They seem to have the planet well in hand—and with a minimum of bloodshed and effort."

"Yeah—largely because we haven't done anything yet.

But their lack of skill is already evident in their inability to adjust their responses to our offensive variations. They only have two speeds in their counterinsurgency gearbox: neutral or double-torque overdrive. They either do nothing—or they launch one of their insane overkill reprisals. Resist them too strongly in an area? They cede the area . . . and then raze it and blast anything that tries to exit."

Ved frowned and cocked his head. "Maybe that's not a weakness. Maybe they've studied the challenges of occupation—particularly in a cross-species scenario such as this—and have decided their current methodology *is* the most effective and economical approach. It sure is a lot simpler. They have one simple rule: immediate, absolute, and dispassionate counterstrikes into any contested area. And we've learned to respect that quickly enough, regardless of any other communications impasse that might exist between our species. So, did they arrive here unprepared to deal with insurgents? Or have they reasoned through the tactical problems of counterinsurgency more completely—and more ruthlessly—than we have?"

Falco held up both his hands. "Okay. After hearing your two different hypotheses, it's clear that we still can't conclusively determine if the Baldy occupation strategies and tactics indicate insufficient, or ruthlessly effective, planning. However, whichever it is, grabbing a bunch of artists makes no sense from a military standpoint."

Ved put up a finger. "With respect, it makes no sense from an immediate *tactical* standpoint. But if it's an attempt to understand us better, it's a long overdue strategic intelligence move. Whether they mean to use their increased understanding to communicate with us or simply control us more effectively remains unclear."

Joe leaned back. "Perhaps not—not when we add in some other data that might indirectly shed additional light on why they came here."

"Which is?" Van Felsen's eyes were focused on Joe.

"My theory is that their military efforts seem so amateurish because they were not at all fixated on combat when they started out on their interstellar journey. Consider their so-called military organization. It follows the same structural lines as all their other social collectives. Their units are really more like semiautonomous work groups. And their vehicles, weapons, and other equipment lack the appearance or performance of purpose-built military machinery. The same is true of their ships."

Falco frowned. "So if they weren't geared up to arrive here as invaders, then what did they have in mind?"

Diane surprised herself by speaking. "Maybe they were thinking of themselves as explorers or settlers."

Van Felsen nodded encouragingly, but her voice held a note of reserve. "Maybe—but this Baldy fleet represents a lot of investment just for an exploratory jaunt, or even for a settlement initiative. All those immense ships . . . Damn, seems to me like they left home because they wanted new turf."

Joe smiled. "Or because they *needed* new turf. Which would explain the extraordinary investment they made in this fleet."

Falco frowned. "What do you mean?"

"Look. I had Toshi Springer and her team track back along the Baldies' approach vector. Nothing interesting for a few hundred light-years, then you hit fairly obstructive nebulae, but right beyond that, you find two novae. Very close to each other. The first, a blue-white giant, looks like it triggered the other one. And probably not more than one or two thousand years ago."

Van Felsen sat straight. "And so you think . . . ?"

Joe nodded. "The Baldies didn't set out on a campaign of conquest. This was a desperate exodus. They are not ravagers on a rampage. They are race of refugees *in extremis*."

Ved smiled. "Maybe. Or maybe not. You've spent so much time thinking about the Baldies that you've become their pal, have succumbed to the Stockholm syndrome."

"Maybe," responded Joe with a matching smile. "Or maybe not."

Jennifer heard Zander throwing his arms around in his crib, lively and happy, but that was just a precursor to his impending discovery that—once again—he was hungry. She tried to refocus on Ankaht, who was evidently trying to ask a question about human relationships or life or experience or . . . something. It wasn't clear: the mind-emotion pulses were not precise enough, and the words that sprayed across the smart-screens were like a random selection of terms from the same page in a thesaurus: all related, but it was impossible to discern the intent. She knew it was a question, because the Baldies had learned the word "interrogative," and they always led with that on its own, and then followed with the vocabulary mish-mash. But the cascade of terms—*life death birth end more again life mate pair life again more*—never made sense, no matter how the Baldies rearranged it. Jennifer watched, almost in pity, as Ankaht became increasingly expressive. Her greater animation was somewhat evident in her face, but more markedly in her clusters' tentacles, which swayed and writhed and stabbed in some fitful attempt to push the words and her mind-speaking into some meaning that Jennifer could understand. Jennifer reflected that it was like trying to communicate with a person who was wearing a mask, and who could only speak a foreign language: she got emphasis and gestures, but the actual content was, at best, uncertain. Sometimes it was just plain noise.

Jennifer lowered her eyes, put her hands up, and said, "Stop."

Peripherally, she saw Ankaht's motions cease. With a sigh she rose—and got to Zander's crib just in time to hear his coos take on a tinge of insistence: time for the next feeding.

She turned and considered the seat next to Ankaht, then the baby in her arms—and thought: *Oh, why the hell shouldn't I bring Zander closer to Ankaht? They could have already killed or tortured us in any way they want, a dozen times over, if that was their intent.*

She reapproached Ankaht, carefully settling Zander at her breast even as she settled herself into the seat. Comfortable and pleased by Zander's determined and successful nuzzling, Jennifer leaned back, very relaxed, waiting to see what Ankaht would do next. . . .

Ankaht had just about decided to give up for the day. After some initial progress on purely primal concepts and emotions, she had tried to push open the *selnarmic* link. She stuck to the simplest of terms and used every gesture of her race, and those she could recall of Jennifer's, to forge a further communicative bond, but to no avail.

When Jennifer rose to tend to her newborn male,

Ankaht feared that the day's efforts were now over, but happily that was not the case. Jennifer came back, more slowly, preparing to provide the Firstling nourishment from her own body, much as did Arduan females for their young. And then the new mother sat, settled in, relaxed—

—And a door opened in Jennifer's rudimentary *sel-narm*. As if looking through a tiny porthole in the side of a vast ship, Ankaht could nonetheless perceive some small part of the interior of Jennifer Peitchkov without significant obstruction. She sent a *selnarmic* tendril through that aperture. "Jennifer Peitchkov, I celebrate your mother-joy. I, too, am a female."

Jennifer looked up, her two mid-sized eyes wide—but not afraid. A wave of (surprise) came back at Ankaht—surprise at the sudden clarity of the message she had received. She had already deduced Ankaht's gender long ago.

Ankaht quickly trumpeted (joy!) at the human. "Yes, Jennifer: hear me!" Ankaht's *selnarmic* roar would have been suitable in one of the ancient parodies, where the Fool was invariably associated with very crude and histrionic *selnarmic* emissions. Embarrassed before her peers, Ankaht doggedly pressed on. "Is it proximity to your progeny that has opened this channel between us?"

From the other side of the porthole, as weak and hollow as a diffident *selnarmic* shrug from the other side of the planet, came the reply. "Maybe. baby. helps. me. do. this. know. not."

It was crude, simplistic, faint. But the intent was clear, and unassisted contact had been made.

However, Ankaht now felt the porthole closing, partly because she herself was becoming too exhausted to maintain it, partly because Jennifer seemed to have drifted past the point of both relaxation and focus where their minds were truly aligned with each other.

Ankaht leaned back and discontinued her enormous *selnarmic* push. She spent a moment recovering, then rose, pointed to the smart-walls that wrote in accordance with her *selnarmic* commands. "Jennifer Peitchkov. Ankaht depart."

As she did, Jennifer looked up and showed her teeth in what the humans called a "smile." Although it could mean many things in many contexts, it seemed to indicate a positive emotion here. And, almost as faint as a feather brushed across her forehead, Ankaht felt a faint *selnarmic* fragment reach out from the human: (affinity).

Ankaht tried to return that emotion, then turned and made for the exit. She hadn't achieved as much as she had dared hope.

But it was a start.

Sandro finally reached the main road back into Melantho and checked the chronometer on the console. He was already two hours late and had another thirty minutes before he'd get to the house. And he hadn't stopped to get the toilet paper yet. Well, there was one roll left. That ought to be enough. And besides, everyone there was a Marine. Nothing was beyond their courage, after all.

He gunned the already-whining engine and wondered if he should vacuum the car to remove any chemical residues of the plastic explosives he had buried—just in case the Baldies started getting smart enough to run spot checks.

✧ ✧ ✧

Heshfet swished her lesser tentacles impatiently. "How long, Lentsul?"

"Soon, Manip. Five minutes, maybe six."

The rest of the Enforcers sat still and stolid in the back of the wheeled security carrier. Two, like Heshfet, had their tentacles snugged through and around the handles of their machine-pistols. The rest—still following the orders of the Council of Twenty—had their own weapons close to their clusters but not clutched and ready.

Heshfet pushed an exhortative wave of (vigilance) through the team and then reached to open the channel to the combat air patrol.

"Heshfet?" asked Lentsul.

(Sardonic.) "Just in case things get interesting. Although we would never be so lucky." She also activated the remote-deployment mode of the vehicle's six defense blisters. So primed, they could be launched to serve as independent aerial weapons platforms at the flick of a *selnarmic* switch. "How long now?" she asked again.

"A minute less than before, Manip."

Which Heshfet rewarded with a brief wash of (amusement). "Not bad. You have some spirit after all, *Ixturshaz*. Now pay attention to the road."

Van Felsen leaned back from the table. "Well, if Joe is right that the Baldies did not set out as invaders—and it seems a reasonable conjecture—we are nonetheless stuck with the fact that they have *become* invaders. If we can get them to reconsider their aggressive posture, that would be wonderful, but we won't know one way or the other until we can talk to them. And I suspect some of them are thinking the same thing in reverse—which is why they took the artists: to find a way to talk to us.

"But in the meantime, we have a war on our hands. And until now, we've concentrated on preparations, not operations. There have been some rogue activities, of course: most notably the bombings in this very city."

Diane, who had been McGee's willing accomplice on two of the bombing missions, tried very hard not to flinch or fidget. Which was fortunate, because she had the distinct, if peripheral, impression that Van Felsen was watching out of the corner of her eye. Falco was openly staring in her direction. *Great, they must know. But keep your trap shut unless they* ask, *Diane.*

Van Felsen hadn't paused. "But just as we're here to find clues on how we might be able to talk to the Baldies, we'd also better make plans for backing up our diplomatic words with some major military muscle. And of course we can't ignore the possibility that the only reason the Baldies want to talk to us is to tell us how to best get in line for our pending extermination. So let's start with an assessment of our current status. You're done correlating all the regional reports, Terrence?"

"Finished just yesterday, Comman—eh, Liz."

Van Felsen almost smiled. "Elizabeth will suffice, Terrence."

"Er . . . yes, Elizabeth. Well, as I was saying right before I put my foot in it and insulted our CO, it's taken a while to get all the regional reports in place and summarized. We've confirmed earlier reports that the Baldies have deorbited large pieces of their space arks to use as citadels for the seven small cities they've established in the Adriagean Archipelago and on the coastlines of Sparta and Sisyphus. We don't have good intel on these sites because of the sparse populations on those continents. However, subsequent covert observation places the estimated population of each Baldy city at somewhere between three hundred thousand and five hundred thousand."

Van Felsen's eyes were narrowed and bright. "But then why put one city—their biggest—right here in Melantho? And why dislocate so many of the residents?"

"Well, of course we only have speculation, but I agree with Ensign Montaño's analysis that the Baldies felt they needed one point of contact with the resident population. Melantho was their logical strategic alternative. It's a deep-water port, has a sizable spaceport, and is the roadway and air-corridor hub for our largest cities—Icarius, Asphodel, and Hallack. By investing Melantho, they put themselves right at the center of the Big Triangle, meaning they can observe, patrol, and of course strike all three from their rather sizable military base right here.

"As to why they felt it necessary to unhouse the entirety of the West Shore District, and give us fifty thousand refugees to deal with, your guess is as good as mine. But Montaño thinks that just as we need to keep tabs on them, so they feel the need to do the same with us. And since they had already decided to make this city their planetside military fortress, where better to keep tabs on us than right here, where they have plenty of force to maintain control?"

Van Felsen nodded. "Okay. Let's stay on the topic of their military. What do we know about its dispersal, command structure, doctrine?"

Falco shook his rather knoblike head. "Too damned little. Their table of organization is—well, it's a damned mystery. We think we've observed NCOs as distinct from line troops, but then the roles seem to change. And sometimes we encounter units made up entirely of the tall, golden ones but other times comprised of a mix of those and the short, dark Baldies. We don't know how they pass orders, but they are a marvel of coordination—particularly in a firefight. While we're shouting orders, trying to track our people on HUDs, and keeping the tactical channels free of needless chatter, the Baldies are moving like a well-oiled machine. Never a misstep. They've got us hands down on operational fluidity and situational awareness of their own people. We make up for it in better tactics and doctrine. If their plans were a tenth as good as their small-unit cohesion and control, we'd be ground meat.

"On the technical side, we've seen short arms, long arms, and what we think are rocket launchers. At the risk of overgeneralizing, I'm happy to report that their personal weapons are just not up to our military standards, either in terms of accuracy or lethality. They seem more like—well, multipurpose weapons . . . which I guess goes right along with what Joe is postulating regarding their origins as refugee-pioneers. They don't have purpose-built military tech. Or maybe their attitude is to simply let their automated stand-off platforms do the heavy work. We all know they are very dependent upon user-directed blisters, which are both well-armored and well-equipped with a variety of passive and active sensors. Almost all their troops—if you can call them that—have laser designators with which they call in support from these blisters or from off-site rocket batteries. And they are pretty aggressive about bringing down the thunder really close to their own positions. The one incident when a Resistance cell actually close-assaulted a Baldy position, the damn no-noses actually called in a broken arrow."

Diane had heard the term before, usually in historical references, but had never quite figured out what it meant. "A broken arrow?"

Ved leaned in her direction. "Sort of like a danger-close fire mission on steroids. 'All tubes and ordnance: fire for effect, my coordinates.' "

Diane swallowed, felt her eyes widen. "Shit . . . Ved," she said.

He smiled at her, caught a nod from Falco. "Okay. The report on our own equipment situation. Here's the bottom line—we can't field true military units. At least, not many."

Van Felsen looked up sharply. "I thought we pulled in a sizable percentage of the caches and stashes. Didn't we get enough?"

Ved shrugged. "Yes and no."

Falco's scowl was as sour as his tone. "Well, that statement was a marvel of clarity."

"Sorry, Cap—Terrence. Here's what I mean to say. Yes, we have a lot of military-grade equipment, particularly weapons, ammo, personal commo and tracking gear, and—thankfully—air-defense systems, including high-velocity missiles. But we had to leave a lot behind at Acrocotinth Main Base. There simply wasn't time for removal. And if we wanted to keep the Baldy anxiety regarding a possible resistance movement low, then we had to be very careful regarding how much we took from the other bases and armories. Any depot or cache that was located in a populated area with other loot-worthy targets nearby—well, we took all the contents in those cases. And we made sure the surrounding area was looted as well."

Joe nodded. "So it didn't look like the military matériel was taken with special care and malice aforethought."

"Right. But isolated bases and armories—that was a hard call. How much should we take? In retrospect, I'm not sure the Baldies would have minded if we took it all, lock, stock, and barrel. But we had no way to know they'd be this clueless about resistance movements. So we figured that we should take no more than ten to twenty percent of the total matériel, with all of the missing items withdrawn in an orderly fashion and due to reasonable causes."

Van Felsen was frowning. "Still, all together, that sounds like a lot of gear."

"It is—if you were to pile it all up in one place. You could comfortably outfit a few battalions of light infantry. Yeah, some of the equipment is almost Rebellion vintage, but what the hell: it's still milspec. Compared to the combat gear the Baldies have shown us, any fifty of our troops could dish out a double helping of whup-ass to any fifty of theirs. But we'll never get that density of military technology in any operation or region. We've got scores of Resistance cells all over the place, and each one of them needs a stiffening core of the heavy punch that milspec weapons deliver. When you start dividing the equipment among all those cells, it gets spread pretty thin."

"So . . . ?"

"So I recommend that we keep a central operational reserve. Maybe about ten percent of the milspec total. We hold that back for the return of the Fleet—that is, when the *big* balloon goes up—or when we get a target with a high enough strategic value to put in all our chips on one roll of the dice. Otherwise, each Resistance cell keeps a small cache of military gear for any operations of major local significance, but only to be used if given authorization by Elizabeth. So until we've got a good reason to bring out the big guns, we keep them quiet and hid—"

"Commander, I've got movement at the east end of the street. Baldy security vehicle, sir. Dismounting troops."

"Shit." Falco kicked back out of his chair and went for his strangely angular overnight bag. Felsen yelled down the stairs, "Private Dalkilik, get on deck," then turned to the other "hunter," who was moving to support their front street spotter. "No, Corporal—you check the back door and see if our path of retreat is clear."

Joe and Ved had each produced old, short-barrel bullpup assault carbines: low-powered by modern standards, but their compact designs had allowed them to fit in the officers' luggage. Diane, tugging at the flap of her holster, stopped when Van Felsen put a hand on her arm and asked, "Corporal Narejko, are you up to date on your heavy-weapons training?"

"Affirmative."

"Good. Then open the big map tube we brought."

Diane did. Instead of maps was yet another tube—an irregular dark green one that was the launcher for a relatively modern fire-and-forget multimissile pack.

"Take up your position at the far left window, Corporal," ordered Van Felsen as she produced and checked her own machine-pistol.

Lentsul almost started when Heshfet leaned over and stabbed a tentacle at the forward camera monitor: the front door of the target house had opened a crack, then shut quickly. The *Destoshaz* Manip sent a pulse of (thrill, interest, aggression) to everyone in her vehicle. "Well, maybe visiting here isn't such a pointless task, after all. Hold here, Lentsul, and launch our drones. All of them."

He complied. The security APC rolled to a stop, its nose just poking into the street that fronted on the house they had been sent to check. In that moment, all six weapons blisters rose up and out of their half-bays, turboprops whining, ducted side fans angling them up and away from the armored personnel carrier.

Heshfet stretched her arm over Lentsul's shoulder and pointed to the screen. "Look at all the thermal blooms inside the house. It has very much been reoccupied. Dramatically so."

Lentsul followed her gaze. "Agreed, Manip. Indeed, there might be too many of the *griarfeksh*. I will send two of the blisters around the back. In addition, I suggest we—"

Heshfet sent the combat air patrol a support request through the *selnarm*-moderated command circuit. Within a second, her message had been acknowledged. Even now, at least half a dozen Arduan strike craft would be sweeping in to put their ordnance at Heshfet's disposal. As she triggered the vehicle's squad-bay door, she instructed (readiness, wariness, ferocity) and also: "The natives that submit, we take captive. All others are to be killed." She rose up to her full height, brandished her machine-pistol. "Now"—Heshfet's *selnarm* surge swept the length of the vehicle—"follow me!"

Diane slid down and into a fire-ready position just as the private—who had taken her watch in the basement—finished pounding up the stairs. He immediately went for his bulky valise.

Ved had snapped off his safety and gone to the window

on the opposite side of the door from the staircase. "Jesu of Old, they must have had this house under observation."

"Looks like it." Falco put his eye to the sights of his own weapon, and Diane imagined she could hear an unspoken addition: *"Yes, the unauthorized bombers operating out of this location must have been sloppy enough to leave a trail. And that's going to get all of us killed now."*

Van Felsen was scanning the room, checking everyone's positions and readiness. He threw a glance at the back door—

—where the hulking Marine corporal she'd sent to check that route of egress had evidently decided to get his rather immense rifle first: he had just stuck his head out the door, leading with the weapon's muzzle.

"Corporal!" shouted Van Felsen. "No—don't show weapons. Not unless we have to, damn it!"

The large Marine, flustered, looked out the back door again as if checking whether anyone had seen him or heard her... then froze for one instant and hastily shut the door.

Van Felsen's voice—and face—was like a slab of bone-dry slate. "Report, Corporal. What did you see out there?"

Lentsul had just maneuvered one defense blister into position behind the target house when the rear door opened and the barrel of a *griarfeksh* military rifle protruded. He quickly dropped the altitude of the blister so that its sensor cluster just topped the roofpeak of an adjoining house. He reached out with (urgency) toward—"Heshfet!"

But she had obviously been monitoring the real-time

selnarm output that converted the vehicle's streaming sensor data into the equivalent of a telepathic command channel. "I see it, Lentsul. Send blister 3 to cover the rear exit, also. Now"—and she widened her *selnarm* projection to include her entire Enforcer-Group—"the *griarfeksh* are armed but not yet prepared. Quickly, rush the building before they can organize themselves!" And, exemplary *Destoshaz* that she was, Heshfet broke into a swift charge toward the target house.

Lentsul—both fearful and aroused by her gallantry—pulsed a warning (desist!) and pleaded with her to "Stop—wait for the air cover! Wait for all the blisters to be in position! Heshfet, you must wait just another—"

But Heshfet's *selnarm* had walled out his reluctance and suffused with (*berserkergang*), she closed on the house.

Joe Adams—usually the most animated of Van Felsen's command staff—was evidently a very cool customer in a crisis. "They're coming," he announced calmly from his position farther up the stairs that were just a step behind Diane. He was using the mid-floor landing as a higher vantage point to see out the same window where Diane waited. "Commander, they are charging with weapons at the ready."

"Shit," hissed Van Felsen, who looked not so much angry as bitterly disappointed. "Corporal, clear us a path of retreat out the back. The rest of you hold them off and disengage in descending order of rank, as possible. You do not wait for anyone else—you run like hell. Stay split up. Make all speed for fallback point delta. If it's compromised, you go into the bush and head for the nearest Resistance cell. Got it?"

Nods and murmurs of assent.

"Good. How close are they?"

Falco sounded tense. "They'll be coming through the door in a five-count. No sign of stopping or any attempt to communicate."

Van Felsen shook her head in what looked like both despair and disgust. "Open fire," she said.

The change in situation was so abrupt that Lentsul hardly knew what to do first. The back door opened, and a stream of murderous fire poured out—and hit the primary rearwatch blister dead-on. Already impressed by the marksmanship, he was utterly stunned when the unit's *protoselnarm* link stuttered and died: that heavy human rifle had been firing some form of hypervelocity armor-penetrating round. He commanded the next blister to rise up and return fire with all munitions, then sent another to the rear as Heshfet had instructed.

But in the same instant, the front windows of the house exploded outward in a glistening wave of shattered glass as multiple muzzle flashes licked angrily out over the sidewalk.

Lentsul felt Heshfet's *soka*—her life force—wink out in the very first moment of that fusillade. All her vitality and energy and raw, primal power was erased instantly, and in its place there was an emptiness so profound and yawning that it felt as if the provocative *Destoshaz* had never existed, had been a figment of Lentsul's fevered sexual imagination.

The others of Heshfet's group were not so lucky, for they did not expire so quickly. The half that did not get to cover first were savaged by multiple hits from a variety of human weapons—all of which fired faster and harder than anything that the Children of Illudor had yet encountered. Limbs trailing, clusters and tentacles shattered or even severed, they fell into writhing, blood-spurting heaps, expiring in an agony that buffeted Lentsul with a *selnarm* wave almost as powerful and piteous as that which had accompanied the burning deaths he had felt during the convoy ambush.

Lentsul experienced a *befthel*—a "three-eyed blink" that was often a sign of impending shock—before he could respond. And then, with (hate, vengeance, bloodlust) suddenly rising up through him and into the nearby *selnarm* links, he gave rapid orders to the blisters. One covered the rear door; a second boosted high on its fans for a bird's-eye look down upon the rear of the house. A third went to the front to provide support for the remaining *Destoshaz* Enforcers; a fourth hung back behind it, lurking low, waiting to pop up, and the last remained back near the vehicle to provide a base of fire.

Then he reached out his *selnarm* to the remaining group members, but an instant too late. They were—

"—charging again, Commander."

"Hit them—hard," said Van Felsen, who, turning, obviously intended to check the back door.

Diane could hardly keep track of events after that: they came so swiftly, that there was no reliable sequence.

All the firepower at the front of the house lashed out again. She popped up to look at the Baldy attackers and was stunned by their utter silence, composure, sinuous dodges, and eerie coordination. There were no delays, no waiting, no double-checking. Their fast leapfrog advance was seamless—but hopeless. The interlocking fields of fire tore the rest of them to pieces.

But a blister—airborne and right behind them—was firing with far greater accuracy. And lethality: the private at the door was literally cut in half by a sheet of small-caliber autofire that roared out of the blister in excess of eight hundred rounds per minute. At the same time, the same drone sent a small rocket blasting into the wall to the right of the door. Falco cartwheeled back into the middle of the room, missing both his left arm and the left side of his head.

Bastards, thought Diane, who brought the launcher up to her shoulder and dropped the crosshairs on the advancing blister. The vertical and lateral bars flashed and were then lined in green: she pulled the oversized trigger.

With a dull cough, the clearing charge put the rocket a few meters beyond the muzzle of the launcher. Diane ducked—just as the roar of the rocket kicked in and sent a back-blast through the window she'd been using but a moment before. A split second later, there was a confused smash, blast, howl of violated metal, and an even larger explosion.

Above and behind, Joe Adams's shout was a celebration. "That's one down, Corporal! Now hit 'em with—"

Then the rotary weapon sound came again, a little more distant—and she looked up in time to see calm, genial Joe Adams blasted into bloody tatters by yet another blister-mounted rotary machine gun.

Fucking *bastards*, she amended, selecting another AP round from the five-rocket magazine sleeve at the rear of the weapon. She shouldered the tube, readied herself to rise into a firing position—

—just as she saw the Marine corporal at the rear of the building go down. Van Felsen, arriving there a moment later, picked up his immense rifle, knelt, and dumped the clip skyward out the back door: there was a shuddering roar over the rooftops. Van Felsen dropped the spent weapon, turned, and shouted, "We're leaving! Everyone on m—"

And then Van Felsen exploded. She literally came apart in a spray of bone and blood and organs that spattered across the room—along with a few pieces of shrapnel that made a zipping sound as they went through Diane's left lung and shoulder. Ved was less lucky; at least a dozen fragments cut through his torso, and—eyes wide and a broad blood smear on the wall behind him—he slid down to the floor and slumped over.

Well, shit, thought Diane through her tears—and she came up to a crouch, firing at the first weapon blister she saw, not even bothering to wait for a targeting lock. She ducked down—and the same sounds of catastrophic destruction filled the street in front of the house.

Clutching the launcher, she low-crawled toward the back door and glanced around; only she was left. And there was obviously another flying trashcan covering the mostly closed back door—the one that had hit Van Felsen. Diane felt her lips pull back even as she pulled back the loading lever to advance yet another 38 mm AP rocket into the weapon's launch chamber. *Well, trash can, you're going down.* She squirmed over and crouched behind the door, ready to push it open, sweep the skies, and take a fast shot—

—when the door before her disintegrated under a typhoon of small, high-velocity bullets. Through the tattered remains of the door, she had a split-second glimpse of a defense blister floating there, just a meter beyond the doorframe. Evidently, it had been waiting for her thermal signature to draw close enough to fire blind through the door itself.

Diane Narejko discovered that she was still, inexplicably, completely lucid, despite the fact that her back was so wet with her own blood that she was lightly sticking to the wall where the inward blast had impaled and pinned her. And as the blister advanced through the doorway, and its rotary machine gun roared again, she experienced a fleeting feeling—rather like a great sadness—as she realized that the red spray now obscuring her vision was her own blood flying up from the bullets tearing through her chest.

And then, after another split second of the dusky red spray, came a deep, permanent blackness.

Lentsul, still quivering with rage and grief and horror, watched the pieces of what had been a human drop to the floor.

The *selnarm* link poked at him. (Urgent. Missiles inbound. Confirm?) came from the combat air patrol which, having been automatically updated on the terrible casualties the Group had suffered, now had precision munitions locked on target. Lentsul considered calling off the strike, sending the weapons to circle back around to fall harmlessly in the bay, but he reasoned—thinly—that there might still be some hostile *griarfeksh* in the house. And there was no reason to take chances that would cost more lives from the ranks of his brothers and sisters. Best let the weapons strike.

But he knew his real reason: he wanted to obliterate the house and the remains of those that had killed Heshfet. Heshfet who had always had contempt for him; who had stretched like a goddess when she emerged from the misting-chamber; who had been impetuous, temperamental, capricious, emotional, and the object of his every waking and sleeping fantasy. These *griarfeksh* would pay—and keep paying—for discarnating her: even if they had already gone to a blank, soulless death in the true oblivion of *xenzhet-narmat'ai*. He would make sure that they were all spinning down that hole of utter nothing, make sure in the most final manner possible: he would wipe the house from the face of the earth.

So it was that when Lentsul sent (confirm) he did not stop to think—nor would he have cared—that he was sterilizing the site of any possible intelligence or forensics value.

And he did not know that, just as surely, he was cremating the remains of what had been the only, and last, nascent hope for peace between Arduans and humans.

Sandro had seen smoke arise with great suddenness over the roofs of his neighborhood as he pulled on to the closest cross-street that would allow him to park near his house. Then more smoke, and he heard the double-crack of distant sonic booms from all points of the compass: Baldy combat flyers going supersonic, and from every side of him. From every part of the horizon.

As he nosed into the intersection with the street that went past his front door, he saw the source of the smoke from three blocks away: his house was aflame. Burning wreckage—some Baldy machinery, some nearby parked vehicles, even parts of the façade of his house—filled the street. He thought he saw bodies as well, and floating objects that looked like upright, round-ended canisters: Baldy weapon blisters in remote mode. Farther beyond that, through the smoke and occasional movement, he saw what looked like the nose of a Baldy personnel carrier—which rolled backward, even as he watched. The blisters stopped their vaguely cyclic movement and fell back directly on the armored vehicle, accompanying it out of sight around the distant corner.

That was when Sandro caught a flash of movement from the corner of his eye. High above the rooftops, a dot—riding a growing column of smoke—was hurtling downward at a sharp angle. Then he noticed five others, each closing from different, and widely separated, points of the compass.

Sandro took his foot off the brake, accelerated smoothly through the intersection, turned back in the direction he had come from, and took a quick look in his rearview mirror.

As he watched, the first missile came down. He saw the roof of his house—and several nearby—fly upward, riding a geyser of smoke and intermittent flame. Then the other five missiles came in, just as the sound of the explosions started rolling over him in one long wave: the concussions rattled the glass of his vehicle's rear window, and shook the roadway enough that he could feel it shift under him as he drove.

And, hands digging into the synthetic leather of the steering wheel, he thought: *This—this is all me. This is* my *fault.*

5

No Task Too Steep, No Step Too Far

No task's too steep for human wit.
—Horace

BuShips Research Station Oscar Sierra Four, Mars Orbit, Sol System

"The Desai prime drive indeed!" Admiral Sonja Desai, TFN/PSUN, gave the sniff that, like so many facets of her personality, not everyone found irresistibly endearing. "They ought to call it the Kasugawa drive, if they must personalize it."

Isadore Kasugawa, PhD, smiled. It wasn't exactly the first time he'd heard this. Nor was he unused to Desai's moods. Old acquaintances, they had come out of retirement in response to the Baldy threat, specifically to collaborate on a major enhancement to the drive technology that already bore her name. "I could hardly cope with more recognition than I already have," he told her gently. An uninitiated observer might have interpreted his smile as fatherly. His face, a thoroughgoing blend of ethnic features even by the standards of twenty-sixth century humanity, looked older than hers. But in fact, he had less than a hundred standard years to her hundred and thirty-six, having commenced antigerone treatments at a later age. "After all, I have the Kasugawa generator named after me."

"It's the least you deserved for discovering what the human race and others have been seeking for almost six centuries—a way around the random natural placement and capacity of warp points."

"But it was really just an offshoot of the principles of your phased gravitic space drive," he rebutted.

"Oh, rubbish! It was a radical new application which had never occurred to me."

Kasugawa laughed and raised his hands in mock surrender. "All right! All right! But if you're going to argue that way, you must admit that the Desai prime drive *isn't* a radical departure, just an extension of the original principle—*your* original principle. I just helped with the details."

Desai knew better than to argue further when Kasugawa's face wore that "*Got* you!" look. She leaned on the rail of the observation deck where they stood and gazed out through the space station's curving transparency at the world it orbited: Mars, Sol IV.

That world's surface stood in sharp relief under its thin atmospheric veil, with craters pockmarking its ocher dryness. A fairly useless world, she reflected. Nevertheless, it had served as the setting for some of the most glamorous and exotic interplanetary adventures imagined by prespaceflight humans. But then, in 2053, the exploration ship *Hermes*, en route to Neptune, had abruptly found itself in the Alpha Centauri system, having blundered through Sol's single warp point. With a galaxy full of Earthlike planets suddenly within reach, Mars had been largely forgotten.

But once BuShips decided to place this particular

test in the Sol system for its security advantages, Mars emerged as the logical candidate to serve as its orbital anchor. Isolated and having ready access to Sol's raw-materials-producing asteroid belt, it was also located relatively close to Sol's Desai limit, within which the phased gravitic drive would not function.

Desai turned to face a battery of screens—and one in particular, displaying the view from a small but heavily instrumented ship out beyond the Desai limit. It showed the starfields twenty light-minutes out, where Sol was little more than a superlatively bright star itself. Occluding some of those stars was an even smaller, unmanned vessel. Desai would have liked to be aboard the observation ship herself, but she needed instant access to the entire array of interpretive computer power here on the station. She ran her eyes over the various screens with heightening anticipation, for the drive should have already been activated; now they were simply waiting for the test data to wing across the light-minutes. Although the imperfectly understood warp network allowed ships to get around Einstein's Wall between paired warp points, nonmaterial energy transmissions were still limited to the velocity of light.

"It should be anytime now," said Kasugawa, eyeing the chronometer. They both fixed their eyes on the robot vehicle in the viewscreen.

All at once, for the tiniest fraction of a second, optical illusion made that vessel seem to stretch out to infinity. Then, in less than an eyeblink, it vanished. At the same time, the various screens came to life, flashing out a veritable explosion of data.

Kasugawa studied it intently. "As predicted. It instantaneously took on a velocity—or a 'pseudo-velocity,' as the purists insist on calling it—of eighty-four point nine seven three five lightspeed." He turned to Desai, and his face looked almost young. "In fact, it matches almost exactly the theoretical figures."

"But—also as theory predicted—it's all or nothing. It can't be slowed down to incremental velocities for maneuvering purposes." Desai looked at another set of readouts. "And, also as we predicted, this speed is beyond the limit of our radiation and particle shielding's ability to protect a crew. We're going to have to work on that." She smiled wryly. "In a way, we're back where they were in the first days of manned spaceflight, before the development of electromagnetic shields, when the effects of long-term exposure to cosmic radiation looked like an insuperable obstacle to interplanetary voyages."

"You might say that." Kasugawa gave her quizzical look. "I never knew you were interested in history."

"I'm not, really. In fact, I used to know nothing about it. But I met someone who was a true enthusiast. His enthusiasm was contagious. . . ." Desai's eyes took on a faraway look. Then, with a jerk of annoyance at herself, she turned abruptly away to study additional data.

Kasugawa smiled. He had heard the stories about the feelings Desai had once held, long ago, for Ian Trevayne, her commanding officer during the Fringe Revolution. Like everyone else, he had found those stories hard to believe. But just maybe . . .

RFNS Zephrain, *Main Body, Rim Federation Fleet, Astria System*

The dazzling light of Astria's type-F primary sun streamed into RFNS *Zephrain*'s cavernous hangar bay as the shuttle nosed through the atmosphere screen and settled down on its landing jacks with a pneumatic wheeze when its drive cut out and the supermonitor's internal artificial-gravity field took control. The gangway extended itself, and the honor guard of *Zephrain*'s Marine detachment came to attention as the Alliance's new supreme commander emerged.

Fleet Admiral Cyrus Waldeck, TFN/PSUN, standing at the foot of the gangway with his staff officers and task-force commanders, reflected that while he'd gone through the rituals of changing commanders many times before, it was especially unnerving when the new senior admiral had not only previously been his CO, but looked so damned *young*. The man descending the gangway looked like an Academy upperclassman dressed up in imitation of a flag officer.

Waldeck pulled himself together. He stepped forward and saluted formally. "Welcome to Astria and Second Fleet, Admiral Trevayne."

The tall young man returned the salute with equal gravity. "Thank you, Admiral Waldeck." Then his dark face formed the lopsided smile Waldeck remembered (although when he'd last seen it, a neatly trimmed graying beard had framed it). "It's been a long time, Cyrus—at least for you!"

It had indeed.

Over eighty standard years ago, in the throes of the Fringe Revolution, Ian Trevayne had become a hero to the loyalist side (and something else altogether to the Fringers who had seceded to form the Terran Republic). He had held the systems of the Rim for the Terran Federation, from which they were isolated by the vagaries of the warp network. The war might have had a different conclusion had he succeeded in ending that isolation by fighting his way through Republic space to reestablish contact with the Federation. But in the apocalyptic Battle of Zapata, he had been stopped and killed . . . almost.

Captain Cyrus Waldeck, scion of one of the Corporate World dynasties whose pitiless exploitation of the Fringe had broken the old Federation apart, had been there. Trevayne had been preserved in a semblance of life by quick-and-dirty measures that had left him in a state of cryogenic suspension from which he could not be awakened without killing him.

However, just prior to the Baldy invasion, it had become possible to transplant Trevayne's brain into a full-body clone of himself—force-grown anencephalic, to avoid ethical issues. Now his fifty-plus mind and personality dwelled in his own early-twenties body—and the coincidental timing of that reanimation had stirred deep mythic wells: Trevayne might not have exactly been sleeping beneath a mountain or on the Isle of Avalon, but he had returned when his people had needed him.

For his part, Trevayne now gazed at a sight that had become all too familiar: the decades-older face of someone he had last seen less than two years ago in terms of his own consciousness, but for whom eighty years had passed.

Although, truth be told, Cyrus Waldeck looked better than many: like all Corporate Worlds old money, he had benefited from the anagathic regimen from an early age. His 130-year-old features remained distinctly those of his plutocratic clan, with a thin, pursed mouth incongruously placed between massive chin and prominent nose. That mouth shifted into a position that suggested an answering smile. "Good to see you, sir."

Trevayne's own smile became a shade more personal. "And you, too, Cyrus." Then he put a brisk edge in his voice: the moment was over. "I'm eager to meet my new staff, particularly since I've only brought one new staffer with me." He indicated the officer who had descended the gangway behind him. "Lieutenant Commander Andreas Hagen, my technical liaison officer."

Waldeck looked slightly puzzled as he returned Hagen's salute—understandably, Trevayne reflected. The title had been cobbled together to justify the presence of Hagen, previously an instructor at the Rim Federation's Prescott Academy, subsequently assigned to Trevayne as . . . there had to be a better word than "nursemaid." But he had fulfilled an indispensable role in the course of Trevayne's eighteen months of intensive study, and Trevayne wasn't quite ready to let him return to the classroom as he would have wished.

As protocol demanded, Waldeck introduced Trevayne to his own staff before progressing to his other unit commanders, and then several of the fleet officers of both the allied and alien contingents: Vice Admiral Alistair McFarland, RFN, of Task Force 21; Least Fang Zhaairnow'ailaaioun, PSUN, of Task Force 22; and . . . "Finally," concluded Waldeck, "for the rebel . . . I mean the Terran Republic elements, Vice Admiral Li Magda of Task Force 23."

For Trevayne, it was as though he were once again in the grand-reception room of Government House on Zephrain, staring into those uncannily black eyes.

"Yes, we have already met. And congratulations on your richly deserved promotion to vice admiral, Admiral Li."

"Thank you, Admiral Trevayne," said Li Magda primly.

Then a twinkle awoke in the ebon depths of those eyes—her mother's eyes. "But I thought we agreed at the time that you'd call me Magda."

"So I recall. I compromised on that, not being quite ready for 'Mags.' But for now, we'd better observe the military proprieties. Oh, incidentally, since then I've spoken to your mother, First Space Lord Li Han. She sends her best."

"Yes, I've heard the story of your meeting with her. Everyone has." She met his eyes boldly. "It's my belief that you and she have written a new chapter into your respective legends."

All at once, Trevayne could feel, in the small of his back, a hangar bay full of eyes focused on him and the daughter of Li Han.

The Fringe Revolution was fresh memory for him, but for the current generations it had receded into the numinous realms of legend, peopled with larger-than-life figures. Figures like Ian Trevayne, who had been forged into a weapon of vengeance by the nuclear fires that had incinerated his wife and daughters—a weapon that had killed his own son, who had joined the Fringe rebels. And like Li Han, who had been Trevayne's prisoner and afterward had battered him to a standstill in the unimaginable inferno of Zapata. Their two names, taken together, had entered into the language as bywords for unrelenting enmity.

"That might be a trifle strong," he said mildly. "But I daresay the sight of your mother and myself, together on the same podium, arguing in favor of the same strategy for ending this war, may have . . . well, made an impression on people."

Her eyes held his and would not permit him to

escape into flippancy. "It's why this alliance is now unbreakable—and committed to that strategy. And you and Mother both know it."

"Well, then," said Trevayne with a briskness that almost succeeded in masking his embarrassment, "perhaps we'd best discuss that strategy. I'm sure you already know it, at least in its essentials, being your mother's daughter. It was, after all, her brainchild. I'm also sure you've maintained security by not revealing it to anyone here. That's what I've come for. Cyrus, lead the way."

They proceeded to *Zephrain*'s auditorium-like flag briefing room. It had a wide viewscreen for the two-dimensional displays that usually sufficed for displays of planetary systems, since planets and warp points tended to occur roughly in a single plane. But at Trevayne's request, technicians had hooked up a holographic projector focused on the stage in front of the viewscreen.

The reason for the holo display wasn't immediately apparent, for what it displayed could have been—and normally was—shown flat. It was a chart looking much like an old-style circuit diagram, with points of light representing stars (and the occasional starless warp nexus) connected by the string lights of warp lines. It had nothing whatsoever to do with the arrangement of those stars in actual three-dimensional space, nor did it need to.

Everyone recognized one segment of the warp network: the Bellerophon Arm, oriented so that the Bellerophon system itself, and its one warp connection to the rest of the Rim Federation through Astria, was at the bottom. Much else was also shown, with the stars color coded for the polities to which they belonged. Somewhat puzzling were two brilliant white star points, one in the outliers of the Bellerophon Arm, the other off to the side of the display among the lights of the Terran Republic, to which its only two warp links ran.

"This, ladies and gentlemen," said Trevayne, "is the way we always look at the universe. Since discovering warp points, it's the only view of reality we've needed. Then the Baldies—whose real name remains unknown because no attempt to communicate with them has had the slightest success—arrived at Bellerophon after centuries of travel through normal space in fleets of generation ships powered by photon drives. It was miserably bad luck that they happened to appear at such a strategic warp nexus, where they've cut off the entire Bellerophon Arm like a tree at its base. As I needn't tell any of you, we have tried twice to break into the Bellerophon system from here in Astria, through our one warp connection. I also needn't tell you what came of those attempts."

"How could it have been otherwise, by God?" Waldeck blurted indignantly. "When their smaller generation ships are designed to be broken down into system defense ships *five hundred times* the tonnage of a supermonitor like this one, carrying four or five hundred fighters? And don't give me any whistling-past-the-graveyard crap about the SDS's inherent design inefficiencies and lack of maneuverability. It doesn't *need* to maneuver when all it has to do is sit on top of the one miserable warp point that is the only way we have of getting at them!" Waldeck suddenly came to the appalled recollection that he was addressing the supreme commander and mumbled an apology.

Trevayne was not offended. "You're quite right, Cyrus. Rest assured that neither I nor anyone else qualified to have an opinion on the matter holds you to blame. Second Fleet has done all that could have been done under the circumstances. And I want to emphasize that this is not, strictly speaking, a change of command. You are still in direct charge of Second Fleet, under my overall supervision as supreme commander of a force that is going to grow to include far more than Second Fleet.

"However, the inescapable fact remains that we find ourselves at an impasse here. And while the more recent incursion by another Baldy fleet into the Pan-Sentient Union has opened a second front in the Zarzuela system, our attempts to counterattack there have not succeeded in creating a war of movement; in effect, it is merely an extension of the impasse.

"It is against this background that First Space Lord Fleet Admiral Li Han of the Terran Republic has proposed a strategy which the Alliance governments have adopted, and which I have been appointed supreme commander to effectuate. To understand this strategy, a certain amount of technical background is in order. Most of it will already be familiar to you, at least in its broad outlines, since you have access to Pan-Sentient Union and Rim Federation classified-message traffic—and Terran Republic intelligence updates." Trevayne accompanied the last with a glare at Li Magda that he suspected probably didn't quite come off, and which she met with a look of bland innocence. "But permit me to recapitulate.

"First of all, by now you have all heard about the new category of warship the Terran Republic is putting into production—the 'devastator.' Fleet Admiral Li gave me a tour of *Taconic*, the first ship of this type to be completed, and I assure you that whatever you may have heard is not exaggerated. At two million tonnes, it is the most massive ship that can transit any warp point."

"But Admiral," Cyrus Waldeck objected, "that must limit its strategic mobility."

There was a general nodding of heads among the PSUN and RFN officers. Warp points differed in their mass capacity. A supermonitor like *Zephrain* could not fit through all of them. And surely this new monster—two-thirds again a supermonitor's mass—would be even more restricted.

"The point is well taken, Cyrus. And that leads to my next item of background information. Here again, it's something of which you're already aware. Kasugawa generators, when activated simultaneously as a pair, can create an *artificial* warp line between them."

"But this would seem to involve what I believe humans call a catch-22, although I have never understood the reference," said Zhaairnow'ailaaioun. The felinoid Orion stroked his luxuriant whiskers in a characteristic gesture of perplexity. "One must position the second generator wherever one wants to establish a new warp point. And how can it be so transported without going through preexisting warp points?"

"That, Least Fang, is the essence of Fleet Admiral Li's strategy. It is brilliant—as I, of all people, have reason to expect of her," Trevayne added dryly, to general laughter and a twinkling smile from Li Magda. He used a light-pencil to indicate the two dazzling points of white light in the holo display. He pointed first at the one in the Bellerophon Arm.

"This is Borden—a lifeless cul-de-sac red-dwarf system connected to the rest of the Arm only through a starless warp nexus. And this," he continued, pointing far across the display, "is ZQ-147, a starless warp nexus in Terran Republic space. And *this*," he finished with a dramatic pause, "is why we are interested in two such worthless cosmic afterthoughts." He made an adjustment to the remote.

With startling suddenness, the lights in the display crawled rapidly together and then exploded outward. The display was now definitely three-dimensional, with lights of all colors intermingled, and the string lights of warp lines had vanished.

"This is the actual distribution of stars in normal space. Normally, we never think about it, nor do we need to. But you will note that the two bright white lights are now almost touching. In point of fact, Borden and ZQ-147 are only 2.21 light-years apart.

"The plan is for a joint Terran Republic/Pan-Sentient Union expedition from ZQ-147 to journey to Borden through normal space—"

"Through *normal space*?" someone blurted.

"—carrying one of a pair of Kasugawa generators," Trevayne continued. "On arrival, an artificial warp line will be opened between the two systems, and Fleet Admiral Li will lead a fleet of supermonitors through it, carrying another Kasugawa generator that can be used to enlarge the mass capacity of existing warp points, thus allowing transit by the devastators. They will be able to liberate all of the Arm short of Bellerophon itself, which will then be isolated and subject to attack through four warp points, not just one."

"But Admiral," McFarland ventured in the Aussie-descended accent of Aotearoa, "even if it's only 2.21 light-years, that's one bloody hell of an 'only'! I mean, across normal space..." He shook his head, clearly having trouble coming to terms with such an unheard-of idea.

"That's where my final bit of technical background comes into play. And this is one which, unlike the others, will come as news to almost everyone here." Trevayne accompanied the heavily stressed *almost* with another attempt at a stern look in Li Magda's direction, with no greater success than the previous one. "Dr. Kasugawa and Admiral Desai are even now in the process of testing experimental prototypes of an improved version of the Desai drive—the Desai prime drive, as they're calling it. Theory predicts that it will be able to instantaneously impart a velocity of 0.85 c, as compared to the 0.50 c of the Desai drive. At this velocity, a significant time-dilation advantage comes into play. The voyage should take only 1.37 subjective years."

"But from the standpoint of an outside observer?" Zhaairnow queried.

"Two point six standard Terran years," Trevayne stated bluntly. "As Fleet Admiral Li pointed out, this is just as well, as her fleet of devastators is going to be a long time abuilding. There are, of course, other problems to be overcome, such as shielding for the crew at such velocities, but Dr. Kasugawa and Admiral Desai are confident that these are solvable. In short, this gives us a war-winning strategy—an alternative to an endless bloody stalemate here at the Astria/Bellerophon warp connection." Stunned silence met his summation. "No questions? Well, then—dismissed," he concluded with a smile.

As the gathering broke up, he found himself—not altogether by accident—facing Li Magda. "Ah... Admiral Li, could you spare me a moment?"

"Of course, Admiral."

"I was thinking . . . since you're the senior Terran Republic commander here, and since the TRN is of course outside the interlocking command structure of the PSUN and the RFN, perhaps it would be useful for us to exchange a series of courtesy visits—simply to establish the closest possible professional rapport, you know."

"It would also create a desirable impression on my personnel, Admiral," she agreed with great seriousness. "Especially given . . . well, your history in relation to my family."

"Excellent point! Well, then, I'll have Commander Hagen set it up. He's acting as my glorified secretary, you see. And . . . I'll look forward to it."

"As will I, Admiral."

As he turned away, Trevayne noted that the room hadn't emptied quite as quickly as he might have expected. In fact, it almost seemed as thought people were dawdling, surreptitiously watching him and Li Magda. He wondered why.

6

Dire Progress

Is it progress if a cannibal
uses knife and fork?
—Lec

Direness, familiar to my slaughterous
thoughts, cannot once start me.
—Shakespeare

Headquarters, Confederation Fleet Command, Luzarix, Hyx'Tangri System

The characteristic flat plains of the Tangri homeworld, with their carpet of tough gray-green *khunillatis* vegetation, stretched away, seemingly into infinity.

Ultraz, gazing out across those plains from the terrace, felt within himself the emotion the sight always awoke in his race—a feeling for which the human word "wanderlust" was a pale and inadequate approximation. He was the Dominant One, the speaker of the *arnharanaks* or "high rulers," the assemblage of the *anaks* of all the hordes. But he was no more immune to the feeling than the lowliest Tangri.

Nevertheless, his position required him to see with longer vision than others. To him, the stars were a vaster plain, on which grazed herds of prey beyond the dreams of his ancestors—prey like the humans.

He leaned on the balustrade, resting the arms of his upright torso on it while stretching out his horizontal four-legged barrel. He had read, in one of the in-depth intelligence reports, that the humans described his race as *centauroid*, a word derived from a legendary creature with the upper parts of a human and the body of their favorite riding animal. He regarded it as a compliment, reflecting the humans' unconscious awareness of their own inadequacy. Their ancestors had needed that riding animal to give them the kind of mobility the Tangri possessed as part of their evolutionary birthright. It had made possible the nomadic cultures of early human history—but it hadn't been enough to prevent the settled agriculturalists and town-builders (*zemlixi*, came the automatic, contemptuous thought) from eventually imposing their mud-bound pattern on all their race.

Which, Ultraz reflected, had probably been inevitable anyway. The humans, after all, were not Tangri, and therefore not truly sentient. Oh, they clearly had some neurological process that served them in place of intelligence, like the Orions and all the others. But nothing could alter the fact that, at bottom, they were merely prey animals.

Very dangerous ones, it had to be admitted.

"It is time, Dominant One," came a diffident but subtly mischievous voice from behind him.

"Thank you, Scyryx," he said, turning. The male who had spoken was slightly smaller than Ultraz, and his short, dense fur had a less pronounced reddish undertone. But a human would have discerned little difference between them, beneath the common alienness of flat, bone-armored head and blunt snout. But to Tangri eyes, attuned to ethnic minutiae, Scyryx was a classic physical specimen of the widely disliked Korvak Horde. ("Greasy, effeminate corrupters with low cunning" came closest to expressing, in human terms, the popular image.) Their association therefore had to be publicly downplayed as a political alliance of convenience. Privately, Ultraz—who was, for a Tangri of the dominant culture, almost uniquely free of Horde stereotypes—valued Scyryx's advice and found his irreverence toward traditional rigidities more refreshing than he dared admit.

They proceeded down one of the shallow ramps that served the Tangri in place of stairways and entered the massive building—even more brutally functional than most Tangri structures, for it housed the headquarters of the Confederation Fleet Command. They passed through multiply redundant layers of security, where guards raised their chins, exposing their throats to Ultraz in the submission gesture of greeting. Those guards all wore harnesses of a uniform pattern—an innovation among the fiercely individualistic Tangri. But then, the Confederation Fleet Command was an innovation in itself, born of the demonstrated inability of the separate Horde fleets to cope with prey-animals as formidable as those that grazed among the star-fields. It was ironic that Heruvycx, its *arnhahorrax* or commander, was by birth a member of the Hragha Horde, whose spectacularly disastrous attempt at independent action had made that inability clear to all but the most reactionary or stupid.

On reflection, though, Ultraz decided it wasn't so ironic after all. Horde origins mattered less and less among CFC officers. That was one reason he spent as much time here among them as he could justify. Their attitude was something else he surreptitiously found refreshing, after days spent wading through the morass of inter-Horde politics.

He and Scyryx entered the vast hexagonal chamber that was the CFC's nerve center. There, surrounded by viewscreens and ranks of control panels, was a large circular table encompassing a holographic display.

Heruvycx and his staffers were reclining on the frameworks that served the Tangri for chairs. Their aides and assistants—*zemlixi* for the most part, descended from the conquered agricultural populations, outside and beneath the Horde society—stood far back in the shadows. Scyryx almost but not quite joined them, taking his place behind Ultraz as the latter reclined, receiving the submission gestures of the officers who rose at his approach.

"Greetings, Dominant One," said Heruvycx. "We have analyzed the latest reconnaissance probe findings and are ready with a report and recommendations."

"Excellent, *arnhahorrax*." Ultraz studied the holo display, recognizing the warp chain its human discoverers had named the Bellerophon Arm.

His attention was particularly focused on the Tisiphone system, nine warp transits up the chain from Bellerophon, and the starless warp nexus BR-07, eight warp transits up and then one transit off into a spur.

It was at those points that the Tangri possessed warp connections with the Bellerophon Arm and the human polity called the Rim Federation that claimed it. Those connections had long since been known, and attempts had been made to exploit them, through the New Hordes (a fiction invented for the purpose of assigning blame for raids that failed—a ploy that would not have fooled anyone but a mental defective or a human politician). But unfortunately, the human admirals had not proven susceptible to such subterfuges. They and their considerable fleets had been a troublesome impediment. Now, however...

"Ever since receiving your policy guidance," said Heruvycx, as if reading Ultraz's thoughts, "we have continued probing those warp points as instructed, to determine whether the Rim humans in the Bellerophon Arm have withdrawn their strength to deal with the new prey animals that have occupied the Bellerophon system."

Ultraz gave a gesture of approval. The appearance of the new arrivals at Bellerophon—through normal space, of all the unheard-of things—had burst open the entire strategic picture and spawned a whole new range of possibilities. After much debate, the options of allying with one or the other of the factions in the new war—for example, allowing the humans access to the Arm through the two warp points—had been rejected. The advantages had not been commensurate with the risks, not to mention with the sheer revulsion aroused by the unprecedented thought of allying (however insincerely) with prey animals. Instead, it had been decided that the Tangri would take advantage of the Rim humans' sudden inability to learn what was transpiring in the Arm beyond the Bellerophon system itself. In fact, the Tangri would reinforce that ignorance by declaring neutrality (a typically gutless human concept) and closing their borders. And then they would begin to implement their longstanding ambition by seizing the Rim's Treadway system and everything beyond it, thus securing all the open warp points of the Arm. Afterward, they could begin to work their way down the Arm toward Bellerophon itself.

Heruvycx indicated a display screen. "These, Dominant

One, are the vessels the Rim humans had deployed in the two systems in question at the time our policy was first put into effect. Since then, as instructed, we have sent reconnaissance drones through the warp points at regular intervals."

Ultraz gestured his understanding. One of the fundamental facts of interstellar travel was that only a fairly substantial physical vessel could transit a warp point. There could be no nonmaterial transmittal of information through one. For centuries, this had meant that anyone passing through an unexplored warp point (or one with enemies waiting on the other side) had been going in blind.

New columns of figures appeared on the screen. "These are the corresponding figures from the later drones, keyed by date," Heruvycx explained. "You will note that there has been little if any rotation among the picket vessels. Instead, they have become steadily less numerous as the larger ship types have begun to depart. Since these systems were never protected by any hull heavier than a light cruiser, the current patrol forces are composed almost entirely of very light units."

"Yes, I see all this."

"Dominant One, these data indicate that the Rim humans are coming under increasing pressure from their enemies, so that they must call on all the forces they can scrape together, even at the cost of inadequate picketing. In the opinion of the Confederation Fleet Command staff, this suggests that the time is growing ripe for us to make our move."

"Furthermore," Scyryx put in, "if the new prey animals are, indeed, advancing up the Arm from Bellerophon, we will be well advised to act without unnecessary delay. The more systems they conquer, the fewer easy conquests will be left for us."

"That is so, Dominant One." Agreeing with Scyryx obviously caused Heruvycx physical pain.

Ultraz considered for a moment. "Very well. I concur, and I do not believe there will be any serious dissent among the *arnharanaks*. Indeed, many of them have been chafing at what they consider our overcaution. If there is any disagreement, it will be dealt with." Ultraz left it at that, without going into what substances some of the *anaks* or Horde leaders used in place of brains. He had long since identified all possible sources of opposition and had arranged in advance for those sources to be humbled in personal combat on the *arnharanaks* floor, in the fine old tradition of Tangri parliamentary procedure.

"Thank you, Dominant One," said Heruvycx. "In anticipation of your decision, we have prepared orders for the redeployment of our fleets."

"Good. I leave matters in your hands, *arnhahorrax*." Ultraz got up off his framework. The staffers rose and then quickly dipped into the departing submission gesture while tucking their *kyeexes*—short-handled ceremonial glaives—well behind them.

Of course, Ultraz reflected, the real challenges to his talents lay ahead. The long-term policy could not be plotted out in advance, for it would depend on whether the humans or their new enemies won their war, and on how badly the winners had been weakened by their victory. Flexibility and adaptability would bear cultivating.

But Ultraz was not worried. A predator who blindly pursued a rigid course of action was a predator who did not live long enough to pass his stupidity on into the gene pool. So there were no such among Ultraz's ancestors.

7

Decrees of the Very Small

How wayward the decrees of Fate are;
How very weak the very wise,
How very small the very great are!
—Thackeray

Aeolian Lowlands, Icarus Continent, Bellerophon

Alessandro McGee stared down the Serrie sight now mounted on a Rimstar Rangemaster hunting rifle. Chambered for the same 8.5 mm ammunition he had been using during his training visits to Upper Thessaborea, this rifle was semiautomatic and optimized for long-range accuracy. And McGee was very pleased with the picture he saw in the scope.

The two Baldies who had been coming here every day for the past week had returned in their floater: a mixture of VTOL and ACV vehicle fused into a smoothly wedgelike fuselage. They had walked away from their craft, comparing data from their forearm computers with what was apparently written on a human paper map they had commandeered, and upon which they'd been scrawling notes for the past two days. Today, they occasionally pointed at the nearby bluffs, the marshland about half a kilometer farther on, and then back in the direction of Melantho, some eighty kilometers to the south. If Sandro had been a betting man, he'd have pegged them as surveyors, assessing water tables and flow patterns—and he was pretty sure he'd have won that bet.

But today was going to be these surveyors' last day on the job. He muttered to Wismer, who was spotting for him just two meters farther along the ridge line, "I make that 620 meters, wind 4.8 kph from north west north."

Wismer looked down his range-finding binoculars again. "I confirm that."

McGee double-checked that the Serrington Arms scope showed the same range and windage information and then carefully pressed the data-accept button in a recessed port on the left-hand side of the weapon's closed action. "I'm on internal processing," he announced.

"Acknowledged. Wind-change reports only, now."

McGee settled in behind the braced weapon, firmed his fingers around both the grip and forestock, and partially floated it off its rest: he wasn't lifting its weight so much as adjusting the rifle's orientation by the faintest slivers of a single degree. He drifted it in the direction of the Baldy who was closest to the vehicle, let the scope's crosshairs slide to a stop on the alien as he held the map steady against the wind. His fellow-surveyor came closer—

—*perfect*, thought McGee. "Check?" he muttered.

Wismer, who had just moved a wayward leaf away from the bushes under which they were concealed, nodded. "Data steady."

McGee let the crosshairs drift up toward his target's head, centering on the large eye that was fixed where the upper bridge of the Baldy's missing nose should be. He squeezed the trigger.

He didn't watch to see what happened to that one: that was Jonathan's job. Instead, McGee immediately drifted the crosshairs over to the other Baldy and put them a bit behind the front of his face.

When the second alien saw his companion go down with a bullet through his primary eye, he flinched back reflexively—and right into McGee's crosshairs.

As McGee had anticipated. He squeezed the trigger, and this time he watched. For the sheer vengeful gratification of it.

In the split second that the bullet took to reach its mark, the Baldy blinked and seemed to realize that he/she ought to hit the deck. But the alien wasn't fast enough: the bullet went into its head just between the lower margin of the large eye and the upper corner of the somewhat smaller and more rudimentary left-hand ocular organ.

Like the first Baldy, this one fell without a sound.

As McGee and Wismer had learned and expected from over twenty prior ambushes and assassinations, the floater immediately lifted up and started orbiting the site where its two passengers had been slain. How each Baldy machine knew when all its operators had been killed was still a mystery: the aliens didn't seem to be equipped with any personal biomonitors or transponders. But up it went. And, if Baldy was following his security-response SOP, high-speed defense sleds would be on-site within ten to eleven minutes. So there was no time to waste. McGee wriggled out of his position, stood, and prepared to head down the slight slope to chase after the pearl of great price.

To chase after the map.

The map was the mission's objective—and possibly the Rosetta stone they needed to begin cracking Baldy's language and his signals. The Baldy computers were as unfailingly unintelligible as the transmissions they emitted. The Resistance's central—and decidedly ad hoc—technical intelligence team (reservists all, but some damned smart ones in the mix) had pulled apart a number of Baldy computers in painstaking detail. In addition to a completely different approach to IT architecture, the team also found some subsystems that seemed vaguely analogous to transmitters but didn't seem to send anything—although they powered up whenever the rest of the system sent information, either by wireless, long-range transmitter, or hard link. God only knew what these mysterious subsystems were, and they gave no clue to their operation, except that they were always quiescent in the presence of humans. However, they seemed to automatically power up when Baldies approached and either sent some undetectable signal to, or involuntarily attracted the attention of, their most proximal masters.

Ah, but the map. For days, the Baldies had been scribbling on it—and a purely written form of their language seemed to offer a better chance at identifying some linguistic constants, some common ground upon which the new communication team could build at least a crude, working Baldy vocabulary. That the Baldies rarely used purely textual sources, and even more rarely uttered any sounds, made the overall challenge just that much more difficult. Which made this map a potential gold mine.

"Sandro," called Wismer as McGee finished scrambling out of the brush that was their overhead cover.

"Yeah?"

"We've got to go. Now."

Sandro had started heading down the slope, but now slowed a bit. "Yeah, just as soon as I—"

"Sandro." Wismer used that flat, level tone of his, which meant he had a must-hear message to relay.

McGee turned. "What's up, Jon?"

"Base. We're to head back. Immediately."

"But the map could—"

"They know about the map. I told them. They want us back now. We're to leave the map and make it back to HQ with all possible haste."

Bloody hell, thought McGee, *this isn't like Cap Peters.* Well, "Cap" was Lieutenant Peters, now—but either way, the Old Man always knew what he was about. McGee sighed, turned, looked back downhill.

The wind caught the map, floated it up as if to torment McGee, and then pushed it onward as it gusted toward the marshlands.

"Sandro?"

"Yeah," said McGee, stalking back up to the observation pit to break down his rifle, "I'm coming."

Resistance HQ was located in what had been a corporate hidey-hole and was therefore not indicated on government maps nor contained in any official directories. Although never a lively place, it seemed more subdued from the moment they arrived. Located directly under a multipurpose materials-processing complex—which saw a heavy and steady stream of traffic varying from bulk containers to trash movers—the gray walls of the complex seemed grayer somehow, as if the color had rubbed off on the HQ staff and standing units.

Moving through the somber corridors with Wismer, McGee offered up the glum joke, "Who died?"

A voice behind him observed, "There are things worse than death, Tank."

McGee turned and saw Harry Li lounging in a doorway. "Light Horse, what's going on arou—?"

But Harry just shook his head. "You're not hearing anything from me, Sandro. But come see me after you get briefed—and if I don't get a visit from you soon, then I'll come looking. Promise." And he rolled off the doorjamb, back into the room, and was gone.

"What the hell?" wondered McGee aloud.

Wismer's lips were tense and narrow. "Let's just get to the CO's office, Sandro."

They did, but once there were redirected to the smaller of the two adjoining conference rooms. *Must be a general briefing of senior NCOs*, McGee thought—but then why had Jon Wismer been included in the summons?

But he didn't have time to voice the question: they went through the doors into the conference room and discovered a very different scene than the one they had anticipated.

They had expected to be met, and briefed, by ex-Major Tibor Peters, who, despite being reduced to a first lieutenant in accord with the late Van Felsen's rank reshufflings, was still addressed (as he had been for almost twenty years) as "Cap"—and was still called the Old Man when he was out of earshot.

Cap was indeed there in the room waiting for them—but not at the center of the table, as they'd expected. Second Lieutenant William Chong, who still had a cast on his right leg, and his right arm in a sling, was also there, but also not at the center of the table. He was active Navy and the only one of the planet-based fighter jocks who had lived to tell the tale of fighting the Baldies. Instead, these two well-respected and competent warriors were seated in flanking positions to either side of—

Julian Heide, as thin and reedlike as ever, cleared his throat. "Sergeant McGee, Corporal Wismer, you will please take the seats that have been provided for you." Two straight-back metal-frame chairs—as hard on the eyes as they were on the posterior—were set in the center of the room.

McGee looked at Cap Peters, who—for the first time in all the years that Sandro had known him, trained with him, and drunk with him—looked away. "What is this, Cap? A trial?"

Heide cleared his throat again. "No, Sergeant. This is an inquest. That means it's an exploratory hearing in which—"

"I know what an inquest is—sir." McGee's lagging addition of the honorific made it painfully clear to all in the room that he had little enough respect for the man he had addressed. "Cap, what the hell is going on he—?"

"Sergeant," Heide interrupted, "I am in charge of this inquest. You will take your seat at once or I will have disciplinary demerits added to your record."

McGee turned back to diminutive Heide, fists balling up—but Wismer tugged him gently toward the chairs. Sitting off to one side, Ensign (formerly Lieutenant) Marina Cheung nodded sad encouragement to follow Jonathan's lead. And McGee conceded that she probably knew best: she was obviously here in her role as the Resistance's only Special Warrant Officer for Legal Affairs—a thoroughly nonstandard position that had been made necessary by the equally nonstandard situation on Bellerophon. McGee felt like spitting as he conceded inwardly, *Oh, Great God on a pogo stick, must I endure this charade—after everything else?* And although he did not want to, McGee dropped down into his chair with a crash, his slouched posture speaking all the contempt he was not allowed to voice.

At a nod from Heide, Marina stood. "Sergeant Alessandro McGee, Corporal Jonathan Wismer, this inquest is now officially convened. You are advised that your subsequent statements will become part of the official record of these proceedings, and that you are presumed bound by your oath of service to answer fully and accurately all questions put to you, to the best of your ability and understanding. Is that clear?" Cheung, who had become the assistant DA of her small township out in the northern wilds of Sparta, looked and sounded as if she were trying to apologize for every word she was uttering.

McGee sighed. *Well, I know what this is about, so I might as well get it over with.* "Lieutenant Heide, there's no reason for all the courtroom drama. I'll admit it. I was the 'Melantho Bomber,' and I was operating alone and without orders. In all honesty, I didn't mean to conceal the truth. I figured HQ had just decided to look the other way. At least that was the impression I got from Force Commander Van Felsen."

"Perhaps, but I have no documentation, nor reliable attestations, that the lieutenant colonel intended to let the matter go unaddressed."

"Of course you don't. Her staff was killed in Melantho just two weeks ago—except Montaño. And you."

"Quite true, Sergeant. And since this matter was not handled or addressed before her death, it falls upon me, as the acting military justice, to resolve it. However, some new information has come to light which compels us to take a more detailed look at your actions."

"Oh? And what information is that?"

"Two days ago, it was confirmed, by multiple report, that both Jennifer Peitchkov and her infant son are alive."

McGee gaped, then grinned and was on his feet to shake Heide's hand. Hell, he'd even consider hugging the little weasel. . . .

But Heide's expression was unsoftened by any fellow feeling or gladness at delivering such news. If anything, his brow was set in an even sterner line. "For the record, it is important to note that the sources of this report were first-hand witnesses. Evidently, a week ago, Ms. Peitchkov's infant developed a cough that, ultimately, turned out to be a routine and easily cured respiratory infection—nothing serious at all. However, the aliens did not know this, and evidently Ms. Peitchkov asked them to provide her with a pediatrician. The aliens complied, abducting the physician in their typical, brusque fashion, and then released him as soon as he had provided treatment and medications for the infant. That same day, he contacted and reported the incident to our new Resistance cell in Melantho, and was also able to prevail upon the two midwives who delivered the infant to corroborate that Ms. Peitchkov and her infant were alive, well, and in alien custody."

"That's great." McGee tried smiling again, but Heide either did not notice it or did not choose to react. Nor did the others in the room, which was even more puzzling. *What the hell is with all the long faces? This is* happy *news.* But after a moment's further reflection, McGee realized that something else had to be going on here: they didn't need all the top surviving Resistance brass just to issue a reprimand, or even convene a routine inquest.

Heide had not stopped talking. "As welcome as the news is that Ms. Peitchkov and her child are still alive, this news has raised an uncomfortable tactical, and even strategic, concern that cannot be ignored."

A strategic and tactical problem stemming from Jennifer's survival? McGee looked to his CO—the man whose job it was to sweat those issues—Captain Peters. "I don't get it, Cap. What's the military wrinkle?"

Heide raised his voice. "Lieutenant Peters is not senior here."

"Just this minute, I'm asking the CO about military matters, Lieutenant. I'm not talking about your inquest."

"Nor am I, Sergeant. The tactical and strategic concerns are now mine as well, since I am, effective today, your new CO."

McGee was not even aware he had leaped to his feet. "You are *what*?"

Heide did not blink. "I am the new commanding officer of the Resistance."

McGee's response was honest, if impolitic: "That's bullshit." He turned to Tibor Peters, who met his eyes this time—sadly. "Cap—Tibe—what the hell is going on here? What is this—?"

Heide rapped his gavel on the desk. "You will resume your seat and address the senior officer when making inquiries as to command structures, Sergeant."

McGee stared at Heide a full second before replying. "I *am* making my inquiry of the senior officer, Lieutenant." He turned back to Peters as Heide scribbled some notes and then started to reach for the paging button—probably to bring in some guards.

Peters spoke quietly. "Lieutenant Heide—sir."

Heide's hand hovered over the button. "Yes, Lieutenant Peters?" He had put a slight emphasis on the word "Lieutenant."

"Sir, this man—Sandro—has been under my command since he joined the Reserves. I think it might be easier—and faster—if I explain the situation."

Heide left his palm suspended over the button for a moment, then removed it with a deferential wave. "As you wish, Lieutenant. He's your man."

Damn right I'm Cap's man, you rat-shit, thought McGee, but instead of saying anything, he bent forward, eyes and ears intent on Cap.

Who looked like he'd fallen into himself and aged ten years since chow last night. "Sandro," he explained, "you know that when Lieutenant Colonel Van Felsen departed for Melantho, she left two of her Intelligence/Communication team behind. Here."

McGee nodded. "Yeah, sure. Ensign Montaño"—*a good kid with lots of promise, but still pretty green*—"and Lieutenant Heide." *Who the Baldies might otherwise have conveniently scragged.* "What of it?"

"Well, Tank, the fact of the matter was that Force Commander Van Felsen used her Intel team as her de facto command staff as well. Hell, we have lots of trained grunts in the Reserves, but not a lot of officers, and there's a particular shortage of folks with staff-officer experience."

"Okay, but that still doesn't explain why Heide's in charge now."

Peters shrugged. "Because he's senior, son."

McGee gaped. "He's—senior? What are you talking about?"

"He's talking about a simple, documented fact, Sergeant." Heide's interruption was cool, level, not quite contemptuous. "When Lieutenant Peters mustered out of active service twenty-one years ago, he had only been a first lieutenant for thirteen months. I have been a first lieutenant longer than that, and therefore—"

"How much longer?"

Heide stared at McGee. "Sergeant, when you address me, you will use the proper—"

"*Sir*, the sergeant wishes to ask a question, *sir*. How long have you been a first lieutenant—*sir*?"

Heide's mouth seemed afflicted by a momentary tic. "Fourteen months. And two days."

McGee looked at Peters. "Cap, tell me this is some huge joke. At least tell me you've logged a protest."

Peters suddenly looked very old and drawn. "Son, there's no basis for a protest. Lieutenant Heide is, by strict interpretation of regulations, completely within his rights. I was an acting first lieutenant for three years, actually—a brevet rank. But the official promotion to the rank took place exactly when Heide says it did. And besides, he's also been active duty now for four years longer than I was."

McGee gaped, worried he'd babble in his growing desperation. "But Cap—all the active service Marines at Acrocotinth, and at Camp Gehenna—there were plenty of captains and majors who—"

But Cap Peters was shaking his head. "All gone, son. All withdrawn—or killed. And we didn't advertise that fact when the Baldies got here. Van Felsen thought it would be bad for morale."

"What do you mean, the other officers were all lost or killed?"

"The training staff and cadres at Camp Gehenna were all pulled back to Astria when it was learned the aliens were going to arrive in the Bellerophon system. And given the furor over their arrival, and the isolated location of Gehenna, it was easy enough to make that withdrawal look like part of the massive redeployments under way at that time. HQ deemed it prudent to remove the Rim's biggest concentration of experienced Marine training staff and cadre. Judging from what happened here, I can't say they made the wrong decision.

"The actual casualties? Well, all our active-duty units were out at the forts guarding the warp points and orbital facilities. We lost ninety-five percent of the formations that had originally been stationed at Acrocotinth out there, along with most of the other active-duty units."

"Good God, Cap, why did they load so many Marines on the forts and orbital stations?"

"SOP when you're dealing with nonhumans, son—but you probably wouldn't have been taught that. It's ancient history now, purged from the training manuals. See, after the Bug War and the earlier dust-up with the Thebans, we had learned that, when your enemy isn't human, you can't assume that they are as sour on deep-space boarding actions as we are. And if you are being boarded, then it's just common sense that if you *don't* have Marines, your ship will be lost—as will all the crew—during the one-sided carnage. So with aliens we'd never encountered on the way, and millions of tonnes of fortresses to defend, General Trinh embarked all the Acrocotinth battalions on our spaceside hardpoints. And he—and almost all our officers—went with them.

"Of course, HQ never envisioned a complete loss of the system, at least not so fast. And although the Intel folks back in Astria made the right call with the withdrawal of Camp Gehenna's staff, they royally screwed the pooch when they presumed the arriving aliens wouldn't have reactionless drives. It's an understandable extrapolation, of course. Since our visitors were arriving by slow sublight speed, it seemed they neither had knowledge of warp points—which was correct—nor an understanding of reactionless drive technology, which was tragically *in*correct. So, by that erroneous logic, it was thought that the naval fight for the system would proceed more slowly, with more time for redeployments, shifting of forces and matériel.

"No one envisioned a two-day collapse, with all space stations lost. Poor Van Felsen was way down on the seniority list before the redeployments to the fortresses. Hell, as a light bird colonel, she just barely had enough rank to be made a Marine force commander. And so, son, what you see in this room is all we've got left, all we've got in the way of a command staff. And in the mix we have left, Lieutenant Heide has seniority."

McGee leaned back in his seat. Jennifer and the baby were alive: the best possible news. Heide was in charge of the Resistance: arguably, the worst possible news. What a day. "Let me guess—that announcement was made earlier today?" Which would explain all the gray faces and dark looks in the corridors of HQ.

Heide cleared his throat. "The officers were informed at 0800. I suspect there has been some inappropriate relay of that information to the enlisted ranks—nonregulation, but predictable."

McGee had to lock his teeth together against the

new CO's prim officiousness. *Heide, you need to get that imaginary swagger stick out of your ass, and the starch out of your jockstrap.* "And so I'm to tell the NCOs of the—change—in command structure?"

"Yes, as master gunnery sergeant, you would normally be responsible for relaying this information to all HQ and special action team NCOs."

"I would *normally* be responsible?"

"Yes. This returns us to the actual purpose of the inquest."

"Wait—wasn't it an inquiry into my bombings?"

"That's how it started, but as I mentioned, Ms. Peitchkov's—and the infant's—survival have added a new dimension to our investigation."

"Which is?"

"That we must reconsider the connection between your unauthorized bombings and the alien strike upon your house, which resulted in the death of your CO and the three most senior members of her command staff."

McGee couldn't see the connection between Jennifer, the baby, and Van Felsen's death, but he certainly understood how the latter was his fault—all his fault. "Lieutenant Heide, allow me to save the inquest board some time. I do not in any way deny that my bombings must have attracted the Baldy attention that ultimately resulted in the deaths of Commander Van Felsen and her—"

"I am not finished, Sergeant. You are relieved of duty, effective immediately. Charges and specifications will be handed down pending resolution of an inquiry into both the degree of your insubordination during your bombing activities in Melantho, and into the now undeniable possibility that you have been suborned by the Baldy occupation forces and have become a willing and active collaborator—"

"*What*?"

"—who may have provided them with both the time and the place where they could ambush Force Commander Van Felsen and her research team."

McGee leaped toward Heide; Jon Wismer's lean—but very strong—fingers clamped down on Sandro's arm, breaking his dive to get his own massive hands around Heide's lying, supercilious neck.

Heide, to his credit, had not even flinched. "Is it your intent to add a multiply witnessed attack upon a senior officer to the list of charges under investigation?"

John tugged at McGee's arm. "Sandro, this won't help. It won't help the Resistance, it won't help you, and it certainly won't help Jennifer. Now take your seat again."

"Thank you for convincing Sergeant McGee to see reason, Corporal Wismer. However, I have the unfortunate duty to inform you that, while you are not being investigated for subornation and treason, your role in the unauthorized bombings is also under investigation. And yes, Sergeant McGee, we will add your perjury from earlier in this session—since you claimed to have acted alone in the bombings—to the charges and specifications currently being assessed. In your case, Corporal Wismer, since we have no reason to suspect your loyalty, you will continue your duties at your current rank, at least until further notice."

"Yes, sir. But at the risk of trying the patience of the board, I can testify that Sergeant McGee had absolutely no interactions with the Baldies. Sir, he hated them—hated them so much that he couldn't just sit by and do nothing. Sir."

"I do not argue with the assertion that Sergeant McGee hates the aliens, Corporal. My concern is that they currently hold two persons who are desperately important to him, personally. It is only prudent to examine whether or not Sergeant McGee is merely guilty of operational ineptitude and disregarding orders—or whether he entered into collusion with the enemy in order to preserve the lives of his family. And Corporal, can you really testify—and I mean *testify*—to the claim that Sergeant McGee never had any contact with the Baldies? Did you have him under constant observation? Did you monitor all his communications?"

Wismer looked down at his hands.

"I didn't think so. So it is needful that we conduct an investigation into the possibility that Sergeant McGee might have been blackmailed into betraying his superiors and fellow Marines."

McGee tried to keep the hateful snarl out of his voice but knew that he had failed. "We were ordered to sit on our hands in Melantho while the Baldies drove fifty thousand men, women, and children out of the West Shore District. We kept sitting on our hands while they killed anyone who disobeyed, and even when they went into some hospices and nursing homes and . . . Damn it, Heide—you can't know what it felt like to be a Marine and watch all that going on right under your nose. You weren't there."

"No, I wasn't there, Sergeant. But did I need to be? Would my having been there change the fact that it looks very much like you were complicit in the deaths of your fellow Marines? The invaders had your significant other and child in their custody. They looked for the Command staff at your house, less than an hour after Commander Van Felsen arrived there. Now, how would the aliens know to do that unless they had gotten to you?"

"No. The timing was a coincidence."

"Was it? Then was it also a coincidence that you were the only person not in the house when the ambush occurred—an ambush that left no survivors who could ever depose against you, in the event they might have seen something during the attack, or in your house, which indicated your complicity? Was it also a coincidence that as soon as Ms. Peitchkov was taken, your bombings stopped?"

"The bombing stopped because the Baldies put me in the hospital. Then I went up to the training retreat in Upper Thessalaborea and Force Commander Van Felsen intimated that I had best stop the bombings. So I didn't resume them when I returned to Melantho, a few days ahead of the commander and her team."

"Possibly—although, except for your injuries, none of that can be substantiated, since all the involved parties are dead. Although—how was it you arrived at the hospital, again?"

McGee looked away: this was not possible, the way random facts seemed to now be gathering together to conspire against him. "I don't remember. I was unconscious. But I'm told the Baldies brought me to the emergency room."

"Which you claim you don't remember. Perhaps. Or perhaps they went back to your house to tell you that unless you cooperated, your pregnant girlfriend would be killed—and then roughed you up to alleviate any suspicion that you were now their willing accomplice. And is that also why the pediatrician was collected as soon as he was requested? Is that just some more *quid pro quo* from your alien masters?"

McGee was almost on his feet again, when he saw Cap Peters staring at him. Staring hard, eyes pleading. Pleading that Sandro stay in his seat.

Heide seemed to interpret the silence and McGee's sullen avoidance of his gaze as indicative of victory. "So, our inquest will proceed to examine if there are sufficient grounds to bring charges of both treason and insubordination against you, Sergeant McGee. Furthermore, I am bound by the express wishes of the late Elizabeth Van Felsen to inform you that, in the event of her untimely demise, she left instructions for you to be promoted back to the officer ranks when your work with her in Melantho was concluded. However, that work was never completed—indeed, it was never begun. Also, since you were absent during the Baldy ambush—"

"*Possible* ambush," corrected Peters.

"—during the Baldy ambush," persisted Heide, "and it is possible that you facilitated that attack, I cannot responsibly act upon Force Commander Van Felsen's recommendation. You shall thus remain an NCO. Furthermore, until we have completed our investigation into your activities in the weeks leading up to the ambush, I am relieving you of active duty and am ordering that you be confined to quarters, and held incommunicado, until such time as we have gathered enough information to decide whether charges are warranted."

Cap leaned forward. "Lieutenant Heide, this borders on the preposterous. Sergeant McGee—"

"Lieutenant Peters, as long as there remains any reasonable doubt that McGee has been suborned by the enemy through his personal concern for his family's welfare, he cannot be safely allowed into the field—and he must be held incommunicado. Any other course of action could compromise this HQ, and our teams in the field, in precisely the same way that Commander Van Felsen and the command staff were compromised."

"Again, *hypothetically* compromised."

Heide again ignored Peters's emendation. "Sergeant McGee, before you leave with the guards waiting outside, do you wish to say anything that you feel might assist in our investigation?"

"Yes. Find Rashid of *Rashid's Sport and Tool* store in Melantho. He will be able to tell you why I was not at my house when Commander Van Felsen's team arrived and will vouch that I was conducting activities vital to *minimizing* the possibility that our operations in Melantho might be compromised. Also, I—"

"Sergeant, since you seem to have a great deal to say, I suggest you write it down. I will see to it that the members of this board all receive a copy."

Peters jerked erect in his seat. "Heide, that is a flagrant violation of inquest procedures. The party under investigation is entitled to speak directly to the—"

"Lieutenant Peters, your carping over insignificant procedural details is an affront to yourself, the board, and the dignity of all Marine officers." Heide stood; for a moment McGee wondered if he was about to smirk. But the new CO only looked at Peters and said, "This board of inquiry stands in recess, pending receipt of further evidence. Dismissed."

8

A Single Step to a Star

A journey of a thousand miles
begins with a single step.
—Lao Tzu

To the stars, through adversities.
—var.

In Geosynchronous Orbit over Novaya Petersburg, Novaya Rodina

Novaya Rodina—altogether Earthlike save for a certain peach-colored tinge to the predominant blue common to almost all such worlds as viewed from space—rolled beneath Fleet Admiral Li Han, TRN, First Space Lord of the Terran Republic, as her shuttle approached the orbital construction dock.

The planet held no little significance for her. Partly it was personal, for this was the birthworld of her friend Magda Petrovna Windrider, godmother of her daughter. But beyond that, it was the site of the atrocity which had given the Fringe Insurrection its baptism of innocent blood and made it irreversible, setting in motion the Terran Republic's eventful early history—quite a bit of which Li Han herself had made.

But she had no eyes for it, or for anything except the titanic shape that lay within the dock, nearing completion as the latest of the TRN's devastators.

Over the centuries, reactionless drives and internal artificial-gravity and acceleration-compensation fields had caused spaceship design to assume a form which pre-spaceflight humans would have found oddly familiar: organized fore-and-aft, with the major components of the drive abaft where they produced the unavoidable "blind zone" that formed the basis of so much naval tactical doctrine. There were innumerable variations, of course—notably in the case of carriers, with their "outrigger" flight decks which enabled fighters to approach from astern for recovery despite that same blind zone. But by and large, the look was one not too unlike that which humans of Old Terra's immediate pre-spaceflight era would have expected to see five or six centuries in their future.

The devastator she saw under construction was no exception, despite her unprecedentedly titanic mass of two million metric tonnes. She still had the lines that had come to embody the transcendent combination of fleetness and destructive power wrapped within the hulls of the capital ships of space. To modern eyes, it meant what the blocky massiveness of a sailing ship-of-the-line must have meant to humans in the age of . . . *Oh, who was that wet-navy admiral Ian Trevayne has so often spoken of? Oh, yes, Nelson . . .*

Her communicator beeped for attention; the voice of her chief of staff awoke in her earpiece. "Admiral, *Goethals* has arrived—with Admiral Desai as a passenger. You asked to be notified as soon as—"

"Yes, of course, Captain M'Zangwe. I will be rendezvousing directly."

✧ ✧ ✧

By the time Li Han's shuttle approached the test station, TRNS *Goethals* lay alongside it, dwarfing it so completely as to reduce it to a tiny irrelevancy. Studying the new arrival's configuration—which the unaided eye could do from a seemingly impossible distance—Li Han was struck by how completely it contradicted all her recent reflections on starship architecture.

The *Goethals* reminded her irresistibly of an épée, its "blade" a thin keel-shaft five kilometers long, with a seemingly tiny tip at the forward end and a disc-shaped shield at the other. Abaft of that was the massive "handle" holding the drive and power plant. On closer inspection, some of the illusion vanished, for the épée-thin shaft was encircled by a series of radiator ribs. And when the Kasugawa generator—currently retracted into a tight ring along the circumference of the shield—was activated almost two and a half years from now, it would expand and unfold into a wagon wheel–like assembly whose rim held secondary power plants and whose spokes were rectifying conduits.

Sonja Desai had already transferred to the test station—which, while fairly Spartan, was considerably more comfortable than the *Goethals*—and she was waiting when Li Han disembarked. A shuttle bay full of curious eyes watched as the two women who had taken it upon themselves to end the war of the Fringe Insurrection greeted each other.

"I hope the trip wasn't too uncomfortable for you," Li Han commiserated after the initial pleasantries. "What I've heard about *Goethals's* accommodations—"

"—is not exaggerated," Desai clipped. As was typical of her, it came out more abrasive than intended. Less typically, she then had the grace to look abashed. "But I shouldn't say so in the presence of her captain, here." She motioned forward a sturdy figure in TRN uniform, who saluted Li Han punctiliously.

"Ah, yes, Captain Cardones, I'm glad to make your acquaintance," said Li Han, returning the salute and studying the man who was to take the *Goethals* across two-and-a-fifth light-years of normal space. Like everyone else who was to make that crossing, he was a volunteer... and something more. It was—*embarrassing* wasn't exactly the word—to talk to a man who had sworn an oath to destroy his ship and himself if necessary to prevent the Kasugawa generator from falling into the hands (tentacle clusters, really) of the Baldies. "I believe you still have a little time before you'll need to return to your ship for the test. Is that correct, Captain M'Zangwe?"

"Yes, Admiral," the chief of staff acknowledged.

"Then let's go to the observation deck while the techs are finalizing their preparations, shall we, Sonja?"

As the two admirals, with M'Zangwe and Cardones in attendance, proceeded through the station, Li Han briefly reviewed current availability and projected construction rates for the Terran Republic's growing fleet of devastators. "So, as you can see," she concluded as they entered the observation deck, "series production is well underway, and on schedule. Our force levels should be as planned when the time comes for the operation to actually commence—even assuming that there are no delays in the *Goethals*'s departure."

"There shouldn't be," Desai assured her. "The Desai prime drive has passed all its tests, up to and including the ones we performed in the course of our passage here. The shielding problem is the greatest single obstacle, but the team assigned to it has concluded that they've worked out the best solutions we're likely to get within the limits of current technology, and that therefore any further redesign studies would result only in pointless delay."

"Do you concur, Captain Cardones?"

"I do, Admiral. We should be ready to depart by three standard weeks from now—four at the outside." Cardones kept his expression blank, but Li Han could sense his frustration. She had already pegged him as an officer of the rather stiff, formal school, and he had a crew consisting mainly of civilian technicians. "I believe any unanticipated delay at this point would have a negative morale effect. Especially—" He caught himself and stopped so abruptly his teeth clicked together. He also exchanged a quick glance with Sonja Desai.

Li Han leaned forward. "Do you have something more to tell me, Sonja?"

"Just this—and it's not really news, because it's what we've feared and expected from the outset. Simply put, *Goethals's* Desai prime drive has only one voyage of this length in it. If they arrive at Borden and the Kasugawa generators, despite our theoretical predictions, prove incapable of establishing a warp connection across interstellar distances—"

"Yes, I think I catch your drift." Li Han turned to Cardones. "Your crew are, I presume, aware of this possibility?" *This possibility of being permanently marooned*, she did not add.

"They are, Admiral."

"I see. My respect for them has just gone up another notch, Captain."

M'Zangwe took on the look of someone who had gotten beeped on his implanted battlephone. He subvocalized his reply, then turned to Li Han. "Excuse me, Admiral, but the technical staffs say they're ready to commence the extended countdown for the test."

Cardones stood up. "With your permission, Admiral, I should return to my ship."

"Of course." Li Han also stood up and extended her hand. "Let me repeat that it has been a pleasure to meet you, Captain Cardones—and an honor. Oh, and... I'll see you in about two point six standard years, in the Borden system."

It was actually as much a demonstration as a test. It was already pretty well established that a single Kasugawa generator could enhance existing warp points to accommodate greater ship tonnages, up to the tonnage of a devastator. ("Dredge" them, in a bit of historical wet-navy terminology that had become common currency and whose origins, Li Han suspected, could be traced back to Ian Trevayne.) She and Sonja Desai sat on the station's observation deck and watched a screen that displayed an effect which Isadore Kasugawa had tossed off as an afterthought. It took the readings from a whole suite of gravitic and other sensors and interpreted them in the form of an entirely specious visual overlay, as though one could see the invisible phenomenon of a warp point.

"Coming up on activation," she heard a voice say. Her eyes strayed to the visual pickup that showed the wheel-like Kasugawa generator and the *Goethals* poised before it. A similar generator was threaded into her round "handguard" that was located well aft on the ship's narrow, épée-like keel. In just over two and a half years, that embedded generator would be one half of the pair that would—hopefully—make history by forging the first artificial warp point.

As this day's countdown went to zero, Li Han's eyes strayed back to the warp-point display . . . but not quite fast enough. She missed the instant of transition, missed the sudden flux and burgeoning of the pattern—but the golden whirlpool she saw was perceptibly larger. And the data were pouring in.

Sonja Desai was watching those data readouts expressionlessly. "Hmm . . . Odd. The warp point's capacity is almost twelve percent larger than the theoretical predictions. And the curve of the gravitic gradient . . . I wonder. . . ."

"Sonja!" Li Han interrupted her firmly. "Please don't tell me that you're suggesting, at this late date, that it might be possible to produce warp points that could accommodate ships *larger* than the figures we've already factored into the devastator design!"

"Eh?" Desai came out of her reverie. "Well, I'm just thinking out loud, you understand. Still . . . if we doubled the capacity of the nodes in the rho quadrant . . . just maybe . . ." Her eyes glazed over again.

Li Han turned away, visions of the trillions of credits invested in the Kasugawa generators and devastators already under construction dancing in her head.

Typical!

9

The Greatest Violence

Opinions founded on prejudice are always
sustained with the greatest violence.
—Jeffrey

Arduan SDH Shem'pter'ai, *Expeditionary Fleet of the* Anaht'doh Kainat, *Achilles System*

Narrok felt the door-boosted *selnarm* pulse that announced a visitor to his quarters. He willed the door open and sent, "Hello, Mretlak. Are you ready for the briefing?"

Mretlak entered slowly, thoughtfully. "I am, Admiral."

"Then why do I *shotan* that your *selnarm* is disturbed and uncertain? This is not the fashion in which you typically radiate readiness, Fleet Second."

(Rue.) "That is so, Admiral. I admit (discomfiture)."

(Reassurance.) "Over what, Mretlak?"

"Over the agenda of this meeting with *Holodah'kri* Urkhot and Senior Admiral Torhok."

"What bothers you about it, in particular?"

"What bothers me is the *lack* of particulars, Admiral. I have read the agenda. It seems like an outline for a—a conversation. I expected there to be more—pressing—reasons for them to have traveled all the way out here for this meeting."

"Oh, there is most assuredly a more pressing reason. They wish to press me—and Second Admiral Sarhan—to move with greater alacrity."

"Perhaps they will facilitate that by summoning fifty new dockyards into existence, so that we will have a sufficient advantage in numbers to break through the human defenses in Ajax."

"Yes—that would be helpful. But I am becoming just as concerned with the casualties among our brothers and sisters."

"So, is that what *you* are hoping to achieve in this discussion with the Councilors, Admiral? Increased operational sensitivity to the casualties we sustain?"

(Resignation.) "No, Mretlak. Not yet. For now, I just want to have the permission to use all the weapons at our disposal—including those of human origin."

"The humans left behind—weapons—that we can use against them, Admiral?"

(Bemusement.) "No, Mretlak. I speak of information, human information, which we must start using immediately."

Mretlak spent a moment (reconsidering, reassessing). "So this 'briefing' isn't really a briefing at all. It is a political *maatkah* match."

"The briefing itself is what Torhok and Urkhot told the Council of Twenty they were coming to hear. But in reality, they are here to pressure us to attack sooner than we should, as well as to assess how dangerous I have become to their plans, and what role, if any, you might also play in their grand game."

"Me?" (Surprise.) "Grand game?"

"Mretlak, Urkhot and Torhok fight against the Pre-Dispersal traditions of our culture at least as much as they fight against the humans. They distrust, and therefore have been attempting to diminish the role and presence of, the *shaxzhu*. They have also almost eliminated the importance of the other castes, and they attempt to argue that as *Destoshaz*, we have little need of *shaxzhutok*—the memories of our prior lives—thereby making the *shaxzhu* increasingly extraneous."

"But Admiral, you and I... as *Destoshaz* ourselves, should we not presume that there is some value and wisdom in their opinions?"

"Some, Mretlak, but there is much intentional misrepresentation, as well."

"So you feel, then, that they are simply liars?"

"Firstly, there is nothing simple about either Urkhot or Torhok. Secondly, I suspect they earnestly believe the majority of what I hold to be their misperceptions. But in their attempt to serve what they believe is the unvarnished Truth of Illudor, they have reasoned that deceit may often be necessary. It is often the way of the overly zealous—their zeal greases the slide downward into greater exaggerations, greater misrepresentations, greater lies... all undertaken to promote the Truth and the Greater Good."

"And so they unmake what they seek to preserve by adopting methods which are its antithesis."

"That is well and concisely formulated, Mretlak. I cannot say how far Torhok has traveled down this slide, but Urkhot has almost vanished from sight into the depths of his own beliefs. In consequence, the more contradictions that arise between those beliefs and the mounting evidence that humans are sentient beings, then the more desperate—and extreme—we must expect Urkhot's convictions to become."

"You describe the evolution of a fanatic, Admiral."

"I enumerate the diagnostic characteristics of obsession, Fleet Second. If they are evinced by Urkhot, and if he frames them in theological terms and concepts, then perhaps fanaticism is an apt term. I, however, am ultimately concerned with how we must interact with him, not with any particular label for his behavior."

"That is a most politic response, Admiral."

"That is a most shrewd observation, Fleet Second. Come, let us go to our meeting. I shall explain how it will unfold as we walk together."

The door closed behind the exiting Second Admiral Sarhan, and Mretlak reflected that so far the meeting with Urkhot and Torhok had unfolded just as Narrok had predicted. There were the initial niceties, the insincere congratulations from Torhok on advancing all the way through to Achilles, and Narrok's muted gratitude for that praise. Sarhan had led off with an update: the humans had been completing their withdrawal from Suwa by the time the two Arduan fleets arrived there and were gone by the time Narrok's and Sarhan's fleets had linked up. After some desultory harrying and delaying actions in Achilles, the humans had ceded that system as well. But when Sarhan made a few initial attempts to probe Ajax, his forces fetched up short. No probes returned to report, and, given the dozens he sent through the warp point, this was a definitive sign that the humans had elected to make the Ajax system a hardpoint. It certainly looked like a reasonable place to do so, Sarhan concluded, but the logic of such a speculation depended upon a datum that he was not officially allowed to accept: the human star charts of this segment of the warp-point pathways. If the human charts in their possession *were* accurate, however, then Ajax was a choke point that controlled access to both the comparatively industrial Odysseus cluster and a long chain of systems that lay along this arm of what the *griarfeksh* labeled "the Further Rim."

Urkhot had simply commented that, indeed, the human data could not be trusted, and therefore, speculation that this was a logical place for the humans to establish a stronger defensive line was indeed unwarranted. Sarhan acceded without comment—and then mentioned that he had urgent business back aboard his flagship. Receiving permission to leave, he had departed to attend that urgent business. What he did not add was that this business primarily involved preventing himself from throttling Urkhot with both clusters. Sarhan had little patience for the *holodah'kri* and had asked Narrok to structure the meeting so that he could excuse himself promptly: if not, he feared his true sentiments would bleed into his *selnarm* and thereby create greater problems for the Fleet. Narrok had gladly acceded to Sarhan's request to make an early departure.

And so now it was just Mretlak and Narrok, sitting across the table from Urkhot and Torhok. And as Urkhot sent forth his *selnarm* toward Mretlak in what was more a probe than an invitation to discourse, the young Fleet Second reflected that this meeting was beginning to resemble a perverse reversal of the duels that were recorded in the annals of Pre-Enlightenment Ardu. There, rival leaders at an impasse often met to decide policy by personal combat; here, although the real combatants were Narrok and Torhok, they were sending their junior proxies into the *maatkah* ring, while they themselves retained a politic distance from the well-concealed war of words and insinuations.

Urkhot's probe rose and coalesced into a question. "Fleet Second Mretlak, I am told that you have prepared an intelligence report upon the *griarfeksh*?"

"Yes, *Holodah'kri*."

"Interesting. Why did you and the admiral conclude that the extensive records on Bellerophon have not provided us with a definitive understanding of the background and intents of our foe? This project of yours seems a strange way for a warrior to spend time, Fleet Second—compiling studies on other species. Are you perhaps a *shaxzhu* in disguise Mretlak?"

The jest elicited a ripple of general mirth that was in fact unanimous agreement to ignore the veiled remonstration, and even more veiled threat, of calling a *Destoshaz* a *shaxzhu*. Mretlak elected to pretend he had noticed none of the implications. "Honored *Holodah'kri*, we felt it wise to compare what we have now found on other worlds—and human-fleet wreckage—with the materials found on Bellerophon. There was, after all, some considerable concern that much of what the humans left on Bellerophon was disinformation."

Urkhot was (surprised, pleased). "This is well reasoned, Fleet Second. And what have you found, out here?"

"Firstly, that the other races depicted in human news and entertainment narratives are not fabrications, but actual species."

"Interesting. Then where are they?"

"For the most part, they dwell in comparatively remote regions of space, *Holodah'kri*, and the species do not share worlds very frequently. However, after the Second Battle of Raiden, we discovered that some of the remains of enemy fighters were of radically different design. We took several of these on board our ships for analysis and discovered that these craft belonged to the species that the humans mislabel the Orions."

"Interesting. But if this is true"—and Mretlak felt a faint undertone of anxiety in Urkhot's *selnarm*—"then it is significant only if these Orions possess *selnarm* and an awareness of Illudor. Do they?"

"*Holodah'kri*, there is no such evidence. Although we had no live Orions to examine, their ships are devoid of *selnarmic* repeaters or receivers. And given the speed of action in a fighter, it is hard to imagine that they would willingly eschew the advantages gained by direct *selnarmic* command of the craft's key operating systems."

"So these are simply *griarfeksh* with much more fur and much larger teeth. Tell me: among the other races that reputedly exist, are there any signs or reports of *selnarm*?"

"No, not as such."

"What does that mean?"

"*Holodah'kri*, the race that the humans have labeled the Bugs employed some form of communication which, like *selnarm*, is not subject to many of the laws and constraints of Myrtakian space. However, it was clearly not *selnarm*. Its manifestation was limited to the system in which the sender was located, and its transmission was not instantaneous."

"And what of the creatures called the Gorm, the heavy hexapeds? Is there not evidence that they have sensitivities which are non-Myrtakian in nature?"

"Yes, *Holodah'kri*, but the Gorm mental exchanges are simply vague impressions, mostly emotional in nature—much as our newborns project—and these transmissions are extremely short-ranged, typically constrained to a few kilometers."

"However, it seems the closest phenomenon to *sel-narm* is to be found in these Gorm."

"Perhaps, *Holodah'kri*, but that is not the parallel the human media have been drawing. We have discovered on each human world we have conquered that we are being compared to the Bugs, which were—reputedly—a ravening hive intelligence that—again reputedly—ate the humans' live infants and children with great avidity."

"So our deeds and our nature are being distorted and vilified through the human leadership's propaganda?"

(Agreement. Faint irony.) "Yes, *Holodah'kri*. They have decided that we are not truly intelligent beings, nor individuals, but dangerous monsters. At least in terms of the opinion they hold of their current adversary, they seem much like us."

"Our view is the correct one, Fleet Second."

"I did not claim nor imply that it is not, *Holodah'kri*: I simply observe that their categorization of us matches our categorization of them."

Urkhot clearly did not feel this to be an appropriately compliant answer, but Mretlak could also sense that the priest could find no fault with what Mretlak had said, and so the *Holodah'kri* moved on. "So, among these many races, the humans are dominant?"

"They are the most widely established, *Holodah'kri*. This is true largely because—"

"—because they are warlike?"

"More because they are curious and acquisitive."

"Tell me, Mretlak, is 'acquisitive' simply a longer word for 'greedy'?"

"With respect, *Holodah'kri*, greed and acquisitiveness

are not interchangeable motivations in all, or even most, humans. Many simply wish to—well, *build* things: structures, communities, institutions. They take a great joy in the act of making, and most then wish to exert some lasting ownership over what they've built."

"As did the *zifrik* colonies of our homeworld. Even those pestilential insects had a great—and aggressive—pride of ownership for their hives and other constructs."

As do we, ourselves, Mretlak thought, carefully keeping that reflection separate from the flow of his *selnarm*. "However, our analysis suggests that the primary behavioral variable that drives humanity's expansion is their thirst for the novel. Humans revel in experiencing new places, new ideas, new challenges."

(Boredom.) "Fascinating. I now understand—in detail—why the *griarfeksh* are the duplicitous, violent vermin I knew them to be before you commenced your briefing."

"Yes, *Holodah'kri*, but this review does serve another purpose."

"And what is that?"

"It provides important new data in the attempt to resolve the matter of determining where, and how much, variance exists between the true nature of our *griarfeksh* adversaries and their self-representations, which we have suspected was largely disinformation."

(Wariness.) "And how does this new data resolve this matter?"

"*Holodah'kri*, in analyzing the human naval wrecks and the archives of the planets we've conquered, we are discovering an extraordinary uniformity of both objective data and of cultural history—all of which makes it increasingly implausible that the humans are engaging in an intricate campaign of disinformation. Not only would the scope of such an effort be unthinkably vast, but all evidence of the organizations and orders which effected these supposed revisions of human history must also have been flawlessly purged from all recent records—another most unlikely occurrence."

"Well, the absence of such evidence is hardly surprising. The government's own agents would certainly have removed it."

Mretlak kept to the point. "But still, *does* such a speedy yet expansive conspiracy seem plausible? It would have to retroactively deny truths which living humans have known for years, or decades."

"Indeed. That any species could be so easily brainwashed is certainly proof of their weak cognitive capacities. And even so, it is nonetheless an astounding feat of propaganda, isn't it? It seems to defy belief—yet what is the alternative?" (Watchfulness. Zealotry. Monomania.)

Mretlak knew he was now on the horns of an impossible dilemma. Either he had to concur with Urkhot that the humans had actually succeeded in mounting such an impossibly sweeping and successful conspiracy of disinformation. Or he had to challenge that view, which in turn meant he was proposing nothing less than heresy: that the human self-representation was fundamentally accurate.

And that would only spawn even more distressing inquiries. For if the humans' self-representations were true, then it raised the further issue of their personhood: whether, in fact, creatures without *selnarm* could be truly sentient. Better to presume that humans were simply a savage pack of clever animals, an ultimate challenge that Illudor had posed to test the worthiness of his own Children. Urkhot's wide, quivering central eye told Mretlak that his interlocutor-become-inquisitor was already committed to this belief with a mania that could not even be fully expressed through *selnarm*. The *Holodah'kri*'s conviction was not merely monomaniacal: it had slipped over into something approaching madness.

Mretlak quickly turned to the military section of his briefing. "I am pleased to report that with our increasing numbers of heavy superdreadnoughts and their Desai drives, we are quickly reducing the advantages the humans have enjoyed in both tactical and strategic mobility. In large measure, this allowed us to keep our losses lower in Beaumont and particularly Raiden—" And Mretlak felt a strong, hot surge of passion rise up in Torhok's *selnarm*. The specific form of passion was suppressed, but Mretlak could guess: the prior, disastrous attempt to take Raiden by frontal attacks—led by the now discarnate Admiral Lankha—had been Torhok's brainchild.

Mretlak hurried on. "Unfortunately, we are still lagging far behind the humans in fighter technology."

Urkhot was (puzzled). "And yet we have made such advances in the drives of our larger ships. What causes this discrepancy?"

Mretlak interlaced his lesser tentacles. "Most of our gains have come through increased efficiencies made possible by the greater scale of the drives in the larger craft. However, the humans are exploiting other technological approaches to achieve their superior performance in the smaller drives. Consequently, although the fighter is a weapon whose tactical significance is swiftly diminishing, it can still be quite dangerous in certain situations. Particularly illustrative of this is the Battle of Beaumont, where the humans deployed their fighters within the Desai limit."

"It was a cowardly ambush," asserted Urkhot.

Narrok intruded. "It was also a shrewd tactic that

capitalized upon our now-predictable doctrine of pursuing all engagement relentlessly and all our objectives directly."

Torhok did not respond. Indeed, he could not do so without also critiquing the source of that tactical doctrine—himself—and the person who had insisted on following it at Beaumont: Urkhot. Mretlak sought to find some oil to pour upon the troubled waters: "Happily, the improved drives of our new SDH class actually provide that class of ship with slightly better speed than their human analogs."

(Relief, triumph) from Urkhot. "Well, this is welcome news. And tell us: what innovation of ours has allowed us to so quickly improve upon the flawed human version of the Desai drive, Mretlak?"

Again, Mretlak found himself mid-stride in a potential misstep, because there was no way to furnish Urkhot with the answer he evidently expected—and wanted—to hear. "Esteemed *Holodah'kri*, our improvement simply arose from being able to compare our system to theirs, and then combining the best features of both. So by partially—copying—the humans, we came up with a better drive."

(Anger. Manic pride. Denial denial denial.) "Are you now claiming that the humans are our technological superiors?"

Careful now. "It is clear enough that our technological strengths are quite *different*. After all, we had never encountered what they call the Desai drive. But they have never managed to create a sustained power source so vast and useful as the one at the core of our pinhole drive."

(Relief.) "Yes. Quite true. We are fortunate enough to enjoy the technological edge—and aptitudes—that really matter the most." (Satisfaction. Suspicion.)

Mretlak elected not to comment on Urkhot's dubious

assertion. "However, in the smaller drives, particularly those of the human 'strike fighters,' the wreckage we've examined suggests that their tuners are more advanced, and that they use instrumentation and third generation quantum computing that we do not have. And do not yet fully understand."

(Disbelief.) "Is not our computing superior?"

"We, of course, have *selnarm* interfaces. Our computers do not merely obey our instructions—they become extensions of our selves, and their responsiveness is absolute."

"So, what is this quantum computing and how is it that we do not have it also?"

"We do not have it because we have not long been students in the needs of space war, *Holodah'kri*. You might say that our peaceful nature has imposed a temporary disadvantage upon us." Mretlak used Urkhot's recession into (mollification) to explain. "Because our *selnarm* is instantaneous across all distances, our ability to share information is faster than the processes that occur within our computers, which are constrained to the speed of light. However, in select human systems—some of those governing the fighters' tuners and point-defense fire systems, for instance—the basis of transmission is in non-Myrtakian space. It exploits certain principles of what the humans call *quantum entanglement*. This gives the humans a profound edge in terms of how fast some of their automated systems may respond."

"I see—but how did our peacefulness keep us from discovering this innovation on our own?"

"With respect, *Holodah'kri*, what need would we have had for such speed? We needed to escape the supernova of Sekahmant and so perfected the pinhole drive, and the many systems and sciences required for our long journey and eventual resettlement. We had not known true war for many centuries. In contrast, the humans stumbled upon and utilized warp points, thereby coming into contact and conflict with other species. They have been driven and defined by an endless round of savage wars. And war rewards alacrity as does nothing else, so they necessarily turned their attention to reaction times, to exploiting aspects of non-Myrtakian space that were of no utility to us."

Urkhot added a capstone to Mretlak's analysis. "Happily, the advantages the humans have enjoyed thus far they shall soon lose. We shall catch and surpass them in all their sciences and technological endeavors. But they can never match our greatest advantage. The knowledge that we are eternal, and thus fear no death. Indeed, as Illudor teaches us, *destolfi montu shilkiene*."

Having watched the casualty lists grow ever longer in the Fleet, Mretlak had come to wonder if, as Urkhot had cited, "Discarnation is but a little thing." However, Mretlak had no permissible reply, and so was relieved when Narrok asked the question he could not. "Is it, *Holodah'kri*? *Is* discarnation always a 'little' thing?"

(Wariness.) "What do you mean, Admiral Narrok?"

"I mean that we *Anaht'doh Kainat* are already much diminished since arriving here in human space. We can ill-afford further campaigns that buy us few gains at the expense of many discarnations of our well-trained fellow Wanderers. We shall not see their replacement for many a year."

Urkhot sent a wave of confident (dismissal). "Illudor would not allow all these discarnations unless they were part of a greater plan. Perhaps it is his will to reduce the number of our bodies, so as to diminish the burden upon this first generation of settlers: fewer mouths to feed, fewer children to teach."

Narrok sent (assent), then "Even if that is true, I wonder if you would indulge my curiosity on a relevant theological point?"

(Wariness.) "Of course."

"Is not Illudor weakened even as we are weakened?"

"Your question suggests that, in part, Illudor's strength is dependent upon us, or can only be measured through our actions. Tell me, Admiral: Do you then also believe that Illudor can commit suicide?"

Narrok avoided Urkhot's attempt to bait him into overt heresy and proceeded with (caution, purposiveness). "Whether Illudor may end his own existence or not is moot. We are taught that he will not. But we are also taught that, as Illudor is the universe, so his destruction would mean the destruction of all things."

"Destruction is a separate matter. You speculated that Illudor might be 'weakened even as we are weakened.' Do you not thereby imply that Illudor might *not* be a supreme being?"

"My question implied nothing. Rather, it invokes simple mathematics. Why do we struggle to preserve the race? To ensure that we are not all destroyed, and thus, neither is the manifestation of Illudor in this universe."

"The youngest of us knows this."

"Very well. So if our population were to be reduced to zero, we, Illudor, and the universe would be at an end. Is this not so?"

"You know it to be."

"Then I put it to you that having two Arduans left alive is a far riskier state of existence than having two thousand. Or twenty million. And so I say further that we have sustained so many casualties already in this war, that I simply wonder at what point we must be concerned with maintaining a safety margin to ensure the continuation of our race."

"This concern has not escaped my notice, but at any rate, it is not *your* concern, Admiral."

"Nor, I suppose, is the single greatest cause of those losses, *Holodah'kri*?"

"You mean the cause is something other than weakness in our fleet leadership?" And as he said it, Urkhot tucked his *selnarm* back in: obviously he had meant to insult Narrok, but only remembered afterward that it was the late Admiral Lankha—as Torhok's proxy—who had suffered crippling losses, and with no gain to show for them. Torhok's *selnarm* rippled, seethed, but did not project into the exchange.

Narrok's response was oddly affable. "Oh, the actions of the Fleet leadership have indeed caused the losses, *Holodah'kri*, but the actions in question were imposed upon us."

"Imposed upon you by what?"

"Not by what, but by whom—for I speak of your own extrapolations of the will of Illudor, *Holodah'kri*."

"My extrapolations of the will of Illudor? How can my theological insights restrain you in your role as admiral, Narrok? I have not the authority to dictate strategy or tactics to you."

"Not directly, honored *Holodah'kri*, but as we enter each new system, we are compelled—as a consequence of your dicta—to disregard the positions of the other warp points as they appear on the human astrographic charts. And in almost every case, we ultimately discover that the warp points were precisely where the human data claimed them to be."

"Which you confirm at your leisure, do you not?"

"At our *leisure*? With respect, we do eventually confirm them, but not at our leisure. Upon entering a system, we lack our enemy's surety of *where* the most strategically imperative regions of that system are situated. Consequently, every plan the humans make starts with a perfect knowledge of the coming battlefield. However, as long as we are prohibited from giving their star charts even a provisional credence, we emerge blind. Because Admiral Lankha was not allowed to accept the plotting of the human charts, she chased after an apparent warp point that was a trap—and which decimated her entire fleet. In Suwa, the humans escaped unscathed because—again—we had to ignore the human data on the system and were duped into interdicting a decoy warp point—as they disappeared through the actual one. In just such ways, they routinely outmaneuver and elude us."

Urkhot gave the *selnarm* equivalent of a shrug. "Illudor compels us to grow by walking in dark and unknown places. And so it is with the *griarfeksh* data. Every one of their purported facts are potential lies, and so we are unable to rely upon any of their information."

Narrok sent (calm, acceptance). "Yes, I see your point, *Holodah'kri*. All their facts are fruits of the same poisoned tree. Which is why I must therefore propose that we immediately dismount all the Desai drives currently in service with the Fleet and cease using the warp-point network altogether."

Urkhot physically flinched. "What? Narrok, are you going mad?"

"No. I am being consistent. Warp-point maps, Desai

drives, quantum computers: it makes no difference. If some of what we have gleaned from human archives must be treated as the fruit of a poisoned tree, then *all* of it must be. Ultimately, won't the theological inconsistency—or caprice—of tolerating some human data and not others prove to be more dangerous to the Children of Illudor? For when the questions begin—when we are called upon to explain why Illudor wills that we must ignore some human 'facts' yet embrace others—how will we answer? Will not the distinctions seem arbitrary? Will they not seem to be the result of pragmatic decisions made by us, rather than as reflections of Illudor's perfect—and perfectly consistent—will? And how will we then undo the damage that has been done to our faith? I readily acknowledge that the human technology we have incorporated has become critical to our survival. However, since—as you have already assured me—Illudor would not commit suicide, and since any losses are therefore acceptable, is it not better that we foreswear these tainted technologies as quickly as possible? The Desai drive and quantum computing and fighter improvements—yes, even the discovery and use of warp points themselves: it seems that we had best renounce them all before the inconsistency they represent becomes so great that it spawns a schism within our unified embrace of the will of Illudor. For surely, that is more dangerous to us than the paltry efforts of the puny *griarfeksh* fleets—is it not, *Holodah'kri*?"

Urkhot's *selnarm* had not merely retracted but had seemingly coiled around itself—leaving Mretlak with a strong impression of the prenatal curl of Firstlings nestled in their mother's birth-sac. Torhok's *selnarm* remained shut but seemed to quiver in rage; Mretlak could not tell if the source of that fury was Narrok or the suddenly enfeebled Urkhot. And Narrok's *selnarm* was like the surface of a high mountain lake, unrippled by wind: it was calm, serene—and completely reflective, revealing nothing of what lay beneath.

When it became obvious that Urkhot dared not open his *selnarm*, Torhok groomed his own and opened a tight, well-defined aperture. "Admiral Narrok, your insight is worthy of a *'kri*."

"I am flattered, Senior Admiral—but why do you say this?"

"Because you have arrived at the very conclusion that Urkhot and his own advisors had determined just a week ago." It was all the purest *flixit* droppings, and everyone in the room knew it, but none dared make such an observation. "In fact," Torhok continued, "you have perceptively anticipated the precise doctrinal change that Urkhot was laboring to complete even as we traveled here. He is no doubt flustered by necessarily having to defend an old view because he has not finished crafting the articulation of the new view."

"Of course. And the new view is—what?"

"As your reasoning suggests: that we provisionally accept the provenance of those human data which had heretofore been rejected. So, then, let us be practical. If the old constraints—specifically, those prohibiting reliance upon *griarfeksh* maps and other data—were removed now, would you be able to accelerate your timetable for the assault on Ajax?"

"Unquestionably, Senior Admiral. It vastly simplifies our planning."

"Then you may disregard the old data prohibitions from this moment forward. This is somewhat earlier than Urkhot had anticipated, but once we return to New Ardu, the new doctrines will be announced. Although not all at once, you understand. Such changes take time."

"Of course, Senior Admiral."

"Very well. The further matters of resource allocation can be arranged through my staff, Admiral Narrok. I believe we are done here. Come, Urkhot. You must complete the articulation of the new doctrine with greater alacrity, now."

Only when the door closed behind the inscrutable admiral and his befuddled priest-lackey, did Mretlak breathe again—and in so doing, realized that he had not done so for almost half a minute.

Two days later, and after what seemed to be a week's worth of logistical wrangling between Narrok's and Torhok's staff proxies, Mretlak stood before Narrok's quarters, wondering how he should tell his commander the latest news—when the door opened unbidden.

(Congeniality, paternal fondness.) "Come in, Mretlak. Your *selnarm* is like a nervous *flixit* warbling on my doorstep."

Mretlak was too surprised to demur or even comment; he entered. And found Narrok poring over projected fleet inventories of consumables—which the admiral put aside as he raised his eyes to meet Mretlak's. "So, I understand congratulations are in order."

(Shock.) "I am—that is, I do not wish—Admiral, how do you know?"

"About your transfer back to Bellerophon? Oh, I was told about it. And I approved it."

(Surprise, hurt.) "You approved—?"

(Reassurance, fondness.) "Mretlak, you misunderstand.

I approved it—after the requisite period and degree of resistance—because it was inevitable. In you, I had too great an ally and helpmate. Torhok and Urkhot were sure to discern this. So they were sure to remove you."

Mretlak sat and radiated (glumness). "Perhaps I should not have been part of the briefing then, Admiral."

"No, that was necessary also. They were going to realize I had a singularly gifted helper here, and they were going to determine the identity of that person, no matter what. By putting you in the briefing, I let them know that I had my eye on you, trusted you, would no doubt follow your progress even at a distance."

Mretlak brightened. "And so that is why they have assigned me to analyze the historical records of the humans, for purposes of 'gathering speciate intelligence of military value.'"

"Precisely. Given your accomplishments, this will seem a wise and natural reassignment when announced to the Council of Twenty. Of course, Torhok and Urkhot intend to bury you in a pointless and endless task. They have no interest in the nature and background of our adversary. However, we made an issue of it in the briefing—and so, we were the ones who opened the doors of inquiry that 'necessitated' your reassignment. All very tidy."

"And, I fear, effective."

"Hmm. Perhaps not so effective as they think. You are not alone in your 'pointless assignment,' Mretlak. As I understand it, the Elder Councilor and *shaxzhu*, Ankaht, is conducting similar researches. Torhok has underestimated her—and the importance of her research. I wouldn't be surprised if you find points of mutual interest and enlightenment with the Elder."

"She is outspoken against the *Destoshaz* resurgence, Admiral."

"She is outspoken regarding its bigoted propaganda, Mretlak. Those are not the same things. My advice is to meet her with an open mind—then judge."

"This is always wise, Admiral. I am guided by your words."

"As I have been indebted to your tirelessness and perspicacity, good Mretlak. More than I can expect from your replacement, Esh'hid."

"She is not capable, Admiral?"

"She is not a creature of her own will, Fleet Second. She is a devotee of Urkhot's caste-and-race destiny rhetoric."

"She is a spy?"

Narrok shrugged. "She is also eager for the glory of victory. When we attack Ajax, I will make sure that she has the opportunity to pursue that goal—by allowing her to command the first wave."

(Surprise.) "You wish her discarnated, Admiral?"

Narrok answered with another shrug. "I wish her off my bridge, and if possible, off my command staff. I hope she finds her duties at the front line diverting rather than discarnating—but that, after all, shall be as Illudor wills it." (Amusement, irony.) "Now, to business, Mretlak. When you arrive at Bellerophon, your official task is to reinitiate something we Arduans have not needed for centuries: an intelligence service. It will be your job to become expert in their tactics of subterfuge and misdirection. In short, we need you to be able to tell us how the humans *think* when they embark upon war-making, Fleet Second.

"But while you are doing this, you will also have

an excellent opportunity—and cover—for continuing to examine the humans' records of their own past, their own nature, their own proclivities and beliefs. And since Urkhot and his ilk have made the human war of genocide against the Bugs the cornerstone of their argument that the humans are neither sentient nor sane, you must endeavor to determine whether the humans might have been justified in their level of aggression. As you do so, take particular care to forensically establish the provenance of older evidence: make sure that you can physically authenticate the date of all documents, printouts, et cetera. If they can be proven genuine, that would utterly refute any assertions that the humans have attempted to rehistoricize their past."

(Dread.) "Admiral, if Senior Admiral Torhok keeps close track of my activities, and discerns what I am doing, I—well, I fear that I may be even less safe than your new Fleet Second."

(Reassurance.) "You are in no danger. Torhok has too much to occupy him to keep track of you once he has consigned you to what he considers a fool's errand. Besides, Torhok leaves here pleased, and unsuspicious, because he got what he came to get."

"And what did he come to get?"

"To get me to promise that we would move against Ajax more swiftly. And he wished to use this visit to continue to deride and resist any growing opinion here in the fleets that the humans might actually be intelligent. And lastly, to remove you from my staff and replace you with a creature of his own persuasion who will watch me once you are gone. Of course, along the way, he and Urkhot were determined to decline several of our requests—just to reaffirm their dominance. And so we had to put forth requests which we knew they would deny."

"Such as?" asked Mretlak, half stunned as Narrok peeled back the unseen layers of interpersonal strategy that had allowed him to anticipate and then orchestrate the briefing.

Narrok shrugged. "Such as a more casualty-sensitive attack doctrine, or permission to construct forts to hold all our warp points. Of course, Torhok—through his logistical officer—was going to refuse that: it would have reduced the resources dedicated to our offensive power.

"So. then what have we gained?"

"Well, there's the support and funding for my special offensive projects—"

"So you think Torhok will actually honor a commitment to build such large hulls?"

"Of course—because he sees it as facilitating the *offensive* operations that are the centerpiece of his vision of conquest. So, since we calmly accepted his rejection of our request to build forts, and then showed an equal willingness to sink that funding into an offensive alternative, Torhok decided to reward our humility and right-thinking by approving our alternate request for the comparatively paltry resources needed to build and seed more defensive mines. Which, quite frankly, are now more essential to our defense than warp forts."

"You feel the mines will serve us better than the forts?"

"No, but we no longer have enough crews to man the forts, and they take too long to build."

"Admiral, until today, I was under the mistaken impression that the majority of one's strategic skill has to be exercised against one's foes. I now begin to suspect that an equal measure is required in dealing with one's allies."

"An equal measure—or more, depending on your allies, Mretlak. And with that last piece of advice, I think you must be on your way."

Mretlak lowered all three of his eyes in a formal gesture of respect generally reserved for parents or beloved mentors. "I would ask one further clarification."

"Of course."

Mretlak struggled to keep his *selnarm* unruffled, for the topic he intended to raise could easily be misconstrued as containing an undertone of criticism. "Admiral, I noticed that as we prepared for, and then during, the briefing, you insisted that we call the enemy 'humans,' rather than *griarfeksh*. I wondered: given whom we were meeting with, was this wise?"

Narrok nodded and sent a pulse that complimented Mretlak on his (shrewdness, perspicacity). "For me, yes, it was wise—or at least necessary, for I must continually push back against the myopic *Destoshaz'ai*-as-*sulhaji* propagandizing. Had you been making the presentation alone, on your own authority, then no, it would *not* have been prudent. So, in the presence of others, it is still usually advisable that we continue to label the humans as *griarfeksh*."

"But is it not safer, then, to continue to so label them even when one is alone? Lest one create a private habit of thought and terminology that might slip out in a public setting?"

Narrok fluttered approving tentacles. "Your foresight and caution serve you well, Fleet Second. And there is wisdom in your pursuit of consistency. But there is a danger in it, and it is this: if you label an adversary as an animal, you will come to think of that adversary as an animal. And if you think of an adversary as an animal, you will expect him to have the limited perspicacity of an animal. In this war, such arrogance could be our downfall. In private, we should acknowledge the full danger of our foe—and perhaps we can remind ourselves of that danger by referring to him with his given name, not dismissing him as some noxious carrion beast of our homeworld."

"Perhaps. But could it not also be seen as, as—?"

"As what?"

"As heresy?"

"Possibly so, possibly not. I can only say: be prudent, be careful, but do not allow yourself to underestimate these humans. They are quite dangerous—and resourceful."

"Admiral, do *you* think they are genuinely sentient?"

Narrok looked at him for a long time. "Remember, Mretlak, be careful in your new duties." And with a kind, wavelike ripple of the raised tentacles of both clusters, Narrok turned his attention back to the inventory reports, signaling that their time was over.

As he left, Mretlak wished that Narrok had answered his question about human sentience.

Five minutes later, as he was boarding the shuttle that would take him to Torhok's flagship, and ultimately, back to New Ardu, Mretlak realized that Narrok had indeed answered his question about human sentience.

He felt a chill pass up his clusters and into his arms as he realized what that answer was.

Urkhot finished outlining the final phase of instituting the Revised Provenance Doctrines. "And as you will see, Senior Admiral, even the last phase of relaxed restrictions should still serve to promote a natural consensus among the *Anaht'doh Kainat* regarding the inherent bestiality of humans."

"Very good," sent Torhok, while he thought: *You are becoming a costly ally, Urkhot. Two days ago, you all but emotionally deliquesced in front of Narrok. That is not acceptable. You are a blade that needs to be rehoned.* "You have done excellent work in a short time, *Holodah'kri*, but what will you do when the next challenge to our authority arises?"

Urkhot stopped: (panic). "What next challenge?"

"Oh, I have no knowledge of the next counter that our political opponents will attempt, but they have been presenting one impediment after another. Do you expect it will stop?"

Urkhot's central eye quivered. "It must stop. I will not countenance any more of it."

Torhok shrugged. (Sympathy, resignation.) "But then what is to be done? How can Illudor's will be expressed so certainly that the voices of nonbelievers will be stilled?"

"I do not know—but those voices must be stilled. Beyond reasonable uncertainty and curiosity, habitual challenges to the wisdom and the will of Illudor are primers for those who would defy him, are encouragements to infidels and heretics."

Torhok (acceded). "So earlier *holodah'kri* have written. But they lived in simpler times, without the difficulties of a people separated from their roots by centuries of interstellar travel and confronted with a species of insane marauders that can mimic intelligence so convincingly that almost a third of our population are ready to consider them sentient. And those earlier *holodah'kri* did not have contentious Elders, such as we do—Sleepers who claim unto themselves the authority of having walked and breathed on our lost homeworld."

Urkhot took up the complaint as a rant. "And they did not have to suffer such authority to be embodied in a *shaxzhu*. For she"—and the image of Ankaht roiled out of Urkhot's *selnarm* like bloody pus from an inflamed boil—"she is the source of so many of these problems. Her infernal insistence that we should seek evidence of personhood in these two-eyed *griarfeksh* drains our strength of purpose, our unity, when we need it most."

"Yes," agreed Torhok, "and with her ready access to past-life memories, her profound *shaxzhutok* which reaches back to the very foundations of our race, it is almost as if she has accrued to herself the credence accorded to our priests, our *'kri*." Torhok paused a beat. "Indeed, perhaps she has already usurped the power and place of our *holodah'kri*." And Torhok waited.

Urkhot's central eye tremored with passion—and then, suddenly, became very still. "Which would of course be heresy of the worst kind."

"Most assuredly so. Perhaps it could even be perceived as treason. For just as surely as Ankaht has arrogated unto herself the authority of the priests, she now has the Council of Twenty tangled in knots of uncertainty over how best to proceed in the case of the humans. She strives to learn how to talk to the vermin. Whereas I have orders to cleanse them from the space in which we must live. And this is not just the Council's mandate, but Illudor's will. He sent us forth when he willed Sekahmant's death-burst. And thus, by extrapolation, sweeping away the *griarfeksh* here is certainly a deed made necessary by His act, and is therefore in accord with His will. Yet the *shaxzhu* would have me delay or desist in that war while she discovers if she can 'communicate' with these furry, two-eyed monsters. And she, like Narrok, would have me fret and count how many *Destoshaz* souls become discarnate in the process. Why should this concern her? Unless, of course, she secretly doubts that we *are* reborn."

"Which would be another heresy—and would also indicate her madness," blurted Urkhot. "For how can one claim past-life memories *and* simultaneously doubt the permanence of our souls? Clearly, she is a danger to us—to *all* of us."

"Your wisdom brings us to that sad but inescapable truth, *Holodah'kri*." And again, Torhok waited—but this time had no doubt of what would follow.

Urkhot opened his *selnarmic* link a bit wider, and Torhok detected a cold, fell resolve that he had never felt before in the priest: the *holodah'kri*'s conversion to a ruthless pragmatist was now as complete as his new purpose. "Senior Admiral, I fear we are perched on the horns of a dilemma."

"In what way, *Holodah'kri*?"

"Our race is in danger—danger from within, Senior Admiral. Yet we have no way to bring this threat into the light for all to view clearly. The clarity of vision—and mission—of the *Anaht'doh Kainat* has been blurred, largely as a consequence of their good nature and open-mindedness. And now, we must save them."

"It seems so. But how, *Holodah'kri*?"

Urkhot's tentacles rippled restively. "The methods are not yet clear to me, Admiral. But suffice it to say that steps must be taken. Steps that are quiet, but decisive." He shook himself, as if out of a trance. "But for now, Senior Admiral, let us speak no more of this. Plans of action will present themselves to both of us, surely."

"Surely," echoed Torhok, who congratulated himself on having crafted so deadly a weapon as the *holodah'kri* and in so short an exchange—and without any trace of blame upon himself. For, after all, it had been Urkhot's words and ideas that had effected his own conversion—and if pressed to reveal it, the priest's own *selnarm* would show no less. Torhok had merely known the right questions to ask, the right buttons to press.

Urkhot imaged (Narrok), considered and weighed (competence, expendability, triage) in the balance. "It is a shame that Narrok has become so increasingly—obstructive. He had been most cooperative and polite, but ever since that fleet second of his joined his staff after the Battle of Charlotte—"

Torhok (concurred) and added: "Yes, this Mretlak is probably a bad influence. Despite his lesser rank, he is quite clever—and manipulative."

"A pity he cannot be more usefully employed at greater range from Admiral Narrok."

"But he can, and will be, *Holodah'kri*. As of today, Mretlak is no longer fleet second to Narrok. He is returning with us to take up new duties sorting through the intelligence archives on Bellerophon. I suspect he will actually be useful to us there—and at the worst, he will be removed from Narrok and consigned to a harmless post among stacks of human data. And in Mretlak's place, I have assigned Narrok a new fleet second who is far more theologically resolute."

"An excellent redistribution of resources, Senior Admiral Torhok."

Whose reaction to the praise was a genuinely diffident shrug. "I am *Destoshaz*," he commented. As if that answered the matter entirely on its own.

10

Two True Women

The first wrote, Wine is the strongest.
The second wrote, The king is strongest.
The third wrote, Women are strongest:
but above all things Truth
beareth away the victory.
—Apocrypha (Bible)

RFNS Zephrain, *Second Fleet, Astria System*

The VIPs from Zephrain looked slightly dazed when they emerged from the shuttle into the hangar bay of Second Fleet's flagship, the supermonitor named after their homeworld.

As well they might, thought Ian Trevayne with a trace of smugness. He had carefully specified the course their ship was to follow after emerging from the warp point into the Astria system. It had taken them past what had amounted to a grand review of the awesome assemblage of naval power the allied powers had poured into this system.

Some had argued against it. Cyrus Waldeck, in particular, had worried that showing them such an incalculable tonnage of concentrated, summated, and distilled death might lead them to demand, in the immemorial way of politicians, why the war couldn't be brought to a triumphant conclusion in time for the next election—ignoring little details like the possession of comparable capabilities by an enemy who had the advantage of position. But Trevayne had remained serene. He knew there were two members of this junket who could be relied upon to gently explain the facts of life to the others.

So it was that the visitors had peered out through their ship's viewports at a succession of titanic supermonitors of the Rim Federation Navy, and also of the Pan-Sentient Union Navy of which it was not necessarily a part (but not necessarily *not*, either). Then serried ranks of fleet carriers and assault carriers, notably the sleekly deadly ones of the PSUN's Ophiuchi allies. Then the dizzyingly innumerable swarms of lesser supporting ships, down to the light cruisers.

Naturally, their course did not take them past the island-sized orbital fortresses that guarded the warp point leading to Baldy-occupied Bellerophon. Not even Trevayne was about to expose them to the risk of an incursion that might, after all, happen at any moment. Besides, they wouldn't have been able to appreciate the minefields, which were so thick around that warp point that the space there could no longer be accurately described as vacuum.

Now their shuttle settled down onto its landing struts on the hangar deck and extended its disembarkation ramp with a hum. Trevayne stepped forward as the sound system broke into the Rim Federation anthem—the kind of uninspired neoclassical farrago typical of such compositions—and the honor guard of Rim Marines in dress forest-green tunics and black trousers came to attention.

"Welcome to Astria, Mr. Prime Minister. I trust your journey went well."

"Thank you, Admiral Trevayne," said Khalid Mulvaney with a not-altogether-steady nod: military reviews were affairs for which his background as an economist had ill prepared him. "Yes, everything went on schedule, although of course the trip was a long one . . . and what we've seen here has been rather, ah, overwhelming."

"You must be quite fatigued, sir," Trevayne commiserated. "I'll have you escorted to your quarters at once."

"No, no, Admiral. I think we're quite able to complete the introductions." Mulvaney proceeded to introduce the members of his war cabinet who had accompanied him. "And in addition, we have with us the Chief Justice, with whom you have . . . er, ahem, worked closely in the past. . . ." He trailed to an awkward halt.

And he thinks he *feels awkward*? Trevayne's heart did not precisely overflow with sympathy. He gave the soft salute appropriate for a civilian lady, then smiled at the woman who could have been the great-grandmother of his current physical self. "Hello, Miriam."

The Honorable Miriam Ortega gave the smile that Trevayne had first seen almost nine decades before on the face of a woman in her thirties. Nine decades, that is, as she had experienced time. Nine decades during which she had served five tenures as prime minister of the Rim Federation and borne two sons, both of whom were now older—in terms of elapsed consciousness—than Trevayne himself, for whom his first glimpse of that smile lay only a few years in the past.

She hadn't been a conventional beauty even then, and now she looked a well-preserved near-seventy despite all that anagathics could do. But that smile had transfigured her face then, and it still did. And for a split second, it was as though he could glimpse the woman with whom he had fallen in love, such a short time ago to him and such a long time ago to the rest of the universe, including her.

"Hello, Ian." It was still the same husky voice. But the moment passed. Trevayne doubted he'd cease to experience such moments, especially on seeing her after an extended absence. But they were growing less frequent, and now he slipped painlessly back into the new, different relationship they had established in his new life. They were both too sane to have done otherwise.

Mulvaney must have sensed something of the sort, for he cleared his throat again. "And finally, Admiral, we are honored to have with us Dr.—and retired admiral—Genji Yoshinaka, Senior Trevayne Fellow at Prescott Academy." The prime minister's lips quirked upward at the title of Yoshinaka's chair at the Rim Federation Navy's academy. "The cabinet has co-opted him as an advisor. He is, I understand, another old associate of yours."

"Indeed he is—not to mention one of the few other natives of Old Terra still running around loose out here." Trevayne grinned and extended a hand to his one-time chief of staff. "Genji, why the hell did you make them bring you along? You'll kill yourself off before your time."

Yoshinaka looked up—almost a foot up, to meet Trevayne's eyes and smiled tremulously. He was coming to the end of the anagathic regimen's capabilities, but his eyes still sparkled. "I wouldn't have missed it for the world, Admiral."

Trevayne gave him a glare whose sternness neither convinced nor was intended to convince. "Well, it would serve you right if this jaunt finished you off, after the 'quote' you let the Rim Federation put on the pedestal of that bloody statue of me while I was getting freezer-burned and couldn't stop them. *Terra expects that every man will do his duty,* indeed!"

"I *told* you I tried to convince them you'd never said that! But as you know, these colonials tend to get their historical figures confused. And besides . . . why don't you just admit that you love it?"

Just outside the range of Trevayne's vision, Miriam Ortega barely managed to smother a guffaw. That sound was probably what enabled Trevayne to keep a more or less straight face. "Well," he said with a final bogus glare at the unintimidated Yoshinaka, "Mr. Prime Minister, permit me to introduce Fleet Admiral Waldeck, commanding Second Fleet."

"Admiral Waldeck." Mulvaney returned Waldeck's military salute with a formal inclination of his head, as was proper. Somebody must have briefed him. The briefing had doubtless included Waldeck's background. But Trevayne decided to risk repetition, for it was worth underlining Second Fleet's character as an allied force.

"As you know," he explained, using the standard formulation for telling one's political masters what they *ought* to know, "Admiral Waldeck belongs to the Pan-Sentient Union Navy but has been seconded to the Rim for some time. This background has been an incalculable advantage to him in commanding what is increasingly an allied fleet."

"Yes, I'm sure. And we've just seen how amply the other members of the alliance have contributed to the buildup of forces here. I'm told that Second Fleet now has more total tonnage than most of the fleets of the Fourth Interstellar War." Mulvaney's voice held a note of awe. The armadas that had been assembled to extirpate the Arachnids a century and a half before had passed into legend.

"Actually, Mr. Prime Minister, that's not the half of it," said Waldeck, whose social background was such that he was unlikely to be overawed by political officeholders, however exalted. "Today's technology can pack incomparably more destructive power into a given tonnage of warships. My staff has prepared a series of informational presentations for you on the subject." Mulvaney looked slightly apprehensive, which Waldeck ignored. "But for now, we have prepared a reception in the wardroom, where you can meet the commanders of the allied contingents."

This was a moment Trevayne had anticipated with a certain amount of concern. Not much concern, to be sure. Genji was an old hand at dealing with aliens, and Miriam had some experience at it. But the fact was that the Rim Federation was an essentially all-human polity. Most, if not all, of the cabinet ministers had probably never met a nonhuman.

Still, they handled Least Fang Zhaairnow'ailaaioun very well. By then, they had gotten drinks. Besides, being from the Pan-Sentient Union, Zhaairnow wasn't just any ally: he was practically family. And the Orions' felinoid appearance (a pure accident of evolution; a Terran oak tree was more closely related to a Terran cat) gave them a certain spurious familiarity; they looked deadly but not really weird.

The same, to a lesser extent, was true of the vaguely birdlike Ophiuchi. And the heavily-built, hexapedal Gorm at least had fairly similar faces. But then came the commander of Task Force 23, the only component of Second Fleet that was truly foreign in the sense that it represented a power not connected to the PSU's network of associations and alliances: the Terran Republic. And that commander was, of course, human.

Yet it was with her that Mulvaney displayed his first real uneasiness. Which, Trevayne, reflected, was to be expected. Between him and Li Magda there was no gap of biology, but a yawning one of history.

"Ah . . . it is a pleasure to meet you, Admiral Li. Be assured that the peoples of the Rim Federation will never forget the help offered to us by the Terran Republic in our hour of need, in spite of . . . er, that is, even after . . ." Mulvaney trailed to a miserable halt.

"Thank you, Mr. Prime Minister," Li Magda said with great solemnity. "And we are pleased to extend that assistance—now that it has been accepted."

Trevayne, standing behind the flustered Mulvaney, gave Magda what he hoped was a quelling glare over the Prime Minister's shoulder. This was hardly the time to rake up the earlier ill-advised attempts by the Rim Federation—with its traditional *more Terran than the Terrans* attitude—to avoid accepting help from the "rebels." The fact that Li Magda was her mother's daughter didn't make it easier.

Miriam Ortega stepped forward, rescuing Mulvaney. "Perhaps you remember me, Admiral Li. We met at the reception on Xanadu, when you stopped in the Zephrain system on your way here."

"Of course, Madam Chief Justice. I recall that reception vividly. It was where I met Admiral Trevayne." For an instant, their eyes met.

For that same instant, Miriam Ortega noted just exactly how their eyes met.

"Well," she said after a barely perceptible pause, "I

want to take this opportunity to offer you my somewhat belated congratulations on your promotion to vice admiral."

"A very well-deserved promotion," Trevayne said heartily. He turned to Mulvaney. "As you know, Mr. Prime Minister, Admiral Li's heroic holding action in the Third Battle of Bellerophon not only enabled many Rim and PSUN units to extricate themselves from the Bellerophon system, it also strengthened the alliance by placing the Orions under a debt of honor to an officer of the Terran Republic—a very serious matter under their code of *theernowlus*."

"It certainly is," interjected Yoshinaka. "In fact, it may have helped reconcile them to being forced to sit here in the Astria system marking time, which comes even less naturally to them than it does to us."

"I've been meaning to bring up that subject," Mulvaney interjected, as though glad to be back in his element. "We've just seen the awesome—and very expensive—power of the Allied fleet here in Astria, Admiral Trevayne. But it doesn't seem to be doing much of anything."

Trevayne groaned inwardly. Hadn't anyone told the man *anything*? "Surely you know—" He caught himself just in time and rephrased it. "As you know, Mr. Prime Minister, the grand strategy proposed by First Space Lord Li Han of the Terran Republic—and approved by every allied government, including that of the Rim Federation—calls for Second Fleet to hold position here in Astria, making only occasional probing raids into Bellerophon, while the fleet of devastators and the paired Kasugawa generators are prepared."

"You do not understand the political difficulties, Admiral. The taxpayers of the Rim are being asked to bear a heavy burden and are not being shown any tangible return for their money. With this tremendous force, surely you could—"

"Launch another frontal attack like Second or Third Bellerophon?" asked Yoshinaka, breaking in as Trevayne could not. "You might recall the losses we suffered on those occasions, Mr. Prime Minister, while we're on the subject of expense."

"Perhaps, Mr. Prime Minister," said Trevayne hastily, "an introductory strategic briefing, in general terms, would be in order at this time. Cyrus . . . ?"

"Of course, Admiral. The full presentations can wait until our guests have had a night's sleep, but my staff is prepared to review the big picture at any time."

"Splendid. Let's adjourn to the briefing room. Genji, you come, too. Miriam, would you like to—?"

"Goodness no, Ian. You *know* how hopelessly unmilitary I am."

"Yes, I seem to recall hearing you mention it once or twice," Trevayne deadpanned. "Well, Mr. Prime Minister, shall we go?" He, Waldeck, and Yoshinaka led the somewhat overwhelmed Mulvaney away.

Miriam Ortega watched Trevayne go. Then she turned her thoughtful gaze on Li Magda. "Admiral, I'd love to continue our conversation. Will you join me in my stateroom?"

"Certainly, Madam Chief Justice."

"Miriam, please. Let's snag a couple more drinks first." She gave Trevayne's retreating back one last glance before he vanished into a lift tube, then turned back to Li Magda. "I think we need a strategic briefing of our own, dear."

11

Illumination, Yet Shadows Before

Coming events cast their shadows before.
—Campbell

Punt City, New Ardu/Bellerophon

When Ankaht came in, Jennifer knew the news was good, because she'd learned how to read the aliens' body language.

That skill had been easier to acquire than Jen had anticipated. Since the Baldies—or "Arduans"—seldom used their bodies as a medium of expression, it made almost any variation in movement noticeable. The variations were simple and few enough that Jennifer had been able to memorize what each one signified.

In this case, Ankaht's unhurried pace, the relaxed set of her eyelids, and the motionless lesser tentacles of both clusters collectively signaled "no anxiety" just as clearly as if she had sent that message by *selnarm*. Indeed, Jennifer was suddenly struck by how much her own perceptions of Arduan kinesiology had changed: originally, their stillness had seemed ominous. Now their minimal movements seemed anything but machinelike or unemotional. Their gait was—well, she decided, *serene* might be the best word. Because there seemed to be a greater range of motion and flexibility in their "elbows" and "knees," Arduans seemed to glide as much as they walked. And once the strangeness of their appearance subsided—along with any fears of harmful intent—they were actually rather wonderful to watch: graceful and sinuous but without any overtones of being snakelike.

Ankaht sat, opened her *selnarm* slowly, expressed her (pleasure, gratitude) to find Jennifer's mind ready to attempt to receive hers; it still took effort, and they spent as much time resting as they did conversing. But now, when she rested, Ankaht usually remained in Jennifer's room, and they sat together in companionable silence, usually with Zander affixed to Mama's breast. Interestingly, little Zander enjoyed feeling Ankaht's smooth, pliant skin—once Jennifer decided to give in to his obvious curiosity. And, in her turn, Ankaht was not only delighted when Zander reached out to touch her, but radiated a luminous (hope, joy, bond) that made Jennifer almost believe that maybe, just maybe, they could stop this war. Because that was their joint project now.

Jennifer sat down and smiled, tried to send. "You. Carry. Good. News."

Ankaht broadcast a pulse of (pleasure, congratulations, encouragement, confirmation). "Well done, Jennifer Peitchkov! Your progress is most wonderful."

(Gratified.) "Good—and I'll remind you again. You can just call me Jennifer."

"Yes, I must remember this. Jennifer. As you have felt, among Arduans names are all one thought, even if they signify several things. It is strange to think of having multiple names, and that there are precise rules governing which different combinations of those names are to be used in which different circumstances. The closest equivalent in *selnarm* is that titles or ranks are appended to, yet remain separate from, names. But I will learn—Jennifer."

"Thank you. And now—you have good news for me, don't you?"

(Curiosity.) "Did you feel that in my *selnarm* or . . . ?"

"I saw it in your motion, your posture, your gestures."

"Really? This is a most excellent development, Jennifer Pei—Jennifer. And yes, I can now confirm our first reports. The male, Alessandro McGee, was not among those killed during the combat at your house."

The first after-action report had pointed toward that conclusion, but hearing it confirmed lifted a great burden from Jennifer's fearful heart and even her tense body. And then she discovered she was crying.

Ankaht sent, "These are what you call 'joy-tears,' Jennifer?"

Jen laughed through her sniffles. "Yes, tears of joy. That's what these are."

"They are . . . strange to witness, Jennifer. But I *shotan* the feeling in you that produces them. We have this feeling, too, although our tears are reserved for sorrow alone. Now, you will want to know how we are sure of this report, of your mate's survival, lest you continue to have doubts."

Hmm. They're getting to know us humans pretty well now, aren't they? "Yes, Ankaht. How was the determination made?"

"Before the Enforcers approached your house, they had conducted a series of thermal scans from a variety of different positions and angles. When the combat was concluded, the Security that sorted through the wreckage also collected all the human remains—which were not very plentiful. Since then, forensic analysis has determined that the number of deceased humans for whom we had remains equaled the number that were detected inside the house at the outset. So, when chemical and physical analysis of all the human remains conclusively revealed that none had belonged to Alessandro McGee, we were also able to finally conclude that he hadn't been a traceless casualty, either."

Jennifer sighed and closed her eyes. "Thank you, Ankaht. I have sensed that this information was not—easy—for you to acquire."

Ankaht was very still. Then: "You sensed this difficulty, Jennifer? How?"

"I'm not sure." Jennifer opened her eyes and looked into the three staring at her; she couldn't figure out which two to look into and wondered if the effort was rendering her cross-eyed. "I really never thought about it. I just sort of . . . knew."

(Eagerness) vied with (composure) in Ankaht's *selnarm*. "This is another excellent development, Jennifer. You are acquiring a sensitivity to that part of *selnarm* which is not strictly thought, but also an attunement to the sender's feelings and conceptual metastructures. The closest word we have found in any of your languages to express this is the German word *gestalt*—but not in the context used by your psychologists."

Jennifer nodded. "More a total message—sort of the way that a work of art strikes you. As a whole package, all at once."

"Just so, Jennifer. Now I must ask you a difficult question. It is rather . . . sensitive, I fear. But I am duty-bound to ask it."

"Go ahead."

Ankaht sent (apologies, necessity). "Do you have any

idea what the humans who were killed in your house were doing there?"

Damn, a fair question—but I can't answer it. Jennifer snapped her *selnarm* link shut, considered lying, then thought more carefully. She opened her *selnarm* again, like turning on the tap so only a thin stream trickled down. "Can you read my entire mind? All my thoughts?"

"No. If that were possible, there would have been other Arduans who—being less patient—would surely have forced open your mind and raided it for any useful information. And frankly, even for those of us who wish to make our discussions with humans consensual, why would we resort to all this mutually exhausting work to establish a *selnarm* link if we could join our minds to yours so easily?"

Jennifer nodded. "Then I must decline to answer the question you asked me about the other humans who were in my house when the Enforcers arrived. I don't want to lie to you. And I probably don't know anything of value. But these are my people—"

Ankaht made a jerky chopping gesture with her arm; the *selnarm* pulse that came along with it allowed Jennifer to understand that it was the Arduan's awkward attempt to imitate a dismissive wave. "I understand, Jennifer. Although I must therefore report to the Council that you are uncooperative with our attempt to investigate those events, I am unperturbed by your desire to keep silent on the matter. Be warned, however, that some of my less sympathetic colleagues may suggest that your refusal to answer indicates you were somehow involved in facilitating the ambush on our Enforcer group."

"Well, I can certainly answer *that* question. No, I was not involved. Not at all."

"I already *shotan* this, Jennifer. Alas, the military

commanders of the Children of Illudor will only care whether or not you answer *their* questions."

"Sounds a lot like some human military types, too."

Ankaht sent a pulse of wry (amusement). "Perhaps our races are not dissimilar in all ways."

Jennifer shrugged. "No, we're not. For instance, like us, you Arduans also evolved from the seas, didn't you? Spent even more of your evolution there than we did, I'll bet."

Ankaht's *selnarm* shut off with what felt like a snap, then quickly reopened with (apology, surprise). "Regrets, Jennifer. I had not expected so quick—or sure—an insight. Tell me: how did you deduce this? You are not a scientist, are you?"

Jennifer laughed—probably the first out-loud laugh she had emitted in four months. "Me? A scientist? Oh, God, no. But as an artist, I have to see how things move. I have to, well, almost get *inside* a thing to really be able to create a piece of art that expresses it." She smiled. "Which reminds me of a word which, I think, even beats *gestalt* as a near-synonym for *shotan*."

"Oh? What is this word?"

"*Grok*. When you *grok* something, you know it as if you were it and it was you."

"Yes, this is the ideal state and purpose of *shotan*. But why did we not find this word in any of your dictionaries, Jennifer?"

"Because it is from a made-up language. A long time ago, a writer used it to describe a way that certain aliens understood things." Jennifer matched the stare of the three eyes. "I'll bet he never thought we'd be using it today—for dealing with *real* aliens."

"I see. But I do not understand why, even if it is a neologism, it is not in your dictionaries."

"A neolog—? Oh, a new word. Well, that's different. We're always having to come up with new labels for new objects or concepts. But this word—*grok*—was part of a fictional universe. It was part of an extensive conceit."

Ankaht struggled. "A—conceit. This is one of your words with many meanings. In this case, your *selnarm* tells me you mean it as a fictional or fantastic presupposition or story. Am I right?"

"Yes, you are. And why is the word *grok* not in dictionaries? Well, I think it was, for a while. Then people forgot it. But not all people. It still gets used in some circles, but not enough for it to earn a place in the dictionary."

Ankaht seemed to take some time absorbing this. "I see. I hope I will *grok* this, too, one day."

Jennifer smiled, inspected Ankaht's "arms": they were long, with the midpoint joint far less pronounced than a human elbow; the same was true of her "knee." The "feet" were broader than a human's, but not quite spatulate. They had probably been furnished with ten tentacles at one time, like the arm-ending clusters, but these digits had become even more vestigial than human toes: they were just the nub-ends of the ten cartilaginous flanges which were the framework for the Arduan "foot." *Yep,* thought Jennifer, *marine evolutionary origins, no doubt about it.*

Ankaht registered (bemusement). "I feel your assessment of our physiology. And you are correct. Ardu had more water than your Earth—almost ninety percent of its surface was oceans. They were our birth sac, and we remained in them until only 150 million years ago, or so it is thought."

Yeah, that much water might complicate the accumulation of a good fossil record, thought Jennifer. "I'd been guessing at your marine origins from the first moment I saw a picture of an Arduan."

"Why?"

"Well, let's see. You've got no nose, and now I've learned that your sense of smell is, as expected, pretty retrograde. Your 'ears' are tucked under those lower-cranial bony ridges—nicely protected, and they allow you to hear if you surface to breathe. But without a dish"—she tugged the loop of her ear—"to trap sound waves, it's pretty clear this wasn't your most important sense. And underwater, why would it be?

"Ah, but *selnarm*! Now, that's perfect for underwater activity—sort of like cetacean echolocation/sonar, except even better. It works without any dependency on the surrounding physical medium, so the way water limits the range and clarity of both sight and sound is completely avoided. And watching the way you move, and the fact that there's a lot of flexibility and cartilage in your body, instead of weight-bearing bone, well, it's pretty obvious that you started out in the ocean. And stayed there for quite a while. But there's one thing I haven't figured out. What happens to an Arduan who is born without the power of *selnarm*?"

Ankaht (surprise, wonder). "What an interesting question."

"Why?"

"Because it has never happened. All are born with *selnarm*. And we would never think to ask what it would mean if one of us were born without it."

"So, as a race, you've never had to deal with physical disabilities?"

"Oh, no, that is not accurate. It is quite rare, but occasionally a Firstling emerges with eyes that cannot see."

"And does their *selnarm* compensate for their lack of vision?"

Ankaht was (puzzled). "I am sorry, Jennifer. Your question is meaningless to me."

"'Meaningless?'"

"Yes, because there are no—" Ankaht suddenly stopped. "Jennifer, I am sorry. Now I perceive where our misunderstanding arose. I think I remember reading that your society teaches the blind how to exist by relying upon their other senses. Is this correct?"

"Yes. Don't you do the same?"

"No, Jennifer. When a Firstling is born blind, he or she is immediately discarnated."

Jennifer felt as though ice-cold ants were racing to and fro under her skin. "You kill your blind infants?"

"Yes. Of course. But the concept you sent me, and the word you thought, for 'death'—*zhet*—is not what happens to a being with a many-lived soul. When a *person* passes to wait for their next incarnation, our word for that is *dest*. *Zhet* is what happens when a soulless creature ceases to exist. It is a death without reincarnation."

"You mean, like what happens to us humans." Jennifer grimaced: this was the crux of the two races' differences—and their misunderstandings. She and Ankaht had had so much to achieve just in order to establish clear and effective communication, that this topic—as profound as it was—had not yet become a focal point of their conversations. Ankaht had explained some basic principles about the Arduan concept of death and reincarnation. For instance, the Arduans really did seem to believe that their souls, while awaiting rebirth, went into some cosmic holding tank that was lovingly tended by a deity they called Illudor. Ankaht herself had referred to past lives and had shared some memories of them that seemed as real and detailed as if she *had* lived them.

And who was to say it was impossible? No one would have believed in *selnarm* before the Arduans arrived, but Jennifer was far beyond such doubt: it was part of her daily experience now. So if one impossible metaphysical phenomenon were proven possible, who could say what others might be realities in the lives of the Arduans? But if they had such wonderful powers of communication and insight, then: "Why didn't you try to find out if we—if humans—had even my kind of limited *selnarm* potential before you started shooting at us and killing us?"

Ankaht spread her lesser tentacles out in a kind of half droop (resignation). "Many of us wanted to pause and do just what you have suggested—but the choice was not ours. And there remains some confusion as to who truly fired first or detected what they thought was a warlike provocation. But either way, by the time the weapons were unleashed, it was too late. The pace of events overcame any other considerations. And you must understand that when we first started receiving your signals, we saw countless images of your war against the Bugs. Those savage images shocked us; they seemed an unabashed celebration of speciate genocide. And since we could not understand the language that gave the images context, it remained hard to believe that such triumphant bloodletting could possibly be vindicated. We sought an accompanying *selnarm* track in an attempt to make more sense of the images, but found none. And, of course, most Arduans deemed this to be further proof of humanity's lack of (apologies) true sentience."

Jennifer leaned back in her seat and reflected. It was sort of like what had happened as the humans of

Bellerophon had formed their opinion of the invaders, but in reverse: there the problem had been too *little* communication. When the Baldies—now, the Arduans—had showed up, they didn't seem to be sending much in the way of discernible signals anywhere on the electromagnetic spectrum. And then, when they landed, it only got worse: no words, no understandable gestures, no body language whatsoever. The Baldies seemed to be nothing more than mute, motionless automatons that gestured, uttered (maybe) single-word instructions—and often killed those who did not obey, or who resisted. But as Jennifer had begun to enter their world, and as her sensitivity to their *selnarm* had at last blossomed, it felt like—all at once—a blindfold had come off, plugs had popped out of her ears, and she discovered herself to be in the middle of a loud ballroom with a wild, rollicking waltz in full swing. And now, just today, she had already begun to discern the whisperings of *selnarms* from the other side of her smart-wall, and in areas even farther away than that—

"You can? You can detect *selnarm* sendings that are so distant from you?" Ankaht's eyes were intense, excited.

Jennifer blinked, looked at Ankaht, and suddenly realized that she'd been feeling all of her thoughts "out loud." "Uh, yeah. The more distant the *selnarm* is, the fainter it gets—sort of like a whisper heard through layers of blankets."

"Yes, but this is excellent news indeed. Most hopeful."

And Ankaht, who seemed distracted by a quick calculation of the importance of Jennifer's newfound level of sensitivity, evidently didn't shut her own *selnarm* down enough—or Jennifer was becoming so attuned to it that she was able to look behind the equivalent of the Arduan's privacy curtain—

—where she saw/felt deep worry, bordering on terror. A slow, costly war in which only one thing was certain: every day, the chances of a settlement, of peace, were slipping further and further away.

—and concern over her own people, the Children of Illudor. But not just in terms of their safety from humans—although that was in there, too—but from each other, both in their factions and as individuals. The Arduans were... coming apart somehow. A schism? A culture war? Jennifer couldn't make it out, but one thing was clear.

She had to do everything she could to help Ankaht. She opened her *selnarm* as wide as she could and with (urgency) asked: "What can I do to help?"

Ankaht responded to Jennifer's extraordinarily strong, clear *selnarm* pulse with a *befthel*—a tri-blink—and an inadvertent glance at the smart-boards that were the opposite wall. The sudden stillness in the collective *selnarm* of her researchers, observing from the other side of those boards, told Ankaht that they had sensed and understood Jennifer's sending. And knew its world-changing—and potentially race-altering—significance: beyond any doubt or debate, Jennifer Peitchkov was a fully functional person. And if one human could be a person, then...

Ankaht turned back toward the human—the *person*—eagerly. "Jennifer, here is the best way you can help me right now. I must understand your people better. Much better. To us, your world and your lives are unthinkable, so much so that many Arduans find it all too easy to decide that, living in such a world, humans cannot be truly intelligent."

"And you need to be able to explain humans to your

own people in order to get enough of them to change their opinion of us. And maybe stop this war."

"Exactly."

"Then tell me what you don't understand, and I'll try to explain—if I can."

"Jennifer, we stand mute and horrified by what, to us, looks like the unbridled chaos of your lives, the almost infinite uncertainties."

"Such as?"

"Such as your bizarre pre-mating rituals, based on what you call secondary sex characteristics. Such as the number of your permanent pairings that end in what you call divorce. Such as the abandonment of countless of your children. Such as the thousands who cling to a life wracked by the pain of terminal diseases or the physical misery and mental anguish of decrepitude. Such as the bizarre means whereby you educate your young, which to us resembles nothing so much as the way some of you still hunt avians: you discharge knowledge and learning like your shotguns discharge pellets, firing bits of data and training again and again into the milling mass of every new generation. All in the hope that enough of those Firstlings are struck, and changed, by these kernels of knowledge. We cannot fathom how you can, or why you would, live with so much uncertainty, wasted effort, and surety of pain and suffering. To us, these are scenes out of a place which, in our culture, is akin to what you label 'hell.' But we never associated such a place with fire or physical torment. For us, hell is more like your legend of Bedlam—a place of eternal, inescapable insanity, barbarity, and chaos. We call it *xenzhet-narmat'ai.*"

Jennifer had wondered how she'd wind up feeling as this less-than-charming depiction of human existence came rushing out at her. However, by the end of it, she found herself to be mostly sad and bemused. She let Ankaht see that, and sent: "I have no argument with any of your depictions. Just this one proviso to apply to all of them: it's as good as we can do. After all, we don't have *selnarm*, and we don't have any evidence of God, the way you feel you do. The way I see it, each Arduan starts life with certainties—of communication and immortality—that each human spends her whole life trying to attain. But that almost never happens, and so we have to accept those uncertainties—and many more—as a burden which we must bear until the day we die."

Ankaht expressed (gratitude, respect) for Jennifer's lack of defensiveness or anger. And she followed with, "It is most interesting that you relate our social differences, in part, to our different perceptions of deity. In your lives, religious thought seems less—how should I put it?—*central* than it is in ours. We are always mindful of how we, and the world, are expressions of the unfolding will and intents of Illudor."

Jennifer shrugged. "Well, given your belief—or, from your perspective, your knowledge—of having many lives and undying souls, that makes sense. But for us"—Jennifer shook her head—"well, lots of people claim that as the domain of science expanded, the domain of spirituality contracted. They say that technology was the inevitable foe of a belief in God and an afterlife. I'm not sure I believe that. But this much seems true: the first religious myths—well, they don't seem to make a lot of sense to us anymore."

"So where, then, lies the ultimate authority for designating what is good and just, and what is evil and unjust?"

"Oh, a lot of that still comes from religion—if only

indirectly. A lot of our governmental structures carry on ideals that began in religions. But not all religions boiled it down to 'good or evil, heaven or hell.' Some, like Hinduism, sort of separated the issues of morality and the issues of existence into two different discussions."

"In what way?"

"Well, I'm not an expert on Hinduism, but you can talk about good and evil as entirely separate from creation and destruction, life and death. In a lot of the other old religions, death was always associated with evil. But in Hinduism, death is a force that is every bit as necessary as life, in order to create a balanced existence and universe." Jennifer smiled. "The old Shiva-Vishnu, yin-yang thing."

But as Jennifer sent these concepts to Ankaht—the duality of destruction and creation, of the Shiva-Vishnu and yin-yang dyads—Ankaht found it equating to a very old, almost forgotten Arduan concept, that of *assed'ai*. And, like a lived epiphany—the kind one experiences before its full significance can be recognized—Ankaht thought: *This is what we lack. This is what is tearing us, the Children of Illudor, apart. We have strayed from this concept of* assed'ai, *of a dynamic equilibrium between countervailing forces. Our troubled* narmata, *our loss of the other castes, our friction between* Destoshaz *and* shaxzhu: *obsessed with polarized conflicts, we have forgotten this simple principle of balance—or worse yet, have evolved in such a way that it is no longer natural for us to embody it.*

Jennifer had detected Ankaht's simultaneous distraction and excitement. "Did I say something wrong?"

Ankaht sent (reassurance, energy, clarity). "Not at all. You have said something very, very right. Something I needed to hear. We have this concept of balance, too, but for us it has become a medical principle, the one you label *homeostasis*. We have allowed its earlier, social meaning to atrophy. And realizing this is a great—perhaps a crucial—lesson for me, Jennifer Peitchkov." And Ankaht physically leaned back, so as to take in the human with all three eyes: it did feel as if she were seeing Jennifer for the first time. "I apologize, Jennifer Peitchkov."

"What for?"

"For my, for our, arrogance."

"You don't seem arrogant at all to me."

"And we did not see it in ourselves, either. For we were convinced that, having no detectable *selnarm*, you were thus a benighted species. But now I see that we have at least as much to learn from you as you have to learn from us. Maybe more."

Jennifer laughed. "Think of that, the mind-readers having something to learn from us—and you furnished with an all-seeing eye!"

Ankaht understood the concepts of *all-seeing* and *eye*, but there seemed to be a metaphoric referent that she was missing. However, she did not miss Jennifer's sudden retraction of *selnarm* and (embarrassment, apology). "Sorry," the human muttered aloud. "That was a little too . . . casual, I guess."

(Reassurance.) "Not at all, Jennifer. But I do not understand. What is this 'all-seeing' eye?"

Jennifer relaxed, brightened (relief). "In a lot of human mythology and symbolism, a single eye was often represented as all-seeing. Sort of the eye of God. In Hinduism, many of their gods were actually represented as having a third eye"—Jennifer stopped in mid-thought, interrupted by a sudden spike of both recognition and reflection—"and yeah, it was always depicted right where *yours* is. Your larger, central eye, I mean."

Ankaht could hardly contain or discipline her outpouring of (wonder, surprise, hope, bafflement). "Jennifer, I must ask to make sure I have understood you correctly. Are you saying that you have images of Arduans in your prehistory?"

"No, not Arduans, but creatures with a third eye. And that eye—if I'm remembering correctly—was able to see into what various mystic traditions have called a 'spirit world': a place invisible to us, where the gods and the truths of the universe were to be seen."

An eye that could see the face of Illudor: Was it possible? Had some long-dead human, gifted as was Jennifer, seen *this? Could it be chance?* Ankaht felt her spine hit the chair's backrest. (Shock.) "Jennifer, this—this is most extraordinary. This whole day has been most extraordinary. And hopeful. Very hopeful. I wish I could continue, but I must report these many new breakthroughs, that we may move forward just that much more swiftly. And I must confess, I am quite tired."

"Me, too." But the human also signaled (gratification, hopefulness).

When Ankaht returned to the observation room, queries and congratulations buffeted her—but she stressed (wait) and sent discreetly: "Let us move to the adjoining conference chamber. Jet'hem, please keep monitoring our subje—our guest."

"Of course, Elder."

As she led them into the conference room, Ankaht could feel the *narmata* wash around her with an undercurrent of something like reverence. "Elder," enthused

Ipshef, the cognitive-science prime, "this is everything you hoped for. Now we can apply these lessons to the other human artists and we will have—"

"We will have not much more than we have now, Ipshef." (Resignation, regret.) "The key is Jennifer. The new vocoder and I were only the catalysts for our breakthrough today. The source of our success, and our hope, is Jennifer herself. Her sensitivity to *selnarm*—and her rudimentary ability to project it—far outstrips any analogs we have observed in her fellow artists. That makes her the most important asset in our attempts to establish full communications with the humans. Indeed, it makes her too important, I fear."

"What do you mean, Elder?"

(Rue, anxiety.) "Ipshef, I have learned a human saying in my reading of their books: 'Don't put all your eggs in one basket.' In this case, I am concerned that so much possibility, so much hope and change, is sited in the potentials of one person. It makes all our efforts for communication, and even peace, far too vulnerable."

"Yes," commented Orthezh of Linguistics, "it is a pity her gift seems so rare, racially. Possibly it is has declined to the point where it is a deeply recessive trait in the human genome now."

Ipshef mused, "It is so difficult to imagine their lives, to picture it as if one of us were condemned to live without *selnarm*. And when I do, I find myself reconsidering the extremes—and the perversities—which we observe in the humans and think: 'I might have to employ much the same methods, were I without *selnarm*, yet wished to make my thoughts known to the rest of the Children of Illudor.'"

Orthezh registered (realization, insight). "Except that

we would mercifully discarnate any such blighted being rather than compel them to live on in a world so dark and so silent. So, of course, we have never had one of our sisters or brothers actually experience the limitations that are the daily reality of the humans."

Ankaht radiated (relief, gratification, pride) in response to Orthezh's insight. "Yes, this is one of the major reasons why the initial phases of interspeciate translation and communication have been so difficult: because we had no analogous experience from which to extrapolate an understanding of their existence. They live in a world so desperately isolated that we would have defined it as a living hell."

The youngest researcher in the cluster, Nektshezh, felt a pang of sudden, terrible (pity). "We must help them."

"The charity of that thought cannot help but bring joy to the face of Illudor," Ankaht thought warmly at her xenobiology prime, "but let us not go from loathing the humans to pitying them. As hard as it is for us to imagine, they feel no lack in their lives. The humans laugh, love, dance—and, I begin to suspect, they treasure their lives as we cannot imagine. And now, I must leave."

"To rest, Elder?"

"To think—and to prepare."

Ankaht struck first with the left foot and followed through with a ripping slash by the *skeerba* claws on her right hand. She then pivoted on her left foot as it landed, pulling her right foot around from the rear in a whiplike sweep.

This *maatkah* maneuver—Hurricane Turns—evolved into Wave Curls Under: she performed a half-cartwheel, half–front-flip that brought both her feet over from behind, sawing radially around her low center of gravity and down through the target in quick succession.

But she landed poorly on the second foot and stumbled, breaking her fall with both arms. Propped up above the *maatkah* mat in her own quarters, she let the sweat run off her body as she thought: *I'm getting better. I couldn't have completed Wave Curls Under two months ago. But better isn't good enough. If I fall like that in a real match . . .*

She shook the image of discarnation from her head—not because she feared that outcome, but because she and her people could not afford it. If she died answering a *maatkah* challenge, then the militants would surely break up her research cluster and, in place of striving to communicate with the humans, might elect to exterminate them. She had felt that solution simmering at the *selnarmic* edge of too many minds that had embraced the *Destoshaz'ai*-as-*sulhaji* caste-cult.

She had felt those suppressed genocidal reflexes most frequently when she used the *maatkah* training circles in central Punt. There she had also felt passing *Destoshaz* notice her, do double-takes, devote sudden close attention to her practice regimen and moves, and quickly withdraw their *selnarm*: furtive, yet sly and pleased, like one of the humans' dogs, eager to run back to its master with a bone of particular interest.

Eager, in this case, to run back to Torhok with a report on her training. It was quite clear that Torhok had begun soliciting reports. Nothing obvious, she was sure. Just the faintest intimations that he had a passing interest in the doings of his fellow Councilors. And so, when she practiced her *maatkahshak* publicly, they spied on her.

Just as she had intended. Firstly, knowing that she was training regularly and ambitiously might give Torhok—or anyone else—some additional pause before challenging her. But it would also lead them to assess her favorite moves, her skills, her weaknesses: having seen her practice, they might believe they knew how she would fight. And she wanted—needed—them to believe just that.

What they did not know was that part of her training involved not merely *maatkahshak*—training in the particular schools of different *maatkah* styles—but regular immersions into deep, almost trancelike states of *shaxzhutok*—the reclamation and reliving of past lives. While all Arduans had some measure of this skill, it was strongest in the *shaxzhu*—those who, like her, practiced it as their primary contribution to the community. In recent generations, this skill had become particularly weak among the *Destoshaz*. It was murmured that even Senior Admiral Torhok himself had no memories of past wars or commands held.

But whatever Torhok's deficit in past-life experience might be, he had vast reserves of power and skill that he had acquired in the *maatkah* ring during the course of this life. He—and many of his devotees—were known to be formidable opponents, and Ankaht did not delude herself in assessing her unaugmented chance of defeating the great majority of them: her odds were, at best, unpromising.

But she had something they did not—past lives—and she planned on using those experiences and skills as well. But today, as she tried to settle into recalling a particularly early life—one in which she had been a warrior in a Pre-Enlightenment island city-state—Ankaht found herself repeatedly distracted by a curiosity that had been provoked by discovering Jennifer's rudimentary *selnarm*, and the following discussion of her being a possible reversion. Ankaht had begun to wonder: *How did Arduans exist in the Pre-Enlightenment "warring states" period? If* selnarm *has always been so uniform, how is it that we Arduans did not have better understandings of each other, that our early progenitors were almost as warlike and contentious as the humans are now? How were we not more aware of each others' true needs, feelings? The only logical conclusion is that, at one time, we were once more akin to the humans: that there was a period in our prehistory when there were great differences of* selnarmic *skill and awareness not only between different groups, but within the same group. Nothing else would explain the lack of unity and fellow-feeling that must have caused the frequent and wanton violence of those days.*

Ankaht pushed with her arms, away from the floor, and rocked back to her knees. She had not often invoked her lives from the early Pre-Enlightenment: they were unpleasant, perplexing, savage. But now she had too many reasons to go back even before the Pre-Enlightenment, to explore past lives—particularly of her earliest *Destoshaz* existences—in order to better understand the humans, as well as to prepare for her own defense. And there was little rationalization for not doing so: it only required a small increase in effort and time to sample from her many lives, which were strung like dim pearls along the timeline of Arduan social evolution. From a short glimpse into each, she could build a mosaic that might show the larger patterns of how her race had changed not merely in the millennia immediately prior to the Dispersal of Sekahmant, but in the Star Wandering generations since.

And so she exhaled, inhaled, exhaled more deeply, curled forward—

—and was flitting through the past, picking up pieces of a life here, an existence there, all the while building a picture of a time that few of the Children of Illudor had investigated since boarding their generation ships.

She found that the Pre-Enlightenment was a riot of diversity, with each small island its own state and culture, and the larger islands gerrymandered into even more, and smaller, polities. The innumerable castes and class stratifications had accreted into a ponderous labyrinth of contending etiquettes, prerogatives, and priorities.

The beginning of Arduan social freedom—which, due to the communalizing tendencies of mature *selnarm* linkages—intruded slowly, rising along with an increased need for the society to perform a greater diversity of tasks. As this Enlightenment edged slowly into existence, it was also comparatively bloodless. Widespread depersonalization was simply not possible when *selnarms* fused to create a truly harmonious *narmata* that linked every rank and caste of society.

New relationships were the lifeblood of the flowering of the new era. Just as Ardu was circumnavigated, charted, and new trade routes sprang up, the rules governing interpersonal association—across class, caste, rank, and clan—became more easily navigated, more relaxed. The polarizing wars between colonizing empires that shaped the course of human history for almost four centuries were not possible on Ardu because of the empathies that flowed naturally, unstoppably, along the links of *selnarm*. Consequently, Earth's religious wars were also unknown. Rather, as cultures contacted and blended into each other, the Face of Illudor was deemed accessible to all of them, but each one was thought to possess a unique perspective upon a particular feature of that godhead, thereby making an indispensable contribution to the complete picture.

It was toward the end of this period that the numbers of *Destoshaz* began to drop. Warfare was a rare, and highly specialized, undertaking. Most *Destoshaz* were consequently diverted into emergency and rescue services.

At the same time, the *shaxzhu* became both more important and more numerous. Their numbers had always been attributed to the direct influence of Illudor, since a powerful ability for *shaxzhutok* could not be learned, nor bred for: its appearance had always been both rare and arbitrary. However, the Enlightenment's increased social complexity and emphasis upon communication and education put a premium on the *shaxzhu*, who quickly became the dominant intelligentsia of modern Ardu. The increase in their numbers was deemed the hand of Illudor at work, providing for the new needs of his Children.

Then came the discovery of Sekahmant's instability. Nations had folded together into vast, monomaniacal instruments of racial survival. There was a sharp increase in centralization and autocracy as Ardu strove to launch as many waves of the Children into space prior to the calamity that was sure to befall it. This, in turn, led to greater militancy, authoritarianism, dogmatism; the principles of toleration, consensus, and the old philosophical whispers of what the *'kri* called *assed'ai* withered. Nuance was as absent as the realization that such absolutism was, in fact, a recidivistic devolution, a return to social primitivisms abandoned millennia earlier—back when Arduans had much more in common with humans. Indeed, many of the developmental parallels were striking—

Ankaht stopped in mid-thought with a self-rebuke:

there were obvious limits to how far she could presume similarities between the evolution of two such disparate species. For instance, human histories depicted a crisis of faith arising along with technology. The Children of Illudor had demonstrated a completely opposite reaction: as technology grew, Arduan cultural uniformity—vested in their *selnarm* and concomitant *narmata*—also grew, further enabled by machinery that shrank distance between peoples and places. They had no crisis of faith; rather, they had an increased surety of it. So it seemed that the parallels between Arduans and other intelligences could not be reliably projected.

Unless, Ankaht heard her inner voice whispering, *unless, of course, the human crisis of faith was not really linked to technology* per se. *Perhaps that kind of crisis is occasioned by the emergence of* any *paradigm that problematizes a culture's early beliefs in the theological wholism of its universe. For my people, technology did not present us with such a challenge: we were still linked by our* selnarm *and felt the will of Illudor and the permanence of our souls in* shaxzhutok. *No, for us, the challenge to our belief in an orderly universe occurred when we first contacted the humans. Because if the humans are truly sentient and yet also lack* selnarm, *rebirth, and knowledge of Illudor, then our cosmology is finally being confronted with a paradigmatic challenge that it cannot answer.*

Suddenly frightened by where her thoughts were leading, Ankaht leaned forward until her short forehead rested against the *maatkah* mats and thought: *Illudor's love, where shall this all end?*

12

A Mixture of Madness

There is no great genius without
a mixture of madness.
—Aristotle

Arduan SDH Shem'pter'ai, *Expeditionary Fleet of the* Anaht'doh Kainat, *Ajax System*

Narrok closed his eyes. But he could still see what the holoplot and the viewscreens had shown him when his flagship, the *Shem'pter'ai,* had emerged from the warp point just ten minutes ago. He saw it as clearly as if all three of his eyes were still staring at it.

The plot was choked with the ocher-colored icons of his dead ships. Here and there, the sigil denoting a vanquished human hull broke the harrowing monotony of the otherwise uniform mass of devastation. The devastation of his fleet. Again. When the day had begun, he'd hoped it would end differently—

Having gone over the order of the coming battle with his entire staff, Narrok had narrowed his *selnarm* link to share the final strategic assessment and intelligence exclusively with Sarhan and Fleet Second Esh'hid. "*This time we know who our adversary is: a human female named Krishmahnta. She is not a legendary leader among the ranks of the human admirals, merely the most senior among those who have been cut off from their main bases when we arrived at Bellerophon. However, for a middle-ranked admiral whose name does not figure prominently in the humans' pre-war dispatches, she has acquitted herself quite well. Questions?"*

There were none. So Narrok gave the order to commence the preparatory operations: clearing the human minefields with *Urret-fah'ah* minesweepers. But it seemed less effective, this time: evidently, the humans had not had enough mines to thickly seed the area immediately surrounding the warp point. Or so Narrok's staff insisted.

Narrok was not convinced, and did not race through with the van of his fleet. Instead, he stuck to the attack plan—and thus allowed the humans to, predictably, decimate wave after alternating wave of recon drones, ever followed by SBMHAWKs. Happily, the latter systems did find and savage several large targets—or so it seemed. Certainly, there were more dead human hulls being detected by each successive wave of RDs.

Consequently, when Narrok felt a strident excitement and urgency underlying Esh'hid's next *selnarm* send, he knew what she was going to request before she pulsed it across the light-seconds to him: immediate attack. Narrok resisted, but chose not to expressly prohibit, that initiative.

Esh'hid, evidently sensing the significance of her admiral's indefinite response, pressed further. "Admiral, this could be the opportunity we have been waiting for—an opportunity to push through a warp point before the humans are fully prepared for us."

"Yes, but it could also be a trap."

"My instincts tell me it is not, Admiral."

Narrok elected not to point out that he had more years and experience with which to refine his instincts. Instead, he eventually consented to Fleet Second Esh'hid's almost piteous pleadings to be given the signal honor of leading an unplanned fast attack against the apparently incomplete human defenses in the Ajax system. With little delay, Esh'hid transferred to the bridge of the largest SDH of the advance assault group and promptly led them through the warp point into Ajax.

Where, drones reported, they were promptly and handily destroyed. The apparent human losses to the SBMHAWKs had been a canny deception: the victims were large, empty bulk-freighters, stripped of everything but their outdated drives and a few electronic suites—just enough to fool the SBMHAWKs into believing them to be valid targets. The RDs had been unable to distinguish the decoys from genuine capital ships: doing so would have required a much closer scanning pass—and the RDs had been unable to get close enough to retrieve that level of detail and still survive to report. Indeed, the few RDs that had returned from each wave spent less than ten seconds on the Ajax side of the warp point.

Esh'hid and her attack force also discovered that a second tier of mines was waiting for them, farther back than the first, and that a surprising number of forts were waiting on the far side of those minefields.

All of which meant that Esh'hid and her advance assault group materialized in the center of a veritable cauldron of lethal human fire. Missile salvos and force beams turned that volume of space into a scintillant collage of overlapping explosions and savagely disruptive energies.

Not that she lived to report it. Narrok and Sarhan got the battle reports from the only two *zhed'bidr*—terminal drones—that survived to limp back through the warp point, seared and semifunctional. And Narrok could not help reflecting that this tragedy did have an upside: he was now freed from Esh'hid's ever-prying eyes, although he had—earnestly, at the last—hoped to convince her to reconsider her impulse to lead an attack that ultimately consumed her and two dozen of the last original-construction SDs like *zifrik* pupae caught in a flame.

So Narrok simply resumed the original attack plan, knowing as he unfolded it that the costs and outcomes were almost as predetermined as the life and death of a star: there might be momentary variations, but the general course of events was unalterable.

With the humans well back from the warp point, Narrok knew that entering the system was not his major problem. Rather, survival of his units, once there, would be a thorny challenge: the forts were predominantly missile-armed, and the data from the terminal drones indicated that they had hammered out densities of heavy ballistic missiles at Esh'hid's SDHs that neither she nor he could hope to match or deflect. So the first hulls Narrok sent through would have to survive the relentless bombardment long enough to not only close on the forts but to cut through the minefields shielding them.

Unfortunately, once away from the warp point, the *Urret-fah'ah* mine-clearers were not only useless, they were too dangerous to employ safely. Their efficacy against the minefields proximal to the warp points was a function of their speed of action: using *protoselnarmic* dead-man switches that were enabled by purpose-bred

Hre'selna biots, each *Urret-fah'ah* did not have to wait for the post-transit electronic disruption to subside. The unicellular *Hre'selna* biots reoriented almost immediately, and, detecting that they were no longer in range of the *selnarmic* links of their controllers (who remained safely on the other side of the warp point) they collapsed, enabling a piezoelectric actuator to launch the minesweeper's missiles almost immediately upon completing transit. But the purpose-built *Urret-fah'ah* minesweeper had modest engines, few defenses, primitive sensors, and no shields or ECM. In short, when crossing open space, it was little more than a thin-skinned chain-bomb, ready to vaporize any ships that were so unfortunate as to be within two light-seconds when it was destroyed by enemy fire.

So the approach to, and path through, the second belt of minefields would have to be blazed by fighters and SDHs. And once again, Narrok had reason to curse Torhok's strategic myopia. Narrok had wanted smaller and more diverse hulls laid down for just this contingency: he needed purpose-built minesweepers and small, fast escorts that could draw some of the murderous fire off the fragile fighters and the SDHs—which were too precious to spend forging an approach through multiply overlapping fields of fire. But no, Torhok and his logisticians had insisted that initiating the design and construction of new ship types would only be an effort-diluting distraction. So the Arduan naval inventory remained limited to SDSs, SDHs, fighters, shuttles, multipurpose tender/transports, and a few of the *Urret-fah'ah* minesweepers. That, Narrok was told, would have to do.

His SDHs went in by the dozens, trying to survive long enough to launch their fighters. And every time one of the heavy superdreadnoughts lasted that long, the fighters were almost immediately consumed by the overlapping white-star eruptions of a constantly churning blast furnace of human antimatter warheads.

But eventually, as Narrok had known it would, the sheer weight of his numbers began to prevail. Presently, messenger drones from Narrok's breaching force carried the story and the pictures of what was clearly a change in the tide of the battle: not all of his hulls were vaporized instantly, and they lasted long enough to divert fire from the next rank of incoming SDHs. The fighters started surviving, closing on the minefields, and clearing them—a tactic that was very nearly indistinguishable from suicide. In time, the human fire fell off—simply because their tenders could not resupply the forts' missile tubes fast enough to maintain their initial salvo volume.

Only then did Admiral Krishmahnta's fleet show up—fully repaired and in superb readiness. Every human hull that had survived the battles at Raiden and Beaumont now confronted Narrok's commanders again, but the humans were evidently better armed and better supplied than before. Their firepower, both missile and beam, changed the balance of the battle back against the Arduans, and, for a few moments, there was even some question as to whether or not the Children of Illudor would keep their tenuous toehold in the Ajax system. . . .

Narrok held his next stroke until the reports were unequivocal—that the human fleet had genuinely committed itself—for that was the moment he had been waiting for. He ordered one last torrent of SBMHAWKs to go streaming through the warp point. They inflicted no damage upon the human ships or forts, but both had to devote the majority of their firepower and attention to counteract that new threat. And hard on the heels of the SBMHAWKs came almost half of the Arduan fleet, led by Second Admiral Sarhan himself.

Over a dozen SDHs were lost, simply to the misfortunes of simultaneous transit, the immense hulls rematerializing in overlapping volumes of space, obliterating each other with blinding glares that made antimatter missiles look like firecrackers by comparison. But most of the dozens that survived quickly swept out of the cauldron, their data nets multiply integrated and cross-patched against any possibility of failure, their defensive batteries cloaking them in an almost unbroken sphere of counterfire. Inside that brief, turtlelike shell of protective energies, Admiral Sarhan pressed through the partial gaps the fighters had cut in the second minefield and closed to effective range with the forts.

The carnage as they did so was unspeakable. At one point, Sarhan lost no fewer than eight SDHs in the space of twenty seconds. But finally attaining close range, several of his SDHs—having been retrofitted with tractor beams—exploited the rigidity of the forts' structures by literally pulling them apart; the beams, once locked on, began to swiftly alter their polarization. It was a desperate tactic, useful only at just such close ranges, but the forts, being immobile, had no means of dancing away from this unanticipated threat. The same reinforced and inflexible structures that gave them such wonderful resistance against missiles and the other destructive energies of most attacks now became their Achilles' heels: unable to run or bend, they broke.

But Sarhan paid the price. In order to keep his ships in place long enough to do this strange execution, they were compelled to endure the full, desperate fire of the forts—and most of them died in the attempt. And when Krishmahnta's fleet came charging forward to intervene, Sarhan's uncommitted SDHs—although terribly outnumbered—screened the others that were still working on the forts. They did not survive—but they lasted long enough to seal the fate of the forts: three were shattered, two more disabled, the remaining three isolated on one flank and unable to bring their fires to bear on the more distant areas of engagement.

Which was when, ten minutes ago, Narrok had transited the warp point with the bulk of his fleet. He moved it quickly out of the last forts' fields of fire and began swinging it through an arc that would ultimately bring it into direct engagement with Krishmahnta's main body, which was still trying to annihilate the last of Sarhan's ships.

But just as Sarhan had expended SDHs to give his ships enough time to tear apart the forts, so Krishmahnta sent a fast screening force of carriers and cruisers to delay Narrok. The human ships were vulnerable but nimble, and although they did more to distract and delay than to inflict damage, their form fit their function: not to close and destroy, but harry and hamper.

As they did, Krishmahnta pulled her main body away sharply, losing three superdreadnoughts and two older, slower monitors in so doing. But her newer supermonitors remained mostly unscathed, and, leaving her last three forts behind to carry out whatever assignment she had given them in the event of her withdrawal, the human admiral made for the warp point to Agamemnon.

Which was what Narrok had anticipated. For Krishmahnta to have fled "north" along this arm of the Rim—to Aphrodite—would have been pointless: she would have been abandoning Odysseus and Tilghman, the two industrial worlds that sustained her forces. To defend them, she had to fall back on Agamemnon.

Which meant there was a possibility—if Narrok kept the pressure on her, stayed hard enough on her heels—that the terrible price he had now paid at Ajax might buy him another system as well. And if he was lucky, as the humans fled before him, using carrier squadrons to delay and harry his pursuers, he might also find the opportunity to cull one of the humans' less speedy fighters from its flock, by damaging it selectively, moderately—and so have a relatively intact model for his technical intelligence specialists to analyze. Maybe some good would come of this day yet. . . .

Willing the recent memories into oblivion, Narrok opened his eyes and saw the viewscreens that ringed the multi-tiered oval of his bridge as if they were the inward-facing facets of a gem turned inside out. More than half of the screens showed wrecks floating in space. These were the proud smooth-shaped hulls favored by his people, the ones he had led into battle: rent, outgassing, some still convulsed with internal explosions that flared from jagged wounds in their sides, sending flame and fragments and his writhing brothers and sisters into the merciless vacuum of space.

Narrok looked away. Half a year ago, when he witnessed such scenes of agony and devastation, he had routinely envisioned a fur-topped human face as the architect of that misery. It was a face he had imagined ripping and tearing and sundering until it could no longer have been recognized even by its own murdering breed.

Now, he did not see a human face.

Now, he saw Torhok's.

RFNS Gallipoli, *Further Rim Fleet, Ajax System*

Erica Krishmahnta rubbed her eyes and leaned away from the tacplot. "We've hardly started fighting, and we're already running. And leaving the forts to fend for themselves."

Captain Watanabe shrugged. "They'll be able to use escape pods when the time comes. That's a better chance than the crews of the other forts had."

"Gods, Yoshi, I just didn't see that coming. I mean, you can find it in the fine print of the training and doctrine manuals: alternating-polarity tractor beams used against the fortresses. And sure, it works—too damned well. But the expense in ships to get that close—I couldn't believe that even the Baldies would stand for losses that bad."

Watanabe shrugged. "Given what they've been losing up to now, it was probably a pretty good trade for them. Which is probably why almost none of us anticipated it."

Erica looked up. "*Almost* none of us?"

Watanabe looked away uncomfortably. "Uh . . . a lieutenant pointed it out in a memo recently. He cited the Baldy willingness to absorb casualties and that the alternating-polarity tractor-beam concept might be the only reasonable way they had to break through our defenses here, since they didn't have the monitors and supermonitors that could stand up to our massed fires long enough to survive."

"And why didn't you tell me about this memo?"

"Because it wouldn't have made any difference. You might be surprised that the lieutenant didn't advise against the placement or design of the forts. Quite the contrary, he thought it was our best option. If we handled it correctly."

"Oh? And did I handle it correctly, according to the lieutenant's expectations?"

"Uh—actually, you followed his recommendations to the letter. Let the Baldies come in, commit to the assault, and use their need for an extended close engagement with the forts as a way of pinning them in place. Their sacrifice of free maneuver is what gave us the opportunity to inflict murderous casualties on them—as long as we remembered to stay light on our feet to avoid the predictable Baldy follow-up strike from the warp point."

"Which of course means we were following a plan which necessarily ends with us running like hell and giving up the system. Again. Damn it, Yoshi, I'm awfully tired of showing the Baldies our heels."

"Me, too, Admiral. But we blew apart almost ninety SDHs back there."

"Yes, but there are almost twice as many again coming after us. And they're close, Captain. Too close."

Watanabe nodded. "Yes, it's going to be tight getting through the warp point, getting turned around, and getting in formation to defend in time."

Krishmahnta looked at the plot, watching the lead edge of the pursuing Baldies pushing at the remaining carriers and cruisers of her covering screens. Those fragile ships were falling back, tucking in behind the main van of her fleet, feinting, striking, harrying in an attempt to delay the attackers. Their success was moderate; their losses were mounting. "Captain, you're going to need to draw up an alternative plan for our arrival in the Agamemnon system."

"Sir?"

Erica closed her eyes and spoke each word slowly, distinctly, hating each one as she uttered it. "I need a contingency plan for making an immediate and orderly withdrawal to Penelope. I need all the fallback points preplanned, all detachments for delaying actions rostered and assigned, so that as we cross the Agamemnon system, we can attenuate our van and get it into a sequence that allows us to get everyone through the warp point to Penelope without breaking stride—and then turned right around into a defensive line on the other side."

Watanabe looked as if he had swallowed a live stun baton. Sideways. "But Admiral, we can still keep them from pushing through the warp point into Agamemnon. It will cost us a bit to keep them from following us through the warp point in force, but once we do, we'll have the time to get our line sorted out and—"

"All that presumes that we can turn and hold them when they're this close on our tails." She raised her voice. "Ops?"

Samantha Mackintosh looked up from her screens. "Yes, sir?"

"I need a hypothetical-evolution timeline for our formation: specifically, our ability to get through the warp point to Agamemnon and reform to meet the Baldies in good order on the other side."

"Already calculated, sir."

Which means the news is worse than I expected. "Let's hear it, Commander."

"Admiral, the Baldy SDHs actually have better speed than we do now. Not much—only about two percent—but better. And their whole formation has the Desai drive. We've still got old-style monitors, sir, and half of our auxiliaries were pulled from mothballs. Most of those were slated for redesignation as target-practice hulls when the Baldies arrived."

"Commander Mackintosh, you have informed me why the news is going to be bad. Now I need to know how bad it is."

"Yes, sir. All metrics remaining constant, the lead Baldy unit will reach the warp point approximately two hundred seconds after our last one goes through." Her voice lowered. "I don't need to tell the admiral what that means regarding our ability to repel their attempts to enter the Agamemnon system."

"You surely do not, Samantha." Krishmahnta turned to Watanabe. "That's it, then. We don't even have enough time to turn and fight. They'll be in among us while we're still milling about, trying to get into our defensive formation. And with all the new forts still back in Penelope, we don't have a ready defensive line to form up on."

"We'd have to deactivate Agamemnon's warp-point minefields, too," considered Watanabe. "We'd be so mixed in with the Baldies when they come through that the mines would be equally deadly to both of us."

"Right. But if we keep moving straight through the warp point, we can leave the mines operational. That will slow the Baldies down some more, maybe inflict a few casualties. Meanwhile, we deploy a sequence of delaying forces, just enough to ensure that we get all our hulls on the other side of the warp point to Penelope in good order and moving straight into a preplanned defensive formation."

"With forts all around us."

"That's the idea."

"Admiral, I'll get Commander Mackintosh to start working right away on a—"

"No, Yoshi. Samantha has received her last assignment on this bridge. I want you to get her on a courier to

Penelope—with a warning about what we're doing—and out of harm's way. Right now."

"Sir?"

"Yoshi, we've been putting off her full-time transfer to Tilghman for too long. She has to take charge of the shipyards and second-phase emergency industrialization throughout the cluster. And don't look so worried, Yoshi; I'll find someone to handle ops just as well as Samantha."

"Oh? And who would that be?"

"I don't have the faintest idea. How about we promote the genius lieutenant you told me about? We could brevet him to lieutenant commander and give him a crack at the big show here on the fleet flagship." Krishmahnta had meant it as a joke—but only partially: top-shelf thinkers were always at a premium in the command ranks, and in a fleet winnowed down by the casualties of almost five months of constant engagement, such minds were either already assigned or in deep denial and hiding.

Watanabe shifted in his seat uncomfortably. "Uh, about this lieutenant . . . you're not serious, Admiral?"

"Well . . . maybe I am."

"Sir, the lieutenant in question—he's in combat right now."

"We all are."

"No, sir. I mean the ship he's on—a carrier—is currently taking fire. It's part of the screen that's covering our withdrawal."

Krishmahnta looked at Watanabe, trying not to look startled or disbelieving. "You're not serious. It's not—"

Watanabe sighed and nodded. "I'm afraid so, sir. The lieutenant in question is—"

PSUNS Celmithyr'theaarnouw, *Delaying Detachment Charlie, Further Rim Fleet, Approaching Myrtilus, Agamemnon System*

Ossian Wethermere finished his update on the Baldy pursuit elements and made his way, datapad in hand, down to where Least Claw Kiiraathra'ostakjo, master of the CV *Celmithyr'theaarnouw* and commander of Admiral Krishmahnta's third and final delaying force, sat brooding over the tacplot.

As Wethermere approached the con, Lieutenant Zhou caught his eye and glanced meaningfully at the distance the Orion staff was keeping from their commander. It was clear that he was not happy, and whereas human COs often showed their mastery by adopting a measure of stoicism that a Spartan would have envied, Orion COs achieved the same result—as well as some stress relief—by, figuratively speaking, biting the heads off of injudicious subordinates. It was rumored that, in ancient times, this rather messy form of decapitation had been a literal, not figurative, punishment.

Wethermere, undeterred, came to stand by the con and hoped that the Least Claw would, as Orions often did, show more restraint when interacting with humans than they did with their own kind.

Least Claw Kiiraathra'ostakjo eventually let his eyes slip sideways toward Wethermere, who stood ready to report, his arm in a sling and his head still wrapped from the injuries he had sustained in Suwa. With surgical stores tight, and his injuries modest, Wethermere had received medical care that would have been as familiar to the wounded at Antietam as at Agamemnon and Ajax. Oddly, Kiiraathra'ostakjo seemed to approve of that.

"Visible wounds are the best testimony of a warrior's spirit," he had pronounced by way of welcoming Wethermere, Zhou, and Lubell to his carrier shortly before the Baldy fleet started pouring into Ajax. Although an Orion hull, the *Celmithyr'theaarnouw*'s crew and fighter complement were now almost one-third human; her own losses had been made up by orphaned TRN craft and crew—and whatever differences existed between the races, they shared a gnawing sense of loss and a burning desire to avenge their lost comrades.

Kiiraathra'ostakjo did not acknowledge Wethermere right away. Whether that was pride, or a mighty attempt at improving his mood before attempting to address a non-Orion, was unclear. "Yes, Tactical?" he asked at last.

"I have the sitrep and recommendations, Least Claw."

"I do not remember asking for recommendations, Lieutenant."

"Yes, sir. You did not. I simply prepared them in the event the captain had an unexpected and sudden need of them."

"Prudent. Continue." Which was also Kiiraathra'ostakjo's way of saying, *You are free to share your recommendations, human—now that you have made it clear you are not trying to suggest that I need anyone to do my tactical thinking for me.*

Wethermere checked his datapad. "The two Baldy SDHs that could still jeopardize the fleet's evolution for fast warp-point transit to Penelope remain in pursuit. However, the rearmost veered off in pursuit of the battlecruiser *Kwajalein*, when she maneuvered to outflank the other Baldy dreadnoughts. The SDH on point, which seems a modified semi-carrier version, is still stern-chasing us."

"Outcome of pursuit?"

"They are matching our speed and course, sir. They will arrive at the main body of the fleet in three hours. The leading edge of their van will be an hour behind them."

Kiiraathra'ostakjo growled.

Wethermere elected not to take that as a warning. "Lastly, we passed the Desai limit twenty minutes ago and are now coming abreast of the outermost planet in the system, the gas giant Myrtilus."

Kiiraathra'ostakjo nodded. "It is here that we must die, then. We will launch all fighters and stand with them within the planet's own Desai limit. Our enemies will be compelled to cease pursuit and engage, lest we take them from the rear when they pass. They will, of course, with their vast superiority in fighters, and even greater superiority in armor and armaments, destroy us—but they will lose crucial time in their pursuit of Admiral Krishmahnta's main van. With luck, the fleet will get through in time to hold Penelope firmly against their lead units."

Zhou, at the engineering board, swallowed hard and blinked at the epitaphic quality of Kiiraathra'ostakjo's pronouncement.

But Kiiraathra'ostakjo seemed to be waiting for something; he turned to look at Wethermere and then a slow, tooth-concealed smile cut an upward curve into the black fur around his muzzle. "Unless, that is, the lieutenant has a different option for us to consider."

Wethermere smiled back: it was always a test with the Orions. At first they tested you to see if you were something better than a cowardly *chofak* (or, literally, "dirt eater"—which they often suspected of humans), then they tested you to give yourself a chance to prove that you could be a creature of honor who understood and embraced the dictates of something at least vaguely reminiscent of their code of *theernowlus*, and at last they tested you because—being their friend—it would be an insult not to give you the opportunity to acquire more honor and refresh your reputation in the eyes of others. So, with the Orions—one way or the other—it was always a test. How Wethermere proposed his idea was the first, but prerequisite test; the utility of the idea itself was the second and final exam. So he'd stick to his notes and the answers he'd prepared. "Least Claw, if we were to follow a conventional concept of engagement, what outcome would you foresee?"

"They will swarm us with their two-to-one fighter superiority while using their SDH to constrain our main hull's orbital path so that we will be unable to retrieve or refit our squadrons unless we come under their fire. Once our fighters are gone, their remaining small craft will pin us in place so that the SDH may close and bring all its weapons to bear. We will be finished. There will be no survivors. But we will at least have given a good account of ourselves."

Zhou looked like he might faint.

Wethermere considered. "So, if some of the alternatives I have prepared for the Least Claw seem—bizarre—he would not feel I was wasting his time or making myself so foolish that I am an embarrassment to his command?"

Kiiraathra'ostakjo smiled, clearly approving of Wethermere's deft navigation of the social challenges implicit in publicly advising a vastly superior officer. "Since convention and common sense show us no path to victory, there is no dishonor in considering alternatives which derive from different sources of inspiration. What do you have in mind, Lieutenant?"

Okay, I've been given a passing grade on the first test. Now Wethermere's tone became more decisive, his syntax less ornately deferential. "Least Claw, how many energy torpedo external weapons packs do we have?"

Kiiraathra'ostakjo nodded appreciatively. "The energy torpedo is a worthy weapon, possibly the best our fighters have, but not enough to make a difference. Besides, we will need something with extended firepower, given how badly outnumbered we are. The ET packs fire themselves dry after twenty launches. And this will not be a short dogfight."

"Maybe it shouldn't be a dogfight at all, Least Claw."

Kiiraathra'ostakjo smiled. "So you suggest—how do you humans put it?—going out 'in a blaze of glory'? You suggest using a weapon that will destroy the maximum number of the *chofaki*, but when empty, shows them our throats and invites them to make a quick end of it."

"No, after a very short engagement with their fighters, I suggest showing them our tails."

Kiiraathra'ostakjo was, for the first time, startled. His tone was only half joking when he began with a chiding, "A typical human response—to run. But here, we cannot run."

"No, Least Claw, we cannot run—not at first. And never to retreat."

"Then why run at all? Your words are riddles, Tactical. Speak plainly."

"Very well, Least Claw." The Orion's injunction to *speak plainly* had given Wethermere even wider latitude with his manner of address and, ultimately, would shorten the time it took to lay out his whole plan.

"Least Claw, the Baldies have hit us and we're on the run already. They know this. They expect it to continue. They probably expect us to veer toward Myrtilus, deploy our fighters, and sell ourselves as dearly as possible. I suggest a slight change in that plan. As soon as we are within the Desai limit of Myrtilus, we scramble all our fighters swiftly and leave them behind, as if we are deploying them to make a desperate run at the Baldy SDH. They will certainly be convinced of this when they intercept us with their fighters and find that our birds are firing energy torpedoes—ordnance which would usually be reserved for use against capital ships."

Kiiraathra'ostakjo frowned. "Yes—but outnumbered two to one, and with a finite number of shots, our fighters would be quickly overwhelmed."

"Naturally—which is what the Baldies would see also. They would also see that our fighters are about to be overwhelmed, and that this carrier is too far out of reach. So they will not be surprised by our fighters' next, desperate course of action: our birds would have to try to lose the enemy squadrons by descending into the upper reaches of the atmosphere of Myrtilus."

Kiiraathra'ostakjo's surprise became horror. "Lieutenant. are you proposing that our fighters should dive into the atmosphere of a small gas giant? Are you mad?" And Wethermere could tell that, this time, the Orion inquiry was not figurative.

"Just a minute more of your indulgence, Least Claw. Firstly, where in this system do our drives have the most advantage over theirs?"

"Inside the atmosphere of the small gas giant." Kiiraathra'ostakjo's rumble was a grudging concession.

Zhou had started nodding, though. "Sure, yeah,"

he added. "The Baldies will be deep inside the Desai limit of a very intense gravity source. Their engine efficiency is going to plummet, and they're already running so close to the red line on their tuners that they're going to have almost no margin for error. As it is, their power curve is going to be fluttering around like laundry in the wind."

Wethermere nodded and turned back to Kiiraathra'ostakjo. "With all respect, Least Claw, given our advantages, why should we not send our fighters into the gas giant?"

"Because, cub of the moiety of Sanders, they will follow us in."

"Which is just what we want, Least Claw."

"Is it? And why is that?"

"Because I'm betting the Baldies have a disadvantage other than the finicky drives on their fighters. I'm betting that they've never trained for gas-giant flight operations. Given where they've come from—untold generations in deep space—how would they have acquired such training?"

Kiiraathra'ostakjo frowned but seemed less agitated by the unfolding plan. "I presume they have flight simulators."

"Yes, I'm sure they do. But this assumes that they had, or kept using, simulations for flying gas-giant operations. And even if they thought maintaining that readiness would prove worthwhile, it's still going to be rudimentary—and we know that simulator training never holds a candle to the real thing. So they'll be at a technical and training disadvantage if they follow us down inside the atmosphere of Myrtilus. And they'll be in the most unforgiving flying environment in all of known space. Awful gusts; down, up, and side drafts; intermittent cyclones; several different forms of precipitation; electromagnetic effects that play havoc with instruments."

Zhou nodded his agreement. "Like flying through chowder in a spinning food processor."

Wethermere kept his eyes on Kiiraathra'ostakjo, whose reluctance was beginning to erode—although he was clearly relenting not because the idea was brilliant but because it was ballsy. "It would be an operation that would be the sire of many long-told tales, Least Claw. The pilots would have to be the best. A moment's mistake gauging the shifting variables of lift, weather, and thrust erosion due to the Desai effects would be catastrophic. And for the Baldies, who are less prepared for this, who have never flown inside the atmosphere of a gas giant, they would find it necessary to spend every second just struggling to stay aloft and alive. That alone represents a decisive advantage."

But still Kiiraathra'ostakjo shook his head, his silky ruff flexing and bunching as he did. "No, the advantage is not decisive enough, Lieutenant—not when we are so outnumbered. They could surely leave a quarter of their squadrons outside the atmosphere, flying a high-guard patrol. So even if our fighters do survive the tempests of Myrtilus, they will eventually have to leave, still with many of the enemy behind them. And as our fighters rise up slowly to reattain orbit, the enemy high guard would intercept them. And so our brave pilots, while pinned from above, would be caught and rent by the claws following them from behind. And if there were survivors, we could not pick them up, for fear of their SDH."

"But what if there were no claws behind our fighters—and what if we only lost one of two of them while they were in Myrtilus?"

Kiiraathra'ostakjo considered. "In that case, the outcome of the entire engagement would change. Without pursuit from behind, our pilots would ultimately smash through the enemy's high guard. If enough of our fighters remain, they could even use their energy torpedoes to make a convincing feint at the SDH while we come closer to retrieve them. Then, as soon as we have come within that distance, they end their feint, come about, land, and we run. If we are done recovering our fighters before the SDH arrives, we will beat them to the warp point and so escape. And we will have bought Admiral Krishmahnta all the time she needs and more. But there is one problem."

"What's that?"

"How do we eliminate all the enemy fighters that would surely follow us into the upper reaches of Myrtilus? And how do we accomplish this in such away that we take negligible losses among our own formations?"

Wethermere smiled. "Well, funny you should ask that, Least Claw, because here's what I had in mind..."

An hour later, after only three losses and ten minutes of heated, long-range dueling, the *Celmithyr'theaarnouw*'s entire fighter contingent broke off from the Baldy squadrons that were trying to pin them down for an in-close dogfight. As the human craft wheeled about, many of the enemy fighters fired flechette missiles in what seemed to be an ill-advised attempt to bracket their delta-shaped human and Orion adversaries with clouds of fast-moving flak. It was not an effective tactic.

The human and Orion fighters danced beyond the edge of the Baldies' weaponry, too fast and nimble for the invaders to catch, whose sensitive drives were severely degraded by proximity to a large planet. The Baldies' logical solution was to launch their reserve squadrons to spread a bigger net. Seeing this, the allied fighters opened their drive tuners even wider, the multitude of pursuers giving wings to their feet as they ran.

Ran straight for the gas giant named Myrtilus.

First Lieutenant Egbert Saholiarisoa's voice was tight and clipped: this was the closest that fighter jocks came to expressing or admitting anxiety of any kind when they were in their cockpits. "Captain, are you sure your tac guy knows what he's doing? We're loaded with energy torpedoes out here. They're not cleared for use inside a gas giant. Damn few weapons are, you know."

Kiiraathra'ostakjo's voice was simultaneously a growl of command and a purr of understanding, reassurance. "Your reservations are prudent and noted, Flight Leader, but I have complete confidence in my tactical officer. Who has a further instruction for you."

Wethermere leaned forward so the general pickup would catch his voice clearly. "Lieutenant, charge the emitters on the energy torpedo packs to full."

"What? Charge them to—?"

"Lieutenant, trust me."

"Not like I have much choice," grumbled Saholiarisoa. "Charging to full, aye."

Kiiraathra'ostakjo's voice became even more soothing. "I repeat, Lieutenant, Mr. Wethermere has my full confidence." Then, cutting off the speaker, he turned to face Wethermere. "You are sure of this?"

"You heard your own meteorologist confirm it."

Kiiraathra'ostakjo shook his head. "This is not fighting—this is trickery."

Wethermere had to close his eyes to recall the axiom. "'No warrior ignores the natural weapons that the battleground itself places in his palm.' The battle-wisdom of H'Zreeaokhri the Cunning, as recorded in the Annals of Jevje'vejesh—is it not?"

Kiiraathra'ostakjo turned to gaze at the human. "It is. How do you know this?"

Wethermere smiled. "My great-sort-of-uncle had a knack for recommending books that caught my interest. He had very—well, eclectic tastes."

"And is it from him that you also learned your pronunciation of the Tongue of Tongues, cub of the moiety of Sanders?"

Wethermere smiled. "He'd be flattered at your question, Least Claw."

"Not so much as you think, human." But Kiiraathra'ostakjo gave a wide, closed-mouth smile after he said it. "Perhaps—if we survive your bizarre scheme—I will teach you the finer points of our language."

The human and Orion fighters had nosed down into the atmosphere of Myrtilus five minutes before. Wethermere was talking Saholiarisoa through the final steps of the operation. "And so you've got to hurry upstairs as soon as you let loose your munitions: the meteorological effects might surprise you."

"Hey, no surprises, please. What the hell is going to hap—?"

"Listen—no time for that. Just trust me, and fly the mission."

"Yeah, sure. Trust you. Great. I'm going open channel now." The audio feed became scratchier and multitracked.

"Okay, everyone, stay on course and don't get out ahead. The Baldies are coming up behind us, and that's just what we want. They'll have to close to a hundred kilometers or less to get a lock on us in this crap."

"You're the boss, boss."

"Damn right, Okuto. And no more chatter. We're ninety seconds from launch, so remember what the man told us on the way in. Watch your intervals and double the pattern size—that means double the distance between all our birds."

"How do we know when to start the party, Ell-Tee?"

"You wait for me to tell you, dumb ass. But we're watching for their trajectory to start getting wobbly. When I see that, I'll give the first order—for us to climb and downtune our reactionless drives."

"Downtune? Shit! With any efficiency drop, we'll fall behind the Baldies and down into the soup."

"Behind the Baldies, yes. Down into the soup—no, not if you climb steeply enough."

The voice of the squadron XO—Cleanth—observed: "Relative to them, it's almost going to look like we're performing a hammerhead stall."

"Exactly," affirmed Saholiarisoa. "With them fighting just to stay airborne, they're going to go past us before they know the game has changed. That's when you run your tuners up, and I'll give the fire order. You'll dip your noses just long enough to let the preprogrammed timer launch a torpedo, and then you pull up hard to port. *Everyone* to port."

"Why?"

"So we don't cross paths flying blind in all that crap, Ensign, and smash each other to pieces."

"What if we don't get a target lock, Ell-Tee?"

"You don't need lock. You just let the system fire."

There was profound silence. "I didn't read that, Ell-Tee. It sounded like you said we don't need target lock."

"That is what I said, Tariq. You shoot blind. Don't aim—you don't need to. And do not stop to look at the pretty lights going downrange. Get your birds over and up as fast as you can. Got that?"

The answering chorus sounded both bellicose and baffled. "Sir, yes, sir!"

As anticipated, the Baldy fighters quickly began to feel the mounting effects of being so close to a major gravity source. Their level flight started to shiver out of alignment, then occasionally stumble, and then, after two minutes, seemed to have degraded into a dogged forward stagger.

Saholiarisoa gave the word: the human and Orion fighters dropped their tuners and raised their noses. The net effect—decreased thrust, but vectored to push them straight up—cancelled each other out for a handful of moments, leaving them in the strange posture of maintaining altitude but skimming forward, belly first, slowing as they went.

The Baldy fighters went shooting past the human craft, which then brought their noses down for one brief instant and, in computer-controlled unison, fired one energy torpedo each before pulling up and pushing their tuners to the max.

The effect was, to put it mildly, dramatic.

The energy torpedo took its name not from its

warhead—plasma superheated to the brink of fusion—but the energy sheath which maintained its brief coherence. The coherence only needed to be brief because the torpedo traveled at almost the speed of light itself.

However, this weapon—intended for use in the airless vacuum of space—reacted most violently with atmospheres, which almost instantaneously began to ablate and strip away the energy sheath. Specifically, that degradation began only five kilometers beyond the weapon's launch point and then took only 0.0002 seconds to complete, but in that time, the torpedo would travel another ninety kilometers downrange at near light speeds.

This meant that the energy torpedoes launched by the human and Orion fighters began to break down shortly after they left each fighter's own drive field. As the fighters' airframes groaned under the stresses of a sudden snap into a vertical climb, riding maximum acceleration up through the roiling gusts of Myrtilus's atmosphere, megaton-level energies were spreading out from their flurry of torpedoes, which, as they broke down and their energy began leaking out, collectively resembled the discharge of a sawed-off shotgun firing stellar-plasma buckshot. At 0.0001 seconds post-launch, the star-hot temperatures of the plasma started cutting swathes through the increasingly ionized atmosphere. At 0.0002 seconds, the leaking energy sheaths ablated fully and the remainder of each warhead detonated. The surrounding atmosphere was annihilated for dozens of kilometers in every direction. The Baldy fighters spun, tumbled, came apart. Two human fighters which had not pulled up quickly enough were buffeted sideways rather than pushed upward by the outrushing shockwaves; they swerved unsteadily out of their vertical climbs.

They—and those few Baldy craft that fickle fate somehow spared—were ripped asunder in the next two seconds: with the gases in the target area utterly and instantaneously vaporized, nature once again demonstrated the axiom that she did indeed abhor a vacuum. The inrushing atmosphere roared back with the force of a dozen converging cyclones, smashing into each other to spawn a clutch of ferocious tornadoes, all capped by the most titanic lightning storm that human instruments had ever recorded.

The climbing human and Orion fighters—their numbers reduced by five since commencing this operation—pulled speedily up and away from the flaring maelstrom behind them and headed toward the now vastly outnumbered Baldy high-guard patrol.

As the last fighter angled gingerly into the portside recovery bay, Kiiraathra'ostakjo gave orders to the *Celmithyr'theaarnouw*'s helmsman. "Best speed to the warp point. Sensors: the enemy superdreadnought?"

"Following—but at a very respectful distance, Least Claw."

Kiiraathra'ostakjo nodded at that report. Then he stared at the red Baldy icon lagging behind their green one in the tacplot and smiled: this time his teeth showed, and Wethermere noticed how numerous, and alarmingly sharp, they were. "*Chofaki* scum," he sneered at the red icon, "now that you've lost your fighters, you seem much less brave. Perhaps we should turn and teach you a lesson . . ."

Then he saw Zhou's panicked expression and Wethermere's carefully neutral one and laughed the snorting, tooth-masked guffaw of his race. "Fear not, humans, we will run as you wish." Then he nodded more somberly. "As is wise." He turned to Wethermere. "Well, you may have some of your distant sire-brother's qualities after all, Lieutenant." The Orion smiled. "Perhaps you would even consent to joint me for a celebratory dish of *zeget* once we have made the warp point."

Wethermere merely nodded; the Orion noted that he was looking intently at the flight-deck relays.

"I offer you a great honor, Ossian Wethermere," Kiiraathra'ostakjo added. His tone was gentler, but had also ceased to be jocular.

Wethermere looked up, as if waking from a trance. "Apologies, Least Claw. I was—thinking."

Kiiraathra'ostakjo sighed—a gesture that was startlingly similar to its human analog—and looked askance. "When you begin to think deeply, I begin to worry greatly. What madness are you conceiving now, human?"

"Not madness. At least I don't think so. Look at this." Wethermere pointed to the relays that were showing the after-action reports being compiled as each retrieved fighter downloaded its mission data.

"Yes? We were uncommonly fortunate. According to those flight records, the Baldy fighters maneuvered less well than usual."

"Yes, there's that. And there's this, also. Look."

Kiiraathra'ostakjo leaned closer. "Odd. They used that many flechette missiles? And always with gaps in their firing pattern? What do you make of this, Lieutenant?" Kiiraathra'ostakjo, although he was made uncomfortable by the unorthodox nature of Wethermere's mind, had also acquired a keen appreciation of its polymathic scope—a trait that was also ascribed to the human's distant sire-brother, the legendary Kevin Sanders.

Wethermere was still staring at the data intently. "I'd say they were trying to cull off one or more of our fighters—like they were working to split up the formation more than they were trying to destroy our craft. That's why they were using the flechette missiles—they were using them as area-denial munitions."

"You mean, to create volumes of space in which our fighters could not fly."

"Yes—but the gaps in their patterns always gave the fighters they isolated an opportunity for evasion."

"Yes," growled Kiiraathra'ostakjo, leaning closer and seeing the patterns in the data, "just as a hunter chooses and culls his victim from a herd ahead of time, separating it from the rest of its fellows. Ossian Wethermere, what does this mean?"

Wethermere looked away from the data and stared into the viewscreen that showed Myrtilus dwindling behind them. "I think they wanted to capture one of our fighters."

"So it seems, but why?"

"Maybe for the same reasons we exploited today—their fighters have too many weaknesses to meet ours on an equal footing."

"So they wish to capture one for the purposes of technical intelligence. Hermph. Most interesting."

"Yes. Interesting . . . at the very least."

From the corner of his eye, Kiiraathra'ostakjo saw that the human was distracted again, thinking his unpredictable thoughts. He seemed to be watching the violently strobing lightning that had been triggered by their fighters' energy torpedoes. The ferocious storm had churned outward from its point of origin to engulf that entire quadrant of Myrtilus' sunward face. Wethermere leaned his left elbow on the console, set his chin into his palm. "Look at all that lightning. The energy torpedoes must have kicked off a chain reaction. There's got to be hundreds of terawatts of electrical energy discharging between those clouds right now." He thought hard. "You know, if there was a way to harness that—"

"Enough!" Kiiraathra'ostakjo's roar contained an undertone of actual fear. "Cease your speculations, Lieutenant Wethermere!"

"But I just—"

"Enough I say, and enough I mean. I know that look, human. You are scheming. And when you scheme in that way, you are always thinking of how to break things. Stop, before you break this, too."

"Break what? The planet?"

"Or maybe the universe. Return to your station at once! Helm, execute course change Feaarnowt-three. Take us away from here before Lieutenant Wethermere can break anything else."

13

Necessary Things

Plots, true or false, are necessary things,
To raise up commonwealths and ruin kings.
—Dryden

Punt, New Ardu/Bellerophon

"Elder, I am pained to say it, but it sounds like it was your incompetence which led to the slaughter of both the human Resistance fighters and my Enforcer-Group." Everything about Torhok's *selnarm*, despite being processed and therefore flattened by an orbital relay station, suggested that he was not pained, but exultant, at being able to accuse Ankaht of incompetence.

"Senior Admiral, your statement presumes much—which also tells me you did not bother to research the event. I merely sent a request to the Enforcer section prime. She handled the selection of the responding unit and any subsequent orders. I am at a loss to see how such a simple request can be 'incompetent.'"

"You should have given special warning that you suspected a Resistance cell to be on the site."

"I had no such suspicion."

"And that is the source of your incompetence, Elder." Ankaht felt the churlish delight Torhok took in combining her honorific—Elder—with the patronizing tenor of his *selnarm*.

"Senior Admiral, I asked for a unit to simply pass by the residence. Not make a contact, much less an entry."

"Perhaps, but when an armed human shows up on our recon monitors, it rather changes the nature of the visit, doesn't it?"

"Most assuredly. And how that change was handled was none of my affair. I was not consulted."

"There was no need to consult you. As you said, security matters are not your affair, Councilor."

"Precisely—which is why *my* competence cannot be in question, Senior Admiral."

Torhok's *selnarm* closed down, and Ankaht dismissed the brief pulse of triumph she felt for having shut him up and beaten him at his own round of the blame game. However, she hadn't the inclination to luxuriate in that small victory—nor had she the time to do so, either, because he came straight back with:

"The flaw is in not involving us sooner—and in failing to provide us with access to this *griarfeksh* 'artist'—"

"Jennifer Peitchkov—"

"—whose house this was, and whose mate seems somehow involved in the Resistance."

"And what good would it have done for your Enforcers to have had contact with Jenni—with our research subject?" But she did not share her deepest retort: *And, had I given you that access, you would have surely, and intentionally, done irreparable damage to our attempts to establish trust and communications with her—*

Torhok scoffed through his *selnarm*. "Elder, our need for access to her is so plain that even you must be able to see it. It is certain that this artist is involved."

"'Involved?'"

(Disbelief, incredulity.) "*Involved.* In the Resistance. Is it not obvious?"

"Admiral, you have been back in-system for just ten days and have been aware of this incident for less than two. Tell me, have you yet had the time"—*or the inclination*—"to read my reports on what the human-research group has produced in terms of communication with the subject in question, Jennifer Peitchkov?"

Silence.

Thought not. "Then let me suggest you update yourself on that data, which will prove to be most relevant to this situation. However, in advance of your detailed study of my report"—*which I'm sure will never occur*—"let me excerpt one or two particularly crucial facts.

"Firstly, most humans are utterly without *selnarmic* resonances, as was projected. Some, however, have residual sensitivities. The subject Jennifer Peitchkov has, even within this small subset, markedly high comparative sensitivities—so much so that we are actually establishing contact with her on complex issues. The sophistication and reliability of that communication has been growing daily.

"However, what we call her *selnarm* is actually quite distinct from what we Arduans experience. One of its most unusual and dissimilar features is that her variety of telempathy permits her no guile or misrepresentation. If she thinks a falsehood, that inveracity registers immediately and unmistakably along with the message itself. As you had requested, I asked her if she was involved in the bombings or other events. This she flatly denied without the faintest hint of prevarication.

Indeed, she was unaware that the human terrorists were in her house. In short, she is not 'involved.'"

Torhok's response carried the faint impress of a dogged defense rather than a confident rebuttal. "Elder, with all due respect for your attempts to understand the *griarfeksh*, you cannot be sure what arts they may have when it comes to concealing the truth. Their own literature indicates that some of them can go through life completely and sincerely convinced that they are not who they are, that they are in direct conversation with their different deities, and, in some extreme cases, that they have multiple personalities, each of which can remain wholly unaware of the actions undertaken by the other personalities within them. How then can you say so surely that the artist-subject's denial of involvement is reliable?"

Ankaht let her smile travel through her *selnarm*. "I must say that you have compiled an interesting—and highly selective—reading list of human literature, Admiral. But I have read these same books and reports, too. All the conditions you cite are profound mental abnormalities, which are inevitably accompanied by characteristic—indeed, confirmatory—clinical aberrations. Jennifer demonstrates none of these aberrations. Therefore, the simplest and most logical answer is that her missing mate is involved in the Resistance, and may be implicated in the bombings, but that she is not."

Torhok was nothing if not tenacious. "These studies of the *griarfeksh* brain and behavior also indicate that many of these mental aberrations can occur acutely, rather than chronically, perhaps triggered by great stress—and some are associated with what the *griarfeksh* doctors call 'post-partum depression.' It therefore seems possible that this species is capable of transient insanity. We have certainly witnessed evidence of this in the humans that we have fought against during our campaign thus far."

Ankaht felt her patience slipping; she did not have the energy to retrieve that leash before it shot out of her grasp in the form of an arch retort. "Really, Admiral? You have observed so much of this transient insanity in your human opponents? Is that why every one of your 'victories' over them has cost us three, five, even ten times the number of ships that they have lost? If that is the nature of human insanity, Admiral, then it must be a mental malady that also imparts supreme tactical inspiration to those afflicted. Now, do you have any other concerns you wish to share?"

"I am finished." Torhok's final sending carried the overtone of being finished with much more than the conversation. Much, much more.

But Ankaht had no time to immediately concern herself with Torhok's wintry and ominous displeasure. She turned to her visitor, who was removing the closed-channel *selnarm* receiver from the base of his skull. She sent (candor, fairness). "So, Cluster-Leader, does that serve to confirm the state of 'amicability' that exists between myself and Senior Admiral Torhok?"

Mretlak placed the band-shaped receiver on the edge of Ankaht's desk with great care. "Indeed it does, Elder."

(Amusement.) "And are you suitably shocked?"

"I am suitably reassured... and unsurprised. Senior Admiral Torhok's mind is occupied by a great vision of our future—so great, that there hardly seems room for any vision other than his own."

(Rue, appreciation.) "You have an aptitude for expressing yourself in very politic terms, Mretlak."

"I had an excellent tutor, Elder."

"Ah. Admiral Narrok. And how is he?"

Mretlak's tentacles rippled restively. "As well as can be expected. Under the circumstances."

(Sympathy, concern.) "And what circumstances are those?"

"Having to follow orders that he knows will lead to the pointless discarnation of so many trained souls at a time when we can spare so few. He is torn between his sworn duty to follow orders and his innate duty to serve the good of our race."

Ankaht nodded soberly, sent (accord), and wondered what quirk of Illudor's wisdom had sent this prize—Mretlak—to her doorstep this day. He was dangerous insofar as he was not under her direct authority or scrutiny, but the natural possibilities for alliance and mutual assistance between them were profound. He evidently saw that as clearly as she did, since it had been he who had proposed their meeting. Yet there was still some reluctance, some reserve in him . . . but perhaps the source of that reserve would soon present itself. In the meantime . . . "Am I right in understanding that, although you technically report directly to Senior Admiral Torhok, you have never met with him since your reassignment? Not even once?"

(Affirmation.) "Even though I traveled on his flagship all the way from Achilles."

"And do you have any conjectures to explain his benign neglect?"

"Obviously, because my assignment to gather and assemble detailed strategic intelligence on both past and present human military behavior was merely an excuse to remove me from Admiral Narrok's staff. In being reassigned, I have simply been shunted to the side and, thereby, administratively contained."

"My sympathies."

"Appreciated, but unnecessary, Elder. This evolution of events is most suitable to my purposes."

"How so?"

Mretlak spread his lesser tentacles loosely: relaxed confidence. "Although the senior admiral presumes little if anything is to be gained by starting a military-intelligence cluster, Admiral Narrok and I anticipate quite the opposite. And if Senior Admiral Torhok is too busy to give specific procedural orders or issue targeted directives, that leaves me free to work on topics—and use methods—without his oversight."

He is self-effacing, particularly so for a Destoshaz—and hence, his own caste will completely miss the shrewd and quiet boldness in this one. "This is well reasoned indeed, Group-Leader. And fortuitous, I think."

"Fortuitous, Elder?"

"Yes—because it would not do to have Admiral Torhok or any of his contemporaries decide upon the staff and operational procedures of our intelligence service. The reactivation of such a—specialty—requires a mindset that is ready to think well beyond the received wisdoms of this day. Our military intelligence, of old, had necessarily been a synergistic enterprise among castes that now frequently find themselves at odds with each other."

"You refer to the friction between the *shaxzhu* and the *Destoshaz*." Mretlak's *selnarm* had suddenly become tense, constrained where it had been fluid.

Ankaht understood: this caste-friction was the source of his restlessness and reluctance. A *Destoshaz* himself, he probably felt that by forging an alliance with

Ankaht—foremost *shaxzhu*, Sleeper, Elder, despised as a *griarfeksh* apologist—he was engaging in something akin to caste-treachery. Ankaht proceeded cautiously with (sympathy, acknowledgment). "That has been the most unfortunate—and pronounced—of the diminished relationships within our community, but not the only one. Consider how the other caste specialties have almost all been wiped away. For instance, one of the groups that was very important to intelligence and research in the past was the *Ixturshaz*."

Mretlak was (bemused, receptive). "A propitious reference. One of my newest cluster members is an *Ixturshaz* himself. He had been serving with an Enforcer-Group."

"Really? And he was released from the group without complaint?"

"Elder, he was the group's only survivor. His Enforcer-Group is the one that went to the house you were speaking about with Senior Admiral Torhok."

Ankaht did not get truly shocked very often: she was truly shocked now. She was cautious, proceeding: "Cluster-Leader, I do not mean to question your judgment—but is such a recruiting choice wise? Can this *Ixturshaz* possibly be objective?"

"I believe so. However, he is most certainly motivated to undertake his duties—and completely impervious to the *Destoshaz'ai*-as-*sulhaji* rubbish that is mesmerizing an increasing number of my caste-mates. And he is very clever. If he has no love of humans—well, I could see how that would be an impediment in your research efforts, Elder. But not in mine."

And Ankaht thought: *Well and fairly answered. Not reassuring, but sensible and sane. These days, who can hope for more than that?* "I am glad you will have an

Ixturshaz on your staff. I could even wish there was a place for a *shaxzhu*."

"As do I, Elder, but there are so few of you—and all so closely watched—that I fear it would bring exactly the sort of scrutiny I hope to avoid."

"Sad, but true. So, no *shaxzhu* in your cluster. Well, that is probably prudent."

But Mretlak's *selnarm* seemed to shift then, as if Ankaht's easy acceptance of his demurral made her easier for him to trust. His sending was obliquely tinctured with (acceptance, cooperation). "However, Elder, it would be most helpful if I . . . or perhaps others of my staff . . . were to know that some specific *shaxzhu* were especially receptive to our inquiries, or requests for unofficial assistance."

And Ankaht allowed a smile into her *selnarm*. "I think that can be arranged." *You will do well at this game, Mretlak. Narrok chose you well.* She moved away from the topic; early alliances are delicate, not to be hammered at: "Have you thought, Mretlak, why the humans seem to have such an advantage over us in this area—in military intelligence?"

"A long, unbroken history of its necessity and use would seem to strike me as the reason, Elder."

"Oh, that explains their expertise—but I suspect they have an innate advantage."

"Oh, why?"

"Because, not having castes, they have remained generalists. Now, in many enterprises, that has been to their detriment. For instance, they cannot so readily accomplish highly specialized tasks, and so they have never been able to organize ship production as quickly and efficiently as the Children of Illudor.

"But their generalist nature arguably makes them

superior in any task that is inherently interdisciplinary—particularly when the matrix of needed skills is such that, if we tried it, we would have to cross caste lines to find an adequate diversity of aptitudes and training. And this unfortunate phenomenon has only grown worse since we left Ardu. Diversity of castes has steadily decreased among the ship-born, even as conformity *within* each caste has increased."

"I have seen this worrying truth myself, Elder. Happily, my project is off to an excellent start, in part because of our caste mix, I suspect. Lentsul—my *Ixturshaz* research prime—is extremely thorough."

"And upon what project has he been exercising his thoroughness?"

"Ascertaining the provenance of human records that date from, and purport to depict or report, what they call the Bug War."

Ankaht sat more erect. "Indeed? And what have you found?"

"We are still some weeks away from processing all the evidence, but the trend is irrefutably clear."

"Which is?"

Mretlak flexed and then withdrew his claws in a gesture of decisive negation. "It cannot be a hoax. The artifacts are genuine, as is proven by the subtle but consistent chemical residues they contain, and which match each other and the atmosphere of Bellerophon as it was at the time of the Bug War, or shortly thereafter."

Ankaht was amazed—not by the findings, which she had already presumed—but by the independent validation and close ally which it promised. "And, by extrapolation, what do you therefore conclude about the human conduct of that war?"

"That their representations of it are fundamentally consistent with what they actually experienced. They were desperate, fighting for their lives—even as we are now. Which must be terribly traumatic for creatures who suspect that they do not reincarnate. But Elder, I have been struggling with one aspect of that belief of theirs—their lack of reincarnation—which seems counterinstinctual."

"Which is?"

"If they so fear and hate discarnation—no, death—then why do they celebrate the horror of war? Why do they torture themselves and cheer at scenes of combat? Why do they wish to broadcast images of these terrible losses?"

"Perhaps because . . ." And Ankaht struggled at the edge of an understanding that required her to embrace a reality at once so alien and so lonely and hope-stripping that she could not breathe as she entered its outer peripheries. "Perhaps because it is the only way their deeds and their identities endure."

"I do not understand."

Ankaht found herself recalling nuances of Jennifer's thoughts as she explored her hypothesis. "Let us presume that their assessment of themselves is not in error, but correct: that, like all living things, they perish, but—unlike the Children of Illudor—they cannot be reincarnated."

"Making them *zheteksh*—animals."

"But what if they are *not zheteksh*? We have always conflated personhood—being truly sentient—with the surety of reincarnation. But what if that is not the standard, not the norm of most intelligent species? What if, rather, it is the exception?"

"The exception? But Elder, how could this be possible?"

"I do not know—but is it any more reasonable to assert that species which create art and satire and starships are *animals*? Consider the other species the humans have encountered, one of which—the Orions—we have met in combat as their allies. All of these species have much the same fear of death as the humans. And all have elaborate celebrations for both marking one's demise and remembering those who died before. Consider the human graveyards, and their desperate clinging to anything touched by, or associated with, the deceased."

Mretlak recoiled in both body and *selnarm*. "If their fears are accurate, then they . . . they . . ."

Ankaht nodded. "They live in perpetual fear of a permanent and all-consuming darkness that not only *can* approach and swallow them—it *must*."

Mretlak stood. His *selnarm* signaled a need to return to his researches."Eldest, if this should prove to be true, then the humans are unthinkably brave—and may prove very difficult to conquer. Very difficult indeed."

Ankaht closed her eyes. "So, if *conquest* is not a viable answer, perhaps we must change the question we are asking."

"That is subtly put. Any less subtle might make it sound treasonous."

"Of which I am well aware, Mretlak. This meeting has been a genuine pleasure."

He reciprocated the (amity, appreciation). "It will be the first of many, if you will permit them."

"I would be happy to work with you again." And then, as Mretlak left, Ankaht added to herself: *Yes,* desperately *happy to work with you, Mretlak. For at last I just might have an ally.*

✧ ✧ ✧

Lentsul remained intent on the trainee's screen. She, Emz'hem, was a *Destoshaz*—tall, golden—but not at all like his discarnated Heshfet. Emz'hem was anything but provocative, and her *selnarm* pulsed with little passion. However, she was a reasonably intelligent *Destoshaz* and had the best record of any Enforcer for dealing peaceably and effectively with humans—both in their dwellings and as prisoners. For that reason, and her modest cognitive gifts, Cluster-Commander Mretlak had recruited her to the military-intelligence cluster, and assigned her directly to Lentsul for training in counterinsurgency intelligence.

For the fourth time, Emz'hem tried to graphically cross-index human production data, inventory records, and pre-war commercial distribution patterns—and failed. "Junior Group Leader," she apologized, "my efforts are unsuccessful."

Lentsul involuntarily succumbed to the tentacular flex-and-droop reflex that was the Arduan equivalent of an annoyed shrug. "Then try again—using a new method." He turned away, resisted the impulse to solve the problem himself. Because if he did that, then Emz'hem would learn nothing and they would not have the necessary personnel to staff a military-intelligence cluster.

Military-intelligence operations had not always been so trying, Lentsul reflected. He had been searching through old records of counterinsurgency operations conducted by the Enlightenment-era city-states of Ardu. Even those scant records drove home the disheartening comparisons with great clarity: there were so many aptitudes and paradigms his predecessors had been able to employ in situations such as this. They had understood covert operations, guerrilla war, and how a freewheeling market economy was the perfect blind for a clandestine resistance movement.

But then, Ardu had learned that bright Sekahmant—the benign central eye of the night sky—had suddenly become a baleful gaze of impending doom. Nations had folded together into massive industrial and research engines in the unexceptioned push to discover and to build the means to leave their doomed, beloved world. During their journey into the great dark between the stars—where only curtains of faint, nebular *vrel* and *crivan* shimmered to remind them of the light they had known when living on a planet's surface—so many souls had returned as *Destoshaz*. Perhaps that was because the simpler, direct, and active nature of that warrior caste was more suited to the demands of the journey. Or perhaps Illudor had willed that his most forgetful children be born to steer the ships, because if too many minds were able to fully experience the *shaxzhutok* of a storehouse of planetary memories—of light-dappled ocean swells and musky, tall ferns—the entire Race might have sunk down past wistful melancholy and drowned in suicidal solipsism.

Lentsul turned back to study the screen and was happy to discover, that, in his prolonged silence, Emz'hem had made yet another attempt. Now the figures stood in useful comparison to each other. At last they might start getting somewhere on the search. "Excellent work, Emz'hem. Now let us find the serial number of the toy in question."

She complied, but her *selnarm* (obtruded). "Why are we searching for the source of this toy, Junior Cluster-Commander?"

"Because this toy"—he pointed to the image of the

blue-red-gold truck that had charged the hopper at the end of the convoy attack—"was not used as a toy. As you see here, it was used to close on, and seemingly attack, the hopper."

"Was it armed?"

"Interestingly, no. But in retrospect, why did it need to be? The humans just wanted to scare the hopper's operator into extracting it—probably so the *griarfeksh* could exfiltrate their control-and-overwatch point undetected. And since every other toy car they used had been rigged with a bomb—"

"—our operator had no choice but to presume that this, too, was so armed."

"Precisely. And that is why one of the Enforcer sleds destroyed it. But they did not completely vaporize it"—he held up a scorched piece of the vehicle's undercarriage triumphantly—"and so we were able to determine the toy's identification number. And if it was purchased recently—"

"Yes, it was. Here is the record."

"Ah. Excellent work." *And long overdue, but I will leave that out of my* selnarm. "Now, has Cluster-Commander Mretlak secured our clearance for full access to monitor all the human computer activity?"

"He did, just before he went to his meeting with Councilor Ankaht. We now have full access to the human systems—at least, to those systems of which we are aware."

"But the data is certain? You are sure that toy in question was purchased? Not declared lost or missing?"

"No, Junior Commander, it was purchased. But this is odd—the price at which this toy was sold is but one-fifth of that which the same merchant charged for a similar unit sold only two days earlier."

Ah. The clue I was seeking. And also an excellent opportunity to test my trainee's perspicacity. "So, what do you conclude from that fact?"

Emz'hem's central eye narrowed; the other two fluttered. "I am unsure, Junior Leader. Perhaps the *griarfeksh* bomber, knowing he intended to destroy the vehicle, purchased one with some defect that was inconsequential to his intents? And the defect resulted in a lowered price?"

Lentsul closed his main eye: there was much work to do before the trusting souls of his own race understood the devious courses that covert operations followed. "Or perhaps the merchant understood the purposes for which the bomber was purchasing the unit."

Emz'hem was (confused, perplexed). "Then if there was collusion between the two, why did the store owner not simply make the toy a gift, or declare it lost from his inventory?"

"Several possibilities present themselves. Firstly, any lost inventory notation is unusual. As a statistical anomaly, it attracts attention. And attracting attention is the last thing a covert operative would wish to do. Also, the reduced price is probably equal to the merchant's expenditure when purchasing the item from his suppliers. As the humans would say, he simply provided it to the Resistance 'at cost.' So the toy in question still registers as sold in the inventory database. Only when we look closer do we see that it wasn't sold for the customary price. And even then, that would not signal much to us—unless we had this piece of incriminating evidence." He waved the charred strip of metal in his tentacle. Now for Emz'hem's next test. "So, how do we proceed?"

"We arrest the merchant. We force him to divulge the identity of the *griarfeksh* bom—" Emz'hem stopped, her abashed *selnarm* confirming that she had noticed all three of Lentsul's eyes closing—slowly, wearily. "You believe I am in error, Junior Commander?" came the timid inquiry.

She has an unsurpassed talent for understatement. Lentsul kept his *selnarm* carefully groomed and utterly blank as he replied, "Even if you could get this merchant to divulge pertinent information, the data will no longer be useful. Once we take him into custody, the Resistance members he supplies will go into hiding, perhaps relocate. No, we must proceed in a far more patient fashion, and so let our enemies reveal themselves to us."

"And how shall we compel them to do that, Junior Commander?"

So much to learn, indeed. "We do not compel them at all, Emz'hem. Rather, if we give the *griarfeksh* enough time, they will show us their faces and not even know that they have done so."

A strong new pulse of *selnarm* entered their conversation. "Lentsul, it seems you have made progress?"

Lentsul started out of his deductive trance and found that it was Mretlak's *selnarm* which was touching his own. "Yes, Commander, it seems so."

"Excellent." Mretlak sent (pleasure, congratulations, encouragement) and hoped Ankaht's reservations about Lentsul would not prove warranted: the little *Ixturshaz* was his brightest staffer, and he had a turn of mind well-suited for the strange mix of detail-checking and free-form analysis that was the rootstock of all counterintelligence work. "I will ask you to let your trainee continue by herself for a moment. I wish your opinion on a technical matter."

"Certainly."

Once Lentsul had followed Mretlak into his office, and the door was shut, the Cluster-Leader reached out a private tendril of *selnarm*. "They have done it, Lentsul."

(Surprise, avidity.) "The vocoder? Already?"

"Yes. I saw it working today. I listened to the communication that the Elder has established with the human artist. It is—very impressive."

"This is wonderful news, is it not?"

"It should be, Lentsul. But before I allow my hopes to move too strongly in that direction, I want one other opinion."

"Whose?"

"Yours. Here, absorb this recording. It will take many minutes. And I want your most skeptical reaction, Lentsul."

"I have no other kind to give, Commander."

And so Mretlak sat silently beside Lentsul as he absorbed the entire day's exchange between Ankaht and the human named Jennifer Peitchkov. When the recording was over, Mretlak asked: "So, what do you think?"

Lentsul squinted his main eye. "I think the operation of this vocoder is akin to having a computer interpret the meaningless screechings and twitterings of a *flixit*. It is a parlor trick. The computer reports meaning? Of course it does—the meaning the programmers and their algorithms have wished into existence. This vocoder is not translating intelligent communication for us, because the human is not uttering any intelligent communication for the machine to translate."

Mretlak smiled. "Then how do you explain the corroboratory *selnarm* exchanges?"

"I can't."

"And the conformity between those and the smart-board lexical translations?"

"I can't—not unless the tape has been altered and edited."

"In short, the entire tape is false."

"It must be, because I cannot explain it otherwise."

"And if I now relieve you of the duty of being an absolute skeptic?"

Lentsul's main eye flexed wide. "Then I would say we finally have the tool we need. Actually, there is more evidence to support that conclusion than the mere matching of *selnarm* to the written language on the smart-boards."

"Oh? Such as?"

"Measure the time that the Elder has had access to subject Peitchkov. Then consider the number and aptitudes of the Elder's staff. Now presume that everything we witnessed-every bit of conversation and *selnarmic* exchange—is all pure fabrication. There's a mathematical discrepancy between the two."

"There is?"

"Yes. The amount of labor required to fabricate the human's seamless references and representations pertaining to her culture could not be completed by the number of workers Ankaht has, in the time available to them. Ergo, even if we were tempted to speculate that this is a meticulously crafted conceit, it is so flawless and extensive that it *cannot* be a conceit. Not given the limited time and resources available for its creation."

Mretlak sent (gratitude, admiration). "Your logic is

invaluable to me, good Lentsul. Now let me show you one other item of interest." Mretlak opened the credenza next to his desk and lifted out what looked like a paper-thin tic-tac-toe grid.

Lentsul's main-tentacle claws cycled quickly in powerful (curiosity). "What is that device?"

By way of answer, Mretlak activated the human machine. After a moment of gray static, a picture appeared in each cell of its three-by-three grid. At first, Lentsul frowned at the disparate images, but then his *selnarm* registered realization: all the scenes were of different locations in Punt City—specifically, the parts which had been taken over from the humans. As they watched, two Arduans crossed the field of view in the lower center screen, oblivious to being observed.

Lentsul looked up at Mretlak. "A monitoring system?"

Mretlak signaled (affirmation). "Yes—an incredibly widespread network of visual pickups. And unnoticeable to the unaided eye." He held up an evidentiary fiber-optic filament that was just slightly thicker than a human hair. "In many cases, the fibers were embedded into the facades of the buildings during their construction. Quite ingenious, actually."

Lentsul studied the images again. "Does the system extend to the human areas beyond Punt City?"

"It may have, but if it did, the humans have disabled the systems there. I surmise that when we took over what they called the West Shore District, they severed all of the links to the areas they inhabit."

Lentsul's mouth edges folded inward. "In that event, Cluster-Commander, may I ask: What need do we have of this system? For security within our city, we have our own *selnarm* repeaters—and so any creature who enters our precincts without *selnarm* will make themselves known soon enough when they fail to interact with our devices, doors, automated security checkpoints."

"Yes, Lentsul—but what if we were to lose control of our compound? Unlikely, yes, but we are on a planet swarming with creatures that mean to annihilate us by any means possible. If they break in among us, how will *selnarm* alone show us where they are and what they are doing? They could be all around and amidst us—and once they have identified and eliminated the *selnarm* checkpoints and repeaters and interfaces, we would have absolutely no means of tracking their subsequent movements."

Lentsul signaled (understanding) if not accord. "Very well, Cluster-Commander. I presume this system is in want of routine maintenance? And that there are more screens and many more pickups to refurbish?"

"Your foresight and deduction are, as ever, excellent, Lentsul."

"I shall set myself to these tasks immediately, Cluster-Commander." And Lentsul left.

Mretlak remained standing. We waited until the faintest murmur of Lentsul's *selnarm* had faded and then manipulated the manual controls on the human viewing unit. All nine pictures changed—and one of them showed Ankaht, in her research lab, working with her Cluster. Another showed Urkhot arriving in his planetside chambers.

Yes, he thought, *and in this time when our leaders share less and less of their* selnarm *with us, and when our* narmata *is frayed, and divided, and uncertain, I shall watch. Watch and record. For what our leaders do not wish to show us, is what we most need to see.*

High City, New Ardu/Bellerophon Orbit

Torhok's personal assistant, Fleet Staff Second Pergesh, probed his *selnarm* gently inward. "Senior Admiral, a communication from Urkhot."

"Very well. Put it on the secure *selnarm* repeater, Pergesh."

"As you instruct, Senior Admiral."

A moment later, Urkhot's boosted *selnarm* rose up to touch Torhok's. "Senior Admiral, I will return to you within the hour."

Illudor help me. "This is excellent news, *Holodah'kri*. Fifteen days is a long planetside stretch for your tastes, but I trust you have now finished briefing the Council on the Revised Provenance Doctrines?"

"Yes."

"And they have accepted these changes?"

"Too eagerly, if anything, Senior Admiral. Predictably, the *shaxzhu* on the Council—and even my own brother-priest, Tefnut ha sheri—wanted even fewer restrictions on document and data access for our general population. I do not think they will be able to compel an immediate reassessment of the dicta we have formulated, but within a year's time—who knows?"

"It is the most we could hope for, *Holodah'kri*. Now, if you have no further—"

"There is one other pressing item of business, Senior Admiral."

Torhok noted the oddly calm and controlled character of Urkhot's *selnarm*. "Indeed?"

"Yes. I wish to know: Are you planning any visits planetside within the next week?"

Odd query. "No. I have none planned."

"Good. Do not change those plans. Under any circumstances. A pleasant day to you, Senior Admiral. I shall see you soon enough." The link terminated abruptly.

Torhok leaned back. And physically smiled.

The weapon he had crafted weeks ago was about to clear its sheath.

Resistance Headquarters, Aeolian Lowlands, Icarus Continent, Bellerophon/New Ardu

Alessandro McGee licked his right index and middle finger and—pinching them together through the fabric of his right pant leg—stripped them swiftly down the length of the crease from knee to cuff. *Enough of that, Sandro,* he thought. *Worry about your presentation, instead.*

The door opened without any knock; pretty typical when you were in the doghouse. McGee rose to attention, and the expected crew filed in: Heide, followed by Cap Peters, Lieutenant Chong and—surprisingly—Harry "Light Horse" Li, a newly-minted sergeant and evidently Heide's new adjutant. Harry waggled his eyebrows at McGee as he entered; McGee arched a dubious eyebrow in response.

"At ease." Heide nodded to the guards outside—Juan Kapinski and Roon Kelakos—who quickly brought in four folding chairs and a table that matched McGee's own.

Heide wasted no time on niceties. "I'll come right to the point, Sergeant. I am not here out of personal interest in your schemes, but because my two senior staff"—he glanced at Chong and then less charitably at Cap Peters—"both insist that you have concocted an offensive plan that is both pertinent and novel."

"It's ingenious," insisted Peters. And McGee thought he could hear Cap's additional words, *And it will get us off our asses and restore morale*. Of course, Cap didn't say any such thing—but McGee knew the look in his old CO's eye.

Heide sat straighter. "Your continued partiality for this man and his schemes—"

Chong spoke. "Brevet Captain Heide, I have no vested interest or prior personal affiliation with Sergeant McGee, but I fully concur with Majo—eh, Lieutenant Peters. This plan is ingenious."

"Preposterous. Besides attracting attention to the Resistance, McGee is proposing an operation that will strike straight into the heart of the Baldy city in the West Shore District. It cannot be anything other than willful suicide, and I—"

Chong somehow interrupted and did not sound rude doing it. "Brevet Captain Heide, hear the man out and listen to the details of his attack plan. And yes, it will attract the Baldies' attention—which is just what we need to remind the Resistance, and everyone else on Bellerophon, that we are a force to be reckoned with and that we haven't forgotten our duty to fight on."

"I agree that we must come up with some plan. But from this man? The full measure of his culpability for the deaths of Lieutenant Colonel Van Felsen and her team is still under consideration."

Cap Peters nodded. "Yes, but the most serious matter—the treason investigation—is behind us now, so—"

McGee was, like the last time, on his feet before he had finished registering his surprise—and relief. "The treason investigation is over? I'm cleared?"

And what should have been a congenial moment

only became darker still. Cap Peters's stunned stare slid away from McGee, and, by the time it had come to rest on Heide's profile, it was a dark and ominous glower. "Brevet Captain Heide, it was understood that Sergeant McGee was to be informed immediately upon our finding that there was no evidence to substantiate suspicion, let alone charges, of treason. That was three days ago."

Chong said nothing but fixed Heide with a stare that was as blank and pitiless as a shark's.

Heide still avoided looking either right or left. "There must have been a communications oversight. It was my intent that he be informed promptly."

I'll bet, McGee almost said—but a cooling look from Harry Li helped him hold his tongue.

Cap Peters pressed on. "With all due respect, Brevet Captain, I must point out that the accumulated record of this command's treatment of Sergeant McGee is beginning to look suspiciously prejudicial. When one considers the severity of the charges you were proposing against the paucity of relevant evidence, the flat denial of any privileges while he has been confined to quarters, and now this unusual failure to communicate the dismissal of the treason inquest, it could be construed that this command has failed to deal equably with Sergeant McGee."

Chong chimed in from the other flank. "And in the midst of this, I have witnessed that Sergeant McGee has been extremely active and effective in helping other NCOs and junior officers plan mineshaft and industrial sabotage. In addition, he personally reviewed and supervised the improvisation of construction explosives into military-grade demolitions charges. In the process of providing this kind of leadership, and through the meticulous analysis and research he conducted to craft his attack plan, he has demonstrated extraordinary growth as a mentor, a tactician, and—if we were to consider his former rank—as an officer."

And all while putting in two hours of calisthenics a day, not including kata, thought McGee, who waited to see what affect these arguments would have upon Heide.

Still Heide looked neither right nor left. His moustache, which he had groomed into an almost invisible line just above his upper lip, seemed carved in stone for a moment. Then, without looking at McGee, he ordered: "Show me the plan."

McGee nodded and unrolled three maps upon the table. At first, Heide seemed unsure of what he was looking at but then appeared to recognize the shoreline of Melantho's Salamisene Bay on each map. But only one of the maps showed building outlines. The rest depicted—

Heide leaned back. "These are . . . are engineers' and contractors' maps of the subterranean structures of Melantho."

McGee nodded. "Specifically, moving from east to west, the Heliobarbus District at the foot of the bay, the Empty Zone, and then the West Shore District."

"Why? Why these?"

"Captain Heide"—McGee longed to put the deflating *Brevet* prefix on like everyone else, but he needed Heide's good opinion now more than ever—"I propose to lead an assault team directly into Baldy Central."

"What? Their deorbited city?"

"No, no, not that part. The part of Melantho they've taken over from us—West Shore."

Heide's smile was one of incredulity, perhaps ridicule. "And what are you planning to do? Assassinate their leadership?"

"No, sir. I plan to exfiltrate at least half of the artists they are holding. And in the process, we'll teach the Baldies that there is no safe place for them on Bellerophon. Even if they're sitting right in the center of their stronghold."

Heide had risen. "And in the bargain, you'll rescue your girlfriend and your infant son. Yes, I see where this is going. And I am not going to commit battalions of our troops to your personal—"

"Sir, I estimate I'll need a strike force of one section, possibly reinforced by a two-man anchor-watch. Plus about ten individual operators who will have no direct role in combat operations. They will be responsible for attack preparations and moving automated assault packages into place. They will either be outside of, or exit, the area of operations beforehand."

Heide did not sit, but nor did he start toward the door. "Thirty-two personnel, total?"

"I could be off by two or three, but no more."

"It would have to be an all-volunteer force."

Cap cleared his throat. "As of today, we have over a hundred volunteers, Brevet Captain."

"And did you solicit them yourself, Lieutenant Peters? I have warned you that your personal attachment to McGee is—"

"Brevet Captain," murmured Chong, "in consideration of how Lieutenant Peters's involvement might appear to you, it was decided that *I* should be the one to selectively share a nonclassified outline of the plan and solicit the volunteers."

Heide started to chew at his upper lip, then stopped himself testily. "I see." He sat. "And so in exactly what fashion have these men volunteered to commit suicide? A frontal charge?"

McGee pointed to the maps. "No, sir. An underground infiltration."

"Sergeant, unless my knowledge of cartography is quite flawed, there seems to be no contiguous subterranean route connecting what is currently the westernmost human area of Melantho—the Heliobarbus District—with the parts occupied by the invaders in the West Shore District."

"Exactly, sir. After they demoed the transport tubes during the first week of occupation, there were no direct subterranean connections across the Empty Zone."

"So, then how do you plan to reach their compound underground?"

"By making some very new openings in a few very old walls. See, Captain Heide, look at these maps in overlay. Basements, access shafts, run-off sluices, sewer systems—in fact, two different sewers put in at different times—and lastly, these big supply lines that used to bring coolant water straight from the Bay and into the mothballed fusion reactors. Now follow this line with me..." McGee drew a semi-tortuous path through the various chambers and tunnels and conduits that riddled the ground beneath the streets of the Empty Zone. "That's only four demolition points, Captain, for which we've got safety surveys less than three years old. And since we're not taking in any dedicated heavy weapons, we'll be able to move very quickly."

"No heavy weapons?"

"No, sir. None are needed. We're going to surface right inside their perimeter. These maps indicate that we'll come up in a building immediately adjacent to the one which is our target."

"Oh? And how have you determined where Ms. Peitchkov and the infant are located?"

Chong placed a report in front of Heide. "The doctor's report, sir—the one who tended to the infant several weeks ago. He fixes the location with certainty, and identifies the complex as one that was used by the university's psychology and cognitive studies annex. Ms. Peitchkov was specifically being housed in the lab accommodations used for sleep-pattern studies. The arrangement—observed living quarters with all the necessary space for long-duration observers, recording gear, et cetera—is optimal for their purposes of either extended debriefing or an attempt to study humans in close proximity. The likelihood that they would move Ms. Peitchkov from this site is deemed negligible. And besides, our current intelligence sources would probably indicate a shift of their operations if it involved relocation to another building."

"Exactly what do you mean by 'current intelligence sources'?"

McGee kept himself from smiling. "Lieutenant Chong is referring to our aerial photo reconnaissance missions." And McGee spread out an assortment of old-style aerial photos on the table: digital 2-Ds, every one. The framing and angle of some of them seemed either inspired or insane.

Heide pored over them. "Where did you get these? How did you do it?"

"Birds, Captain."

"Birds? What do you mean?"

Cap Peters was smiling. "This one really takes the cake, Heide. McGee starts asking about the folks who used to work in the behavioral labs in the University's West Shore annex—the ones the Baldies have commandeered for their own use. It turns out there had been a long-standing project to determine how Terran transplant species—like gulls and sparrows and geese—still manage to orient themselves and travel despite the fact that they're no longer inside the magnetic fields where they evolved. When I heard that Tank was asking questions about it, I figured he'd cracked under the strain of—well, I figured it was just nonsense. But no, he wanted to know how they were trained to fly from point A to point B and so forth. Three weeks later, I'm sitting with two underemployed professors who've been reduced to adjuncting at the main campus of Philomena University, arranging for undercover 'student volunteers' to help them train gulls and crows to fly from the hills beyond West Shore to one of three visible landmarks across the bay in downtown Melantho. These experiments were integrated into their ongoing research program, which was rubber-stamped by the Baldies as part of their hands-off policy. And so, by releasing these birds on flight paths that took them right over the objective, and rigged with continuous feed micro cameras . . ." Cap Peters waved a hand at the photos on the table. "Voila."

Heide frowned. "You were very lucky to get such good images, and of the places you wanted."

McGee kept his voice level. "Captain, with respect, luck had nothing to do with it. For every one of the pictures on the table in front of you, we had twenty thousand that were utterly useless. This was just a lot of repetitious work. But then again, I had a lot of time on my hands."

"And do these photographs fix the location of your objectives?"

My "objectives"? Huh. When your girlfriend and child are your "objectives," it certainly gives new meaning to the word. "Sir, our objectives' locations are fixed by solid operational inference. The traffic in and out of this building shows it to be, beyond doubt, the site where all the hostages are being held. This is the same building the pediatrician visited. In addition, we've detected live-crewed defense emplacements here, here, and here, and charted the eight weapon blisters that can bear on our area of operations."

"They will send more."

"Unquestionably. But their stand-off heavy weapons will probably not be as effective here. The Baldies are not really rigged for dedicated military operations, and their laser designators do not seem to be multi-spectral."

"Meaning?"

"Meaning when we go in, we should carry a good supply of prismatic anti-laser aerosol grenades, which will also give us a smokescreen. The reflective and refractive qualities of the aerosol should play holy hell with their laser designators."

Heide nodded: a breakthrough in his demeanor. "Which will deeply compromise, or even eliminate, their ability to call in pinpoint fire support from the blisters."

"That's our thinking."

"Those anti-laser aerosols are milspec gear, you know—special use only."

McGee met Heide's gaze squarely, but without allowing any confrontation or defiance to creep in. "Yes, sir. I am aware of that."

Heide seemed to study him closely. "Good. Just so you're aware. We can't spend them like party favors."

Significant looks passed between Chong and Peters:

against all odds, Heide seemed to be buying into the plan. Light Horse grinned widely for one second—and then reacquired his perfect poker face.

"Now, Sergeant," Heide continued, "let's walk through this by the numbers, presuming you make it into the compound. Let's assume limited defensive contribution from the weapons blisters, but what about their on-site troops?"

"Captain, we're going to take casualties, but I suspect that most of them will be from chance encounters as we're following along to the lab/observation areas where Jennifer and my son are being held. Since we're minimizing milspec use, we're only going to have light armor—nothing more than Kevleuron Two torso protection. So if we get hit, it's a roll of the dice."

"What kinds of personal weapons has your reconnaissance observed on site?"

"Pretty much the usual Baldy mix. The ubiquitous machine-pistol, which has that weird donut magazine—they wear the contraption like a bracelet. Their standard long-arm is only seen in full military detachments, but we're sure to run into it, since it seems to also be the standard equipage for crew in the emplacements and on any fast-response teams. For those of you who haven't seen it, it resembles a high-tech multipurpose rifle. Old-style brass cartridges."

"Brass?" said Juan Kapinski, who had remained inside the room after bringing in the chairs—and whose monosyllabic query now earned a stare from Heide.

"Yeah, Juan, I know. Brass was old before we hit the stars. But it has advantages—and for folks who expect to be pioneering rather than conquering, it's a natural. Easy reload, easy to handle, stable in most conditions—which means that the weapon which fires it can be kept simple also. All of which reduces the logistical drain on a start-up colony. It's about as good a model of this kind of rifle as has been made: rugged, light, reliable. Wide diversity of ammunition types: in addition to basic ball, we've seen discarding sabot, dum-dum, and SLAP. It's selective fire, but in the autofire mode it's pretty anemic—about 220 rounds per minute. Not great for close assault or high-volume suppressive fire, but easy to control and, with its recessed bullpup drum magazine, they won't have to reload often. The most sophisticated part of the weapon is its gyroscopic barrel stabilization and rather extensive scope/sensor suite with an integral laser designator. We have seen a few—a very few—fitted with variable wavelength lasers, but most are pretty much one flavor.

"Hand-carried heavy weapons are pretty rare in their formations, and we've never observed them being deployed inside their compound, only on the perimeters."

"So the invaders do not have heavy weapons in those three emplacements?"

"I'm not sure about that, sir. They've got overhead cover, and we never have managed to get a peek under their roofs. I suspect they have point-defense weapons for engaging incoming missiles. But they can't have a lot of heavy weapons, either way, and we can hit all three of them from this point right here." McGee pointed to a broad marble pavestone with an inset *X* pattern that fronted the building which contained their ingress point. "Using pre-prepared munitions from that exact point, I believe we can suppress or kill all three of the crewed emplacements that bear upon our area of operations within ten seconds."

"Ten seconds is a long time in combat—or so I'm told," admitted Heide. Who, by dropping any pretense of being an experienced wartime officer, was actually seeming a little less like a complete prick with every passing second.

McGee nodded. "I've only been on a few suppression missions at the edge of Tangri space, sir, but yes—ten seconds in close ground combat is pretty much eternity. But many of our other bird's-eye pictures strongly suggest that the Baldies do not keep their most capable and seasoned ground troops in these positions, or in this part of their city at all."

"Where are they?"

"Their true Security units are billeted near their airfield and motor pool, sir. Again, best guess only."

"But eminently sensible," muttered Heide. Cap looked like he was ready to fall out of his chair at the cooperative tone the Hider had adopted. "They'll want to position their best troops to protect their primary ground-engagement assets—their airpower. They'll also want those same troops proximal to airlift mobility in order to be able to project force quickly beyond their city."

"Yes, sir," McGee agreed, "that was my thinking."

"So, what are your intentions for dealing with a counterattack from their Security troops? They're sure to have a ready-response team on standby."

"I've had some volunteers who've observed the Baldies' scramble and flight times, Captain. I don't think their airmobile assets are going to catch us."

"They do seem to have an uncanny knack for communication and coordination, Sergeant."

"Yes, sir. During my—unauthorized operations—I got a chance to see that firsthand. They are very, very fast.

But they spend longer than we do coming up with plans, almost as if they don't have a very diverse playbook and have to invent a lot of their tactical responses on the fly. Which is why our best tactical approach is to keep them off balance. We move quickly once we're inside the target building and shoot anything that's not human. We don't have any time for finesse, because they seem to be able to signal to each other with a speed and precision that is far beyond anything we've ever dreamed of. So if we can put their lights out before they can deduce our strategies and fix our position, that's what we'd better do."

"But once you're in the building, you are blind, Sergeant. You have no idea of their security defense points, or on-site guards."

"True—but fortunately, the pediatrician the Baldies brought in to look at my son wasn't a complete newb. He volunteered time with Reserve units on maneuver. He knows his way around a defensive installation just enough to be able to tell us that they didn't seem to have anything other than their magical equivalent of keycard readers. But those were not defensive. They were traffic monitors and intrusion-detection systems. And we won't be trying to maintain a stealthy approach by the time we've run into those scanners."

"So your biggest worry is chance-met hostiles as you advance along the corridors."

"Yes, sir. I'd say that sums it up pretty well."

Heide leaned back. "Well, you have an interesting plan, Sergeant. But I still see some problems."

McGee kept his spirits and shoulders from sagging. "May I ask what those might be, sir?"

"Certainly. Firstly, let's go back to your initial underground approach. I'm sure they've got many, if not all, of these subterranean passages monitored. Audio pick-ups, at the very least. So as you start blowing your way through foundation walls and sewer tubes, they will hear you."

"Yes, sir, I've thought of that."

"And it will take a lot of time to maneuver through those old subterranean levels—gaps in the floors, cracks and shifts in the foundations, lots of debris to climb over. It could be very rough—and very slow—going."

"Yes, sir. Thought of that, too."

"And perhaps the biggest problem is that once you've entered, how will you get out? The same way? They have scanners, and they'll take a look at the data. It may take them a few moments, but the Baldies will quickly deduce how you got inside their perimeter, and their fast-response teams will move to cut you off from your egress/ingress building long before you are done securing the objectives. Have you thought of that, too?"

"Actually, sir, I have. And strangely enough, there's one additional detail to this operation that provides the answer to all of those problems."

Heide leaned back. "Indeed? And what is that?"

McGee smiled. "Well, Captain, there's one thing the Baldies have overlooked. . . ."

14

Multum in Parvo

"Much in little."
—Latin motto/saying

Melantho & Punt, Bellerophon/New Ardu

As Emergency Response Chief Menachem Guzman watched, two more fires sprang up, one only a block away. The Baldy Security sleds escorting his convoy of fire and rescue vehicles stopped and seemed to put sensors on the closest conflagration, which had started right at the border of the Heliobarbus District but was now spreading quickly into the Empty Zone. What the Baldies were inspecting was unclear, since even they knew that all these fires had to be premeditated acts of arson. Maybe they were trying to discern if there was an ambush waiting nearby. An ambush: Menachem leaned his head down on the steering wheel; this day was either going to be very long—or very, very short.

Mtube Ventrella, who ran the pressures and volume board for the Water Supply Section of the Public Works Department, looked at the red-lined digital gauges nervously. "As per your orders sir, water pressure is at max, plus six percent, in all lines running into the western fringe of the Heliobarbus District."

"Outflows?"

"They're sealed, sir. This is not going to hold for long."

Mtube's supervisor looked over at the much-scarred man that neither of them had ever seen before this morning. He nodded. The supervisor turned back to Mtube. "Not long, now."

Mircea Basarab first thought that a large chunk of the flying plasticrete fragments had struck him on the left shoulder, but then he felt the light blow again. He turned and discovered Modibo Jones preparing to thump him a third time. Modibo stopped, jabbed an urgent finger at his watch. Mircea released the portajack's power bar: the deafening hammering ceased.

"One minute," warned Modibo.

Mircea nodded and turned back to face his adversary: a sealed section of Bellerophon's oldest sewer system. Located beneath the western extents of the Heliobarbus District, and three hundred meters back from the Empty Zone, the old sealing wall now looked like a pincushion. The two courses of old-fashioned cinder blocks, capped at either end by a good layer of plasticrete, had been intact when he had arrived just an hour ago. Since then, Mircea and Modibo had drilled dozens of equally-spaced holes through to the open space on the other side. Mircea set the portajack's bit into the last, half-drilled hole, depressed the power bar, and leaned into the resistance. After fifteen seconds of pushing, he felt that split-second of give which meant he was about to break through. He backed off the power bar—just as the bit plunged easily into the hole it had drilled:

its point had cut out into open air on the other side. Mircea checked his watch and discovered the past fifteen seconds had really been thirty. Slinging the portajack over his shoulder as he yanked out the power feed, he hustled over to the steel ladder and fast-handed it upward, right after Modibo. Like a dozen other similar teams throughout the area, they made a quick ascent to the street level just above them.

One of Salamisene Bay's ubiquitous Richthofen fish—a triple-winged sea-ray—started and plunged into the black-blue depths, its three rippling planes now pulsing in unison to accelerate its dive.

A moment later, a submersible repair bot churned through the space just vacated by the fish. Its tired old prop housings gimballed fitfully as its remote human operator kept it on course. Eventually, it reached the sheer face of what the locals called the Drop: the two-hundred-meter submarine cliff that also extended upward beyond the crashing waves, providing the high bedrock upon which the Heliobarbus District—and the Empty Zone—were perched. The ROV's prop-cans swiveled a bit, stabilizing; then the fans slowed, counterspun, and stopped the unit just two meters from the vertical rock face. Along that rock face, a set of gray plastic conduits ran east to west. The ROV swung west, following the dim, cliff-hugging line.

Ten seconds later, the bot's maneuver lights snapped on, revealing the intake fairing of an immense tube. The bot angled around the rim of the fairing, turned to face directly into the tube; it was plugged by a smooth surface, almost as smooth as the fairing itself.

Esmerelda Chin, senior ROV operator in the Remote

Maintenance Section of the Public Works Department, turned to the swarthy, silent, muscular woman who was watching over her shoulder. "The seal on the primary cooling intake is still solid," Esmerelda said.

The woman nodded. "So we go under. As we discussed."

Esmerelda tilted the ROV's nose down and sent it diving under the lower rim of the tube's fairing. When the bot leveled off again, the fairing was directly overhead—but after a few meters of forward progress, it seemed to vanish upward into blackness.

Esmerelda checked her instruments. "I've got to be careful—it's unfinished rock in here, from when they blasted into the cliff face."

"Crude method," commented the woman.

"Old method," corrected Esmerelda. "The colony's first settlers built this fusion plant. Back then, the plants were big, cumbersome, crude. That's why the big water intakes for cooling."

The woman nodded; her short, tight ponytail bobbed. "And that's good for us now. Snug us up under the tube."

"Okay."

"And now reverse—gently—until the rear of the ROV makes contact with the back side of the fairing. Good. Can you angle up the nose a bit?"

"Sure." Esmerelda complied. "Okay, now what?"

"Now you kill the lights—and wait."

"Wait? For what?"

But the short, dark, and very serious woman—who had become Esmerelda's one-day boss just two hours earlier—only checked her watch.

The operator seated next to Esmerelda—Section Head Odile Djabwurrung—looked over at the woman. "Time for me to start?"

The woman didn't look up from her watch, but said, "Go ahead."

Odile adjusted her earbud, tapped her collar mic. "Everybody with me?"

Green affirmation lights blinked on her board: the other nine ROV operators scattered throughout her section were good to go. "Okay, everyone: watch your intervals. Keep your speed low and be prepared to back fans at a moment's notice. Here we go." She looked to the short dark woman, who was now watching the video feed from the ROVs, arrayed like a tic-tac-toe board on Odile's auxiliary screen. The woman pushed out her slightly scarred chin. "Seal and flood the lock."

Odile tapped a virtual button on the margin of her own control screen—which showed the door behind the waiting ROVs descending as the water level in the chamber began to rise rapidly. As it did, yellow lights started pulsing at each end of the chamber, the ones in front revealing a sign above the two-meter-wide iris valve centered in the far wall: Caution: Sewage Interface Valve.

Mretlak entered his office and performed his newest morning ritual: he checked the security-monitor activity log.

The red light at the bottom of the human device was flashing urgently.

Ill'sblood, he thought profanely, *how long has that been on?* He had wanted a *selnarm* alerting module added to the surveillance system, but there just hadn't been the time or experts available that quickly. And now, time had run out. He commanded his computer via *selnarm*: (Download surveillance data. Locate anomaly. Display. Analyze.)

His primary Arduan computer spent half a second accessing and then played back the footage of the atypical activity the human surveillance system had detected. The scene was Urkhot's outer chambers, the room that the *holodah'kri* alternatively used as a private shrine, place of meditation, and site for highly confidential meetings. Urkhot was not present, but eight other Arduans were. Mretlak immediately recognized two as being among the dozen or so *hwa'kri*—or acolytes—that Urkhot was mentoring personally. Mretlak also recognized three *Destoshaz* hard-liners who had, at various times, served as aides and bodyguards to Torhok, Urkhot, or both. As Mretlak watched, they all raised bowls to their lips and drank deep; when they lowered the bowls, their lips were a bright red.

Mretlak snapped upright out of his chair: assassins. They had all drunk from a Death-Vow Cup, which meant that they fully intended to symbolically drink the blood of their enemies and also to let their own flow freely and finally in the completion of their intended murders. Illudor's holy face, they had dredged up this ritual from the distant Pre-Enlightenment, and Mretlak—having no *selnarm* recording—could not be entirely sure that they were using the juice which, from the Enlightenment era onward, had replaced the actual blood used in the original ceremony.

Without any further gestures or interactions, the eight filed out of the shrine, and, on the belt of each, Mretlak saw the small pouches in which many Arduans—but unfailingly, all *Destoshaz*—carried their three-clawed *skeerba* when going to a *maatkah* practice or a match. Or an execution.

Mretlak brushed aside the morning's pending status reports—arson in the depopulated zone; increased rodent activity noted by the subterranean monitors within the zone; joint emergency response operation commenced with humans; airmobile Security reserves reduced to minimum in order to provide close anti-terrorist security for response operation—a busy day indeed, and only an hour into it. But it all paled in comparison to the ceremony Mretlak had witnessed—

—which, he learned from his computer, had occurred almost seven minutes ago. Seven minutes. They could be anywhere by now. But they would have had to walk to reach any of the automated shuttles that served Punt City. *Which means,* Mretlak thought as he started using both the human dynamic-control tablet and the *selnarm* relays in his own computer, *that I have a lot of camera feeds to check from the past seven minutes.*

The eight *Destoshaz* garbed in black tunics—five males and three females—ignored the stares of the passengers of the third automated shuttle that passed them by. *Selnarm* tendrils reached out, grazed their consciousnesses faintly, as if to tap them lightly and point out that they did not need to walk: a passenger vehicle was approaching. They did not return the looks, did not acknowledge the gentle prompts.

A block farther on, they began to see the ugly concrete boxes of Old Punt rising over the sweeping pylons and supports of their deorbited citadel-city. Moments later, more *Destoshaz* began to emerge from the alcoves and recesses that gave True Punt, Inner Punt—*Arduan* Punt—its intrinsic character and intricate architectural beauty. The first eight did not acknowledge the new sixteen, who formed up in pairs on each member of the original group.

As they crossed the boundary into what the humans had called the West Shore District, the foremost of the original eight, who walked at the point of this rough wedge of formidable warriors, tossed aside an object that was much like a handkerchief, stained half-red with blood.

It hit the ground and began blowing about in the sea-brewed breeze, an enigmatic white-and-red warning.

Which no one was there to see.

Mtube Ventrella was surprised when his supervisor leaned over his shoulder and activated the control relays for the interfaces, which, in an emergency, could link or flush the new water-supply system into the old one. "Sir?"

"Now, open the pressure-relief valves into grid blocks G-14 through I-12."

"Sir? With our water pressure at max-plus-six, that's going to be like turning on a fire hose throughout the entirety of the old system. Some of those walls may not hold."

The superintendent almost seemed to smile. "They might not," he conceded. "Open the valves."

"Yes, sir." And, swallowing down his anxiety and misgivings with an audible gulp, Mtube pressed the red virtual button that would unleash the underground equivalent of Noah's flood upon walls and culverts and sluices that were, in many cases, three centuries old.

In the same control building as Mtube, but two floors overhead, the short muscular woman raised a finger and held it poised. Then she jabbed it at the control screen for the ROV waiting patiently under the long-sealed tube in Salamisene Bay. "Now."

Esmerelda released the waldo-safety and maneuvered the manipulator arms of the ROV into an upright position. In the screen, she could see the large black waterproofed bundle clutched between them, held out like an ominous offering. She pushed the activation button: a short flash, a dying data squeal, and her screen went black.

Twenty-seven seconds after Mircea and Modibo reached the street level and ran for their lives, the roaring, high-pressure plume that was Melantho's pent-up water supply slammed into the sealing wall which they had thoroughly perforated with their powerjacks. The wall—centuries old, unmaintained, and now deprived of structural integrity—let go with a sound like an explosion, chunks and fragments propelled hundreds of meters down the abandoned sewer lines that led into the Empty Zone. The torrent howled through the opening, blasted its way westward. Rusted access doors buckled and gave; more walls washed away; bricks stripped off and tumbled down into the roiling cataract like hordes of cubist lemmings diving to their watery deaths.

With the full pressure of Melantho's entire water supply pent up behind it, the lateral geyser continued to blow a wide, west-streaming pathway through the long-abandoned subterranean warrens of what was now the Empty Zone.

But the full pressure of Melantho's water supply was a Lilliputian force compared to the titanic blast of seawater that thundered and screamed into the defunct fusion plant's main coolant intake: the payload carried by Esmerelda's ROV—ten kilograms of top-shelf plastic explosive—had completely torn off the sealed end of the tube. The inrushing jet of seawater roared south and hit the old plant's outer restraining wall. The wall lasted just long enough to double the pressure pushing outward against the sides of the tube—which bulged, seamed, and split in dozens of places. What had begun as one massive lateral geyser became a dozen lesser but equally forceful ones. Access doors and emergency run-off hatches were simply blasted out of the way. The foaming cataract expanded in all directions, speeding east, west, and south into almost every conduit that honeycombed the ground beneath that part of Melantho.

As it went, it carried down walls, toppled stanchions, ruptured pipes—and, significantly, caught up and shattered the several dozen Arduan audio sensors with which the invaders had monitored the subterranean passages that joined West Shore to Heliobarbus across the otherwise interdicted Empty Zone. Those two or three sensors that survived the deluge by dint of fortuitous placement or a quirk of fate were deafened and then drowned by the roar of rushing water and crumbling walls.

Emergency Chief Menachem Guzman felt more than heard the faint rumble beneath the street. His driver slowed; the Baldy vehicles ahead had come to a dead stop: humans and aliens alike were looking around, unsure of both the cause and source of the sound.

Menachem reached to toggle the command circuit that would allow him to speak to the rest of the vehicles in his convoy; he preferred manual controls, having learned not to trust voice activation or other commo frills when in the midst of a genuine emergency.

Just then, the rumbling abruptly grew louder. "What the hell—?" he started.

The old-style manhole cover in the intersection ahead of him was suddenly blasted upward, riding a vicious geyser of green-gray water up beyond the fourth story of the surrounding buildings. The nearest Baldy defense sled panicked and blasted the gushing hole with a quick rip from its remote pintle-mounted autocannon—which then fell silent, almost as if embarrassed to have been seen shooting at a geyser.

But a moment later, more manholes—one at every intersection—came flying off. A muffled—probably underground—explosion reverberated somewhere farther inland, farther south. And then, starting with a deep growl that was audible above all the other noise, a five-story building collapsed into the street just two blocks north of the convoy, the crash and dust rolling on longer than any sound of destruction that Menachem had ever heard.

However, the long, final groan of the collapse didn't end: rather, a similar sound had seamlessly taken its place, rolling suddenly louder. And then Guzman realized why. He gripped his assistant's arm. "The water—it's rising!"

As he said it, water started gushing and moaning up through the long-disused grates of Melantho's first, and long-decommissioned, sewer system.

The short, powerful woman with the ponytail leaned over Odile's shoulder and activated the remote address system. "Your avenue of approach is now fully flooded, Tank. The ROV's are on their way. By the time the pressure lock recycles for your team, they'll have scouted your waypoints and demoed through the four separating walls you've identified—and any other obstructions that we might find. By the time you've water-checked your gear, the backwashes should have steadied out. So when the interface valve opens, you'll be heading into still water and fully-immersed passages."

A deep voice answered. "Roger that, Haika."

On an adjacent screen, which was monitoring the surface of the access pool where the ROVs had started out, twenty-three black-suited divers rose to stand next to the slime-edged reservoir, small tanks and gear bags strapped to their backs. One by one, they stepped out over the ledge and plunged down into the murky water, hands held over facemasks.

Ankaht sent a (farewell, fondness) to her two most talented primes, Orthezh and Ipshef, and—somehow—managed not to teasingly intimate that she was quite aware of the romance that was blossoming between them. She managed to remain completely professional. "Do you feel comfortable overseeing the other human subjects on your own?"

Orthezh was confident, perhaps a little proud. "Certainly, Elder. With the vocoder, we are beginning to make some genuine progress. Not anything such as you enjoy with Jennifer"—*significant: they all call her "Jennifer" now, not "the Peitchkov subject"*—"but we'll manage. And we'll do better every day."

Ankaht sent them (pride, joy) and began a leisurely walk to her next session with Jennifer, enjoying the view from a bank of windows overlooking the foot of the bay and the Empty Zone. She noted multiple plumes of smoke curling skyward from that part of the city, stopped, and watched the darting, *zifrik*-sized Security sleds weaving in and out of the buildings. Human emergency vehicles were scattered along the streets, lights pulsing stridently. She closed her lesser eyes, half closed her main one: so much violence, so little reason. She felt a sudden urge to mourn—for both her people and Jennifer's—but then straightened her spine with a whiplike motion. *You are shaxzhu, you are a Councilor, you are an Elder, and your researches may be the only hope we have of stopping this senseless carnage. So do not waste time and energy regretting the violence: rather, devote them both to ending it.*

She turned away from the smoke plumes and walked briskly toward Jennifer's quarters.

McGee heard the link from the Department of Public Works Control Center open with a sputter of static. "Tank?" asked Haika's voice.

"Right here."

"I'm opening the iris valve now. Fair warning, folks: there's a lot of lighter debris in the water. A couple of buildings went down up near the edge of the Bay."

"Side flows took out basement support beams?"

"Looks like it. And because of how that junk spread downstream, I suggest rerouting your avenue of approach to alternate Baker Two. Thirty meters longer, but you should then be able to use your sea-scooters with wide-open throttles the whole time."

"They're not 'sea-scooters'—they're DPVs," said Harry as he adjusted his thermal imaging/LI monocle. "Diver propulsion vehicles." Perceptive Harry didn't seem to realize that he mercilessly corrected and annoyed Haika because he was utterly smitten with her. "Sea-scooters are kids' toys."

"Call 'em whatever you like, jackass. Dilating the valve now. Good luck, Tank. Only fourteen hundred meters and then it's show time."

The iris valve in front of McGee's assault group began opening like the shutter of an old-fashioned camera, but in slow motion. A light current—a thermal—pushed in at them: the water out there was colder. It was also both cleaner and greener: sea-water from the bay. There was still a slow sway in the water, the last backwashes equaling out.

Sandro toggled the open channel and turned to face the first rank of his team: Wismer, Li, and Battisti. "Okay, here we go. Keep a good interval; these sea-scooters"—he glanced at Li and had the satisfaction of seeing an annoyed eye-roll—"run faster and hotter than the ones we had when we trained for underwater ops at Camp Gehenna. Watch you don't snag on doorways or downed beams: you've got less clearance than you think. Any questions?"

Twenty-two faces, hunched low behind the handgrips of their bullet-nosed DPVs, looked back at him. There were no comments.

"Okay then, follow me." Turning, McGee thumbed the sea-scooter's throttle forward. Its fans spun up, and McGee let himself be tugged out into the cool green waters. He started steering toward the first way point. It was, he estimated, approximately eighty seconds away.

And approximately six minutes more to the West Shore District—and Baldy Central.

Mretlak had spent too many fruitless minutes hunting between different security camera perspectives. *Why are the Death-Vowed on none of the main thoroughfares? And although I have many observation points, there are so many places they could be going—*

And then Mretlak felt his spine become gelatinous with dread. No, there were some places that were far more likely to be their destinations. If, that is, one were willing to think the unthinkable—

Mretlak manipulated the controls hastily; the screens cleared, then showed new pictures—all of them in the immediate environs of the old University complex that the Council had released to Ankaht for her researches. For a moment, Mretlak felt relief: nothing suspicious on any of the screens.

But then three groups of three tall *Destoshaz* in featureless black tunics appeared, approaching the main entrance from a side street. Two seconds later, three more of the black-garbed triads emerged from an alley, approaching the secondary entrance on the side of the building. Two more of the teams rose into view on the steps that ascended toward the broad asphalt skirt that fanned out around the loading bays at the back of the building.

Three separate entry forces. All formed into teams of three. Mretlak heard the old dictum of his earliest training, remembered that tripartite axiom of three-to-one odds which had been taught to all *Destoshaz* since the savage dawn of their caste in the Pre-Enlightenment epoch.

Encircle.

Engage.

Eliminate.

They were entering the building. There was only one thing he could do in time.

He thrust a *selnarm* spike into his secure channel repeater and sent a long, strobing pulse:

"Ankaht. Respond. Urgent. Urgent. URGENT."

The site security for the human-research cluster—a team of less militant *Destoshaz*—started in surprise when their unusually tall and uncommunicative caste-mates entered their ground-floor operations center unannounced, the newcomers' *selnarm* so suppressed and narrow that it faded into the background of the communal *narmata*.

Ulshev, the junior manip in charge of Ankaht's dedicated Enforcer team, rose and extended a respectful tendril of *selnarm*, for he recognized the *Destoshaz* in the lead: Khremhet. Once a bodyguard of Urkhot, Khremhet was a most redoubtable warrior and superb *maatkah* opponent. (Surprise, gratification, welcome.) "Greetings, Khremhet. How may we help you, brother?"

(Sorrow.) "You may help by accepting my apology, brother."

Ulshev never knew he had been discarnated: Khremhet's *skeerba* came out and up so quickly, and cut through one side of his spine so expertly, that Ulshev was dead before he even saw the motion that ended his life.

The other Death-Vowed *Destoshaz* spun into action, their lesser brethren stunned, all three caught in the middle of a great, collective *befthel* as they died, most still in their seats.

At that moment, from the Empty Zone's forgotten dumpsters, from under half-collapsed awnings on rooftops, from covered cargo beds of several "rescue trucks" now abandoned in the flooded streets, clusters of 78 mm self-guiding rockets roared skyward, fanned out, leaned quickly over into level flight, and oriented themselves toward their preprogrammed coordinates. A few of them added jinks and jerks to their trajectory: just enough to complicate the intercept calculations of the Baldies' automated defense systems.

The smoke-trailing swarm leaned over even farther, starting to aim down into the West Shore District.

The Arduan weapon emplacements all along the bayside extents of Punt sputtered into life. Rockets began exploding in midair—brief orange rashes bright against the blue tegument of the sky—but the inbound weapons had spread out far enough that the destruction of one did not cause the loss of any of the others. Even so, by the time the rockets had closed half the distance to Punt, seventy percent of them had been destroyed.

But that was also the moment when two more mass launches took place: two more flocks of missiles climbed quickly up and then arced over toward Punt.

The Baldy defense emplacements fired continuously now. The point-defense lasers spat out short, crackling, invisible bursts that burned and ionized their way through the atmosphere. The emplacements at the south end of Punt, particularly in the vicinity of the University's former extension campus, were hard put to sweep down the rockets. With those defense systems overburdened, the leading edge of the surviving mass of rockets edged closer to that zone with every passing second. For those weapon sites, there was neither rest nor respite.

Matthew Maotulu retracted the sensor filament back down through the grapple hole in the metal access plate overhead. "All clear."

McGee nodded and turned to Li. "Harry, you and Simonson secure the first interior way point, then Mei goes on to unlock the door into the lobby. Kapinski, Battisti: you're responsible for carrying two sea-scooters each until we reach the target building."

Harry was already halfway up the short ladder, a

6 mm bullpup carbine in his right hand as rested his left palm against the underside of the access plate. Then he pushed lightly and mounted the rest of the rungs, weapon at the ready, the plate hinging upward as he went.

Evidently, Maotulu's sensor sweep had been accurate: Li signaled all-clear to Simonson, who—small and lithe—was up the ladder in less than two seconds. She carried a complete set of the building's prewar mechanical keys in her left hand.

McGee muttered his orders to the rest of the team. "Just as we practiced: dump your fins and tanks here, but keep your masks. Don't unbag your gear until you get to the top. Then arm, toss your bag, and reform. Double-quick, after me."

And despite his size, McGee's actions fit his own instructions. He was up the ladder almost as fast as Simonson.

Scuttling away from the sewer-access shaft, he looked to Harry, who, peeking quickly into the janitor's lounge and locker area, gave a single big thumbs-up.

McGee turned, sent the same sign back to his gathered Marines, and led the way up the stairs.

They caught up to Mei Simonson at the top landing, where she was peering out the door that opened onto the lobby. The wiry little Marine pointed at her eyes and then joined her index finger and thumb into the universal "okay" sign: all looked clear. *And all according to plan*, thought McGee, *which, oddly, makes me worry*. He nodded to Mei: she slipped out the door, followed by Li—and then McGee himself.

Simonson advanced to the first of the lobby's grid of mirror-paneled support stanchions. Li peeled off in the other direction and ducked behind one near the elevators to cover their rear. McGee loped past Mei and snugged up against the next stanchion in sequence: one more to the main exit, and beyond that, a clear sight line to all three local weapon emplacements.

Which were, as he had expected, beehives of partially seen but obviously frenetic activity. The rapid strobe-sparking near the bayside periphery of each emplacement marked the nonstop activity of the expected point-defense lasers. Well, the skulking part of the operation was at an end: hell, there really wasn't any cover left. Besides, at ranges this close, surprise and speed would be better friends than stealth. McGee raised his right hand and looked behind; his team stared back like a pack of Cyclopi, a combo monocle blocking each one's shooting eye. McGee nodded, turned to face their objective, and then dropped his hand sharply.

The Marine section charged out the front doors of the lobby of the Sociology and Special Education building. McGee waved Danilenko's team forward to the "X marks the spot" pavestone they had identified in the overhead photographs. Jon Wismer and his team started heaving prismatic aerosol smoke grenades in a semicircular pattern around their current position, the arc flattening and extending so that it also covered the twelve meters of open ground to their objective: the entrance of the Psychology Lab Annex. McGee waited a two-count, letting the smoke build, and then rushed across that space.

Igor Danilenko had already dropped down into a kneeling position, left knee centered on the "X" of the marble pavestone, even as he was releasing the safety on the rocket-propelled grenade affixed to his rifle's under-muzzle shoot-through launch ramp.

He looked down the Alliant-Rimstar's Serrie scope, watching the bearing and elevation numbers change as he adjusted his aim with them: although thermal imaging still showed him a few murky outlines, the wall of smoke was already opaque. When the Serrie scope's telemetry counters hit the numbers that indicated his aimpoint was directly upon the first weapon emplacement, he hit the *encode* button. The grenade's computer chip now knew where to fly. He checked the weapon's preset detonation range—another piece of data derived from the bird's-eye photographs—and saw that it matched the Serrie sight's multispectral laser ping against the target. Danilenko pulled the trigger.

The clearing charge boosted the grenade off the launch ramp with a dull cough. A millisecond later, and five meters into the obscuring cloud, the weapon's actual rocket kicked in: a bright flare illuminated the near edge of the smoke as it did. An eyeblink later, the concussive wave and sound of a ferocious explosion came buffeting over the hard stone expanse of the esplanade.

"That's one down," muttered Danilenko as he handed off the rifle to one teammate and took a new, identically rigged and armed Alliant-Rimstar battle-rifle from another. His left knee still planted firmly at the center of the X, Danilenko rotated around that pivot point until the new azimuth bearing in the Serrie scope matched the position of the second emplacement.

As McGee reached the entry of the Psych Annex—a broad glass-faced lobby with five wide doors evenly spaced along its front expanse—he heard Danilenko's second grenade go off. He had expected some blind fire into the smoke from the third emplacement by this time, but no: nothing. Probably because the Baldies were not going to fire blind while they were on their own turf. Meaning any of their Security personnel who were not manning the air-defense laser were probably closing on foot—

"Jon," he ordered Wismer. "Scan south. Drop any thermal signatures. Now."

Wismer and his team, having finished with their grenades, dropped into kneeling positions, scanned into the smoke—and evidently discovered the anticipated outlines of approaching Baldies. The Marines' weapons stuttered, stuttered again—just as Danilenko's third and final grenade went off.

"Clear," announced Jonathon.

"And clear," supplemented Danilenko regarding his own three targets.

McGee toggled his com-link. "Li, rejoin main body. Fire-team leaders, leapfrog advan—"

And then there was movement in the lobby—lots of it. Baldies, almost a dozen, were running every which way—but none of them had weapons, and all were scattering toward either the side or front entrances as though they were fleeing something *inside* the building. *What the fu—?*

Then Matto opened fire. The odd-even mix of discarding sabot and dum-dum rounds disintegrated two standing panels of glass an instant before two of the Baldies went down, one still thrashing. The other Baldies who had been heading for the front entrance—arms waving wildly—swerved toward the sides. Other Marine carbines were already up and tracking.

"Cease fire," McGee shouted over the unit channel. "They're not targets."

"Wha—?" started Wismer.

"They're civilians."

"*Shto*? How can you know?"

"Stow it, Igor. It's my command, it's my call. Now we go in, hot and ready—but something smells funny here. Wits and guns ready, Marines—but just as we drilled it. Simonson, are you and Chakrabarti ready?"

"We've got the backdoor, Sarge." The two of them were already moving to enter the lobby on either side and take up their out-facing flanking positions.

"Good. Li?"

"I'm on your six—and waiting."

"Fine. Here we go."

Ankaht reapproached the observation labs, signaling (urgent, all, urgent).

From several dozen meters away, the *selnarm* of Ipshef reached out to touch hers. "Elder, what distresses you?"

"Quickly, Ipshef, gather the staff and the humans together. All staff split into teams of two; each team take four humans. And then run. Do not tell me where. Do not tell each other. Run as far and as fast as you can. Stop for nothing."

Orthezh intruded. "Elder, why—?"

"Assassins. Death-Vowed. They are coming for us. Mretlak showed me. And now our Security detachment does not respond."

She entered the observation lab's lounge. All the humans and Arduans were already together, in mixed groups. There was something terribly reassuring about the sight, but also something poignant, as if it were a tableau of impending tragedy. Ipshef involuntarily radiated (horror) when she saw Ankaht arrive, saw the *skeerba* that was already in her right cluster. "No, it cannot be—"

Orthezh overrode her with a sort of loving brusqueness. "There is no logic in denying the truth we can feel in *shaxzhu* Ankaht's sendings. We are wasting time." In the next instant, he was giving orders for dispersal.

Ankaht sent a tender tendril across Ipshef's gentle and terrified soul, and ran back the way she had come, straining to get to Jennifer.

And hoping it was not too late.

Leading from the front, McGee reached the back staircase. They'd greased two more Baldies on their way back here, and although he never thought he'd feel such an emotion for the three-eyed monsters, McGee actually experienced a pang of regret: the two they'd vented had popped out of doorways, unarmed, hapless, and panicked. But on this kind of op, there was no time to check intent. You had to presume it was kill or be killed. And so his team had efficiently and swiftly gunned down two harmless Baldies who had been wearing what might have been the alien equivalent of lab smocks.

But now, as the Marines reached the backstairs, they heard the approach of something or someone from down below. McGee waved his two squads back against the side of the corridor and listened. Faintly, rising up out of the stairwell, came the sliding, gliding sound of Baldy legs swiftly mounting stairs—but these were not the sounds of panicked movement. No, these steps were sure and purposeful.

McGee pulled one of the older frags off his web-gear

and nodded to Matto to do the same. McGee pulled the pin, counted down two seconds and lobbed the grenade down the stairwell. Matto's arced in right after it.

A second of silence, the briefest moment of frenetic skittering—and then a double blast. McGee and his team were at the railing, aiming over the side, before the last bits of shrapnel had fallen. Three Baldies were sprawled on the landing below, all cloaked in black. Without checking for movement, McGee and his team tagged each of them with a short burst. One twitched. Another flopped and cough-howled like a junkyard dog getting kicked in the ribs. Then there was nothing but stillness.

Li came to look over the banister. "Lucky we heard them coming up."

"Damned straight. Kapinski."

"Sir!"

"The animal-behavior labs are right under us, so proceed downstairs with your team and secure that position. Confirm our egress point, set the charges, and have our exfil gear ready and waiting. We're going up to the human-observation labs—and we could be coming back with trouble right behind us."

"Yes, sir." Kapinski looked over the railing. "Think there are more of those black-robed Baldies down there?"

"Can't tell. But they weren't running scared."

"Which means what?"

Damn, logically, that would normally mean that they're *what the other Baldies were running away from*—but the Baldies were unfailingly loyal to each other, so that made no sense. "I don't know what it means, Juan—except that something's off-center, here. Expect the unexpected."

"Gee, thanks, sir. Any more words of wisdom?"

"Yeah—don't sass your boss." McGee returned Juan's smile. "Move out."

As Ipshef reached the intersection where they had planned on turning left toward the lobby staircase, she felt Orthezh reach out to her, both physically and through his *selnarm*. "What, beloved?" she asked.

"We must separate."

She halted. "Separate? Why?" The four humans with them, detecting the pause, were already growing restless, anxious.

"We will make less noise and hide better if we go as two separate groups. And if one of us is found—"

"The other might not be. It is logical but—"

And that was when a black shape loomed out of the right-hand branch of the intersection. Ipshef gasped, reached out to Orthezh in (love, panic, fear)—but the shape slid past his back. Deliverance?

No, The shadow was a *Destoshaz* that had simply slipped behind Orthezh to get to the humans. She pulsed out to them to (Run!), hoping they would hear her *selnarm* scream—

She did not feel the *skeerba* as it cut into her from behind, severing her spine and tearing through her heart, all in one savage, sinuous twist. She recognized that attack, in a strange moment of pre-mortem lucidity, as a death strike also used to impart a final insult to the one attacked: its message was *You are so inept at* maatkah *that I can kill you without any fear that my claws will snag within your harmless body.*

And, obligingly, Ipshef died as harmlessly and gently as she had lived.

Orthezh had seen the Death-Vowed that swept in

behind her and was already moving as her torso bulged obscenely outward, distended by the interior ravages of the deeply penetrating back-strike. His own claws sprang from their tentacle sheathes, vengeance and agony surging out of him in a ferocious wave of *selnarm*—

—which ended as abruptly as it had risen. Another Death-Vowed assassin, following the first that had slipped behind him, cleanly slashed the back of his head free from the top of his spinal column.

The first Death-Vowed had already reached the humans, who fled, screaming. But rather than attack, he swerved around and then ahead of them; then he wheeled about, *skeerba* ready. The *griarfeksh* stumbled to a halt, the ones in the front falling in their panic to stop. The other five Death-Vowed came loping up behind. Arms whipped out, *skeerba* met flesh with a sound like hacksaws slicing at a tarpaulin; the rear two humans went down, one spraying blood out of an arterial wound. The Death-Vowed clambered over the fallen bodies, the last two humans cowering and whimpering—

A ragged chorus of staccato weapon reports filled the corridor. Three of the Death-Vowed toppled, one thrashing as if its brain were already dead but the body refused to believe it. The other two in the rear spun and leaped toward the new threat—

—which turned out to be two teams of Marines, shooting high to avoid hitting the cringing civilians. The two Baldy heads and torsos shredded into tattered ruins of flesh, bone, and cartilage. The last Death-Vowed at the rear, realizing it had but seconds to complete its mission of assassination, swept both arms back. With *skeerba* ready in one cluster and claws snicking out of the other—

—the Baldy blinked its main eye shut, suddenly

motionless at the sound of a single, thunderous report. Igor Danilenko lowered his Alliant-Rimstar battle-rifle and spat. The Arduan's central eye opened again—a bloody, oozing ruin—and the alien toppled over, as limp and heavy as a slaughtered steer.

McGee raced forward, checking bodies, sad for the losses but relieved that Jennifer was not among them. He lifted one of the human survivors—a balding, rather frail man—and said, "Sir, you've got to focus and give me information."

"Wha—yes? Yes?"

"Are you one of the artists the Baldies abducted?"

"Well, not really abdu—"

"Yes," interrupted the other human survivor, a thickset woman of middle age who lifted herself stiffly from the floor. "We're the artists."

"And where are the rest of you?"

"Don't know. Ankaht split us up."

"Ankaht?"

"She's the Arduan in charge of the translation project."

"Uh . . . okay. Are some of the humans—eh, subjects—still in the sleep-study lab area?"

"Don't know anything about that. But Ankaht evacuated the general-observation labs. I guess she heard that these other Arduans were coming after us."

Shit. My neatly packaged cluster of objectives has now fragmented into various, moving pieces. Shit and shit. I knew this op started too smoothly. "Where might the Baldi—the Arduans try to hide themselves?"

"Maybe in our quarters?"

McGee shook his head. "That's probably the first place the attackers will look, so anyone who's there is probably already—eh, anywhere else?"

The thickset woman thought. "The safest place would be the discreet-observation room in the library. It's on the sixth floor."

McGee knew the blueprints of the other floors pretty well, but her description wasn't ringing any bells. "What discreet-observation room?"

"The Psych staff put in a hidden observation room so they can watch social interaction in a non-laboratory setting."

"Can you show me where it is?"

"Sure."

"Good." McGee toggled the command circuit to Li. "Harry, you hear all that?"

"No, I was napping."

"Figures. Listen, this snoop room sounds like our best bet. But just in case they've taken Jen somewhere else, I want you to continue on to the Sleep-Observation Labs."

"Got it. If I find her, should I—?"

"No, Harry. We maintain radio silence as much as possible from here on out. I've got your position via transponder on the HUD. You just check the lab and follow any leads you might find. As you go, watch out for hostiles coming back from the main human dormitory area. Rendezvous in eight minutes at the exfil point."

"Roger. We're moving."

McGee toggled the channel for Simonson. "Mei, how're you doing?"

"Some company on the way."

"Radio silence unless your position is compromised."

"Yep. Out."

McGee turned to the stocky woman, who was looking up at him, hands on her hips. "Ma'am, what's the least obtrusive way to get to the library?"

✧ ✧ ✧

Khremhet sent calm (approval) out among his fellow Death-Vowed as they spun, tumbled, and slashed their way through the last three Arduan researchers and five *griarfeksh*. One of the humans—a large, hirsute creature—surprised the Death-Vowed who attacked him: nimble for his size, the fur-faced male spun to avoid a lethal slash, rotating all the way around through his spin so that he was now behind his Arduan attacker. The *griarfeksh*'s two hairy arms caught his would-be executioner about the neck, pulled him close and did not simply squeeze: they cinched tight, like a pair of short-stroke pistons compressing. The snap of the *Destoshaz*'s neck vertebra was audible throughout the room.

There is some training in this one, thought Khremhet, who crossed over to the human in a single, high-arcing leap. The human turned, hands at the ready—but Khremhet twisted in midair and landed short of the human. As he did, he tucked down into a tight, fluid roll that brought him up behind his adversary. Without stopping to uncurl fully, Khremhet swept his talons across the back of the human's knee even as the patch-furred *zheteksh* was turning to attack. Tendons severed, the human fell, stifling a howl of pain down into a harsh gargle—an act of profound self-control for which Khremhet felt a pulse of respect, just as he struck upwards with his *skeerba*, slashing deep into and across the *griarfeksh*'s pale throat. The animal's dying blood-spray spattered across the First Blade of the Death-Vowed, who shuddered at such a soiling of his person. Arduan blood was arguably an honor, but the reeking spume from a two-eyed animal such as—

His lieutenant sent (respect). "We are done here, First Blade."

"So we are." Khremhet tried to shake off the *gri-arfesksh*'s blood. "Guzhgef, conduct a search of the upper floors and other locations where any stragglers might hide."

"Yes, First Blade. If any remain unfound, we shall find them."

"Excellent, Second Blade. The rest of us will now follow in support of the first team that went to the Elder's quarters."

Fighting the instinct to cradle her baby in both arms, Jennifer shifted Zander so that his spine lay along the inside of her forearm, which she clutched tight against her body. She needed the other arm for balance as she ran, following Ankaht through the maze of narrow office corridors. When they reached the central bank of elevators, Ankaht paused, thought, signaled "Wait here," and, moving to the left, opened the fire door leading to the staircase. She slipped inside, evidently listening and sensing for any movement above or below.

That was when three Arduans, all in black tunics, came trotting around the right-hand corner. They stopped, looked at Jennifer, who looked at them and clutched her baby close. She was about to send a *selnarm* cry after Ankaht, when the *shaxzhu* Elder's pulse came clear and tight—and through what felt like an armored tube, as though she was trying to limit its reception to Jennifer alone. "Jennifer. Flee into the office behind you. Then hit the fire alarm."

And without question or thought, Jennifer did just that, sprinting and panting, Zander giggling as he was jounced. She could hear the three *Destoshaz* behind her, slow and wary at first. But by the time she reached the office door, they were coming hard. She shut and locked the door, looked for the fire alarm but couldn't find it. The first *Destoshaz* crashed into the door, trying to break it down. Jennifer saw the office had another door, one that opened into an open space with an infinitude of cubicles. Maybe if she ran that way—

Ankaht's thought interrupted hers. "No, Jennifer. Trust me. Trip the fire alarm and wait there."

Which was when Jen saw the fire alarm—and the tip of the bit of a small hand drill that one of the assassins was using on the door's lock. Every primal instinct told her to run and keep running. But Ankaht had said otherwise, and after all, Ankaht was—well, she was Ankaht.

Jennifer pulled the lever of the fire alarm that was mounted next to the door.

The triple-time shrieking of the alarm system started immediately. The three Arduan assassins paused, looked baffled for a moment, and then went back to their drilling. The drill bit came through the lock, the door swung open, the first black-garbed killer stepped through—just as Ankaht came soaring, literally soaring, through the air behind them.

She landed with her full weight on the rearmost of the three Death-Vowed, riding his back down to the ground and tumbling him into his two co-conspirators. The second one—the one with the drill—fell. The other stumbled but turned it into a shoulder roll that took him into the room with Jennifer.

From what Jennifer could see, Ankaht had somehow used her claws to kill the one whose back she had leaped upon. The one with the drill tried rising but saw he was about to be struck down by the strange three-clawed weapon that Ankaht—like the assassins—was wielding in one of her clusters. He raised one cluster to block Ankaht's oddly imprecise roundhouse cut while his other cluster swung back, clutching his own three-clawed weapon. But he had let his attention slip away from Ankaht's feet. Her left leg snapped out and caught him low in the chest. He went back with a grunt. In a second, she had leapt upon him and buried the claws of her unarmed cluster into his throat. Scissoring her claws together sharply, she then yanked them upward with a twist. Her adversary fell aside, clutching the long, jagged hole where the front of his neck used to be.

Ankaht had ridden the momentum of her backward ripping motion into a rearward hop, just in time to narrowly dodge a powerful cut from the weapon of the third assassin. The flurry of blows and blocks that ensued was too fast for Jennifer to follow—but as it progressed, Ankaht gave ground slowly, slowly, until they were halfway back to the elevators.

And then Ankaht emitted a wide-open, desperate *selnarm* scream. "Now! Run!" And Jennifer almost did—before she realized why the pulse had been sent out as an open message, not through the tight private tube that Ankaht had used the first time. Jennifer was just starting to smile as the last assassin spun to check on the flight of his human target—who, oddly, was standing very still. Staring at him. Jennifer could see in those alien eyes that he, too, had figured out Ankaht's trick, but a second too late. He spun about, arms rising into a cross-block defense—

But discovered a *skeerba* already sliding deep into his chest. He twitched, drew his own weapon back for a final strike, but Ankaht yanked her *skeerba*—still deep in his upper torso—upward sharply. The last assassin breathed out, blood gargling up over his narrow lips as he slumped down, quite dead.

"Shit," said Jennifer looking at the bodies.

"Yes," agreed Ankaht, "that was very close."

"No, I mean your fighting. Can you teach me that?"

(Amusement, fondness.) "Probably not. It is based on the principles of our more flexible joints and spines. But enough. We must hurry."

"Where?"

"The Extreme Environment Trauma Lab."

They started running. Jennifer, carrying Zander as if she were running with an ancient rugby ball clutched tight against her, asked, "Why there?"

"That Lab connects to an entirely separate wing of the building—the Post Abaria Recovery Center—through a single shared resource."

"Which is?"

"A hyperbaric chamber. The safety seals of which cannot be overridden without special command codes, once it has been sealed and activated."

Jennifer smiled slowly. "I get it."

"Good. Then run faster."

She did.

Neither of them noticed that Ankaht had not fully avoided the third assassin's first *skeerba* sweep: emerging lazily from a nick not much bigger than a paper cut, droplets of her blood seeped and fell after every fourth or fifth step.

Second Blade Guzhgef entered the library quickly, scanning with eyes and *selnarm* both. Too many of the researchers and humans were unaccounted for—and they had checked almost every other wing of this building. Perhaps the *griarfeksh* were sheltering in a stairwell, or one of the service rooms accessed through them. He motioned to the two Death-Vowed behind him, reached for the handle of the fire door that led into the staircase—

Which burst open, revealing two rows of flickering muzzle flashes that sent a deafening wave of explosive, chattering gunfire breaking over and through him.

"Cease fire," called McGee.

The two Marine fire teams—one standing, one kneeling—lowered their weapons slightly.

"Deploy."

At that command, the two teams sped out into the second tier of the library, moving at a half crouch, weapons held up close to their cheeks, pace steady as they checked the flanks and then the path to the snoop room using a hurried leap-frog advance.

"Clear." Wismer's voice, from the point position of the lead team, was as certain as it was calm.

"Hold your positions. Cover us in and out of this level, Jon."

"Roger that. Whenever you're ready, Tank."

McGee waved for the other eight Marines to follow him, and he sprinted to the concealed door of the snoop room, hustling the two rescued artists along with them.

Breathless, the thickset woman knocked on the door. Nothing. She knocked again, waited, then spoke loudly. "Matilda, get your fat, quivering ass over here and open this door. The Marines are breaking us out of this dump."

Unless Matilda was, in fact, a gaunt, hairless man

who stood as tall as McGee, it was someone else who opened the door. "Marines!" he exclaimed, as if he hadn't believed his own eyes—or what he'd been told.

"Yes, sir," confirmed McGee as he pushed past and into the room. Six translators—and two Baldies. McGee snapped his weapon up to his shoulder—just as the Baldies lay down, limbs spread out, clusters open and empty. *Well, hell.*

"They don't mean any harm," supplied a rather dumpy woman with a head of wild, flowing blond hair.

"The hell they don't," muttered Matto.

"Well, right now," said the gaunt, depilated man, "they seem more worried about their own kind."

That seems true enough. "Everyone up."

Danilenko shouldered into the doorway. "The Baldies, too?"

"No. They stay here."

"Permanently?" asked Danilenko, hefting his rifle and preparing to enter.

Ready to do the job yourself, eh, Igor? "No. We secure them and leave them."

"Alive? They seem to be able to—well, to signal each other. If so, then that leaves us in grave danger."

"Yes, Igor. But unless I'm wrong, they've probably been signaling for quite some time—before we arrived, in fact. So they're not going to be bringing down any more heat than what they've already called in."

At which moment, the command circuit toned: Simonson, at the front door. *Well, speaking of heat coming in*—"Mei, sitrep."

"We've got company, Tank. A defense sled."

"What? Haven't any of the ready defense blisters tried rushing the building on their fans?"

"Nope. Never a sign of them."

Well, that didn't make any sense—unless the Baldy assassins had been aided and abetted by a little treasonous sabotage of the local defense units. If that's what had happened, then someone in the Baldy security organization might have forced the local weapon blisters to stand down. Or maybe some sympathetic officer had sent the blister operators off on the Baldy equivalent of an extended coffee break. Either way, the weirdness the Marines had encountered during their attack thus far had just become more weird, more unpredictable, and therefore, definitely more dangerous. But for now, all McGee needed was few more minutes to exfil. "Mei, are you telling me the Baldies have sent only *one* sled?"

"Affirmative, and this bunch looks more like they are from an Enforcer group, not a Security unit. Either way, they seem pretty unsure what to do next."

"Have any of the Baldies dismounted?"

"Yeah—and now it looks like they're trying to get manual control over two of their own vehicles' defense blisters—neither of which seems to be responding."

"How many Baldies have come outside the sled?"

"I'd say all of them—except the driver. And maybe a weapons/sensor operator."

"You've got a good angle on the Baldies outside the hull?"

"Straight and unobstructed."

"Then burn 'em."

Mei Simonson looked out around the side of what had once been the security desk in the lobby of the Psych Annex. The Baldies were still milling around near their sled, trying some kind of direct override on the two portside defense blisters. If they suspected that any humans were watching them from inside the lobby, they gave no sign of it.

Well, that makes my job a lot easier, thought Mei as she removed the HEAT rocket grenade from her rifle's under-muzzle launch ramp. She replaced it with a high-explosive fragmentation grenade. "Okay, Bart," she whispered over the team channel to Chakrabarti, "Let's light 'em up. On three. One, two, three—"

The two grenades jumped off the two Marine carbines. Then their rockets kicked in, and they rushed out the shattered glass expanse to explode in the midst of the Baldy Enforcers. Several were blown—quite literally—to bloody bits. The others toppled, missing pieces. None moved or made a sound.

A fraction of a second later, the sled seemed to flinch back a few meters. Then it lifted on its thrusters and circled up and away. Simonson watched it go as she put the HEAT grenade back on her weapon's launch rail, and thought, *Well, son of a bitch.*

Visible beyond what looked like two treatment bays in a hospital emergency room was the massive door of the hyperbaric chamber. The chamber itself looked like a pint-sized version of the radiation-hardened habmods that Sandro used to shelter in when Bellerophon's flares interrupted his off-world mining stints. At last, safety—

But then Ankaht spun in mid-stride, guiding Jennifer past her with one cluster and raising the other—

Just in time to lock *skeerbas* with a Death-Vowed who had noiselessly drawn so close in his pursuit of Jennifer that he had been able to strike at her. Over her shoulder, Jennifer saw that the strike was an awkward one—overextended—and as the two Arduans broke apart, little Ankaht managed to get a claw strike into the vicinity of the attacker's groin. He stumbled back; Ankaht sprinted the other direction, trying to catch up to Jennifer.

Who, in reaching the hyperbaric chamber, found it closed. The heavy handle resisted her tugging: she didn't have enough leverage with one hand. Put down Zander? Was there time? She turned to check—

—just in time to see all three of the black-garbed *Destoshaz* swarm around Ankaht, who stood, broad-legged, at the last choke point in the corridor. Once they pushed Ankaht back from that position, Jennifer could see that the Death-Vowed would be able to reach both herself and Zander.

As she put Zander down, Jennifer caught another glimpse of the furious melee taking place only a few meters away from her. Strike, block, counterstrike, bits of flesh flying free—some of it Ankaht's—as the assassins fought with utter disregard for their own safety. However, what made them most unnerving was their utter silence. Because, Jennifer realized—even as she cinched both hands around the lever that opened the hyperbaric chamber—when such boundless ferocity was also perversely calm, it suggested a governing intellect so monstrously alien that no human could ever hope, or want, to fathom it.

Jennifer got the door open and spun back to sweep Zander into her arms—but saw that the combat had entered its final second. Ankaht, bleeding from at least three significant wounds, had finally taken down the Death-Vowed she had wounded at the beginning of the fight. But, exhausted now, she had not managed to withdraw her *skeerba* in time: as her opponent slumped over, she was tugged sideways, and then had to release her weapon. The last two—one of them an uncommonly tall and bright *Destoshaz*—reared up, arms back to deliver bone-severing death blows—

—when, behind and to the side of the large one, she saw the small, fine figure of Harry Li wearing a wetsuit, shiny where it was still damp. Single shots spatted archly: 6 mm rounds went through both of the assassins' torsos. The first exit holes that Jennifer saw were small, crisp: pass-throughs by discarding sabot rounds. But the next bullets fairly erupted as they cut through the Arduan bodies, blasting out craters that spewed blood and chunks of flesh and bone.

The *Destoshaz* fell. Harry and the two Marines with him advanced at the ready, weapons still leveled—

—at Ankaht.

"*No!*" shrieked Jennifer, who jumped up from her crouch next to Zander and landed beside Ankaht.

"Jen—" Harry's eye was down along the barrel.

Jen moved so that her midriff was between Harry's unblinking brown eye and Ankaht's spent, bleeding body. "No." Jennifer's voice was sharp, ragged, even brutal in its insistence.

Harry looked up, stared at her, then looked at his two men. Who—smiling smiles that were anything but smiles—began to move around and to either side of Jennifer. Harry kept his eyes on her, but his focus flicked away for an instant, evidently noting that Ankaht was finally rising to her feet. "What's wrong with you, Jen?"

"Nothing's wrong with me. She—Ankaht—is our friend."

"That's crazy talk, Jen. And I don't think Sandro will want to hear it."

"Sandro? He's here?" She felt tears well up and a sob surged out of her gut. "He's here?"

"Sure he is. He's right back there." And Harry turned to look behind. She craned her neck to stare over his shoulder—and realized her mistake at the same moment she hated her gullibility. The Marine to her right side made a grab in her direction, the one on the left brought up his weapon to bear on Ankaht—who had chosen the moment of confused motion to leap backward into the hyperbaric chamber, out of his field of fire.

But she was still well within Harry's, who had stepped forward, sighting along his barrel, and was directly in front of Jennifer—

Who pitched backward against the Marine clutching her arms, shrieking "My baby!" The sudden shift of focus, and the desperate cry, froze the three Marines for a fraction of a second: obeying a prosocial male impulse as old as humanity itself, their lethal intent was momentarily overridden by an impulse to shield the child against some unseen threat.

A threat which was not there. Jennifer, still struggling backward, pitched sharply forward; the sudden reversal of momentum caught the Marine by surprise, carried him over with Jennifer. They half fell, half stumbled into Li, knocking his carbine aside.

"RUN!" Jennifer both shouted and signaled at Ankaht—who quickly reached over to grab the door's handle. Harry untangled his carbine from Jennifer's desperate grasp, leveled it, and fired—just as Ankaht slammed the door. The DS round cut a deep gouge in it, but failed to penetrate. Ankaht had not stopped moving: she leapt out the other side of the chamber;

she was now in the Post-Abaria Recovery Center. Harry bounded after her, stretching for the door he had just dinged—as Ankaht slammed the far side door shut.

Harry had his hand on the near-side handle—just as Ankaht smacked the control panel on her side: lights flashed, alarms sounded—and the emergency-depressurization indicator illuminated.

Even as Harry was trying to yank open the door on his side, he heard a fateful clank: activated, the chamber had autolocked—and could only be overridden by a manually entered command code. A command code which he did not know.

Through the tiny windows centered in the chamber's two hatchlike doors, they could see Ankaht already fleeing down the corridor in the other Recovery Center.

Harry rounded on Jennifer. "Open it. Now." Zander—never having heard such a sharp and threatening tone—promptly wailed.

Jennifer looked up at Harry from the ground. "I can't."

"You mean you won't."

"I mean I *can't*, Harry. I don't have the code. Anyway, it doesn't matter. You won't catch her. It takes thirty seconds for the chamber to complete a full cycle, and the door won't open before then. She's gone."

"And you helped her get away."

"She's our only hope for peace."

"She's a damned Baldy."

"Yes—and she's my friend."

McGee checked his watch: Harry was a minute overdue. He looked at the rest of his team, clustered in the Marine Species Behavioral lab, down on the basement level. The artists they'd retrieved—eight in all—were being given simple instructions on how to use the essential escape gear. All but two of them—Mr. Gaunt and Ms. Thickset—alternated between looking bewildered and petrified. Back near the empty holding tank, Kapinski and Battisti were affixing puttylike demo charges around the circumference of a large hatch.

Damn it, Li. A minute and a half overdue? Gotta risk the com-link. "Harry—"

Who interrupted as if he'd been waiting. "Coming. And I've got Jennifer. We're half a minute out, at most."

Somehow, McGee gave the necessary orders even as his brain refused to think about anything other than the image of Jennifer and her blue bundle. To his own ears, his voice sounded miles away as he rapped out, "Final test on the gear, and then equip it. Everyone in exit sequence. Sea-scooters ready. Kapinski, I need that sedative and the child-sized evac ball." He toggled the command circuit over to—"Simonson?"

Static.

Damn it. "Simonson?"

A new channel opened. "Chakrabarti here, Sarge. Mei is—she's KIA, Tank."

McGee thought he might throw up. "You okay?"

"Yeah, but not for long. About a minute ago, the local blisters came back online. All at once. Six of them rushed us. We were ready, blew 'em all down—but there were so damn many, shooting so damned fast, and so damned much ordnance—"

"You did Bravo Zulu, Chakra. And Mei, too. Can you hold on for another thirty seconds?"

"Hell, I might manage forty. They're quiet right now."

"Good. Sit tight, get the smokes out to cover your fallback on the exfil point."

"Got 'em lined up like apples ripening on the sill, Sarge."

"Good man. Hold on."

Harry came through the door. And Jennifer was with him. McGee felt a rush of both elation and vertigo and his vision tunneled down so that all he could see was her face. *One second,* thought McGee. *One second can't hurt anyone.* He reached out, grabbed and hugged Jennifer so hard he thought he might break her. But he didn't—and she had rotated the baby to the side of her body: although whimpering a moment before, the infant grew suddenly and strangely quiet. McGee looked up to thank Harry—but saw that Light Horse and his fire team were wearing long faces and dark looks. "Harry? What's wrong?"

Li's eyes—hard and unfriendly—flinched away from the back of Jennifer's head. "I'll tell you later."

"Okay. Well, it's time to go." McGee raised his voice. "Everybody ready. Exfil in fifteen seconds." He toggled back to Chakrabarti—and got what sounded like a mix between a car crash and a firefight. "Bog in heaven—Chakra, report. Chakra?"

"Sarge—damn, shit. Sarge, I'm—" Then a gasp, a roar of rotary machine guns at close range... and static.

McGee swallowed and closed the link. *My one second—the one second that couldn't hurt anyone—just cost Chakrabarti his life.* McGee turned away from his team, his loves, himself. "Everyone down." He nodded at Kapinski and Battisti. "Blow the valve."

As Kapinski sprinted away from the valve—but staying close against the wall in which it was mounted—Battisti shouted, "*Clear! Fire in the hole!*" Battisti pressed a button on his wrist-comm. A circular blast sent fragments of plaster, paint, and plasticrete jetting against the inner glass of the empty tank, cracking and star-shattering it in a dozen places. A roughly circular part of the wall tipped forward, slowly at first, and then faster as the weight of the water behind shoved it out of the ragged gap. Kapinski and Battisti snugged their diving masks back down and attached their thirty-minute chemical rebreathers. McGee rose. "Everyone stand. Up the ladder into the pool. Marines—dump your weapons and assault gear. Now it will only slow us down. We're getting the hell out of here." *All except Simonson and Chakrabarti, that is.*

All except for the Marines I failed.

Jennifer hugged the evac ball—usually used on spacecraft—tightly and used her fingers to grope and locate Zander's head within it. She told herself he was just drowsy, not suffocating in the half-inflated sac which, if fully deployed, would have been about the size of a medicine ball. The infant sedative—its safety assured by the pediatrician's labwork—was just doing its job, she told herself, and forced her attention back to the tasks of their escape.

Which was terrifying enough. Although never claustrophobic, Jennifer had been ready to vomit as they went, one by one, breathing apparatus on, into the dim tunnel and cold water that, according to the maps, would ultimately lead them out into Salamisene Bay. Jennifer's mouth had become dry with fear as they began to navigate the narrow, blind passageways, but the Marines seemed both able to see in the dark through the monocles inside their masks and were fully conversant with their exit pathway. Also, no one was required to swim: the entire party had been broken into four equal groups, each towed like a string of sausages behind one of the sea-scooters that the Marines had brought with them. It was slow going in the tight tunnel, but other than holding hands with two people, and using one's own feet to keep a little distance from the walls, the tasks were not particularly strenuous or complex.

The underwater caravan turned right twice, left once, and then Jennifer lost track. But eventually they came to a thin-barred grate, covered with tide-moss. Beyond it, the water was blue and the light was dappled. The sea? Salamisene Bay? Two Marines went ahead, placed charges, and then led everyone back around the last corner they had turned. The same Marine who had overseen the demolitions in the empty sea-life tank—Battisti—manipulated the buttons on his wrist-comm again: there was a sudden backrush of water along with an uncomfortably loud—yet muffled—blast. Harry led them back around the corner and toward a now-jagged opening where the thin-barred grate had been. They kept their bodies well away from the twisted metal fangs that were the remains of the grate and then were out into the waters of Salamisene Bay. And there, barely visible farther down in the dark blue water and somewhat offshore, was a small submarine. Well, what a neat escape plan.

As they approached the sub, Jennifer saw that its hull was equipped with racks carrying larger versions of the sea-scooters that were towing them now. But, rather than preparing to enter the sub, the Marines unlatched the sea-scooters. There were enough so each two persons could share one—and in the case of the artists, each one of them was teamed up with a Marine.

Sandro got Jennifer to hold on to a handrail on the side of the scooter and then carefully situated her and the baby so that he could see and reach out to them with maximum ease. He held up his left hand, waited until all his Marines had seen him and done the same, and then aimed his sea-scooter down into the depths. Jennifer looked behind and then forward, confused and a little scared: they were moving away from the sub and down into the benthic dark. Why?

As they descended, Jennifer looked back again. The sub was now moving, gaining speed as it headed out to sea on a shallow but steady dive. Then, rather suddenly, the dark blue around her deepened into near-black and blotted the vehicle from sight. She shut her eyes against the sensation of being sucked down into the watery pit of a submerged hell.

She didn't know how long she kept her eyes closed; it seemed like hours that she clutched the increasingly restless Alexander closer and closer, even as the water grew colder and colder—and then they stopped. Using a sense she was not aware that she possessed, nor could have named, she felt quite sure that they had reached a sheer wall of some sort, that they could not swim farther south. *We've come to the foot of the bay,* she thought, just as a dim blue light seemed to flare out of the darkness beside her. It was Harry Li, opening what looked like a black-painted hatch. At first it appeared to be a doorway into the cliff-face itself. But closer inspection revealed that it was centered in a bulge protruding from a gap in the stone: an inset habitation module? Probably so, because Sandro's large hand—gentle on her elbow—began to tow her toward the light.

Moments later, Jennifer swam into the pressure lock

of the cylindrical habitat module and waited while the others maneuvered in after her. The walls of the module were festooned with various military markings and stenciled haphazardly with emergency procedure lists. Then the outer hatch closed and there was a slow gurgling noise. Centimeter by centimeter, the water level dropped lower and lower, and when it went beneath his waist, Sandro tore off his mask, and then gently removed hers. He took the rebreather out of her mouth—only to put his lips where it had been. "Jen," he sighed, holding an arm in either bearish paw, staring intently as if to make sure it was really her.

"Yes, Sandro, it's me. But where are we?"

"Marine Reserve training modules. They didn't start out that way, of course. They were put here when the first colony built the fusion plants and had to monitor and routinely repair the coolant pipes and other open-water interfaces. Then the habmods were shut down when they put the old reactor in mothballs—and we took them over for training purposes."

"Training?"

"Yeah, sure. If we're issued new EVA qualification standards, we come down here first to train with the real gear in the pseudo-weightlessness you get with submerged neutral buoyancy. And we also come down here to maintain our readiness for actual undersea assault ops. The regular-duty Marines used the really nifty facilities out in Camp Gehenna. We Reserve grunts in Melantho and the Big Three had to make do with these. They're not too pretty, and they smell awful—but they'll be fine for the next seventy-two hours."

"And then?"

"Then, in twos and threes, we return to Melantho.

First, an easy swim beneath the bay. At the end of that, we come up under the docks, dump our gear, change into the clothes waiting there, and blend back into the street. Before we relocate."

"Relocate?"

"Jennifer, this city—this entire metro area—is no longer safe for me, or for you, or for..." And he looked down with a wide smile.

Jennifer wanted to tell Sandro that she couldn't leave Melantho, not now, not when she and Ankaht were making such progress. But she also wanted to let that urgency fade for just a moment, to steal a private moment from the respective duties of their lives, and so, instead, she undid the seams of the emergency ball. Barely audible whimperings became infant squallings—that faded just as quickly when Zander's small hands reached up and found his mother's familiar and beloved nose. Sandro made a noise that sounded like something between a gasp, a sigh, and a wordless prayer. Jennifer smiled at him. "Sandro, I'd like to introduce you to our so—"

At that moment, there was a dull *thrump* against the outer hatch, even as the last of the water was gargling its way out of the chamber. "Have they found us?" Jennifer asked, fearful but strangely glad that if she and the baby and Sandro were to die, they would do so together. It didn't seem quite so bad that way.

But Harry shook his head. "No, but they found the sub."

Jennifer looked back at Sandro. "And so—"

"And so they've destroyed it—and think they've destroyed us." He smiled. "Which is just the way we want it."

15

Save in His Own Country

A prophet is not without honor,
save in his own country.
—Matthew 15:57

Prisoner Holding Facility, Resistance Regional Headquarters, Charybdis Islands, Bellerophon/New Ardu

Jennifer woke up, moved languorously . . . and found nothing in her arms—

Zander! She sat bolt upright, arms sweeping a desperate circle around her—the circuit of which knocked over the glass of milk they had given her: half finished, she had returned it to a precarious perch half on and half off the coaster. Yeah, they had drugged her, all right: had put something in the milk to knock her out. She remembered barely getting the glass back to the night table. Folding her arms, she sardonically hoped one of the Marines was also a wet nurse or that they had some baby formula in stores, because she was not about to allow Zander to suckle on her barbituated breast milk for at least forty-eight hours.

If, of course, they returned Zander to her at all.

Some welcome for the homecoming hero, she thought. But then, she had returned with attitudes and knowledge they really hadn't wanted to hear. Harry and the team that had rescued her—and almost killed Ankaht—had been kind and savvy enough not to say anything about what had happened while the Marines and rescued artists spent their time crowded in the hab module embedded into the side of the Drop at the foot of Salamisene Bay. That had been the happiest of times, just watching Zander play with his dad, evincing that fast, almost mystical affinity that infants have for a parent they have not yet met. There had been no talk of war or captivity: just of the three of them, as if they were suspended safely in the timeless moment of a perpetual Now. Jen and Sandro had even, fleetingly, readopted the personas they had played long ago in a historical-reconstruction troupe: she the brassy tavern wench Bess, he the ne'er-do-well Highland border reiver Ruari Mac Ruari. It had been sheer silliness and sheer bliss. No one tried to debrief her; no one pierced the invisible social cocoon that the little family had spun about itself.

But then the time to complete the after-action exfiltration had come, and, in pairs and threes, the artists and their Marine escorts had begun the two-kilometer swim to the docks of East Shore Melantho. There they would transform back into civilians and immediately make for destinations far outside the area of influence projected by the planetside Arduans—whom the Marines and Resistance still insisted on calling Baldies.

Jennifer and Sandro had been the fourth group to go, with Zander sedated again. Up until a year ago, the two of them had swum frequently in the summers, so they knew the local waters and each others' pace pretty well. It was an uneventful crossing.

And it was the last uneventful activity that Jennifer had been a part of. As they reached the docks, Harry Li—who had been the first to swim back—was on hand and pulled Sandro aside. Meanwhile some other folks—dressed as surveyors and inspectors from the Public Works Department—not only fitted Jennifer out with new clothes but with all the mommy gear that she needed: a baby backpack, diaper bag, umbrella. In five minutes, they had her looking like a semistylish, middle-class *hausfrau*-in-training, rather than the edgy, funky Earth-Mom she would have opted for if left to her own devices.

But they were not leaving her to her own devices—in any fashion. She looked around for Sandro—saw him being "invited" into the back of a big-wheeled overland rover. She and Zander were guided to a taxi with two female fellow-shoppers: taciturn and smileless bodyguards who treated her as if she were one-half foreign dignitary, one-half death row inmate. Nothing was said—indeed, conversation remained at the level of monosyllables—but the vibe was unmistakably cold and suspicious.

And it remained so until, after six switches between cars, overland cargo-haulers, buses, ATVs, and a two-day hydrofoil journey, she and Zander were deposited—most unceremoniously—in this plain room here on Hylas Island. She had asked to take a walk. Request denied. Swim in the local waters. Request denied. Permission to contact her family, to let them know she was okay. Request denied. To see Sandro, damn it. Request under consideration.

And when the questions started—posed by a weak-chinned, officious popinjay called Heide—she realized that she'd already been judged and tried by the opinion of the Resistance and thereby determined unreliable, certainly a collaborator, maybe even a traitor. The questions that Heide insisted on asking—about numbers and locations and force dispersals in Punt—were not the right ones to be asking her, which she kept trying to point out. They only wanted to know how best to kill the Baldies; she wanted, strove, to tell them that not all the Arduans were hostile and that the whole war—the whole thing—was just a big mistake. Their looks only got harder, their questions more clipped, their eyes more distant. And last night, they had come and taken away her baby. She hadn't seen that coming: after all, were any of them trained in Close Quarters Mommy Ops? Judging from their looks when she changed Zander's diapers, efficiently cleaned his spit-up, or even breast-fed him, she thought not. Well, these *Marines lead the way!* bitches and bastards had better be "leading the way" regarding the needs of her son, or she was going to—

The door opened and a shock of red hair poked in. "Sandro?" she breathed, hardly able—or, more accurately, hardly daring—to believe it was him. Then she was on her feet—"Sandro!"—ready to race into his arms.

But he either missed those physical cues or elected not to see them. He moved directly toward a chair located well away from where she stood—and the farthest from her bed.

Jennifer stopped in mid-stride and stilled a growing sense of both panic and rage. *Okay, don't jump to any conclusions, Jen; this is a completely unnatural environment and there's no knowing what he's been told, or whether we're being watched, or . . .* She again stilled her racing mind and started to move toward him, hoping to be drawn more slowly into his embrace. But she saw that might not be the right move, not just yet. He was tense—terribly so: his hands and forearms were sharply corded by broad veins. And gone was any sign of the playfulness that had made their most recent hours together so golden: neither the accent nor the swaggering posture of Ruari Mac Ruari had returned with her beloved. Well, maybe a little nudge at the memory of that persona—and how it had facilitated their meeting and courtship—was a useful approach, a means to rekindle some of the personal intimacy they so desperately needed to bridge this gap now.

"So, where's me Ruari?" She put a hint of sass into her broad and burlesqued Geordie accent.

Sandro shrugged.

She kept herself from blinking in surprise and persisted. "What? All I get is a shrug when I'm wantin' a buss? Come now, where's that great oaf of a Highlander?"

Sandro didn't look at her. "Dead, I guess."

Jennifer let herself sink into the chair across from his and felt some desperate hope sag within her; she suddenly felt more alone among humans than she had for months amongst the Arduans. All she knew was that she needed Sandro—to talk to, to hold—now more than ever. "Sandro," she whispered, "please tell me what's wrong. How are you?"

Then he looked at her and smiled—and he was absolutely not there. The expression could not have been more artificial had it been painted on a mask. "I'm fine, Jennifer. How are you?"

Hurt by an acknowledgment so impersonal that it was infinitely more painful than a complete silence, Jennifer fired an arch reply. "Well, I was better before you came in with that plastic smile. And before I woke up without my baby. Where is Zander, Sandro?"

She had hoped he'd act surprised, outraged, grief-stricken: something that would indicate he hadn't known this was coming, or that it tore him up inside. But instead, Sandro just looked away. "He's someplace safe, Jen."

"Someplace safe? You won't even tell me where he is?"

"Jen, I don't know where he is—not exactly."

"And why the hell not?"

He turned to look at her. "Because what you—and the rest of the hostages—have been revealing about mental contact with the Baldies means we don't really know the limits of their powers. Maybe they can read our minds through yours—and maybe you wouldn't even know it. Maybe they can locate us through minds they know—maybe even little Alexander's, who'd be too young to know to resist them."

Jen leaned back and laughed. "Sandro, this is nonsense. Pure bullshit and nonsense. None of what you've said has anything to do with how *selnarm* works, or how the Arduans use it."

"Maybe, but how do *we* know that?"

"You know that because—because I've told you so."

Sandro kept looking at her.

And that's when she understood. "Oh, so that's it? Now it's presumed I'm on *their* side?"

"Not just you, Jen. All the artists. You've got to see it from our side. We just don't know if—"

"No; you—all of you—have to see it from *my* side. I was in captivity. I had a baby . . . with aliens all around me. I saw humans twice—*twice*—during the whole time I was there. And the Arduans were good to me, even kind, once they started understanding us humans a little more. Oh, Sandro, you have no idea how much they don't understand us—and we them. That is why it is so important for us to—"

But Sandro had risen. "Jen, look. We are so in the dark about the Baldies' mental powers that I can't even be sure, when my feelings or opinions start to shift, that it's me—my own mind and heart—that is changing. How do we know it isn't some mind trick they're exerting through you? So when I start feeling sympathy toward you, or being convinced that maybe I should consider your claims, how do I know—*know*—that I'm not being tricked by them?"

"Meaning that you think I've become their agent? That I *am* a traitor?"

"Jen, how could we determine that, either? What we have learned is that they have a method of communication that simply leapfrogs everything we know. The only people who have any details about its operation are the same ones the Baldies have had in captivity for months. So how do we know they haven't brainwashed you? You might believe that everything you tell us about them is true because they *programmed* you that way. If that's the case, what happens to us if we start believing the intel you've brought us on the nature and limits of what you call *selnarm* and telempathy? We'd be believing what the Baldies *want* us to believe—which means they'd probably be setting us up to walk right into a trap, or to make plans based on critically flawed information. Jennifer, we've got no means of independent verification, of determining the truth of what you and the other artists are telling us. And until we do—I'm sorry." And with that, he rose and started toward the door.

Jennifer was too surprised, enraged, terrified, and hurt to cry or do anything other than scream at his retreating back. "My baby! God damn it, you can at least bring me my baby, you fucking bastards!"

Sandro stopped: he did not turn around. "I told them that removing Zander was extreme. I'll make them return him—soon."

"Well, thank you so much, lover," she spat at his back. And then collapsed into the chair, sobbing.

Sandro closed the door so quietly she did not hear him leave.

Sandro turned the corner that led away from the observation rooms—and almost ran into Heide, with Harry Li in tow.

Heide stopped and looked up at him. "I'm sure that was difficult, Sergeant. Or should I say"—and he proffered a black box—"Lieutenant?"

So, the Hider had promoted him. "I don't need—don't want—these."

"You may not, but this is wartime, McGee, and you do not have the luxury of refusing. We all have a job to do, and you did yours flawlessly."

Heide thrust the box into McGee's hands, who reached it back toward his CO. The Hider did not make a motion to take it back; McGee let it slip from his hands and hit the floor. "A flawless operation doesn't come back with two casualties, Captain."

"McGee, you know better than I that we were expecting thirty- to fifty-percent casualties, best-case estimates. There was a reasonable chance that you'd all be lost. Instead, you acquired the objective, disrupted their counterintelligence operations by reclaiming the artists, inflicted no small number of casualties, and—if the survivors are to be believed—uncovered evidence of dissension within the enemy ranks. All in exchange for two personnel. That, Lieutenant, is—by any standard—quite a bargain."

A bargain. "Yeah, I'm sure Simonson and Chakrabarti would be gratified to know that because they were willing to get blown to bits, we got to go shopping for some real great deals at Baldy-mart."

Harry's voice was soft; for once, not a hint of teasing or irony was in it. "C'mon, Tank. You know they wouldn't blame you. We all know the rules of this game, this uniform. We put ourselves at risk to move the fight forward."

"Except they didn't have to die, Harry. If I had pulled them back the first second I knew there was any possibility of new trouble, if I hadn't stopped to—" And McGee could not go further: his jaw muscles bunched and his teeth ground. He started to walk away.

"You mean because you stopped to kiss Ms. Peitchkov?" finished Heide with inhuman smoothness. "Understandable, that. You are, after all, only human. Besides, that may not have been your doing, McGee."

"What?"

"McGee, watch your tone—and a little more decorum please, now that you are an officer again. As I was saying, your succumbing to the urge to kiss your girlfriend may have been an example of enemy mind-manipulation. Using her as a 'transmitter,' so to speak, they may have seen this as a way to try to delay you further, so that their response teams could catch up with you. She was quite possibly their geisha-marionette."

McGee turned to face Heide directly, his immense fists in knots on either side of his body. "Go ahead, Heide. Say that just one more ti—"

And Harry was around and between them. "Captain Heide, I think this may be a little too hard for Tank to hear. The news that his girlfriend might be an enemy asset—willingly or unwillingly—is very disturbing to him. He's likely to get . . . er, emotional."

The Hider seemed completely unaware that his continued existence had been anything but certain for the past ten seconds. "Very well. But McGee, be warned. I will not stand for any more insolence. You will address me by my rank, or I will throw you in the brig, regardless of your recent record. Now, get some rest. Dismissed."

"On one condition. Put my son back with his mother."

"McGee, this is not wise. We need some separation between the two in order to assess if there is any linkage we are missing, which could be a control mechanism that the Baldies—"

"Captain, you don't even know what to look for. Meanwhile, with every passing minute, you make Jennifer more hostile and intractable. And if it's determined that she is *not* under Baldy influence, then you'll want her to be happy and cooperative when it comes time for her to be fully debriefed on Baldy procedures, communication, et cetera. She's an intel gold mine—but if you withhold her baby, that gold mine will have collapsed and you'll have no chance of digging it open again. Trust me—I know."

Heide considered Tank's weary but earnest face and nodded. "As you suggest, then. Go to bed, McGee."

Tank turned without saluting; slump-shouldered, he headed toward his bunk.

Heide crooked a finger behind him. "Li?"

Harry came closer, not enjoying the proximity. "Yes, sir?"

"Pass these orders to the security-oversight team. The infant is to be restored to his mother. But she is to be watched carefully. And so is he. Be ready to intervene with the child at a moment's notice."

"Why? Are you concerned that Jennifer might attempt to attack her own child?"

"No, I am concerned that he might attack us."

"Sir?"

"We already have plentiful evidence that the enemy has managed to alter her thoughts, has managed to get deep inside her mind. Do we know they haven't done the same to the boy?"

"But the boy is an infant, sir!"

"So what? The enemy is evidently capable of psychic manipulation, possibly communication. He might be their ears, their eyes, even their remote-weapons platform. Whatever powers they might have and be able to confer, we can only guess."

"And if the boy is doing something that the security observers think might be dangerous?"

"Then he is to be dealt with as any other captive attempting to attack us or break out."

Li laughed, not believing. "You mean, lethal force."

"I do indeed, Sergeant, I do indeed."

Li gaped after Heide's receding back.

Ankaht felt as well as saw the two pirates close in, their dual-bladed knives flashing in the dreaded Summer-Lightning pattern that was the trademark of their *zhetshotan* Renegade Brotherhood. She saw and felt herself begin the traditional parries—the same ones she had rehearsed upon waking up from her long cryogenic sleep to New Ardu, hundreds of lifetimes after the last of the *zhetshotans* had been hunted down and purged from the Inner Sea of Qez'em'frek.

But then this vivid *shaxzhutok* avatar of her earlier self moved differently than she would have. Instead of a tumbling semicartwheel away from her attackers, her ancient incarnation had feinted at a backflip that turned into a falling twist: she went sideways as the pirate blades came in, slipping between them. As she went beneath the insufficiently down-corrected sweep of their knives, she crouched low so that she remained poised on one foot only; a precarious stance, not maintainable for more than a second. But in that second, she swept her other foot into the back of one opponent's knee, even as she swiped at the other's heels with her *skeerba*. With a pair of shrill cries—Arduans had been far more vocal in the early Pre-Enlightenment—they both went down. She rolled up to her feet, all claws out and diving for the one whose legs she'd swept—

—and Ankaht fell to the mats, sweating, suddenly pushed out of her *shaxzhutok* recollection of a fighting style that had been lost from all memory and record. And understandably so; it trafficked in moves that were very risky, but very lethal if successful. The style had fallen from use as the *Destoshaz* caste became more uniformly populated by the tall, golden variety of her species. This *maatkahshak*'s prevailing strategies—of close maneuver and sudden inversions that rewarded a low center of gravity and shorter limbs—had been a useless discipline to the tall, lean, deadly physiology of the increasingly uniform *Destoshaz*. And so this fighting style had been forgotten, lost in a history that was becoming all the more dim, given the small number of *shaxzhu* awake to impart it and the disinterest of the majority *Destoshaz*.

But it had not been the strangeness, and yet odd suitability, of the forgotten *maatkahshak* that had ejected her from immersion in the *shaxzhutok*, but the repetitive persistence of her last full memory of Ipshef and Orthezh. For some reason, it intruded itself with greater frequency the closer she came to this afternoon's meeting with the Council of Twenty—the first since the chaotic incidents of last week. The fact that she did not choose to linger upon the memory, but that it was nonetheless increasing in frequency as she came closer to the meeting, suggested that it was telling her something, was guiding her to a true and powerful *sulhaji* that she had either not yet seen—or did not want to see.

And, as she lay panting in the circle of her private *maatkah* ring—the only place she ever practiced old, forgotten moves that she had reclaimed from past memories—the sweet yet horrible memory washed over her again—

—Ankaht had returned unannounced to the primary observation laboratories, retrieving some human books out of a storage closet. She intended to have Jennifer explain the puzzling concerns of human thinkers such as Erasmus, Nietzsche, Kierkegaard, *'kaiKri* Augustine, Emerson . . .

Ipshef and Orthezh, thinking themselves alone, were slightly indiscreet in that they had simply retracted the field of their *selnarm* rather than making it direct and exclusive—which had the side effect of making it less emotionally rich and expressive. Therefore, to limit the radius of a *selnarm* field, rather than create a tight pipeline, was the traditional choice of lovers, and so Ankaht had sensed their exchange as they prepared to resume their tasks with the humans.

"I am but *Ixturshaz*. Why would you want to have anything to do with me, anyway?" Orthezh wondered.

"Beloved," Ipshef almost purred through her link, "do you not see that here, on New Ardu, the caste of one's origin is of no import to our choice of life-partners? Indeed, in most regards, castes have ceased to matter."

(Irony.) "Unless you are *Destoshaz*."

Ipshef, who was *Selnarshaz*, thought, "Better to be nothing. Better even not to be *shaxzhu*."

Orthezh was surprised. "But *shaxzhu* are our memories, are our culture, are the fingers that touch the mind of Illudor himself. They are—"

"They are not safe to associate with. Not anymore."

"But that is nonsense."

"Not to many of the *Destoshaz*. They want to fight a war to the last claw and grinder with the humans. The *shaxzhu*—such as Elder Ankaht—want to ask if it is necessary. But the *Destoshaz* are stronger—*much* stronger. Even stronger than her. Who do you think will win?"

"Who will *win*? Ipshef, we are all the Children of Illudor. We are linked in our *narmata*—"

"Are we?"

Orthezh, who was usually the dominant and outspoken of the two, stopped, too stunned to respond. "What do you mean? Of course we are of one *narmata*."

(Sadness, dispassion, negation.) "Then what do you make of the *Destoshaz* who claim that the *shaxzhu* no longer touch the mind of Illudor? That their interest—or obsession—with understanding the humans indicates that they are putting the defense and survival of all the Children at risk? That, therefore, their *selnarm*, their *narmata*, is no longer that of the Children, but of their own collective perversity? And that therefore, our race's *narmata* is no longer uniform and ubiquitous? Are not the *Destoshaz* at least right when they say that the unity of our *selnarm* has been compromised?"

"Perhaps, but it wasn't the *shaxzhu* who've disrupted it!"

"I didn't say it was. But if we put aside blame for a second, are they not right in at least this much: that our *selnarm* is truly ruptured? Are we not at a greater distance from each other than ever before?"

Orthezh was still for a long moment. "Yes. There is so much filtering, withholding. But that is because of *Destoshaz* censorship, accusation—"

"Feel this well, cherished Orthezh. You may share that opinion with me. But it is no longer safe to share it with others."

"But—"

(Urgency. Love. Insistence.) "It is *not* safe to share with others. Do you understand, dear one?"

(Bewilderment, appreciation, fugue.) "I . . . understand, beloved Ipshef."

"Good. Now let us return to our tasks."

But they had never returned to their tasks. Ankaht had, only minutes later, returned to urge them to flee, and they had died, defending their love for each other—which was gone now. And they had also died defending their subjects: intelligent *zheteksh*, human artists who never had any chance to understand or avoid the Death-Vowed assassins that had been sent to eliminate them.

Indeed, they had been sent to eliminate the entirety of Ankaht's human-research cluster. Ankaht had thought nothing, no threat or perfidy, could have aroused a greater passion from the center of her soul. The treachery—in both its scope and intent—was monstrous. But one thing had proven to be even more ghastly and paralyzing than that treachery.

In defending Jennifer's life—and that of her infant—Ankaht had accepted a responsibility more onerous and horrifying than she had ever known before. For Ankaht to contemplate her own death merely stimulated misgivings for the social tragedy that might follow: without her work, this war would continue, possibly disastrously, and thus the path whereby Illudor and his Children would persevere was difficult to imagine. But to protect Jennifer had filled Ankaht with a desperate, primal terror, because if Ankaht had failed—failed her *friend*—that friend would not be reborn. When the being that was Jennifer Peitchkov was gone, there was no consolation of knowing that one day she would return: instead, she would plunge straight into the screaming chaos of *xenzhet-narmat'ai*, utterly and eternally irretrievable. And her infant . . .

Ankaht discovered she was shedding tears—for humans and Arduans shared that physiological anomaly—and watched them spatter down upon the fresh scabs creasing her arm. Jennifer had put her improbably finite existence on the line to save Ankaht, whereas Ankaht had placed one of her infinite lives on the line for Jennifer. In retrospect, the human's gift was so much greater than Ankaht's that they hardly warranted comparison. But both had risked discarnation at the hands of their own species to save the other. Lasting friendships—and alliances—had been built on far less than that.

The door's *selnarm* repeater pulsed. "Yes?" Temret, her most junior researcher, entered. He was armed. "Yes, Temret?"

"Most revered Elder, it is time for the Council."

"Very well." She rose. "You are armed."

"I stand ready to guard my Cluster-Commander and our greatest Sleeper, Elder Ankaht."

She sent (appreciation, ease). "I have no need of a bodyguard, Temret."

But Temret, a most intellectually gifted *Destoshaz* who had not found an easy role within her cluster, was (resolute). "With respect, Elder, you need a friend—a friend who is armed and willing to discarnate and be discarnated many times over to ensure your safety."

Ankaht felt her amusement ebb and she sent (accord). "Perhaps you are right, my young Temret." And, leaving the chamber, she thought, *perhaps you are very right indeed.*

Torhok rose as Ankaht entered. "Ah, greetings, Elder. We trust you are recovering from your injuries?"

Ankaht did not seat herself. "Injuries, Senior Admiral, are what one might sustain in an accident. I am recovering from wounds inflicted during an assassination attempt."

"So you have said."

"And upon which I will say more, when you have finished your presentation."

The cool reserve of her *selnarm* sent a ripple of alarm through the room: among her supporters and the moderates, this was not the gentle Ankaht they had come to know and cherish.

If Torhok noticed any of this mood change, he gave no indication of it. "So, to conclude, the losses inflicted by the *griarfeksh* were light. But it must be concluded that we were very fortunate. As I have outlined for you, their method of infiltration exploited our lack of knowledge of their systems. I am pleased to say that we have just recently initiated a dedicated military-intelligence unit, led by Group Commander and First Prime Mretlak, formerly fleet second under Narrok. We expect great things from that new analytical resource."

But Ankaht felt the subtle disjuncture between the enthusiastic words and the disinterested support. *Of course, Torhok will be just as happy if the military-intelligence cluster doesn't produce any useful results, because then we have only one choice: widespread suppression of the humans.*

"In the meantime," Torhok continued, "I have instructed the security-advisory cluster to cut all public services for Melantho. This will give the *griarfeksh* too many domestic worries to consider further offensive operations against us. It also provides an example to the other, larger cities of the planet, since we have issued an edict indicating that the same suspension of services will befall any city in which an act of rebellion occurs. Since we presume that the humans would attempt to employ what they call 'plausibly deniable' disasters against us, we have further announced that we are not concerned with evidence or protestations or explanations. So if an event affects us adversely on this planet, we will employ the same shutdown of all services in the human cities of the stricken area."

Amunherh'peshef's eyes widened. "So the humans are to be blamed for the damages inflicted by hurricanes and floods, as well?"

"Unless we can concretely assert, based on our own researches, that the *griarfeksh* had no conceivable means to generate such disasters, yes, they will be held accountable."

"This is madness."

"This is what their own perfidy has wrought. They attacked us even while setting fires that drew our emergency vehicles to the depopulated zone. They used our most charitable impulses to distract us from the treacherous strike they were launching. There were many among the security-advisory cluster who recommended a wholesale elimination of the population of Melantho, but more moderate voices—such as my own—prevailed."

Oh, you source of boundless mercy, though Ankaht. Aloud: "So, now we are considering genocide as an appropriate means of reprisal."

"Not all of us, Elder. Clearly not you. But we would hardly expect otherwise, given your research cluster's role in all this."

Ah, here we go. "And what role is that, Senior Admiral?"

"I wish we knew, Elder. Perhaps you could enlighten us yourself."

"I would—if I had the faintest notion of what you are referring to."

"I am referring to the many indications that your so-called human-research cluster has produced only one significant result thus far—it provided the one possible pathway for a *griarfeksh* strike team to bypass our precautions and strike into the very heart of Punt."

"You say that as though you suspect that my cluster was somehow in collusion with the attacking humans, Senior Admiral."

"Well, was it?" Torhok's *selnarm* rippled with chilling (pleasantness).

"Of course it was!" roared Urkhot, as fiercely as a double-fanged *yihrt* suddenly released from its mating-season restraint pen. "She—the *shaxzhu*—has gone over to the *griarfeksh*. She is all but one of them. She is a traitor—a traitor!"

"Is that why you sent eight Anointed Death-Vowed—and sixteen lesser Unanointeds—to kill not only me, but all of my staff and all of the humans in our laboratories, esteemed *Holodah'kri*?"

No one had ever heard Ankaht use such vitriolic sarcasm before, nor accuse a Council member of conspiracy to commit murder or of abusing the privileges of not just one, but two offices: priest and councilor. The Council sat still, dumbstruck; eight of the twenty *befthelled,* all their eyes shut against the shock.

Urkhot had risen, but his *selnarm* had closed down. Ankaht doubted he would come after her here, in the Council chambers, but events and accusations had taken such a dire turn that she started a quick calculation of how many of those gathered might support her—physically—if *skeerba* were drawn.

Amunherh'peshef's deep, layered *selnarm* descended on all the others, quashing them all beneath its bulk. "Last week's events were most peculiar indeed," he soothed. "However, accusations of treachery or murder will do us no good—certainly not before we have more facts before us. Senior Admiral, you have given us a most comprehensive assessment of the human plan of attack. I am less convinced that it was only made possible by inside help. It is significant that the humans constrained their attacks to areas that they had great familiarity with—which, indeed, they themselves had built and maintained for centuries. Their ability to swiftly locate the human subjects is not mysterious but plainly manifest in the historical record: the midwives and the infant-physician had adequate knowledge of the research cluster's facility to report the necessary information to the human Resistance. And their choice of targets was logical: they wished to rescue their own kind."

"There may have been yet another motivation, Esteemed Amunherh'peshef," added Ankaht.

"And what is that?"

"I have had an opportunity to look at the records of the events made by our security and recording devices at the site of the attack. The leader of the humans is the mate of Jennifer Peitchkov."

"How do you know this?"

"Because at the outset of our researches, we had to confirm his survival—and therefore, his identity—to secure her compliance. And because she has shown me his image in her mind."

"So you say," Torhok dismissed airily.

"So I can show you." Ankaht boomed out the assertion through her *selnarm.* And in its wake, she gave them Jennifer—not all of Jennifer—but enough of what she had learned of the human so that the *selnarmic* nature of the facilitating link between them was beyond question.

Again, the Council sat in profound stillness. Urkhot made a disgusted sound not unlike an episode of indigestion.

"If you have achieved so much," wondered Amunherh'peshef, "why did you not share it earlier, Elder Ankaht?"

"With respect, honored First Councilor, you may recall that I tried to present my findings at an earlier Council meeting. That was declined by a slim majority of this body"—she stared around the table—"whose objection was that their caste-leader, Senior Admiral Torhok, should be present to inquire about, and possibly vote upon, any matters pertaining to such momentous evidence. Senior Admiral Torhok was returning from his visit to Admiral Narrok in the Ajax system, if I am not mistaken."

"You are quite right. Please continue."

"The next meeting was to have been last week—but five hours before it was to be convened, the two attacks began. So, with respect, honored First Councilor, I did try to present these results earlier, but fate decreed otherwise—possibly aided by those who do not want us to further consider the issue of human intelligence."

Amunherh'peshef raised and lowered two tentacle tips. "Yes, I remember thinking how unusual the timing was. Now, Torhok, I wonder if you could explain your reason for accusing Ankaht of treachery."

"With respect, esteemed Amunherh'peshef, I did not make that accusation. That was—"

"*Holodah'kri* Urkhot, yes—but you baited the hook, asked the Elder Ankaht if she or her cluster had abetted the humans, and while you set it in the guise of a facetious jest, there was purpose in it, as well. So I will hear this from you, Torhok. Why do you suspect the *shaxzhu* Elder of treason?"

Ankaht could feel Torhok tighten: he had not thought he would be pinned down on this, but rather that he would be able to redirect the inquiry to the ever-intemperate Urkhot. Amunherh'peshef was shrewd, but if he wasn't careful, Ankaht wondered if he might also be visited by a cohort of Death-Vowed.

But Torhok was not easily rattled and turned the moment to his own advantage. "Since the Eldest of the Council asks, I have no choice but to share my full mind on this matter, with no implication of having contemplated or undertaken actions which would follow from these thoughts."

Amunherh'peshef closed his eyes slowly and accepted the ancient rite of legal immunity from suspicion simply based on a revelation of one's deepest passion and motivations. Which meant that Torhok had maneuvered himself to get a pulpit from which he could say anything without fear of retribution or accusation. Shrewd indeed. Had this been his objective all along?

The senior admiral stood. "From before we entered this system, Elder Ankaht has shown marked sympathies for the *griarfeksh*. The numerous times, reasons, and methods she sought to limit, constrain, or end my war against them is on the record. There are no less than thirty such interferences with Council-decreed military policy or initiatives. She also sought—and was granted—Council approval to research the *griarfeksh*. What has she produced? A 'vocoder'—a talking box which converts their subcognitive screechings into sensible speech. Or so we are told."

"She has been trying to present it to us for analysis, Senior Admiral."

"Nonetheless, we have no evidence in hand. And I must point out that those claims are not only highly suspect, but quite frankly heretical. She tells us that there are intelligences in this universe which have no knowledge of Illudor. These intelligences also lack *selnarm*, or any hint of *shaxzhutok*. Yet they are sentient, we are told. I find it nothing less than astounding that Elder Ankaht sees fit to not only be a voting member of this Council, but also to revise holy writ autonomously. These definitions of soul and selfhood—knowledge of Illudor, *selnarm*, and *shaxzhutok*—are not folklore, not conjectures. They are oft-proven theological and cosmological facts that have been the bedrock of our race for dozens of millennia.

"And let us not overlook her behavior during the *griarfeksh* attack, which we have by her own report. She abandoned the research workers of her own cluster to the savage attacks of the human warriors, only to protect one *griarfeksh* female from harm. And that *griarfeksh* female is the one who is mated to the human war captain who led the infiltration of our city and the slaughter of our brothers and sisters. These events make Elder Ankaht's motivations clear: she promised the *griarfeksh* that she would liberate the female artist into the custody of her mate. She has sold her birthright in this race for a passing alliance with the patch-furred murderers indigenous to this world."

The Council chamber was utterly without sending; no one dared express anything lest a deluge be released.

Ankaht stood slowly. "Your lies mark you as an orphan from Illudor's love and estranged from his face."

Several of the Councilors gasped and looked nervously at Torhok. Ankaht knew they were wondering if he would now challenge her, given the depth and severity of so public a rebuke. Only by calling him a *zheteksh* could she have made the insult any worse.

But she had decided upon almost as severe an approach. "I call Torhok a liar before all gathered here and insist that he refute what now I call to your attention." Now it was her turn to play an ancient legal card, since refuting any challenge to a Councilor's veracity was also an activity that was free of constraints. "Torhok's first lie is that he characterized my actions of last week thusly: 'She abandoned the research workers of her own cluster to the savage attacks of the human warriors.' Ah, but it was not the humans who killed—or even attacked—them. We found only two pair of our workers dead of wounds inflicted by the human weapons. In both cases, the implicit combat scenarios involved surprise, not intent."

"But you cannot prove that."

"Oh, but I can. Firstly, there is the after-action forensics report of the event."

Torhok almost preened. "You can hardly reference a document that does not exist. As I informed the Council earlier this week, a computer failure—ultimately a residual glitch caused by one of the human rockets' aftereffects—blanked that report out in its entirety."

"Yes, so you did inform us. Most unfortunate. However, with esteemed Amunherh'peshef's permission, I took the precaution of requesting that another, contemporaneous analysis of the attack be conducted."

"By your researchers, Elder Ankaht?" His sneering contempt for non-*Destoshaz* methods was palpable.

"No, Senior Admiral. I requested the military-intelligence group—and Group Commander Mretlak—to conduct an independent analysis. After all, they are trying to learn how the enemy operates, and the aftermath of the human attack at our facility was an extraordinary research opportunity. While the focus of his investigation was not predominantly forensic, happily his methods and sampling were similar enough that he was able to compile a separate post-action report."

Torhok's *selnarm* shut fast, and his color went from gold to a glowing, jaundiced yellow. Ankaht wondered: Would the challenge come now? She continued.

"Mretlak discovered the following: that it was the

Death-Vowed who slew all but four of my researchers. This was not something Torhok's forensic report could have missed. The wounds were all inflicted by *skeerba* and claw, and many of the death strikes were ritual—and derogatory—in nature. Even if the humans had wished to imitate our general weapons, they would have no way of knowing these death strikes and their meaning.

"Mretlak also determined that the humans could have shot many, many more of my support staff when the first wave of workers fled the building initially. Only two were killed, at which point the lead human—Jennifer Peitchkov's mate—evidently gave an order that prevented an attack upon the rest. The humans *were* responsible for killing one group of Arduans, however."

"Oh, which?"

"The Death-Vowed. They killed almost all of them."

"And the others?"

"I killed. In self-defense. It is also worth noting that when the humans—again led by Jennifer Peitchkov's mate—found two of my researchers and six humans hiding in a secret room in the library complex, the human called Alessandro McGee restrained his men from killing the two Arduans, compelling them to be bound instead. An interesting behavior for a race that—since the attacks—Torhok and Urkhot have been publicly and loudly decrying as 'irreclaimable savages that show no sign of mercy, quarter, or intelligence.' But my researchers did forward our ongoing reports of the humans' true natures to Torhok's staff investigators—"

"Reports which were never received."

"No, Senior Admiral. They were registered as delivered by the special trace I had put on them. This trace indicated that each one was delivered, read, and erased. All within the same five-minute interval. So your most recent claim is yet another lie, Torhok. Now: rebut or recant. It is my right to hear—this instant—which you will do."

The eyes in the room turned upon Torhok. "If you are saying I sent the Death-Vowed, I deny it," he jetted out through his *selnarm*.

Amunherh'peshef brushed that indignant outburst away. "You have not been asked about the Death-Vowed, Torhok. And although I doubt you recruited them yourself, I suspect you were anything but surprised by their appearance. However—for now—our interest is restricted to hearing your response to what the Elder *shaxzhu* has lawfully requested regarding your accusations of her treason and disloyalty. Rebut or recant."

It looked, for a moment, as though Torhok's skin was going to rupture, explode into a fuming, acidic yellow spray. But then he said—in *selnarm* and aloud, as the ancient custom required—"I recant."

Amunherh'peshef tipped two tentacles aloft for a brief second. "Interesting."

Ankaht could feel the suppressed rage of the slight *Destoshaz* majority simmering higher: a little more irritation and a *coup d'etat* was not out of the question.

Amunherh'peshef continued, apparently unruffled. "For now, I believe this business is concluded. We have a functional forensics report. We have cleared Ankaht of charges of treason. Torhok has recanted. If any wish to advance similar charges or others against Ankaht, based on the evidence Torhok claimed, you must do so now." No response. "Then all questions pertaining to the relevant actions of Elder Ankaht are prohibited as the basis of, or precedent for, further charges or inquiries. Councilor Torhok, having lied and recanted, your vote is held null in this Council for a minimum of three months, the full period of which will be determined by this body at its next convocation. An investigation will be launched into the origins and mission of the Death-Vowed."

Urkhot spread his beneficent *selnarm* out like a tablecloth. "I will pursue this inquiry with a vigor unlike any—"

"*Holodah'kri*, your zeal is noted. But since Death-Vows are, properly, religious in nature, we must exclude you and all other *'kri* from the investigatory board. And insofar as Admiral Torhok may or may not have knowingly and therefore perjuriously concealed the fact that the Death-Vowed, not the humans, were responsible for the deaths of most Arduans during the attack, I cannot have any of his personnel involved in the investigation."

"Which leaves no one to investigate, Honored Amunherh'peshef," observed Councilor Felnarmaht.

"Perhaps so. But I see a different solution. Senior Admiral Torhok, rather than order this, I will give you the opportunity to volunteer an accommodation to the Council as a matter of good faith. Will you consider a request from the Council that you release the military-intelligence group from your authority and place it at the sole service of, and reporting only to, the Council of Twenty, until such time as we deem it suitable to be returned to direct military authority?"

Torhok's *selnarm* opened up a crack; Ankaht sensed the senior admiral's relief at having been given such an inexpensive means to reinstate his good opinion in the Council. "Of course, Esteemed Amunherh'peshef."

"Excellent. I shall inform Mretlak myself."

And I shall dance for joy when I am alone in my

misting chambers, thought Ankaht as she maintained a thoroughly aloof and detached exterior, *both for having Mretlak in a position where we might work together more closely, and also for getting out of this meeting alive.* She hadn't been sure whether she wanted Torhok to challenge her or not, but now that the heat of the moment was passed, and she reassessed his size and thews, she was glad that the moment had indeed passed.

That night, alone in her room, preparing for sleep, Ankaht tried one last time to stretch out her *selnarm*—beyond Punt, beyond Melantho, beyond the entirety of the continent of Icarus—reaching, probing, grasping to find the smallest tendril of what might be Jennifer's mind. But no: her human equivalent of *selnarm* was too different to be detectable at greater ranges. In the days after the attack, Ankaht had requested a sled to fly in wide circles around the region, searching, searching. There had been a few indistinct readings here and there; none seemed likely to be her, and there were too many of these faint signs to check individually. Besides, having the admirable caution and canniness which their long experience with insurgencies had taught them, the humans would surely have anticipated such sweeps and—if Jennifer was still alive—would have moved her to a more distant locale.

Of course, even if—against all odds—she had survived the escape, Jennifer might not be having a very easy time of it. Her fellow humans had seen her save one of the leaders of the perfidious "Baldies"—at the risk of her own life. *Jennifer, Jennifer,* she thought, *becoming half-sisters has not made our respective peoples very happy with us.*

✧ ✧ ✧

The ride up to High City had been almost entirely without a single ripple in the *selnarm* that existed between Urkhot and Torhok.

As their shuttle sped away from the sun over New Ardu's terminator, Urkhot sent out a tired surge. "This was unfortunate. Disastrous, even."

"The meeting?"

"That, too—but more what Ankaht revealed to us. She actually did touch the mind of that *zheteksh griarfeksh*. And, even worse, it does seem intelligent."

(Wry.) "Are you becoming a heretic in your own temple, *Holodah'kri*?"

(Impatient.) "Of course not. But the appearance of this seeming intelligence will confuse too many of our soft-hearted—and soft-headed—Star Wanderers. And we cannot afford that confusion . . . not when we are in the middle of a war where the outcome remains uncertain. And now Mretlak is being put at her disposal—"

(Dismissal.) "Do not concern yourself there, *Holodah'kri.* Mretlak is but a little fish in all these waves and troughs. Just yesterday he sent another request for a meeting, even though he had 'nothing momentous' to report. He is a functionary, over his head, and I do not think the Council will know how to use him—but nor will they make a gift of him to Ankaht. So he is too small a variable for us to include in our calculations."

"Very well. I had been worried that, with his special access to restricted human materials, he might perhaps be facilitating and accelerating the speed with which Ankaht is able to disseminate a more sympathetic cultural understanding of the *griarfeksh*."

Torhok offered (disinterest) and replied, "There is

no evidence that Mretlak has been any kind of information conduit for Ankaht up to this point. But either way, that situation has slipped too far beyond control for us to worry ourselves over such minutiae. What is more ominous is that Ankaht's researchers have started going into the human community—with help from the humans she still has. Together, they are getting access to books from public libraries, universities, even schools for the very young."

Urkhot twitched his major tentacles on both clusters. "Can we not control these sources of... disinformation?"

Torhok grunted and signaled (flat negation, futility, resignation). "Out of the question. There are too many of these book repositories, dispersed all over the planet. And this does not take private collections into account. Amongst these humans, the distribution of key documents, histories, and information is almost as wide and diverse as the population itself."

Urkhot mused darkly. "So if we cannot stop the speed with which this sewage of lies and disinformation is rising..."

Torhok sent (conviction). "Then we must cut the pipeline that has brought this pollution into our community. It started harmlessly enough—just a trickle around our ankles. But now it is gushing in, up to our necks, and threatens to drown us all. In short, brother *'kri*, I think I must now take a direct hand in stopping it once and for all, and, along with you, sever this polluting pipeline—before any more treasonous poison can come gushing out of it."

Urkhot was suddenly (troubled). "Senior Admiral. The Death-Vowed were volunteers. True, they had long ago given me their hearts, and so it was easy to get their ears and convince them that their deed would be for the good of our race. But I remained out of the planning. Carefully and completely out of the planning. In contrast, what you are talking about now is, is—"

"Execution."

"No. It is premeditated murder."

"Murder is what civilians do, *Holodah'kri*. We are all soldiers fighting a war. And we have an enemy—a traitor—in our midst. When you kill under those circumstances, it is not murder. It is execution."

Urkhot wrung his clusters together. "What would the Council say if they knew?"

"I do not know. But in the years to come, subsequent Councils will say only one thing."

"What is that?"

"They will thank us for taking action when others were too timid—for being the saviors of our race."

"Do you think they'll say this of us? Really?"

Torhok carefully concealed his contempt for the priest. "Certainly. Particularly of you. Now let me nap."

16

Presuppositions Perturbed

Injury, violation, exploitation, annihilation,
cannot be wrong in themselves, for life
essentially presupposes injury, violation,
exploitation, and annihilation.
—Nietzsche

Arduan SDH Shem'pter'ai, *Main Van, Expeditionary Fleet of the* Anaht'doh Kainat, *Treadway System*

Narrok flicked a *selnarm* tendril toward his sensor prime as they came within ten light-seconds of the Treadway system's Desai limit. "Any sign of human craft?"

"None, Admiral Narrok. We have apparently—" And then the prime's *selnarm* emission became momentarily sublexical: (hold, change, data) he pulsed in a sequence so fast that it was almost one thought.

Three *murn*-colored icons flashed into existence in the holotank at the same instant that the prime identified them. "Three human vessels, sir. All light cruisers. On a high-speed intercept course."

Narrok paused: that he had not expected. He double-checked the plot: no planets nearby, no emissions that suggested a new human cloaking technology concealing a flotilla. He had had his fighters scour the light-hour of space surrounding the warp point that was his route of withdrawal back into the Mercury system relentlessly. No, there was no chance that this was some kind of ruse, that another human force was nearby. Indeed, it was more or less a certainty that no significant enemy formations had survived to flee this far on the warp-line that extended "northward" from Bellerophon. It was just three human cruisers heading directly for his immense fleet at their best speed. They could not reasonably hope to ram his vessels or get close enough to explode a widely destructive warhead akin to that which the humans deployed in their AMBAMMs. Therefore, this suicidal rush by three light ships made no sense.

But Narrok's course of action—and duty—was unconfused by the perplexing behavior of the human craft. "Targeting solutions?"

"Calculated and locked, sir."

"Range?"

"Forty-eight light-seconds and closing."

"SDHs *Memref*, *Tumpep'f*, *Herres* forward to engage. Fleet signal: maintain best uniform speed."

"Yes, Admi—the humans are reversing course, sir!"

And so they were . . . in a manner of speaking. The three *murn* icons had come to a complete halt. Then they started moving again, but now they were veering off in three radically different directions, mostly aiming themselves directly up out of the system's ecliptic plane.

Odd, thought Narrok. But obeying his general orders and taking advantage of an easy kill had priority over—and compelled him to put aside—the faint curiosity aroused by what the unprecedented human scattering might portend. In the tacplot, this three fastest SDHs were closing on the light cruisers.

"Lock confirmed. Missile launch," his operations prime signaled.

Somewhere out in space, too far ahead for it to be detected with the unaided eye, the bows of Narrok's three pursuing SDHs had sent forth a rippling sheet of flame that quickly resolved into a dense spread of missiles. The human ships weaved slowly in the tacplot. Another, more faint *murn*-colored icon appeared briefly, then flickered away: a sensor ghost generated by a human ship's image-making ECM package. None of the Arduan missiles were distracted from their target icons.

Ten seconds later, those target icons faded, changed to a dark *crivan* color, and were then blanked from the holoplot. "Enemy vessels destroyed," affirmed Narrok's tactical prime.

But Narrok kept staring at the plot. The tactical prime's *selnarm* touched his deferentially. "Admiral, you seem—distracted."

"I am, Prime. Tell me. What do you think those human ships were trying to do?"

The Prime groomed his *selnarm* and responded carefully. "One cannot always ascribe reason to the actions of *griarfeksh*, Admiral Narrok. For they are not true thinking beings, after all."

Narrok gave no response. It would take time, even in his own fleet, to wean his crews away from such propaganda. Instead, he poked a lesser tentacle at the glimmering silver-white hoop from which his own fleet had lately emerged. "They were going there, Tactical. To the Mercury warp point. Without question."

"With respect, sir, they were headed straight toward us."

"Were they? Look at their course trajectory: straight out of the inner system to the warp point. Not the smallest bit of deviation. We just happened to lie right along that line."

The tactical prime looked again and, as if throwing off a cloak of orthodoxy, seemed to see the plot anew. "Yes," he affirmed after a few seconds, "and our sensors clearly detected them before they detected us—which was why they seemed at first to be on an intercept course but then suddenly pulled away, as if they were surprised by our presence."

"Yes, they pulled sharply away from us—but not *directly* away from us." Narrok looked at the three vermillion icons of his returning SDHs, watched them reapproach the system's ecliptic. "The human cruisers could have turned 180 degrees, possibly made us chase them all the way across the system to one of the other warp points. But rather than choose the most promising escape option, they angled up out of the ecliptic."

The tactical prime (agreed, wondered). "Why would they do such a thing, Admiral?"

Narrok looked back toward the inner system and understood. "Because however much they feared us, they feared something coming from the other direction even more." He opened his *selnarm* wide. "Operations Prime, the van of the Fleet is to deploy for broad engagement. Assign twenty SDHs—with the latest generation cloaking systems—to follow us at a range of twenty light-seconds as our hidden rearguard. As soon as our lead elements cross the Desai limit, fighter patrols are to launch immediately to establish a hundred light-second picket radius. The van is on us. Helm Prime, take us directly toward the main world—flank speed."

✧ ✧ ✧

Narrok was not sure—or, more accurately, could not believe—what he was witnessing until his advance elements had drawn within thirty light-seconds of Treadway. Two small auxiliaries, modified for maximum speed and carrying cloaking systems, observed what was transpiring in the vicinity of the human world, recorded it, and sent it back to the Fleet as quick, fluttering laser pulses and *selnarm* bursts.

These were instantly decoded and integrated by the powerful computers on board the *Shem'pter'ai* and projected into the bridge's holoplot. The human world of Treadway—a mottled orb of browns, blues, and occasional green—appeared in the tank, turning slowly. In orbit around it were a large array of indigo-colored icons: ships unknown to the computer, and thus, unknown the Children of Illudor. But there was no mistaking the activity of the ships: they were bombarding several sites on the planet. There was no evidence of active opposition, or even defense.

The tactical prime edged closer, sent, "Are the *gri-arfeksh* fighting amongst themselves? Even though news of our threatening approach must have reached them, might they still—?"

But the question died before the prime could finish projecting it: a cluster of yellow spheres bloomed on the planet surface.

"Immense explosions, sir," explained the sensor prime. "I estimate their nominal yields to be—"

And then the yellow globes became black, then yellow again, then black: they pulsed their dire message out to the silent bridge.

"Illudor's tears," breathed the tactical prime. "Nuclear detonations."

"Over twenty megatons each," confirmed the sensor prime.

The mysterious ships altered their orbit slightly, leisurely—and struck again: a new crop of yellow, then black, spheres sprouted in the center of the planet's largest land mass.

Narrok swallowed; his throat was so dry he almost gagged. "What have the ships been targeting, Sensor Prime?"

The sensor prime visibly trembled before he sent his response. "No targets of military value that we can detect, Admiral. The impact points are centered on—on population centers."

Narrok stared, shocked beyond comprehension. "No shipyards or facilities of any kind?"

"No, sir. But we have intercepted this communication from one of the ground sites."

The sensor prime lifted a slow tentacle toward one of his bridge display screens. After a moment, the static resolved into a disheveled human male, his head's top-fur in disarray, his face smudged, a blasted room tilted oddly behind him. Smoke hung in the air; fires could be seen through shattered windows. The man was screaming something, and although Narrok was no expert at discriminating among the chaotic array of human facial expressions, this male was clearly desperate, fearful, pleading. Then billows of flame geysered into the room, filling it; scintillant plasma rushed in a moment later, and the flesh of the human's body seemed to be flashing away from his bones—just as the video feed flared and died.

Narrok discovered that he was rasping his grinders together so hard that it was audible. "Sensor Prime, the ships in orbit—are they *human* ships?"

"Admiral, I cannot tell if— No! Intelligence has just finished correlating the data on their drives. The tuner signatures of the unidentified ships are not consistent with human drives, nor are the shape and bias of the reactionless envelopes they generate."

"Could they be ships from one of the other human polities—the Republic or the Union?"

"Not if our comparative technical intelligence on their ships is accurate, sir. And these ships' communication frequencies—both microwave and laser—seem to be modulated in a manner inconsistent with human equipment."

Narrok looked at the plot again, watched the unidentified ships begin to spawn smaller motes that plunged planetside. Within moments, a patch of smaller, but more numerous yellow-black-yellow blooms erupted on the surface. Narrok narrowed his eyes. "Operations."

"Yes, sir?"

"Take us in."

Tangri SD Styr'car'hsux, *Raiding Fleet of the Dagora Horde, Treadway Orbit*

Not even the military technocrats of the Confederation Fleet Command had succeeded in imposing a rationalistic rank structure on the Tangri—not that their hearts had ever really been in the attempt, for they were Tangri themselves. So Atylycx's title was simply fleet leader. And in theory, he wasn't even acting for the CFC at all, but for the Dagora Horde, to which he belonged. Not that he felt any particular identification with it, for it was one of the synthetic "New Hordes." Some of the members—notably Hrufely, the horde's *anak*, or chieftain—actually took the farce seriously. They were the ones who gave the horde its reputation for stupidity. Atylycx didn't care about the stereotype; he knew what the real purpose of the deception was.

Now he stood, all four legs squarely planted in front of the viewscreen, and watched the nuclear rash spread across the tortured face of Treadway. He could have gotten a more precise appreciation from a computer simulation. But that would have been no substitute for this deeply satisfying spectacle.

The looting had been disappointing. This had been a small base, whose unimportance was reflected in the fact that it had been unarmed. The landing parties had had fun—Atylycx had even permitted himself the indulgence of joining in himself—but had garnered little more than the minimum loot required to qualify this as a worthy raid. And now that the shuttles had returned, bearing the blood-sated but somewhat surly raiders, the bombardment had followed as a matter of course. After all, there was no reason *not* to do it.

His reverie was interrupted by the voice of Hurvaz. "Your pardon, Fleet Leader," he said, making the submission gesture, "but a large incoming force has been detected."

Atylycx restrained his instinct to snap his teeth and perhaps deal a buffet for the interruption. Hurvaz was the intelligence officer—a position whose importance was reluctantly appreciated among the Tangri—and his news was vital.

"Humans?" he demanded, already striding toward the navigational holotank.

"No, Fleet Leader. From their energy signatures and other indicia, that can be ruled out. So—with only slightly less confidence—can the possibility that they belong to any of the humans' allies."

"Would you then conclude that they belong to the newly arrived prey animals here in the Bellerophon Arm?"

"I would stake my life on it, Fleet Leader."

"You just have." Atylycx glared down at the holo simulation of Treadway and its immediate vicinity. Its scale had been expanded to include the newcomers, approaching the planet where his own main fleet lay in orbit, marked by burgundy icons. The yellow dots of the newly arrived fleet, supplemented by ever-more-detailed readouts on a board overhead, showed a formidable force, but not an overwhelming one. At any rate, Atylycx was not alarmed. This contingency had been foreseen and preparations made for the inevitable encounter.

"Prepare the translation program, Hurvaz."

"At once, Fleet Leader." Hurvaz turned to a figure that crouched in the background—a figure with the drab harness and ethnic features that denoted *zemlixi*. He snarled a command, and the functionary scuttled off, with the instinctive cringe of his kind.

Essentially nothing was known about the new breed of prey animals, beyond the extraordinary fact of their arrival after crossing interstellar distances through normal space. But certain things could be inferred. One was that, having spent some time ruling over conquered human populations, they had acquired some familiarity with the common human Tongue—Standard English as they called it. So when Atylycx spoke to them, his words would be transmitted in that beast-language.

Something else could be inferred from their conquest of Bellerophon. That they were prey went without saying; they were *not* Tangri, so it was a matter of simple definition. But it seemed at least possible, on the basis of performance, that they were somehow less preylike than the humans, and that they had instincts that might make them easier to deceive with a pretense of alliance. At least it was worth a try.

And if it *didn't* work... Atylycx shifted his gaze from his main fleet to a second cluster of burgundy icons, on the opposite side of the planet. Cruisers, and ships comparable to what the humans called fleet carriers.

The Tangri had developed strikefighters just in time for the Shiratsuuk Horde's blundering incursion into the human system of Lyonesse almost two centuries earlier. Atylycx sometimes wondered why his race still used them. After all, modern naval developments—improved defensive screens, reduced relative speed and maneuverability advantages over larger warships, more deadly anti-fighter shipboard weaponry, and all the rest—had robbed the fighter of the terror-weapon status it had once enjoyed. And the Tangri physiology had never been well suited to it.

But maybe that last was part of the reason. All Tangri fighter pilots used the drug *sacaharrax* to make what they did tolerable. It was quite effective. It was also quite addictive. And its side effects included a shortening of life. All of which created a cult of the fighter pilot as doomed hero, cheerfully accepting a short but glorious life like a brief but intense flame. The consequent mystique was sunk too deep in Tangri myth to be easily uprooted.

And in this case, it might prove very useful. A simple mental calculation showed that, by the time he was done with his prepared speech, those carriers would be sweeping around the limb of the planet on their current orbit, coming in astern of what seemed to be the rather unwary formation of yellow icons, in perfect position for the classic fighter tactic of attacking in the blind zone of spatial distortion created by ships' drives. Then, if the speech proved unavailing, a sudden launch . . .

"Raise the leader of these prey," he commanded.

Yes, he thought as the image appeared on the com screen. Bipedal, like most prey animals that had somehow stumbled onto to use of tools. And even uglier than the humans, in their repulsive hairlessness. (Atylycx stroked his own auburn pelt with unconscious complacency.) And the large central eye between the two smaller ones was truly repellant. Nevertheless . . . he launched into a well-rehearsed speech.

Arduan SDH Shem'pter'ai, *Main Van, Expeditionary Fleet of the* Anaht'doh Kainat, *Treadway System*

Narrok listened to the intricate and repetitive jabber that was pouring out of the alien's wide mouth. And these creatures were, indeed, startlingly alien compared to the humans—alien in their quadrupedal and distinctly predatory physiology, as well as their actions. "They are communicating in the human tongue?"

"In English. Yes, Admiral. I think they presume we must know it, too."

Although the language still sounded like hyperactive gibberish to Narrok, he could assess the expressive posture of the alien. The creature speaking had been caught off guard by the Arduans' arrival, perhaps—but it was still collected, measured. There was no evidence of utter shock or alarm. "They didn't expect to meet us in this system, or in this way, but I think these creatures have heard of our existence."

"That would be my conjecture, Admiral."

"Which may also explain their presence here, as well—and the methods they are utilizing to 'subdue' this planet."

(Perplexity.) "Admiral?"

"I refer to their use of nuclear warheads against the surface."

"Yes, sir—but still, I do not understand how this leads you to deduce that they are only here at Treadway, and using these weapons, because they know of our existence."

"Reason it through, Fleet Second. If these creatures have heard of us, it means they have also learned that the humans are now struggling against a massive, unexpected invasion that has cut off this arm of what they call the Rim. Like the pack predators this race obviously descended from, they have discerned that Treadway—and systems like it—are now the weakened members of the humans' interstellar herd. According to their nature, these predators, smelling an easy kill, have attacked in force." He looked at the screen and the strange, long-headed creature still babbling and gesticulating there. "And so, with the humans removed or subjugated, this would be the face of our new neighbors."

Narrok felt the effect of that observation ripple through the *selnarm* on his bridge: all of a sudden, the humans looked neither so alien nor repulsive, by comparison. "Have you a translation yet, Intelligence Prime?"

"Pending, Admiral. But Tactics and I have noted an interesting—development—in the alien fleet."

"Oh, and what is that?"

Tactics came forward, and compelled the holoplot to shrink inward; slightly more of the space surrounding

Treadway came into view. Out near the far shoulder of the planet, in a tight retrograde orbit, a large number of medium-sized craft—cruisers and carriers, from the look of them—were tucking around the far side of the mottled globe.

"If they keep that heading, Admiral—"

"They will come upon us from the rear, just by remaining in that orbit. Yes, I see it, Prime. Tactics, are our twenty rearguard SDHs still trailing the van at twenty light-seconds?"

"As per your orders, Admiral."

"Excellent. They are to hold position and maintain cloaks."

Intelligence shifted; his *selnarm* was cautious. "Admiral, I do not mean to presume, but wouldn't these creatures expect us to have a cloaked rearguard? It is, after all, our standard fleet doctrine."

"Yes, but they do not know our doctrine. And unless their reports of us include a complete description of how our *selnarm* functions, and how we use it in battle, it is not a tactic that would naturally occur to them. The limitation of fully cloaked ships for other races is, after all, that they can neither receive nor send signals through the cloak they project. But this has no effect upon our *selnarm*, and so we can summon our cloaked ships to engage at the precise moment when it would be most advantageous for them to de-cloak."

"But this plan presumes, Admiral, that these creatures have sensors that are unable—or at least unlikely—to see through our cloaking technology."

"True, and a well-considered point, but I note with interest how close we approached before these creatures detected our presence. I conjecture that their sensors are somewhat less sophisticated than ours—or the humans'. From what little data we have, I would speculate that their ship-design philosophy emphasizes speed and simple, overmastering firepower, but at the cost of more sophisticated ancillary systems. Does that match your current assessment, Sensor Prime?"

"Yes, sir. From what we have seen of their sensor probes, their odds of detecting our cloaked ships would be small. Perhaps very small."

Tactics sent (accord, admiration). "Any orders to the cloaked rearguard, sir?"

"Yes. Apprise them regarding the fast force of unidentified ships that are apparently working their way behind us, using the planet as a screening mass. Send the relevant telemetry and all the data we have on each craft, but inform the commander of the rearguard that we in the van will give no sign of our awareness when these ships approach us. However, the rearguard must be ready to act in concert with us at a moment's notice."

"Very good, sir. But what kind of coordinated action are you anticipa—?"

Communications' *selnarm* cut through Tactics's. "We have a translation, sir—crude, and only a summary."

"Share it, Prime."

"They announce themselves as the race the humans call the Tangri, Admiral. In short, they bid us welcome. They observe we have a common foe: the humans. Pardon, I correct: the 'weak and irresolute' humans. The Tangri commander indicates that he has already eliminated the Rim Federation naval complex on the planet."

"Which our intelligence indicated was unarmed, did it not?"

"It did so indicate, sir. He therefore invites us to

discuss our common interests. He is proposing an alliance, from the sound of it. And he suggests we could certify and celebrate that alliance by continuing to subjugate Treadway together."

"He proposes a joint administration of the planet?"

"No, Admiral. He is requesting that we join him in the continued bombardment of the surface. He has gone so far as to provide targeting coordinates for the humans' most populous—and undefended—cities, sir."

Narrok felt his blood pumping hard and fast behind all three eyes. *So, the spade-toothed Tangri commander is offering me the unsurpassed delights of joining him in the decimation of a planet of civilians—of mothers and young, of the old and the weak. And if I am too—unenthusiastic—in my response, he has sent a poisoned dagger around the planet to strike me in my uncooperative back. Oh yes, one could hardly ask for more charming allies—*

The communications prime pulsed (reminder, pardon) as he prompted: "The Tangri commander is awaiting your response, Admiral."

"Is he?" Narrok looked up at the expectant alien face staring at him from the communications screen. "Then here is my reply. Operations, fleet signal: all units, flank speed and transfer fire coordination to data-hub vessels. Data hubs, once you have acquired target lock on the Tangri flagship, the order is: all weapons, open fire."

Tangri SD Styr'car'hsux, *Raiding Fleet of the Dagora Horde, Treadway Orbit*

Atylycx staggered back to the feet from which he had been thrown by the latest and worst of the rapid series of concussions. The teeth-hurting squeal of the damage-control signal made it hard to think. So did the reddish mist of fury through which he scanned the readouts. The outside viewscreen had shut down automatically at the intolerable glare of antimatter annihilation from the missile-storm that lashed his fleet.

"Are the carriers in position yet?" he demanded.

His flag captain, as humans would have called him, looked even more shaken than Atylycx felt. "Almost, Fleet Leader."

"I don't want to hear that 'almost' shit! Order them to launch right now!"

"At once, Fleet Leader!" The flag captain turned to obey, looking into the holo display... and his voice trailed to a halt before he had finished speaking the order.

"What's the matter with you?" Atylycx bellowed, swinging around. Then he followed the flag captain's gaze.

Astern of the burgundy icons of his carriers and their cruiser escorts, a cluster of twenty yellow lights had sprung into being. The readouts showed the indicia of heavy superdreadnoughts.

Tangri CVL Anyx'hrruzn, *Raiding Fleet of the Dagora Horde, Treadway Orbit*

Squadron leader Rytaz settled his body onto the framework that allowed a Tangri—however awkwardly—to pilot a fighter. It should have been uncomfortable, but Rytaz didn't care. Not with the *sacaharrax* singing in his veins. He luxuriated in it, as immune to discomfort as he was to the thought of defeat. He strapped himself in, waiting to launch first, as it befitted a squadron leader to do.

A voice punctured his euphoria—a panicky voice,

aborting the countdown and ordering an immediate launch. He still didn't care—the sooner the better! An opening dilated in front of his fighter and he stared down the long tube of the launch catapult at the few stars visible in the black circle that was its far end. Then the electromagnets kicked in, and he was pressed back against his padding, the walls of the tunnel seeming to rush backward. Yes, this was better than possessing a female . . . even an unwilling female.

But then, for the second time, something was wrong. The launch tunnel shuddered slightly, and behind him was the glow of an explosion.

Still the catapult continued to fling his fighter forward—just ahead of the flames that burgeoned astern, seeming to pursue him.

The fighter cleared the tunnel and was abruptly in space. Ordinarily, at that moment, Rytaz would spend an instant of *sacaharrax*-enhanced exaltation among the stars. But for a split second, his gaze went to the view aft . . . only to see the carrier breaking up in a holocaust of secondary explosions. And before that split second was over, a jet of superheated flame shot out of the launch tunnel's mouth, consuming Rytaz and his fighter like a moth caught in the flare of a blowtorch.

Rytaz would never know it, but his was the only Tangri fighter to get clear of its carrier that day.

Tangri SD Styr'car'hsux, *Raiding Fleet of the Dagora Horde, Treadway Orbit*

Atylycx tasted blood as his teeth gashed the inside of his mouth in his impotent rage.

He had watched as the last of the burgundy icons of

his carriers and cruisers flickered out, caught between the totally unexpected cloaked rearguard of SDHs and the units—roughly a third of the enemy's main force—that had turned back to form an anvil for the rearguard's hammer. As he had watched, the other two-thirds of that main force had inflicted significant losses on his fleet. And now, both hammer and anvil were turning about and coalescing into a single weapon that could have but one purpose.

At least, he reflected, forcing his paralyzing rage to ebb, he must have the advantage of speed. Those SDHs putting out such devastating missile salvos were larger than anything he had, and Tangri ships were built for fleetness.

He needed it now.

He spoke over his shoulder to the flag captain without looking at him. "Set a course for the Tisiphone warp point. Get us out of here."

Arduan SDH Shem'pter'ai, *Main Van, Expeditionary Fleet of the* Anaht'doh Kainat, *Tisiphone Orbit*

Five days after chasing the last of the Tangri out of Tisiphone's orbit—and system—Narrok stared down through a half meter of glassteel at the blue-white world and reflected that the humans had misnamed it. The planet should simply have been called "Typhoon." The observation deck of Narrok's orbiting flagship *Shem'pter'ai* afforded him an excellent vantage point from which to watch no less than five hurricanes bluster around and against one another like five enraged and overstimulated *yihrts* in rutting season. And, as with *yihrts*, the gargantuan tempests of Tisiphone were only interesting when observed from a great distance: he had lost three shuttles to a brace of thrashing monsoons, 200 kph winds, intermittent waterspouts, two immense tornadoes, and ferocious near-ground windshear.

But, he reflected, those three losses had been arguably the most productive of the campaign thus far. Because those shuttles had all been lost on a mission of mercy. Scattered among the most remote archipelago of this ninety-two-percent-water world, a number of small human communities had been compelled to seek higher ground at the approach of this multi-celled storm front. Their homes and goods washed away by a sequence of cyclones that were severe even by Tisiphone's standards, the locals had called the main continent for help. However, Tisiphone's civilian air assets had already been crippled by Tangri strikes, since the Tisiphonian Air Militia had operated its fighters out of the co-located—and pulverized—spaceport. The haggard remains of Tisiphone's air services were both scattered and grounded by their own meteorological challenges.

At which point Narrok had offered to intercede on behalf of the endangered humans: he would provide air transport for the necessary humanitarian aid. He had sent ten shuttles planetside to carry survival shelters and comestibles to the stricken pelagic communities. The human freight handlers and relief coordinators, waiting at the edge of the airfield's main tarmac, had gazed, silent and suspicious, at the "inscrutable" Arduans who landed at their savaged spaceport, loaded the rescue shipments into their bays, and flew off into the growing thunderheads.

Three of the shuttles ended their journey as debris at the bottom of Tisiphone's endlessly roiling seas. But the other seven got through and delivered enough needed supplies to allow the stricken communities to weather what was left of the storm that had isolated them from the rest of the world.

And in the days that followed, there were two sea changes. One involved the weather: the storms became squalls, which died down to calm and bright skies. Almost as though they were announcing, and an omen of, the second sea change: that which involved the human attitudes toward the Arduans who had come to Tisiphone. Although invaders, they had also shown compassion, and Narrok had been determined to shape his actions to meet the crudely phrased assurances he had given the humans during their surrender proceedings. However, the change in human attitude had not ultimately been effected by the seven shuttles that had pushed through the storms to bring succor to the human survivors. Rather, it was the three shuttles that the Arduans had lost in the attempt which had clearly purchased the changed opinion of their unwilling hosts.

Narrok stared down into the southern hemisphere of Tisiphone, the spawning ground and creche for the planet's worst storms: a new one—a tight, angry white spiral—was being born as he watched. Against this turbulent backdrop, the strange social calm of this one planetary occupation, secured by the death of six Arduan pilots striving to help humans, only further underscored and proved Ankaht's mounting evidence (which Narrok received through Mretlak's surreptitious updates) that humans feared death so intensely because, for them, it *was* final. When they discarnated, they did indeed tumble, dwindle, into the oblivion that was *xenzhet-narmat'ai*. So when three Arduan shuttle crews tumbled down to their own temporary deaths in an attempt to save a few thousand horrifically finite human lives, many of the inhabitants of Tisiphone became less overtly hateful and began to consider the few Arduans who passed among them with stares that were more curious than hostile.

And that curiosity had now led, it seemed, to a tentative attempt at contact. A human cargo handler, who had assisted one of the doomed Arduan shuttles before it had lifted from the tarmac to begin its fateful mercy flight, had passed a handwritten note to one of the surviving shuttle pilots just a day ago. Once submitted to the analysis of the newly arrived vocoder, it simply said:

> Even mortal enemies can respect each others' courage. Thank you for your sacrifice.

Narrok closed all three eyes slowly, composing himself. *And these, these are the "creatures" that Torhok would have us liken to* griarfeksh, *as mere beasts to be exterminated?*

Extermination. Thanks to the Tangri, Narrok had now seen what that policy looked like when put into practice. His gaze slipped sideways to where his fleet's auxiliaries were hard at work repairing battle damage to an early-mark SDH. If only Torhok had been present for the battles with the Tangri, he might not be so quick to call the humans "beasts." Where humans died bravely for the love of their duty, their ideals, their homes, and each other, the Tangri seemed to be creatures wholly driven by self-interest. They fought well enough when the odds of success seemed promising, but as the tide turned—as it always had—one could watch how their flanks began holding back, how their reserves started dropping farther behind, how the formation of their van started changing—albeit only subtly—as each captain began to angle toward a trajectory that gave him a slightly better escape route. They were opportunists, cowards—and Narrok had taken a carefully hidden but savage pride in driving them back from the human systems they had occupied. The systems that they had, for all intents and purposes, brutally raped.

The Tangri were every bit as faithless and brutal as the human reports claimed them to be. Whereas the humans themselves were . . . were . . .

They were people.

And, having at last admitted this to himself so frankly, Narrok discovered the emotions that had been hiding behind his growing hatred of Torhok, behind his resentment at having to send so many of the Children of Illudor into premature discarnations.

He also grieved for the brave humans he had killed and felt remorse for the ones whom he would yet have to send to *xenzhet-narmat'ai*.

For, he admitted as he folded the hand-scrawled message reverently, there would be many, many thousands of human lives that he would still have to consign to that terrible fate.

17

Comrades

We need the comrade heart that understands,
And the warmth, the living warmth of human hands.
—Clark

TRNS Taconic, *Warp Nexus ZQ-147, Deep Space*

No one had ever been able to fully account for the warp network that enabled space travelers to get around the lightspeed barrier and, as Li Han's ancestors would have put it, fool the gods into thinking their laws were being obeyed. The fundamental force of gravity was somehow involved, all admitted. The fact that most warp points occurred in proximity to the gravity wells of stars reinforced this view, in addition to being highly convenient in practical terms. But some warp points didn't, and every attempt to formulate a general theory accounting for the phenomenon had come to grief on that irritating fact. It was a source of endless frustration to physicists, who devoutly wished that starless warp nexi didn't exist.

Li Han had moments when she felt the same way, albeit for different reasons. This was one of those times, as her flagship TRNS *Taconic* emerged into the starless warp nexus ZQ-147 and, for the first time in decades, she found herself in true interstellar space, without the comforting hearthlike glow of a local sun to serve as a reference point.

She reminded herself that the all-volunteer crew of TRNS *Goethals* had been in the gulf between the stars for over two and a half standard years. *No*, she automatically corrected herself, *about a year and a third as they themselves have experienced time, traveling at relativistic velocities.* The psychological and physical dangers of the voyage had been explained to them. So had the mandatory oath to blow up the defenseless *Goethals* if, contrary to expectations, they encountered Baldy forces in the planetless red-dwarf system of Borden that was their destination.

Still, they had volunteered. They had brought their ungainly vessel here to ZQ-147 and plunged on into the void at 0.85 c, thanks to the Desai prime drive, thereby leaving the warp network behind and becoming the first human beings ever to attempt an interstellar voyage through the normal space of Newton and Einstein.

The 2.6-year length of that voyage had been no particular disadvantage in terms of the Alliance's war plans, for it had taken almost that long to construct the fleet of devastators Li Han now commanded. But within three months of *Goethals'* estimated time of arrival at Borden, she had begun moving that fleet toward ZQ-147. It would not do to miss the prearranged instant . . . and besides, she had a rendezvous to keep.

"Pardon me, Admiral," said Captain Adrian M'Zangwe, her chief of staff, interrupting her thoughts. (She had forbidden the use of any form of address more exalted and pompous than "Admiral.") "*Kazin* has just transited, and the first of the Kasugawa generators should be appearing directly."

"They will not be an improvement to the scenery,"

Li Han muttered. Her fleet had departed from Novaya Rodina with thirteen of the ungainly things. Three pairs had been left behind along the way, for they had been used to make possible the passage of the devastators through warp points that could not have otherwise accommodated their monstrous masses. The varying tonnage capacities of warp points was something else that wasn't fully understood about them, but the Kasugawa generators could widen, or *dredge*, them.

"They may be hideous and slow," M'Zangwe agreed, "but they enabled us to get our devastators this far. Eventually, they'll be able to cross-connect the entire alliance."

Li Han cut him off with an impatient gesture. "I know. But for now we only have seven of them left."

"They ought to be enough, Admiral," M'Zangwe reassured her, not for the first time.

"Yes, yes. It's one more than we need. Assuming that all goes well. Which it almost never does." She turned away from the viewscreen. "Well, present my compliments to Captain Estrada and ask him to get the recon drones deployed and headed toward the other local warp point. It wouldn't do for us to be late in detecting the arrival of Admiral Trevayne . . . and Admiral Li."

From the earliest stages of the planning process, it had been evident that they would need a force of capital ships lighter than the devastators once they were in the Bellerophon Arm. The BR-06-Mercury and Demeter-Charlotte warp lines could not be dredged for the devastators until Kasugawa generators were in place at both ends, and by that stage of the operation the Baldies would surely be aware of the Allied Fleet's presence in the Arm.

Wherefore it had been decided that a powerful Rim

Federation/Pan-Sentient Union Force, accompanied by Li Magda's TRN task force (but with nothing larger than a monitor; the warp line between BR-06 and Mercury was impassable to anything more massive), would proceed from Astria and rendezvous with Li Han here in ZQ-147. However, whereas this combined armada's date of arrival had been relatively predictable, the outcome of the initial meeting with its overall commander had been somewhat less so. But the lingering trepidations that Li-Han had harbored turned out to be groundless.

"Well, I could hardly be expected to pass this up," said Ian Trevayne after the initial greeting ceremonies were behind them.

"Your behavior," said Li Han primly, "is more commensurate with your apparent age than your actual one. For the supreme commander of the Rim Federation to appoint himself to—"

"Oh, tosh! Cyrus Waldeck is more than capable of handling things in Astria. He's been doing so all along, as commander of Second Fleet. Now he just won't have me looking over his shoulder."

"As you'll have me looking over yours." For an instant, Li Han wondered if she'd said more than she should. She looked around the circle of faces in her quarters: Trevayne, Mags, and Adrian M'Zangwe. She looked into Trevayne's eyes—not, strictly speaking, the *same* eyes she had looked into across his desk after spending months in his POW camp. Those eyes had looked out of a neatly bearded face in its fifties. She had never seen that face again. Indeed, she had destroyed the body—the original body—to which it had belonged. "Does the idea of being my second-in-command for this operation present a problem for you, Admiral?"

There was the barest pause before Trevayne replied. "I'd be less than honest if I didn't say it seemed a trifle odd at first. We were, after all, enemies—legendary enemies, in fact. And those days are relatively fresh in my mind. Remember, it's been more than eight decades in terms of your elapsed memory, but only a few years in mine."

Li Han let the silence stretch. M'Zangwe obviously wished he were somewhere else. But Magda only looked very serious, as her gaze shifted between her mother and . . . what? Her "colleague"?

"But," Trevayne resumed, "having fought against you, I'm in better position than most to know that serving under you is a unique honor. And you've never had a more loyal subordinate. There's just one thing . . ."

"Yes, Admiral?"

"Well, the force I've brought here is an allied fleet, and considering the political implications of that fact, I'm wondering if perhaps it would be a useful gesture if I were to transfer my flag to Admiral Li's flagship, rather than a Rim Federation ship." He gestured, with completely uncharacteristic awkwardness, in Li Magda's direction. "After all, inasmuch as my command includes Terran Republic units as well as—"

And of course that's the only *reason*, thought Li Han.

"I have no objection," said Mags with an equally awkward aversion for eye contact.

Well, thought Li Han, *I'm supposed to be the older and wiser one here, by even more of a margin of life experience in his case than in hers. . . .*

"I think that would be an excellent idea, Admiral Trevayne."

18

An Innocent Fighter

Look like the innocent flower,
but be the serpent under 't.
—Shakespeare

Arduan SDH Shem'pter'ai, *Expeditionary Fleet of the* Anaht'doh Kainat, *Agamemnon System*

Narrok looked down at the surface of Agamemnon and watched a dust storm emerge from the dark side of the terminator, sweeping across the uninhabitable equatorial desert-belt. A pulse emanated from the *selnarm* repeater embedded in the observation deck's main hatchway. "Enter," sent Narrok.

His new fleet second, Nenset, entered. (Apologies, regret) preceded his lexical pulse of, "Admiral, we have received the answer to your request."

"And Senior Admiral Torhok has refused to postpone the attack date?"

(Regret) preceded "Yes, Admiral. You are instructed to begin the attack upon Penelope at the agreed H hour, M minute."

Of course I am. "And is there any word on the progress of my offensive enhancement project?"

"*Rin* station's yard engineers report all construction is

on schedule. They indicate that they have had less problems with the modular interfaces than they expected."

Well, at least one thing seems to be going right back in the New Ardu system—despite Torhok's incessant meddling. "Thank you, Nenset. Fleet signal: commence pre-assault operations. Send it at once. You may go." Nenset seemed grateful to leave. Narrok stared at the surface of Agamemnon again, but three seconds later, the planet's sere surface seemed to plummet away from him: the fleet was moving.

Moving to undertake an attack that Narrok knew would be disastrous.

Further Rim Fleet and Expeditionary Fleet of the Anaht'doh Kainat, *Penelope System*

Admiral Erica Krishmahnta looked at the plot and was unable to decide: should she feel despondent or elated?

The reason for despondence was there to read in the holotank's icons: there were more green icons trailing omega symbols than in any engagement since the very first with the Baldies. And in that mix were two of her precious supermonitors and three of her monitors, to say nothing of the last of the fleet's cruisers and most of its lighter pickets. Thousands upon thousands of crew were dead, many of whom were officers she had known for years, shared a meal or a drink with. Gone in the space of two hours.

But her eyes slid to the other half of the tank, and she felt the elation rise: the sea of red icons that floated there—dead, motionless—was what she had hoped to achieve. She knew she couldn't hold Penelope forever. She wouldn't have enough forts in time. Oh, the components of the forts had been ready, but they took time to move from the yards in Tilghman to their final destinations, even when it was only two transits away, like Penelope.

But she had still had twelve forts at Penelope, dense minefields, lavishly supplied ships, and a different objective: kill so many Baldy ships that she was sure to cripple them into a three-month delay in their offensive operations. Because in three months, the first new ships would be sliding out of the spacedocks in Tilghman, and the minefields in Odysseus would be so dense that even the Baldies couldn't suicide through them successfully.

So, Krishmahnta was retreating, but she felt the satisfaction of knowing—finally knowing—that this was the last time she had to draw a line in the sand. Today, when she led her battered but still capable fleet through the warp point to Odysseus, she would at last be able to give her peerless crews and cadres a rest. And the Baldies could not break the defenses, because throughout all these months, Admiral Krishmahnta had been buying the time needed to ready what had at last been fully assembled in the Odysseus system: a phalanx of no fewer than forty-four forts, modified so that their missile-resupply systems could be fed from the rear of their superstructures while the launch bays continued to vomit death from their relative bows. Never before had such a defensive edifice been constructed outside the Home Worlds in order to protect a single warp point. And with a solid fleet left to support this defensive network, breaking it would take far more assets than the Baldies had spent thus far throughout their entire campaign. Which meant that, in three months, Admiral Erica Krishmahnta could begin to think about mounting the best and most satisfying defense of all: a strong offense.

Yoshi Watanabe joined her, returning from debriefing the fleet's senior squadron leaders; he nodded greetings as he looked in the tacplot. "Well, there's a first for everything."

"Which, in this case, is what?"

"That everything went according to plan."

Krishmahnta looked at the plot, worried that she'd missed something. "Yes, they danced to our tune all right. Makes you wonder."

"About what?"

"Can't they learn? I mean, this is almost exactly what happened to them in Ajax—just worse. Much worse."

Watanabe frowned at the tacplot. "We paid heavily, too, in our fighter squadrons."

"Yes, but in a way, it was the fighters that won this battle. With all of our fighters deployed early—to keep theirs from working at our minefields and from getting too close to our forts—the Baldies had to spend and spend and spend to break our line." Well over two hundred icons denoting dead SDHs attested to the price the invaders had paid. "Anything left for us to do?"

"We're in good order for transit, if that's what you mean. Looking at what remains of Baldy's forces, he doesn't look ready to mount a new frontal assault, anyway—not unless he can sneak something through the warp point right on the tail of our own transits."

"You mean like he tried when we were withdrawing from Agamemnon."

"Yes—and which he might try again."

"Yoshi, I know that look and that tone: what am I missing on the plot?"

Watanabe shrugged and pointed at a single red icon trailing Krishmahnta's van, which was strung out like the beads of a green necklace; pacing the human ships, the Baldy was moving briskly toward the Odysseus warp point.

Krishmahnta tried not to snort her disdain. "A single ship? What can they do with that?"

"Maybe nothing. But maybe they could give our defenses in Odysseus trouble by mixing their units in with ours long enough to force the minefields to stand down while what's left of their fleet's van follows through."

"And how is one ship going to do that? The forts in Odysseus would maul it."

"As we've been observing lately, Baldy has been field-modifying a lot of his SDHs for special-purpose duty. Like this one."

"And this one is modified to do what?"

"Carry pinnaces. Seems like they've taken a page from the Bugs' playbook. They're looking for a way to inundate a warp point by putting through a stream of the smallest ships possible. And they just might have found it."

"And given what we've seen of the Baldy tactics, the pinnaces could be just big antimatter bombs on a suicide run."

"Exactly. And if the minefields have been deactivated, and the Baldy pinnaces get in among our forts—"

"Right." Krishmahnta frowned. "So we have to delay them."

"Yes—and happily, the unit which detected and ran the sensor sweeps that identified the special design of this SDH also has a plan for delaying, maybe even destroying, it."

"Is it a sound plan?"

"It's—well, it is. But it's also unorthodox. Very unorthodox."

Krishmahnta rested her forehead in her raised palm. "Not again."

"Yes, it's from Wethermere, on the *Celmithyr'theaarnouw*. We're getting the details of his plan coordinated with Fleet Tactical now. They're having to confirm some of the specifics with Engineering."

Krishmahnta looked at the icons of her fleet. It was limping home, this time: not badly, but with enough of a hitch in its gait that almost any hull she'd send to help the *Celmithyr'theaarnouw* would be at risk of not making it to the warp point in time, particularly if it took further damage. And, sad as it was to say, the *Celmithyr'theaarnouw* was of increasingly marginal value: with her squadrons down to forty-five percent, she was a proud, fierce Orion *zeget* which had lost too many teeth and claws to be fully effective. *So if I have to lose something...*

She hated even thinking that thought, hated giving the dogged and ever-reliable crew of the *Celmithyr'theaarnouw* the short end of the stick one more time. And Wethermere—was this his reward for always living to fight another day? To finally be given up to the insatiable maw of war as just so much expendable cannon fodder? It wasn't fair. But war never was.

Krishmahnta felt Watanabe's eyes scanning her profile. "Well," he drawled in an excessively nonchalant tone, "it seems that Least Claw Kiiraathra'ostakjo and his Tactical Officer get to save the day once again. I wonder if Wethermere fully appreciates the honor we're bestowing upon him."

Krishmahnta stared down at the green speck that marked the position of the Orion carrier *Celmithyr'theaarnouw*. "You can ask him yourself. If he lives."

Least Claw Kiiraathra'ostakjo rested his muzzle in both handlike paws and didn't care that his own crew saw him in that position. Because, once again, they were all following one of Wethermere's schemes, which usually seemed to be the product of a mind either insane or suicidal, or both. But that they were following it at all was Kiiraathra'ostakjo's fault, and he knew it, because he had done the one thing that he absolutely, positively knew he should not do: he had posed Ossian Wethermere a problem for which there was no conventional solution.

The conversation had started innocently enough. Thirty minutes earlier, Lubell, another human late of the *Bucky Sherman*, and an excellent new ops officer, delivered the integrated report on the SDH that they were attempting to delay. It was running its tuners over the red-line, and the surface of its hull was laden with small-craft mooring racks, which were in turn laden with pinnaces. Clearly, this was a Baldy bid to compromise the Fleet's clean escape through the warp point to Odysseus, and one which might prove successful, for as Lubell had concluded, "We can't hold this SDH back: it keeps pressing us too hard, and we're overdue for maintenance. They're going to steamroller us before we can get through the warp point ourselves. And if they make it to the warp point just behind the fleet, and let loose all those pinnaces—"

Kiiraathra'ostakjo interrupted the human with an expressive nod. "Yes, Lieutenant. I understand. Thank you for your report. Well, it seems we have little choice. We will have to redeploy our fighters en masse if we are to slow them down enough to do our duty to the Fleet. They clearly do not consider our intermittent sorties reason enough to slow their advance." And from the corner of his slit-pupiled eye, Kiiraathra'ostakjo saw Wethermere turn to stare into the tacplot. And he kept staring there.

That, Kiiraathra'ostakjo reflected, was when he had made his fatal mistake. Almost as a rueful admission that there was nothing else to be done, he had addressed the human. "Lieutenant Wethermere, as our Tactical officer, do you have any alternatives to that option?"

"I might. With respect, Least Claw, the enemy does not fear our current offensive operations enough to make him halt his advance, yes?"

"Yes."

"Then what if we gave him a new reason to slow down?"

"You suggest that we give him a taste of a full-frontal assault with our main hull, as well?"

"No. I suggest that we give the Baldies a gift. A gift that they can't resist stopping to pick up."

"A gift? And what sort of gift do you think they might stop for? Perhaps to receive our surrender and take possession of our ship?"

"No—not our whole ship, anyway."

"Human, when you begin to speak in riddles, I begin to choose the hero-lays I wish chanted over my pyre. What madness are you conceiving now, Wethermere?"

"Last month, in the Agamemnon system, during the fight near Myrtilus—the Baldies clearly wanted one of our fighters."

"I recall this."

"Then what if we gave them one?"

Kiiraathra'ostakjo paused, making sure he had understood the human correctly. "You would purposely give them an intact model of one of our fighters? You would propose to sacrifice our entire fleet's advantage in fighter technology?"

Wethermere shook his head. "Firstly, we give them an older fighter with a tuner three marks out of date. That might help them a bit, but not much. Their problem is that they don't know how to best miniaturize their tuners." Wethermere looked to Zhou, who nodded in confirmation. "A model three marks out of date is only going to give them marginal improvements. Instead of throwing off five times our rads, and burning out their engines ten times as fast, they might manage to reduce those rates to three times and six times, respectively."

"Hmm—not so great an advantage to them, but still too great a price for a brief interruption of their advance."

"I agree. That's why, if the plan actually works, their technical intelligence services will never get a chance to surgically dissect the fighter at all."

"Oh, and how do we ensure that?"

Wethermere smiled. "I thought you'd never ask."

So, mused Kiiraathra'ostakjo, *here I sit, without a single fighter left on board, my squadrons and even my hull in dangerous proximity to a massively armed and armored heavy superdreadnought, a body missing from the lockers of the burial detail, and everyone's life depending on the outcome of an utterly insane scheme.*

The fighter squadrons' main command channel crackled. "*Celmithyr'theaarnouw,* this is Polo Two, over."

The Orion equivalent of the strike group commander, a particularly taciturn male named Threk'feakhraos, replied, "Receiving. Status?"

"Polo One is KIA, but we still have control over Medicine Ball. We have handed it off to Polo Three, with backup remote control transferred to Polo Six. Rugby and Ak'kraastaakear flights are still on my flanks."

"Has the enemy begun using flechette missiles?"

"Nothing but, for the last twenty seconds."

"Stand by for orders and activation of Medicine Ball, Polo Two." Threk'feakhraos looked to Wethermere. "Tactical?"

Wethermere glanced at Kiiraathra'ostakjo, who nodded.

Wethermere grinned and said loudly enough for Threk'feakhraos's pickup to register it, "Toss out the Ball, Polo Two."

"You heard the man, Polo Three. Time to put the Ball in play."

Polo Three—otherwise known as Vera Demetrikos—responded crisply to Polo's brand-new flight leader, Jakub Varshov. "Throwing in the Ball now, Polo Two. Don't you guys be too far behind me."

"I'm right on your tail, Polo Three."

True to form, Jake, thought Vera, who could hear the subtle leer in her flight leader's voice. Vera steered her fighter off to the relative left and down with two jerky twitches of the controls, as if a malfunction—or panic—had compelled her to fall out of formation. Her apparent wingman—Medicine Ball—followed her faithfully; Polo flight was a bit farther back, being protectively screened by the still more distant Rugby and Ak'kraastaakear flights.

The Baldies pounced, reacting to the break in their enemy's formation by firing a torrent of flechette missiles. Moments later, large swathes of space became impassable due to the expanding clouds of those lethal, mite-sized darts.

Spaceside flechette munitions were, fundamentally, misnamed: their resemblance to the lethal in-atmosphere flechette munitions was purely superficial. In space, and among craft using reactionless drives at relativistic pseudospeeds, a flechette missile's method of operation recalled ancient caltrops more than it did a modern shotgun. The warhead of the flechette missile detonated a fraction of a second before its drive burned out: in that fraction of a second, the warhead sent a sleetstorm of hard, grain-sized projectiles out in every direction. While within the missile's drive-field—which bubbled out in a final overpowered and self-annihilating pulse—the projectiles kept their relativistic velocity. But when the missile was destroyed, and the drive field with it, the flechettes fell back into normal space-time. The result: a sphere of mite-sized tetrahedrons, which, if hit by a fighter at pseudorelativistic speeds, was sure to destroy or at least disable the small craft.

Within seconds, the volume of space around Vera was filled with just such globes of flechettes. Some were peppering the area around Medicine Ball as well. *Perfect.* She called up Medicine Ball's remote-control system on her dynamically reconfigurable board and tapped the virtual button labeled "RPV match-course autopilot: OFF." The green button lost its color, became gray. Then she hit the button beneath it, labeled "Demo Command Circuit," and whispered, "Godspeed, Sven."

From a distance of 32,162 kilometers away, Polo Twelve—redesignated Medicine Ball for its last flight—swerved erratically, its pilot's hands still on its suddenly undirected controls. A second later, the fighter quaked—first from a blast back near its fuel tanks and main bus, and then again when a small, externally mounted explosive charge blasted in the exposed glassteel portside cockpit panel. The hard vacuum pulled the air out in a single cyclonic rush, sucked out papers, tugged at the pilot's hands, attacked the flesh of his face—which had been exposed by the shattered faceplate of his flight helmet. But the form of the pilot remained motionless—even as Medicine Ball tumbled out of folded space, suddenly motionless since its drive field was gone.

Already many light-seconds away, Vera Demetrikos brusquely wiped a tear off her cheek; Sven Pugliotti had been a nice guy, a quiet guy, a brave guy—and she hated leaving one of her own behind. But, safely bracketed by the survivors of Polo flight, and further protected by Rugby and Ak'kraastaakear squadrons, she followed the last orders of the mission:

Return to the barn.

On the bridge of the *Celmithyr'theaarnouw*, the strike group's commander growled through the tally of his squadrons' losses. "We lost eleven fighters." He cut his eyes quickly at a blinking silver-white icon in the tacplot. "Not counting Medicine Ball, of course."

Lubell leaned forward over the ops board to peer into the holotank. "The question is, have the Baldies seen it?"

As if to answer him, the red gnats in the tacplot—the Baldy fighters—quickly split into two separate groups: one swarmed around the bright white icon that marked the position of Medicine Ball; the rest formed a wall between that position and the *Celmithyr'theaarnouw*'s retreating squadrons.

Lubell leaned back, still watching. "Well, son of a bitch."

"Sensors," commanded Kiiraathra'ostakjo, "report."

"Half of the enemy fighters surrounding Medicine Ball have shut down their reactionless drives. The SDH has altered course toward those same coordinates. Now she is slowing, slowing . . . and she has shut down her drives as well."

"Helm, best speed to rejoin the rearguard of the Fleet's van. Execute immediately." Kiiraathra'ostakjo leaned back with a look at Wethermere. "As you humans say, 'so far, so good.'"

Wethermere, still focused on the data readouts, simply nodded and told Zhou, "Start the clock."

Zhou hit the timer, glanced at the clock, and read what it showed. "Ten minutes. And counting."

In the space surrounding the motionless Medicine Ball, Baldy fighters adopted postures that were both aggressive and protective. Sensor-equipped shuttles approached, measured, scanned, scanned, scanned again: no sign of power emanations. No sign of computer activity. No sign of mechanical movement of any kind. And no signs of life.

When Zhou's operations clock on the bridge of the *Celmithyr'theaarnouw* showed eight minutes, two heavily modified Arduan shuttles came forward and reached out with robotic arms and tentacles that secured the human fighter in their steely clasps. Using standard fusion-impulse rockets, they began towing the crippled remains of Medicine Ball toward their looming mothership: the Arduan heavy superdreadnought, its back, belly, and sides bristling with scores of pinnaces. A brightly lit vehicle bay opened in the warship's immense side: altering course slightly, the two shuttles dragged their precious cargo unceremoniously in that direction.

When Zhou's clock hit seven minutes, just before Medicine Ball was drawn inside the SDH, the *Celmithyr'theaarnouw* focused one last, wide-spectrum, high-gain active scan upon its opponent, with particularly strong pulses in the radio and microwave frequencies. Indeed, those pulses were not only strong, but unusually repetitive.

At six minutes, the bay doors began to close and the SDH's reactionless drive reinitiated. She had lost ground in her pursuit of the Orion carrier, and would still have to lose a bit more, since going straight from cold drives and full stop to hot drives and full speed would severely damage, and possibly destroy, her engines' tuners and coils. However, as the superdreadnought picked up speed, her outreaching sensors detected small new signatures: the *Celmithyr'theaarnouw* was depositing mines, a few at a time, as she gave ground before the stern-chasing leviathan.

At five minutes, the SDH's reactionless drives had folded space enough so that the Arduans were no longer falling behind the Orion carrier. They swept the first cluster of mines out of their way with defensive lasers and pressed on, bold and direct.

Four minutes. In the vehicle bay of the SDH, an all-clear buzzer—both audial and *selnarmic*—pulsed to announce that the vast cavern had been repressurized and that the final set of chemical, thermal, and radiation scans indicated that the human wreck was truly inert. However, as the commander of the technical-intelligence cluster waited for the doors to open so he could inspect his prize, he noted that the "Emergency purge" override control remained illuminated. The hangar's senior manip, who stood ready at the controls, pulsed (regrets) but, "At the first sign of trouble, I must purge the whole bay."

"I understand."

Three minutes.

The last of the carrier's mines out of its way, and its engines now warmed to be able to attain maximum speed, the Arduan SDH pushed its tuners to the limit. The carrier continued to speed away but was now slowly losing ground.

Meanwhile, the access hatchways into the heavy superdreadnought's bay opened at last. The entirety of the ship's technical-intelligence cluster swarmed out, leaping around and past the withdrawing sensor bots and converging on the human fighter.

Eager and sinuous, the Arduans surrounded the vehicle, sweeping it with more reliable, individual sensors. Still no sign of any threat. But it was not the prize that the cluster-commander had been hoping for: in addition to the damage done to the vehicle, it was also a very old model of fighter—the oldest still used by human formations. But its tuner and entire engine were still far beyond what the Children of Illudor had at their disposal for small craft.

Two minutes.

The human-biology junior group leader sent a pulse

to the cluster-commander, signifying that he had something (interesting) to report.

"What have you noted?"

"The pilot is—was—a human male. The effects of the explosive decompression seem to have been very severe. The flesh is more desiccated than I would have expected."

"Did the cockpit lose all air?"

"Yes, and his suit was breached in multiple locations, including the faceplate."

"Well, does it present any danger to us? Is the body some kind of ruse? Are they trying to infest us with a geneered virus?"

"I seriously doubt it, Commander. If anything, the extreme desiccation makes it unlikely that any biot would have survived to be capable of infecting us—that is, if we were so stupid as to bring the human's remains out of the hangar."

"Very well, then. Remove the remains to the sealed med module for analysis, once its jettisoning charges have been primed. Are any identifiers attached to the body?"

"Yes, Commander, it has a name patch. Sven Pugliotti."

"Record it, and put the remains in storage."

"Yes, Commander."

One minute.

The engineering prime who entered the bay with the disassembly team was new to the operation; she was a last minute replacement from Fleet, arriving earlier that day. She quickly found and inspected the high-gain fuel cells that were used to start the reactionless engine system. She looked up at the cluster-commander. "Excellent news. The engine and its starter are completely intact. Should I begin to remove them?"

"Do not touch the engine components! That is for sequenced technical analysis, one piece at a time, in the lab clean-rooms. Just uncouple the power leads and make sure all the controls are inert."

Thirty seconds.

The engineering prime, unseen beneath the savaged belly of the human fighter, signaled, "Group Leader, this craft's systems are damaged—and unfamiliar. It is a very old model, and it has been extensively modified."

"Yes? And the significance of these facts?"

"It is hard to tell exactly what needs to be removed, Group Leader. In the places where it is most severely damaged, I cannot always tell if those systems were original or modified prior to being hit."

"Well, let us be maximally cautious. Start by removing anything with live or residual electric potential. Other than the power core itself—that is part of the engine."

The engineering prime sounded cautious. "Could the power core be weaponized?"

"Impossible. Their reactionless drive is fundamentally the same as ours, so the power core only retains a starter charge for the drive. It cannot discharge as anything other than a brief gigawatt pulse. Just disconnect it from the fuel cells and the master controls, to be safe."

"Yes, Cluster-Commander."

Fifteen seconds.

"The electrical systems have been neutralized, Cluster-Leader."

"Excellent. I will signal the ship prime that the human fighter has been secured."

Zero seconds.

Buried deep inside a lightly pressurized, modified

coolant sleeve, two objects—both of which were needed to resist the expansion of a coiled trigger-spring—finally completed the changes that had begun when they received the activating microwave and radio pulses from the *Celmithyr'theaarnouw* seven minutes earlier.

One object was a bio-decay capsule, usually designed for the precision-timed release of targeted drugs. Its synthetic bio-gel suspension reached the end of its activated life cycle and swiftly deliquesced. The capsule collapsed.

The second object—a timed mechanical-resistance actuator—gave way at the same instant. A restraining tab—stressed to breaking by the constant pressure of the coiled spring beneath it—finally tripped: the tab's precisely calculated nanomatrix resistance was designed to fracture when the accumulated force exerted upon it exceeded its miniscule lifetime load rating.

Released when the two objects collapsed, the trigger-spring shot forward, slamming a primed actuator rod into the butt plate of a piezoelectric cell.

The cell's discharge both activated the power core's test probe—which swung immediately back into contact with the drive's direct power feed—and also sent a conducting arc through the now-linked systems.

Suddenly hot-wired into connection with the drive coils, the power core discharged.

The twenty-nine gigawatt ignition pulse hit the tuner coils, activating the engine for under 0.5 seconds before the sustained heat vaporized the test probe and the power level in the core was exhausted.

But only 0.02 seconds into that discharge, and therefore, 0.48 seconds before the power ran out, the crippled fighter's reactionless drive kicked briefly into life.

At that moment, Medicine Ball's entire fifty-one-ton mass was instantaneously accelerated to 0.12 c, cocooned within its engine's momentary drive field.

However, the Arduan heavy superdreadnought's own drive field refused to share folded space with this unexpected internal interloper. Contrapolarized gravitic forces, normally used to bend space selectively, tore each other asunder—a split second after Medicine Ball proved just how much energy is released when fifty-one tons of fighter impacts the interior of an armored hull at a speed of 20,500 kilometers per second.

Sixty-three seconds later, on the bridge of the *Celmithyr'theaarnouw*, a small star flared briefly into existence at the center of the stern-looking viewscreen. Kiiraathra'ostakjo looked down at Lubell, who smiled his huge, toothy smile—and earned a warning growl in return. Orions only showed their teeth when they meant business—bloody business—and the one courtesy they invariably expected from humans was to remember, and follow, that custom. Lubell closed his mouth so tightly and so quickly that he seemed to have swallowed his teeth.

"You may report now, Ops," muttered Kiiraathra'ostakjo.

"Target destroyed, Least Claw."

"This I surmised. But thank you." He turned to Wethermere. "Congratulations, Mr. Wethermere. In truth, it will be a pity to see you go." Kiiraathra'ostakjo had the gratification—finally—of saying something which surprised Wethermere, rather than vice versa.

"I'm going? Where?"

Kiiraathra'ostakjo looked at the ship's chronometer. "I suspect you shall find out in about two hours. Until then, you will join me in my quarters for what I expect to be a mutually unpleasant experience."

"Which is?"

"Teaching you how to improve your pronunciation of the Tongue of Tongues. Consider it my parting gift to you."

Two hours and fourteen minutes later, Ossian Wethermere was standing at attention before Admiral Krishmahnta in her ready room. She had a new memo in her hand, and waved it at him. "And here's another 'anonymous' and harebrained plan—this one about energy-torpedo battery reconfiguration for capital ships. It's yours, isn't it?"

"Uh . . . yes, sir. How could you tell?"

"How could I not? This kind of inspired insanity doesn't cross my desk every day—and certainly not as an anonymous memo. Which is why I've got to get you the blazes out of my fleet."

"Sir?"

"You're to report to the courier *Darcy Maisson* as soon as you leave this ward room, and make straight for your new assignment."

"Yes, sir." Wethermere tried not to look too relieved, but—for a few seconds—Krishmahnta's tone had made it sound as though his next duty station was going to be in a small, secure room in the *Gallipoli*'s brig. "You did say I have a new assignment, sir?"

"A *very* new assignment, Commander. Yes, you can get your jaw up off the deck whenever it suits you, Mr. Wethermere. For now, your promotion to lieutenant commander is merely a brevet rank—but if you're successful on this assignment, I just might be able to make it stick for good."

"Yes, sir. And, again—what's my new assignment?"

"Why, to get these new energy-torpedo batteries installed in the new hulls we're laying down back in Tilghman."

"Sir, with all due respect, I'm no engineer. I'm just a—"

"You're a person who makes things happen, who gets things done, Commander. I've got hundreds of engineers, but not a lot of—well, whatever the hell kind of specialist *you* are. And you have got to—*got to*—make this armament upgrade happen."

"But, sir—"

"Commander, as I dismiss you, I will give you two choices. You either turn yourself around, head to Tilghman, and get to work—or, if I hear another peep out of you, I will have you taken off this ship in irons. And you'll stay in those irons until you get to Tilghman."

Wethermere snapped a salute, about-faced, and exited.

At best speed.

19

Virtue Upon the Scaffold

Curse on his virtues! they've undone his
country. Such popular humanity is treason.
—Addison

Truth forever on the scaffold,
Wrong forever on the throne.
—Lowell

Prisoner Holding Facility, Resistance Regional Headquarters, Charybdis Islands, Bellerophon/New Ardu

"Sergeant! We're not done yet!"

Harry Li was glad he was facing away from the Hider; that gave him the momentary relief and luxury of rolling his eyes. He finished his ocular acrobatics and turned to face his CO. "Sorry, sir. I thought that was all."

"You'll know when we're done. I'll say 'dismissed.'" Heide smiled wanly; for him, this was the very paragon of pithy wit. Li managed not to sigh.

"Yes, sir. How else can I help you, sir?"

"Not help me, Li. I just need you to be aware of certain—developments."

When Heide became vague and mysterious, it usually did not signify anything good. In Li's growing experience, it was a sure sign that Heide's better nature (if such a thing existed) was not completely reconciled to a course of action his brain had decided was incumbent upon him, as per his improbably exacting interpretations of the Marine Corps' Practices and Procedures Manual. "Developments, sir?"

"Yes, Li. I'm sure you're aware that, in the months since the rescue operation in Melantho, the surviving artists we did not successfully extract have been making all sorts of outrageous claims regarding the actual history, intents, and nature of these so-called Arduans."

"Yes, sir. I've heard." *Just like everyone else who lives on this planet, jackass.*

"Unfortunately, the artists we *did* successfully rescue are saying almost exactly the same things, despite our best attempts to undo their brainwashing. This is making our position difficult, Sergeant."

"Difficult, sir?" *And what do you mean by "our" position, Captain Weasel?*

"Yes. You see, our best analysis shows that the public is beginning to show signs of actually dignifying these lies with some credence—largely because they have heard, by the grapevine, that the artists in our custody are making similar claims."

"I see, sir."

"I'm not sure you do, Sergeant. If we let this type of muttering go on, it is likely to undermine the resolve of the general populace, even the Resistance. So we have to stop it quickly, before it gets any worse."

"What did you have in mind, sir?"

The Hider seemed to almost take umbrage at the somewhat conversational idiom Li had employed to ask his question. "What I have in mind, Sergeant, is to approach this with the directness and decisiveness that it has warranted from the first. I propose to convene a court-martial to begin reviewing the evidence pertinent to bringing a charge of treason against Jennifer Peitchkov."

Li started. "Treason, sir? But she—she's a mother."

"That will only serve to better illustrate our resolve and the extreme seriousness of the matter. After the proceedings are made public, of course. In the meantime, we will properly consider and organize the evidence, and send the message out among our own ranks that we do not believe that there is the faintest bit of validity to her preposterous claims regarding a large peace faction within the Arduan governing body, or that this war is all the result of 'cultural misinterpretation.' This is just the nonsense of collaborators and apologists."

"Yes, sir. But, be that as it may, sir—*treason*?"

"Are you hard of hearing, Sergeant? Yes, of course. The charge would—must—be treason."

"But you just referred to the artists as 'brainwashed.' Wouldn't their compromised self-control excuse them from the presumption of malicious intent that is the basis of any charge of treason?"

"That is why I do not propose to try all the artists, Sergeant Li—just Peitchkov. Her case is . . . different. The degree of detail she recalls and recounts, the degree of mind contact she claims to have willingly made with the Arduans: I doubt all the understanding and sympathy she professes for them could be imposed by outside conditioning. She must have come to these conclusions by her own free will. And that, Sergeant Li, furnishes us with the basis for a charge of treason."

Li nodded, and thought: *He's actually serious. And he*

actually thinks it will be for the good of the Resistance and the planet. God help us all. "Captain, if I may?"

"Certainly, Sergeant. I have time for a quick question."

"Captain, why are you telling *me* about this?"

"Ah. Yes. Well, it seems to me that you are, historically speaking that is, a frie—a close associate—of Lieutenant McGee." When Li made no comment, Heide had no choice but to press on. "Because of that relationship, I thought it might be a kindness to—well, prepare him. Things could get . . . quite difficult, I expect."

Li couldn't keep the frown off his face. "Captain, you're not thinking of taking Zander away from Jennifer again, are you? That didn't have any effect on her stories or claims, and it wasn't good for . . . for morale, sir." *Or for your life-expectancy, you rat-shit; during that week, if I had a credit for every late-night convo I heard involving a grenade in your latrine . . .*

But Heide looked genuinely surprised. "Removing the infant? No, I hadn't even thought of that, Sergeant. Actually, I think it would be unreasonably cruel. Given the probable outcome."

Li's initial reaction—to feel reassured—quickly evaporated. "Sir, what probable outcome are you talking about?"

"Why, of her trial, of course. Treason is, after all, a capital crime."

"You . . . ? Sir, you—you intend to *execute* her?"

"Well, that's the whole point of a treason conviction, isn't it? And in this case, execution is not just deserved, but is a social duty. As the French said, the execution of one well-known traitor—*pour encourager les autres*—may reform lesser offenders. Sergeant, are you well? You look quite pale."

Li came to stiff attention. "I am well, sir."

"Excellent. It wouldn't do to have a namesake of the dreaded Admiral Li of the Terran Republic show anything less than true spartan endurance."

Li kept from rolling his eyes. "Sir, I wasn't named after the admiral. Among very traditional Chinese, like the admiral, the *family* name comes first. My family is more relaxed, so we followed the European tradition and put our family name last. But when it comes to the admiral and me both being named Li, there's no more special intention behind it than two guys who both happen to be named Mr. Jones. Just coincidence, sir."

"Ah, yes, of course. Still, noteworthy sharing a common heritage with such a military giant."

"Yes, sir. I'm sure that the other Li's must feel the same way—each one of the several hundred million of us."

Heide looked stymied. "So many? Really? That's quite . . . interesting."

"Yes, sir," Li said with a nod, even as he thought: *He's even worse at conversation than command. What a loser.* "Now, Captain, if you have no further need of me, I have an urgent matter to attend to. Crucial Resistance business, Captain."

"I see. Very well, then. Dismissed, and on your way."

Li saluted and was, very quickly, on his way—directly to Alessandro McGee's quarters.

When Jennifer's voice came from behind the door—"It's open"—Alessandro McGee found himself ready to run, to yell, to weep, to do anything but go in and speak with her. But he did.

Bearing a glass of water like a peace offering, McGee

cracked the door, looked in, and spoke the best, deathless monosyllable of eternal love that came to him. "Hey."

"Hey," Jennifer answered.

"Baby asleep?"

"Yes. In the other room." She looked up from under her very straight bangs. "It's good to see you, Sandro."

McGee slipped into the room, went to the seat across from hers, and fumbled with its backrest as he looked down at her. Jennifer Peitchkov was not the most beautiful woman in the world—her nose was a little too long, her cheeks a little too full, her shoulders a little too narrow—but he had long ago stopped seeing imperfections. He only saw his Jennifer. "Hey," he said again and tried to keep the tears from welling up in his eyes.

She looked at him . . . and rose quickly. "Sandro, what's wrong?"

He looked away. "Harry Li came to see me about half an hour ago."

"Oh, he did, did he? Well, what poison has good old Harry been spewing about me this ti—?"

McGee turned back and held her face in both his hands. "No, no, Jen. You've got it all wrong. Harry came to—to warn me. To warn us."

But even as McGee made his enigmatic, ominous announcement, Jen's face lit up like the dawn. Indeed, she looked happier than he had seen her in a year—since before the invasion. "What?" he said, puzzled.

"You love me. You love me again," she answered, her arms up and around his neck they way they used to be, fast, smooth, and effortless. "You do, don't you, Sandro?"

Did he? Of course he did. Had he stopped? No.

Had he *forgotten* that he did? Not exactly. But with her constant, desperate plea that he understand the Arduans, that he consider their side of the tragedy, it had been very hard to stay in touch with his feelings for her. But now . . .

"Of course I love you, Jen. You're my—my Jen," he finished eloquently.

She laughed, and it was like music, like water tumbling over tiers in a fountain. "Then everything else is going to be okay," she said. She drew him to the seat closest to hers. "Now, tell me what Harry said."

McGee told her. She listened quietly, nodding occasionally. "You know, I do see Heide's point."

"You do?"

"Well, sure. But it's going to backfire on him. And kill me."

McGee felt as though he were corkscrewing down from a high-altitude drop with both chutes tangled and blood pounding in his temples. "You seem pretty calm about all this."

"I've had a lot of time to think, Sandro. And I realize that I can't convince people about what happened to me, of how the Arduan telempathy works—and what it can and, more importantly, *can't* do. Because all of you can't really *hear* any of it, not when you are already convinced, deep down, that having me around is like having a bomb under your bed. Sure, while I'm talking, I'm only a minor annoyance. But if you believe that the Arduans are able to control me, to 'detonate' me, at their will, then . . ." Jennifer shook her head.

McGee put his hands together between his knees, like a worried little boy. "I wish I knew what to tell you, Jennifer. I guess I'm no help, because you've tried so hard to convince me of who and what the Baldi—er, the Arduans are and what they want. And look at me. For all your arguments, I haven't changed one bit. I'm still—"

But McGee saw that Jennifer's eyes had widened, and then she shook her head as if trying to rouse herself from a mental fog. "That's it. That's what I've been doing wrong. Sandro"—she grabbed his face and kissed him hard, once, on the mouth—"Sandro, my love, you are a bona fide genius."

"I am?"

"Yes, you saw the problem—the problem I've been struggling against all these months."

"I did? I have?"

"Sandro, it's there in what you just said—that I've been trying to *convince* you, and to use arguments to make people understand. But of course that was never going to work. Not with something as strange and unprovable as *selnarm* and mind-links. No, what I have to do is *show* you how it was, not *tell* you how it was."

She sat again and folded her hands in her lap, and although she seemed very composed now, she also seemed excited, the way she used to be when she had finally figured out how to get a sculpture to work the way she wanted it to. Her voice was quiet, almost difficult to hear, as she started. "Sandro, let me tell you how it was while I was with the Arduans—and I mean the day-to-day details, the little things and the big things together. Maybe then you'll better understand what I did and why I believe what I believe now. I'm not saying you'll accept it—I just want to work at having you understand it. After all, people who love each other don't—can't—agree about everything all the time.

Even things as important as this. But understanding each other, why we do what we do . . . that's essential. Don't you think?"

McGee nodded, and leaned forward to listen to her and gaze at her wonderful, expressive, quirky face. At the face of his Jen.

Two hours later, McGee remembered the glass of water that he had brought with him, and handed it to Jennifer, who had been talking almost nonstop. As he watched her drink down the water and admired the cycling of her long, smooth neck, he reflected: *She sure as hell doesn't sound like a traitor. She doesn't even sound deranged, deluded, or brainwashed.*

She just sounds like she's telling the truth.

20

None So Blind

There's none so blind as they that won't see.
—Swift

West Shore District, Punt City, New Ardu/Bellerophon

Ankaht assisted Tefnut ha sheri to his seat in the speech lab's observation chamber. He waved off her arm and pulsed (gratitude, regret, dismay) at her. "I had thought to be discarnate by now. But with so many of our trained brothers and sisters gone down the gullet of war..." He made a gesture of feeble futility.

Thutmus—rejoined with Ankaht for the first time in four months—rested the lesser tentacles of his left cluster gently upon old Tefnut ha sheri's arm. "We appreciate your continued wisdom, *Holodah'kri'at*. We wish your body was not such a discomfort."

"It is long past the time I should have been rid of it—but these times force changes and sacrifices upon us all. No matter. Besides, we have not come here to share the *narmata* of my infirmities and woes! Where is this—human—translator?"

Ankaht sent (fondness, amusement) and gestured with a lesser tentacle. "You will note the two humans in the—"

"*Ankaht!*"

She jerked erect. It was Mretlak, on the secure *selnarm* repeater. "I am here."

"Leave the floor, and then the building—now."

"Why?"

"I will show you."

And then Ankaht was seeing—imperfectly, since the visual perceptions and memories of another were not so complete nor clear as those experienced directly, personally—her concealed security station down off the lobby. The image was flat, gray, as though imparted by a, a—

"Yes, this is a human surveillance camera," intruded Mretlak.

In an eerie reprise of the Death-Vowed attack of just weeks ago, her double-staffed Enforcer detachment was dead, sprawled about. Not all had been killed by *skeerba*; some were dead from what looked like gunshot wounds. But there had been no report, and she had not heard—

"The assassins are using commandeered human infiltration weapons—machine-pistols with what they call sound suppressors. Crude, but effective."

"Why haven't the alarms gone off?"

"They have been deactivated."

"Deactivated? But how? The anti-intrusion systems are all controlled by the Enforcers and Secur—"

"Yes, Ankaht. And those who in turn control the Enforcers and Security are obviously a part of this conspiracy. Now go."

Ankaht had already drawn the rather frail Tefnut ha sheri back to his feet with a pulsed warning of (danger, flight, now), and Thutmus—wonderful mate that he was—had taken the rest of the observers from the Council in hand, as well as the two humans.

Ankaht passed Tefnut ha sheri off to Thutmus, who led the way. "Temret," she pulsed as she found and donned her *skeerba*.

"Here, Elder."

"I have a situation to share." He signaled (ready) and she flooded the images at him, including one that arrived from Mretlak in the midst of her sharing: an image of the new assassins, all *Destoshaz*, but not displaying any of the garb that would be the hallmark of warriors who had taken the Death-Vow. Instead, the five she saw were dressed in ballistic armor; four had firearms, two of which were the humans' suppressed machine-pistols. A fifth was unarmed. They were gliding swiftly up the north stairwell.

Temret signaled (coming, hide) as Mretlak commented. "I believe there are two other teams. We are conducting a five-minute look-back into the buffers now."

Ankaht sent (gratitude, life-debt) and moved to get back to the head of the group as they reached the double bank of elevators. She signaled Thutmus to "Turn left."

"Where do we flee?"

"Toward Temret and his team. They are coming from—"

The left-hand elevator chimed, began to open—and a flurry of automatic-weapons fire came pouring out. Marcus Chin—the most promising of all the remaining human translators—caught half of the spray directly in his chest. His body tattered and bloody, he fell back, quite dead before he hit the floor.

Thutmus, well to the left of the elevator, leaned back into a crouch that was the attack posture known as Tentacle Poised. Ankaht dodged farther back to stay out of the line of sight, and sealed her *selnarm* entirely within her; she was surprised at how complete her withdrawal was.

The assassins—two, bearing the typical Arduan machine-pistols—came out of the elevator low, one to either side.

As they did, Thutmus unleashed from Tentacle Poised into Wave Curls Over: throwing himself forward, he boosted off the floor with both feet. As the assassins emerged, he was already airborne and nearly over their heads; he reached down, a *skeerba* already in his cluster.

The assassin on the right thrashed spasmodically as Thutmus's blow landed, clutching at his severed spinal artery with both clusters. The other assassin, ducking, perceiving the overhead threat without fully seeing it, spun, tracking with his gun, which had almost come to bear on Thutmus—

Three *skeerba* claws came slashing through the front of his neck. The assassin's blood sputtered out and bubbled as he wheezed and died. Ankaht stood behind him and let the body's weight drag it off her *skeerba*.

Thutmus, who had not landed squarely, picked himself up with a small limp.

Ankaht felt a strange desperation as she rushed to him. Why should Thutmus's discarnation mean so much more now than it would have a year ago? But she only asked: "Beloved, are you hurt?"

"No. I am unharmed—thanks to you." He picked up one of the Arduan machine-pistols. "I see, by the way, that you have been training."

"I have been prudent. Let us go."

They did.

✧ ✧ ✧

"Elder."

"Temret. Where are you?"

"Approaching with my volunteers, Elder. Are you in a safe place? Can you remain there?"

Ankaht peered into the atrium before her: she could see all the approaches. The corridor behind her was long, and—other than the deactivated service elevators—the only entry into it from another floor was at the opposite end. "We are safe here—for a minute. Perhaps."

"I will be there in fifteen seconds."

(Gratitude) radiated out of her as the link closed: to think that she had been tempted to reject Temret's offer to provide her with an independent security force.

A distant, amplified *selnarm* spike startled her. "Ankaht."

"Mretlak. We are—"

"No time. Attend. The hallway behind you has an access shaft that follows up alongside the service elevators. I believe that one of the assassination teams is—"

As Mretlak started explaining, Ankaht took the precaution of getting the surviving human translator behind cover. Tefnut ha sheri, trying very hard not to dodder and fall behind, either failed to see or understand the Elder's hurried gesture that he should follow her, out of the corridor's line of sight.

Only ten meters behind him, an access panel—set flush with the wall—fell outward, and five assassins came out in a rush. Thutmus had his machine-pistol up swiftly and ripped a long burst down the hall: the last of the five sagged and hung limp in the mouth of the access shaft. Another spun around and fell, and a third was knocked backward—but those latter two immediately attempted to rise. Thutmus's fire had evidently not penetrated their ballistic armor. The last pair—one with a machine-pistol, the other unarmed and unclothed except for a long formal robe—charged at them.

Thutmus tried bringing his aim over to the last of the armed assassins—but that one had already gone down on one knee, a steady laser-point bead drawn on Thutmus's torso—

A loud report reverberated from across the atrium, and the kneeling assassin pitched backward.

Ankaht spun, saw one of Temret's *Destoshaz* volunteers still sighting down the barrel of his rifle. Temret and two of his other private-security contingent were racing toward her across the ramp from the other side of the atrium. *Good. We may yet—*

As she turned back toward Thutmus, she saw him attempt to get the last assassin to halt—but that attacker kept racing forward, eyes wide, mouth open and emitting a rising roar.

What happened next occurred so fast that Ankaht had trouble reconstructing the sequence later on. Thutmus lifted his weapon as he pulsed out one more "Halt now!" The charging assassin's robe fluttered open, revealing the bricks of plastic explosive that fronted his body like a wire-laden wall. Thutmus leaned slightly forward and squeezed the trigger; two rounds spat outward—which hit, and slowed, the suicide bomber—but then the machine-pistol jammed. Thutmus tossed it aside, pushed Tefnut ha sheri to the side with a mighty shove, and then leaped straight at the bomber.

Ankaht felt an emotion she had not known before—a desperate, aching fear of loss—and leaped after Thutmus to stop him—

Just as Temret tackled her from behind . . . so hard

that she was carried sideways, the two of them airborne: they landed behind the opposite corner.

A columnated fury of flame and debris exploded outward from the corridor's mouth and into the atrium behind them. The building shook; windows in the atrium shattered; tumbling bits of prefab, doors, and wall fixtures ricocheted down the wide skylight shaft to the lobby level.

Ankaht screamed—the first time in her life—and clutched outward with her *selnarm*. "*Thutmus*!?"

But his *soka*, his lifeforce, was gone. As if it had never been.

"Elder, are you hurt?" Temret's inquiry also contained an assurance that Tefnut ha sheri was safe, having been sheltered to the other side of the corridor mouth.

Strange, Ankaht thought, aware but not particularly cognizant of the chaotic and hurried activity around her, *I know that Thutmus's soul continues. I know that he has but experienced* dest—*discarnation—not the endless oblivion of* zhet. *But now, for the first time in my life, that offers little consolation. Now, in this time of trouble for me, for this city, for our race, I need him: I need Thutmus. And he is gone. And because I thought eternity was ours, I had not even thought of him once in the past four months.*

And as tears ran down her face—strange tears, tears that grieved a death—she realized: *This is what they—what the humans—feel every time one of their loved ones dies. This is the dagger of bitter loss which we have been ceaselessly jabbing into them as we destroy their fleets, their families, their infants. Illudor's Tears, how will—how can—they ever forgive us?*

Ankaht stretched her full length upon the floor and wept for all the dead.

✧ ✧ ✧

Torhok had, in the course of his career, seen many colleagues and subordinates crack under the strain of their positions, their responsibilities, their duties, even their guilt. He had acquired a fine-honed ability to distinguish the signs of mere anxiety and anger from those that presaged the peculiar and complete shedding of decorum and restraint that typified an individual who had at last exceeded their limits of psychological or emotional forbearance.

Urkhot was showing those signs now, as he stood before the Council of Twenty. Thutmus's vacant seat was filled by the injured Tefnut ha sheri, who was acting both as the slain *shaxzhu*'s pro tem replacement and as a witness to the assassination attempt that had compelled the emergency convening of the Council.

"Do you refute the testimony of the witness?" Senior Councilor Amunherh'peshef asked again.

And again Urkhot refused to meet his inquisitor's eyes or open his *selnarm*. "I am not bound to answer that until I may confront the witness myself."

Amunherh'peshef tapped a single, negating claw. "Incorrect, *Holodah'kri*. The law on this matter is not subject to interpretation or challenge. When a sole witness is either physically incapable of appearing before a Deliberative Collect, or the Collect has reason to suspect that the witness might be a target for preemptive discarnation, the accused's right of Disputation is set aside. So it is here. The sole surviving assassin—Qes'shah—is still recovering from the wounds inflicted by Temret's volunteers—"

"You mean, Temret's traitorous thugs." Mahes of Civanrock stared out beyond the ring of the table to impale the tall *Destoshaz* with all three eyes. Temret, standing behind Ankaht, remained impassive.

Amunherh'peshef pulsed a reproof. "Mahes, if it was not for Temret, we would have had two more seats to fill—and no clear evidentiary path. Which leads us back to you, *Holodah'kri*. Do you deny Qes'shah's accusation that you personally approached her—and her co-conspirators—with what you called 'the urgent mission to rid ourselves of the race-traitor Ankaht'?"

Urkhot's body seemed to tremble.

"*Holodah'kri*, do not make this more difficult than it is. We also have the testimony of the Enforcer manip who followed orders coming from your highest-ranking *Destoshaz hwa'kri* to shut down the security sensors and *selnarm* repeaters in Elder Ankaht's research complex. We have a clear video record of the covert entries made by the assassination squads, thanks to the human surveillance system that Intelligence Prime Mretlak discovered and has been using to watch for further human intrusions. And we have indications that the leader of the assassins—the Security second for all of Punt—was provided by you with a copy of the privy notes of this Council. These included the official itinerary of Tefnut ha sheri, indicating the time that he would be at the Elder's research complex to conduct an independent assessment of *shaxzhu* Ankaht's vocoder."

Urkhot's *selnarm* quivered, as did his body. "And of what possible relevance is that last item?"

"Given that you have chafed under Tefnut ha sheri's nominally superior position as *holodah'kri'at*—the senior high priest—and his insistence upon more liberal access to human documents and the use of the vocoder in understanding them, it would be ingenuous of us not to consider the possibility that you were attempting to remove all your political opponents in a single blow, Urkhot. About which I have yet to hear your answer. Do you deny the testimony of Qes'shah? Did you or did you not conspire to assassinate your fellow Councilors, and also aid and abet the persons who attempted to carry out that assassination?"

And still Urkhot did not respond.

"You have been asked three times, *Holodah'kri*, and you have closed your *selnarm* and self to the appeals and questions of all the Children of Illudor. You know, better than most, that in these cases our law compels us to construe your silence as consent—and as a hostile act against our community. So, in accordance with our oldest laws, I give you one last chance to—"

"You puppet. You prating puppet. Do you not see the abyss of your own destruction yawning wide at your feet? Do you not see how you yourself are helping to dig it, this very second? You compel me to answer for murder? *Me*? How many of our brothers and our sisters have met untimely discarnations because of this, this—Elder's—*griarfeksh*-loving apologetics?"

Amunherh'peshef narrowed his eyes. "This Council still does not have your direct response to its questions."

"You will—after I exercise my ancient right of Challenge first. Who brought forward these accusations against me?"

Amunherh'peshef radiated (displeasure, annoyance, impatience). "*Holodah'kri*, you know very well that the charges—and evidence—were compiled as a collective effo—"

"Ill'sblood and be damned, I will know the identity

of the person who initiated this defamation of my name and character."

Ankaht sent without moving. "I did. As you know."

Urkhot swiveled his eyes to look down on the small, dark Elder. "At least you have the nerve to admit it."

Torhok had a sudden twinge of misgiving: the *holodah'kri* was not reading the unfolding confrontation correctly. Torhok knew, from the confident coilings and uncoilings of Urkhot's *selnarm*, that the priest was interpreting Ankaht's lack of affect as grief over her loss, or fear, or both. *But, unless I'm very much mistaken, the Elder's quiet does not signify weakness—*

But Urkhot was pushing his *selnarm* directly at the contained, quiet figure of Ankaht. "You are the one who should be on trial here, race traitor. From the first, you have asked questions that were not merely pointless, not merely distracting to our efforts to survive, but actively pernicious to our faith. They were heresies cloaked in the guise of scientific investigation. Your questions were as deadly as they were interminable."

"At least I asked questions, *Holodah'kri*. Illudor gave us three eyes to see, and in seeing, to explore and inquire. You have not done so. You see the humans, are surrounded by their handiwork, have been ignominiously defeated and outsmarted by them in battle, and yet you do not see them as what they are, and do not ask questions. You simply assert that they, and all their works, are flawed, wicked, valueless—and all without ever investigating or considering their possible worth. But I will concede this to you, *Holodah'kri*: you have a most pressing reason to vilify them—and to do away with anyone who would challenge your campaign to do so. Such as me."

"So you accuse me not of mindless, but sagely premeditated, murder? How charming."

Ankaht pulsed (accord). "Your act was indeed premeditated, *Holodah'kri*, because you understand—all too well—that our resolve to defeat the humans will be greatly weakened if we come to identify and accept them as true, thinking beings."

"Which they are not!" Urkhot's retort—hot and desperate—was more a confirmation of her conjectures than if he had admitted them directly.

"You propose to know—without research—that the humans are not intelligent?" It was Tefnut ha sheri who asked the question. "To make a decision before gathering and reviewing evidence is, at best, unwise."

Urkhot's *selnarm* stormed out at both of them. "Illudor tells us we are his only Children, and that our link with him, each other, and our past lives, is what makes us thinking beings—true *persons*—rather than just another species of bestial *zheteksh*."

Ankaht still had not moved, but she sent: "So Illudor has already said, and shown us, all that is to be said or shown? We have nothing left to learn, no questions left to answer?"

Urkhot's *selnarm* lashed back at hers. "*Shaxzhu*, do you suggest you know the will of Illudor better than I do?"

"No. I suggest that it has become unclear where the will of Illudor ends and the will of Urkhot begins. Indeed, I wonder, *Holodah'kri*, have you confused yourself with your god?"

The room was very quiet and Urkhot was, suddenly, very still. Then he sent: "I can abide your heresies and lies no longer. I make a formal challenge of *holo'ai maatkah*—here and now. I will have the satisfaction of having the Elder withdraw her accusations—or I shall slay her as surely as we are Illudor's Only Children."

Selnarms rippled and quaked. Temret stood, his tentacles ready at the flap of his *skeerba* pouch. Tefnut ha sheri emitted a tired grunt of dismay. Torhok raised the lid of his central eye: a *holo'ai maatkah*? A challenge to be resolved right here in the Council Chamber, this instant? Torhok's earlier misgivings about Urkhot's state of mind rebounded and coalesced into self-recrimination. *If I had seen this coming, I might have prevented it*. Because no matter the outcome of this challenge, Urkhot had gone too far by issuing it, had done irreparable damage to his own cause. If he won, the accusations of assassination could still come from another source. Furthermore, he had now made an ogre out of himself by invoking one of the Council's most antediluvian and barbaric conventions.

Torhok watched the motionless tableau of the stunned Council Chamber. It was as if all its members were suddenly remembering why they always *had* to sit in a circle, why three concentric rings were inscribed within the inner periphery of their round table—and what those rings signified: the limits of the de facto *maatkah* ring that was situated like a hub at the center of their deliberative wheel.

Torhok glanced sideways at Urkhot and reconsidered: this situation might not be as unfortunate as it had first seemed. Urkhot had become much less useful of late. His theological edicts to the hard-line *Destoshaz* had taken on the quality of distracted rantings. So, on second thought, there was nothing to be lost in a mortal contest between Urkhot and Ankaht. It would certainly eliminate one problem or another. Torhok even allowed himself a small pulse of optimism: in the best of all possible worlds, they would both expire on each others' *skeerba*. That was too convenient an outcome to hope for, of course, but there was no harm in fantasizing.

Urkhot was still looking down at Ankaht. "Well?"

Ankaht still did not move. But she sent: "I accept your Challenge."

Temret started forward but was stayed at a gesture from Amunherh'peshef. "Urkhot, if you proceed with this—"

"Our course is set, Amunherh'peshef."

"Ankaht is not alone in making this accusation. It was a majority decision."

Urkhot vaulted the table, flexed his body in one long ripple as he entered the *maatkah* ring that they had all forgotten existed. "Then I shall challenge each member of that majority, one at a time, and in the order that they recorded their accusation against me."

"*Holodah'kri*, this is madness. In the interest of our Race and Traditions—"

"You simpering idiot, I do this to *preserve* our Race and Traditions! It has been the sole motivation for all my actions. You have forgotten you are the Children of Illudor. You have forgotten what that means. Very well. I shall remind—or teach—you. Starting with you, Sleeper." He had aimed the points of his left *skeerba* at Ankaht. "And consider this a long-overdue repayment for your treachery. You let the humans into your labs, encouraged them, coaxed them to attack us in Punt itself."

Ankaht had stood, swung up onto the conference table, and lowered herself into the ring slowly, carefully—like an elderly person navigating a tight room overfilled with sharp-cornered furniture. "You can no longer even hear yourself, Urkhot. Your desperation to keep our race from a crisis it cannot avoid—the redefinition of personhood—has driven you to delusion."

"I am driven by one thing—the protection of our Race and the continuity of Illudor. Prepare yourself, *shaxzhu*."

Ankaht drew both her *skeerba* and knelt, head lowered. Urkhot knelt also, his lesser tentacles writhing eagerly, wildly, about the cross-palm hilts of his own ritual blades. His head was up, his eyes wide, quivering. He was immense and fiercely ready. She was small and completely motionless. The outcome, Torhok observed, did seem preordained. . . .

The mechanical chime announced the start of the match. Usually, *maatkah* contests began with a struggle between the duelists' *selnarms*; usually it lasted only a few seconds. In some celebrated instances, it had lasted for hours.

But Urkhot went straight into motion. He leapt directly toward Ankaht in the attack known as Wave Breaks High. Jumping up and out, his left *skeerba* was slightly forward to attack or parry, while his powerful right was held back, coiled and ready to unleash a lethal blow.

Ankaht seemed late rising to her feet; Urkhot's long, golden body had unfurled halfway into his leaping arc, his *skeerba* descending. Ankaht—short, compact—had no way to stand her ground and strike back at him: his reach was too great, particularly in this leap that extended his whole body. The best she could do, Torhok thought, was go into the defense known as Shifting Winds, a sequential set of forceful blocks, usually conducted while retreating.

But Ankaht did something entirely different—something Torhok had never seen before, had only read about: she pitched forward into a fast but low front-flip. She could not have done it if she had had the typical *Destoshaz* body: her low center of gravity and short limbs allowed her to put herself into this tight forceful spin with extraordinary speed, even as it minimized her size as a target.

Urkhot, three-quarters of the way through his leap, tried to compensate—but couldn't, not entirely. He tried turning his leap into a flip of his own—thereby modifying Wave Breaks High into Wave Curls Under—so he could attempt to rake her as he passed. But Ankaht's positional change was so fast and tight that he only got a glancing blow at her as he went through his longer, larger flip, which carried him well past his target. To his credit, he landed on his feet, started to turn—

And saw, quite distinctly, the front of his torso bulge and writhe outward, a moment before he felt a white-hot burning in his back. He tried to complete his turn, couldn't, realized he couldn't even feel his legs. Then he felt Ankaht's *skeerba* twist deep inside him.

And then he felt nothing at all.

Ankaht eased Urkhot's body to the ground with some difficulty. She felt the Council's *selnarm* close around her: a taut, quivering necklace of entities that ringed her with an intensity of focus that was almost uncomfortable.

Finally, there was a slow probe. Temret, reimaging her flip—the one that had made Urkhot overshoot her and expose his own back. "What was that maneuver?" Temret asked, almost timidly.

Ankaht tried to summon enough interest or energy to respond, but before she could, a reply emerged from the careful, assessing *selnarm* of Torhok. "Unless I am much mistaken, that was a riposte from an old, indeed forgotten, *maatkahshak* that was called *Ran'zhetshotan.*" His *selnarm* swished like a predator's tail as he added with (rue, constraint), "Forgotten to all but a Sleeper *shaxzhu*, evidently." And behind his sardonic observation, Ankaht could feel—almost as clearly as if he had sent it—Torhok's true emotion: *Thank Illudor I was never foolish enough to challenge her.*

She straightened, noticed blood trickling from her shoulder and upper arm: Urkhot's grazing *skeerba* tooth had opened a long, leaking seam there. "Yes, it was a discipline used against Slaughter-Sworn pirates of the Inner Seas, during the Pre-Enlightenment." She turned, looking round at the Council. Of the eighteen *selnarmic* resonances, six were decidedly hostile, seven decidedly favorable, and five neutral and distressed but clearly happier with this outcome than had Urkhot won. *Well, that's a more promising mix of attitudes than when we all entered the room.*

"Councilors," she sent, "this tragedy must not be repeated, must not spread. This suspicion of each other—to the point of duels and assassinations—must be decried and discouraged in the strongest possible terms."

"A strange exhortation from one who holds the bloody victor's *skeerba* after a challenge, and who accused the slain of murder." Mahes stared at her, his eyes rigid with accusation and hatred.

"Clever words—which sidestep my point. In both cases, I had been marked for death—all in the name of race-loyalty and necessity. That I am alive is a testament to the friends I have, good fortune, and the will of Illudor."

"And a most impressive command of *shaxzhutok,*" added Torhok with a pulse of (irony), "to be able to so thoroughly excavate past knowledge for present purposes."

"Yes, that, too," conceded Ankaht, "which reminds us that all castes have something to offer. This is an illustration of why we must not lose the *shaxzhu*. In our past lives, our memories, there are lessons that may be essential to our present or future survival. But there are also the special skills of the *Ixturshaz* and the *Selnarshaz* and the other castes as well. The *Destoshaz* are our indispensable bulwark—but they are not the model for our entire race. *Destoshaz'ai*-as-*sulhaji* is only the path to enlightenment for one caste: the *Destoshaz*."

Torhok stood. "Yes, well should we speak of the honored and cherished *Destoshaz*. For what is the present proof of the appreciation and high regard enjoyed by the warrior caste?" He physically gestured toward Urkhot's twisted body. "There is your answer. He who was both a noble *Destoshaz* and a revered *holodah'kri* slaughtered in our midst. But only after he was first pushed to near-madness by false accusations of assassination—"

Amunherh'peshef's *selnarm* bristled. "The evidence and the charges—"

"—were never admitted to by the deceased, and are now moot."

Ankaht reflected that this outcome was actually extremely fortunate for Torhok and his supporters. Which was perhaps why the senior admiral had said nothing to support his staunch ally: seeing the possibility of such a scandalous outcome, Torhok had studiously maintained a pronounced distance from Urkhot.

But Tefnut ha sheri was not so easily deterred by Torhok's dismissal of the importance of the charges.

"Senior Admiral, if your legal expertise is as great as your naval ability, it is news to me. It would also be a matter of some worry, since the fleet losses you have sustained do not seem a sign of strategic perspicacity. Either way, it is not for you to decide whether further investigation into these matters is moot. While it may be true that the accountable parties are now beyond the domain of legal redress and recourse, it does not logically follow that we must turn our attention away from the origin of their deeds. Indeed, until we fix accountability for the events, we cannot be sure that all the offenders have been identified . . . and neutralized, Senior Admiral." Tefnut ha sheri's implication—that Torhok himself might somehow be implicated—hung like a gathering thunderstorm in the air of the Council Chamber.

But Torhok—true to form—was not easily perturbed. Instead, he sent a strong pulse of (accord), to which he added: "I am glad to hear of this resolve, revered *Holodah'kri'at* Tefnut ha sheri, for if the investigation is pursued with all the diligence it deserves, it will not stop with the particulars of the assassination attempt, but will probe its causes, will ask what ultimately inspired and impelled it. For there are further questions—troubling questions—of causality that must also be asked, unless you have determined that all the reputed assassins were simply Urkhot's automatons. If this is your conjecture, you are welcome to it—but it ignores the greater possibility: that our brothers and sisters did not enter the Elder's research complex at the prompting of anything other than their own martyred consciences."

Amunherh'peshef's response was stiff, cold. "This, too, we shall consider and investigate."

"Do. Do indeed consider and investigate this. And while you are doing so, consider what these 'assassins'—and their comrades—have endured as they fought to protect our Race from the *griarfeksh*. And all the while, they were forced to endure a rhetoric that would have us promote these savage aliens as our equals, as persons, as Illudor's lost children. And that rhetoric had one source." He turned to look at Ankaht as the *selnarm* of the *Destoshaz* members of the Council swelled with fierce and unpleasant passions. "The Elder has made much of being the voice of truth. I ask this: Would a voice of truth—of Illudor's truth—become so ardent an apologist for the most deadly enemy our race has ever known? Would she go so far as accusing, and then killing, its most vigilant and inspired *holodah'kri*, as she has done here today? Is there any way in which common sense tells us that this Sleeper is still an ally to her own people?"

Rage flared out from the *selnarm* of Torhok's *Destoshaz* faction. Which gave him the opportunity to portray himself as the much-beleaguered voice of reason. "Calm now," he gently remonstrated his followers, "we cannot presume that the Elder's treachery is willful and malicious. After all, tragic insanity is another possible source of her actions, for did not the builders of our ships warn that they could not be sure what centuries of cryogenic suspension might do to the minds of Sleepers?"

"I am quite sane," averred Ankaht quietly.

"When has a victim of insanity ever claimed otherwise?" Torhok's retort was almost fey. "But at any rate, I wish to hear assurances—now—that the Council will also investigate the possibility that the Elder's behavior has become pernicious to the welfare of her own people.

And that an awareness of this danger may have had a decisive role in compelling those *Destoshaz* whom you have labeled assassins to take corrective matters into their own hands." The Council's *Destoshaz* faction sent out a forceful wave of (approval, insistence) in support of this ultimatum.

Amunherh'peshef was quiet for a long moment, as if coming to a difficult decision. "Councilor Torhok, you know we can promise no such investigation. Elder Ankaht has conducted her researches with the sanctions of this Council—including your own. That she has uncovered potentially disturbing facts is not a pernicious act. It is the consequence of following where one's research leads. She has initiated attacks against no person, but has now twice been the target of attacks that were almost entirely *Destoshaz* enterprises. And while it *may* be entirely circumstantial that her most ardent opponents in this Council have been supporters of the *Destoshaz'ai*-as-*sulhaji* movement, it seems probable that this is *not*, in fact, merely circumstantial. Therefore, this Council must investigate the persons who might have instigated one or both attempts upon her life. At a bare minimum, her personal safety cannot be assured until we have identified all those parties who participated, directly or indirectly, in these attacks.

"However, I have absolutely no grounds for mounting the investigation you suggest be brought to bear upon Elder Ankaht. For it is not an investigation—it is merely an attempt to validate your contention that the attacks against her were carried out for the good of the Race. The Council has tolerated this species of insinuation and political bullying long enough. We will do so no longer."

Torhok's anger flared briefly, but Ankaht felt it was almost an act. And then, as Amunherh'peshef leaned back from completing his rejection of Torhok's motion, she understood who his intended audience had been.

Three of the *Destoshaz* Councilors rose to their feet. Torhok acknowledged their *selnarm* with (sadness, gratitude, fellow-feeling) but kept his eyes down on the tabletop: a tragic figure, a spurned warrior. "I see. Then if this is what passes for evenhanded justice on this Council, I cannot both serve my conscience as a Child of Illudor and dignify this governing body with my continued presence. To do so would be an affront to His Truth and to the millions of our brothers and sisters who have died for it. In their name, and in honor of their sacrifice, I must boycott this Council."

Torhok lifted his head and strode from the room. The three *Destoshaz* who had been on their feet already were close on his heels. The last three *Destoshaz* radicals rose—one quite hesitantly—and then they, too, followed the senior admiral out of the Council Chamber.

Ankaht counted and considered. A Council of Twenty. Two of its members—Thutmus and Urkhot—were recently killed, reducing it to eighteen. Now it was boycotted by Torhok and his six remaining devotees, reducing it to eleven. The inevitable response of Senior Councilor Amunherh'peshef? To reassign the seats of the boycotting Councilors with pro tem members—which the *Destoshaz* would contest as an illegal act, and thereby attack the legitimacy of every subsequent guideline and dicta issued by the Council.

Ironically, the Council had put the specter of a possible civil war in Torhok's hand like a doomsday device. And instead of a lunatic fringe that had been whipped up into a homicidal frenzy against Ankaht alone, there was now the possibility of a far more sweeping and dangerous reaction: a general hatred and distrust of the Council. *Better if we had also had a showdown with Torhok now,* reflected Ankaht as she allowed Temret's gentle clusters to guide her from the Council Chamber. That would have left the *Destoshaz'ai*-as-*sulhaji* extremists leaderless, which might have been a far better outcome.

Or much worse, she realized with a quick pulse of almost paralyzing fear. And suddenly she hoped—desperately—that in his coming trip to the front lines, nothing would happen to Torhok. *Because,* she realized, *a wild and furious beast without a head to control it is the most dangerous beast of all. . . .*

"Thank you for seeing me on such short notice, Mretlak."

"Thank you for being a bastion of sanity amidst the madness that seems to have descended upon the Children of Illudor, Elder." Mretlak sent (approval, sympathy, appreciation), and then he sent what he knew Ankaht had also come to learn: he relayed his full (support, determination, accord, loyalty). Her *selnarm* brushed his like one weak friend leaning against another's arm for support. Mretlak was gratified, humbled, suddenly awkward. "Revered Elder, this intelligence cluster remains at your service. Indeed, I was informed mere minutes before you arrived that I have been permanently removed from Senior Admiral Torhok's chain of command. I am now a security asset of the Council itself."

"Excellent. And how is your cluster—which I understand is soon to be expanded into a Section—taking this news?"

"Without much distress. Many of my staff have no love of humans, but none of them are infected with the *Destoshaz'ai*-as-*sulhaji* fanaticism. I screened any such candidates out of the initial selection pool. So—for the moment—we are not merely safe, but finally free to work on our own broader researches. Which have produced a most interesting result."

"Indeed? What is it?"

By way of answer, Mretlak passed a data token to Ankaht, who slipped it into her forearm-mounted reader. She let the *selnarmic* data streams flood into her. Mretlak watched for her reaction.

He was almost disappointed by her calm as she turned off the unit and turned to face him—until he realized that her stillness was a byproduct of the immense self-control she was exerting. "This is true? This is not a comedic fancy concocted by some bored analyst in your cluster?"

Mretlak was genuinely hurt. "Elder, if you think I would waste your time with lies, and right after you have suffered such losses and tribulations..."

She sent (apology, shame, apology). "Good Mretlak, I am sorry to have insulted your offices and your integrity. But this is—"

"It is rather stupefying, is it not? This human legend—of a third eye which possesses or signifies enlightenment, true seeing, and mystic powers such as clairvoyance and telepathy—is actually extremely widespread. But it is in Hinduism—as we have detailed here—that it has its most powerful and startlingly parallel presence."

Ankaht signaled (accord). "Jennifer Peitchkov mentioned this to me, but I never had the time to explore it. I presumed that it was merely an inchoate, ancient myth. But the exacting scholarly attention lavished upon the topic—"

"Yes. Its theological centrality is at least as arresting as the degree of detail in which it is set forth. This third eye—called the *gyananakashu*, or eye of knowledge—is a feature possessed by all noteworthy Hindu gods, and many of the lesser beings in the myths surrounding them. It also plays a central role in the outcome and end-story of creation, for the universe is said to end when the goddess Shiva finally opens her third eye."

"But if I read the material correctly, this annihilation is also the catalyst for rebirth, for creation."

"Yes—and for souls to be restored."

"So the Hindus believe in reincarnation as well?"

"For them, reincarnation is far more than a belief, Elder. Again, it is central to the Hindu cosmology. As with the teachings of Illudor, Hinduism teaches that the human soul attains enlightenment—we would say *holodah*—in its journey to and through higher states of being, with its end destination being a peculiar concept that they call Nirvana. And yes, I note the phonetic similarity of that term to our word *narmata*. Indeed, the similarities between our lived reality and Hinduism's faith-based myths are, quite frankly, disturbing in both their quality and quantity. If there were any other reasonable explanation, I would sincerely doubt that all these parallels could be dismissed as mere coincidence."

"I'm not sure they are coincidence, Intelligence Prime."

Mretlak had not expected that response. "I do not understand, Elder."

"Nor do I, Mretlak, but in the process of our research we found yet another disturbing human-Arduan parallel which exponentially increases the significance of your discoveries. As you know, in the course of creating the vocoder, we had reason to study every aspect of human communication. This involved studies of their physiology and biochemistry, with particular focus on their brain and related neurology."

Mretlak sent (accord). "Of course. To have ignored these physical variables would have been an unforgive-able oversight."

"We felt so, also. And in the process of closely examining their books on anatomy, we discovered something called the pineal gland. It is located in humans exactly where the neurological network for our main eye is located, and its phylogenic characteristics have caused many human anatomists to designate it as a latent, unexpressed, or evolutionarily lost third eye."

Mretlak had thought that he was the one who would proffer startling news during this meeting. Now he found himself on the receiving end—worse, arguably, because he had taken smug comfort in thinking that he was to be the sole purveyor of a shocking new perspective. "This cannot be . . . can it?"

"The structure is there, Mretlak, inside their bodies today. And there is still more evidence that supports the theory of it being a vestigial third eye. In higher Terran vertebrates—such as a number of their homeworld's reptiles—an analog of the human pineal gland actually asserts itself as a rudimentary light sensor. This means that directly on the humans' genetic tree there is not merely an ancestor but a plenitude of present relatives in the same phylum—*Chordata*—that have a third eye. And therefore, buried deep in the humans' own genome, there may still be a residual but deactivated code for it."

"So what does this mean, Elder? That there is some... some convergent evolution at work? Is this some challenge that Illudor has put before us—to find His Blind Children and reclaim them to His vision and awareness of His manifestation in the universe? Are we to be missionaries, then, to aliens—no, not aliens, therefore, but to long-lost and distant cousins?"

Ankaht projected (uncertainty, distraction, perplexity). "Mretlak, who can say? But I see now why Urkhot fought so desperately to keep the human histories, myths, and old religions hidden from us."

"Why? Do you suspect that he had come across these parallels in his readings of the human materials?"

"No, I doubt it. But I also doubt he needed to, in order to realize that it was only a matter of time before some evidence arose which was sure to topple his contention that humans are merely *zheteksh*."

"And he hasn't really lost that battle, Elder."

"You are absolutely right, Mretlak. His ludicrous propositions are now protected by the aura of his martyrdom. So now—for all of us—it is a race against time. Since he has imparted his desperate fanaticism to his followers, the more contrary evidence we unearth, the more frantic and intemperate their zealotry will become. In time, I fear..."

Mretlak saw it. "They will resort to genocide."

Ankaht shrugged. "They would then be able to claim that the question of human personhood was, at last, moot."

"Except that there are still uncounted billions of humans that exist beyond the limits of this star system."

"I'm sure the theological heirs of Urkhot would be happy to extend their genocidal policies to the rest of human space."

"Yes, that seems probable. It would also mean our ineluctable doom."

"So it would seem." Ankaht rose. "I must return to my tasks, Mretlak. You have given me much to think about. I shall continue to update you on any matters that seem pertinent."

"And I you, Elder."

As Ankaht left, Mretlak felt a new *selnarm* aura approaching, carefully matching her withdrawal. So he knew who it was. "Lentsul. Come in." Mretlak's promising counterinsurgency group junior commander entered, casting eyes back in the direction of Ankaht's withdrawal. "Do not worry, Prime. She will not return. Why do you avoid her so?" Mretlak knew the answer, of course, but needed to get the situation out in the open if it was to be resolved.

"She has protected the humans, Commander, and they are our enemies."

"This is incorrect, Lentsul. The Eldest Sleeper has—rightly—explored the humans and, in the process, uncovered facts that make our course of action less clear and our present position morally ambiguous. But she has not betrayed the People to champion the cause of the humans. If she had, I would not be her ally and this cluster would not support her activities."

Lentsul's *selnarm* seemed to settle, as if reassured. "I feared, given the recent events in the Council, that we might be ordered to discontinue our attempts to locate the headquarters of the human Resistance."

Mretlak felt the suppressed thirst for vengeance that throbbed at the back of Lentsul's dedication to his duty. Clearly, the humans had discarnated someone quite dear to him—an issue that was too nebulous and private for

Mretlak to address. But he could offer the reassurance the small *Ixturshaz* obviously wanted. "Be unconcerned, Lentsul. Your search continues. Even if we cannot now see the ultimate use to which your intelligence findings will be put, we do need to have it, regardless. Perhaps upon finding the human Resistance headquarters, we will simply keep it under observation. Perhaps we shall obliterate it. That is to be determined in the future—and by persons other than us. But our job remains unchanged. Now what do you have to report?"

Lentsul signaled (gratification). "We have finally back-tracked the purchase records for the remote detonators the humans used to trigger their charges in the Empty Zone's sewers. Most lead back to a number of construction supply companies, but there were also several lots that—once again—passed through the inventory of Rashid's Sport and Tool."

"Excellent. And who purchased these detonators?"

Lentsul pulsed (satisfaction). "The Department of Public Works."

Mretlak sent (dubiety). "This sounds like a completely legal transaction."

"Yes, it would seem so—except that the passive monitors we placed on the store provided us with images of the individuals who picked up the detonators, all of whom arrived in Public Works trucks and uniforms. However, we ran a comparison of their pictures against the photo ID records of all Public Works Department employees."

"And you found that none of the humans who picked up the detonators were actually employees of the Public Works Department."

"Exactly."

"Who are they, then?"

"Our first efforts to establish their identities were fruitless. With so many official records and databases having been purged by the humans before we arrived, we had little to work with. But we started finding the faces we were seeking by searching through other photo lists that belonged to ID databases that hadn't been purged—records of memberships to sporting facilities, hunting licenses, special vehicle registrations. And all of the IDs had a code on them which revealed what they all had in common."

"And what was that?"

"They were all affiliated with the human military services. Their current status of involvement varied widely. They might be active duty, reserve or retired—but they all had that in common."

Mretlak nodded. Now, at last, they had touched the core of the organization that opposed them. "Excellent work, Lentsul. And now we must track their movements. If we do so assiduously enough, they will lead us to our next objective—the location of the Resistance's headquarters."

"And how do we track their movements?"

"By giving them something we can track."

21

Ex Nihilo—Omnia

"Out of nothing—everything."
—Latin proverb (revised)

TRNS Goethals, *Detached Duty, Deep Space*

Against the backdrop of interstellar space—not the abstract circuit-diagram–like warp network to which humans had become accustomed—TRNS *Goethals* was a submicroscopic mote.

But on any normal scale of human engineering possibilities, *Goethals* was huge. And within her multimegaton depths, life-support systems and cryogenic sleep cells fluttered into activity, and began filling the small crew section of the behemoth with living warmth—a much greater warmth than that radiated by the dim red star that had begun to wax in her forward viewer.

Captain Javier Cardones once again tried to shrug off the cold-spasms in his larger muscles: a common side effect upon awakening from cyrogenic sleep. Unlike most of his crew, Cardones was career Terran Republic Navy. He wasn't always comfortable dealing with the civilian technicians under his command, even though they had, for this voyage, enlisted and placed themselves under military authority. Now he stood before them and stiffly went through the requisite platitudes about what they had accomplished, before getting down to business. "Our recon drones have completed their preliminary swing through this system, and it appears that, as expected, the Baldies have not picketed this star."

There was a general release of breath. Everyone knew what it would have meant if there *had* been pickets. The Baldies could not, under any circumstances, be allowed to capture the Kasugawa generator, or even to know of its existence. Hence the codes, known only to Captain Cardones and a few others, that were set to trigger an immense antimatter scuttling charge that would reduce *Goethals* to subatomic plasma.

"Now," Cardones continued, "the drones are continuing on the next stage of their programmed course, toward this system's single warp point." He pointed at the small holotank in the wardroom; they all crowded around it, peering over each other's shoulders. The red dot of Borden glowed at its center. The green icon of *Goethals* was to one side—about three o'clock, by the arbitrary "clock" overlay, roughly seven light-minutes out from the primary. The smaller icons of the recon drones crawled across the system, and one of them approached the purple circle that lay fifteen light-minutes out along the nine o'clock axis, marking the solitary warp point that led to Trebuchet, the next system in the Bellerophon Arm. The drone would closely inspect the space proximal to that warp point and determine if it was picketed. And if it was, then it was also possible that the drone might be spotted and elicit a response from the Baldies. . . .

But that did not occur: the space around the warp point was empty.

They all looked at each other, and the meeting broke up in the uneasy knowledge that they had gotten, if not a full pardon, at least a temporary reprieve.

And for the duration of that reprieve, they had a crucial task to finish: it was time to prepare the Kasugawa generator.

Naturally the planners hadn't wanted Li Han's armada to have too tedious a voyage between Borden's warp point and the new one it was about to acquire. At the same time, they wanted to leave room between the two for organizing and maneuvering—and for defensive depth, in case things should go sour. So a compromise had been worked out before *Goethals* had departed, using old survey charts of the Borden system.

Thus it was that *Goethals* now lay twelve light-minutes out from Borden along the twelve o'clock axis, with her clocks ticking toward an instant determined by atomic decay, in unison with other clocks ticking in the ZQ-147 starless warp nexus 2.21 light-years away. Her crew worked with a long-practiced smoothness that almost muffled the steadily rising suspense.

They could only assume that the matching Kasugawa generator was in place in ZQ-147, just as its operators could only assume that *Goethals* had completed its voyage on schedule and not found itself faced with the imperative of self-immolation. But neither could be certain until that approaching instant arrived, when both generators were to be simultaneously activated.

"T minus ten!" Captain Cardones called out. All at once, the pervasive low rumbling sound increased in pitch and volume, while all around the chamber displays lighted up with a jump in power levels. It seemed much longer than it was before he called "Mark!" and the noise rose sharply.

The crew watched the corresponding change on the big screen: a swirling pattern of golden light like a very slow whirlpool, down whose funnel they all stared into what appeared to be infinity.

They all knew it was spurious, and that the figures told the real story. But for a time no one could stop staring at the first artificially generated warp point in history.

TRNS Hochblitz Azhanti, *Combat Group November, Allied Fleet, Borden System*

First Space Lord Li Han's diminutive stature made her holographic image look even more ghostlike: she seemed like a diaphanous, aging sprite whose calm radiated a sense of patient yet immovable eternity.

"Captain Torrero-Suizas, do you have any questions?"

"None, Admiral. We advance with all speed until we detect the Baldies." He almost stumbled over the last word. The term—picked up from the intelligence relays received during the two abortive attempts to retake Bellerophon—had, like the rest of those communiqués, only recently made the jump from need-to-know suppression to common knowledge. Torrero-Suizas hardly missed a beat, however. "Once we've detected the Baldies, we are to send signals to you and send them to hell. And if we can, we keep pushing straight on through."

"Colorfully expressed, Captain, but a bit incomplete. Your combat group is to push through to Mercury. At each system prior to that destination, you stop, assess, and report. Once you are in Mercury, you secure the warp point for the safe passage of the fleet. As soon as the van starts coming through, and assuming there is no resistance, you take all your monitors to the Athena warp point. Being the gateway to the alien base of power back in Bellerophon, it is our primary objective. At the same time, send your light elements to patrol and hold the Treadway warp point. Once we have secured all Mercury's warp points, we will reassess. However, be prepared to receive new orders anytime after the van starts arriving in Mercury. This is a fluid situation, Captain. So, for the immediate future, flexibility must be Combat Group November's watchword and greatest virtue."

Torrero-Suizas saluted smartly and suppressed a smile. "We are ever virtuous, Admiral."

"If you would be a liar, Captain, at least endeavor not to be such a poor one. You have your orders. Carry them out."

"Yes, Admiral."

Li Han's hologhost faded out.

Torrero-Suizas turned to face both his bridge staff and the holograms standing at either of his rear flanks: Captains Oleg Skorinkov of the *Thunder Child* and Petra Ganjaring of the *Devourer,* respectively. "Start your op clocks on my mark . . . *mark.* Scout elements begin transit in five minutes."

Armed Auxiliary Enset-shef-rahir, *Detached Picket, Expeditionary Fleet of the* Anaht'doh Kainat, *BR-06 Warp Point*

The *selnarm* repeaters began stabbing "URGENT. ALARM. URGENT. ALARM." at Junior Commander Hers'hetr just as she emerged from her misting chamber after a double shift at the con. She sent a spike of her own into the repeater and pulsed at her XO, who was currently on the bridge. "Met'hir, report."

"Sir, I—" Evidently at a loss for words, Met'hir simply linked the visual relays into the *selnarm* repeater, so that Hers'hetr could see the source of the alarm for herself.

A veritable mountain of armor and weapons had emerged from the warp point—and now ponderously turned toward her. It dwarfed her own tiny craft, which was little more than a repair frigate that Admiral Narrok had retrofitted with some external missile racks and a few force beams. She reflexively fired off a *selnarm* command that both launched her hull's ready terminal courier drone and also sent an update across the system via *selnarm* booster—which triggered an automated courier to dive through the warp point into Mercury, raising the alarm as it went.

But even as she turned her attention back to her adversary, whose immense hull now loomed over her craft, Hers'hetr found herself frozen on the horns of an ethical dilemma. Yes, she had to do her duty to the Children of Illudor—but which interpretation of that duty should she follow at this crucial juncture? Torhok always urged his warriors to fight, but Narrok exhorted them to survive: to live to observe and report at least, to harry and hamper if practicable.

She was still in the process of deciding which course of action truly defined her duty to the Race in this circumstance when a force beam cut through her stateroom's bulkhead and sliced her freshly washed body cleanly in two. Two seconds later, the beam performed an analogous vivisection on the *Enset-shef-rahir*'s fusion containment rings and, in that same instant, the late

Junior Commander Hers'hetr's first humble command transformed itself into a brief, tiny replica of a star.

The other two Arduan ships near the Trebuchet warp point—a shuttle tender/transport and a fighter—were similarly reduced to subatomic particles within the ensuing twenty seconds. By that time, the three monitors, eight heavy cruisers, two light carriers, four scout cruisers, and two destroyers of Combat Group November had all transited the warp point and were making best speed for their objective: the BR-06-Mercury warp point.

Deployed in their rapidly receding wake, four courier drones plunged back into the warp point to Trebuchet to send the word:

The way is clear. Advance the fleet.

"Do you think they know we're coming?"

Captain Marco Torrero-Suizas cocked an eyebrow at his tactical officer of one month, Lieutenant Brian Lewis. "Of course they know."

"Well, I thought that we got all the Baldy ships and drones so fast that—"

"Listen, what little we know about these Baldies from the intel squeaks we snatched during the last two Battles of Bellerophon tells us one thing clearly—they have some kind of very fast communication, possibly something on the order of telepathy. If that's the case, then their first response to an attack coming through a warp point would be to send a message as far and fast as they can to their rear areas."

"But we hit all their drones, Captain."

"Yes—all the drones that we *saw*. But what if their hoodoo mind powers reach back as far as twenty light-seconds... or more? If they do, then they could have rung the alarm on us before the second of our ships completed transit. Face it, Lewis—we're going to have company as soon as we transit."

"Which is imminent," Helm chimed in. "Coming in four, three, two, one—transit!"

The *Hochblitz Azhanti* plunged into the warp point in BR-06, where it was instantly yanked out of one part of the space-time continuum—

—only to be hurled back into it, and out of the linked warp point, in the Mercury system—where force beams and lasers immediately began peppering the *Hochblitz Azhanti*.

"See what I mean?" Torrero-Suizas grinned sourly at Lewis.

The young tactical officer, ashen-faced, gripped the edge of the holotank as the monitor shook around him. "Our electronics are back online, sir. Orders?" The viewscreen blanked: overloaded. Lewis looked at his terminal again and reported, "Our defensive batteries are going to be overwhelmed soon, sir. They just intercepted twenty-nine capital missiles in the space of four seconds. More inbound."

"But not just at us anymore," Torrero-Suizas muttered around a grim smile. For in the tacplot, a second green icon had emerged into the Mercury system, where approximately three dozen red specks faced them.

"Their weapons are adjusting to hit *Devourer*, sir."

"And split between us, they will do less than half the damage to each." Not that the aliens had much choice, Torrero-Suizas allowed. If they failed to attack one of the two human monitors, the other, unharried ship would surely use that freedom to concentrate its many batteries on—and thus, savagely gut—one alien craft after another. "Tactics, hold missile launch until we've got *Thunder Child* with us and the datalinks established. In the meantime, concentrate all beam fire on the most proximal enemy ships and launch our fighters. Let's keep the Baldies busy and take our lumps, as we planned."

Ops nodded into the holoplot. "*Blackwyrm* intercepted a salvo meant for *Devourer*. Too many missiles got through her active defenses. Major damage in most sections—"

The stricken cruiser's green icon acquired a yellow limning: in naval parlance, it had been marked by a damage pennant.

"Rotate *Witchbane* into *Blackwyrm*'s place. Try to get her—"

But the yellow-ringed green icon fluttered, disappeared, and became an omega symbol.

"Captain Torrero-Suizas, *Blackwyrm* is Code Ome—"

"Thank you, Ops. My eyes still work. Unfortunately. *Witchbane* is to continue forward and plug the hole left by *Blackwyrm*." He stared at the most recently arrived large green icon—that denoting *Thunder Child*—and tapped an impatient finger. "Datalinks?"

"Coming sir . . ."

Now *Witchbane* began to flash bilious, as Torrero-Suizas's own hull tossed around him. "Communications, I need those—"

"Datalinks are up, sir!"

Torrero-Suizas turned to Lewis. "Target the cluster of SDHs bearing 34 by 300, thirteen light-seconds range. All monitors fire all tubes: salvo external racks. Maintain your fire."

"How long, sir?"

"Until all the bastards shooting at us are dead."

TRNS Cimarron Rebuke, *Allied Fleet, Mercury System*

Flying his lights from a monitor reminded Ian Trevayne of the early days of the Fringe Rebellion, or whatever the Terran Republic now called it. In those days, a monitor had been the largest warship type available. He had led a battlegroup including four of them on an epic flight through rebel-held space and the benevolently neutral Khanate of Orion to Zephrain, gateway to the loyal systems of the Rim. There, he himself had organized the construction of the first supermonitors, which had come as a nasty surprise to Li Han when the rebels (*I really must stop thinking of them as that*, he chided himself, not for the first time) had made a second attempt to take Zephrain.

Of course, TRNS *Cimmaron Rebuke* was very different in many ways from those ships. Those differences were part of the reason he still had Andreas Hagen, now a full commander, on his staff. Nevertheless, he felt increasingly confident of his ability to cope with the multiple revolutions that had overtaken military technology while he had lain in biotechnological limbo.

After a courier drone from Combat Group November had announced the way was clear, he had led the vanguard through to the Mercury system, deploying Mags (Li Magda had finally worn him down) ahead with her carrier-centered task force, adding her fighter strength to Torrero-Suizas's firepower as they pushed the remaining Arduans back from the warp point. He himself hung back for now with the monitors and superdreadnoughts, forming a shield wall around the BR-06 warp point and the unprepossessing thing that had just emerged from it.

As he watched the image transmitted from a remote pickup, the voice of the *Cimarron Rebuke*'s captain intruded on his thoughts. "Excuse me, Admiral, but the technicians report that the Kasugawa generator is now in position with relation to the warp point."

Trevayne glanced at the navplot and saw that the generator's rudimentary reactionless drive had brought it to a halt. "Excellent, Captain. Tell them to make preparations to activate at the prearranged time." Prearranged in conjunction with the identical generator Li Han was watching even now in BR-06. "And don't bother giving me a countdown."

Cimarron Rebuke didn't have Dr. Kasugawa's artsy visual representation of warp points, and Trevayne hadn't asked for it. He merely watched the pickups until he heard the background hubbub that indicated successful activation.

And, very shortly thereafter, the inconceivable mass of TRNS *Taconic* appeared in a warp point which hitherto could not have accommodated her, or any of the other devastators that now appeared, one after another.

Arduan SDH Hrun'pah'ter, *System Defense Force, Expeditionary Fleet of the* Anaht'doh Kainat, *Mercury System*

In the *Hrun'pah'ter*'s holopod, Fleet Second and System Commander Unshezh stared as the hoop denoting the warp point to BR-06 seemed to shimmer, flicker, wink out for a second, and then reassert.

"What happened?" she insisted of her sensor prime on the open *selnarm* link. "What caused that energy spike? Did another human craft materialize within this strange vessel of theirs?"

The sensor prime pulsed (urgent, wait) and kept studying his results.

"Sensor Prime! I must have the information, or your best estimate, immed—"

"Fleet Second, I . . . I cannot say with certainty, but I believe the humans have—have *modified* the warp point."

"They have *what*?"

"Modified the warp point, Fleet Second. Its entire signature has changed, and its gravitic flux wave has drastically increased."

"Hypothesis—and fast. What do these alterations signify?"

"I am not sure, but the warp point's overall distortion of non-Myrtakian space is far more profound than it was beforehand. By two orders of magnitude. At least."

Unshezh stifled the impulse to declare this impossible. Something extraordinary had occurred—and with all the human hulls that had already streamed out of the warp point, it seemed a certainty that the humans had some trick, some technology which had either allowed them to hide an entire fleet in the open expanses of the Trebuchet Trace, or which enabled them to somehow—

And then the beginnings of understanding came to her. She commandeered a system-ranged *selnarm* repeater and sent an urgent message to one of the drone launcher/tenders hovering at the very edge of the Mercury-to-Athena warp point. "Urgent. Prepare for immediate relay. Message begins: 'The humans have modified the warp point joining Mercury to BR-06. I conclude that it is extremely improbable that the immense human fleet now attacking Mercury could have been concealed anywhere in the Trebuchet Trace. I therefore conjecture that the humans have found a way to link other regions of their space with one or more systems within the Trebuchet Trace. Urgent. If this is true, Mercury is now a strategic bottleneck and must be held at all costs.' Message is for immediate *selnarm* relay and warp-point transmission, both to New Ardu and the current Flag Command site of Admiral Narrok. Send immediately." With any luck, given *selnarm*'s instantaneous transmission, the drone that was already plunging back into Athena would immediately activate its cousin that was waiting on the other side of that system, poised to dart through the warp point to Hera. And so, from one system to another, the *selnarm*-linked drones would trigger each other like a string of firecrackers going off. Conceivably, the message would be received at both terminal destinations within the hour.

But in the meantime, what did the human modification of this warp point portend: What advantage did the humans expect it might confer upon them?

At that moment, an impossibly huge green icon emerged from the warp point in the holotank and furnished a stupefied Unshezh with the horrifying answer to her question.

TRNS Taconic, *Allied Fleet, Mercury System*

Li Han stood on the flag bridge of *Taconic* and observed the Battle of Mercury unfold.

In the holotank, the main body of her ships moved inexorably from the newly enhanced BR-06 warp point in the direction of the Athena warp point, obli°terating anything that stood in its way. Her devastators were organized into datagroups of four, with two escort cruisers armed exclusively with anti-fighter weaponry stationed in the traditional flanking-and-astern position to cover the capital ships' blind zones. Any target of four devastators' firepower, datalinked into a single time-on-target salvo, did not need to be targeted a second time. The devastators' limited maneuverability scarcely mattered as Han advanced steadily through the center of the frantic Baldy defenders.

She turned to the tactical plot. Her daughter's carriers flanked the phalanx of devastators, streaming aft in a skirtlike fashion, providing fighter cover that so far had barely been necessary. Trevayne, with the remainder of the vanguard, was off to the left (in terms of the system's ecliptic plane), which placed him more or less in the direction of the Treadway warp point, guarding against the possibility of any fresh Baldy incursions from that direction.

"Admiral," Adrian M'Zangwe called from the ship's bridge, "the Baldies seem to be breaking up into two bodies. One is continuing to resist us. The other is withdrawing in the direction of the Treadway warp point."

Li Han expanded the holotank's scale and understood. Her irresistible advance had split the Baldies' system-defense force in two, and her force now stood between the retreating elements and the Athena warp point, which was doubtless where they would have preferred to go.

"Raise Admiral Trevayne," she ordered. While she waited, she sent a series of orders to Mags. Soon she began to see the skirt of carriers sweeping forward, reconfiguring into a net with which to trap the Baldies who still showed fight.

"You are in the best position to deal with those retreating elements," she told Trevayne. "Of course, your monitors aren't as fast as their heavy superdreadnoughts, but—"

"But this won't be a stern chase," he completed her thought. "At the course they must follow, we'll be able to intercept them at a converging angle. Don't worry. They will be attended to."

Han wondered if the hormones of Trevayne's youth were inducing excessive cockiness as she watched Mags's fighters herd the Baldies into the furnace door of the devastator formations. Meanwhile, Trevayne's monitors, armed predominantly with missiles, began to savage the Baldies well before the two forces slid together and interpenetrated. Finally, like a prey animal tormented beyond endurance, the Baldy commander had his ships turn sharply, in echelon, and roar toward their pursuers. But Trevayne's superdreadnoughts included a number of Pan-Sentient Union ships with a better short-range weaponry mix, and these were in his van. They and the Baldies had an exchange of fire whose intensity Han could barely imagine, before the Baldies flashed through them and neared the monitors.

But Trevayne had pushed through an innovation in Rim monitor and supermonitor design—partly inspired, Han recalled with pride, by what Mags had done to the Baldies at Third Bellerophon. He had decreed the removal of most of their limited beam weaponry and its replacement by energy torpedoes. These came as enough of a surprise to disrupt the Baldy attack, giving Trevayne's lighter ships time to come about in the manner possible to reactionless, inertia-canceling drives, and attack from astern. The battle dissolved into a chaos of engagements, which could have but one conclusion.

No, Han thought. *Trevayne hasn't lost his edge.*

Arduan SDH Hrun'pah'ter, *System Defense Force, Expeditionary Fleet of the* Anaht'doh Kainat, *Mercury System*

The long shudder that rippled through the hull of Unshezh's flagship was an ominous sign.

"Fleet Second, we are losing antimatter containment for the powerplant. In two minutes or less we will—"

"Time to repair?"

"Repair is not possible. We must fight our ship or abandon her."

"That choice is no choice." Unshezh looked carefully at the holoplot. Harried by fighters, her tattered system-defense force was either dying in place or being pushed back toward the Treadway warp point. She doubted any of them would make good their attempted escape. But she had to hold the humans here a little bit longer, make them pause, at least, so that reinforcements might arrive from Athena. . . .

She stabbed a greater tentacle into the plot, impaling the closest *murn*-colored icon. "This monitor, the one from their initial breaching force."

"The second warship that entered the system? Yes, Fleet Second, what do you wish to know about it?"

"If we run our engines at max plus twenty percent—"

"We will overtake the human warship in approximately seventy seconds. Our engines will probably go critical about twenty seconds later."

"And if your other estimate is correct, our antimatter pile will detonate thirty seconds after that. We have a choice of cataclysms, Helm. I choose the one that serves the Race."

The helm—and the entirety of Unshezh's bridge staff—sent (accord, joy, ferocity, resolve). Unshezh's helm prime set course for the large *murn*-colored icon.

Unshezh settled back into her command-pod and happily anticipated being reborn into a world where these patchy-furred humans had either been tamed, contained, or eliminated. In consequence, her next life would surely be a far more pleasant one. "Tactics, all priority to defensive weapons. Communications, signal our sister ships

In'sehert'tepsh and *Sho'ahah'fikir* to concentrate their main batteries on the other two human monitors to draw return fire. Then signal the remainder of our van: regroup around Fleet Third Sefet'hes and exploit any surprise our attack might generate in the humans. Helm: no evasive maneuvers. We go straight in. Ops: launch all small craft to help shield and screen us. Systems: all secondary and auxiliary command nexi are to be manned and operational. If this bridge is hit before we complete our run . . ."

"Understood, Fleet Second. For the Race."

"For the Race," Unshezh echoed proudly and watched as the vermillion icon of her beloved *Hrun'pah'ter* leaped toward the speck denoting the sluggish human warship. Beneath her, she felt the beginnings of a tremor that originated back in engineering, back in the overstressed tuners and coils that were pushing her forward. Like the heart of a great predator that refused to stop throbbing during an arduous pursuit, they would eventually burst.

But not before she took down this final prey.

TRNS Hochblitz Azhanti, *Combat Group November, Allied Fleet, Mercury System*

Lewis gaped. "I don't believe it, sir."

"Believe it." Torrero-Suizas's grim confirmation sounded more like a snarl than a statement. "Ops, who do we have that can—?"

"No one, Captain. *Devourer* was our outrider as we turned to provide flank support for the admiral's push toward the Athena warp point."

"And you're sure that Baldy superdreadnought is trying to ram?"

Helm confirmed it. "Range closing, bearing constant."

"Damn. General order to the Group: concentrate all batteries on that Baldy. Continuous fire."

Lewis swallowed loudly. "Sir, if we ignore the other two SDHs that are—"

"Dispatch fighters and two cruisers to engage them directly. If the other two SDHs ignore those attacks to stay focused on us, we'll let our giant-killers bag them."

Lewis, ashen, nodded and passed on the orders.

Torrero-Suizas felt his ship begin to quake as the missiles began running out in a steady stream at the enemy ship that was closing on the *Devourer*. The human monitor, having the maneuver characteristics of an overloaded dross barge, was executing its inevitable, and pitiful, attempts at evasive maneuvers.

The *Hrun'pah'ter*'s bridge—and with it, Unshezh and her entire staff—were reduced to subatomic particles twenty-eight seconds later. Five seconds before their incandescent discarnation, however, helm control had passed to Auxiliary Station Two. Auxiliary One had already been replaced by a very big hole in the SDH's savaged sides.

Twelve seconds later, the *Hrun'pah'ter*'s last shields went down and pieces of her started coming away in chunks as beams gouged at her sides and antimatter missiles almost reached her hull.

But four seconds after the *Hrun'pah'ter*'s shields went down, she reached her ponderous, wallowing target: she struck *Devourer* just aft of amidships.

The two vessels were suddenly gone, and in their place, a miniature analog of a blue-white sub-dwarf star flashed into sudden, blinding existence and sent out a glimmering wave-front halo of energies that ran the gamut of the electromagnetic spectrum.

Then the mini-star guttered, winked once, and died back into the blackness of space.

Torrero-Suizas rested his forehead in his hand and noticed, peripherally, that his ship's abrupt, arrhythmic bumps and jolts—near misses and partial hits—had dropped off sharply. He looked up: Lewis was staring down at him, pale but—finally—composed. "Sir, sensors confirm that *Devourer* was lost with all hands. All three enemy SDHs were destroyed. The remaining Baldy forces are attempting to regroup. Should we change course to—?"

"Negative, Tactics. Monitors and superdreadnoughts are to hold their headings. We are going to keep Admiral Li's flank secure. Cruisers and carrier squadrons are to screen us, but also try to maneuver to the rear of the Baldies' remaining forces. If the bastards have to keep turning around to protect their asses, they won't be coming after ours."

"What if they turn to reinforce the elements slipping back toward the Treadway warp point?"

"We let them go. The pursuit force Admiral Trevayne left behind will, I'm sure, happily add them to its many-toothed meatgrinder."

"Yes, sir. Any other orders, sir?"

"Yes. Once we secure from general quarters, pipe this down to all decks: ten seconds of silence for the crew of the *Devourer*."

The Baldy reinforcements had been emerging from the Athena warp point for about fifteen minutes when Li Han's main body drew into range. That force didn't concern her particularly, as she scanned the readout showing the ship classes involved. She crisply issued firing orders and settled back. Over patient, steepled fingers, she watched a wave of change sweep across the icons of the hapless Baldy SDHs. One after the other, they transformed into enemy omega symbols.

In the end, slightly less than half of the Baldy force from Athena had made it back to that system. Li Han's scout ships and drones began to pick over the wreckage, gathering data for the post-engagement briefing.

Li Han turned toward her holograph-convened staff after her ops officer had finished reeling off the post-action statistics. "So, Commander Rijksdottir, am I correct in concluding that this system can be declared secure?"

"You are, Admiral."

"Then we can start launching recon drones into Athena."

"They'll be launched immediately, Admiral."

"Make it a little sooner than that. I intend to commence the assault in twelve hours."

Many of the more junior, flesh-and-blood staffers looked taken aback, but the two holo images of Trevayne and Li Magda showed nothing but predatory eagerness. "Bloody right!" the Trevayne-image exclaimed. "They're still reeling—not just physically, but from the shock our devastators must have been, to say nothing of our expanding the warp point. Hit them while they're still off balance, before they have time to recover and reorganize."

"Then let's get busy, ladies and gentlemen," said Li Han in meeting-adjourning tones. Before the holo images of her two senior admirals winked out, she noticed them glancing at each other. She ordered herself not to draw any conclusions from their expressions.

22

Nothing Half So Melancholy

Nothing except a battle lost can be
half so melancholy as a battle won.
—Wellington

Arduan SDH Shem'pter'ai*, Main Van, Expeditionary Fleet of the* Anaht'doh Kainat*, Achilles System*

Narrok closed his eyes slowly and stole a moment of complete solitude . . . just as one of his staffers—Communications—approached, *selnarm* primed but withheld.

Narrok sent (permission). "I would not delay you in your duties, Communications Prime. What message?"

"Update from Mercury, sir . . . well, actually from Athena."

So: his units had been driven out of Mercury and back to Athena. That suggested the human flotilla was every bit as large as early estimates had indicated. Furthermore, since a full-sized fleet could not have remained hidden in the Trebuchet Trace, this news indicated that Unshezh had been right regarding its origins and the humans' ability to alter a warp point. "I will assimilate the message now, Prime."

"Yes, sir."

And Narrok immersed himself in the streaming data, which took him about ten seconds to absorb.

It told him what he had already surmised: those forces of his that had sortied into Mercury from Athena had been lost. Significantly, no Arduan response had been noted coming into Mercury from Treadway, which meant that the commander there—Fleet Second Nejfel, who oversaw the task-force monitoring and preventing any further Tangri incursions—was mulling over the situation and his options. And whatever course of action the fleet second ultimately chose, Narrok felt that Nejfel, above all the other commanders he had been compelled to scatter along the various highways and byways of the Arm, would understand that his objective was not to inflict damage, or to display ferocity, or to repel the attackers.

It was to buy time.

Because having too few hours, thought Narrok as he looked at the warp-point matrix in his holotank, *will be far more deadly to us than having too few ships.* He looked at the links and calculated: he had less than two days to get there.

Of course, Torhok would be on his way up the Arm, presumably bringing the main Fleet reserves from New Ardu. Given the smaller number of warp points he had to traverse to reach Charlotte—only three—Torhok had every apparent reason to arrive first. But a fleet already in the field—such as Narrok's—was poised and ready for response in any direction. By contrast, a home fleet at its moorings was a creature much slower to stir. At least, Narrok consoled himself, Torhok was more astute at grand strategy than operations or tactics: he would understand the need to reach Charlotte with all possible alacrity.

And perhaps he would even remember to thank Narrok for being the voice that insisted on sowing minefields in the Arm's various choke points and preparing a new surprise for any human—or Tangri—thrusts toward New Ardu. Yes, Torhok might remember that Narrok had been the architect of these plans—

But he probably wouldn't admit it, even if he did.

TRNS Taconic, *Allied Fleet, Mercury System*

Admiral Li Han checked the ops clock: twelve minutes remaining before it ticked down to the row of zeroes that meant S-Second had been reached. She looked around the main plot of her chart room; fourteen holograms of her senior officers stared down at the holographic specks and icons that depicted the Fleet's current—and coming—dispositions. "Any questions?"

Li Han waited for the two-way transit time to elapse. When it had, there was still silence. "Very well, then. Fleet Operations Officer Rijksdottir, your final update, please."

A tall woman with olive-toned skin and startling red hair rose and surveyed the ghostly simulacra of the Fleet's senior officers. "Sirs, the tankers, tenders, and ammunition carriers of our supply train have all reached their groupment point, here." She indicated a dense cluster of small green icons slightly above and beyond the Desai limit on the side of the system opposite the warp point to Athena. "They are currently configuring their formation to establish what will be the equivalent of a semi-mobile depot and refit base for supporting operations farther down the Arm. It has been positioned farthest from the Athena warp point to provide maximum warning and withdrawal time in the event any counterattacking forces manage to reenter the Mercury system."

"That presumes the threat from Treadway is less imminent," observed Captain Tanner, whose ship, the DT TRNS *Fionna MacTaggart*, was only two light-seconds away.

Fleet Ops shrugged. "We have no means of assessing that risk, Captain. Our holding force—Combat Group Sierra—is too low on drones to mount a good recon effort. They are simply tasked with contesting and delaying an intrusion. We have other forces in reserve for repelling any such counterattack."

"What forces are those?" asked Tanner.

At a nod from Li Han, the tall woman sat and a short, stubby man—dark of skin, hair, and eye—rose. Li Han invited his answer with a graceful gesture. "Fleet Tactical Officer Sarimanok?"

Sarimanok pointed to a dense cluster of larger green icons positioned above the vertical arc of the Desai limit halfway between the supply train and the bright sphere representing the system's star. "This, for lack of a better term, is our all-purpose reserve. With the exception of one DT, it is comprised of our older, slower craft—predominantly MTs and BBs that are two or more marks out of date. In their current position, they have equal response times to either support the assault into Athena or prevent a serious incursion from Treadway. What they lack in speed and technological recency, they make up for in numbers, armor, and firepower.

"The assault into Athena itself is the next step on our march to the warp point linking Demeter to Charlotte. Unfortunately, it's going to be a hard-fought step. Advance recon indicates defender forces of almost 140 SDHs in the Athena system. We are also detecting minefields, which the Baldies have shown no tendency to employ before now. Our attack into Athena will begin with a sustained barrage of SBMHAWKs, followed closely by a rapid sequence of AMBAMMs. We will lead with a number of DTs to absorb the first wave of defensive fire. We anticipate considerable damage, but no immediate Code Omegas." Sarimanok sat abruptly.

Li Han rose and looked at the ops clock. Eight minutes left. "Thank you. Gentlemen, ladies: stand to your cons." One after the other, the hologhosts snapped salutes and disappeared. Within thirty seconds, the chart room was quiet, empty, unhaunted by the spectres who were soon to carry flame and death to the enemy.

Arduan SDH Nelsef's'hed'rem, *Tangri Containment Task Force of the* Anaht'doh Kainat, *Treadway System*

Fleet Second Nejfel considered the battle recording as it unfolded in both his holopod and over his *sel-narm* link. Unshezh's vastly undergunned force in the Mercury system had held as long as it was able but ultimately shattered when the very warp point itself seemed to change—and then truly immense warships emerged. According to the last courier that had come to his command in Treadway, four surviving SDHs had been within thirty minutes of reaching the safety of that same portal. But now almost half a day had passed and those SDHs had never come through.

Not that that had been a surprise. Shortly after the expected arrival time of the last four SDHs had elapsed, Nejfel has sent an RD back into Mercury. The area immediately around his own warp point was deserted, although a small human force was detected inbound: a pair of SMTs, a few DD's, and about a dozen battleships—relatively old marks from what the sensors showed of their drive efficiencies. Clearly, not an assault force: just enough to keep an uncertain attacker from Treadway occupied for a while. However, because Nejfel's reconnaissance drone had seen this detachment, and because one of his relay drones had promptly apprised him of it, he would not be an uncertain attacker—not if he struck within the next few hours.

Meaning that Nejfel now had a most difficult decision to make: sit tight and defend his side of the Treadway-Mercury warp point or advance to engage the humans. The matter had been debated among his primes and seconds for thirty minutes already, and the accelerated recordings of the battles and deployments in Mercury had been played three times. But now Nejfel let his subordinates feel his *selnarm* coalesce, like a gas cohering, compacting, gathering into a liquid that would soon roll its will down upon them and set the task force on whichever course he might choose.

"We advance," he radiated. Those members of his staff who were devotees of Torhok signaled (pleasure)—from which they could not purge a faint halo of (surprise) as well. Nejfel was known to be a favorite of Narrok, and his deft prosecution of constraining actions against the Tangri resonated with that admiral's doctrine of measuring the force required for a task so as to minimize the losses taken. Consequently, Torhok's advocates had expected Nejfel to hunker down and defend the warp point from this side.

Predictably, Nejfel's decision to attack had the opposite effect upon his most dedicated supporters. "Admiral," asked his ops prime, "may I ask what leads you to this decision?"

"The inevitability of the situation, Ops."

"I do not understand. We have reasonable minefields here in Treadway, and our combat tonnage vastly outmatches what we have seen the humans commit to the warp point into our system. Granted, we could probably defeat them even if we assault across the warp point, but we can *surely* hold them here, with minimal losses, while Admiral Narrok sends a sufficient force up the Arm. With no place left to run, these human ships will be crushed by our numbers."

Nejfel signaled (appreciation) but thought: *How much this war has cost us already, that this precocious Youngling is the best advisor in my task force. Heaven help us against the seasoned command staffs of the humans.* What he shared with his staff was: "Would that these were our only worries. But the appearance of this human force gives us a new, and very dangerous, variable that we must factor into our plans: Where have they come from? Alas, I suspect discarnate Unshezh's surmise is correct: that either the humans have discovered a new warp point leading from a seat of their power to one of the systems beyond BR-06 or have been able to manufacture one. If this is the case, then we could be faced with the thankless task of trying to stem a flood, a tidal wave that has no end. And we cannot do it from here. The surge is coming at us out of the Trebuchet Trace and has already broken free into Mercury. Even if Admiral Narrok arrives with the entirety of his fleet, there is no surety that they will be able to compel the humans to withdraw back that way. Meaning that we are cut off, without hope of reinforcements. We must do what we can with what we have."

"But if you are right, Fleet Second, then how will our attacking into the Mercury system manage to deter this armada of enemy ships? We would be a pebble challenging a mountain."

Nejfel radiated (serenity, certainty). "Then we must not challenge the mountain, Ops. We must remember this: our actions will be without efficacy if we do not first carefully consider how they will mesh with the actions being undertaken by the rest of our forces."

"And what actions do you conjecture they are undertaking, Task Force Commander?"

"Nothing unusual, Tactics. Just as our drones have reported to us, those waiting at the Athena warp point have certainly reported back as well, and their alarum is even now racing down the arm—toward Narrok and Torhok. They certainly have enough ships to halt this human invasion—but will they have enough time? Any relief forces coming up toward Mercury will be in a desperate race to intercept the humans before they get far enough down the Arm that they could come between our two greatest force concentrations: the Home Fleet under Torhok in New Ardu, and the Expeditionary Fleet under Narrok, who has returned to Ajax. So what our brothers and sisters need is time. That is what we must purchase for them."

"But if we abandon this warp point to carry a full-scale attack into Mercury, the Tangri will—"

(Agreement, exception.) "At this moment, my primes, all other considerations pale beside this: we must do what we can to buy time so that our fleet that can contain this incursion. I have already instructed the forces in Tisiphone to leave only light elements there and to take our place, defending this side of Treadway's warp point into Mercury. If, as a consequence, the Tangri sense the withdrawal of our task forces in Tisiphone and beyond, then it must be so: our first and only duty is to the survival of our Race. And that duty calls us to meet the humans in the Mercury system. Are there any questions or uncertainties?"

"A curiosity, Admiral."

"Yes, Ops?"

"What will we do, once we meet the humans in the Mercury system?"

"An excellent question. I wish I had an excellent answer. But since we have elected not to send through further RDs—thereby hoping to lull the humans into believing it as a sign of our quiescence—I cannot know what we will find when we get to the other side. Once there, I will choose among a variety of alternatives."

The group was still. *Selnarms* pulsed with (accord)—some eagerly, some with that species of regret that typifies a person who has lost a debate . . . and knows that the right of the argument was indeed with the other side.

"Very well," Nejfel projected, "we are finished. Ops, alert the task force: flank speed, closest intervals, *Urret-fah'ah* minesweepers in the lead. The order is: all hulls through the warp point into Mercury."

TRNS Scarlet Reaper, *Combat Group Sierra, Allied Fleet, Mercury System*

"Captain! Warp-point activity!"

"What? Evasive and all batteries, fire."

"Yes, sir, but—they're pinnaces. Dozens, all running heavy ECM and image makers. And, sir—"

Commander Simone Aswan-Parimbo had learned

what that tone of voice meant when uttered by her seasoned ops officer: disaster on the hoof, and closing in. "Facts. Fast."

But before Ops could speak, Simone's ship—the supermonitor TRNS *Scarlet Reaper*—bucked, the tacplot blinked, and when it came back, half of her command—Combat Group Sierra—was gone. "Shit," she muttered, "what the hell just hap—?"

Simone was vaporized in mid-syllable, along with every other person onboard her SMT. Having positioned her hull close to the warp point so as to be able to put immediate, murderous fire on anything that came through, there was one gambit she had not anticipated: that the often uninventive Arduans would discover a new use for their stickhive minesweepers. Retrofitted with advanced ECM and far more powerful engines, three of the glorified cluster bombs had come through the warp point, recovered almost immediately, and darted forward at almost 0.23 c toward the closest hulls of Combat Group Sierra. One Stickhive had been intercepted in time. The second got most of Captain Aswan-Parimbo's light hulls. But the third one survived long enough to come within 32,000 kilometers of the *ScarletReaper* and discharge its omnidirectional spray of immense antimatter warheads.

Into the superheated cloud of discorporated human ships emerged a fast flurry of SDHs from the Treadway warp point. And by the time the remnants of Combat Group Sierra reformed, the Arduans had managed to activate a datahub. Missiles—guided with one mind and purpose—reached out toward the human ships that were still struggling to respond. . . .

TRNS Taconic, *Allied Fleet, Athena System*

Riding her own gargantua of metal, composites, weapons, and death out of the warp point into Athena, Li Han nodded to her staff: she needed updates. Immediately.

And because she needed so much information so very quickly, she closed her eyes as they surrounded her: this way, the collage of excited faces did not distract her from the voices that contended with each other, weaving the chaotic tapestry and tale of a battle already in progress.

The AMBAMMs had done their work well, igniting as a rapidly advancing cascade of blue-white actinic spheres: each seemed to spawn another, stretching across the insufficient Baldy minefields like a string of annihilatory pearls.

But as the human ships started coming through, the enemy missiles came in from all points, unerringly guided by the Baldies' innumerable data hubs. These hubs demonstrated surprising resilience, able to rebuild faster than Li Han's ships could break them up: the enemy had multiply cross-patched their ships' computer control systems like an ancient telephone switchboard. The human point-defense batteries were eroding the consequent waves of antimatter warheads, but not fast enough: the first smaller ship that had come through the warp point—the fleet-footed battlecruiser TRNS *Greyhound*—was not able to handle her share of the deluge and was consumed by a cluster of antimatter explosions.

The devastators of Li Han's command, and now the supermonitors as well, were holding their own, reaching out and squashing the Arduans with overwhelming firepower. But they had to advance slowly, wielding their immense batteries like battle-axes. In contrast, the enemy SDHs were fast and agile, stabbing here and there with their épée-like armaments. When the human craft struck, the blows dealt death; when the Baldies jabbed or slashed, they always drew blood. But there were far more épées than battle-axes on this battlefield, and Li Han foresaw that pressing forward into the Athena system was going to be akin to hacking through a veritable thicket of just such nimble blades.

She opened her eyes. "Send back word: the Fleet Reserve is needed. It is to make best speed for the Athena warp point."

Then she turned her eyes to the plot she had avoided looking at for as long as possible, forcing herself at last to witness the carnage depicted therein.

Arduan SDH Nelsef's'hed'rem, *Tangri-Containment Task Force of the* Anaht'doh Kainat, *Mercury System*

"Junior Admiral, we have lost all thr—"

(Known.) Nejfel had seen the three crippled SDHs at the leading wedge-point of his van blink away in rapid sequence. The few human SMTs that had been in ready response range when he came through the Treadway warp point were now being aided by one of the new human DTs. This mountainous human ship could not be resisted, could not be held, could not even be delayed. And if there was not some way to deter it, then not only would Nejfel's own task force die—it was, he frankly admitted, dead already—but the one in Athena might be lost as well, if the humans attacking there perceived no dire need to leave these reserves behind to guard Mercury. So, using the eight

SDHs he had kept carefully cloaked, and veering away from the main engagement with the human warships, he acknowledged—as he had thought from the very first—that there was but one way to effectively strike at such a seemingly impervious adversary.

Upon entering the system, he had recited an old *Destoshaz* axiom invariably taught in the first week after the Caste-choice Ceremony: "There are enemies too great to contest, let alone defeat. Accept this—and search for their weaker associates. Threatening those lesser proxies may allow you to shape the behavior of a foe you could not hope to influence directly." And so, good *Destoshaz* that he was, Nejfel had found the weaker associates of his unassailable foe.

"Helm, all cloaked SDHs on us. Bring us to 342 by 317. Tactics, if we make directly for the auxiliaries the humans have deposited at the edge of the Desai limit, how close will we pass to that behemoth and its escorts?"

"Twenty-five light-seconds, sir, and that presumes they will alter course to engage us. If they do, they will be able to hit us with missile barrages. However, their cruisers and fighters will probably reach us first and work in around our sterns if we don't change course. Both of those problems will arise just about the time we start engaging the human auxiliaries."

"Yes, I see it. Shortly after we attack their supply train, they will bring the great ship to bear and their missiles will make quick work of us. And those of us which survive that will certainly be annihilated by their fast craft. So I speak truth to you, Tactics—and all the rest: we will be discarnated within the hour no matter what course we set, so let it be one that diverts the humans from their focus upon Athena. Helm, all cloaked ships on us, flank speed plus ten percent, ready all missiles. Let our names be remembered until we are embodied again! Engage."

TRNS Taconic, *Allied Fleet, Athena System*

Li Han knew, from the metronomic regularity of the flat-soled, ungracious footfalls, that Sarimanok was approaching, steeled to deliver a message he knew would displease his superior. "Yes, Commander?" she asked over her shoulder. "What is the bad news?"

If Sarimanok was surprised that she knew it was him, or that he was the bearer of ill-tidings, he gave no sign of it. "Admiral, we have had a signal from the Reserve in Mercury. There was an enemy attack in strength from Treadway—it wiped out Combat Group Sierra. The Reserve had to make best speed to engage, and then retake and secure the warp point."

"So the Reserve will be unable to reach us in time."

"Yes, Admiral. But there is more."

There always is. "Report, Commander."

"Admiral, the Baldy attack force from Treadway was destroyed—every last hull—but a number of them eluded initial detection and penetrated almost to the Desai limit."

Li Han closed her eyes. "The depot?"

"Yes, Admiral. The Baldies reached launch range. Because the ships were already forming into *ad hoc* space docks, and had already affixed stabilizing booms and tethers, they were unable to maneuver. Losses among the tenders and missile supply ships were disproportionately heavy."

"And the Kasugawa generators?"

"One was lost before their tugs could pull all of them out of range."

Li Han nodded, opened her eyes and looked at her tacplot. The news was not much better here in Athena: the enemy was managing to hold together longer than had been expected. The Baldies had obviously anticipated and prepared for losses: their data hubs were furnished with multiple redundancies, fresh hulls waiting to take the place of others that had been lost or crippled. This, and whatever mind contact they used, evidently provided them with many swift contingencies for rerouting. She turned to Sarimanok and looked him straight in the eyes. "So, the Reserves are not coming. In that case, it is all upon us."

Arduan SDH Tesnu'hep'heb, *Hera System Reserve Force, Athena System*

Fleet Second Sentersep studied the holopod and watched the evolution of the engagement replay at 100:1 speed again. After punching through the minefields, the humans' leading wedge of behemothic warships had made straight for the Hera warp point. *Of course: they want to roll us back as far as possible. Probably they're hoping to reach Charlotte. And if they take Charlotte, then the question is no longer* if *they will be able to carry an attack into New Ardu, but* when. *And that is not acceptable.*

Ebrenet, her long-standing tactical officer and second commander, sent a gentle tendril, as was his wont. "You must prevent them from reaching Charlotte."

She sent (amusement, amazement). "Old friend, how is it you read my mind, even when our *selnarm* is not linked?"

Ebrenet, despite the carnage of the day, managed to find a mood that was a bit (fey, ironic). "Ah, Fleet Second—I have my ways."

"I am sure you do." She turned her attention to the tacplot again. "We will need to slow them even more."

"Difficult."

"Challenging. But not impossible. We have seen how ponderous these great ships are."

"To be charitable, they turn quite slowly. What of it?"

She spoke in the code that long association produces. "We send our SDHs to the far flanks, outside the Desai limit; all fighters gather inside the Desai limit. They both use the same tactics: work toward the humans' rear, keep them turning to protect their own sterns."

"Yes. This is best. And it will allow us to minimize our casualties. We will not inflict many either, of course."

"Of course—but we are fighting for time, not exchange ratios."

"So true." Ebrenet turned to the ops prime, whose eyes were goggling: even sharing an open *selnarm* link with the other two did not help him penetrate all their shorthand. "I will explain. The ships at the leading edge of the human attack are slow; this makes them vulnerable to rear attacks. Faster craft, such as our SDHs, if pushed out to the flanks, will compel them to slow down, to angle their heading so they both keep their bows to our SDHs and their course obliquely toward their destination—the Hera warp point."

"And so, we gain time."

Ebrenet sent (accord), adding: "And by giving ground slowly, we minimize our losses, which will in turn allow us to hold them at the Hera warp point for a longer interval."

The ops prime pulsed (accord, appreciation) and sent the necessary orders.

Five minutes later, Sentersep watched as her strategy unfolded. Her blocking force of SDHs had scattered out and away from the relentless path of the human DTs. In the tacplot, a diaphanous ring of her flotilla's vermillion specks had formed around the leading edge of the lateral column of *murn*-colored icons that marked the advancing van of the human fleet. And as predicted, the lead elements of that van slowed, angling their courses so as to turn their engine decks slightly away from the SDHs which were now flanking them. Faster SDs emerged from the human van to engage and attempt to drive off the Arduan SDHs. And all the while—as each engagement resolved—the humans were losing precious time, turning away from their direct advance to the Hera warp point.

Tactics observed the evolving engagements as human SDs traded dire damage with Arduan SDHs, most hulls limping away from the combat like exhausted pugilists. "We will kill only a few of their ships this way. Our bases of fire are now too scattered, and our ships are too far apart to maintain their data hubs."

"All true. But I am not interested in how many hulls they have left, Tactics."

Tactics sent (accord, rue). "No, you are interested in how many hours they have left."

"Just so, Tactics: just so."

And as they watched the tiny, luminous fireflies chase each other slowly around the tacplot, the space beyond the hull of the *Tesnu'hep'heb* was being made bright with the sudden comings, goings, and dyings of the actual ships represented. Inside the Desai limit, hundreds of Arduan fighters were destroyed by their vastly superior human and Orion analogs in futile attempts to threaten the flanks of the leviathans. The pilots of the Allied Fleet shouted or howled in victory, counted their kills, imagined further glories—but all of it took time. Too much time.

Meanwhile, the van of the Allied Fleet continued to grind forward, vaporizing any Arduan SDHs that were foolish or unfortunate enough to come within its missile range. Those SDHs that attempted doubling around the devastators had to be cut off, herded away, and since that task fell to the speedy human cruisers, losses among that class of ship were high—along with lighter carriers, which were plugging any gaps that opened suddenly, unexpectedly. They were dispatched like fire brigades, sent out from the safe body of the van whenever an engagement did not go as planned. And too often, in their race to put out one such fire, they attracted and fell victim to another.

The minutes and the hours went by. Hulls great and small dodged, plunged, flared, and died—leaving either trails of debris or monomolecular dust to mark the site of their vaporization. And those ships that were not slain were almost all wounded, seamed and scarred by the brief glances of beam weapons and the close detonations of warheads. By the time Sentersep gave the order for a final withdrawal to, and through, the Hera warp point, her fleet had been reduced by fifty percent. The human fleet followed stolidly, much less diminished than hers, but too spent to give chase. It was merely ensuring that Sentersep did not change her mind and round on them once again, ensuring that she was indeed conceding the system.

And so she did, as the bow of her battered flagship *Tesnu'hep'heb* headed for the warp point to Hera.

Having outrun their supplies—Ian Trevayne had made a characteristically obscure reference to someone named Patton—the three senior human admirals could afford the luxury of an in-the-flesh meeting . . . the first they had had in a while, and perhaps the last they would have in an even longer while.

Thus it was that the three of them sat in *Taconic*'s otherwise empty flag lounge. The debriefings and staff reports were over, and now they shared a moment of companionable silence, with Trevayne sipping his trademark single-malt Scotch. Li Han's eyebrows had risen as high as they ever rose when Mags had asked for the same thing. *He's corrupted her!* She told herself not to follow the thought out to wherever it might lead. Instead, she sipped the white wine that was all she ever permitted herself and gazed surreptitiously at the two youthful faces and the looks they occasionally couldn't help exchanging.

Isn't life strange? Her lips quirked upward at the reflection.

"Well," she finally said, breaking the silence, "I suppose the first wild ride is over."

Mags stared down into her Scotch. "What really disturbs me is the loss of one of the Kasugawa generators."

Li Han could barely bring herself to nod. "Indeed. Our margin for error with the generators is now paper-thin. And you both heard Fleet Ops's report on the recon drones we've sent ahead into the Hera system."

"Yes." Trevayne scowled into his Scotch. "Of the fifty or so, none have come back. I'd say that ominous silence is as articulate and telling as any sensor readout could have been."

Li Han finished her wine. "Well, I'll have to ask the two of you to excuse me. There's a final set of reports I need to receive from my chief of staff."

Trevayne met her eyes. He knew the exact nature of the grisly rite to which she referred. He tossed off the last of his Scotch and rose to his feet. "Yes. I should be getting back to *Rebuke*." But he paused, and there was a moment of what, if it had been anyone else, would have been instantly recognizable as awkwardness. "Admiral Li . . ."

"I think you can call me Han by now, don't you?"

He looked almost startled, but recovered quickly. "Yes, I suppose so. Ah, Han . . . History is real. It can't be undone."

"You mean, of course, *our* history."

"Yes. It's still there. But it no longer has to matter. And . . . you were worth having as an enemy, Han."

"As were you, Ian," she heard someone who sounded remarkably like herself say.

Mags looked from one living legend to another, and her expression said she wanted to look away but could not.

Trevayne tried to say something, but nothing came.

Well, I've lived long enough to see him speechless, Han thought. But then his eyes met Mags's, and this time their eyes held each other for a long moment. Then they both turned and met Han's eyes unflinchingly.

What can I say? "Bless you, my children?" No. Impossible. Absurd.

So she said nothing. Neither did they. No words were necessary.

Li Magda went to her mother and hugged her with fierce intensity. Trevayne gave her a salute that would have done credit to the junior officer his apparent age suggested.

As she returned the salute, Li Han suddenly remembered the bearded, fiftyish version of that face. She had stood in prison garb and looked into that face with more hate than she had ever known she could feel. It had been the last time she had ever seen it. She hadn't dreamed that she would never see it again. And now...

What am I thinking? Of course I'll see him again.

And then they were gone. And she had to attend to that final report that every commander dreaded.

The list of ships—and crews—that had been lost.

23

Nothing More Unpleasant

Nothing is more unpleasant than a
virtuous person with a mean mind.
—Bagehot

Prisoner Holding Facility, Resistance Regional Headquarters, Charybdis Islands, Bellerophon/New Ardu

Alessandro McGee insisted on being the first person into the room, but by the time Heide looked up from the desk, Lieutenant "Cap" Peters and Lieutenant Chong had already entered and come to stand in front of him. Igor Danilenko slotted into the second rank right beside McGee, and both Juan Kapinski and Roon Kelakos slipped in behind them. Thus, in a column two wide and three deep, they faced the Hider, at parade rest.

Heide had looked up when McGee entered, had returned to shuffling the papers for the hearing, then looked up again as the unprecedented parade of personnel filed into the small makeshift courtroom that had been set up for the day's proceedings. "What is the meaning of this?" he asked just as Harry Li trotted through the door and up to Heide's desk, where he saluted the CO and then turned smartly to look out over the six men gathered before them. Heide, evidently surprised and a bit baffled by the unexpected crowd, repeated, "What is the meaning of this? Lieutenant Peters?"

Cap Peters looked straight ahead. "Captain Heide, I have been informed by the sergeant of the guard that detainee Peitchkov has disappeared from her cell."

Heide jumped to his feet so quickly that his chair tipped over behind him. "She is what? She has escaped?"

"Sir," repeated Peters, "she is not in her cell." McGee wondered when Heide would catch on to the significance implicit in Peters's avoidance of the word *escape*. But the captain was too busy trembling with—what? Rage? Frustration? Fear? Something else? McGee wasn't sure.

"How did this happen?" The Hider jutted his almost nonexistent chin out. "Who was the sergeant in charge?"

"Sir, that was me, sir." Danilenko, like Peters, stared straight ahead, not meeting Heide's quivering eyes.

"How did this happen, Sergeant?"

"I do not know, sir."

Heide's eyes seemed to bulge outward for a moment, while his mouth soundlessly repeated Danilenko's answer. Then his eyes stopped quivering and his face grew expressionless. "Sergeant, that explanation is not sufficient. As you know. Recount the events leading up to her escape."

"Sir, we have no knowledge of how she exited her room without authorization and without being seen."

Heide stepped back, almost tripped over his fallen chair, seemed ready to kick it, then continued slowly extricating himself from behind his desk, slipping behind his special warrant officer for legal affairs, Marina Cheung, to do so. "At what point was the detainee discovered to be missing, Sergeant?"

"Just a few minutes ago, sir—when we opened her room to bring her to this hearing, sir."

Heide now stood before his men directly. "I see. And who reported her missing?"

Roon Kelakos cleared his throat. "I did, sir."

"And were you alone, Sergeant?"

"No, sir. As per orders, I had two guards—originally active-duty off-worlders—present as a security detachment to escort the detainee to this court. When we opened the door to the detainee's quarters, she was nowhere to be found."

"And these two Marines are—?"

"Right outside the door to this room, sir."

"So, how long had you been standing guard outside detainee Peitchkov's room, Sergeant?"

"Less than ten minutes, sir. We relieved the previous watch and waited until the time appointed to remove her from her quarters—exactly five minutes prior to the convening of this hearing."

"And while you were waiting, did you think to check the room, Sergeant? To make sure that the detainee was present and prepared to accompany you?"

"Sir, by your order, the standing protocol was to isolate the prisoner as much as possible before this hearing. Since there is no other means of egress from her cell, it was deemed an unnecessary security risk to open her door at the change of each guard shift. Besides, we had been able to rely on fiber-optic monitors to maintain oversight on the detainee's physical status."

"So, then, who was guarding the room before you arrived?"

"Sir, I was, sir." Kapinski sounded every bit as young as he looked.

"And did you have any occasion, during the course of your guard duty, to leave your post?"

"Sir, no, sir."

"Did you ever open the door?"

"Sir, yes, sir."

"For what purpose?"

"To feed the pris—the detainee, sir."

"I see. And did she like her meal?"

"S-sir?"

"I said, Corporal"—and the Hider stalked down between the two files of his men to reach Kapinksi at the back of the room—"did she enjoy her meal?"

"Sir, I—I don't know, sir."

"You don't know? Did she finish the food?"

"Sir, our protocols indicated we were not to open the door simply for the purpose of removing the dishes. They were to be removed at such time as another opening of her quarters was required, sir. I had no opportunity to inquire whether she enjoyed her meal, sir."

Heide came to a halt directly before tall, lean Kapinski and stared up at the gray eyes that were staring fixedly at the far wall. "And you're sure that's all that happened, Corporal? If you are found to be lying now, the punishment is severe—but much less so than should any prevarication be disclosed later on."

"Sir, I did not open the detainee's door except to deliver her meal, sir."

Heide turned away sharply and marched back to the head of his men. "Well, since we have a fiber-optic monitor in her room, what does the playback of her last few hours of confinement show?"

Lieutenant Chong's voice was as cool and still and low as Kapinski's had been high and jittery. "Sir, the video record of the detainee's room has been compromised."

The Hider visibly struggled to maintain an even tone.

His face was almost purple as he asked, "What do you mean, 'compromised,' Lieutenant Chong?"

"Sir, it seems the computer dedicated to the brig's overwatch system experienced a power spike just about fifteen minutes ago. All recent electronic security transactions—camera feed, keycard access, transponder tracking—have all been corrupted. The files are still present, but unreadable, sir."

Heide was utterly still and silent for five whole seconds. McGee had never realized—even in combat—just how long five seconds can be. "So, the recent security-monitoring records for all the detainees are corrupted?"

"Yes, sir."

"And have you personally checked on the status of the other detainees?"

"Yes, sir. They are no longer present in their quarters, either, sir."

Heide looked at Chong for a very long time. "I see. And have you begun a search of this facility and beyond?"

Cap Peters, still looking at the far wall, answered. "We made inquiries throughout the facility, sir. No guard posts report spotting the detainees. And while we don't have full reports from all sections and bays, sir, no other personnel have yet reported encountering them. And, of course, we can't conduct an exterior search, sir."

"And why not?"

"Sir, that would violate our security and concealment precautions, which stipulate that, to prevent detection by either satellite or local—"

"Lieutenant Peters, I know the base security OpOrds. I wrote them. But if the detainees have escaped, then they could be warning their Arduan contacts—"

Peters's eyes shot over to lock on to Heide's. "Captain Heide, are you saying that you have acquired evidence which proves that one or more of the detainees actually is in active, willing collaboration with the enemy?"

Heide started as though stuck with a pin, then considered. "Well, no, not exactly—"

"Sir, the wording of your last statement suggested that it was predicated on just such a presumption."

"My last statement, Lieutenant Peters, is motivated by a desire to exercise some damage control over this unprecedented disaster."

"And you are therefore instructing us to initiate an extensive, open-air search for the missing detainees, in broad daylight? Regardless of the possibilities of detection by the Baldies?"

McGee saw Chong's gaze rotate quickly toward Heide as well: the captain was close to giving an order that might become grounds for charges of incompetence. Behind the Hider, Marina Cheung looked up from her briefs, her old-fashioned pencil poised to record the time and take a note.

Heide, oblivious, plowed on. "Damn it, Peters. They—the detainees—are the greater threat. They must be found. And not just to prevent them from revealing this base's location to the Arduans, but because they are the only ones who can indicate who the other traitors are."

Chong's voice was very measured. "Other traitors, sir?"

"Why, of course there are other traitors involved. How else could all the detainees have escaped?" When no one responded, Heide raised his voice, staring round at the impassive faces. "Can't you see it? They clearly had inside help—they *had* to." And then—as McGee had known he would—the Hider stared straight at him.

"After all, detainee Peitchkov's significant other is one of our own officers."

Chong nodded. "Yes, sir, that's true. But in anticipation of today's treason hearing, Lieutenant Peters and I decided that it would be prudent to confine Lieutenant McGee to quarters last night, so as to—er, disincline—him from considering any rash actions in support of Miss Peitchkov. Until we sent for him to join us here, he has been under Marine—not Resistance, but *Marine*—guard. I have the list of personnel who remained in his quarters with him, sir, should you wish to interview them."

Heide swallowed, looked from face to face, seeking—guilt? Help? Compassion? But the only eyes that met his were McGee's. Heide's narrowed in response, and he brought up an accusing finger. "It's you. You may have been confined to quarters, but you still had a hand in it, McGee. I know it. I can feel it."

McGee did not avert his eyes. "Captain Heide, for the record, I was in my quarters from 1950 hours last night until just fifteen minutes ago."

"But they escaped. They must have had help. How else could they have exited their rooms, and this base?"

Li cleared his throat. "Perhaps the Arduan mind powers also include teleportation, sir?"

Heide spun about, surprised—but, when he saw that Li was also looking straight out into the room, rather than meeting his eyes, he became very still. He turned slowly back to his men and looked at them, face to face to face.

And McGee thought, *Now he knows. Took him long enough.*

Heide's voice was very quiet. "This is mutiny."

Peters, senior in the room, was the one who had to respond. "Sir?"

"You heard me, Peters. All of you heard me. This is mutiny."

Chong cocked his head very slightly. "I'm sorry, sir, exactly *what,* in this situation, constitutes mutiny?"

Heide became purple again. "This . . . this charade."

"Charade, sir?"

"You know where she is, where they all are." He turned and screamed—finally—at Harry Li. "And you, too. You're in on it, too! I order you—*order* you—to tell me where they are!"

Harry did not look at Heide but only said, "Sir, I don't know what you're talking about."

McGee thought that the Hider might fall over, but then he corrected the slight tilt that Harry Li's denial had evidently inflicted, and he turned back upon his men. McGee saw the knowledge clearly in his eyes: he knew they were all against him. And that they had discovered that he had insufficient grounds for convening hearings of treason proceedings against any of the hostages they had extracted from Melantho. And now he had no one left to carry out his orders—at least not among his most senior and popular officers and NCOs. But he almost seemed ready to smile when he straightened up and said, "And what is the status of the infant, Alexander Peitchkov?"

"Still in our care, Captain," Harry reported promptly. "He was removed and kept separate from his mother to—to ensure her compliance with the hearings, as per your orders." McGee heard Roon Kelakos's teeth grinding behind him; to his front he saw Cap Peters's back-clasped hands clench into a white knot. Unwittingly, in mentioning Alexander's removal from Jennifer, the Hider had touched upon his own fatal misstep, the straw that had broken all the strong backs of the Marines now gathered before him—and hundreds of others, besides.

The image had stuck with everyone who had seen—and later whispered the tale of—it: little Zander wailing, shrieking as Heide's private team of especially doltish Resistance members pulled the toddler from Jennifer's grasping hands. Then came the tersely worded general announcement that declared the child's "special welfare" completely dependent upon Jennifer's abject compliance with the farcical treason hearing Heide had summoned into existence by autocratic *fait accompli*.

When Marine faces were at last free to turn away from those sights and pronouncements, their jaw muscles had been bunched and hard. Alternatives were considered and then, slowly, shared—at first obliquely, then more openly, then in surreptitious groups. Part of defending humanity, they decided at last, meant protecting its most innocent members from the delusional abuses of those leaders who happened—by chance rather than merit—to be in power.

Leaders like Heide, who was even now letting his possession of the infant float in the air like an unuttered threat. "So although we do not have the accused, we do have her offspring. And I will point out that it has never been conclusively proven that the child has not been influenced—even modified—by the Arduans. So you might want to send word that if detainee Peitchkov wishes to ensure our continued attention to the special welfare of her child, she should voluntarily return herself to this facility at once."

McGee had sworn to be silent—had promised all

of them that he would—but he had not foreseen that Heide would stoop to such base extortion. "What does all that double-talk mean, Captain Heide, sir? Are you going to try Alexander in place of his mother? Are you saying that you're ready to take it all the way? Are you really up to executing an infant, Heide?"

As the last line came out of McGee's mouth, Heide turned pale—and the big Marine knew that he had won. But, in the same instant, he had the terrible certainty that Heide had not gone pale because he had been confronted with the idea of killing a child for the deeds of its parents, but because he knew he had irrevocably lost his authority. He had overplayed his hand and thus stepped right into McGee's trap.

Marina Cheung thankfully broke the silence—and also provided a segue into a conclusion that might allow Heide to withdraw and save face. "Captain Heide, since I'm sure you didn't mean to suggest that the child should be considered as a candidate for execution or euthanization, I see no reason to retain these remarks on the record."

Heide's initial relief quickly changed to trepidation. "The record? What do you mean?"

"Captain Heide, you gave me express instructions to run the court recorder from the time the detainee entered the room. When the door opened, I naturally presumed . . ."

Heide looked trapped: his shoulders tightened, his head came forward into a posture that somehow looked dogged and cowed all at once. "You misunderstood my orders, Ensign Cheung. I meant that—"

"Yes, Captain Heide, I realize that now. Of course, given the rather extraordinary report we now have on tape, it would seem necessary that all present parties would have to explicitly agree that its erasure would not constitute the destruction of what might become essential evidence in a later hearing on either misconduct, mutiny, or fitness for command. It seems to me that all of these issues were directly or indirectly raised during the exchange we now have recorded. But if all the parties can come to a suitable understanding, I'm sure we could all agree that this recording was made in error and need not be part of any legal proceedings, current or anticipated."

Cap Peters nodded. "That sounds like a good plan, Ensign Cheung, but it sounds to me like there's a problem as long as we've got a treason hearing pending. After all, it's still on the docket—and here we are to see it carried out."

Heide straightened up, hearing the alternative being laid out for him. "Lieutenant Peters makes an excellent point. Perhaps the best way to handle this impasse is to simply use this occasion to announce that the hearings are dismissed for want of sufficient evidence to support an investigation of treason. That would save us all a great deal of time—and it might induce the detainees to return of their own accord."

Chong nodded thoughtfully. "I believe that if we can get the message to them, it would almost certainly have that effect. I suspect it would also make them far more willing to provide intelligence on the Arduan city of Punt, and Baldy SOPs in general."

Heide stared at McGee. "Would it have that effect?"

McGee did not respond. Instead, Cap Peters offered his opinion. "I think we can rest assured of that, Captain. I also think if the detainees were housed in regular quarters as intelligence specialists, rather than isolated in the brig, that might further encourage them to help us come up with a viable plan for a decisive strike against the Baldy command structure."

"*Da*," agreed Danilenko, "but for safety's sake, I think a general announcement needs to be made among the rank and file that the persons in question are no longer detainees or prisoners. All our soldiers have been taught to think of them as possible security risks for so long, that if these people were now to be encountered in the corridors, unescorted..."

"Yes, Sergeant, I see your point," agreed Heide with a rapid swallow. "I will make a general announcement that all hearings and charges contemplated against the detai—the *former* detainees, have now been dropped for want of any substantiating evidence. And that with their help, decisive offensive operations are now being contemplated and planned."

Harry chimed in from the side. "I'll send that at once, sir. I'm sure the announcement will not only prevent any confusion regarding the former detainees but raise morale, as well."

Heide nodded. "And would that settle the matter, do you think?" His tone—and complexion—had both returned to normal.

The six men in front of him nodded as Cap Peters said, "I think so, sir. Which means, I guess, that Ensign Cheung can erase the recording now—sir."

Marina Cheung mouthed "Thank God" and did so. Heide saluted his troops. "You are dismissed. Report to me when you locate the detainees. That is top priority."

Cap Peters followed the others in returning the salute and affirmed, "Will do, sir."

And, with the negotiations concluded and Heide's command intact but constrained, the six Marines filed out and prepared to start breathing normally once again.

Jennifer Peitchkov rubbed her arms to get the chill out of them and dispel the unsightly goose bumps she didn't want Sandro to see: the access passages for the subterranean base's embedded sump pumps had been damp and cold. But they had been perfect for the purpose of hiding the detainees. With the base on the coast, and the flood table high, the labyrinthine network of runoff pipes, filtration and collection traps, overflow tanks, and interconnecting maintenance shafts and service crawlways had offered absolute concealment.

She looked from Tank to Cap Peters. "And Heide bought it—all of it?"

Cap shrugged. "Hard to tell. And it's hard to tell what he'll do in the aftermath."

Jennifer rubbed her arms vigorously, angrily. "Yeah, well, I guess that's partly up to me."

Sandro stroked her gooseflesh. She wanted to flinch and crawl away; he evidently didn't even notice the Braille epic that was pushing up through her skin. "What do you mean by that?"

"Well, I suppose the more helpful I—and the rest of the former detainees—turn out to be, the happier he'll be, and the more he'll feel like he got what he wanted and that his itty-bitty officer manhood has been left uncastrated."

Cap winced but said nothing; Chong looked away politely; Danilenko's sudden grin went from ear to ear. But Sandro simply eased closer and took both her hands in his great, red-furred paws. "Jen," he said softly, "I know you don't like Heide—God knows I don't, either. And I know you feel that the Arduans deserve better from you than helping to plot an attack against them. But right now, that's the price of your freedom, and Zander's, too. And don't forget—you can't change things sitting in a jail cell, an object of suspicion. Sometimes you have to be a part of the system, to work inside and with the system, in order to change it."

At those words, Jen leaned far back to look Sandro full in the face. "Alessandro, is this really you? Are you a duplicate? Or has Heide finally gotten to you with all his charm and smooth talk?"

"Huh? What?"

"Tank, did you just hear yourself? Are you really *you*?"

"Why?"

Jen smiled, drew her hands out of Sandro's, and placed one long, thin palm on either side of his irremediably hairy face. "Tank McGee tells me to 'work inside the system to change the system'? *You?* Saying *that*? You don't hear a little change there?"

Sandro looked away, looked sheepish. Standing to the other side, Cap Peters smiled down with palpably avuncular pride. Sandro let a small smile escape. "I guess that's probably not how I'd have reacted a year ago."

"Or a month ago, Lieutenant." Cap slapped him on one immense shoulder, and his eyes twinkled. "It's always gratifying to see a full-grown man grow up."

"Hey!"

But Jen laughed, and Sandro's smile widened. Chong had allowed himself a small, constrained, upward crinkle of his lips, but that was already fading. "This is a good outcome. But we've still got plenty of challenges."

Roon nodded. "Yeah." He looked at Jen. "Most of

the junior NCOs are still on the fence about you and the detainees—but when Heide took your child hostage to secure your good behavior, the general feeling seems to be that he went too far. But that isn't because they support your view of the Baldies—they don't. It's because they couldn't stand Heide's implicit threat to a civilian, and worse yet a baby, to compel your cooperation."

Kapinski nodded. "Rule one amongst us grunts—a CO can yell at us, cuss at us, even whack at us. But if a CO resorts to blackmail, he's finished. Period."

Chong nodded. "Perhaps . . . but there's still rumbling and unrest in the rank and file over your loyalties, Jen. They still don't understand—or believe—the nature of the interaction the detainees had with the moderate elements of the Arduan leadership. And Heide can—and will increasingly—use that suspicion and fear to maintain his position."

Kapinski made a sour face. "So, what are you saying, Lieutenant? That we shouldn't have pulled Heide up short?"

Chong shook his head. "No. That had to be done. And not just to save Ms. Peitchkov's life, but to save our morale and cohesion as a fighting force. A set of treason tribunals would have had the exact opposite effect that Heide was hypothesizing. The division of opinion would have been a mortal blow to the Resistance, as we all debated and disputed whether it was conscionable, let alone right, to levy such charges against civilians who had been taken and held against their will. It had gone too far, and the officers and NCOs knew it had to end. And this way, Heide still gets to say he's in charge."

"*Da*," affirmed Danilenko grimly, "and as long as the rank and file believe he is, he is."

Cap Peters nodded. "There's truth to that, Igor. But Heide also knows now that we can—and we will—check him if he goes too far."

"Yeah," Kelakos agreed with a sigh, "which also means he's watching us now. All of us."

Sandro shrugged, returned his eyes to Jen. "That couldn't be helped."

Jen looked into Sandro's eyes while speaking to all of her rescuers—all save the absent Harry Li, who was still trapped with the Hider and suffering through God-only-knew what kind of vituperative, or utterly silent, passive-aggressive bullshit and abuse. "Getting Heide to drop the treason charges—that isn't really a win. It's a trade, a negotiation. My life, and the lives of the other detainees, in exchange for action, some kind of action that Heide—and an awful lot of you, too—want."

Sandro nodded, but said, as the others discreetly exited, "Hey, you're alive—and you're going to stay that way, Jen. And for me, that's a win. Hell, it's the only win that matters."

And seeing Sandro's eyes so wide and innocent and guileless and full of her—nothing but her—Jen could not help smiling, throwing her arms around his neck, and whispering in his ear, "I love you. Damn it. I love you."

24

How Sleep the Brave

How sleep the brave, who sink to rest
By all their country's wishes blest!
—Collins

TRNS Lancelot, *Allied Fleet, Demeter System*

Entering the Demeter system, Ian Trevayne was not as surprised as he knew he ought to be to find it completely undefended.

Not after what they had found at Hera.

The results of the entry into Hera should have been a relief, but in fact it had been an anticlimactic letdown. Li Han had refused to move until her savaged fleet train had built up a stock of SBMHAWKs that could burn a path through those defenders. Finally, Trevayne and Li Magda had taken the vanguard into Hera in the wake of that death storm, only to discover wreckage. Analysis had revealed the truth. Hera had been held by twenty heavy superdreadnoughts and a swarm of fighters, whose function had been to gobble up recon drones and create the illusion of a strongly defended warp point. In short, the Baldies had been buying time. At the cost of what was, by their standards, a token force, they had bought it rather cheaply.

It was a purchase that Li Han was resolved not to let them repeat. She had ordered Trevayne through the Demeter warp point after only the most perfunctory probing by recon drones. For a moment, it had been as though Li Han's "wild ride" had resumed.

But now he and Li Magda stood on *Lancelot*'s flag bridge and studied reports that confirmed those drones' findings: save for its primary—a close G5v/M7vi binary—and its one colonized planet, the Demeter system was empty.

"Well," Trevayne sighed, "we may as well send word to your mother to advance the Fleet while we're sending recon drones through this system's other two warp points to probe the Polo and Charlotte systems."

"Yes." Mags chewed a knuckle in a rare display of perplexity. "They're obviously pulling their assets back—leading us on. But leading us on into what?"

"A more defensible position, from their standpoint." Trevayne turned to a flat screen that gave the strategic display and pointed at Demeter. "Both the Polo and Charlotte warp lines are impassable to devastators. If the Baldies' intelligence analysts are as good as I suspect they are, they understand that limitation as well as we do."

Mags nodded. "So wherever we go from here—and Charlotte, of course, is where we *want* to go—we're going to have to enter the next system without the benefit of our devastators. Until, that is, we dredge the warp line to accommodate them. Surely the Baldies know by now that we can do that."

Trevayne had never seen Mags this way. She was not normally given to brooding. But now it was as though she lay under a cloud of foreboding that blocked the sunlight he had come to know so well in her.

✧ ✧ ✧

"Well, Ian, it appears that you were right," said Li Han crisply as she paced in her ready room on the *Taconic*'s flag bridge and addressed the two holo images from *Lancelot*.

"Yes," said Trevayne, with no evidence of feeling vindicated. "There's a fairly sizable force in Polo, but the main body is quite obviously massed in Charlotte."

"Which, of course, makes sense," Li Magda put in. "They assume Charlotte is our next stepping-stone on the route to Bellerophon. And, once again, they're right."

Li Han was getting better at reading Trevayne's expression through the unavoidable distortion of even the best holo imagery. "You seem preoccupied, Ian. Are you seeing something in the data that I've missed?"

"No, nothing in the data. But . . . well, I know I have nothing standing behind this statement except a very strong gut feeling, but I can't rid myself of the impression that we're facing someone new."

"A command shakeup among the Baldies?"

"It would be a natural reaction to the shock of our arrival in the Bellerophon Arm and our initial successes. And the change is clearly not good news for us. We've come to expect to be one step ahead of them tactically. I believe that expectation is no longer justified. There's *someone* over there who has a shrewd sense of our strengths and weaknesses, and is altogether too bloody inventive in taking advantage of the latter and neutralizing the former."

"And," Li Magda interjected, "this hypothetical personage may have a special advantage." She paused a moment to gather her thoughts. "It's been obvious for a long time that the Baldies can communicate in some way we don't understand. I've heard terms like 'hoodoo' among our people. Whatever it is, we have no way of knowing what its limitations in range and speed of propagation are. We also don't know whether they have technology for enhancing it."

"So," Trevayne said slowly, "you think they enjoy a significant advantage over us in communications—possibly on the strategic as well as the tactical scale?"

"It would certainly be a powerful tool in the hands—or whatever—of someone like you're postulating, who's smart enough to take full advantage of it."

Li Han let the thoughtful silence last only a few seconds, then drew herself up. "Well, if all this speculation is correct, I don't want to give them any more time to prepare whatever it is they're preparing in Charlotte. So I'm going to take a calculated risk and hit it with almost everything we have. That means you two will have to clear the way—using supermonitors, at most—for the Kasugawa generator so our devastators can go through. Ian, will you want to transfer your flag to one of the Rim Spruance II class that are configured as command ships?"

"No, I'll stay where I am. I've grown rather fond of *Lancelot.*"

"Well," Li Han said primly, "I'm going to have to transfer *my* flag—and my combat command staff—from *Taconic*, because I intend to personally lead the bulk of our supermonitors through directly behind you, just before the Kasugawa generator makes transit." She held up a hand before they could protest. "I can't delegate this—it's too crucial. While you engage the enemy, I'm going to form a defensive globe of supermonitors around it."

Neither Ian nor Mags liked it, but they had no answer. Han could see that in the look they exchanged.

She could also see the real reason Trevayne was fond of *Lancelot.*

Arduan SDS Unzes'mes'fel, *Consolidated Fleet,* Anaht'doh Kainat, *Charlotte System*

"Admiral," sent Narrok's communications prime, "a Fleet signal."

Narrok reluctantly linked his *selnarm* to his flagship's command repeater-receiver and found himself in contact with a mind he had learned to loathe.

Torhok's.

"So, Narrok, are you ready to do your part?" asked the senior admiral.

(Reassurance.) "Quite ready, Senior Admiral." *An ironic question, since it's been you who's been ceaselessly contacting me to get familiarized with my battle plan. To no avail, of course. You are a* bilbuxhat *in a crystal-cutter's shop, Torhok: you'll no more attend the nuances of this plan than that oafish beast would avoid shattering the glassware. And it will be everything I can do to keep the plan on course—while you get all the credit for it.*

Torhok was signaling (appreciation) for Narrok's considerate behavior even as he chided: "There can never be too much coordination between subordinates and their superiors, Narrok. How else am I to know if you are, in fact, prepared for battle? At any rate, you seem to have done a most passable job readying these ships."

"So you are happy with the results of my offensive initiative?"

"Yes. I do not know how you managed all the disassembly in Bellerophon, and then all the portage to and reassembly here in Charlotte. But I must also wonder just how truly aggressive these system-defense ships can be. They carry as much—more—firepower and armor than a warp-point fort, but are so very slow, and too big to transit a warp point."

"True, but unlike a warp-point fort, these SDSs can still maneuver. Not swiftly, but enough to keep up with a fleet—and, as we have seen, their firepower is more than a match for anything the humans can bring to bear. I believe that even several of their so-called devastators would be overmatched. And having these SDSs available also frees up most of our SDHs for more mobile operations."

"Yes, I appreciate that—although I find what you have done with the SDSs' fighter wings most unsettling. All of them are to be piloted—well, remote-controlled—by *selnarm* link?"

"Why not, Senior Admiral? *Selnarm* is instantaneous. The advantages gained by having the pilot actually in the fighter are minimal. This way, we will no longer lose our senior pilots—and as soon as one fighter is destroyed, another can be deployed to instantly take its place, and in the hands of the same expert pilot who directs it from the safety of the SDS on which he is stationed. Also, by stripping out the life support, rad shielding, and cockpit accommodations, we have lightened our fighter craft. This brings the performance of our fighters to a point that approaches parity with the humans."

Torhok's response was not praise, merely: "That achievement is overdue. My main concern is our distance from the warp point, Narrok. Are we not too far off to engage the humans in time, if they bring through one of their—er, warp-point modifiers?"

"I share your misgivings at the distance we must maintain—but maintain it we must. Keeping the massive signatures of the SDSs cloaked is a difficult job under the best of circumstances—but if we were to put them any closer to the warp point, we would surely lose the element of surprise. If we are to use these twelve SDSs to crush their entry into the system and disrupt their expansion of the warp point, we must begin well back, entirely out of their detection range."

"It is not to my liking," complained Torhok. But he did not disagree nor change the plan.

TRNS Lancelot, *Allied Fleet, Charlotte System*

At least the Baldies, for reasons best known to themselves, hadn't emplaced orbital forts at the Charlotte end of the warp line, and their mobile forces were deployed farther from that warp point than Trevayne had expected. So the SBMHAWKs he had sent ahead were still speeding toward their intended prey when *Lancelot* entered the system. They were also speeding into the local sun, which the Baldies had behind them.

Then they watched as clouds of fighters flashed past, over, and under and to both flanks on a sunward course. The need to clear the warp point for Li Han's oncoming formations of supermonitors had precluded the traditional carrier tactic of making transit, launching fighters, and then returning to safety. So the assault carriers and fleet carriers followed behind Trevayne's phalanx of monitors and supermonitors, from which wings of superdreadnoughts and battlecruisers extended and were now sweeping forward in an enveloping motion. The deck vibrated under their feet as *Lancelot*'s HBM launchers, like those of the rest of the heavy capital ships, sent forth their great missiles in a salvo timed to coincide with the SBMHAWKs. Mere seconds passed before the Baldies' own missiles were detected.

Andreas Hagen, who more and more filled the role of a general staff liaison for Trevayne, approached. "Admiral, the Kasugawa generator has made transit. Admiral Li is forming her defensive globe around it as it moves into position."

"Ah, thank you, Commander. That evolution should be complete by the time we close to beam-weapon range."

Then the enemy missiles arrived, and the viewscreens stepped down even further to preserve human eyes from the stroboscopic eruption of innumerable antimatter warheads. Most were detonated short of their targets by point defense, but all too many worked their way in and delivered their shattering discharges close enough to rock even supermonitors. Those big ships were clearly the Baldies' primary targets—which was just as well for mere monitors like *Lancelot* in this cataclysmic combat environment.

"We seem to be getting somewhat the better of the missile exchange," Mags remarked, studying readouts. "Our fighters are doing their job of disrupting them by threatening to work around into their blind zones."

"And taking serious losses doing it," Trevayne added.

Then they were past the long-range missile envelope and using their external ordnance racks and backup launchers to engage with intermediate-range missiles. Meanwhile, the battlecruiser "wingtips" of the formation had curved around and were at optimal energy-weapon range.

Less than a minute later, the central formations

of big ships crunched together. Trevayne's lead ships blasted a path ahead with energy torpedoes at short range. Space was racked with the inconceivable energy expenditures, and Code Omega transmissions began coming in with sickening rapidity. Only to be expected, of course: without the mass of supermonitors under Li Han's direct command, Trevayne was at a disadvantage in numbers and tonnage.

But he was doing his job of clearing the way. Things were going according to plan. Or seemed to be. . . .

He knew better than to be surprised when Mags read his expression. "Something's bothering you," she stated rather than asked.

"The Baldies' tactics bother me. They just don't seem to make particularly good sense. They must know by now that we can dredge the warp line and bring in our devastators, after which they will have to beat a retreat. So what's the point of this battle? Why don't they draw us even farther along the warp chain, lengthening our supply lines and shortening theirs?"

"In short, it seems out of character for the new Baldy commander you've been postulating."

"It certainly does," Trevayne muttered.

Arduan SDS Unzes'mes'fel, *Consolidated Fleet,* Anaht'doh Kainat, *Charlotte System*

Narrok felt the tentative probe from the sensor second whom he had tasked to watch for anything unprecedented or unusual in the human fleet. "Yes, Sensor Second?"

"Admiral, this is probably nothing urgent—"

"Do not so assume. Tell me at once."

"Amidst the cluster of enemy ships which just made

transit in rapid sequence, I detect a craft—or possibly an object—that seems to be different in configuration. Unlike any of the other ships in their formation, or any others that we have seen."

"And this craft's drive signatures?"

"Again, different, Admiral. Its tuner is running unusually high for a human craft, but its power output is somewhat low."

As if they are running a lighter engine at higher speeds, unconcerned that it will burn itself out quickly—because it was never meant to last very long at regular maneuver speed. A logical design feature for a self-consuming warp generator . . . but Narrok had to be sure. "What about anomalous gravitic readings or non-Myrtakian emissions?"

"Sir, I can't be sure abou—wait. Yes, sir. This is odd. There are gravity fluctuations which are starting to counterpoint those of the warp point."

"Counterpoint?"

"Yes, sir. In any given period of time, when the gravitic-distortion waves generated by the warp point's own cycle are at peak intensity, this object is sending out the very opposite. Its distortions are at an inversely symmetrical nadir. Conversely, when the warp point's fluctuations are at nadir, the object's are peaking."

So, a countervailing force that takes its inverted shape from, yet also works directly against, the signature of the warp point itself. This was it then: the human warp-point modifier preparing to discharge. And sooner than he had thought. Narrok pulsed a brief (gratitude, excellent) at the sensor second and then opened his *selnarm* to the bridge. "The humans have brought in their warp-point device and are preparing it for activation. Communication Prime: alert Admiral Torhok. Navigation Prime: best speed toward the warp point. Tactics: call in Fleet Second Memshef's battlegroup to come along our flank and interpose herself between us and the human advance force. The human vanguard will no doubt turn back and try to intercept us. Bear this uppermost in your mind at all times: our target is the human warp-point generator. We cannot allow any detours or deviations from that objective."

His staff signaled (understood, resolved, ferocity, race-pride), and he returned it all—just as his communications prime intruded a less stirring note of (apology). "Admiral, on the Fleet command-repeater—Senior Admiral Torhok."

Of course. You can't just follow along, can you? Narrok slipped a tendril of his *selnarm* into the repeater as willingly as he would have handled *griarfeksh* droppings. "Yes, Senior Admiral?"

"Narrok, what illogic and impertinence is this? How dare you advance the SDS echelons without consulting me?"

"Sir, I thought our plan was clear enough. We now have multiple data points that suggest the humans are readying the device they use to modify warp points. We have no time to waste. Our ships are very slow."

"All the more reason to let the human vanguard move slightly deeper into the system. They would have been so far behind us that they might not have caught up to us before we engage their warp-point force."

"Unfortunately, waiting that long might also make us too late to prevent the humans from activating their device—and that is and must remain our primary objective. Besides, had we let the human vanguard go farther, they would still have turned and caught up with us . . . from directly behind. I suspect that vulnerability might even have proven fatal to these twelve SDSs."

Torhok obviously did not want to be distracted by either facts or the dictates of tactical prudence. "Admiral Narrok, your reasons may or may not be sound—but you were to consult with me before ordering an advance. This is the nature of command. You are relieved of your post."

So, Torhok was determined to try that gambit. But Narrok and the remaining Council of Twenty had prepared for this eventuality. "Senior Admiral, I am sorry to point out that you no longer have the the authority to relieve me. The prerogative to dismiss your second-in-command vests in your holding *two* positions simultaneously, that of senior admiral and that of councilor. In boycotting the Council, you left its remaining members no choice but to reassign your seat there. Consequently, you can no longer relieve me. You can of course contest my orders—and supplant those you feel wiser." Before he finished on that note, Narrok had checked his plot: all twelve SDSs were still moving at best speed toward their objective in four echelons of three upright triads—including Torhok's own flagship.

Torhok was still for a long moment. "Slow your echelon, Narrok. I will close distance so all our weight of metal arrives together. And after this battle is done—should you survive it—be assured that I will discarnate you in personal combat. Which I anticipate most eagerly."

The link broke.

Narrok smiled. He had read a human axiom some months ago that was most suited to this moment: Violence is the last recourse of the incompetent. That wisdom applied just as readily to his own species, it seemed. He opened his *selnarm* link to his bridge staff again.

"Maintain course, speed to three-quarters. Launch all fighters. Missiles to pre-launch mode. Now we triumph for the unity that is the Race's embodiment of Illudor!"

TRNS Lancelot, *Allied Fleet, Charlotte System*

Shock can be so overwhelming that it defeats itself. Li Magda's moment of stunned immobility lasted only a couple of heartbeats before she burst out, "What in the hell are those things *doing* here?" Her tone reflected too much indignation to leave room for panic.

But Trevayne was already responding, barking out a series of orders that would send the reinforced vanguard into a fighting retreat. Only afterward did he reply, in a voice that was almost too composed.

"It's obvious in retrospect. We've always *known* that something massing a billion tonnes—five hundred times a devastator—can't possibly transit any warp point God ever made. So we've comfortably assumed the system-defense ships are confined to Bellerophon, where the Baldies created them by breaking up some of their generation ships." His smile held absolutely no humor. "Why didn't it ever occur to us that if they can break up a generation ship they can also break up an SDS? That must be how they did it. They sent the things through in pieces and reassembled them here."

"What a colossal effort!" she breathed. "But the one thing we know for certain about the Baldies is that they don't think small."

"*I'm* the one who's stereotypically supposed to be given to understatement!" Trevayne permitted himself another quick, humorless smile, then turned toward the comm station. "Raise the First Space Lord."

It had been a long time since he had referred to her as that.

"Well," Li Han said briskly, "we can stop wondering why they positioned themselves so far from the warp point, can't we? It was necessary to conceal things that size with cloaking ECM."

"We can also stop wondering why they didn't try any tricks with our recon drones," said Li Magda bleakly.

Li Han's tone grew even more clipped, and it was as though she were donning a robe. "Self-reproach is useless. Let us consider our position. Given what we know of the weaknesses of the SDS—its extreme slowness and and even more extreme lack of mobility, and its seeming fragility—I believe we can still win this battle if we can bring our devastators into this system." For a split second, the robe seemed to flutter. "At any rate, we *have* to act on that assumption. The two Kasugawa generators will activate at the preset moment, which defines how long we have to hold out. And that moment can't be advanced, given the requirement that the generators be synchronized. Ian, you've done exactly the right thing by falling back ahead of the SDSs, which can't catch you."

"Especially," he added with a glance at the navplot, "given their position. They're not aligned in the same axis as us and the warp point. They're starting to converge from about a thirty-five degree angle, and we're ahead of them."

"Good. We'll combine forces and defend the generator as long as it needs to be defended."

There seemed nothing else to be said.

✧ ✧ ✧

Trevayne's force was far faster than the SDSs. But it wasn't faster than their heavy bombardment missiles, and it wasn't faster than their fighters—about five hundred fighters each. Trevayne's fighters were better, but they had already taken losses, and he hadn't had time to recover and rearm all of them, so some of them had already expended their depletable munitions. Still, they gamely kept up a running duel, and the point defense of the capital ships and their escorts was for the most part capable of dealing with the repeated flurries of long-range missile fire.

But, as Trevayne came to realize, what he really had going for him was that those titanic ships weren't really interested in him. They were lumbering inexorably toward the warp point, and their extended-range missile fire was already erupting in voracious fireballs against the shields of Li Han's ships.

"It's obvious," he reported to Li Han, "that they're resolved to close with you."

"Which means, close with the generator," she replied emotionlessly. "They must have identified it. I've detached practically all my escort cruisers to globe up around it, practically shield-to-shield, and do their best to fill the volume of space surrounding it with an inferno of point defense."

"There's only one thing to do," Trevayne said. "Mags and I will abruptly change course to intercept them short of you. We'll break up their formation, force them to maneuver to deal with us."

Han shook her head. "You don't have the tonnage and firepower. There's no guarantee you'd be able to delay them until the activation sequence is completed. No, there's only one alternative." For the barest instant, she locked eyes with her daughter, and her eyes shone with a strange intensity, as though desperate to memorize every detail of that face. "I'm coming out."

"*What?*" Li Magda's voice rose to falsetto and then broke. "But—"

Li Han made a decisive chopping motion with her hand. "No time. We're all going to have too much to do. Signing off."

The comm screen went black. And in the tactical plot, serried ranks of supermonitors were surging out from the vicinity of the warp point, for all the world like charging knights.

Trevayne gave a quick series of orders that wrenched the vanguard into a tight turn of the sort possible to inertia-canceling drives. A furious battle raged as the remains of the lighter Baldy units fought to keep him off the SDSs. He and Mags were thrown off their feet as a near-miss shook *Lancelot*'s tonnage, showering the flag bridge with ruptured metal and plastic and filling it with acrid smoke. Damage-control klaxons whooped, and the saturnalia of destruction went on.

But it paled beside what was happening as Li Han's force and the leading SDSs slid together.

As they approached, the intervening space was criss-crossed by rapid-fire missile exchanges. Then, as they drew closer, they belched out missile salvos at ranges where interception grew more and more difficult, and the antimatter fires seemed to merge into a quasi-solid mass of lightning, a ravening energy expenditure that must surely strain the metrical frame of spacetime itself.

It was, Trevayne thought in awe, a battle that was itself an astronomical event. He found a moment to wonder if, on any undiscovered planets nearby in Newtonian space, there were alien astronomers who in few years would watch this bright star momentarily grow even brighter, and wonder why.

Then the supermonitors—not as many as there had been—were actually in among the leading echelon of SDSs.

By most standards, supermonitors were neither fast nor maneuverable. But among the SDSs they were almost like fighters weaving around capital ships, working their way into the blind zones.

And then, all at once, *Lancelot* was through the tatters of the Baldy mobile forces, and more and more of the vanguard's survivors followed her into the brawl of the titans.

The SDSs were predominantly missile and fighter platforms. They were at a disadvantage at close range. And not even a billion tonnes of matter is immune to a contact antimatter explosion.

Their relentless progress toward the generator was thrown off as they maneuvered clumsily to evade their attackers. It wasn't always enough. Trevayne heard Mags—and himself—cheering as he watched one of them go up in an explosion beyond the powers of any gods humankind had ever imagined.

Then they identified Li Han's flagship—limping, streaming air—as it doggedly worked its way around into beam-weapon range of an SDS's blind zone.

"Raise the First Space Lord!" he commanded.

"Yes!" Li Magda said in tones of desperation. "Tell her to disengage. It's almost time for the generator to—"

"Fleet flag isn't responding, Admiral," said the comm officer.

But then the supermonitor and its giant prey practically vanished in an insanely suicidal short-range exchange of fire. The SDS began to erupt in a series of secondary explosions that blew it apart—but it flung out chunks of debris huger than starships. One of them collided with the supermonitor in a holocaust that consumed both and sent their mingled wreckage tumbling sunward.

With a sobbing wail, Li Magda fell into Trevayne's arms.

"She did it!" he breathed into her ear as she clung to him. "Look, Mags, she did it! See, the attack by the leading wave of SDSs has been broken up, lost its momentum. And now . . ."

He pointed to a telltale, in which energy readings jumped. The Kasugawa generator's final activation sequence was beginning.

"She *did* it!" he repeated. Magda looked up, and her eyes blazed through their film of tears.

Arduan SDS Unzes'mes'fel, *Consolidated Fleet,* Anaht'doh Kainat, *Charlotte System*

"Admiral Torhok's flagship is . . . is gone, Admiral. So is Commander Ums'shet's SDS."

Narrok (affirmed) sent. "I see it, Prime. Tactics: Range to target?"

"Sixteen light-seconds."

"Data hubs?"

"Intact sir, but the humans are inflicting considerable damage on our—"

"All missile tubes: continuous launch. Flush external racks."

"Any targets other than the unidentified object, Admiral?"

"No other target. That one target only. Fighter wings Two, Seven, and Eight: close on the target, tuners at max."

"They will not get through, Admiral."

"They are not supposed to. They will draw fire from all the nearby enemy defense batteries. Because of that, the humans will not be able to destroy all our missiles."

Narrok felt the tremor—very faint in the massive SDS beneath his feet—as the torrent of missiles began rushing out toward the single human construct.

His ops prime signaled anxiously. "Sir, the human vanguard ships are now in among our echelons. They are—"

"Continue firing. All other fighter wings sweep through this arc"—he drew a glittering path in the holoplot with his light-stylus—"and attempt to engage the human vanguard from the rear."

"Sir, the humans have ample time to turn and—"

"—and in turning, they will be less of a threat to us for a few more minutes. By which time, our job should be done."

"Yes, sir."

Tactics called for (attention) to the plot. "Sir, intercept in ten seconds."

"Very good, Prime. The human defense batteries?"

"They have eliminated almost all of our fighters."

"Anticipated. The effect of the batteries upon our missile salvos?"

Tactics checked his readouts. "Negligible, Admiral. And intercept in two, one . . . now."

It took about ten seconds for the flash to reach them—a flash that seemed to writhe and pulse as over four hundred missiles detonated one after the other in the same cubic light-second of space. After four seconds, the angry, roiling glow dimmed down to occasional flickers, then a vaguely luminous haze. And then, the dark, infinite stillness of open space reasserted.

"Target destroyed," announced Tactics calmly.

TRNS Lancelot, *Allied Fleet, Charlotte System*

Trevayne and Li Magda thought they had no room for any additional horror and despair after watching the immolation of the generator. But then the telltales pitilessly showed a huge, meaningless energy pulse that abruptly winked out. They knew what it meant. The generator in Demeter had also activated, uselessly, wasting itself. Their paired generators were gone.

Trevayne gently disengaged Mags's arms and stood up. "She won us the chance to beat a retreat to Demeter and rejoin the devastators there. Let's not waste that chance." He straightened, then paused for a moment and looked at the viewscreen, toward the blazing white sun of Charlotte. They had last seen the wreckage drifting toward it, to be caught in its powerful gravity well.

"It's not enough," she heard him say. "It's not a sufficient funeral pyre. Not for her."

Then he shook himself and began giving orders. And his face, for all its firm flesh and thick hair, was no longer the face of a young man.

Arduan SDS Unzes'mes'fel, *Consolidated Fleet,* Anaht'doh Kainat, *Charlotte System*

Narrok watched the last *murn*-colored blip withdraw through the warp point, signifying that the human attack on Charlotte had ended. As usual, the humans had inflicted more casualties than they had taken. Not counting the two SDSs, he had lost fifty percent more hull tonnage than the humans had lost. However, the Children had also lost many times more fighters (although none of those losses had inflicted any pilot casualties).

But the humans had been repulsed, sent fleeing back to Demeter for want of their decisive devastators. Furthermore, the warp-point modifying device had been destroyed, and prior to that had been subjected to a number of fairly detailed scans—detailed enough to facilitate ready and positive identification of such objects in the future. And the humans had left a treasure trove of information behind them: wrecks whose data banks would tell—either directly or by implication—where this new human fleet had come from, how it had arrived here in the Arm, how large it was, and, possibly, how large it might ultimately get.

Narrok let his shoulders relax, his tentacles uncoil—and was suddenly aware of the utter stillness around him. He turned—and found the entirety of his bridge staff staring at him expectantly. "Yes?" he pulsed at them.

He felt a barely suppressed surge of (admiration, approval, loyalty, exultation) behind their collective *selnarm* as his ops prime asked (with deference): "Your next orders, Senior Admiral?"

Narrok blinked all three eyes—for once, a pleasant *befthel*—and reflected: *Me? The* Senior *Admiral? Yes, I guess I am, now.*

25

Marked Destiny

Our hour is marked, and no one
can claim a moment of life beyond
what fate has predestined.
—Napoleon

TRNS Lancelot, *Allied Fleet, Demeter System*

The mind-shattering violence had subsided. The blinding dazzle of antimatter warheads had died away, leaving only a galaxy of black dots in the eyes of any who had seen it in the view screens. The space around the warp point held only dissipating debris.

Ian Trevayne, standing on *Lancelot*'s flag bridge and keeping his exhausted body erect by sheer force of will, surveyed it all with a look of grim satisfaction. He had managed to extricate the Allied Fleet from the holocaust of Charlotte, though not without heavy losses. Now, with the fleet securing from general quarters, he permitted himself to turn to the straight, slender figure beside him.

Li Magda had held together through the nightmare retreat from Charlotte and the smashing of the Baldy pursuit, dutiful beyond grief, her face a solid but brittle mask damming up a tide of unshed tears. And now, here on the flag bridge in the sight of so many eyes, she still couldn't let the dam burst—not yet. And he couldn't do as he longed to do and take her in his arms and comfort her.

Instead, he approached her as closely as he dared let himself, and spoke carefully. "Mags, you know what I have to do."

"Yes. You're in command of the Fleet now." Her voice was too calm.

"And you're my second in command, as well as succeeding to command of the vanguard. I don't want to leave you now, of all times. But we no longer can afford to risk both of us in the same ship—especially when it's just a monitor. I have to transfer my flag to *Taconic.*"

"I know." She kept her face carefully expressionless, as though fearful to crack the dam.

"I'll be taking my own staff with me, of course." *Almost all your mother's staff died with her,* he did not add. "But I'm soon going to be making some reassignments, to add some Terran Republic people and make it a joint staff and not just a Rim/PSU affair. I'll need your help with that."

"I'll get you a list of names." Still no expression.

Trevayne stepped closer. Bidding military propriety be damned, he put his hands on her shoulders. "Mags, when I go over to *Taconic*, I want you to go with me. I'm going to be taking command of a predominantly TRN force. And they've just lost Li Han. And I'm . . . who I am. I need your help."

At those last, simple four words, she looked up at him, and her eyes, which had held nothing but dead hurt, awoke with something else: the need to be needed.

"The night we first met," he pressed on, "you told me the peoples of the Terran Republic looked back on me as a historical figure along the lines of Erwin Rommel. Well, what if Rommel had been reborn after eighty years—and a group of Israeli officers had been called on to serve under him against a common enemy? How should he have dealt with them?"

She spoke slowly, but with a perceptible quickening of life. "He should have let them know that he understood, and appreciated, just exactly what it meant to command an outfit like the Israeli army."

"Yes . . . Yes, you're right."

She continued to hold his eyes. "We don't have to leave just yet, do we?"

"No. I don't suppose we do," he answered, recognizing her need.

They departed the flag bridge, oblivious to all the eyes that were ostentatiously not watching.

Adrian M'Zangwe's face was like ebon lava frozen into a mask of grief. But the chief-of-staff-become-flag-captain rose to his feet smartly enough and called out, "Attention on deck!"

The officers filling *Taconic*'s flag briefing room rose as Trevayne entered, followed by Li Magda, and proceeded to the dais. They were all in space-service grays, pretty much the same for everyone, but trimmed with the colors of the services to which they belonged. For Trevayne's staff and a few others, it was the black and silver of the Rim Federation and the Pan-Sentient Union. But for the majority it was the deep-blue, white, and gold of the Terran Republic. It was the latter group that Trevayne watched keenly as he received a series of more-or-less routine reports, which gave him time to observe. He found no surprises. These people were behaving with every evidence of professionalism, but also with a mechanical quality, as though they had awakened into a new reality they had not yet accepted.

"Before I issue any specific orders," he said after the last of the reports was in, "I wish to speak in general terms about our position here. Our immediate priority, of course, is to secure this system. Then we can turn our attention to the portions of the Bellerophon Arm behind us, on the far side of Mercury, while waiting for reinforcements—especially the new superdevastators, and the additional Kasugawa generators we now need, including the new ones that can allow passage of those superdevastators. Only then will we be able to resume this campaign as originally planned, and complete the liberation of the entire Arm, up to and including Bellerophon itself."

"But . . . but, sir—" M'Zangwe began.

Trevayne overrode him, and his deep baritone, without getting any louder, somehow filled the room to the exclusion of any possibility of other sound. And now he frankly spoke to the TRN contingent. "Yes, we all know what we've lost, *who* we've lost. But in a very real sense, it's not going to matter. Not when we resume our advance. Because wherever the Baldies face us . . . in every Terran Republic officer, they will find a Li Han."

An electric current seemed to run through the room.

He's made them his, thought Li Magda. *Mother always said he had a way of doing that. She said a room seemed to get bigger when he left it. I never knew what she meant until now.*

M'Zangwe stood up, and now his was a living face again.

"What are your orders, Admiral?"

Arduan SDH Shem'pter'ai, *Main Van, Consolidated Fleet of the* Anaht'doh Kainat, *Charlotte System*

For the first time in weeks, Narrok luxuriated in solitude. And his brief sequestration was not just a means of finding relief from the demands of being the new senior admiral. It was a necessary moment of privacy so that, in the stillness of his own mind, he could touch and explore a thought that it was unwise to approach in the presence of others, for fear that they would get some hint of it, or the associated sentiments.

Torhok was discarnated.

Narrok was not given to profound displays of emotion—not even as a Youngling—but now, for the first time in many years, he had to acknowledge (albeit easily suppress) an impulse to jump, trot about, shout, and otherwise cavort in joyous triumph and relief.

But soon enough, he became solemn, considering the small holoplot in his chambers: yes, Torhok was dead—but had he died soon enough? Narrok reviewed the staggering losses in combat hulls and trained personnel, as well as the withered industries and engineering staffs who had no new ship classes or other technologies on the way because Torhok had forbidden expenditures on any initiative other than the one he had decreed: attack, attack, always attack.

The fool, the utter fool, thought Narrok. The strategic holoplot of the Bellerophon Arm showed the immensity, and dire consequences, of Torhok's megalomaniacal follies. If his limited information was correct, the humans would not be able to bring their DT-class hulls through seven strategically significant warp points. And among these seven systems, his strategic goal was to hold Ajax,

Charlotte, and Polo, which formed a protective umbrella around the approaches to New Ardu—but only if their warp points remained unaltered.

Of the three systems, Charlotte was the linchpin: if it fell, the enemy had a straight run through two other systems to Bellerophon—and all of the warp points on that path were already navigable by the humans DTs. So Charlotte had to be defended at all costs. Looking to his left flank, if Ajax fell, Narrok could withdraw to Achilles, fight there as circumstances permitted, but ultimately could withdraw to Suwa, behind the safety of another DT-proof warp point.

However, on his right flank, Polo was of greater concern. It had no forts in it yet, nor SDSs, and if the humans could hit Polo before those defenses were improved, then the fallback would have to be BR-02, which had even fewer ready defenses that Polo.

This presented Narrok with a thorny choice. If he pushed all his new defensive assets into Polo, he might be able to hold it against even an all-out attack. But if the humans struck before his defenses in Polo were truly impregnable, then he would lose everything he had committed there—and BR-02 would be profoundly vulnerable.

The conundrum of how to divide his limited defensive assets had no definitive, quantitative solution, but the humans had a saying: "Never put all your eggs in one basket"—and Polo was but one basket. And after all, that basket was also in ready reach of adversaries who, when it came to breaking eggs with their technological and strategic surprises, had already proven themselves quite adept.

Quite adept indeed.

26

The Avenging Sword

To arms! to arms! ye brave!
The avenging sword unsheathe,
March on! march on! all hearts resolved
On victory or death!
—de Lisle

Headquarters, Confederation Fleet Command, Luzarix, Hyx'Tangri System

The Tangri didn't use carpets, so Atylycx couldn't be called on one. But that was the general idea.

He stood in the great hexagonal chamber at the heart of the Confederation Fleet Command's fortresslike headquarters and sweated—Tangri did do that—under the pitiless gaze of Ultraz, the Dominant One, speaker of the *arnharanaks* of Horde leaders, and Heruvycx, *arnhahorrax* of the CFC. Other high CFC officers surrounded the circular table, reclining on the frameworks that served their race for chairs, but he himself was ostentatiously left standing. Slightly back from the table was Scyryx, well known to be a devious political ally of the Dominant One even though he belonged to the widely despised Korvak Horde. *He would sell himself for a pile of shit,* Atylycx thought. *And he would thereby make the better bargain.*

Aloud, Atylycx protested, "But I followed the plan to the letter!"

Heruvycx half rose to his feet in fury. "Are you implying that the plan itself was at fault?" *The plan that I authored and the Dominant One approved*, he did not need to add. "Is that how you are attempting to excuse your failures, Fleet Leader?"

"If, indeed, what you lead can still be dignified by calling it a fleet," Scyryx added with their species' equivalent of a sneer.

Atylycx's belly seethed with his desire to go for the oily, supercilious Korvak's throat. But Scyryx was too well protected. So Atylycx had to be content with conspicuously ignoring him and answering Heruvycx as though the interjection had never occurred or was beneath notice. "I merely point out that the behavior of the new prey animals—the *Baldies*, as we've learned the humans call them—was not as we anticipated. They did not respond favorably to our proposal of an alliance."

"A proposal which you obviously bungled! Then they went on from Treadway to take not merely Tisiphone and the BR-07 starless warp nexus, but even our outpost just beyond BR-07."

"But," Atylycx objected, grasping at straws, "they have made no further advances since then."

"Yes," said Scyryx with disdain too blatant for any male to pretend to ignore. "Their intelligence must be at fault regarding the quality of the opposition they would encounter."

"You miserable Korvak male cu—"

"Enough!" roared Ultraz before Atylycx could finish saying the unsayable. Startled, they all adopted submissive postures in the face of the Dominant One.

He shot Scyryx a quick warning glance, then resumed in a normal volume. "Bickering serves no purpose. Let us turn our attention to the reality in which we now find ourselves.

"First of all, it is clear that we have profoundly outraged the Baldies and must consider the possibility of further counterattacks by them. Since they have evidently become our implacable enemies, should we consider the possibility of making a similar offer of alliance to the humans?"

Scyryx spoke up diffidently. "First of all, Dominant One, I am by no means certain they would accept it, given their past experience with us. The stupidity of human politicians is not infinite, appearances to the contrary. Second, even if they did accept it, the result would be disadvantageous to us no matter who won in the end. If the Baldies win, the disadvantage would be obvious: we'll find ourselves on the losing side. If the humans win . . . well, they'll reoccupy their colony worlds, and what they find there will reveal that we attacked the Bellerophon Arm while the Baldy incursion enabled us to do so without their knowledge. They might well . . . ah, resent this. It will also reveal that we engaged in nuclear attacks on planetside human population centers. My studies lead me to believe that the humans have strangely strong feelings on that subject."

"Well, then, what alternative do you offer?"

"Simply this, Dominant One: we do the obvious and drive the Baldies out of Tisiphone and Treadway. And then we complete the extermination of the human populations that we have encountered in the Bellerophon Arm."

"Complete extermination was never part of my orders, Dominant One!" protested Atylycx.

"Of course not," said Scyryx with renewed contempt. "It wasn't cost-effective. Slaves, and even meat animals, are worth more than irradiated corpses. But thanks to your incompetence, it has now become unavoidable. After we've killed all of the offended populations, *then* we can make the humans the offer of alliance. And whether they accept or not, we can blame the Baldies for the attacks, and there will be no one alive to contradict us."

Ultraz considered it. From his studies of the humans, he recalled an uncharacteristically sensible proverb: *Dead men tell no tales.*

"Very well. We will proceed along these lines." He swung his gaze to rest on Atylycx, who had blood connections with Hrufely, *anak* of the Dagora Horde. So having Atylycx's throat ripped out, however deeply satisfying, would have been more political trouble than it was worth. "You will be permitted to keep your command, Fleet Leader, and you will be reinforced with all the CFC units that can possibly be spared from elsewhere. Also, the individual Hordes will be persuaded to contribute. Your part of our new strategy should be within the scope of your talents: drive out the Baldies and exterminate all life on the human planets you previously attacked. Only afterward will we make our approach to the humans, and that will be done at higher levels, so this time you will have no opportunity to mishandle it. This is your final chance. Do I make myself clear?"

"Yes, Dominant One!" said Atylycx, frantically exposing his throat in the submission gesture.

Touchstone, Provisional Capital, Treadway

"So, you really are Admiral Trevayne." Commander Stanley Fraser, RFN (ret.) shook his silver-white head slowly, then continued in the distinctive twang of the Rim world of Aotearoa, where he had been born well over a century before. "We heard about your return, of course, even out here in Treadway. But it seemed unbelievable."

"Especially to you, I imagine," Trevayne speculated with a grin. He liked this tough old bird who had become a leader of the human survivors here.

Fraser nodded and chuckled. "Yes. I was an enlisted spacer back during the Fringe Rebellion—I served under you at Second Zephrain, and in Operation Reunion. I was a youngster then, and you were in your fifties. Afterward I stayed in the Rim Federation Navy and moved here after retirement."

Trevayne nodded. Fraser had the look of someone who had started on anagathics relatively late in life. He probably didn't have too many years left. But his mind was still sharp.

"And now," Fraser concluded, "I'm an old sod, and you . . ." He gestured at the man in his physiological twenties who sat across the table where they had been sipping Scotch from the latter's private stock, and gave his head another shake, as though contemplating the inscrutable workings of destiny.

This town currently served as the provisional capital of Treadway, most of whose larger population centers were radioactive pits. It was in the tropics and therefore spared the worst of the prevailing nuclear-winter effects. So today was mild enough for them to sit on the verandah of the large building that was the administrative center. Treyayne gazed out over the valley, which must have been lovely once but was now clogged with refugee camps. At least those camps now had everything they needed in terms of supplies and medical assistance. As he watched, yet another shuttle from his orbiting fleet settled down to join those already parked on the outskirts of the town.

With their advance toward Bellerophon stymied until the new Kasugawa generators were available, he and Li Magda had led major elements of the fleet back to Mercury, and onward to the liberation of the human populations in the Arm beyond it. Thus it was that they had entered Treadway . . . and made a discovery with which they were still trying to come to terms.

He turned his attention back to Fraser. "I'm still having trouble crediting what everyone here has told me."

Fraser shrugged, eyes averted. "The Tangri landed and . . . did what the Tangri generally do. Then they took off and began nuking the cities from orbit. Not that there was really anything you'd call a city here. No, they just did it for the sake of doing it." He trailed to a halt and took a pull on his Scotch.

"But then the bombardment stopped," Trevayne prompted gently. "And after that . . . ?"

"We had no idea what was going on in space, of course. People tried to tell themselves that the Rim Navy had arrived and driven the Tangri off. But then when the shuttles started landing and they obviously weren't ours, people thought the Tangri were back. But I knew it wasn't them, even if my ship recognition is a few decades out of date. Then *they* emerged, and we . . . well, we were too despairing even to panic. But then . . ."

"Yes, this is the part I find hard to believe."

"It's true, though. As you know, they can't communicate with us, so it all had to be just a matter of gestures and actions. But . . . they left food and medical supplies. Then they went elsewhere and did the same thing." Fraser gave Trevayne a look that was almost beseeching. "Admiral, after all we've heard about the Baldies . . . I just don't understand."

"I don't, either," Trevayne admitted. "But I *do* understand what the Tangri did—what they've always done. And this is the last time they're going to do it. Ever."

Fraser stared at him. "That's a mighty big oath, Admiral."

Trevayne smiled thinly. "I have a mighty big fleet, Mr. Fraser."

27

Seeming Otherwise

But I do beguile the thing I
am by seeming otherwise.
—Shakespeare

Novaya Petersburg, Novaya Rodina

It hadn't been all that long since Magda Petrovna Windrider, in her capacity as a director of Seinfeld Starship of Novaya Rodina, had been aboard the test station orbiting the planet. The installation was, of course, physically unchanged. And people were scurrying about in their usual numbers, performing their usual duties. But something was different.

Her husband put his finger on it. "They're numb," said Senator Jason Windrider.

"How could they not be?" she muttered. Since the news had arrived from Charlotte in the Bellerophon Arm, a wavefront of shock had spread outward to the uttermost limits of the Terran Republic, leaving in its wake a region of dull hurt where everyone awoke every morning to the knowledge that Li Han was gone.

That Ian Trevayne now commanded the predominantly TRN fleet Li Han had led only added to the stunned sense of unreality.

"And yet," her husband persisted, "there's more to it than that. It's more than mere grief. It's also more than a lust for vengeance. It's a calm, grim determination to see this thing through—"

"—as Li Han would have wanted it," she said, finishing his sentence for him in the way of old married couples.

They continued on to the familiar conference room, into which they were passed with only the most perfunctory security. A man and a woman rose. The woman they knew, but not well; the man not at all save by reputation. Sonja Desai stepped forward, armored in stiffness, clearly dreading having to do that which she did least well.

Magda tried to ease it for her. "Hello, Sonja. It's been a while."

"Yes, it has." Desai swallowed hard. "Magda, I . . . I'm so sorry. I know how far back your friendship with Li Han went, and how special your relationship with her was. After all, being the godmother of her daughter—"

"Thank you, Sonja," Magda said quickly, sparing her the need to go any further.

Desai's eyes dropped, and she mumbled something inaudible that might have been "Thank you." Then she turned briskly to her male companion. "I'd like to introduce Dr. Isadore Kasugawa."

"Senator . . . Admiral," the elderly-seeming man murmured.

"Just Magda, please. I've lost track of how many decades I've been retired. And let me say what an honor it is to meet you, Doctor."

"The same goes for me, only more so," declared Jason, extending his hand. "I'm merely a senator—not a genius."

"That's one way to put it," said Magda with a twinkle.

Sonja Desai, reverting to type, plowed straight into the business at hand. "As I mentioned when you asked for this meeting, Dr. Kasugawa and I have been turning our attention to ways of speeding up construction of new generators—especially the improved ones which will be necessary when your superdevastators become operational. I assume you've already had the opportunity to review the summary we sent."

"Yes," nodded Magda. "You're quite right about the need to dredge warp lines to accommodate the SDTs. But in the meantime, Admiral Trevayne's fleet is going to have to fight its way through a certain number of warp points that can't accommodate the SDTs—or, for that matter, DTs—until after the way has been cleared for the Kasugawa generators to transit. Isn't this so?"

"It is," Desai acknowledged glumly. "It's the basic tactical problem we've been up against from the first. Ian—I mean, Admiral Trevayne—would call it a catch-22."

"Well," said Magda, "we think we may have found a way around that."

She could tell that she had their undivided attention.

"We've naturally been concentrating on series production of the new SDTs," she continued. "But ever since it became apparent that the smaller warp-point assaults are going to become a lot tougher, we've assigned additional priority to the construction of the supermonitors which can transit them prior to dredging. But the real problem is getting the Kasugawa generators through those warp points. So I sat down with our chief designers, who've determined that, by ripping out practically everything else, we can cram a Kasugawa generator into one of those same hulls. The crew could be extremely small, and the ship would be equipped with specially designed escape pods for them. They would simply take the ship through the warp point, then abandon ship when it's time for the generator to activate."

"In the middle of a warp-point battle?" Sonja Desai breathed.

"The crew would, of course, be volunteers?" Kasugawa tentatively asked.

"Of course," said Jason. "But I don't think we'll have much trouble finding volunteers from the Terran Republic Navy." He glanced at the black mourning banners draping the peripheries of the briefing room. "Not now."

28

Stubborn Things

Facts are stubborn things.
—Smollett

Punt City, New Ardu/Bellerophon

Ankaht sent a *selnarm* command to her lexigraphic vocoder: *turn page*. Expecting yet another sheet filled with an unbroken phalanx of human characters, she was stunned when the dense, even turgid, prose of the book—*The Cosmology of Ethics*, written in 2346 AD by the Martian hermitess Farzaneh Adenauer—suddenly relented: in its place was a single iconic image. It was the interpenetrated black-and-white-waves disk known as the *taiji* symbol—the hallmark of the Terran philosophy/faith known as Taoism.

Ankaht leaned back and felt the thread of Adenauer's argument dissipate, felt the looming omnipresence of the symbol—and its import—grow and fill her mind. The basic notion behind it was not an isolated feature of just one strain of human thought; it was arguably one of the species' most central and universal concepts, albeit represented in different ways in different cultures. Health, understanding, reality itself: all a product of contending forces that were also utterly interdependent and, ultimately, engendered by their seeming opposite. And returning to Adenauer's prose, Ankaht discovered the pearl of insight she had begun to despair of finding in this book: "In societies and nations, as in individual organisms, the lesson resident in the *taiji* holds constant: to be *in extremis* is to veer further away from balance; to veer further away from balance is to place oneself *in extremis*."

In extremis. Like an ominous antithesis of the *taiji* symbol, this phrase had also leapt out at her again and again from human documents on philosophy, on law, on war. For individuals, to be *in extremis* was the harbinger of disaster; for societies, it was the herald of the Four Horsemen. And the cautionary tales of both history and fables were always the same: when situations got too desperate—or beliefs or behaviors became too extreme—tragedy followed, just as the ear-splitting thunder of annihilation followed a warning flash of lightning.

In contrast, while the humans' exhaustive analyses of every war and crisis rightly examined the historical particulars that gave each one its shape, they too often became seduced and blinded by those same particulars. In so doing, the otherwise learned experts and academics too often lost sight of the core truth that was the common seed of all the dire events they examined: when humans find themselves *in extremis*, they rarely extricate themselves via peaceful, productive, or prosocial means. The urgency and immediacy of any crisis—having been allowed to develop unchecked—left little time to choose among, let alone consider, alternatives when at last the claws of mortal peril came close.

And this has fueled our own war-making here, just as surely as any of the examples I have found in the annals of human history, Ankaht thought, *for we are both—Arduan and human alike—now* in extremis. *Two years ago, the humans were suddenly confronted with invaders who are intractable, inscrutable, unstoppable. They are invaders who care little of death, who take no interest in communicating, who believe that—being the Children of Illudor—they do what they must in accordance with divine will. The humans—rightly—believe themselves to be* in extremis.

And us? We, no less than the humans, find ourselves in extremis. *We are refugees from our blasted world, lost in the dark and thrown upon these strange shores like castaways upon an island. And—with no way to leave, and no home to return to—we discover these islands are inhabited by wild, Pre-Enlightenment savages. Without benefit of* selnarm *or* narmata, *they live in contentious chaos. Without knowledge of Illudor or the surety of rebirth, they roil about in a desperate terror of death, even as they spend their lives trying to eject us from the islands they infest.*

Except that they are not a savage infestation, any more than we are soulless invaders. But if we do not learn to communicate, truly communicate, our desperate fears—our respective states of being in extremis*—then we may well be each others' annihilators.*

Ankaht sat back upon her flexible legs and hung her head. *Jennifer, Jennifer; you and I. We could have stopped this. But now—*

A gentle wisp of *selnarm* probed at Ankaht. It was Temret. "Eldest, it is time. The Council is convening."

Ankaht arose, found an attenuating tickling sensation spreading down one check, lifted her cluster—and found that she had been crying. Again.

"Are you ready, Eldest?"

"I must be, Temret. Let us go."

"And so this concludes my integrated findings on the humans. We now have built enough dual-purpose vocoders that you may all assess my conclusions for yourself. Lacking our capabilities of *shaxzhutok* and the communal data pool of *selnarm*, the humans have committed much more of their collective experience to the written word than we ever felt necessary. And some of their creative forms—for instance, their 'poetry' and its emphasis on meter and rhyme—may seem particularly odd, until you recall that, relying upon speech in the place of *selnarm*, they have developed various rhetorical forms and mannerisms that are entirely dependent upon sound."

"This is quite remarkable—and quite odd. Tell me, was there a reason you did not report this—and all their philosophical overlaps with our own beliefs—earlier?"

A delicate question—and made more so since it was being asked by one of the two *Destoshaz* who remained on the Council. The rest, following Torhok's lead, had openly declared a political moratorium regarding their participation in, or recognition of any dicta from, the Council of Twenty. "Councilor Hetfeln, some of these data come from studies that we have only recently completed. However, to be frank, I have often attempted to present key portions of this data to this Council. But my research cluster's work was always suppressed as premature, prejudicial, nonessential, or—according to the accusations of the late *Holodah'kri* Urkhot—intentionally pernicious to the welfare of our Race."

Hetfeln inclined his head slightly. Among Arduans, the physicalization of his response made it extremely profound. "I do recall this. And you are kind in your obliquity, Eldest."

Ankaht radiated (fellowship, appreciation). "Your receptivity does us all honor and shows us all the path back to balance, to *assed'ai.*"

Tefnut ha sheri tapped two claws on the table in alternation; it was a contemplative metronome that also called for attention. "Yes, the path to balance. The conditions of the humans has made me reflect upon something I have not thought of in many years. When one becomes an initiate *kri*, he or she is taught that our impulse to join our *selnarms* together in *narmata* is simply an expression of our impulse toward unity in Illudor. The metaphor they teach acolytes—*hwa'kri*s—on that first day is that the multitudes of us are akin to billions of molecules of glass, but cast together in a perfect sphere. The sphere is both Illudor and *narmata*, and the true perception of all three is the attainment of *holodah*. Because, in that perfect sphere—the most perfect of geometric shapes—all is held in perpetual, crystalline, pellucid balance."

Hetfeln suppressed (incredulity). "And this reminds you of the *humans*?"

Tefnut ha sheri waved a tentacle that seemed to call for patience and also beckoned to follow him into deeper reflection. "Yes, in a way. For the humans seem to have the same instincts, the same desires, for oneness that we do—but their lack of *narmata* leaves them all separate and innately out of balance. It is as if the glass globe of the human community had been shattered at the outset and ever since—as distaff and disparate parts—they are all trying to find their way back to reconstruct and rejoin that whole. Consider what Eldest Ankaht put before us about their beliefs. The Taoists find and express a human analog of our principle of *assed'ai*. The Hindus discover and focus upon reincarnation and the special sight which they envision as a property of a third eye that is actually latent in the human body as the pineal gland. The Western philosophers struggle with the necessity of reconciling the universe's cyclic processes into its linear relationships and vice versa, in an attempt to create a concept of the whole that is greater than the sum of its parts. These are all attempts to bridge the gaps of isolation, of separation, which is the consequence of their lack of *selnarm* and *narmata*." Tefnut ha sheri shifted listlessly in his seat, as though very tired. "It both encourages and discourages me."

"What encourages you about this, revered *Holodah'kri'at*?"

"That the humans are, in so many of the traits and impulses that matter, so very like us."

"So, then what discourages you?"

"That the humans are, in so many of the traits and impulses that matter, so very like us."

Hetfeln blinked. "I do not understand."

Ankaht let her feelings of (accord, insight) rush out as she experienced them. "Revered *Holodah'kri'at*, you fear that our way is made more difficult by this similarity between our races?"

"Difficult in ways even you have not yet foreseen, Eldest Sleeper. But for now, we must use the human translators to attempt to forge more and better communicative links between ourselves and the humans inhabitants of New Ardu."

Ankaht sent (rue). "I fear that the translators we possess now are not sufficient for the task you would set them."

"Are their powers of pseudo-*selnarm* too weak?"

"That, too, but there is also the matter of their reception in the human community. They have been our mouthpieces, whereby we explain our methods of enforcement, dictate our expectations, and convey our threats. Naturally, the rest of the humans are now innately suspicious of them, believing that they are in fact our puppets—and thus will not speak with them. Our best hope to establish true contact with the local humans—for so many reasons—was Jennifer Peitchkov. But she is gone."

Treknat, her fellow *shaxzhu*, queried: "Can we not at least use the others to initiate some feelings of trust and amicability between ourselves and the Resistance?"

"Establishing an atmosphere of cordiality—or at least, mutually assured safety—should not be too difficult. The question is: How do we know if we are being understood once we have entered the thornier areas of negotiation and specific agreements? We must know that they understand us, and that we understand them—precisely. We need to be able to create and enact detailed agreements with specific conditions and timetables, and a clear understanding of each others' intents. Without this degree of communicative surety, it may well be more dangerous to initiate a peace process than not."

Tefnut ha sheri tapped his claw a single time. "And the intransigence of the *Destoshaz* radicals has now made it impossible to even promise the humans a cease-fire. The warrior caste is becoming increasingly autonomous regarding their security missions. It seems as though they are actively provoking conflict with human communities."

Hetfeln (agreed). "It saddens me to concur, but I must. Almost all of my caste-siblings remain both distrustful of, and disgusted by, the humans."

Amunherh'peshef turned to Narrok, who had arrived only minutes before the meeting started. "Senior Admiral Narrok, are you finding that this problem is still prevalent in the fleet?"

"It is still present, but decreasing, First Councilor. In the Expeditionary Fleet, we had the occasion to encounter humans under a variety of different circumstances. We experienced both their cleverness of mind and greatness of heart on many occasions. It was therefore somewhat easier to wean that fleet away from radical opinions once Admiral Torhok was no longer there to reinforce them."

Amunherh'peshef sent out a brisk wave of (practicality). "Senior Admiral Narrok must return to his fleet, but has returned to brief us on the latest intelligence reports regarding the new human technologies we have observed, and our altered strategic situation."

Narrok stood. "First matters. The newly expanded military-intelligence cluster under Intelligence Prime and Cluster-Commander Mretlak has recruited our leading physicists to investigate the device the humans have used to expand several warp points, and its principles of operation.

"According to analysis of the computers in the latest human wrecks, they designate these devices as 'Kasugawa warp-point generators,' which also seem capable of making a smaller warp point more capacious. Unfortunately, this achievement is so very much at the forefront of human warp-point science and technology that we can find no theoretical clues as to how they have achieved this effect.

"However, we have made strides in other areas, including improvements to our fighters. We assess that two of our fighters are now roughly a match for any one fielded by the humans. We have adapted some of the SDS-production pathways so as to create modular warp-point forts, albeit very small ones.

"But these are not truly innovations. They are simply evolutions and adaptations of extant designs. We no longer have the time or luxury to develop new ships or weapons. That opportunity is now irretrievably lost. It probably slipped through our tentacles about five months ago."

The *narmata* of the room was quiet, somber, almost grim. Ankaht could feel that although they appreciated Narrok's candor and deference, they were unaccustomed to such frank and dire portents.

Tefnut ha sheri was the first to break the stillness. "Then what does this bode for the Children of Illudor, Senior Admiral Narrok?"

"Simply put, we stand a reasonable chance of holding any system in which I have been able to construct a good number of SDSs. So, with enough time, we should be able to create nearly impregnable defenses."

"However, with your recent victory in the Charlotte system, we are secure. For now."

Narrok delayed sending a response. "We are secure in the Charlotte system, First Councilor."

Amunherh'peshef sat more erect. "Share your fears with us, Senior Admiral."

"I fear our vulnerability in Polo, and beyond that, BR-02."

"But these systems are both protected by warp points that the largest of the human ships cannot traverse."

"This is true. But it is also true that we do not yet have SDSs in those systems, and, as I said, a density of those ships is the key to successful system defense. We are, I fear, in a race with the humans. Can we can build SDSs faster than they can recover to mount an attack?"

"So, do you suggest that we abandon Polo and concentrate all our new defense assets in BR-02?"

Ankaht sensed the hesitation in Narrok: he was clearly of two minds on the matter. "Collecting all our defenses in BR-02 is a prudent, but final, step. There is no defensible warp point to fall back upon if we are driven from that system. Obversely, if we manage to retain control of Polo, then we continue to possess two assault pathways into the key system of Demeter. Should fortune favor us, that position will allow us resume offensive operations far earlier, and with a far better prospect of success."

Ankaht felt the dutiful but unenthusiastic undertone with which Narrok ended his review of their strategic situation. She kept her sending modest, almost gentle. "But you do not favor this alternative, Senior Admiral?"

"Eldest Sleeper, I would like to suggest a third alternative."

"Which is?"

"Which is that we seek ways to extricate both ourselves and our foes from our current, mutual condition of having no choice but to fight. In short, so long as we are both—to adopt your usage, Elder—entities *in extremis*, it will be difficult for either of us to consider alternatives other than victory or death."

Tefnut ha sheri leaned back from the table. "It is refreshing to hear such a perspective from an admiral on the Council. Your hope for an easing of tensions may be beyond our power to make manifest, but it is worthwhile to consider it—and it is always important to wish for a life that is not simply endless war."

Hetfeln shifted uncomfortably. "I concur, revered *Holodah'kri'at*, but I must remind you that it matters very little to the radical *Destoshaz* what we think laudable or not, anymore. Senior Cluster-Commander Iakkut, a reactionary who was a close friend—and *maatkah* partner—of Torhok's has now become a powerful voice among the *Destoshaz'ai*-as-*sulhaji* faction. Even with Torhok and Urkhot gone, the religious and race fanaticism they engendered and amplified continues to escalate—in large part because they are now martyrs to the cause."

Ankaht sent (accord, regret). "I have it on good authority that Urkhot's final exhortations to genocide have now evolved into an ideological fashion among his most ardent followers. They wear the concept of that atrocity like a badge of honor, a way to memorialize their fallen leaders."

"Yes." Tefnut ha sheri signaled (rue) "One of whom lost his life against the humans. And the other lost his life at the hands of a race-traitor—while a Council full of other race-traitors looked on." The old priest closed all three eyes slowly. "These are dark times, full of dark tidings."

Mretlak leaned back from the security feed coming from the multisensor he had had installed in the Council's gathering chamber—at their behest—and let his eyelids droop for a moment. It had been a long day—and it promised to get longer. With his cluster recently expanded to a section, and being the only collective that possessed the means of reliably keeping a surreptitious eye on the *Destoshaz'ai*-as-*sulhaji* zealots, once-insignificant Mretlak had become arguably the most important Arduan whose position was known to virtually no one outside the Council itself. He had also become arguably the busiest.

A familiar tendril of *selnarm* brushed across his own: it was Lentsul. "Yes, Lentsul. Enter."

The small *Ixturshaz*, who had risen quickly to become the Intelligence Second, shuffled into Mretlak's office—who knew all too well what that gait signified: disappointment. "Very well, Lentsul. What has gone amiss?"

(Annoyance, frustration.) "Nothing amiss—just another defeat in locating the Resistance base."

"What now? The potential site you identified did not prove to be accurate?"

"Well, yes and no. We kept the site—an old warehouse complex in Upper Thessalaborea—under distant surveillance for four weeks before we decided to go in and search it."

"Prudent. What did you find?"

"Absolutely nothing of use. Oh, there was ample evidence that it must have been one of their training bases in the early days of the war. Close inspection indicated soil samples from all over the continent: dirt kicked loose from many boots, I suppose. But we estimate it was last used over two months ago."

"Do you have any reason to suspect the Resistance abandoned it because they learned of your surveillance and investigation?"

"No, there's no indication of that. My hypothesis is that they simply processed as many new recruits as they were able to handle and then closed up their base."

"So they didn't dodge us."

"No. We were just too late."

"Which is why we needed a military-intelligence section from the very start of this war."

(Accord, weariness.) "So, with that lead cold, how do we locate them?"

Mretlak sent a coy (reassurance). "Oh, I've seen to that, Lentsul."

"You?"

"Yes, me. Do you think I just sit behind this desk all day?"

"Well, I—"

Mretlak could feel that Lentsul did indeed suspect that, but he pressed on. "Do you recall what I said several months ago, that we only needed to give the Resistance something that they would covet and that their own actions would lead us to them?"

"Yes."

"Well, about four weeks ago, I determined what objects we could thusly put out as bait and could also easily track."

Lentsul was (amazed, intrigued). "What?"

"Batteries. Power cells."

Lentsul was (perplexed, doubtful). "But, Commander, everyone uses batteries. With so many of their power plants shut down or on reduced operation, the humans are *all* desperate for them."

"Yes, everyone needs them. And everyone is running out of them. But the Resistance cannot afford to. They are a military unit, and they rely on batteries in all their portable communications, their sensors, computers, targeting devices. More unusual still, many of the batteries used by the human militaries must be

EMP resistant, so the Resistance will also require a disproportionately large supply of the more advanced and expensive power cells. Using this strategem, we shall not catch them with a single decisive trap, Lentsul, but with a thousand statistical snares which will stick to them and their logistics flow like *zifrik*-pupae in molting season."

"And how soon can we expect the first results, Mretlak?"

"Any day now, Lentsul. Any day now."

29

Vae Victis

"Woe to the vanquished."
—Latin proverb

Tangri SD Styr'car'hsux, *Reconquest Fleet of the Consolidated Hordes, Tisiphone System*

Atylycx rounded furiously on his intelligence chief. "What do you mean they're not the Baldies?"

They stood in the mingled light of Tisiphone's binary suns that streamed in from the flag bridge's large, curving view screen. The Tangri fleet that Atylycx had elected to personally lead, while entrusting the simultaneous attack on BR-07 to subordinates, had emerged from the warp point and set a course for the planet they were charged with rendering uninhabitable. Of course the occupying Baldies would have to be dealt with first, but Atylycx was confident that his reinforced fleet was up to it, given the tactical lessons he had absorbed and analyzed from his previous unpleasant encounter with them.

But now...

"They're not Baldies, Fleet Leader! The energy signatures admit of only one interpretation. These are ship classes of the human polities known as the Rim

Federation and the Terran Republic. The majority of the monitors belong to the former, but—"

Atylycx's self-control, worn thin by the stress he had lived under since his visit to the homeworld, suddenly gave way. He reared on his hind legs and brought his arm down in a blow to his subordinate's head. The intelligence officer staggered, then immediately assumed a submission-posture. Everyone on the flag bridge pretended not to notice.

"Idiot! Cretin! They *can't* be humans. There are no human naval forces in the Arm except scattered pickets and other light units left stranded by the Baldies' conquest of Bellerophon." He waved an arm at the display screen, where new readouts were appearing with staccato rapidity. "Where could all these monitors and assault carriers and the rest have come from? Answer me that, imbecile!"

"I have no explanation, Fleet Leader."

"It's obvious. The Baldies must be using electronic countermeasures to disguise their ships as human ones." *For what purpose?* came the whispered query at the back of his mind. He could tell the intelligence chief wanted to ask exactly the same thing but didn't dare. "To confuse and disorient us," he answered the unspoken question. "Yes. That's it. And they've succeeded completely in your case, fool!" He turned away contemptuously, now able to think clearly, and studied the readouts.

Unless the Baldies—they *must* be Baldies!—had ECM capabilities beyond everyone else's, they couldn't be simultaneously falsifying both their identity *and* their tonnage classes. So they had outsmarted themselves: he knew what he was up against. He didn't relish facing that array of monitors with the characteristically lighter Tangri ships. But he outnumbered the force he was facing by a margin sufficient to make him willing to trust that his ships' equally characteristic superior maneuverability would offset the monitors' bone-crunching firepower.

Of course he would take some losses before getting in among them: he first had to pass through the missile storm they could put out. But at the same time, his fighters might prove an equalizer. Judging from the number of assault carriers he was seeing in the emerging enemy order of battle, they should have a substantial numerical advantage. And intelligence analysis indicated that Baldy fighters (unlike the humans ones, which of course couldn't be here) had no qualitative advantage over his.

"Ah . . . Fleet Leader?" The tentative voice was that of his intelligence chief. "I mention this only to remind you of the full scope of your tactical options. But our ships *are* faster than theirs, and we are currently—though only for a limited time—in a position to return to the warp point before—"

Atylycx rounded on him, and he instinctively flinched back. "You're a coward as well as a fool! Baldies or humans, these are *prey animals.* Get out of my sight, you . . . you . . . *female!*"

Atylycx turned away, not bothering to watch the effect of the ultimate insult he had delivered in the hearing of the entire flag bridge. What he had said was true, of course. And besides . . . after the directive the Dominant One had given him, retreat was not an option. Better to die here.

TRNS Lancelot, *Allied Fleet, Tisiphone System*

Li Magda was still getting used to being, for the second time, alone on *Lancelot*'s flag bridge.

When the recon drones had given warning of an impending attack on Tisiphone, Trevayne had brought in a few more monitors (the largest ships that could reach it through the warp lines) and carriers. But judging it likely that the Tangri would also hit the BR-07 starless warp nexus, he had gone there himself, along with as many of his heavier units as he felt he could spare from confronting the Baldies at Demeter.

Now she watched as the datagroups of her monitors—mostly missile-heavy RFN ones—sent one smashing salvo after another into the advancing Tangri ships. Already the fighters from her assault carriers were entangled in a snarling series of dogfights with their more numerous but less effective Tangri analogs.

And now, she decided, it was time to play another card: her lighter fleet carriers, which included some Orion-crewed ones from the PSUN contingent, and which were now in the position she had wanted, behind the unsuspecting invaders.

She turned to her chief of staff, who had remained in that billet long after promotion. "Captain De Chaleins, send word to Small Claw Khzhotan. Tell him to drop cloaking ECM and launch his fighters."

"At once, Admiral. That should be a welcome order, given how he and his personnel feel about the Tangri."

"Yes. I seem to recall hearing the term '*chofaki*-spoor.'"

Tangri SD Styr'car'hsux, *Reconquest Fleet of the Consolidated Hordes, Tisiphone System*

There was no longer any possible doubt. There hadn't been since the initial fighter engagements. These were not Baldies. The now-unambiguous energy signatures merely confirmed that.

And some of the fighters from the now-decloaked lighter carriers that danced maddeningly in Atylycx's rear weren't even human ones. They were Orion. Which was not good news.

It was impossible. But there it was. And with his ships exploding all over the sky, there was only one thing to do. And surely the Dominant One would understand. He gave the order to retire on the warp point.

But it was easier said than done, with the datalinked missile-storms still breaking over his collapsing fleet—another concussion shook the flagship's bones, sending Atylycx staggering—and the Orion fighters corkscrewing through what could no longer be described as a formation, mercilessly seeking his ships' blind zones.

Another hit, and another...

Just before the reactor went, Atylycx glimpsed something in the dim emergency lighting. It was the expression on the face of one of the *zemlixi* orderlies. The two of them both lay on the deck, and for just an instant their eyes met.

I've never seen a look like that on one of their faces, Atylycx thought. *I don't think I like it.*

It was his last thought.

TRNS Imperious, *Task Force One, Allied Fleet, BR-07 System*

BR-07 had no local sun to relieve its stygian interstellar darkness. But now its spaces were illuminated by another kind of flame.

Ian Trevayne had once read what the American author F. Scott Fitzgerald had written about the futile waste of his own British ancestors' offensive at the Somme in the First World War: "A whole empire walking very slowly, dying in front and pushing forward behind." Now he was reminded of that as the Tangri emerged from the warp point into the concentrated fire of his devastators and supermonitors. The leading elements simply disintegrated in that inferno, which consumed them as fast as they could appear and rush into it.

Trevayne harrumphed to get the attention of Andreas Hagen, who had been staring awestruck at the massacre. "Andreas, I think we can anticipate a chance to have a staff meeting shortly. But first I want courier drones prepared, to be dispatched to Demeter via Mercury and also to Admiral Li at Tisiphone."

"Ah . . . yes, Admiral," said Hagen, pulling himself together. "And the messages?"

"To Admiral Li, a request for confirmation that the Tangri advance against Tisiphone has been stopped." Trevayne's confidence that this was indeed the case was palpable. "And a further request that she send us as many monitors and carriers as she feels she can spare. Beyond that, we'll need overall logistical support for our advance beyond this system."

"Uh . . . our *advance*, Admiral?" This was the first Hagen had heard of it.

"Precisely. We're following the Tangri remnants through this warp point as soon as practical. That's why we need some of Admiral Li's monitors. We don't know how far we'll get before we reach warp points that our devastators and supermonitors can't transit. And we don't want to let that slow us down, any more than we want to outrun our supplies." He strode off abruptly, and Hagen could only scurry to catch up. "And, oh, yes," he said over his shoulder, "we'll need additional courier drones, to be dispatched to the home governments."

"All of them?" asked Hagen faintly.

"Yes—the Republic and the PSU as well as the Rim. They need to know that now is the time to begin putting pressure on the Tangri wherever our warp networks abut theirs. This is a unique moment—we can't let it slip away."

Headquarters, Confederation Fleet Command, Luzarix, Hyx'Tangri System

The air of the Confederation Fleet Command headquarters was heavy with repressed panic.

Ultraz had felt it as he had passed though the shadowy corridors where little knots of staffers conversed in hushed tones or moved about in frenetic futility. Over everything hung a sense that the course of events had passed beyond control.

And everywhere the *zemlixi* functionaries stood in the background, diffident as always . . . but there was something different about them.

Now he sat in the great hexagonal chamber at the architectural mountain's heart and listened to reports that all added up to one thing: the attack on Tisiphone had been a fiasco redeemed only by the fact that they would no longer have to endure Atylycx's incompetence. But what had followed was far worse.

"The appearance of the new human ships of unprecedented size and power at BR-07 was, of course, an unanticipated factor," the intelligence analyst droned on. "Our offensive there could make no headway against them, and the local commander withdrew as losses reached unacceptable levels. Equally unanticipated was the promptness with which the humans followed him. And now—"

Ultraz cut him off with an impatient gesture. "Is there any explanation yet of the even more unanticipated factor of these immense human forces' presence in the Bellerophon Arm, which the Baldies' conquest of Bellerophon was supposed to have isolated?"

Heruvycx answered that himself, for the CFC high command. "No, Dominant One. It remains a deep mystery."

"The resolution of mysteries is supposed to be the function of your intelligence branch," said Scyryx acidly.

"It was totally unforeseeable!" Heruvycx glared at the hated Korvak, then appealed directly to Ultraz. "We speculate that the humans have achieved some heretofore unknown capability to manipulate the physics of the warp network, but this is no more than speculation. What is beyond speculation is that their counteroffensive from BR-07 has now taken six of our systems." He pointed to the holographic warp line diagram that floated above the center of the table.

"Without even slowing down, it would appear," said Scyryx. There was a quaver in his voice that Ultraz had heard more and more lately, as the news of disaster had grown from a trickle to a freshet to a flood. "Why has our defense been so ineffectual?"

Heruvycx's reply was scrupulously correct, but his look of hatred now held an element of contempt. "The human reaction was so unexpectedly swift that we had no time to organize one. Remember, we have never emphasized fixed warp-point defenses."

No, brooded Ultraz. *Of course not. We always relied on subterfuges, ploys . . . and the fact that our enemies were, in the end, nothing more than prey animals.*

"Furthermore," the intelligence analyst resumed at a gesture from Heruvycx, "it appears that the humans are proceeding in accordance with a preexisting plan once they enter our systems. They are distributing weapons to the *zemlixi* in those systems and inciting them to rise in rebellion. And not just the *zemlixi* but also the conquered populations of inferior animals."

"I have received reports," said Ultraz with deceptive mildness, "that the rebelling *zemlixi* have, in several cases, made common cause with those populations."

An unvoiced shudder of revulsion ran around the table.

"What more can be expected of *zemlixi*?" someone muttered disgustedly.

"Finally," the intelligence analyst concluded, "our routine recon drones show disturbing indications of force buildups in all the human polities along our borders. This, combined with input from our political intelligence sources, leads us to believe that a general offensive is in the offing."

"While our forces are concentrated in the approaches to the Bellerophon Arm," Ultraz added. It was the corollary no one wanted to hear.

"And inadequate even there," added Scyryx. The

instability was unmistakable now. His voice nearly broke with it.

Ultraz looked around the table, and no one met his eyes. "So, the question becomes: What do we do now?"

With a suddenness that shocked almost everyone into immobility, Scyryx cracked. He leaped to his feet and stared wildly around the table.

"Do? Do? If we want to have any hope at all of surviving, there's only one thing we can do—surrender!"

Every Tangri officer of the CFC or the Horde fleets carried, hanging from a part of his harnesslike *anharichu* just behind the base of the torso (a human would have thought of it as the "withers"), the traditional weapon called the *kyeex*—a short curved blade attached to a three-foot staff that gave a greater torque for sweeping blows delivered at a gallop. The fancy modern-dress versions weren't as heavy as the ones that had spread slaughter across the plains centuries before, but they were still functional.

With a flesh-tingling cry, Heruvycx reached behind him, swept his *kyeex* out and around in a single motion, and brought it down in a diagonal slash across the front of Scyryx's torso, slicing on down through the chest muscles below that protected the vital organs and cutting open the heart. A gout of blood shot out and spattered in a long line across the table. While there was still blood in the already-dead Scyryx to taste, Heruvycx reached out barehanded and tore out his throat. Then, breathing heavily, he turned to Ultraz with a level gaze.

Ultraz sighed inwardly. It was too bad about Scyryx; he had been a useful advisor, and Ultraz had found him more refreshing than he could publicly admit. But there was no help for it, of course. *He must have gone insane,* Ultraz thought. By advocating surrender to prey animals, he had made legitimate prey of himself, and Heruvycx's act was irreproachable.

"We will," Ultraz said, as though nothing had happened, "alert all the Hordes that they are responsible for the defense of their own domains. The CFC will provide as much help as can be spared from the Bellerophon Arm. The objective, of course, is to inflict the maximum possible casualties. We must never forget that we are dealing with what are essentially herd animals—even if they are stampeding at the moment—and they will not be able to equal our ability to endure heavy losses."

A rumble of agreement—a little too loud—ran around the table.

"It shall be as you command, Dominant One," said Heruvycx. His voice held the near-dreaminess of satiety.

"Have the corpse removed," Ultraz added as an afterthought, then stood up and departed, ignoring the submission-gestures.

As he left the chamber, he passed within a meter of one of the *zemlixi* menials. Ordinarily, one didn't even notice them. But for some reason, he glanced at this one. And for a split second he thought he saw something in that face, instantly smoothed over.

I don't think I like it, he thought.

30

Tecum

Tecum vivere amem, tecum obeam libens.
("With you I should love to live,
with you be ready to die.")
—Horace

Resistance Regional Headquarters, Charybdis Islands, Bellerophon/New Ardu

Newly minted Sergeant Jonathan Wismer pushed the agitator through the sewage catch tank one more time. The various gathered discussants either gagged, went pale, or both. But as an untrafficked site in a hermetically sealed base, the sewage backflow tankage room was perfect. This was the group's seventh meeting in the reeking gray pit, and they had yet to be interrupted by a single unwanted visitor. Hardly a surprise: there had been guffaws and snickers when the well-known (and well-respected) officers and NCOs of this group each drew a short-straw in the—carefully rigged—rank-blind lottery for cleaning the dreaded chamber. That the lottery had been instituted only a week after the showdown with Heide was a subtlety lost amidst the general chortles and enthusiastic hootings.

McGee watched Jon's long-handled tool move through

the viscous swells and wished, at that particular moment, that he didn't have a nose. "So, it's not just rumor, Jon?"

"Nope. Toshi Springer and the others at the observatory confirmed it before they got shut down. The Baldies are going into ship-building overdrive. Eyeball astronomy lenses aimed at their geosync industrial-belt show that bigger hulls are starting to show up in the ways, too—or maybe small forts. Kind of hard to tell the difference, with university-grade optical scopes."

Cap Peters nodded. "But it all makes sense, and goes along with everything else we're hearing. The Baldies are shutting down a large number of their own facilities. In particular, they're pulling back from a lot of their recent public-outreach offices that were evidently designed to make them seem more accessible and likable to us."

"Good luck to them with that project," muttered Kapinski.

"Yeah, those were not big successes, but the Baldies' reasons for folding up their tents seem to have less to do with local outcomes than with something else happening outsystem. Our observers are reporting a huge upflux of the same Baldies who used to work in these outreach projects. Most of them are outward-bound, evidently."

"Casualty replacements?"

"Well, it doesn't seem like they're trying to swell the ranks for the victory parade, given the mood."

Roon Kelakos cocked an eyebrow. "You can tell a Baldy's mood?"

Next to McGee, Jen took the handkerchief away from her nose long to enough to retch, and then explained, "Actually, you *can* tell an Arduan's mood. It's hard to see, for us. The physical signs are very, very subtle. But they're there. And the observers are right. The intel footage you've shown me recently makes it pretty obvious that something awful has happened to them, something that—*gak*!" She slapped the handkerchief over her face and spun away from the sewage tank. McGee put an arm around her spasming shoulders.

Chong—impassive and stoic except for his tightly pinched nostrils—nodded. "Cap is right. It all adds up. The outsized, automated defense blisters they've been emplacing around their own cities, the remote missile sites they're putting deep underground, their withdrawal from our population centers, the shutdown of one power plant after another until they've got our civilians rationing electricity . . . Yes, they're expecting an attack. Not today, not next week, not even next month—but they're digging in."

"*Da*, and they are digging in right next to where our families live." Danilenko spat. In the sewage-backflow room, that unclean habit provided both a hygienic and aesthetic improvement.

Harry Li sighed. "I hate to say it, but maybe this one time Heide is right. Maybe we need to attack sooner rather than later." He looked around the group. Igor nodded vigorously, Juan a moment behind him. Roon Kelakos and Cap Stevens seemed a little less enthusiastic. McGee noticed that only Chong seemed to share his own reluctance. Jen shook her head in a vigorous negative—a motion that evidently induced a new surge of nausea.

Cap broke the uncomfortable silence with a tone that was the very epitome of reasonableness. "We know how you feel about this, Jen, and some of us are starting to sympathize. But we could be running out of time. The Baldies are getting pretty short-tempered with our civilians again."

"That's the *Destoshaz*," Jen gagged out. "Fanatics."

Igor—who demonstrated an almost chivalric deference to Jen in all things—nodded gravely. "*Da*, Jennifer. Clearly, not all the Baldies perform atrocities. This you have helped us see. But we cannot fight some of the aliens and not the others. When we strike to save ourselves, they will all fight against us. So we must fight against all of them. It is sad, but it cannot be changed."

Cap nodded. "Igor is right, and whatever course we take, it's not going to be pretty. As I see it, we've got two choices—cripple the Baldy command echelons or wait until the Fleet shows up. And when the Fleet makes orbit, and if the Baldies are still in uncontested control of the surface of this planet, then the Fleet will have no choice but to follow the pre-invasion SOP."

Jen coughed out, "What SOP is that?"

Cap Peters frowned and looked away. "Pre-landing bombardment. Neutralization of all enemy infrastructure, including all known or suspected defense installations and force groupments. In the case of Bellerophon, that is going to mean a whole lot of cities will get pretty roughed up. And Melantho will be slagged into trinitite."

Jonathan Wismer leaned on his long-handled tool. "Couldn't we try to organize a general evacuation once we knew—?"

Cap shook his head. "A noble idea, Jon, but it won't work. The Baldies have now shut down all our communications, dismantled all our observatories, confiscated every bit of radio equipment they could find. So, with no way to receive or send a warning, how do we know it's time to evacuate before the first missiles start raining in? And by that time, it's too late."

Jon nodded, sadly resigned to Cap's logic. "What's our move, Cap?"

"Well, given the irregular nature of our command structure"—Cap looked around the *de facto* strategy council and was greeted with sour grins—"I'm open to suggestions and new ideas. But I can't see many alternatives that don't start with an assault into Punt itself. It will be costly, but they don't have any awareness of what a full-readiness, milspec-equipped attack will be like."

Jen shook her head. "I wouldn't count on that, Cap. They've seen all our documentaries and movies." Jen held up a pausing hand as a wave of nausea passed; McGee rubbed her back gently. "The Arduans didn't believe any of our self-representations at first. But when you rescued us, that was already starting to change in a big way. Ankaht and her group were realizing that actual footage of events, as shown in news programs, could be taken at face value. So if any other Arduans are listening to her research group, your equipment won't come as a complete surprise."

Cap nodded thoughtfully. "That's useful intel, Jen, thank you. But did you have any sense of how much milspec equipment they thought we had?"

Jen shrugged. "It never came up."

Cap kept nodding. "I can see how it wouldn't. But we've also watched how they extend their vehicles and aerial patrols beyond their safe zones without a lot of overwatch. I think if they knew—or even speculated—that we have as many high-tech toys as we have, they'd be a lot more careful once outside their cities and bases."

Jen tilted her head, then matched Cap's nod. "Ankaht never thought of it that way, exactly, but there's something in what you say. The Arduans weren't concerned about these issues because they didn't think it possible that you had the numbers of sophisticated weapons that you've got in reserve. That would certainly be the radical *Destoshaz* conclusion. Their contempt for humans makes it unthinkable to them that we'd withhold such powerful systems from deployment for so long. They think we are completely ruled and governed by our most violent instincts."

"Huh. Sounds like they were looking in the mirror, rather than looking at us." Juan's remark earned him a quick smile from Cap.

Harry's face was uncharacteristically earnest as he leaned forward. "Look, in the end, Cap's right. The only way to minimize civilian casualties is to seize the Baldies' cee-four nexus and then start a general guerrilla strike against all their assets. If we can create an interval of chaos in their defenses, that should open a window for the Fleet—and it will show them that Baldy control is being actively contested. There's a good chance they would send forces down into friendly areas, rather than directly assaulting—or leveling—our cities."

Roon frowned. "That's still a lot of bodies you're talking about piling up, Harry. Hey, are you an officer now?" The joke didn't go over as well as Kelakos had obviously hoped—particularly with the officers. McGee didn't mind it that much. Officer or not, he remained an NCO at heart.

Chong showed no appreciation for Kelakos's jibe at officers, but that didn't stop him from agreeing with the sergeant's central point. "Yes, it will indeed be a lot of bodies. And I think we might be able to avoid that if we try taking the Arduan leadership hostage, rather than decapitating it. We might be able to briefly paralyze the militants by threatening to kill their Council of Twenty, unless they agree to a parley. Meanwhile, our Fleet continues to land forces. We wouldn't need to delay the Baldies very long for this tactic to work. Even an hour's hesitation as they consider their options could turn the tide."

"Except you won't get even one minute's hesitation," interjected Jen. "Look, I'm going to say this one more time." She laid aside her handkerchief and leaned forward to go nose to nose with Harry Li. "If the Baldies believe their Council has become a liability, they will destroy it themselves. Without flinching."

"From what you've told us," observed Cap, "it sounds like the *Destoshaz* radicals are thinking about it already."

"Exactly. And if they do stage a coup, it won't be politically motivated—not in the way we think of it. They'll do it because they feel that the Council is jeopardizing the survival of their race. And when they kill the Council, it won't be with the thought that they are permanently annihilating those leaders. It's more like they're sending them to stand in the corner because they were making trouble. They're not gone for good, just for now. They'll be alive again later. Heck, maybe they will all be reincarnated together. I can just see it. They'll all have a reunion, laughing over how they were silly enough to kill and assassinate each other when they first arrived on Bellerophon."

The eyes of the Marines surrounding her were wide with a mixture of bafflement, amusement, and horror. "For real?" asked Juan Kapinski.

"For real," affirmed Jen. "This is the core of what I keep trying to tell you, and why they find it as hard to understand us as we find it hard to understand them. The communication stuff—the speech versus *selnarm*—that's easy. That's just mechanics. The real difference is in what *we* mean when we use the words 'life' and 'death,' and what *they* mean. For the Arduans, 'death' is not an absolute term or condition, so neither is 'life.' They don't have anything as profound and absolute as our self-preservation reflex. Their only analogous reflex is a desperate urgency to ensure the safety of their race, because if their race dies, then so do they—for good. So if you take their leaders hostage, and send the message 'Capitulate or we will kill them,' the Arduans would be as likely to send a bomb down your throat as ignore you—but they won't negotiate. They won't even consider it."

Harry Li sat back; Cap frowned deeply; Chong rested his chin in his hand and seemed to be staring into an infinite nothingness located about a foot in front of his face.

Roon Kelakos shifted uncomfortably. "So, Ms. Peitchkov, are you telling us that we should just attack Punt City—straight on?"

"No, that won't help, either. If they're threatened, the Arduans will call in a missile strike on the very edge—maybe inside—their own perimeter."

"So we sit on our hands and let the Fleet kill us with their pre-invasion bombardment?" Juan was aghast.

"God, no—look, I'm not saying I support that alternative, either. I don't. I'm just saying that the plans you've proposed so far won't work."

McGee ran a hand down her back. "We know that's what you're trying to tell us, Jen. But we're going to need a plan—awful or not—soon. If we don't have one to propose, then Heide will come up with one of his own, and that's sure to be a disaster. He's talking about a general uprising. All cities, all at once, civilians in the streets, led by the Resistance."

Jen blanched. "That's insanity. It would be a bloodbath. The Arduans would just withdraw and—"

"—and blast every site of the uprising clean off the map. *Da*, Jennifer." Danilenko nodded. "I have seen them do this. I know they will. But tell me, please—if none of our plans will work, what plan do you suggest?

Because if we do not do something, then we will be bombed out of existence. Or Heide will send us all to our deaths in the bloodbath you predict. We must propose something ourselves, or one of these things will be done to us."

Jen shook her head and looked pained. "I don't know. I don't—look, I'm not a soldier. I don't think about plans and strategies. I don't know about all your weapons and all your—"

"Jen." McGee tugged her closer with the hand he had encircling her far shoulder. "Jen. It's okay. No one is expecting you to be, or think like, a soldier. Maybe you could think about our problem a different way."

"Oh, yeah? Like how?"

"Well"—McGee rubbed a soothing hand up and down her taut, wiry triceps—"don't think about the situation in terms of weapons or strategies. Or even information. You've given us all the information about the Arduans and Punt that we could want. Even Heide is happy with what you and the other specialists have provided us. Our problem is that complete information isn't getting us any closer to a workable plan. Because what all that information doesn't tell us is this—how do we get leverage? What would make the Arduans pause, think about negotiating, or at least stop to talk? How do we influence them—in any way?"

Jennifer looked at McGee; at first her eyes were wondering, and then they were very, very glad. "Thank you, Sandro," she said.

Cap cleared his throat. "Jen, I know that coming up with new ideas isn't work that can be done on the clock. Ideas come when they come—or not at all. But here's our reality. Heide is getting antsy. I think we have two weeks—maybe a month—before he decides upon a plan of action. He'll probably try to implement it no less than a month after that."

McGee watched Jen nod, even as she kept her eyes on his. "Thanks, Cap. Nice not to be working under pressure." Cap made a vaguely apologetic rumbling sound, which Jen brushed away. "Not your fault, Cap. Don't worry about it." She turned and looked at the group. "Now, before we break up, do any of you have any other questions for me? Or any more surprises?"

McGee pressed her arm gently. "Uh—I have both."

She turned back. "Both? A question and a surprise?"

McGee nodded.

"Well?" she said.

"Jen," McGee said through a long swallow, "will you marry me?"

Jen laughed, disbelieving, then looked at him again—closely. Her mouth dropped open, and her eyes flickered across the pools of sewage and the ring of grimy Marine faces. Even Chong was smiling. She turned to McGee. "Will I marry you? Damn it, Tank McGee, you just try and stop me!"

It was probably the first time anyone had hugged, let alone passionately kissed, in the sewage backflow tankage room.

31

More Than Force

Our patience will achieve more than our force.
—Burke

TRNS Taconic, *Allied Fleet, Demeter System*

Ian Trevayne remembered his reaction, years before, on his first sight of TRNS *Taconic*. Now he could only chuckle as he recalled the awe he had felt at that first devastator as he watched the superdevastators emerge from the newly dredged Hera warp point into the light of Demeter's G5v sun.

"Twice the tonnage," he heard Adrian M'Zangwe breathe. The voice of *Taconic*'s captain held decidedly mixed emotions.

Li Magda said nothing. But Trevayne knew her emotions were even more complicated—and decidedly more primal.

They stood in the flag observation lounge of *Taconic*, which had once again become Trevayne's flagship when he had returned to Demeter after the campaign against the Tangri was well enough in hand to entrust it to subordinates. Li Magda had also returned, for the same reason. Now Trevayne was about to transfer his flag once again.

"We probably ought to be going," said Li Magda.

"Yes," nodded Trevayne. "After all, we have a special visitor."

They departed and went to the shuttle that would take them to TRNS *Li Han*.

Trevayne had never met Magda Petrovna Windrider. And he stayed in the background while she and Li Magda fell into each others' arms. The older woman whispered words he could not hear into her goddaughter's ear, and he caught sight of a glint of tears on Mags's cheek.

After a time, they released each other, and Trevayne thought the moment right to step forward. "Welcome to Demeter, Admiral. It is an honor and a pleasure to meet you."

"Retired Admiral, to be precise—and please call me Magda, even though it could get confusing. I, too, am privileged to finally meet you, Admiral Trevayne—although in a sense I almost feel I know you already, if only from a distance, having studied you with great care during the . . . the . . ."

"The late unpleasantness," Trevayne supplied.

"Which isn't nearly as late for you as it is for the rest of us, is it?" The warm but sharp brown eyes in the quintessentially Russian face grew even sharper.

"You're most understanding . . . Magda. As was she for whom this tremendous ship is so appropriately named."

For a moment, they regarded each other in silence. And the last wisps of tension and awkwardness evaporated and were gone.

"Well," Magda said briskly, "you're probably wondering why I came out here to the Bellerophon Arm—aside from wanting to see my goddaughter. And why I asked for this private meeting."

"I admit to more than a little curiousity about it," Trevayne acknowledged.

Magda regarded him levelly. "I hope to persuade you to delay your offensive into Charlotte."

Trevayne met her eyes squarely. "You realize, of course, that the longer we delay, the longer the people of Bellerophon—all two hundred and thirty-five million of them, or however many of those are left by now—will have to continue to live under the Baldies' occupation."

"I'm only too aware of that. And yes, if you attack Charlotte, using existing Kasugawa generator applications, you may win through and shorten the war. But you must first enter Charlotte with nothing larger than a supermonitor—before you can bring in the generator that will allow transit by devastators and superdevastators—the possibility also exists that you will fail, and by your failure lengthen the war."

Trevayne didn't reply directly, and his momentary silence was acknowledgment of the truth she spoke. "You said 'using *existing* Kasugawa generator applications.' Does that imply that there's another kind?"

Magda nodded and briefly outlined the concept of supermonitor-concealed Kasugawa generators.

"So," Trevayne said in tones of grim satisfaction, "we wouldn't have to use our smaller ships to defend a helpless generator in the teeth of a counterattack by SDSs and hordes of their other craft."

"And," Li Magda added excitedly, "the Baldies' tactical calculations are now based on that assumption. So this will catch them completely off balance."

Trevayne gave a quick nod. "All right. We'll wait until we have these new units. But in the meantime, we'll use the generators we already have to continue dredging the warp lines we already control." He rose eagerly to his feet and smiled at Magda. "Let's get the staff together and work out the details while we have the benefit of having a recognized expert here!"

32

The Secret of All Victory

The secret of all victory lies in the
organization of the non-obvious.
—Spengler

RFNS Gallipoli, *Main Van, Further Rim Fleet, Odysseus System*

Admiral Erica Krishmahnta looked around her bridge. "Are we ready?"

The eyes of her bridge personnel and section heads already told her what Yoshi Watanabe's voice announced. "All sections report ready and awaiting the word, Admiral."

Krishmahnta, eyes steady but heart racing with eagerness to finally—finally—give the Baldies a taste of their own medicine, leaned back in her chair and lowered the shock harness slowly into place over her slim torso.

"Captain Watanabe."

"Yes, sir?"

"The word is given."

RFNS Excalibur, *Strike Group Sigma, Further Rim Fleet, Odysseus System*

Leopold Kurzweil didn't need to hear the incoming Fleet signal to know that, in an instant, everything had changed. One moment the bridge had been abuzz with last-second preparations, communiqués, quips: now it was utterly focused, silent except for the voice of the ship's CO, Commodore von Tscharner.

"Mr. Wethermere," the commodore said, turning to his temporary tactical officer, "this is your show from here on. For the duration of your special operations, I cede restricted command of this vessel. In accordance with the special terms set out by your orders from Admiral Krishmahnta, I say three times: you have the con expressly and only for coordinating the initial attack of Strike Group Sigma."

Wethermere stood. "Sir, I say three times, I have the con, to the extent it may be relinquished to me by Admiral Krishmahnta's special orders."

"Very good, Commander. Now what?"

Wethermere smiled. "Sir, I will not be getting in your way any more—or any longer—than I have to. First we let the SBMHAWKs go in—and wait."

In a waist-high alcove just below von Tscharner's uncommonly large feet, the tacplot showed an impossibly slow trickle of green specks entering the warp point. The codes that announced their transits alternated between those of a recon drone and those of an SBMHAWK every five minutes—a pace that had been set thirty-six hours ago and had continued ever since. It was the eighth time in the past three months that Krishmahnta had pushed the interval so tightly. On the other side of the warp point, the Baldy forces—noticeably diminished in the past two weeks—would have little reason to suspect that this time, however, Krishmahnta's strategic equivalent of Chinese water-torture was not merely intended to fray their nerves and make them uncertain if an attack might follow. This time, hulls amounting to almost a year of ceaseless industry were poised to flood back through the warp point and drive the Baldies out of the Penelope system—either by a brilliant display of tactics or a brute-force display of tonnage.

But as Kurzweil watched, still trying to get all his recording gear up and running, the trickle of SBMHAWKs ceased—and eight larger icons began leaping dutifully through the purple hoop that signified the warp point into Penelope: AMBAMMs, off to blast their way through the Baldy minefields and any ships that happened to stray too close to the other side of the interstellar portal. A covey of RDs followed them by a second, and then the SBMHAWK transits resumed—but as a biblical flood, not a trickle. Eight at a time they disappeared into that rift in spacetime, and, no doubt, many destroyed each other upon emerging—interpenetrated—in Penelope. But those that survived were, even now, chasing the Arduan ships on the other side. In the holoplot, Kurzweil looked at the tiny icons denoting the SBMHAWKs, expecting to see them almost exhausted: instead, untold masses of them waited motionless near the warp-point icon.

Next to him, Wethermere reached up and tapped the shock harness that was hinged aloft behind Kurzweil. "You might want to think about putting that on, Leo."

"Yeah, sure. Listen, I wanted to say how grateful I am that you're letting me come along on this mission.

The folks back on Odysseus and Tilghman will really appreciate hearing and seeing what all their work has made possible."

Wethermere shrugged. "Don't thank me. Thank Admiral Krishmahnta. This was her idea."

"Yes—and not all her staff was particularly fond of it, I hear."

Wethermere looked away. "I wouldn't know anything about that."

"Wouldn't you? You've been in charge of this special weapons project for the last six months. Seems to me you would have inevitably been in on any discussion about a media request to witness the weapon's first combat application. Or at least you would have heard the shouting that supposedly went on between Admirals Krishmahnta and Yoshikuni."

Wethermere looked at Kurzweil and smiled. "You know, you're not going to bait me into making a comment, Leo." Then he glanced at the tacplot. "Commodore, I think it's time we take our place in the transit line."

Von Tscharner nodded. "Very good, Commander. Helm, at my mark, take us toward the warp point, ahead slow. Comms, apprise Admiral Krishmahnta that we have the ball and inform her when we start the clock. Ops, start the clock on my mark . . . and three, two, one: mark."

Kurzweil detected no change in motion, not even a tug. That only happened when a craft was traveling at the upper limits of its pseudo-velocity envelope. At that point, real space started breaking through in a manner that felt remarkably like drag, or the rearward push of acceleration. The tri-vid action shows still liked the drama of showing people pressed back by what they dramatically labeled "gee-forces." Despite some superficial similarities in appearance, they had entirely different causes—and sometimes, startlingly different effects.

But although the physical sensations of the *Excalibur* remained unaltered, the mood on the bridge had changed again. The crew exchanges were quiet, clipped, efficient. Kurzweil glanced up at the ops clock: they were one minute in. Which meant that, as per the stipulations put in place by Admiral Krishmahnta, he was now allowed to ask Wethermere about the "big surprise" they were going to spring on the Baldies. Krishmahnta's chief of security had insisted upon that one-minute mark because, at this point in the countdown, all nonsecure commo links were terminated: Kurzweil no longer had any way to transmit off the supermonitor *Excalibur*—even if he had wanted to. He looked over at Wethermere—who was already looking at him—and waiting. "So, Commander, I know that whatever secret project you've been working on involves the five supermonitors of this task force, and that it involves energy torpedoes."

Wethermere's left eyebrow climbed a bit, but he didn't look too surprised. "Oh? And how did you learn that?"

"Yard talk, sir. Consider the details you couldn't keep a lid on. Five ships being modified in lockdown. No news about the armaments going in. But it was easy enough to find out which batteries were being dismounted—almost all the force beams. It was harder to find out what might be taking their place."

"And how did you do that, Leo?"

"By keeping an eye on where other projects fell short of parts, Commander. Your plans—whatever they were—hit the shipyards late. Caused a stir. Grumbles rose up wherever parts designated for a project or a hull got diverted into yours. And it was always energy-torpedo batteries. But more than that—well, I haven't a clue."

"For which I'm thankful, Leo. As it is, you managed to get through one or two clearance layers. You are to be congratulated."

"Well, rather than congratulations, I'd like answers."

"Fair enough. Tell me, Leo, what do you know about energy torpedoes?"

Two months ago, Kurzweil had known nothing about them, but by now he'd become a minor expert. "Pre-fusion plasma wrapped in a very short-lived drive envelope. Travels very close to the speed of light. Almost as much punch as an antimatter warhead. Starts losing some accuracy beyond ten light-seconds but can still reach out beyond twenty. Hard to intercept because it's moving so fast and because most defensive arrays find a blob of plasma harder to target than a regular solid object, like a missile."

Wethermere nodded appreciatively. "Very good. So, if the energy torpedo is such a wonder weapon, then why haven't we phased out other weapon systems?"

Kurzweil frowned. "Because of that limited range. And at close range, although the energy torpedo does a lot of damage, the studies say it would have be about twenty percent more powerful to offer destructive performance equivalent to an equal volume of force-beams. So missiles are superior at range, force-beams superior at close range."

"But what if you double-fire the energy torpedoes?"

Kurzweil leaned back. "Double-speed fire burns out about twenty-five percent of the capacitors—every time you try it."

"Yes—that's why it's not done. But what happens when you *do* actually fire that many torpedoes?"

"Oh—that's pure lethality. Double-firing an energy torpedo battery makes its other failings insignificant. Sure, each torpedo is still less accurate than a missile—but now you've got twice as many of them heading downrange. Except at very long ranges, the aggregate hit possibilities are now all on the side of the energy torpedoes. And at short range, you're putting so much hurt so fast on an adversary that they easily outperform the force-beams. And at middle ranges, where they're already superior, they become—"

Kurzweil stopped, noticing how broad Wethermere's smile had become. And then he knew. "You've found a way to reduce the double-fire burnout of ET batteries."

"No," answered Wethermere, "we've found a way to *eliminate* the burnout entirely."

Kurzweil started to stand, eager with the reflex to send the story—and suddenly realized why Krishmahnta et al. had insisted he not be told until the operation clock was a minute in. Wethermere's hand was on his shoulder.

"Have a seat, Leo—and last warning: swing that harness down and seal it. It just might save your life."

Kurzweil complied absently. Like the true newsperson he was, the story had wiped any thought of his own safety from his mind... for now. "But this—this changes everything, Commander. Energy torpedoes on perpetual double-fire? God, that will obsolete so many other weapons so quickly, that..."

Wethermere shrugged. "I wouldn't rush to any conclusions, Leo. They said the same thing about the fighter almost a hundred years ago, and here they are, still helping to decide the fate of this war. But yes, it's going to change a lot of things—one day."

"What do you mean, one day?"

"I mean we only managed to convert these five supermonitors to the new ET armament suite."

"I see. Well, how did you do it? What was the breakthrough?"

"Oh, there wasn't any breakthrough, Leo."

Von Tscharner, evidently eavesdropping, snorted out a quick laugh.

Kurzweil fixed Wethermere with a stare. "The commodore doesn't seem to agree."

"Well, look, I just had a harebrained scheme. It was really the engineers who—"

Kurzweil jabbed a finger at the countdown chronometer. "Enough with the semi-genuine humilities, Commander. We are, quite literally, on the clock here. The facts—and fast, if you please."

"Okay. Look, an energy-torpedo generator is about two-thirds capacitor and one-third launcher. In the double-fire mode, the capacitor is twenty-five percent overtaxed, meaning about twenty-five percent of the systems burn out. So you'd need twenty-five percent more power to get fully reliable function in the double-fire mode. Follow me?"

"Uh—yeah, I think so."

"So I just sat down and asked some engineers: What if we could provide each ET generator with twenty-five percent more power? 'Fine,' they said, 'that would keep the weapons from frying. But where are you going to get those extra gigawatts? Every system on the ship has its own closely balanced power supply, so there's not a whole lot of surplus, even from the engines.'"

"So what did you do?"

"Well, I asked if we could remove one weapon from

every battery of five generators. That put us down to four generators, but in place of the missing weapon, we put in an extra capacitor, with room to spare. That extra capacitor is like having an extra one hundred percent power surplus to spread around each battery. And since each of the four remaining ET generators requires a twenty-five percent surplus over their own output . . ."

Kurzweil gaped. "So now each generator has access to the extra twenty-five percent power it needs for double-fire! My God, that's so—so simple!"

Von Tscharner smiled without looking over. "Which is probably why nobody thought of it before—and because naval designers rarely think about reducing armament, even if that would mean an increase in total offensive power. Leave it to a non-engineer—a guy who thinks outside that box because he has to—to come up with that solution."

Kurzweil nodded. "Okay—but it's got to put a hell of a strain on all the support systems. Is that why you also had to draw so much extra coolant from supplies? Does the system have a tendency to overheat?"

Wethermere smiled. "Oh, you heard about the coolant, too, did you? Well, actually the system doesn't have an overheating problem. In fact, we're using the coolant for—"

"Approaching warp point," announced the helmsman crisply.

In a tone he might also have used to ask a messmate to pass the salt, von Tscharner instructed, "Sound general quarters. Mr. Wethermere, your instructions?"

"Missiles ready. Energy torpedo generators charged to full. All cargo bays designated for coolant venting, stand by."

Von Tscharner nodded to Commo, who passed along the orders.

Kurzweil looked in the plot, saw the green blip of the *Excalibur* approaching the warp point, one similar speck ahead of her, three more behind.

"*Caladbolg* transiting, sir," Ops reported to von Tscharner.

"Very good. We're next. Shock harnesses down, Mr. Kurzweil. Combat has a tendency to get a bit—kinetic."

Kurzweil swallowed, pulled down the cuirasslike seat restraint, and suddenly realized: *Holy God above, I'm about to go into combat.* Forgetting himself, he murmured, "I could be killed."

Von Tscharner looked down from the promontory of his con. "Indeed you could, Mr. Kurzweil, indeed you could. All stations, rig for transit. Shields full. Restoration of PDF and data links have first priority upon arrival. And now—in we go."

And then they were gone.

A moment later, the *Excalibur* blinked into existence in the Penelope system and was immediately surrounded by a seething storm of antimatter explosions. But the shields were already coming up and bore the brunt of those detonations.

"Tactics: report."

"*Caladbolg* bloodied but steady, sir. *Dyrnwyn* just coming out behind us now."

"The minefields?"

"A clear path through them, sir."

Von Tscharner looked in the plot, saw dozens of Baldy SDHs equidistantly ringing the mouth of the warp point. "Range to threat forces?"

"Between twelve and fifteen light-seconds, sir. Seems that last, pre-transit rush of SBMHAWKs really caught them off guard. It certainly backed them off the warp point."

Von Tscharner turned to look at Wethermere and nodded down at the plot in something like admiration. "So far so good on your tactical soothsaying, Commander. What next?"

Wethermere looked in the plot as the last two green icons of Strike Group Sigma emerged. "Gotta wait for the data links to come up, Commodore." As he spoke, Wethermere started tapping his targeting stylus into a dense cluster of the red enemy icons on the left flank of the half-globe of Baldy hulls.

Von Tscharner snapped orders. "I need those data links up now." He turned to Tactics. "Shields? PDF systems?"

"Shields up and holding, sir. PDF just coming online. And—*Tyrfing* is in the net, sir. The Strike Group's data links are complete. Shall I—?"

But Wethermere was already shouting. "Fire control, acquire lock on the eight targets I just designated."

"Already done, sir."

"Then all missile tubes: salvo at max rate for fifteen seconds."

Kurzweil felt the deck beneath his feet and buttocks begin to tremble, as if the precursor tremors of an earthquake were repeating endlessly, stuck just shy of the culminating seismic spike. Tactics made what seemed a redundant announcement. "Missiles launching, sir."

Kurzweil was about to ask a question, then noticed the sweat beading Wethermere's brow as he watched the ops clock. When eight seconds had elapsed from the beginning of the missile salvos, the commander said—in a loud, sharp tone: "Now—vent ready coolant tanks to space. And energy-torpedo batteries: prepare to double-fire. . . ."

Arduan SDH Unshesh'net'ah, *Odysseus Cluster Containment Flotilla,* Anaht'doh Kainat, *Penelope System*

Fleet Third Kez'zhem watched his PDF systems begin to pick off the first of the human missiles that were coming into range. It had been a massive salvo, although it was curious that more of the enemy supermonitors did not keep streaming in after these first five. But there wasn't time to wonder about that now. Surviving this salvo was the first order of business. "Will our PDF systems intercept all the missiles?"

(Uncertainty) tinged his sensor prime's rapid send. "Hopefully, Fleet Third. But if it wasn't for our datahub coordination, we'd surely be—sir!"

"Yes, what is it?"

"The human vessels are—are venting gases and liquids, Fleet Third."

"What? Have we damaged them?"

"Maybe—but that can't be the cause, sir. They are *all* venting the same amount of volatiles—and at the same time."

"Analysis of the volatiles?"

"Spectrography says the vapor is . . . is a coolant, sir. The standard human coolant for their high-energy weapons systems."

Coolant? And all at once—?

That was when the long-range remote sensors not only conveyed quantitative but visual proof—instantaneously, due to the *selnarmic* relays—of a terrible and ominous spectacle: the space around the human ships sudden flashed alive with blue-white beams, stabbing toward Kez'zhem's combat group with murderous speed. But the actinic shafts only looked like beams: instead, moving so swiftly that the eye could not see each as a discrete object in motion, they were in fact—

"Energy torpedoes, sir," reported Tactics. "But—"

"But what? Quickly!"

"Sir, this is impossible. They are firing without stopping. It is as if the armament of two supermonitors is contained in each hull."

A cool finger of regret for impending failure traced Kez'zhem's spine, followed closely by an icy surge of race-dread. "Time to missile impact?"

"Seven seconds, sir."

"Energy torpedoes?"

"They're much faster, sir. Given their launch delay—also, seven seconds."

Kez'zhem pulsed the order to Helm and Engineering (URGENT. REVERSE. URGENT. REVERSE.) along with the permission. "Do it, even if you have to burn out the engines." Then he switched back to Tactics: "PDF intercept ratio?"

Tactics was too overcome by surprise to create lexical *selnarm*. Instead he signaled (despair, hopelessness).

Kez'zhem did not change the targeting of his PDF systems: the missiles were slower and easier to hit—not that it would really matter. He simply sent his thanks—to the entirety of his staff—and pulsed "For the Race" even as Engineering was slamming the engines into immediate reverse, thereby risking their complete burnout.

As it turned out, a flurry of eighteen energy torpedoes from the *Durendal* handled the job of incinerating the *Unshesh'net'ah*'s engines—and all the rest of her—an eyeblink later.

RFNS Excalibur, *Strike Group Sigma, Further Rim Fleet, Penelope System*

Leo finally realized his mouth was open: he shut it with an audible snap. "Holy hell," he breathed.

No one seemed to be paying any attention to him—or evinced any reaction other than a series of fierce, tight grins when the eight SDHs Wethermere had targeted simply vanished all at once from the tacplot, wiped away as if they had never been there. In their place, a large gash gaped in the thin fabric of the Baldy containment force.

Tactics reported the enemy fleet evolution as it was unfolding in the plot. "They're moving away, Commodore."

Von Tscharner's voice suggested a desire for a more precise report. "Are they retreating, Tactics?"

"No, sir. I'd say they're giving ground—grudgingly."

"Good enough, Mr. Wethermere?"

"Almost. Send the all-clear drone back through the warp point. Maintain rate of fire and ahead three-quarters. Push 'em, make them give more ground."

"Very good, Mr. Wethermere. Helm, you heard the commander: make it so." Von Tscharner's pale blue eyes went back to the plot, and he grinned broadly. "And here comes the Grand Dame Herself." And sure enough, in the tacplot, more SMTs had started to pop into the system, immediately arraying themselves into a loose but evenly spaced skirmish screen with two layers. Within half a minute, twenty-three SMTs were in place, advancing slowly while Strike Force Sigma pushed generally at the Baldy center, but angling so as to widen the edges of the hole they had made in the enemy line.

Von Tscharner looked at the growing distance between his strike group and the van that had come in with Krishmahnta. "Commander? We're getting a little exposed out here."

Wethermere was watching both the ops clock and the distances in the tacplot with almost monomaniacal focus. "Let's press them a few more seconds."

"It's your show, Commander. But tell me—why push them so hard?"

Wethermere looked at the plot intently, evidently measuring distances with great precision. "I don't want them to get too close a look at our next trick."

Von Tscharner looked perplexed for a moment, then smiled. "Ah, I see. You know, you're not half bad at this, Commander."

"Not half good, either, sir."

Von Tscharner looked away, still smiling. "Oh, you'll do."

Tactics' next report sounded a bit nervous, Kurzweil noted—which made him even more nervous. "Commodore, the Baldies are still backing off, sir, but they're slowing down. I think they might be preparing to—"

Wethermere interrupted. "Are they twenty light-seconds from the warp point yet?"

"Just now, sir."

"Then signal Admiral Krishmahnta. It's time to spring her half of the trap."

Arduan SDH Ateth'te'senmir, *Odysseus Cluster Containment Flotilla,* Anaht'doh Kainat, *Penelope System*

Fleet Second Sems'shef, who was still busy trying to dress his line and transfer command data to his new fleet third, saw the spectrography scanners probing at the main body of the human fleet even before his sensor prime could alert him to the activity. "Prime, those new SMTs: are they—?"

"Yes, sir. They are all venting vapor and gas."

"The same gas that the first five emitted just before they fired?"

"Identical, sir!"

Sems'shef glanced quickly into his holotank: twenty-three more SMTs. If they salvoed missiles the same way the first five SMTs had, and then opened up with the same impossible density of energy-torpedo fire, that meant those twenty-three ships had a short-term firepower equal to almost seventy normal ships of their class. And even if they ran out of normal missiles, they would still have this miraculous energy torpedo firepower, making them equal to more than forty of their fellows. The math was not merely unpromising: it was brutally conclusive.

Sems'shef sent his *selnarm* orders out with typical briskness. "Fleet signal: all about and full speed back to the Agamemnon warp point."

"We are fleeing, Fleet Second?"

"We are saving ourselves so we may help save the Race, Tactics. We need to warn Agamemnon to ready their defenses, and they will need every hull—including all of ours—if we are to stand against this kind of compact firepower. It is unclear to me if we can even hold that warp point." Then Sems'shef cleared his mind. Spiking his *selnarm* into a system-wide repeater, he reached out toward one of the commo drones waiting at the edge of the Agamemnon warp point, preparing to initiate a cascade of similar relays that would soon find and furnish Admiral Narrok with the dire portents of the Second Battle of Penelope.

RFNS Excalibur, *Strike Group Sigma, Further Rim Fleet, Penelope System*

Kurzweil watched Krishmahnta's SMTs spread out, slow and surly as if disappointed that they had not been given the opportunity to fight. Fifteen seconds ago, the last of them had finished venting coolant: five seconds ago, the Baldy flotilla had—literally—turned tail and run for the system's far warp point.

Kurzweil turned toward Wethermere with a crooked smile. "Well, I guess I can't trust you any more than the other military types, Commander."

Wethermere raised an eyebrow. "What do you mean, Leo?"

"Don't give me that. You told me you had only been able to convert five SMTs over to the new boosted energy-torpedo system."

Wethermere smiled. "That's right."

Kurzweil jabbed an indignant finger at the phalanx of large green icons in the tacplot. "Oh? Well, how do you explain these other twenty-three ships? They vented the coolant, too."

Wethermere's smile became broader. "Yes, they did, didn't they?"

The reporter frowned, annoyed, and looked over at

von Tscharner—who was smiling at least as broadly as Wethermere himself. And then it hit him. Kurzweil turned back toward Wethermere. "The coolant. It isn't... isn't really coolant. I mean, that's the compound, sure—but you don't actually need to vent it before you fire."

Wethermere nodded. "Right. That was just some theater for the benefit of the Baldies."

"So, when they saw the next rank of ships do the same thing that your first five had done—"

"They drew the inevitable conclusion. But this time they had to concern themselves with twenty-three more supermonitors firing all that ordnance. I figured that when they did the tactical math, they wouldn't like the answer very much."

"And if they had stopped to question whether the coolant was real or a trick?"

"Well, the outcome wouldn't have been much different, although our casualties would have been significantly higher. But we crafted our tactics so that the Baldies didn't have the time to stop and question anything. They were confronted with a situation which was going to hell in a handbasket, and they had to act quickly."

Kurzweil changed topics but kept his recorder running, all the while calculating the increased circulation this story was going to generate. "And so how far back do we push the Baldies, Commander?"

Wethermere shrugged. "I don't know—and I'm no longer in a position to speculate on that pursuit, let alone order it." He faced von Tscharner. "Sir, it has been an honor and a privilege. As of now, my special orders have been discharged in full, so I cede my operational prerogatives. And I say three times: you have the con in full, sir."

Von Tscharner nodded. "I say three times, I have the con. You are dismissed. Now go get some rest. And Commander..."

Wethermere, already headed for the lift, turned back. "Sir?"

Von Tscharner smiled. "As they used to say in the wet navy that defended the land where you were born, 'Bravo Zulu,' Mr. Wethermere."

RFNS Gallipoli, *Further Rim Fleet, Agamemnon System*

A day later, Erica Krishmahnta watched the last Baldy SDH's red icon dive into the purple hoop of the Ajax warp point and whispered, "Good riddance."

Captain Watanabe nodded enthusiastically, but his tone was wry. "Admiral Yoshikuni does not seem to share your sentiments, sir. Comm just told me she's hopping mad that the Baldies wouldn't stand and fight. She's champing at the bit to lead the vanguard when we go to Ajax."

"Tell her she's welcome to the first chair, Yoshi—when we go to Ajax. Which might not be so very soon. I'm betting they've had enough time to prepare some better defenses there. And they've fallen back with almost seventy percent of what they started with in Penelope, and all their assets from here in Agamemnon."

"True. A pity we didn't inflict more casualties."

Krishmahnta glanced sideways at her chief of staff and confidante. "Now you're starting to sound like Miharu, Yoshi."

Watanabe literally recoiled. "Me? Sound like the Iron Admiral? I should hope not. I'm simply pointing out that, since we didn't fight them in these systems, we're going to have to fight them later on—and probably all at once. And that's going to be a lot more costly."

Krishmahnta nodded. "Yes. But we won these two systems back at an incredible bargain: no ships lost, fewer than four hundred crew dead. We'll be back up to full supply on our SBMHAWKs within the week. And the civilians back in the cluster are just going to love this victory—and the way we won it—when Kurzweil files his story."

"Yes, about that. Aren't you a bit worried about how it might make Wethermere a bit of a—well, a celebrity?"

"Worry? Why should I worry? Look, Yoshi. Until someone gets out here to rescue us, those people are all we've got, and we're all they've got. We need each other. And we needed this win. And now we get to send the happy news home with less than a thousand body bags and no hulls lost? If they want a hero, let them have a hero."

Watanabe shrugged. "Personally, I think von Tscharner's the real hero. It's not every officer who can stomach having a lieutenant commander in charge of his strike group and ship—not even for ten minutes."

"Well, I'm glad von Tscharner did so well, because he's next in line for rear admiral." She looked at Watanabe with a bit of melancholy. "Right after you, of course."

"Me? But I don't want—"

"Yoshi. You of all people should know that this war has never been about what we *want*. You're too valuable to the effort to be here with me. With all the new ships and crews we finally have available, I don't have enough seasoned group leaders. And you're in line and overdue. Besides, we've got our hands full of real problems. Such as the way the Baldies have changed their game: whoever we're fighting against now is using different tactics, thinking more strategically." She mused, resolved not to chew her lower lip, which was almost devoid of its customary swelling. "I wish I knew more about him or her."

Watanabe leaned back. "Well, I can tell you one thing about your adversary."

"Oh? What's that?"

"Today, he's really pissed."

Arduan SDH Shem'pter'ai, *Consolidated Fleet,* Anaht'doh Kainat, *Charlotte System*

Narrok considered the reports from Ajax again. "We must not panic."

Sarhan's response was as laconic as ever. "Why not?"

Narrok spontaneously pulsed out (amusement, rue). Although Admiral Sarhan's body had been blasted by fire and radiation at the Battle of Ajax, he was still the shrewdest intellect, and most refreshingly sardonic peer, that Narrok had in the fleet. "Do you really think this news from Penelope and Ajax indicates that the humans who pushed in from the Mercury Trace have recontacted those in the Odysseus Cluster?"

"How can we eliminate the possibility, Senior Admiral? Since we know next to nothing about how their Kasugawa generator works, we have no way of knowing if, perhaps, they have opened another new warp point into the Tilghman system, for instance."

Narrok nodded. "I would agree—if we were to constrain our speculations to the science alone. But from a strategic and logistical standpoint, it seems unlikely."

Sarhan lifted a half-amputated cluster; the tentacles he

waved in speculative curiosity were withered, scorched smooth and pasty. "How do you deduce this from their strategy and logistics?"

"Consider, good Sarhan. If the groups had made contact, would they not have coordinated actions more closely? As it is, they have given us challenges in a manageable sequence, not all at once. And why would they not equip the forces in the Odysseus Cluster with their new devastator class? Similarly, if this near-miraculous energy-torpedo battery was brought in from outside the Odysseus Cluster, why did the Allied Fleet not have it to use in their offensive down the Arm? It might have turned the tide of battle at Charlotte. No, I am convinced that the human groups are still separate, are still operating in mutual ignorance."

"Perhaps so. But it will not long remain the case, I suspect."

Narrok sent (accord, appreciation) for Sarhan's perspicacity. "Probably not. And with the humans emerging in force from Odysseus, I feel we have little choice but to withdraw from Ajax."

"And give up that system's two warp points?"

"Frankly, I am more worried about splitting my forces between the two warp points of the Ajax system. And that situation would be all the worse if their devastators arrive, fitted with these new energy-torpedo batteries—"

"Senior Admiral, I am frail. I should be discarnate. Please do not shock me into my demise with such speculations. But yes, of course, we must anticipate that, too. Although I confess I have also wondered: Did the humans perhaps trick us at Penelope?"

Narrok sent (appreciation, camaraderie) to the old warrior. "You are thinking that the vented coolant was a ruse? That the larger group of ships was not actually armed as the first?"

"The timing and structure of the engagement makes it impossible not to entertain the hypothesis."

"I agree. But we will never know. And by the time we face the humans again, it probably will not matter. Unless they are in a terrible rush, they will have enough time to retrofit even more of their ships with this new weapon system."

Sarhan sadly (concurred). "Either way, our job of holding them has become more difficult—which means it is all the more urgent that we fortify the systems you have selected as our minimum safe perimeter. About which: Is the assembly on schedule?"

Narrok signaled (affirmative). "Slightly ahead of schedule, actually. SDSs are entering the final phases of construction in Suwa, Polo, Andromeda, BR-02, and Raiden."

"And if the humans attack before they are all completed?"

"Then, friend Sarhan, we shall truly *shotan*—live and taste—the meaning of this human term which Ankaht now routinely utters. We shall indeed be *in extremis*."

33

In Yon Smoke Concealed

If hopes were dupes, fears may be liars;
It may be, in yon smoke concealed,
Your comrades chase e'en now the fliers,
And, but for you, possess the field.
—Clough

RFNS Gallipoli, *Further Rim Fleet, Agamemnon System*

Admiral Erica Krishmahnta frowned into the plot. "No, Yoshi, I don't think it's a trick. I think the recon drones are showing us the real situation: the Baldies are ceding Ajax."

Watanabe looked at the 1:1000 time-ratio recording from the recon drones—all of which had returned unscathed. In their holoplotted representation of the Ajax system, the last flickering hints of red enemy icons were seen departing and, judging from their heading, were making directly for the warp point into Achilles. "Let's assume you're right, Admiral. What in Terra's name would make them want to abandon a crossroads system like Ajax?"

"Maybe *want* has nothing to do with their actions. Maybe *need* is the term that would help us understand it."

Watanabe frowned. "So, why would they *need* to withdraw from Ajax?" His frown deepened. "Well, unless it's a trap—which I still suspect—the only need that might drive them to abandon Ajax would be—" And he stopped with his mouth open.

Krishmahnta nodded. "Yes—that they've got trouble somewhere else. Big trouble."

Watanabe clearly couldn't allow himself to contemplate the unthinkably joyous possibility; he posited an alternative. "The Tangri?"

Krishmahnta shook her head and watched the last red icon wink away from the plot. "No. The Tangri couldn't handle a fifth of what we've seen the Baldies bring to the field. And I just can't believe the Baldies could be in a civil war, not given their suicidal dedication to whatever common cause they're serving."

"So you think . . . ?" Watanabe still couldn't say it.

Krishmahnta nodded, staring down into the blank holoplot. "Looks like we've got friends on the way."

"But—but how?"

Krishmahnta shrugged and leaned back. "I don't know, Yoshi. Maybe they found a warp point from back home to someplace else in the Arm. Maybe they're assaulting nonstop into Bellerophon from Astria. If that's happening, the Baldies could be taking so many losses that they have to draw down their garrison flotillas out here and are retracting their perimeter to feed that meat grinder. But either way, this is the opportunity we've been waiting for. Ajax has a population of almost eighty-four million. I want to liberate those people—and get them working to build a fleet that can liberate even more worlds."

Watanabe offered a broad smile. "Then what are we waiting for?"

✧ ✧ ✧

RDs went in; the half that were supposed to come back did, and showed the other half spreading out to picket points in the Ajax system. So far, no unexpected contacts, no anomalies that might be a cloaked Baldy ship.

SBMHAWKs followed, entering the system and taking up ready-response positions, but half asleep in standby mode. Thusly spread out, they formed a thin protective sphere around the warp point from which the fleet in Agamemnon would emerge. Their hawk-eyed sensors scanned, sought targets, found none. They waited.

First in was a lowly courier, retrofitted with an extensive sensor suite. She probed further, poked harder: still nothing. She sent back the all-clear drone.

In response to that summons, three cruisers (among the last Krishmahnta had) and two of her new SDHs (copied and then improved from the Baldy designs) edged through the warp point—just before Least Claw Kiiraathra'ostakjo's much-patched but still sturdy carrier *Celmithyr'theaarnouw* made transit. The Orion ship immediately began disgorging fighters, which streamed outward, seeking the far corners of the Ajax system.

Which, except for its perplexed human inhabitants, they found completely empty.

Two days later, Krishmahnta commenced the same process of delicately probing and then investing the Aphrodite system—and got no farther than the first phase of the operation. The first wave of drones returned—all of them—which meant that they had detected movement outside the Desai limit of the system.

As their reports came in—accumulating as lines of

cyan characters floating in midair beside the tacplot—Krishmahnta and Watanabe gaped. The captain was the first to speak. "Could this be a trick?"

"Anything is possible, Captain."

"Those transponders and call signs—that's TRN commo traffic, alternating with our own."

"Right down to the identifying and confirmatory crypto-codes embedded into the transponder beacons. If those RFN signals are counterfeit, they're absolutely indistinguishable from our own—and no one has ever broken the kind of multiply trapdoored authentication ciphers that are woven into them."

"And look at the size of those mass returns. Admiral, some of those ships must be twice the size of our largest supermonitors."

"*At least* twice the size," amended Krishmahnta. "This is either someone trying to succeed with an ECM version of the big lie—or it's no lie at all. Given that the Baldies left this system heading the opposite direction—southward into Achilles—I'm betting on the latter."

"Then let's go visiting."

"Better yet, Captain, let's send them an invitation to visit us."

Eight hours later, the supermonitor TRNS *Doomwhale* turned smartly away from the Kasugawa generator it had deposited at the lip of the Aphrodite warp point and moved off—just in time to clear the counterspinning gravitic vortex that sensors registered as swirling down into, and then pushing back up out of, the interstellar transit point. Which had grown immensely.

"Nice trick," commented Wethermere, who tugged his dress blacks straight.

Krishmahnta nodded—and then sucked in her breath as a literal mountain of steel, composites, and superdense armors emerged from the newly dredged warp point, bristling with weapons.

"That must be one of the new devastators," offered Watanabe after a long silence.

Miharu Yoshikuni, svelte yet still curvaceous in her own night-dark dress uniform, turned a baleful eye upon Watanabe: "You think?"

Watanabe reddened a bit. "I was just making conversation."

Krishmahnta turned back to smile at them. "Come on," she said. "Let's go meet a living legend."

Shortly before the Baldies had appeared and turned the universe upside down, Krishmahnta had heard the story of Ian Trevayne's rebirth in his own younger body. She had tended to discount it as sensationalist rumor. Even when reliable confirmation had arrived, she'd had trouble coming to terms with the idea.

She was still having trouble even now, after the initial hoopla of reunion was over and she and her staff were settling down to business with the tall, incongruously young but instantly recognizable version of the legend they had all grown up with.

There had, she decided, been simply too much to assimilate. Those tremendous new ships . . . the Kasugawa generator and its overturning of all conventional thinking about interstellar travel . . . the death of Li Han . . . Too much.

"Now, then, Fleet Admiral Khrishmanta," Trevayne began.

"Er," she dared to interrupt, "that's Vice Admiral, sir."

"No, it isn't." Trevayne smiled easily. "We're a bit isolated out here, you see, and I have an unusual degree of latitude. I believe a promotion conferred on my own authority will probably be confirmed. Don't you? As will...oh, we'll decide on a decoration later. Whatever you care to name."

For a moment, she had trouble breathing, let alone speaking. "Sir," she finally managed, "I don't...I can't possibly..."

"Yes, you can." Trevayne's voice was still pleasant, but there was a new firmness in it. "You can do a great many things, Admiral, as you've shown. Left in isolation, and to to your own devices, you've held the Odysseus Cluster for the Rim Federation." She found that she could not look away from his suddenly somber eyes. "I'm not altogether unacquainted with that sort of thing, you know. With all due modesty, I must claim a better appreciation of it than most."

For a moment, legend filled the room.

Krishmahnta finally ended the moment. "Sir...if you're resolved on this, may I make a request? It concerns Lieutenant Commander Wethermere, whom you met earlier."

"Ah, yes, I'd been looking forward to making his acquaintance, after reading some of your reports. He reminds me of someone I once knew."

"Kevin Sanders?" she suggested.

Trevayne blinked. "How did you know? At any rate, he's a very refreshing young man—and clearly deserving of the brevet promotion you gave him, given his contributions to the success of the Further Rim Fleet."

"That's what my request concerns, sir. I'm asking you to make that brevet rank permanent—and give me authorization to brevet him again, to full commander."

"Agreed," said Trevayne without hesitation.

"Furthermore, if his designator turns out to be a problem—frankly, I've never been entirely certain of his status in that respect—"

"He does seem to be rather *sui generis*," Trevayne interjected with a smile.

"—then I'd like to have it changed to unrestricted line, and any other administrative changes made that are necessary for giving him a command. I believe that his potential is one we owe it to ourselves—and to him—to exploit to the fullest."

"I'm sorry, Admiral Krishmahnta, but I can't give this man a command of his own. Despite his exemplary performance, he's simply not trained for that role—not yet, anyway—and you can't afford the risk. Or ask another ship to accept it in your stead."

Krishmahnta had her mouth open to object—but Trevayne wasn't done. "You also can't afford *not* to have him working Intelligence for you. And Tactics. Both."

Krishmahnta goggled. "You mean—make him my chief of Intel *and* Tactics? Admiral—that's too much."

"It is indeed, which is why he probably can't officially perform in either role—solely. So let's approach the problem from a different angle. If I'm not mistaken, you just lost your chief of staff and flagship captain to a promotion also, didn't you?" He smiled at Watanabe, who visibly swelled with pride.

Krishmahnta nodded. "Yes, sir."

"And your old ops officer is still keeping the yards humming back on Tilghman."

"That is also correct, sir." Krishmahnta wondered how Trevayne could not only have read through, but retained, so many details on her staff in so short a time.

Trevayne looked at Krishmahnta's tatterdemalion cadre roster. "Looks like you have enough bodies, but not enough experience, on your staff. A fellow like this young commander could help get them working in the same direction if he was your deputy chief of staff—assuming he has authority commensurate with a full commander."

"With respect, sir, then I still don't have a *chief* of staff."

"I recommend you give that position back to Admiral Watanabe."

"But he's no longer on my flagship, sir."

"And where is it written, Admiral Krishmahnta, that your chief of staff needs to be on your flagship with you?"

"Ahem . . . eh, nowhere, sir."

"Precisely. This way, Wethermere's role as *deputy* chief of staff—a post suitable to his rank—won't ruffle any feathers on your flagship. Of course, he'll be operating as your actual chief of staff, while Admiral Watanabe will simply fill the slot on the table of organization, thereby furnishing that august position with all the rank and gravitas it requires. And young Wethermere—well, not so young after all, judging from his files—will be able to work as a filter for, and thereby adjunct to, both your fleet intelligence and tactical officer."

"Well, I suppose so, sir—but as the Admiral knows, putting the actual chief of staff on another hull—well, that's a pretty radical departure from the routinely observed manners and fashion of how to structure the command ranks during wartime—"

"My dear Admiral Krishmahnta, as a great playwright of Old Terra—and, in fact, England—approximately put it, 'you and I cannot be confined within the weak list of our profession's fashion: we are the makers of manners and the liberty that follows our places stops the mouth of all find-faults.'" Trevayne stopped and smiled hugely. "How satisfying. I've been waiting a long time to use that line."

Krishmahnta mastered her boggled officers with a stern look, then pressed her point—gently. "Still, Admiral—Shakespeare's wisdom notwithstanding—I can already hear the rest of my staff muttering over how my actual, functional chief of staff is only a lowly brevet commander."

"And what do you imagine they will they say about this?"

"That it's just not done, sir."

"Oh, but it is—if I say so." Trevayne smiled—but there was steel behind it.

34

While Ye May

Gather ye rosebuds while ye may,
Old Time is still a-flying:
And this same flower that smiles to-day
To-morrow will be dying.
—Herrick

TRNS Li Han, *Allied Fleet, Demeter System*

Ian Trevayne and Li Magda stood silhouetted, alone in the *Li Han*'s observation lounge, arm in arm, oblivious to the star-dappled vista before them—indeed to everything except each other.

She finally broke the silence. "Are you sure you really want to do this now?"

"Too bloody right I'm sure!" said Trevayne. And then he hesitated: for a fleeting instant he seemed not a day older than he looked. "That is, if you're willing . . . ?"

"You know you don't need to ask that." She raised her face to his, and they kissed.

"Well, then," he said afterward, very briskly, "this is the perfect opportunity. Since your godparents arrived with the latest Kasugawa generators, they can stand in for your mother!"

✧ ✧ ✧

"There are any number of things I never imagined I'd live to see myself doing," said Senator Jason Windrider in what he thought were inaudible tones. "This is one of them."

"Shh!" hissed his wife, jabbing him in the ribs. He subsided as the ceremony drew to its close.

Everyone had expected Ian Trevayne to insist on a Rim Federation Navy chaplain. But he had surprised them. *The master of the unexpected,* Magda Petrovna Windrider thought, and certain recollections brought a wince even across the gulf of more than eight decades. He had agreed to let the *Li Han*'s chaplain officiate.

Not that it greatly mattered. The Terran Republic held so many religions—all of those that humanity had carried with it from Old Terra and also a dizzying variety of new ones—that the idea of providing a chaplain for each was absurd. The chaplaincy function in the TRN was a unified one, requiring its practitioners to master—in addition to a great deal of applied psychology—a set of conventions, ceremonies, and terminology that couldn't possibly give offense to anyone. They might not give much in the way of inspiration to anyone, either, but at least they enabled everyone to get on with business like that currently transpiring in *Li Han*'s observation lounge, with the firmament as a backdrop for the two figures in full-dress uniform, the woman in the Terran Republic's deep-blue, white, and gold, and the man in the Rim Federation's comparatively austere black and silver.

"And so," concluded the chaplain, "by the authority vested in me by the Terran Republic"—he cast a slightly apprehensive glance at Trevayne, who remained serenely impassive—"I pronounce you husband and wife."

They kissed, and the small audience of staffers and

task-force commanders applauded. Andreas Hagen looked relieved that he had carried off his duties as best man without a hitch. The godparents took turns hugging Admiral Li-Trevayne Magda, and Jason Windrider extended his hand to her husband.

"I was just philosophizing to my wife about the unfathomable strangeness of the workings of fate," he said, his brown, high-cheekboned face wreathed in a smile. "Now I've decided it isn't really so strange at all."

"You're probably one of the few people who think so," said Trevayne ruefully.

"Well, anyway, let's get busy celebrating." Windrider indicated the bar and buffet that had been set up. "For a while, anyway. I know you two will want to depart on your honeymoon."

"Yes," said Mags. "Probably the shortest honeymoon on record."

Her godparents knew what she meant.

The assault on Polo was scheduled to begin in two standard days.

Allied Fleet, Polo System

Intensive probing with recon drones had revealed that the Baldies had managed to get a few system-defense ships built in Polo; several others were detected still under construction. The SBMHAWK bombardment that preceded the attack by targeting those SDSs was not the most intensive such bombardment in history, but, as Trevayne put it, nobody was likely to get rich on the difference.

Still, the fact remained that *anything* the size of an SDS could absorb a lot of hits. And they did so now, as the space around them became an almost continuous stroboscopic eruption of antimatter warheads. The barrage did not destroy them, but it did rock them back as the supermonitors began to emerge from the warp point.

The SDSs held their distance, pouring missile fire into the leading waves while launching clouds of fighters. Those fighters, like the arrays of heavy superdreadnoughts, moved into position but also held back, awaiting the appearance of the Kasugawa generator that would be the target of their single-minded, casualty-oblivious attack.

They were beginning to wonder what was keeping the generator when certain of their sensors began to pick up some very strange energy readings from the warp point. . . .

They hadn't noticed the sudden emergence of a swarm of escape pods from one of the SMTs, indistinguishable from the rest. And even if they had noticed, it wouldn't have meant anything to them. They wouldn't have dreamed that the Kasugawa activation sequence had been going on all along inside that nondescript SMT hull.

And suddenly they had other things on their minds as the first of the superdevastators materialized in the newly blown-open warp point.

They had seen devastators before, and were no longer taken aback by them. But their almost wholly unannounced arrival was a shock. At once they scrapped their plan and launched an all-out, but somewhat disorganized, attack.

Waves and waves of fighters—five hundred from each SDS—went in first, like a swarm of locusts around a herd of elephants. But after the initial wave, the SDTs were accompanied by assault carriers, and some of those were Orion hulls from the PSU that had been joining

Trevayne's force in ever-increasing numbers. Although steeply outnumbered, their pilots burned lanes of death through the dense Arduan formations, filling the comm nets with eerie, flesh-crawling howls of triumph as they did their warrior's work.

But the SDTs were now the primary targets of the missile salvos from the Arduan SDSs. They advanced steadily through that torrent of death, and the heavy superdreadnoughts that came within range of their searing firepower died like moths in a flame. They were not maneuverable ships by most standards, but compared to the SDSs they were positively nimble. And by drawing the SDSs' fire, they had allowed many of the still more maneuverable SMTs to survive and come into knife range of the behemoths, working their way into blind zones and delivering gutting strokes.

It was a protracted, brutal outpouring of violence, almost inconceivable in its intensity. But in the end the SDSs died, unable to escape due to their slowness, succumbing like mastodonic beasts that took toll of their tormentors while sinking to the ground. Some of the lighter Arduan units fled across the system to the BR-02 warp point when it became clear that their crews could accomplish nothing by their discarnation, harried by the fleeter ships that had entered from Demeter with the later waves.

Admirals Trevayne and Li-Trevayne stood on *Li Han*'s flag bridge and tried to concentrate on the reports flooding in, despite the noise of the ongoing damage-control work. *Li Han* was in no danger, but she had taken enough hits to shake even her titanic frame. As had so many others. And still others had been less lucky.

Trevayne's eyes strayed to the viewscreen. They might as well have been in a starless warp nexus, for Polo's primary was an M5vi red dwarf, barely visible from here: a sooty stellar cinder with only a few lumps of uninhabitable frozen rock for planets.

His wife of a few days read his thoughts. "How many died for this worthless cosmic afterthought of a system?"

Trevayne drew himself up and shook off the mood. "This wasn't what they died for. They died to bring the end of this bloody damned war a little closer."

"Yes. And so now we'll have to choose among the options of how best to achieve that."

Their eyes met. They had discussed this enough to have thoroughly explored the strategic implications of a reconquest of Polo. And to know that some hard choices now had to be made.

35

Wisdom of the Monstrous Regiment

"The First Blast of the Trumpet Against
the Monstrous Regiment of Women."
—Knox (pamphlet title)

TRNS Li Han, *Allied Fleet, Polo System*

Li Han's flag conference room was appropriately large, with a long table in the form of a hollow rectangle surrounding a holo-display tank. One had to be at least a task-force commander to rate a seat at the table, but each had brought two or three staffers. Erica Krishmahnta had brought the newly minted Commander Ossian Wethermere. Looking across the table, she noted that Li-Trevayne Magda wasn't present, although her ops officer was. Trevayne's staff was already arrayed behind the chair at the head of the table.

At a quiet "Attention on deck!" from a master-at-arms beside the door, they all rose to their feet. Admirals Trevayne and Li-Trevayne entered together. The latter went to her place at the table, near its head where Trevayne sat down with a curt "As you were." He activated the display, which showed the relevant portions of the Bellerophon Arm. "I have called this meeting to discuss our next step. Our liberation of the Polo system"—he manipulated controls, and the newly green icon of Polo flashed for attention—"has burst open the strategic picture and opened up new possibilities."

"Yes!" Claw of the Khan Khzhotan leaned forward avidly on the specially designed chair provided for him, luxuriant whiskers quivering. "Now we have a war of movement again—an alternative to inevitable assaults on a single front, in which these *chofaki* can optimize the defensive firepower of their SDSs."

Trevayne nodded. "Quite. But now that we have alternatives, we must choose among them." He exchanged a quick eye-contact with his wife before resuming. "From here in Polo we have two further avenues of advance open to us. The first is to return to Demeter and assault Charlotte with as little delay as possible. The second is to proceed onward from Polo and attack the BR-02 starless warp nexus."

Trevayne ran his eyes around the circuit of the table. "After all the battles we have been through together since entering the Bellerophon Arm, you all know that you are free to contribute your own ideas without fear of disfavor. So I will tell you forthrightly that the Charlotte option is my personal choice.

"The Baldies will be expecting us to follow up our success here by continuing on to BR-02, and I'm willing to wager that they're rushing every available mobile unit there. So this is just the time for an unexpected assault on Charlotte. If we take it, we open a direct line of approach to Bellerophon.

"However, as I said at the outset, we need to consider all options. And there is a case to be made for

BR-02 as our next objective. I will now ask Admiral Li-Trevayne to set forth that case."

"Thank you, Admiral," said Mags into the general stunned silence, fully equaling her husband's deadpan propriety. "Bluntly, no matter how many of their mobile units the Baldies may be deploying away from Charlotte, we know that they have at least a dozen system-defense ships there. On the other hand, we found the Baldies still in the process of assembling SDSs here in Polo, with only a few completed. This indicates that there will probably be few if any of them in BR-02. Furthermore, capture of BR-02 would open up two axes of approach to Bellerophon: one through Madras and Pegasus, and the other through Elein. Of course, capture of Charlotte would also give us a second axis of approach, but that one is far longer than either of these, and is impassable for DTs without the use of Kasugawa generators."

"A most able presentation, Admiral," said Trevayne, and the two exchanged a barely perceptible smile that most of those present didn't even catch. Krishmahnta, seated directly across from Li-Trevayne Magda, did.

Trevayne looked around the table. "Under the circumstances . . . ," he began—and let the words linger.

Everyone, Krishmahnta was sure, understood what *the circumstances* were without having to be told. Trevayne was fleet commander and could, in theory, simply overrule his wife and impose his view. But—completely aside from their marriage—the politics of the situation were more complicated than that. The fact of the matter was that his heavy striking power—the devastators and superdevastators—was all provided by the Terran Republic. And Li-Trevayne Magda was the natural (if unofficial) spokesperson for the TRN here.

"Under the circumstances," Trevayne repeated after a moment, "it seems prudent to do more than simply solicit the opinions of our own experts. There is one group of seasoned officers—arguably the most experienced in dealing with this enemy—from whom we have not heard. I refer to the veterans of the Further Rim Fleet, Admirals Krishmahnta and Yoshikuni." Ian Trevayne and Magda Li-Trevayne both turned to face Krishmahnta. Erica commanded herself not to bite her lip: after all, she had known this moment was coming when she got the summons to the meeting—and the request for her opinion—two days ago. But that advance knowledge hadn't made this moment any easier.

Trevayne nodded at her. "Admiral Krishmahnta, what is your opinion on this matter?" Among Trevayne's staff, the postures all bespoke easy confidence; after all, Krishmahnta was a fellow RFN officer. Li-Trevayne's Terran Republic staffers were, obversely, rigidly motionless.

Krishmahnta managed not to swallow loudly before saying, "Admiral Trevayne, both plans have obvious and powerful merit, but I am in favor of Admiral Li-Trevayne's approach. The attack on BR-02 seems the most prudent path."

If Trevayne was shocked, he did not show it: he simply nodded. His staff was not so restrained. Several of them jerked forward in their seats; more than a few brows lowered and remained fixed there, deep, resentful scowls building around them. In Admiral Li-Trevayne's staff, eyebrows headed the other direction: they rose into quizzical surprise.

"I see," said Trevayne. "And your staff?"

"Sir, I only had time to consult directly with Admiral Yoshikuni and Commander Wethermere, but we were all of the same opinion, Admiral." Krishmahnta wanted very badly to add *I'm sorry*, but nothing could have been more against decorum. So she tried to put the regret she felt into her unblinking eyes.

Trevayne nodded again. "Well, I believe this decides the matter. Our next objective is the BR-02 warp point. I promised a short meeting, and I mean to keep my word, so I will not ask Admiral Krishmahnta or her staff to detail their analyses at this time. Rather, a synopsis of their rationale will be circulated within the next day or so." Trevayne rose and looked back to Krishmahnta. "Pursuant to compiling that synopsis, I will ask you and your staff to join me in my ready room, where you can brief me in detail—and where I might officially welcome you to the van of the Allied Fleet. I hope, Admiral Krishmahnta, that you will not mind that I have tasked you to take overall command of our smaller capital ships—the supermonitors and monitors—but you do have a singular degree of experience commanding them against the Baldies."

"I consider the assignment an honor, sir."

Trevayne's gaze softened just the faintest measure. "It means you're first in—and without support, Admiral. As you know."

"Knowing that makes the honor that much greater, sir. We'll get the Kasugawa generator in place and dredge that warp point, sir. You may rely on us."

"I do, Admiral Krishmahnta. Indeed, all of us will be relying on you." Trevayne swung his gaze around the perimeter of the conference table. "That will be all. Dismissed."

Ian Trevayne poured the drinks himself; he did not inquire as to preferences. It was a double scotch for everyone: his ship, his rules. And since they had all rejected his choice regarding the next step in the campaign strategy—well, he was at least going to choose the drink of the day.

He put the tray in the center of the table and took one of the amber-laden tumblers. He took an assessing sip, leaned back and looked at the faces around him. "Very well, let's hear it."

Yoshikuni looked surprised. Krishmahnta was unreadable. And that blasted Wethermere looked almost a bit relieved—as if he had seen this coming and was glad to get it over with.

"Hear what, sir?" asked Krishmahnta. The tone wasn't quite innocent, but Trevayne reflected that, at this very moment, clarified Hindu butter would not melt in her mouth.

"Admiral Krishmahnta, you bloody well know what I mean. Your staff's unanimity is a bit of a surprise—and I'd like to understand what led you to your conclusion."

Out of the corner of his eye, Trevayne saw Mags dip her nose into her own drink and then indulge in a smile which, had she been a cat, would surely have signified that she had gulped down a canary.

"Admiral," replied Krishmahnta, who had taken a polite sip of the scotch and now pushed it away with an almost completely suppressed shudder, "our conclusions were all the same, but they were not a product of unified deliberation."

Oh, and that's supposed to make me feel better? *Three separate reasons for rejecting my plan?* Trevayne resisted the impulse to take another defiant pull at his whiskey. "Then perhaps I'd better hear them. Separately."

"Yes, sir," answered Krishmahnta. "My reason was

pure math, sir. Your SDTs and DTs enjoy their greatest advantage when they are dealing with the Baldy SDHs and smaller—and that means going to BR-02. Yes, it takes time to chase all those nimble enemy ships down—but with respect, sir, where are they going to go? Whether we win BR-02 in a day or a week or a month probably doesn't alter the final equation very much. Once we've dredged that point and secured that system, the Baldies know their days are numbered. And then there's the issue of probable losses. We'll need all the big ships we can get when it comes time to assault into Bellerophon. If we go back to Charlotte, we have no choice but to slug it out, our heavies against their heavies: our DTs and SDTs against their SDSs. A lot of big hulls—and big crews—will be lost. I say avoid that."

Trevayne nodded. Not exactly his wife's logic, but a close cousin, at least. "Admiral Yoshikuni?"

The heretofore unperturbable Iron Admiral sat up very straight, and her eyes opened very wide. "Permission to speak freely, Admiral."

"Granted."

"Sir, we adapt to new conditions and situations more quickly, and more successfully, than Baldy. To me, that means that a war of maneuver—tactical maneuver—favors us, because it plays to our strengths. Baldy has shown a lot more inventiveness in situations where he's on the defensive, has had time to consider his options and lay a trap."

"So you feel that Charlotte holds more traps, Admiral?"

"It might. There's no way to know that for sure. But we *can* be sure that we're going to get into a set-piece slugging match there. It will be a war of attrition, not surprise or tactical exploitation. Will we win? Sure.

Probably. But can we control the costs?" She shook her head: her fine, straight hair swept from side to side like a shining wave of black silk. "I doubt it—and the butcher's bill is going to be high. Very high."

Trevayne nodded. Yoshikuni's analysis wasn't based on quantifiable data, but then again, not all decisive truths could be boiled down to numbers. Trevayne let his eyes roll around to Ossian Wethermere. "Mr. Wethermere, I'm going to hazard a guess that not only did you have your own opinion on this matter, but that it is the most unconventional of all three."

Wethermere nodded. "Yes, sir—but I'm not sure that its difference vests in its unconventionality."

"No?"

"No, sir. I guess I looked at the question from the opposite end of the strategic pipe."

"I beg your pardon?"

Wethermere spread his hands. "Admiral, I think all our battlefield confidence is richly warranted—but what if the upcoming attack *fails*?"

Trevayne found himself caught between two reflexes. The first was the seasoned commander's instinct to immediately quell any talk of defeat or failure: the Fleet had had only one genuine setback—the First Battle of Charlotte—and now had the necessary momentum and strategic initiative to remain victorious. But Trevayne's equally powerful, and converse, reflex emerged as a sudden insight: *Damn it, Wethermere's right. We're all so close to the turning point that none of us is thinking about a reversal, about failure. It's almost as though we are presuming success. But this Wethermere chap doesn't seem to presume anything—for which I guess I should be grateful.* "Very well, Commander. So, tell me—why is it better to attack BR-02 if we should find ourselves repulsed?"

"Well, actually, the key factor is something you pointed out during today's presentation."

"Something *I* pointed out?"

"Yes, sir. I made a note of it. You said, 'The Baldies will be expecting us to follow up our success here by continuing on to BR-02, and I'm willing to wager that they're rushing every available mobile unit there.'"

"And you disagree with that assessment?"

"No, sir. I completely concur. *Completely* concur."

And that was when Trevayne saw it. "Of course. So if we attack Charlotte and lose, the mobile units the Baldies rushed in to *defend* BR-02 can suddenly change roles and go on the *offense.* They would be free—and already in position—to launch a counterattack into Polo when we're at our weakest."

"Exactly, Admiral. And if we've spent ourselves heavily in Charlotte, or if they surprise us with something new there, and turn the tables on us—"

"Then they'll guess—rightly—that we probably don't have enough forces to be holding on to Polo with maximum strength. So they'll go on the attack and push us out—and we'll have lost all the ground we've gained since recovering from the Battle of Charlotte. And they'll have bought more time to invest Polo, and BR-02, and Charlotte with forts and other static defenses."

"That's what I'd fear, sir. So, all other things being equal, even if we were to lose, I still want to inflict damage upon their mobile forces in BR-02. That way, even if we take severe losses during our attack there, the Baldies still can't really follow up their victory. So

I think that attacking BR-02 minimizes our risk by safeguarding our strategic gains to date."

Trevayne nodded sharply and regarded the three officers from the battered and well-seasoned Further Rim Fleet. They were all very different, yet their analytical styles were oddly complementary: Krishmahnta thought like a line admiral, Yoshikuni like a knife fighter, Wethermere like a chess master. Trevayne turned to Mags. "Well, it seems like your plan has a decisive mandate, Admiral."

"Thank you, Admiral," she said with a nod. Mags shared a small, brief smile with Krishmahnta and Yoshikuni. "I'm glad we—the Admirals and I—were able to convince you."

"'Convince' me?" Trevayne harrumphed as he refilled his tumbler. "As if my plan ever had any chance—or I any choice."

"Sir?" Yoshikuni's perplexity seemed genuine.

"Admiral Yoshikuni," said a suddenly too-solemn Ian Trevayne, "do you think the demography of this council of war has escaped me? My plan was not overthrown in a fair test of wits and merits. No, it was a victim of the oldest of all wars: the war between the sexes. It seems, judging from the intelligences arrayed against mine, that for now I am, to misquote Knox, sadly subject to the 'monstrous regiment of women' here deployed against me." He toasted the ladies with a mischievous smile.

Before Krishmahnta or Yoshikuni could figure out how to respond to their CO's fey waggishness, and before Mags's eyes had stopped rolling, Wethermere started backward with histrionic shock and outrage. "Sir! You are including me in the ranks of that 'regiment' of *women*? Really? Sir, I don't have the appropriate—credentials."

Trevayne shook his head and tried not to smile. "Nevertheless, your gender allegiance is under question, sir."

Wethermere smiled back. "With respect, sir—*I've* never worn a skirt. But, sir, I've seen a picture in which *you* were doing so."

"That, son, is a kilt."

"That, sir, is a matter of terminology."

"And that ends this discussion." Trevayne turned to Krishmahnta. "I say, Admiral, what dunderhead approved the promotion of this insolent young pup, anyway?"

36

Diminution

The martial character cannot prevail in a whole people but by the diminution of all other virtues.
—Johnson

Punt City, New Ardu/Bellerophon

Narrok, flanked by a double gauntlet of guards—not all of whom were *Destoshaz*—approached what Ankaht's *selnarm* told him was today's meeting site.

Narrok did not try to hide his (surprise). "We are not convening in the Council Chambers?"

Ankaht sent an abashed (negative, regret, despair). "No, Senior Admiral. It is no longer safe to do so. We must choose new locations for each meeting—and the site remains undisclosed until a few hours before the gathering itself."

Narrok, inspecting the small, windowless chamber they were ushered into, queried, "How can the human Resistance hope to penetrate this far into Punt City?"

"Oh, no. They are not the danger, Senior Admiral."

"Then who is?"

She turned all three eyes upon him and sent (apology). "The radicals of your own caste, respected Narrok: the *Destoshaz'ai*-as-*sulhaji* Martyrs' Movement."

"Martyrs?"

"Torhok and Urkhot."

So it had come to this. Battered at the front lines, and breaking apart behind them, the Children of Illudor were indeed a race *in extremis*. And he had only one answer to the dilemma.

Amunherh'peshef was waiting for them, and seemed anxious. "Our apologies, Senior Admiral, but every minute we tarry in one place increases our vulnerability to possible attack. So, if you would not mind beginning immediately—"

Narrok complied. "I will be blunt. We are losing the war. This statement is true on both the tactical and strategic levels, and in both the short- and long-term projections.

"The arrival of the new Allied Fleet immediately changed our strategic picture from secure to severe, and the improvements made to our forces may prove to be too little, too late to change that. Also, the Allied Fleet now recovers its losses more quickly than we do. After its defeat at Charlotte, it rebuilt more swiftly than we believed possible. It also showed up with three new innovations at, or just before, Polo: the superdevastator category of ship, the Kasugawa generator concealed within an SMT hull, and the double-firing energy-torpedo battery. If the humans can use these technologies to breach our secure perimeter at either Charlotte or BR-02, our strategic position becomes almost hopeless. We lack the combat power to retake either system, and the humans would then have a direct line of warp points to New Ardu."

Amunherh'peshef's *selnarm* burst like a bomb. "But surely New Ardu itself is secure!"

"For now, yes. But the humans are not shackled to an admiral whose imperative is 'always advance.' Rather, they will first methodically drive us from every system. They will then have four warp points leading here into New Ardu and will eventually batter us down as we divide our forces between the warp points. The endgame of such a contest is inevitable: our extinction."

Tefnut ha sheri tapped two claws on the table to refocus the stunned Council. "Senior Admiral Narrok, would that your news were as welcome as your candor. There is one thing you have not told us yet."

"And what is that, revered *Holodah'kri'at*?"

"What we might do."

Narrok stood as straight as he could. "I see two options."

The Council's collective *narmata* quailed before the turbulence that they could feel churning behind their senior admiral's *selnarm*. Ankaht's own *selnarm*—clear and fearless—broke through that morass to touch his own. "Tell us, Admiral."

"Both the alternatives I suggest are extreme choices. The first alternative is to fall back upon both our and the humans' weapon of last recourse: biological agents. Intelligence Overseer Mretlak has identified several humanocidal viruses that could be produced fairly quickly. If we elect to pursue this course of action, we recommend a sleeper virus—one which lays dormant for weeks, even months. In order to spread it, we would strike back through to human systems wherever we might—particularly out from Suwa up the left side of the Bellerophon Arm. Not only would the human relief units and the local population become carriers, but the naval crews debarking for recreation or cargo exchange would carry it back up into the Fleet. After a few months, the disease would become manifest and destroy them, and we would then be able to reestablish our defensive perimeter."

"Assuming we, too, are not victims of this virus." Tefnut ha sheri clicked a single claw lightly on the table-top. "Many such organisms seem to be indiscriminate."

Narrok nodded at Tefnut ha sheri. "This is why the humans, their many allies, and even their most vicious enemies have never employed such weapons."

Amunherh'peshef had recovered enough to resume control of the meeting. "And the second alternative, Admiral?"

Narrok steadied himself. "Make peace. Humans are not faithless *griarfeksh*. Nor, of course, are they flawless *'kaiKri*—'saints,' in the human tongue. They can become mindless in their pursuit of retribution . . . and we have given them many reasons to exact it from us. But they are also capable of great leaps of faith: faith in what is right, and in the better qualities of others—even in their adversaries."

Amunherh'peshef was very still as he asked, "And what would we hope to gain by negotiation from a position of weakness, Senior Admiral?"

Narrok sent (rue). "Thankfully, that is in the province of politicians, First Councilor, and I am but a military professional."

"Yes, Senior Admiral, but you are also a member of this Council, and having long fought against the humans, you may have a better understanding of them."

Narrok was (dubious). "A better understanding of them, First Councilor? No. If that is what you seek, then here in this room are both Elder Ankaht and

Overseer Mretlak, at your disposal. However, I understand my own caste well enough, and this I must tell you. The closer we come to defeat, the more desperate the radical *Destoshaz* will grow. And, among those *Destoshaz* who have lost faith in this body, their first order of business will be to remove the Council with maximum speed and finality."

"So, you are saying that our precautions here today are prudent?" Amunherh'peshef gestured to the austere chamber in which they were meeting.

"Prudent. But also insufficient. First Councilor, I suspect the radicals are long past attempting to bomb or assassinate this Council. You have made it too difficult, and it is altogether too predictable. They will seek other methods with which to bring about your dissolution. They will seek a weakness you do not even realize you have, and will strike you there—hard and fast." Narrok sat, glad to be done.

Ankaht rose. "I, too, have something to say that will be difficult for us to hear. Particularly for our *Destoshaz* brothers and sisters." She glanced at Narrok, who cycled all three of his eyelids, once, slowly: among acquaintances and friends, it was a wordless assurance of patient and willing acquiescence. He felt Ankaht's quick but intense send of (gratitude, apology, purpose) like a quick clasp of reassuring tentacles between siblings. "This theory is not mine alone. Several weeks ago, Overseer Mretlak and the senior experts of my research cluster approached me—independently—with almost identical causal explanations for the many social problems with which we are now faced."

"Proceed," sent Amunherh'peshef with (weariness, encouragement).

Ankaht bowed her thanks. "From the first generations of the Dispersal of Sekahmant, it became obvious that the demographics of our birthing clusters were changing. The number—and ratio—of Younglings whose only conceivable casting was for the *Destoshaz* increased sharply.

"But as an Elder—as one who walked upon the surface of Ardu and then slept the long centuries until these past few years—I must tell you that the caste changes have not merely been in terms of numbers. The few *Destoshaz* I knew as a Youngling—for that caste was by then almost a rarity on Ardu—were reminiscent of Narrok, or Mretlak. They were persons capable not only of great focus and decisive action, but also of discernment and sagacity. Among the human authors I have read, the ancient war-philosopher Sun Tzu captured the essence of this ancient *Destoshaz* archetype when he wrote, 'To fight and conquer in all your battles is not supreme excellence; supreme excellence consists in breaking the enemy's resistance without fighting.' "

Ankaht looked around the room. "Why, when we have more *Destoshaz* than in any recent epoch, do we have so few of this kind of wise warrior? The more I pondered on this, the more I explored back past the recent millennia through my *shaxzhutok*, and in those past lives, I believe I found an answer.

"It is my hypothesis that the membership of today's *Destoshaz* caste does not merely recall the *quantities* associated with its Pre-Enlightenment demographics, but recalls its behavioral *qualities*, as well. Their rapid reflex toward violent resolution of conflicts, their impetuous embrace of physical peril, their predilection for hero worship, their dismissive attitude toward *shaxzhutok* and past lives: these were the tendencies that the Pre-Enlightenment *Destoshaz* had to overcome in order to share in our communal *narmata.* Many of us have noticed what we have haltingly called the current 'atavistic' tendency of the radical *Desotashaz* to reject these harmonizing elements of Arduan society. But it is now my group's hypothesis that this signifies a deeper, more physiological change: a reversion to an earlier evolutionary form."

Tefnut ha sheri started. "But is this possible, Elder? After all, there is nothing genetic that determines one's casting as a *Destoshaz.*"

"Revered *Holodah'kri'at*, that very presumption was why we dismissed this hypothesis at first. But lately, our investigation of human science has revealed that our understanding of genetics remains somewhat rudimentary. And the reason for this is obvious: we simply euthanized the unfit and congratulated ourselves that, with the coming of the Enlightenment, we had achieved an evolutionary zenith.

"But the humans pursued genetics far more assiduously than we did. After all, for them it was their only hope for significantly expanding their finite lifetimes. And in so doing, they happened upon a set of genetic relationships which are not mappable in the simplistic one-to-one correspondences that assign a given trait to a given gene. No, they pressed onward into what became the key to all their greatest genetic accomplishments: epigenetics—where less obvious traits are expressed, or marginally amplified, by subtle variations in the genetic structures around them."

"The structural pattern of the codes, rather than the codes themselves, induce traits," supplied Mretlak smoothly, orienting the few Councilors whose *selnarm* still registered (perplexity).

Ankaht gestured toward Mretlak. "It was indeed Mretlak who first brought this element of human genetic science to my attention. I then began to wonder if an analogous feature might be present in our own genetic makeup."

Amunherh'peshef seemed filled with (anxiety) as he asked, "And is it?"

Ankaht let two minor tentacles from each cluster droop to underscore her (uncertainty). "We do not have a reliable methodology to determine this yet, and due to the drains of the war, we will not soon rectify this. However, we long ago observed on Ardu that, in other species, environmental crises can spark reversions—particularly if an older form of the species is more suited to the new, adverse conditions."

"But," objected Amunherh'peshef, "among our homeworld's species, a profound reversion required a proportionately sustained crisis. That is not the case here, Elder. We have been at war for less than three years."

Ankaht sent (accord) and added, "Yes, but our current state of crisis dates not from our arrival on Bellerophon, but from the First Dispersal of Sekahmant. For centuries now, the sole survivors of our race have been hermetically sealed in controlled environments, fleeing through the harsh medium of interstellar space. And what transpired in the society that was compelled to endure this trauma? The emphasis upon *shaxzhutok* waned, and intensive technical training increased. The mix of castes came to resemble those of the Pre-Enlightenment, and among the *Destoshaz* there was a continually intensifying trend back toward the tall physiotype of our species."

Tefnut ha sheri drummed all his claws on the tabletop in a slow, even cascade. "Elder, this hypothesis has much to commend it, but is it not also possible that the *Destoshaz* resurgence is more a matter of what the humans call 'natural selection,' that the *Destoshaz* were simply the caste most likely to survive and thrive amidst the challenges of our long, harsh journey between the stars?"

"Perhaps, revered *Holodah'kri'at*, but consider this also: among all the castes and skill-groups, only the incidence of *shaxzhu* has declined to Pre-Enlightenment levels. Which is quite strange, since that group's particularly strong gift for experiencing *shaxzhutok*, while genetically determined, is also a random mutation rather than an inherited trait."

Amunherh'peshef sent puzzlement. "What do you feel this signifies?"

"First Councilor, it suggests that it is not just the *Destoshaz* that are in regression. It is the whole of the Children of Illudor. After all, in the Pre-Enlightenment, *shaxzhu* were by far the rarest of all groups—and they have become so once again."

"And now you reconceive those ancient changes—to both *Destoshaz* and *shaxzhu*—as evolutionary consequences of the social change wrought by the Enlightenment, rather than acts of divine grace?"

Ankaht bowed slightly. "I think we must consider the possibility, at the very least."

Amunherh'peshef sat back, his *selnarm* settling. "If this hypothesis is true—what then? How should it factor into our deliberations . . . if at all?"

Mretlak's ever-subtle *selnarm* uncoiled into the main current of the Council's *narmata*. He had been brought in to fill one of the chairs left vacant by the departure of the radicals. "At the very least, this hypothesis gives us a clearer understanding of why the *Destoshaz'ai*-as-*sulhaji* movement has worked like a magnet, attracting the most regressed of my caste like iron filings. This also compels us to accept that a large cohort of my caste-mates are being driven by perceptions, emotions, and reactions that are simply not akin to ours."

Tefnut ha sheri signaled (realization, accord, sorrow). "Meaning, therefore, that we may need to despair of ever reclaiming them to the Body of Illudor."

"Very probably. It also means that, reciprocally, they have long since abandoned any thought of rehabilitating us, or this Council. Indeed, they may be operating in accordance with the more ferocious principles of the Pre-Enlightenment *Destoshaz* caste, whose methods were often quite brutal."

"So, you feel they will begin to massacre us?"

"I fear for us less than I fear for the humans."

"Why?"

"Because if the radicals can provoke the humans into such a fury that they would prefer certain death to continued occupation, the *Destoshaz* will have created the unremitting and genocidal war they want. In such a polarized conflict, we would have no choice but to side with the radical *Destoshaz*."

Amunherh'peshef tapped a sharp claw on the table. "Then what do you recommend, Councilor Mretlak?"

"Containment of the human Resistance. And then—strangely—the guarding of it."

"What? I do not understand."

"Consider. In containing the Resistance, we neutralize their ability to make a sweeping response to any atrocities by the radicals. In simultaneously guarding the Resistance, we also show our general interest in mediating the harshness of our occupation, and our specific resolve to protect them against *Destoshaz* extremists. If the humans become aware of our struggle to protect them, it might make them more amenable to negotiating with us."

"Which would furnish me with an opportunity—perhaps—to make successful contact through our lesser translators," added Ankaht.

The Council was still and then began polling opinions. Narrok, detached, felt the deliberations flow around him and let the various councilors read his thoughts and assessments like a book propped open for their convenience.

Amunherh'peshef stood. "It is decided then. Admiral Narrok will spare no effort to halt the advance of the human fleets. We will attempt to contain—and protect—the human Resistance here on New Ardu. Mretlak, have you been able to determine their location?"

Mretlak sent (assurance). "There seem to be two bases. By tracking their flow of logistical needs, particularly those relating to electronics, my Counter-Insurgency Prime Lentsul has narrowed their location down to two regions 100 kilometers square, each . . ."

Lentsul watched the live feed from the Council Chamber and could not repress the thrill he felt when Mretlak credited him with locating the Resistance bases. In actuality, it had been a joint effort, but Mretlak was uncommonly generous to his subordinates.

Arriving at the doorway to the office Lentsul now shared with Mretlak, Lentsul's assistant Emz'hem send a tendril of *selnarm* at him, inquiring. It was a tender tendril, somewhat desperate and forlorn, darkly fixated on the bittersweet rejection it anticipated from him. Lentsul responded, discomfited by this contact even more than Emz'hem's customary shadings of unrequited love. "Yes?"

"Good Lentsul, I felt your—pleasure. Has Overseer Mretlak relayed the approximate location of the Resistance bases to the Council?"

"Yes, yes." Lentsul tried not to be snappish, but it was difficult. The memory of strong, passionate Heshfet was like a constant reproach to the ineffectual passivity of Emz'hem. "Why do you ask?"

"I know it was important to you," Emz'hem answered simply, "and also that it means that your estimates passed Mretlak's independent review. Which means they were also confirmed by orbital reconnaissance."

Lentsul sent affirmation. "Yes, we've finally got the Resistance pinned down. We've done good work, you and I. Why do you not cease your labors for this day, Emz'hem? They will always be here when you return in the morning."

"Thank you, good Lentsul. I will do as you suggest. Perhaps when you are done . . . you might wish to join me?"

There it was again: that same pathetic longing, bleeding out around and through her *selnarm* like sweat out of distended pores. What was it that she—she, a *Destoshaz*—saw in a small *Ixturshaz* like himself? It made her even more contemptible, somehow—but he resolved to be kind. "Regrettably, I am unable to comply with your request. I must log the recording of the Council session immediately, and so will be working late this evening." He congratulated himself for being the very epitome of charm in constructing this suave demurral.

"I see," sent Emz'hem and withdrew, her *selnarm* trailing injury and longing like a wounded animal bleeding during mating season.

Resistance Regional Headquarters, Charybdis Islands, Bellerophon/New Ardu

McGee was sitting on the edge of their bed when Jen returned from dropping Zander off with one of his 'aunts' among the former abductees. She started when she saw him. "Well, you're home early. Our date doesn't start until—Sandro? What's wrong?"

McGee had learned a great deal about how to be a better communicator, particularly with his fiancée, but he grimly acknowledged that he had made almost no progress in the fine art of approaching a topic obliquely. "Jen, the amateur astronomers coordinated by Toshi Springer have detected changes in the Arduan satellite grid."

Jen came to sit on the bed next to him and put her slender hands over the great hairy fists that were knotted in his lap. "What kind of changes?"

"The Arduans have retasked their satellites, changed their orbits. To fixed lookdown positions. Pretty much right overhead here, and at the main base in the Aeolian Lowlands, back on Icarus. We also confirmed reports that the Arduans were poking around our old virtual training facility in Upper Thessalaborea. They're looking for us, Jen, and from what you've told me of them, they're going to find us—very soon now."

She nodded somberly. "Yes, once they decide something is important, they're both clever and relentless. And so now I'm guessing everyone here is pushing for an all-out attack. Again."

"They've got to, Jen. All the rank and file know that the debriefings ended months ago, so there's no basis for claiming we're still gathering intelligence. We've got all the intel we're going to get, and the gruntiest grunt of us knows it. And everyone's been getting cabin fever. You can't have a Resistance movement that doesn't resist the enemy."

Jen looked up at McGee, who suddenly wished that they had gotten married the same day he had proposed. "Sandro, who's making the attack plan?"

"Cap Peters and Chong, with tactical input from me. They're going after Melantho, like we discussed. And it's going to be a bloodbath—on both sides."

"They're not going to wait for the Fleet?"

McGee shook his head. "They can't—not anymore. There's too much unrest, too much impatience. And now, with the Arduans coming so close in their search for us—"

"But what about hostages? Will the attack at least try to take hostages—or prisoners? If we could just get our hands on Ankaht—"

"Jen, no one really sees any value to that option now. Taking hostages is a delicate operation. It puts a lot of added risk on our side—and for what? You yourself argued that there was no value in taking the Council hostage. Besides, we've come to a point in this war where it may simply boil down to kill or be killed. No quarter asked, no quarter given."

Jen stopped as McGee uttered those concluding words. She stared off intently for a second. Then her eyes turned back toward him; a smile played at the corners of her mouth. "You know," she said, "I've just changed my mind. Maybe taking hostages isn't such a bad idea after all. Just so long as it's done correctly. . . ."

Punt City, New Ardu/Bellerophon

Iakkut stood. "And so we have access to the nuclear warheads?"

"It is so, *Destoshaz'at*." Former-Councilor Mahes sent his (affirmative, savor, exultation) along with the ancient formula of address reserved for the caste's high warlord: a position and title that had last been used half a millennium before the Dispersal of Sekahmant. "We have secured the cooperation of most of the Security forces in possession of our bombardment munitions. Most of the others will stand aside. The few that resist will be overwhelmed so quickly, they will not have time to act."

"And you are confident that you can deliver the two strikes in a convincing sequence?"

"Absolutely, *Destoshaz'at*. The first strike will come from our craft and annihilate the two *griarfeksh* bases—once we have located them. The second strike will appear to be a wave of *griarfeksh* reprisals—by secretly planted nuclear munitions—against all our remaining outreach installations in the major *griarfeksh* cities."

"It is imperative that no race-loyal Arduan be killed in this second strike: *griarfeksh* and race-traitors only. We will need all our true-hearted brothers and sisters to help us control the planet—and the Fleet—after we strike."

"*Destoshaz'at*, you need have no fear of killing the race-loyal among the Children of Illudor. However, arranging the 'reprisal strike' here in Melantho itself did present us with some difficulties. We have no way of evacuating all our race-loyal brothers in time."

"No matter. I presume you have planted smaller warheads here, have you not?"

"Yes. None larger than fifteen kilotons. And all in the south-central area just east of the Heliobarbus District."

"Why there?"

"It is more than a mile from Salamisene Bay. The initial shock and plasma emissions of the detonations will first have to sweep away the dense urban areas—"

"—and thus will be greatly diminished by the time they reach the Bay's open waters. And so will not flash across and reach us here in Punt."

"Not much, *Destoshaz'at*."

"The plan is well-conceived and sound. I could not hope for more. Our Martyr-Brothers Torhok and Urkhot would be proud. The *griarfeksh* will be incensed against us. Those of our brothers who can still be reclaimed will join us in exterminating them. We will naturally ensure that the *griarfeksh* fleets hear of this. They will feel compelled to attack before they are ready, to save their *zheteksh* littermates—and so our immense defenses will have a singular opportunity to deal them a crippling blow in space, as well." Iakkut stood. "And now, you must excuse me. I have further business to attend to."

Selnarms slid against each other in sly appreciation of the innuendo: they all knew the nature of Iakkut's next business.

Eager to be the first to open the door, Mahes led the way out.

Waiting just beyond the doorway was a *Destoshaz* female, eyes down in shame, yellow-mud colored in embarrassment and strange excitement.

Mahes went past her, staring. As did all the rest. When they were gone, she entered the room, slide-shuffling toward Iakkut. Coming near him, the tentacles of her left cluster writhed fitfully toward the *Destoshaz'at*, then retracted. She looked up, looked away, her *selnarm* tortured and desperate, striving toward his yet also somewhat repulsed. Timidly, she sent: "Shall we join now?"

"Not yet. You have information for me?"

Iakkut smelled how her mating musk redoubled as he held her off, made her wait upon the resolution of the business that had brought them together in the first place. She had been exactly what he—what the entire *Destoshaz'ai*-as-*sulhaji* movement—had needed: an informer inside the cadres that helped the Council with its deliberations and planning. But that had only been half of what made her ideal. The other half was her low sense of self, her *selnarm* troubled by a constant ache of loss or rejection—Iakkut could not tell which and hardly cared. For a *Destoshaz*, she was contemptibly weak: providing information from arch-traitor Mretlak's so-called military-intelligence section only made her doubly deserving of scorn. She had gone to work for a traitor and had become, in time, a traitor within his ranks. That she seemed to find titillation in the brusque treatment Iakkut showed her here—and in his mating pod—only served to make her a perfectly disposable and depersonalized object for the movement's purposes and his own dark passions.

He felt her *selnarm* reach out toward his; he ignored it, and smelled the musk become thicker as a result. "The information?"

"What—what do you wish to know?" Her mating urge had obviously addled her wits. She was intelligent, but in the limited way of persons who are only gifted with manipulating set quantities and bases of knowledge: activities which reward maximum focus and minimal imagination.

"You know the information we need, Emz'hem," Iakkut said, making her work for his compliance.

"The coordinates for the Resistance bases—that is what you want most, yes?" Emz'hem's agitated *selnarm* writhed and bulged like an animal straining to get outside its own skin.

"Yes. What do you know?"

"Lentsul does not know the exact positions. But he and Mretlak have narrowed their locations to these two map grids. . . ."

37

Pendragon in Hell

> I am tired and sick of war. Its glory is all moonshine. It is only those who have neither fired a shot nor heard the shrieks and groans of the wounded who cry aloud for blood, more vengeance, more desolation. War is hell.
>
> —Sherman

TRNS Li Han, *Allied Fleet, Polo System*

Both of the Trevaynes turned out to have been right, each in his or her own way.

Li-Trevayne Magda had correctly foreseen that there would be only a handful of operable SDSs in BR-02. There were a surprising number of incomplete ones, festooned with machinery and showing their titanic ribs. But the robot brains of the SBMHAWKs were sophisticated enough to distinguish those from their real targets, and the torrents of missiles raced off to blanket the operable SDSs with rippling sheets of antimatter flame Or so it was hoped. Erica Krishmahnta's monitors and supermonitors would only begin to emerge after the missiles—and the AMBAMMs—had prepared the ground for them.

But Ian Trevayne had, it seemed, correctly predicted a redeployment of mobile Baldy units to BR-02, judging from the shocking number of heavy superdreadnoughts lurking at some distance from the warp point, protected by belts of minefields. At least that was how it looked: any RD that stayed in BR-02 long enough to get definitive information never returned. In sum, the SDHs and the mines were a vindication that Trevayne could easily have lived without.

Still, he permitted himself to hope that this would be no worse than a repeat of Polo. The Kasugawa generator would soon follow Krishmahnta's SMTs through the warp point, and the subsequent waves included what was now the standard mix of assault carriers to deal with the Baldy fighters screaming in from the SDSs.

At least that was what Trevayne told himself as he watched the lead elements of Krishmahnta's oddly named Task Force Vishnu disappear through the warp point.

RFNS Gallipoli, *Task Force Vishnu, Allied Fleet, BR-02 Warp Nexus*

Upon emerging into that part of the void designated BR-02, Fleet Admiral Erica Krishmahnta immediately conceded that she had been mistaken in her estimates about how very bad the first minutes of the assault were going to be.

They were going to be much worse.

Gallipoli, fresh out of the ways which had effected her energy-torpedo upgrade, immediately began quaking under a constant buffeting of near hits by dozens of missiles. "Tactics?" she called—and wondered why that officer was not already at her elbow.

"Ma'am—sir," stammered Lieutenant Witeski, "I was just helping—"

"Damn it, Witeski, I don't have time for excuses. I barely have time to hear your report." He didn't take—or hear—the cue. "Damn it, I need a sitrep, incorporating best sensor data—now." Witeski, flustered, jumped to do her bidding; she peripherally noticed Ossian Wethermere moving to intercept him. Krishmahnta suppressed a sudden impulse to reassign Witeski immediately—and pull Wethermere away from his duties as acting chief of staff: *he* would have had all the information in hand already. . . .

However, the holoplot told her much of what she needed to know: the Baldies had finally learned how to properly defend a system. What the few surviving recon drones had reported as proximity mines just beyond the lip of the warp point had evidently been signal-producing junk—and the AMBAMMs which had preceded her task force into BR-02 had apparently achieved little more than trash removal. Beginning five light-seconds back from the warp point was a thick, almost solid hemisphere of actual mines—and judging from the yellow damage shading already beginning to limn the icons of her smaller MTs, those weren't just outsized laser-buoys: the Baldies had seeded force-beams into the mix.

Beyond this dense protective shell were stationary defenses, but not full-fledged forts: more like pillboxes. Each was only the size of a small monitor, but there were at least three dozen of them, and they were emitting a nonstop stream of missiles. Beyond them were the inevitable enemy SDHs—hundreds of them—and five large signatures that could only be SDSs.

It was either going to be a long day for Task Force Vishnu—or a very, very short one.

Gallipoli bucked savagely; next to Krishmahnta, freshly minted Fleet Captain La Mar snapped orders to the finally linked data-net operators: energy torpedoes started streaming out at the Baldy pillboxes.

"Here's the sitrep, Admiral—"

Krishmahnta turned, stunned because the voice was not Witeski's: it was Ossian Wethermere. She was too glad to dare show it. "Commander Wethermere, your duties as acting chief of staff—"

"—include reassigning Fleet staffers at need, and as advisable. Mr. Witeski also shows excellent aptitude for Commo, so I put him in special oversight on maintaining our nets. They're going to be crucial, don't you think, Admiral?"

He smiled at her, and she felt a wave of relief so great that she had to repress a shiver. "Yes, Commander, I think you're right." *And you were right to make the switch with Witeski—because you know as well as I do that once we're in combat, I need you on Tactics and coordinating with Fleet Ops. When we don't have time to retire to a briefing room, I need a real-time war-thinker, not a chief of staff. So—*"Let's get to work."

Arduan SDH Shem'pter'ai, *Main Van, Consolidated Fleet of the* Anaht'doh Kainat, *BR-02 Warp Nexus*

"Senior Admiral, you asked to be notified when over forty human warships had come through the gate."

Narrok sent (appreciation). "And are they all SMTs or MTs?"

"Yes, sir."

"Any gravitic fluxes?"

"None detected, sir. Most of the human ships are starting to move away from the warp point, sir—and their fire against our small forts is beginning to get worse."

"As we expected. Their energy torpedoes will become more effective as the range drops under twenty light-seconds."

"They are approaching that range now."

"Yes," sent Narrok with a surprising twinge of regret mixed in, "which means the humans are about to discover the trap we've laid for them—once they bring in their Kasugawa generator."

RFNS Gallipoli, *Task Force Vishnu, Allied Fleet, BR-02 Warp Nexus*

"Entering outer minefield belts now, Admiral." La Mar's voice was tight; so far, *Gallipoli* hadn't taken any major hits, but two omega icons already hung motionless in the holotank, marking the loss of RFNS *Caladbolg* and TRNS *Briareus*, respectively. "Starting to cut through now."

In the forward view screen, blue-white afterimages of energy torpedoes hammered out like long-tailed tracers into the sunless void of BR-02; at the end of each, a small yellow-white blossom told of the destruction of another laser or force-beam buoy.

"I don't like it," muttered Krishmahnta.

"Too easy," Wethermere said with a nod.

"Exactly. Only a few of their SDHs are tossing in their weight of missiles, and the SDSs are staying back."

"Maybe they don't want to get too close to our energy torpedoes," La Mar offered over his shoulder. Krishmahnta's former fleet tactics officer, he sometimes slipped back into his old job.

"I'm sure they don't—but then why aren't they pounding us to pieces now, before we can get through the minefields?"

Wethermere rubbed his chin meditatively, but his voice was firm and certain. "To trick us into thinking it's time to bring in the Kasugawa generator."

"Which means they're hiding something up their sleeve."

"Yes."

"And we've got to find out what it is before we risk the generator."

"Agreed, Admiral. But I think we should send a drone back to inform Fleet about the delay. And sending the drone may also trick the Baldies into thinking that we are calling for the generator."

"And so they'll wait a little longer than they should, if we press forward."

"Because they don't want to play the ace they're holding up their sleeve if they think their *real* target is about to come popping out of the interstellar rabbit hole."

Krishmahnta smiled at the younger man who was so adept at completing her thoughts and sentences without seeming presumptuous or importunate. "It's karma, you know."

Wethermere—who, in the preceding weeks, had been brushing up on the finer points of Hinduism with his admiral over tea—quirked an eyebrow. "Karma, sir? What is?"

"Our working together. And doing it so easily, so well."

Wethermere grinned. "Perhaps, in an earlier life, I was your kid brother."

Krishmahnta smiled. "Or maybe I was yours. Who knows?" Then the brief respite from imminent death and destruction was over. "Send the drone. And Commo, signal Admiral Yoshikuni to move into the lead and pick up the pace."

Lubell, at Fleet Ops, half turned toward Krishmahnta. "Sir, if we go any faster, we won't detect all the force-beam buoys in time—and they will cut hell out of us if we get that close."

Wethermere interceded, giving her the time she needed to reassess the tacplot. "Lieutenant, the warning is appreciated," he said calmly, "but the admiral knows the costs of her order. All too well."

Arduan SDH Shem'pter'ai, *Main Van, Consolidated Fleet of the* Anaht'doh Kainat, *BR-02 Warp Nexus*

"Senior Admiral Narrok, they have sent back a drone. It could be the sign that they are about to send through the Kasugawa generator."

Or it could be a trick. Or the Kasugawa generator could already be here, in one of the SMTs that is providing a base of fire from closer to the warp point.

He assessed the increasing speed with which the enemy van was cutting a path through his coreward minefield—and the math was most unpromising: unmolested, they could conceivably bore a tunnel through his defenses if he continued to hold his fire, waiting for the generator. And perhaps the drone was merely a ruse to get him to delay even longer. . . .

Narrok straightened. He'd have to spring his first surprise now; it was crucial that he prevent the humans from opening a navigable aperture in his defenses, so that he could instead keep them bottled up close to the warp point.

Close to the kill zone he had so painstakingly prepared.

RFNS Gallipoli, *Task Force Vishnu, Allied Fleet, BR-02 Warp Nexus*

"Admiral, Baldy missiles inbound! Dozens—no, hundreds of them!" Lubell's voice almost cracked—but not quite.

Krishmahnta watched her task force reconfigure to optimize its defensive-fire assets. "If this was poker, I'd say we've called their bluff."

Wethermere didn't respond.

"You don't agree?"

"I do, Admiral, but I suspect whoever is running the Baldy fleet now has more than just one trick in store for us. I think—" And, staring into the holotank, Wethermere fell silent.

Krishmahnta followed his gaze and saw what had stilled him: the tiny sparks denoting inbound enemy missiles began fragmenting into chips of light so small that they were almost invisible.

"Multiple warheads separating from their buses," explained Lubell. "Analyzing now..."

"Do all those warheads have lock on us?"

"Admiral, they—no, sir. None of them do. In fact, they are—"

The wave-front of actinic pinpricks suddenly vanished—and in its place, a mustard-colored blotch hung in the display.

Krishmahnta blinked. "Is that a holotank malfunction? Or is there really—?"

Wethermere nodded, looking through the reams of data streaming in midair before him. "It is just what it looks like, Admiral. A navigation hazard."

"But how—?"

"Each of those submunitions was a flechette warhead, sir. They've just turned the open space before us into a pea soup of BB-sized rubbish."

Krishmahnta looked at the plot and saw more mustard blotches hemming her task force in as others arose at various points within the Baldies' defensive hemisphere. "Best speed through that junk, La Mar?"

La Mar turned back from consulting with his helmsman. "Zero point five c, sir—assuming we divert all our defensive systems to navigational sweeping duties."

So, to get through that crap, we have to slow to a crawl, following a predictable course—and remain defenseless while doing so. Meaning that all their real missiles will shoot us to pieces, one by one, as surely and methodically as if they were plinking bottles off a fence.

La Mar's voice was tight. "Orders, Admiral?"

Krishmahnta pushed through a brief wall of mind-blanking panic to confront and solve a battlefield challenge that she had never read about or even imagined. "We form into two data-linked combat groups. The lead group conducts navigational clearance. The follow-up group extends its defensive fire envelope to protect the lead team." *Like providing sappers with cover fire as they advance across no-man's-land to carry through an assault—and probably every bit as costly.* "It's going to be expensive, and slow, but we'll—"

"Admiral," muttered Wethermere, "if I may."

"Please do, Mr. Wethermere—but quickly."

"Admiral. I recommend that each vessel continue to contribute to the general navigational clearance effort. And that we stop firing our missiles at the pillboxes."

"How does that help us?"

"Because instead of shooting our missiles at the enemy, we'll use them to blow a clear path through the junk instead." He evidently saw her startled expression. "Sir, when an antimatter warhead goes off, what is left in its blast radius?"

Krishmahnta smiled, understanding. "Nothing. Empty space."

"Exactly. So we'll use our missiles to dredge a path through the silt they've put in front of us."

"They will, of course, pound us with *their* missiles."

"Recommend we split our energy-torpedo batteries between defensive fire against those missiles and selective elimination of any force-beam buoys we detect. We'll still be taking damage—"

"—but we'll get through their junk a lot more rapidly."

"Yes, sir—and we'll achieve one more thing."

"What's that?"

"We'll give the Baldy admiral who surprised us a big surprise in return. And that just might push him into showing us whatever else is up his sleeve—before we bring the Fleet in."

Arduan SDH Shem'pter'ai, *Main Van, Consolidated Fleet of the* Anaht'doh Kainat, *BR-02 Warp Nexus*

Narrok saw it before his fleet second could send an update by *selnarm*. The humans' rate of advance—stalled for a minute or so—had resumed, almost regaining its former rate of advance, literally blasting open a tube-like passage through the flechette-cluttered space. And although the humans would take more losses—another of their supermonitors and two of their monitors had been vaporized in just the past five minutes—they would emerge from the far side of his defensive ring with an effective fighting force. There was no doubt that he could easily obliterate that force, but once committed to such a combat, he might find himself too heavily engaged to respond to the appearance of the Kasugawa generator in time or with enough force.

Crafty, these humans, he thought, *and terribly, terribly brave, to stare so determinedly at the onrushing black abyss of* xenzhet-narmat'ai *and yet not flinch aside. They can—and do—teach us much about courage. But today, I must make sure that their heroic sacrifices are all in vain.*

"Fleet Second."

"Yes, Admiral Narrok?"

"We cannot withhold our Eyes of Illudor any longer. Notify the ROV pilots to activate their *selnarm* links to the suicide drones in grid cells F 16 through K 14."

"Rate of attacks, sir?"

"Maximum. Constant. Engage."

RFNS Gallipoli, *Task Force Vishnu, Allied Fleet, BR-02 Warp Nexus*

One moment, Erica Krishmahnta was looking into a tacplot where her wagon train of green icons was making steady, if not swift, progress through the minefield which separated her from surly red swarms of waiting enemy blips—and the next moment, her task force was thronged, inundated by a sea of much smaller scarlet specks, closing in around the larger green icons of her task force like piranha going after steers crossing a ford.

"What the hell?" barked La Mar.

Lubell had the answer first. "Sirs—small vehicles, going active. Most of them are much smaller than mines. I make them out as . . . uh, orbital transfer gigs, remote tugs. Our sensors returned them as debris, but now they're—"

"Kamikazes," summarized Wethermere flatly. "Admiral, I suggest—"

But Krishmahnta was way ahead of him. "Fleet signal: one-half of all ET batteries are to shift to small-craft intercept." Krishmahnta turned to Wethermere. "You have something to add to that order, Commander?"

He smiled. "Not a thing, Admiral. Do you think we'll make it through in time?"

"I don't know, but I know we can't call for the Kasugawa generator—or bring in the Fleet—until we've cut a hole through the minefield and drawn more of their missile fire."

"I agree. Which is exactly what we're going to draw if they can't stop us with these—"

That was when the first kamikazes started to hit. Lubell read off the casualties as they mounted. "*Hastings* and *Fafnir* are Code Omega. *Harrier*, *Balaclava*, *Tyre*, *Kraken*, *Drake*, and *Tormentor* are all code yellow. Code Omegas were direct hits by kamikazes. The others impacted debris from proximal intercepts. Estimating over two hundred more—"

The deck pulled out from under Krishmahnta in a rush, and for a second she seemed to sleep; then she found herself surrounded by the swirling lights of the tacplot, into which she had fallen. She resisted the impulse to giggle; from here, she could swat all the red icons into oblivion, godlike—just like Vishnu. Except the angry, bloody gnats kept coming back. . . .

Then Wethermere and La Mar were helping her up, one hand from each lifting at both of her armpits. What nice strong men they were. . . .

"Admiral? Admiral?"

Wethermere had such a nice voice, too—soothing in a way; just the way an Old Soul should sound. . . .

"Admiral?" She felt a light tap on her cheek—

—and Erica Krishmahnta roused out of the mental fog with a spine-crackling jerk. "Sitrep," she ordered.

Wethermere and La Mar looked at each other, then back at her. "Admiral, are you quite all right?" The hand that La Mar raised to steady her was stained with blood.

She put a hand to her wet forehead—and found the source of the stain. "I'm fine," she said. And looking over at Wethermere, she grinned. "Do you think we have the Baldy admiral's attention now?"

"I don't know, sir—but he sure does have mine."

She laughed. In the middle of it all, she laughed. "Old Soul," she said fondly at Wethermere.

"Ma'am—uh, sir?"

"Nothing, Commander. Stand by for new orders. Captain La Mar, how's *Gallipoli*?"

"Holding up, sir. No need to transfer your lights to another hull."

"As if I could—or would. La Mar, keep us moving forward. Lubell, how are our data nets?"

"Witeski just brought them back online—but all this damage is breaking our links faster than we can repatch."

"Do the best you can. Now, Commander"—and she

turned to Wethermere, who, somehow, looked both concerned and a bit wistful—"I need you to get down to the auxiliary bridge."

"Sir? With all due respect—"

"At this moment, 'due respect' means you hear me out, mister. You get down to auxiliary, you get Zhou to join you from Engineering, and be ready to take over this hull at a moment's notice. Alert all the third-chair bridge-crew replacements and send them down to the emergency control center in Engineering. Tell Lieutenant Nduku to put that shop in order and have it ready as a third bridge. With these kamikazes, Commander, we are particularly vulnerable to targeted attacks—meaning they'll be aiming for our control centers. If they manage to hit us here on the main bridge, we have to have another nerve center ready and running. Now go—Old Soul."

Wethermere lifted an eyebrow, then saluted and jumped away from the con to get about carrying out his admiral's orders.

At that moment, an orbital debris sweeper that had been built seventy-one years before on Astria, and had been put to work (and, more recently, commandeered) in the Madras system, received the focused *selnarmic* pulse that activated it. Following the commands of its SDS-based operator, it swung toward the nearest enemy object and accelerated in that direction at twelve percent the speed of light. Pure chance put it in the wake of a larger kamikaze—a small robotic tug—that was headed for the same object.

When the tug was destroyed less than 50,000 kilometers away from the human craft, a modicum of luck favored the smaller kamikaze: it sped through the sparse remains of its larger cousin without incident. However, its own, smaller drive field was finally revealed, now that the larger one in front of it was gone.

One point three seconds later, the little kamikaze was finally detected and destroyed only three kilometers away from the human object it had targeted.

The RFNS *Gallipoli*.

As the lift to the main bridge opened, Ossian Wethermere was suddenly blasted forward and into the passenger car as if an immense hand had smacked him on the back. Within the space of a single second, he felt flame wash near him, heard the damage siren abruptly dueling with the explosive-decompression klaxon, felt his left leg—still outside the elevator car—spattered by hot debris.

And then—as suddenly as the chaos and destruction had swirled up behind him—it was over: fire-fighting gel frothed as it sprayed down, hull-breach foam burgeoned into a temporary seal, and the alarm and klaxon both went silent.

And in their place arose piteous moans.

Wethermere scrambled to his feet and jumped back onto the bridge.

Or rather, what was left of it.

Obviously, some distaff piece of a destroyed kamikaze had struck them: probably nothing larger than a pinhead—because anything that was much bigger or faster would probably have resulted in *Gallipoli*'s immediate and complete annihilation. But some fragment from a close intercept had probably burrowed into the three decks above them and sent a shock wave down far enough into the hull to reach—and rupture the bulkhead around—the bridge.

A cursory glance confirmed his hypothesis: the starboard-quarter ceiling plates were either half swallowed by the anti-breaching foam or as buckled as water-warped plywood. La Mar, who had been standing close to the rupture point, was in three separate pieces, along with the navigator. The sensor operator was still in her chair, but a split-second glance told Wethermere that she'd never leave it: a support strut had gone through the back of her seat, impaling and pinning her to the console that had been her daily duty station. Helm had already picked herself up, and Lubell was limping back to his station, dragging a useless left leg behind him. And Admiral Krishmahnta—

Wethermere scrambled over wreckage toward her bloodied, prostrate form—and discovered, against all odds, that she was still alive—probably due to La Mar's placement. As if by a miracle, the deck to either side, and both before and behind her, had been riddled by high-velocity debris. Relative to the breach point, she had been in La Mar's shadow—and it had saved her life.

But that life was rapidly ebbing out of her. Wethermere saw the steadily widening pool of blood spreading out from a ragged, deep wound that had cut through to her right femur, just above the knee. Her other injuries—penetrations in the left arm, cheek, and right shoulder—were not immediately life-threatening, but she would bleed out from the leg wound in less than a minute.

Wethermere barked an order at Lubell as he moved. "Get Zhou up here—now! Send Nduku to take his place on the auxiliary bridge. Helm, can we still fight this ship from here?"

"Aye, sir."

"Then get Witeski back up here, and replace the other casualties as well. And get a med team, on the double. The admiral is down."

Arduan SDH Shem'pter'ai, *Main Van, Consolidated Fleet of the* Anaht'doh Kainat, *BR-02 Warp Nexus*

Narrok studied the human ships closely and compared the patterns he saw to the data scrolling past. Yes, the Eyes of Illudor had inflicted many losses upon them, and yes, the enemy formation was no longer moving in perfect unison: in all likelihood, their deadly data-nets were down, meaning that they would no longer be able to coordinate their maddeningly effective energy-torpedo fire. But singly, and in pairs, many of the ships from the less damaged rear of the column were moving to take up the places—and tasks—of those in front of them, doggedly pushing through the minefield with a grim determination that could only be attributed to creatures that were wholly insensate—or arrestingly courageous. *Griarfeksh*, indeed.

Regardless of the source of their tenacity, however, if the humans were not stopped—and soon—they would ultimately breach his defensive envelope. And that could not be permitted. With a reluctance that bordered on strategic dread, Narrok sent to his XO: "Fleet signal to SDHs and SDSs: ready to salvo missiles on my command."

"We will cease to pre-target the warp point, Senior Admiral?"

"We have little choice, if these humans continue onward. Send the signal, Second."

RFNS Gallipoli, *Task Force Vishnu, Allied Fleet, BR-02 Warp Nexus*

Wethermere—using the strut he had been compelled to yank out of Sensor's body—turned the makeshift tourniquet tighter: the bleeding from Krishmahnta's left leg finally diminished to a slow leak. But the tourniquet was twisted so damned tight, that the Admiral's leg might—

The bridge lift opened and new crew poured out. Most scattered to their stations, several of them growing suddenly pale as they sat in pools of blood or brushed away singed bits of hair, bone, and organs. One—a whey-faced kid of maybe eighteen—lagged behind, looking around like a lost toddler in a supermarket. "Medic—for the admiral?"

The accent told Wethermere everything he needed to know: the kid was from the backcountry of Odysseus, one of the thousands of recruits pulled into service when Krishmahnta was compelled to militarize as much of the Cluster as she could. He'd have had—maybe—six weeks of training. "Over here," called Wethermere, trying to sound confident and calm all at once.

The kid approached and stopped two meters from the admiral's savaged body. "Gosh," he breathed. He did not resume moving. And his aid pack looked heavily depleted.

Great. "Corpsman, do you have any tourni-quiks left?"

"No, sir. I used my last ten minutes ago."

Damn. "Listen. The admiral is stable. But you're going

to have to use field expedients to get a real tourniquet on her. I don't know if this one will hold. Either way, you have to lash it down for high-gee maneuvers. Do you understand?"

"Uh . . . yeah."

"Corpsman—repeat back what I told you."

"I . . . uh, sorry. What did you say?"

Wethermere forced himself to be very patient. "The admiral needs a real tourniquet. Use the best materials you've got, and rig it for high-gee stresses. Now, what did I tell you?" *And meanwhile, ships and crews are dying while I try to get this poor frightened kid to help save the admiral.*

"Uh—put on a real tourniquet if I can. Rig the tourniquet for high-gee stresses."

"Right. When you're done, get the admiral into bridge escape pod 1A." When the kid started looking around wildly, Wethermere pointed it out. "It's right there. And before you seal her up, administer a mild, long-duration sedative. Got that?"

"Got it, Skipper."

Good grief, I'm "skipper" again? Please no—

But looking up and seeing himself ringed by urgent, waiting eyes, he knew the answer. As before, he was the right guy in the wrong place at the wrong time. He sank into was left of the XO's chair. "Sitrep?"

Lubell started speaking as Zhou emerged from the lift. "Commander, Task Force Vishnu's data links are all down. Commo is spotty. I can't raise Admiral Yoshikuni."

"Is that because of our equipment?"

"I don't think so, sir. Looks like her hull, *Jellicoe*, has been pretty roughed up. We're holding our own against the kamikazes. There seems to be a lull as they're bringing in more bandits from farther off in their defensive belt—but at the rate the task force is taking damage, we're not going to get through the minefield before they reduce us to scrap."

Wethermere looked at the flickering and blood-spattered tacplot: not much minefield left to cut through. And with a lull in the kamikaze attacks— "Ops!" he snapped.

"Sir!" Lubell sounded startled but somehow more confident. Indeed, the slumped postures on the bridge all straightened out admirably.

"Here's the plan. We're going to get through the minefield in about three more minutes."

"Sir?" Lubell—and the rest—gaped.

"Here's how. All energy-torpedo batteries are to join our missile tubes in blasting the rest of the way through the mines and the flechettes. I figure we've got about five minutes before the next wave of kamikazes gets to us. Commo, signal whoever you can raise that they are to join our effort. For any ships that aren't in the comm net, I need active sensors to pulse them the message in Morse code. Between that, and our example, we'll have to hope that the remaining hulls know to follow our lead. And let Guard Group Excalibur know that they are to expect our signal soon."

Lubell's voice was very quiet. "Commander, you know what's going to happen when we redirect our energy torpedoes away from defensive fire, don't you?"

Wethermere leaned back with a sigh. "Indeed I do, Mr. Lubell. Indeed I do."

As Commander Wethermere's voice faded into a staccato stream of unheard orders, Medic's Assistant Junior

Grade Rupe Colom saw that Admiral Krishmahnta was starting to stir: her face twisted in sudden, semiconscious agony. *Damn it. If she starts squirming, I'll never finish lashing down this new tourniquet.* So he reached into his kit and pulled out a pre-surgical autoinjector: not the mild sedative that the commander had wanted, but there just wasn't time—and Rupe needed the admiral unconscious fast.

The injector went in with a hiss, and in a moment the admiral's face relaxed.

At the same moment, the deck shook, and loose fixtures showered down on Rupe, one cracking him solidly in the head.

Disoriented, flushed with a suddenly resurgent fear of his own imminent death, the young quasi-medic checked on the admiral again: her respiration was good and the tourniquet was holding—and now that he was done, he could seal her up, get off the bridge, and get ready to abandon ship.

Once he had placed Krishmahnta in her escape pod, he hit its autopriming button: the pod's door swung back down with a sigh and sealed with a sound like a wet, pneumatic kiss. Rupe collected his gear and made for the lift.

And never realized that the falling debris had distracted him from completing his primary task: securing Admiral Erica Krishmahnta's new tourniquet against the high gee forces that would be imparted by the pod's escape charge.

Arduan SDH Shem'pter'ai, *Main Van, Consolidated Fleet of the* Anaht'doh Kainat, *BR-02 Warp Nexus*

Narrok stared at the holoplot in both wonder and dread. Once again, the human ships—sluggishly and scattered at first—had resumed their deadly passage through the minefield. And although their data links were clearly gone, the sheer volume of fire generated by their energy-torpedo batteries was both breaking through the minefield and vaporizing the floating drifts of flechettes.

"How can they do it, Senior Admiral? Surely they must know that they will all be—"

"They know, Fleet Second, they know. And they have forced us to commit our full force." And having sent that, Narrok wondered if, in another life, he might recall those words as the eulogy for millions of the Children of Illudor. Maybe for all of them—in which case, he would recall no eulogy, for his incarnations would be at an end.

Feeling a moment of utter, paralyzing fear at that concept—and reflecting, *this is what* they *feel, all the time*—Narrok mastered himself and gave the order he had wanted to avoid giving. "All SDHs and SDSs: salvo all missile tubes at the human column. Continue until they are all destroyed. And maneuver Reaction Group Zep'tef to confront any human ships that might survive long enough to break through the minefield."

RFNS Gallipoli, *Task Force Vishnu, Allied Fleet, BR-02 Warp Nexus*

"Commander Wethermere!"

"I see it, Lubell. I make that—over four hundred missiles inbound."

"Yes, sir—and I don't think the salvos are going to stop."

And once they've committed, why would they? Until we're monoatomic vapor, that is. Aloud: "Commo, send the signal to Guard Group Excalibur: *Pull the sword from the stone*. Keep repeating."

"Yes, sir."

"Sensors?"

"Yes, sir?"

"Time to enemy salvo impact?"

"Leading edge hits us in about ninety seconds."

"Lubell, time remaining before we get through the minefield?"

"Uh . . . ninety seconds. Give or take."

"Commo, signal this to all the ships you can reach. In eighty seconds, half of all energy-torpedo batteries are to shift back to defensive fire. And send this shipwide on *Gallipoli*. Nonessential crew are to report to evacuation pods in one minute."

"Yes, sir."

Back near the warp point to Polo, the four remaining supermonitors of Guard Group Excalibur received the message they had been waiting for: they immediately sent a flurry of recon drones plunging through the warp point.

A moment later, they began moving out into a rough defensive screen—and started coming under slowly growing fire from the laser and force-beam buoys. Missiles were inbound also—but only a fraction of the obliterating torrent that would have saturated the area had much of its force not already been directed against the crippled van of Task Force Vishnu.

TRNS Li Han, *Allied Fleet, Polo System*

"My God!" breathed Andreas Hagen as displays exploded into life with a flood of reports from Guard Group Excalibur's courier drones. "Almost fifty percent Code Omegas, and some degree of damage to all the survivors."

Ian Trevayne ordered himself to disregard those data for now. There would be plenty of time for horror later. At the moment, he must fixate on the one item that made the nightmare now transpiring in BR-02 worthwhile. Krishmahnta had given the go-ahead to send in the Kasugawa generator. That was what mattered. Now the sword would come from the stone.

"Task Group Pendragon will commence transit," he said in a harsh voice that brought Hagen out of shock.

The order was transmitted, and in the tactical holotank an array of green supermonitor icons began to vanish into the warp point. One of them—the shell with the pea under it—contained the generator.

RFNS Gallipoli, *Task Force Vishnu, Allied Fleet, BR-02 Warp Nexus*

Wethermere looked at the clock: impact in twenty seconds.

"Sir!" Lubell's shout was an exultation. "Sensors indicate that *Jellicoe* has cleared the minefield. Admiral Yoshikuni's done it! She's—"

He stopped. The *Jellicoe*'s icon—already yellow—began to flutter, and then became an Omega icon. The cause of its destruction loomed ahead of *Gallipoli*'s icon in the plot: at least thirty enemy SDHs were waiting at the end of the tunnel they were trying to exit.

"Escape pods from *Jellicoe*?" asked Wethermere.

"Can't tell at this range and through all the debris, sir. Our energy torpedoes are now shifting to defensive fire."

"Commo, send shipwide. All nonessential personnel into escape pods and abandon ship."

The hull shook: the first missile—and it had been way too close. *Gallipoli*'s icon was ready to exit the minefield:

the enemy SDHs—fresh, lethal—loomed large in the tacplot. No way out of the tube now—except through them. And the next wave of kamikazes was beginning to show up as tiny scarlet chips converging on what was left of the column from all points.

"Sir." It was Zhou.

"Yes?"

"It's looking pretty bad."

"It is indeed."

"So . . . what trick do we pull this time, sir?"

Wethermere shook his head. "No tricks left, Zhou. Now all we've got is guts." More shaking as missiles detonated—closer still. Wethermere stared hard at the holoplot and the thirty red icons in front of them.

Helm's voice quavered. "Course, sir?"

Ossian looked up at her. "Right down their throats."

Arduan SDH Shem'pter'ai, *Main Van, Consolidated Fleet of the* Anaht'doh Kainat, *BR-02 Warp Nexus*

Narrok saw the new wave of human supermonitors flooding through the warp point and retasked his immense missile assets to fire all tubes on that target. But even as the new, retargeted salvos streaked forward with their payloads of utter annihilation, his sensor prime uttered the words he had feared hearing for weeks. "Gravitic fluctuations near the warp point, Senior Admiral."

"Given the observed activation time of the Kasugawa generator, will our missiles get there first?"

"Yes, sir—but the new human SMTs and MTs have integrated into the datalinks of the ships that were already on this side of the warp point. I estimate it will take three salvos to bring them down."

"Because they are using the energy torpedoes in missile-intercept mode?"

"Yes, sir."

Of course. Each step the humans had taken was the one he would have pursued, in their place.

"Orders, sir?"

Narrok forced himself to stand very straight. "Fleet signal: general advance. We must bring everything that comes through the warp point under the full weight of our fire."

And as he sent it, the warp point's whirlpool of energy emissions pulsed, fluxed—and then expanded dramatically.

RFNS Gallipoli, *Task Force Vishnu, Allied Fleet, BR-02 Warp Nexus*

The *Gallipoli* groaned and shook—and the shaking did not entirely go away.

Zhou looked over at Wethermere urgently. "Tuners are destabilizing, sir. Too much peripheral damage."

Wethermere nodded to the entire bridge crew. "Thank you, everyone. Commo, all remaining crew to pods. Sound abandon ship. But Zhou, you stay with me for a second longer. I need you to automate *Gallipoli*'s battery activity."

"Easy." Zhou pressed three virtual buttons on his console. "Done. The old girl will now hammer away at fixed targets as long as she can." The bridge was now empty except for them. "Can we go?"

"No, there's one last thing to do. I need you to rig the computer in engineering to monitor our pod status."

"Okay." Zhou started working. "What do you want the engineering computer to do, exactly?"

"Once it sees that all pods are away, the computer is to wait until both the main bridge and auxiliary register as 'destroyed' or 'off-line.' When that condition is met, *Gallipoli's* engines are to boost to max"—Wethermere checked the distance and time to the center of the enemy SDHs—"and then, after thirty seconds, the computer is to lower the primary containment field in the main power plant."

Zhou stared at Wethermere for a second. "What is it with you and destroying your own ships?"

Wethermere jerked his chin in the direction of the tacplot. "Look at those SDHs in front of us, Zhou. They're a plug with which Baldy is trying to reseal his defensive wall. We've got to push that plug out—for just a few minutes—so that the main van of the Fleet can come in and bust the tube we made wide open."

"Okay, but I think that by charging forward like that, *Gallipoli* is only going to attract even more Baldy atten—"

"Zhou."

"Yeah?"

"Shut up and finish."

Zhou rose. "I'm done."

"Already?"

Zhou smiled. "I had half the programs written already. I'm starting to understand how you think."

"Then get to your escape pod."

"Well," observed Zhou as the little capsule's hatch hissed open, "this is just like déjà vu—all over again."

Wethermere watched Zhou dive into the pod and hoped that wouldn't be the last bad joke he ever heard from the stubby engineer. Wethermere leaped into his own pod—and as its straps grabbed and pinned him, *Gallipoli* gave a great wrench and started shuddering apart in time to the shrill screams of multi-layered armor being sheared into strips.

TRNS Li Han, *Allied Fleet, BR-02 Warp Nexus*

Ian Trevayne had sometimes quipped that ever since the Battle of Zapata, where his original body had been nearly destroyed, he had no particular fear of death, having already experienced Hell.

Now, emerging from the dredged warp point into BR-02 just in time to witness the catastrophic destruction of *Gallipoli,* he realized he still had a great deal left to learn about Hell.

He stared into the plot and, despite many long years of service, could scarcely credit what he saw as reality. Omega icons littered the plot like fallen autumn leaves, and their numbers continued to creep upward as Task Force Vishnu's van was ground to pieces within the breaching tube of clear space it had drilled through the Baldies' cloud of space junk. Most of the survivors were battered and torn in various degrees, staggering on like blood-dripping prizefighters who simply didn't know how to quit.

"Escape pods from *Gallipoli*?" he demanded harshly.

"Quite a few, sir," Hagen reported. "But no identification of individuals yet," he added, reading Trevayne's mind without difficulty.

"Of course not." Trevayne told himself that there was at least a chance that Erica Krishmahnta still lived, then filed that thought away and concentrated his entire being on fighting the battle she and the rest of Task Force Vishnu had, by appalling sacrifices, enabled him to fight.

"Admiral," he heard from the comm station, "we're being hailed by *Taconic.*"

Trevayne saw that the devastator—from which Mags was now flying her lights—had just made transit. Her face appeared on the comm screen. She said nothing about

Krishmahnta's fate, knowing he would be able to tell her nothing definite. She was merely awaiting orders, as their great ships' active and passive defenses shrugged off the missile-sleet that was now targeting them.

"We know what the basic condition of battle here is," Trevayne stated. "There's no local sun, hence no Desai limit. Which means that fighters—including those employing kamikaze tactics—are at a disadvantage vis-a-vis full-sized ships, which can use their Desai drives. Therefore, we're going to rely on that—and on our own fighters—and press forward to come to grips with the SDSs."

"Without spending any more time in their missile envelopes than necessary," Mags added. As though for emphasis, she steadied herself as the vibration of a near-miss shook even *Taconic*'s mighty frame.

"Right. The SMTs of Task Group Pendragon can use the same tactics Krishmahnta's people did—I've had time to scan the reports from the recon drones—and clear additional paths for us." He paused for a moment and looked at the face of the woman to whom he'd been joined for so short a time in a marriage which might well be dissolved in minutes by the death of one or both of them . . . and found himself unable to say anything except, "All elements of the Fleet will advance."

Arduan SDH Shem'pter'ai, *Main Van, Consolidated Fleet of the* Anaht'doh Kainat, *BR-02 Warp Nexus*

Narrok watched the holoplot carefully; several of the human DTs flickered and went dark, but most kept coming—and their missiles would be upon his forces in minutes. In addition, the new wave of supermonitors, evidently copying the strategy improvised by the first task force that had breached his defenses, were using their energy torpedoes to cut even more pathways through the defensive hemisphere. If the gargantuan human ships were able to exit his cauldron of concentrated fire too quickly...

"Fleet signal: all remaining Eyes of Illudor—activate for sustained wave attack plan Izref."

TRNS Li Han, *Allied Fleet, BR-02 Warp Nexus*

The locustlike swarms of kamikazes came on—now including actual fighters—as though actuated by a new will and armored in the Baldies' usual inexplicable indifference to individual survival.

But as Trevayne soon saw very clearly, their very single-mindedness gave his human and Orion pilots an advantage. As long as they were fixated on self-immolation, the Baldy fighters could not deal with the slashing attacks of pilots equally fixated on killing them: the Alliance fighters swept through the dense formations of their opponents, mowing them down in windrows.

Not even the Baldy fighter pilots could endure this: they could not complete their suicide attacks if their craft didn't live to reach their intended targets. So they turned aside to fight off their tormentors. And whatever it was that had granted them their newly enhanced capabilities allowed them to put up a better fight than they once would have.

But once they did, another problem presented itself....

Arduan SDH Shem'pter'ai, *Main Van, Consolidated Fleet of the* Anaht'doh Kainat, *BR-02 Warp Nexus*

Narrok watched the plot and saw the fighters—his and the humans'—wheel slowly: in this battle, fought at the speeds enabled by the Desai drives of the larger ships, the small attack craft were functioning almost like mobile minefields, more effective at denying areas than they were at delivering killing blows to enemy hulls.

At last his fighters had enough qualitative parity so that now, along with his advantage in numbers, he was able to contest the human flights for dominance. Of course, the price of doing so was reduced numbers still available for suicide attacks. And there was a new variable which further undermined his fighters' conventional combat improvements: the unceasing torrent of human energy torpedoes. Whenever Narrok's craft managed to wrest a positional advantage from the human fighters, they would retreat back behind the incandescent protective skirts of that inexhaustible base of fire—and shortly after reemerge, reformed and largely recovered.

"Sir, the humans have breached the defensive ring in sectors X 9 and W 13. Devastators in the lead, superdevastators right behind them."

So, containment had failed—despite the terrible losses the humans had suffered thus far. And now, Narrok knew, the tables were about to turn. "Signal Sarhan," he sent. "Tell my old friend to lead us in."

Narrok watched as Sarhan's command, the SDSs of the Fleet, began moving forward to commence their final death-duel with the leviathans of the human armada.

TRNS Li Han, *Allied Fleet, BR-02 Warp Nexus*

As the slaughter progressed, Ian Trevayne could be little better than a spectator. His task-force vice-admirals, his squadron leaders, his ship captains all knew what they had to do. It had all been discussed before, and reduced to tactical doctrine and training routine. His work was done.

"Ironic, isn't it, sir?"

Trevayne shot a sharp glance at Andreas Hagen. "Would you care to explain that remark, Commander?"

"I think you know what I mean, sir. You know why you're here. When you were, so to speak, restored to life at a time when the Rim Federation faced a new threat, it tapped into some very deep mythic roots."

"Yes. Madam Chief Justice Ortega said something of the sort to me," said Trevayne, his eyes focused on something far away and long ago.

"Well, sir, you've done it—you've emerged from the magic mountain, or the Isle of Avalon, when your people needed you. And now—"

"And now the very code names we've assigned to this operation seem to underscore that, don't they?" Trevayne finished for him. "'Excalibur,' indeed! Well, Admiral Krishmahnta has enabled me to draw the sword from the stone." He closed his eyes at the unwelcome recollection and sternly reminded himself that there was still no word as to Krishmahnta's fate, which left room for hope. "But now that I've drawn it—"

"Other hands have to wield it." Hagen stopped, swallowed, resumed. "Sir, it is a privilege given to very few men to be part—however menial—of a legend."

Li Han shuddered from a near miss. They both grabbed stanchions. Trevayne stared at Hagen. "It is given to all too many men to die today, Commander. If that should befall us, I want you to know that the privilege has been mine."

Then he could only watch, sending out occasional general grand-tactical directives, while with mind-shattering, space-wrenching discharges of elemental energies of destruction his devastators and superdevastators did what they had been created to do.

The Brobdingnagian system-defense ships did not die easily. But die they did.

Arduan SDH Shem'pter'ai, *Main Van, Consolidated Fleet of the* Anaht'doh Kainat, *BR-02 Warp Nexus*

The fleet second's *selnarm* was riddled by (disbelief, shock, horror). "Senior Admiral, the system-defense ships—the last of them is gone, sir. And Admiral Sarhan is—"

"Thank you, Second. I felt his *selnarm* terminate a few seconds ago."

"What do we do now, Admiral?"

Narrok looked at the plot. He had lost the battle. The question was, how much more of his force should he spend before he conceded the field? He still had seventy percent of his SDHs left, and they represented a credible threat to the humans. He had preserved his mobile assets not merely by choice, but because he could protect them, whereas the SDSs could not flee, and thus their fates were tied to the system's. The humans would still take damage from the remaining small forts and mines—and would take more if he kept his SDHs at the very edge of extreme range, harrying them. Naturally, the humans would then temporarily weaken their forces arrayed against the small forts in order to chase his SDHs out of the system. During which interval, the small forts would not be so outnumbered and could inflict greater damage on anything that came into range—which, given their proximity to the warp point, meant just about all the inbound human traffic. It was a small victory—to help the pseudo-forts sell themselves more dearly—but at least it wasn't very expensive, either.

Narrok sat in his pod and sent the order that meant eventual retreat. "All SDHs fall back on our lead. We will harry the enemy for as long as we can."

TRNS Li Han, *Allied Fleet, BR-02 Warp Nexus*

Li-Trevayne Magda's shuttle had barely docked in *Li Han*'s boat bay before she hurried off to the flag bridge, moving through a scene of regimented damage-control chaos.

She found Ian Trevayne in consultation with staffers. Seeing her, they hurriedly concluded their business and went away. When he turned to meet her eyes, he looked every hour of his actual age.

"Eighty percent of Task Force Vishnu Code Omega," he began without preamble. "*Eighty percent.* And all the survivors are almost too badly damaged to tell the difference. And . . . Admiral Krishmahnta didn't make it. At least Admiral Yoshikuni survived." A fleeting smile. "So did Wethermere."

It was like a blow to the forehead for Mags. "I'd heard that Admiral Krishmahnta was badly wounded but got off *Gallipoli* in time."

"She did. But it seems she had a tourniquet that couldn't endure the gee-forces of the escape pod. So she died of good old low-technology exsanguination." Trevayne paused, seemed to search for words. "I didn't have the chance to know her for very long," he finished simply.

"No. Neither did I. I wish I had." Mags's lips quirked upward as far as exhaustion and grief would permit. "After all, she was a fellow member in good standing of the 'monstrous regiment of women.'"

"So she was." Trevayne gave a momentary grimace, as though in pain, then lowered his head and spoke in a voice that could barely be heard. "I will have my little quotes, won't I?"

She laid a gentle hand on his arm. "If you didn't, you wouldn't be you."

Through the contact of her hand, strength seemed to flow into him—enough strength to raise his head and speak in his customary tone of brisk authority. "The toll of ships actually destroyed is bad enough, but they're almost all SMTs and smaller. What's actually more serious is the number of DTs and even SDTs that have taken damage too severe for routine damage control to cope with it. We both wanted so badly to follow this victory up without delay. But we can't risk it. We have to bring ourselves back up to strength in the heaviest ship classes—the ones that do the business."

"That's what Erica Krishmahnta would have wanted," she agreed "A job done right."

"And that's just what we owe her." Trevayne looked at the omega icons littering his holotank. "And to ensure that the next offensive is the last."

38

Striking True

Power is not revealed by striking
hard or often, but by striking true.
—Balzac

Icarus Continent, Bellerophon/New Ardu

As Iakkut's Security sled lifted from one of Punt airfield's thirty landing pads, he gazed briefly out the cockpit window. Beyond the nose-racks—which were, like the rest of the vehicle, bristling with conventional munitions—he saw the bodies of those brothers and sisters who had not elected to join him and the rest of the Martyrs' Movement in this strike against the human Resistance bases. The tragedy was that they had not been race-traitors: he could feel the sympathy in them, but greater than that had been their misguided sense of duty, of obedience to the Council. Unfortunately, there had been no time for a debate: Iakkut hoped they would reincarnate soon, and into a world purified of the trouble and stench of *griarfeksh*.

Iakkut's vehicle followed the last of Punt's ready Security sleds and half of its more heavily armed Enforcer models, quickly joining the rest of the flight. From that vantage point, he could see the human regions around

Punt—and the five-hundred-meter security margin that had been cleared by the Security forces. It encircled the Arduan precincts like a belt of devastation, sweeping in a long semicircle from the abandoned marinas of the *griarfeksh* North Shore District, then paralleling Punt's western extents, and ultimately curling slowly back to connect to the much-scarred Empty Zone between the occupied West Shore and Heliobarbus districts. The security margin had originally been a filthy *ranarmata* warren of buildings and businesses that the *griarfeksh* labeled "suburbia." It was now a dead, flat expanse—buildings razed, obstructions leveled—that mutely declared itself a killing ground separating the Children of Illudor from any would-be *griarfeksh* attackers.

Scattered along the edges of this zone was the haphazard and haggard caravansary that had arisen to serve the needs of the native towns ever since the Council had finally seen sense and restricted the *griarfeksh* power-plant operations. No longer able to maintain delivery schedules to their gargantuan multipurpose stores, the *griarfeksh* transport companies had resorted to using the meager output of the reduced power grid to provide energy for only a few score of their largest vehicles. Fully laden, these wheeled argosies then ponderously circulated between the various human communities. At each, they unloaded their diverse cargoes into an immense market that tarried for a week or two, then repacked and moved on.

In Melantho, they usually chose to tarry in the Southern Extents, just below the Heliobarbus District, but a week ago the grimy vehicles and their even grimier wares had debouched in a long arc that followed the northern half of the security zone. The diminished population of the further western suburbs had treated the rough market crescent like a grand promenade, spending their days strolling along the improvised boulevard of tables and truck beds. Iakkut repressed a shudder at the thought of all the milling humans: unwashed, coarse-furred, jabbering, and bickering.

Not that it mattered anymore, he consoled himself with a sudden inward pulse of (satisfaction), because after today, there would be no more human markets, or caravans, or gatherings.

And soon enough, he thought as the outline of Melantho dropped out of sight through the clouds, *there will be no more humans at all.*

Alessandro McGee watched the last Baldy sled rise up, bulging and bloated with external ordnance, and followed it with his eyes until it had disappeared up through the low-lying clouds. On the far horizon, the upper rim of Bellerophon's yellow star had just started sending rays of yellow light across Salamisene Bay like wave-dappling spear-shafts, which were apparently routing the clouds away before them.

Danilenko looked skyward and cleared his throat. "You think we are safe now, Sandro?"

"It's not us I'm worried about."

"*Shto?* Who then?"

The other members of McGee's assault team—already wearing their sensor-grid undersuits—stopped to listen.

"I'm worried about our bases. That last flight of sleds was so overloaded with ordnance that they can't be going too far. Probably no farther than our main base in the Aeolian Lowlands."

Harry looked off to the west, behind them. "And so you think that smaller flight that took off two hours ago—"

"Is headed for the regional HQ in the Charybdis Islands."

Kapinski looked at Jen and seemed to grow anxious. "Maybe we should break radio silence, warn them..."

McGee shook his head—and knew full well that the firm "no" was directed as much at himself as at Kapinski. In preparation for the attack, he, Jen, and Zander had relocated to the main base in Icarus's Aeolian Lowlands. Zander was still there—meaning his safety was now dependent upon Heide. McGee wanted to vomit but resolved not to show his anxiety. If Jen learned that the outgoing Baldy air assets were speeding to put Zander's playpen at the center of their intended ground zero...

Jonathan leaned forward, kept his voice low. "Are there any landlines left, or wireless?"

McGee shook his head again. "The Baldies terminated all of those services—even here in the cities. We've got no way to warn our people."

Danilenko frowned. "You are not calling off the attack, are you?"

McGee looked between the torsos of his gathered NCOs: just beyond them, Haika was helping Jen into a sensor-grid undersuit that was too big by half. "No," McGee declared. "We don't even have a choice now. There might not be any bases left to return to. So we have to drive the spearhead of this attack home and make it stick."

Jon Wismer nodded. "Final orders?"

McGee lifted himself up by one of the many straps securing half of a modular house to its precarious perch atop a flatbed truck. Shielding his eyes with his hand, he scanned the long curve of caravan trucks and abandoned houses that lined the outer edge of the Baldy kill zone. Once home to a bustling commuter nexus, the population of the remaining suburban sprawl had diminished almost as much as Melantho's own, due to the sharply diminished influx of staples.

Consequently, there hadn't been many inhabitants left in the suburbs before this very special caravan had arrived eight days ago. Which meant that despite a startling paucity of goods for a market so large, there had nonetheless had been enough genuine goods to go around—until yesterday, when the legitimate caravan organizers left their vehicles and wares behind, convincing as many of the local residents as they could to come along with them. Where are you bound? the residents had asked. Anywhere but here, was the answer. Most understood that it was time to go. Far away.

But as the organizers made their way to the hills in the west, the many manual laborers who had arrived with this peculiarly overstaffed caravan remained behind. And once their lookouts told them that they were unobserved, these remaining workers began unstacking the heavy, unmarked crates that had been stored far in the back of the trucks. Always under cover, several battalions of weapon-calloused hands began opening those containers, which disgorged military gear of divers types and vintages.

That had been yesterday. Now, as McGee scanned it with binoculars, this outer rim of the Baldy security zone—cluttered with trailers and trucks and abandoned houses and all the detritus of the caravan—was quiet, like the in-facing blade of a scythe held poised and still.

And then, high overhead, a muffled boom. And then another—and then a tremolo of them. McGee's Marines glanced upward: only Jen craned her neck to search for the source of the sonic booms. A futile task.

McGee looked around his command staff. "That's it,

then. They're calling down fast movers—transatmospheric craft—from orbit. And they're not inbound toward us. Meaning they're part of the strike bound for our bases."

Matto Maotulu shrugged. "Could be worse, El-Tee. With all that heat going elsewhere, we stand a much better chance here."

McGee nodded, deciding not to point out that better for them meant worse for everyone back at the bases. Probably much, much worse. "Let's move to final positions. Kapinski, Kelakos, put out our yellow pennant and then motor on down to Cap's CP. You're with him for the main assault. Igor, keep a watch with the binoculars. Let me know when all other CPs are showing their colors in response to ours. Jon, I need a final check on the fixed Baldy weapon sites. Look for anything that suggests they might have altered their traverse arcs." They nodded and went to perform their duties.

McGee nodded to the rank and files of his fast assault section, who started undraping the armored carapaces that they would soon be wearing. Harry turned to start overseeing their suit-up process, but McGee put his hand on Light Horse Li's shoulder. "Harold."

Li started at McGee's tone and use of his given name. "What is it, Tank?"

McGee looked back at Jen, who saw him, smiled fearfully, and gave a brave but wilted thumb's up. McGee returned the smile with one of sunny confidence and mimicked her gesture. Then he turned to Li. "I've trusted you with my life, Harry. But now I have to trust you with something really important. Stick with Jen. No matter what."

"Tank, won't she listen to reason? Does she really have to come on this—?"

"Harry, shut up. And the answers are 'No, she won't

listen to reason' and 'Yes, she does have to come on the assault.' And I don't have time for debates. Just tell me—will you stick with her, no matter what?"

Harry looked down and muttered. "Shit, Tank, you know I will."

McGee patted Li on the shoulder and hoped his small friend would still be alive in thirty minutes.

And then he silently beseeched a god he did not particularly believe in to preserve his son's life as well.

Distracted, Lentsul did not detect the *selnarmic* page at first. When he recognized Mretlak's *selnarm*, he responded, unsheathing his own as he rose to his feet.

Mretlak did not engage in his customary welcoming prattle—which would have been oddly welcome this day. "Lentsul, we have a crisis."

Lentsul's mind sharpened, as much because of the dread he felt in Mretlak's *selnarm* as the words that arrived through it. "What has happened?"

Mretlak communicated in the bulleted form that was the best high-speed transmission mode of *selnarm*. "Nuclear munitions commandeered from orbital reserve bunkers. Transatmospheric attack craft hijacked, now planet-bound. Tomorrow's Security readiness training exercises for Punt were rescheduled for predawn, today. Munitions load-outs on those air assets were in excess of operating standards. No authorization sought or given for any of these actions. Command overrides sabotaged for all deployed craft and munitions. No replies to attempted *selnarm* and radio contact. All known *Destoshaz'ai*-as-*sulhaji* leaders missing. Dozens of Security and Enforcer personnel found discarnated by weapon fire at the site of each violation."

Lentsul sent (consternation). "Not a coup—"

"No. They are heading toward the coordinates of the Resistance bases."

Lentsul saw it now. Iakkut and his Martyrs' Movement had learned of the plan to protect the humans and were inverting it. In using nuclear weapons against these sites—and their proximal civilian populations—the *Destoshaz* radicals had every reason to suspect that they could trigger an all-out and irremediable war of mutual genocide. Although the byproduct of a monstrous brutality, it was a perversely elegant stratagem.

"Lentsul, I will work to restore our override systems and our internal *selnarm* relays so we can identify, organize, and deploy the Enforcers and those few Security personnel who remain loyal. I am no longer in my quarters but am traveling with twenty of our combat specialists as a mobile headquarters. We are carrying a portable *selnarm* relay pack and will keep moving. I have also summoned the Council to gather in auxiliary meeting chamber E. You are to collect as many military-intelligence section combat effectives as you can within the next five minutes and then move to rendezvous with the Council. You are to protect them until you hear otherwise from me. Trust no units unless I have cleared them."

"It shall be as you instruct, Mretlak."

"A final word of caution, Lentsul. I still have no leads on how the Martyrs' Movement learned of our plan to protect the Resistance, much less the location of their bases. So I am concerned that some of our own people may be cooperating with the radicals. I just wish I knew—"

"Overseer, I think you may consider that mystery solved."

"What? Why?"

"Because," sent Lentsul, looking down, "when I

came in early today, I found Emz'hem already here. In our office."

"Emz'hem? What was she doing? Relaying classified information to the radicals?"

"No, Overseer. She was dead." At his feet, Emz'hem lay in a limp, compactly coiled position, all three eyes open and staring, her neck riven by the distinctive three-talon slash of an expert *skeerba* blow.

"And you think . . . ?"

"I think that she was the leak. And I conjecture that her contact within the Martyr's Movement decided to silence her. I suspect that her conscience made her arrive early today, possibly to confess her actions to us. If her movements were actively monitored by the radicals, then, arriving here on this day—before dawn—also probably sealed her fate."

Mretlak's *selnarm* seemed frozen for a moment before he sent. "My regrets. I know you and she worked closely."

"We did." *Not closely enough for her, however—which may have played a role in this, somehow. She was a fragile creature, particularly for a* Destoshaz.

"I promise you, Lentsul, we shall find who did this to her, and he shall face the stern wisdom of the Council."

To which Lentsul replied, "Thank you, Overseer." But, withheld from his *selnarm*, Lentsul thought: *I already know who is responsible for this. And it is not he who wielded the* skeerba*. Because a year ago,* none *of us were capable of this deed. Killing, yes, but not this skulking, dishonorable assassination. No, the culprit in the murder of Emz'hem is essentially the same one responsible for the death of Heshfet, my entrancing Heshfet.*

Humans. They have all but destroyed us. So the sooner we destroy them, the better.

✧ ✧ ✧

"*Destoshaz'at?*"

Iakkut made a gesture of permission with the least tentacle of his left cluster. "Inform me."

"All transatmospheric attack craft confirm rendezvous ETA, and full function of all nuclear warheads and short-range launch buses."

"Acknowledge receipt of their status. Transmit final launch protocols in the event that forward control and target designation is eliminated."

"Sending." A pause. "Overseer Iakkut, do you actually believe the *griarfeksh* could eliminate us? They do not seem to have any weapons capable of intercepting our attack sleds."

"Communications Prime, just because we have never *seen* the *griarfeksh* use such weapons does not conclusively prove that they do not have such weapons. However"—and Iakkut added a satisfied tinge of (contempt)—"I remain unworried. Profoundly unworried."

"Captain Heide?"

Heide stabbed peevishly at the receiver. "Yes, Montaño? What is it now?"

"Sir—they're coming. The Baldies."

"Coming? From where? How many?"

"From Melantho and low orbit. Sleds and fast attack craft. Numbers unclear—but lots."

"Montaño, has there been any signal from Peters or any of the attack force's cadre?"

"No, sir. And no heliograph relay from the Melantho Baldy-watchers. Sir, I think the timing—their attack coming the same day as ours—must be a fluke."

"So it seems, but let's not assume anything, Montaño.

Maintain a close watch on all frequencies for any squelch signals. Our attack force may be getting jammed. Either way, it seems that we are going to have visitors." And suddenly, Heide found a surprising sense of relief wash through him like a purgative. He had lived through weeks of annoyed ambivalence. He had been grateful to be deemed "too essential" to lead the assault on Punt, yet also chagrined at his universally recognized superfluity. But now, despite his best, deeply concealed, and self-denied efforts to avoid war, it had come seeking him. Now there was only one course of action, and—deprived of any chance of fleeing it—Heide felt strangely unburdened. "Mr. Montaño."

"Sir?"

"Orders. Contact Ensign Cheung. She is to oversee the emergency evacuation of the main base. She is to direct all personnel not tasked for intercept response protocol Bravo to safety using the secret tunnel that follows along our underground river."

"Yes, sir, the old corporate smuggling tube. Cheung is already on her way there."

"Good. Tell her I am making her personally responsible for the safety of Alexander Peitchkov-McGee. She is to report her progress to us regularly. Next, relay a similar evacuation order to the regional base in the Charybdis Islands. However, they are to abandon the base without—I repeat *without*—any attempt at intercept. Lastly, you, Mr. Montaño, are to relocate posthaste to our off-site auxiliary ops. Remain online there as long as you can, maintaining communications between all our elements to the best of your ability."

"Yes, sir. But what about you? Where will you be?"

Heide had already risen and was strapping on his

completely pointless sidearm. "I'm going topside, Ensign. To direct our intercept of the Arduan attack. I will buy the base as much time as I can. And Ensign, you are to order one modification to intercept protocol Bravo."

"Yes, sir?"

"Our defense batteries are not to reserve any primary munitions for a second engagement."

"Sir—are you ordering me to fire off *all* our Hyper Velocity Missiles?"

"Yes, Ensign. Given the composition of the Arduan attack force heading at us, I suspect we're only going to get one chance to use our HVMs—so we had best use them all now."

Alessandro McGee scanned the human edge of the Baldy security zone for the yellow or purple streamers—or tents or pennants or awnings—that would serve as a company's or a battalion's all-ready sign. As he watched, the final signal—a faded gold tarp—was unfurled from the side of a truck as an ostensible sunscreen. "We're good to go all along the line," McGee called out. "How are you doing, Haika?"

The short, powerful woman looked up at him as she banged her considerable fists at either side of a Marine's breastplate. "Finishing the last checks on the powered armor now, El-Tee. Seals are tight, servos are good."

McGee nodded at her and the dozen Marines standing like Impressionist granite statues in their combat armor, then shouted into the window of the half-house perched on the flatbed trailer next to his overwatch perch. "Matto, how's the PDF system on B mount?"

Matto's velvety bass came rumbling back in answer. "Tank, the targeting arrays are just not hitting spec.

They took too much wear and tear when the mount was used for training, and the civvie electronics we used to refurbish it can't keep up with the rest of the system."

"How badly degraded is it?"

"Twenty percent off clock-time, maybe thirty. Won't know 'til we're running hot."

Tank nodded. "Then we have to run with A mount in the lead."

Danilenko jerked upright from where he was hand-checking a small rocket-propelled grenade. "Sandro—Lieutenant—this choice is not wise. Miss Peitchkov must be in the second vehicle, where she will be most prot—"

"Igor, I appreciate your concern, but I'm way ahead of you. If we put B mount in the lead, that carrier and all its troops are as good as dead. We need the lead vehicle up to spec so it can burn a clear cone through their anti-armor missiles. That means A mount has got to take the lead. Besides, we can't risk Jen in any mount with a slow point-defense fire system, because even if it's following on the flank, it will still be the more vulnerable vehicle of the two. So, whether I like it or not, she's in the lead with me—in A mount."

Jen's teeth chattered as she averred, "Which is where I should be." She didn't look much braver than she sounded—or McGee himself felt.

However, McGee mustered a reassuring smile even as he wondered when he had become such a good actor. He hopped down to slip into his own armor under cover—just in case Baldy satellites were tasked to conduct full-time look-down surveillance of the perimeter around Punt. As he wriggled into the stiff suit, he called the others to him. "Okay, listen up. Last review. We go in hot, dismount, leave the driver plus one with the troop carriers to provide a base of fire and act as a beacon for the main attack force. We follow our Baldy specialist"—he rubbed the immense, smooth pauldron perched atop Jen's narrow right shoulder—"wherever she leads us. We've got no maps, so stay alert and be prepared to improvise. As soon as we're inside, you activate your UV dye dispensers. That's how the follow-up assault will find our trail and follow us in."

"Lieutenant," asked Ramirez, who was a last-minute replacement, "why not just radio back the coordinates as we go?"

"Good question, Ben. Sorry we didn't cover that for you. Without maps, coordinates aren't going to help much inside a city. Second—and probably more important—we can't count on our radios working more than thirty seconds after we turn them on. We may have milspec transceivers and scramblers in these suits, but Baldy will be all around us, with big fixed ground stations and honest-to-god specialists manning them. I expect we'll lose the EW battle in one minute or less, so we don't go active until we are at target." McGee looked around the group. "Which is why we can't assume that any com-links are going to work. No biomed updates, no telemetry, no personal transponders. Which, in turn, is why we can't start relying on our HUD displays for squad-position data. We could find ourselves relying on info that we could lose at any second. So we do this old school—hand signals, verbal commands, and your best sensor is the Mark I eyeball."

Roon Kelakos's comment was more grumble than words. "At least with our hardened goggles, we can see in the dark if they turn the lights off."

"Maybe, Roon—but maybe not."

"Whaddya mean?"

"I mean if things get bad, they may call in EMP strikes on us—and then we might lose all our electronics, night-vision goggles along with the rest. And that includes any of our weapons that require juice."

Battisti clucked his tongue once. "Ah, so that is why no plasma guns, and only a few of the coil guns."

"Right. Baldy can't turn off chemical propellants. So that's why you're almost all carrying the old-fashioned cannons"—he nodded to their almost uniform armament: 10 mm magnum caseless assault guns with Serrie Sights and an underslung grenade launcher—"with a triple load of ammo, hand grenades, and not much else. Those ten-millimeter rounds go straight through Baldy drones and blisters, and you won't even feel the recoil inside your armor, so you can shoot on the run. And speed is going to be our watchword, Marines."

Wismer hefted his coil gun, the flexible ammo cassette bunching slightly. "So if Baldy hits us with EMP, I use this as a club?"

Jen held up a pair of very short, caseless carbines. "No, you come get a working gun from me, Jon. But Tank, what about our suits?" She moved her arm—which made a faint whirring noise. "If the EMP knocks out *all* electronics . . ."

McGee smiled at her, glad to see that her nerves didn't keep her from thinking straight. "The suit works like a big Faraday cage for everything inside it—which is already triple-hardened. Don't worry, Jen. As they tell us in Basic: 'Even if the enemy uses nukes, your suit will still work when everything else is dead.'" He left off the end of the training axiom: "—including *you*." Instead, he offered what reassurance he could. "With any luck, Baldy won't EMP us. Their equipment doesn't show much evidence of being hardened against a big pulse. But then again, there's a lot about their military circuitry and control mechanisms we don't understand because of their machine-mind interfaces. So it's all guesswork, at this point. Any questions?"

The twenty-three Marines—and Jen—were silent. "Okay, then, strike teams into the mounts. Outriders, strap on. It's time to start the party."

As the Marines disappeared up into the two half-houses sitting on trailers with flat tires, Sandro stretched out one arm, holding aloft a second yellow pennant to flutter alongside the first. He held them both there for fifteen seconds, then lowered the one he was holding and pulled down the first.

Before he had hopped down from his covered watch-post, a swelling, ragged susurration arose from about a kilometer behind the edge of the Baldy no-man's-land: more precisely, it was a sustained rumble of dull, fast-paced coughs, and a constant sputtering of rushing skyward whispers. The sounds—generated by hopper-fed mortars and 78 mm vertical disposatube rockets, respectively—continued to grow as their first salvos began raining down toward Punt.

The Baldy positions seemed stunned for a moment, then responded. The distant sparkling crackles of their PDF lasers began a split second before dozens, and then hundreds, of the human munitions began exploding in mid-air, filling the sky above the no-man's-land with smoke and thunder. Enforcer sleds—far fewer than originally anticipated—began rising up from Punt's airfield and spaceport, swiveling defense blisters and turrets in the direction of the human attackers.

As they rose up, the shattered edge of human suburbia seemed to discharge a veritable wall of volleyed fire, much as had the serried ranks of Napoleonic infantry. But instead of a fusillade of muskets, this was a horizontal torrent of anti-armor rockets with self-seeking warheads. The Baldy sleds tried to evade and destroyed dozens of the inbound missiles with their own PDF systems—but dozens more of the weapons got through. White and orange flashes denoted stricken sleds, some exploding to fragments in mid-air.

The perimeter PDF systems of the Baldies shifted, reallocating some of Punt's overall intercept capability to cover the remaining sleds' attempts to withdraw back under the defensive berm that ringed their hangars and landing pads. But as soon as the Arduan PDF systems shifted their efforts, a second barrage of "fire-and-forget" rockets rushed outward—this time, directly toward the PDF emplacements themselves.

Those Baldy defense systems tried to retask to handle the new threat—and did, partially. But many of the Baldy weapon emplacements were overtaxed, or caught in that instant when they were changing from one set of targets to another—and jets of dirt and flame marked their destruction.

At the same moment, rocket salvos leaped out from the edge of Punt's defenses, and deeper in the city as well, unerringly targeted at the human launch sites. Which, if the Marine-led Resistance was doing their job, had nothing left in them but now-emptied control-by-wire launchers, their human operators located at quiet points along the line, or in second- and third-story observation points well back from it.

As the bow-wave of the murderous Baldy salvo began

savaging the edge of the no-man's-land perimeter, a last flurry of human rockets jetted from those launch sites—and only covered half the distance to the city before they vaporized themselves in a brief, actinic flare. At that exact instant, the running lights on the house-trailer winked out.

"Our EMP strike went in," Tank called down to his assault team.

"Yeah, but did it work on the Baldies?" Harry Li's question was borne up toward him on a chorus of guttural, curious mutters.

"Well," McGee shouted down to his Marines as a dust cloud—kicked up by human vehicles—began rising from the southernmost edges of the no-man's-land, "we'll be the first to know."

As the rumble of Arduan rockets rose up, and half the lights in Punt went out, Ankaht felt Mretlak's *sel-narm* spike abruptly into her own. "Elder, the human attack is in earnest."

The sturdy deorbited bulkhead that was the outer wall of Punt City quivered as she sent (worry) but with a (wry) twist. "This I have surmised, Overseer."

"Then you are to immediately evacuate to Safe Point Three."

"Farther north into the center of Punt? But why—?"

"Elder, I only have time for the briefest update. Human vehicles have been sighted heading toward your old facility in the West Shore District, beyond our primary walls. Perhaps they still expect to find you there, and eliminate you."

"That makes little sense."

"I agree. The other reason they may choose that as

the starting point for the attack is because they are familiar with the area's layout. They may believe they can exploit their native knowledge of the district to their advantage a second time."

Ankaht doubted that, too, but continued to attend to Mretlak's report. "At any rate, they launched an EMP assault against the city."

"But I thought they had no such—"

"Evidently, our estimates regarding the weapons available to the humans were in serious error."

"How propitious. We choose to employ doomsday devices on each other on precisely the same day."

"I doubt it is luck, Elder. I suspect the timing of the radicals' move was determined by our own timetable for isolating and then protecting the Resistance. At any rate, the human EMP attack has had only a moderate impact upon us. Our reinforced systems were undamaged. However, secondary and retrofitted systems may have been compromised."

"Such as the doors that were added planetside," amended Ankaht as she unsuccessfully ordered one of the lighter, nonbulkhead portals in her meeting room to open.

"Yes, such as new doors and lights and other fixtures that were added after we deorbited Punt. Perhaps this is another reason their main attack seems to be focused on West Shore. All the electronics there did overload and no longer function."

Ankaht still found the focus on the human-built southern extents of Punt suspicious. "How many troops do the humans seem to be advancing toward the West Shore District?"

"Impossible to say yet, Elder. Although we have taken—and continue to take—losses to our overburdened defensive systems, we remain prepared to intercept any human movement across our security zone—particularly in the south."

"And have they made no attacks elsewhere—not even feints or probes?"

She could feel Mretlak pause. Since the normal Security leadership had deserted to join the strike against the Resistance bases, this was probably the first time he had stopped to consider the human attack from a broader perspective. "Yes, Elder, it is most curious that the humans have not also—"

But then Temret was tugging urgently—physically—at her. "Revered Sleeper, we must go. Our route to Safe Point Three is now twice as long. The missile and EMP damage has blocked our primary pathways. We must improvise—and therefore, must start now."

"Understood. Mretlak, I—"

"Go. I perceive—and concur with—your suspicions regarding the pattern of the human attacks. Now relocate yourself quickly."

McGee watched ten seconds count down on his mechanical watch and looked up.

As he did, a growl of additional motors drowned out the almost-stilled sputter and crump of human rockets and mortars. That growl crescendoed and then broke free of the long, smoke-lined periphery of the no-man's-land in the shape of dozens—no, hundreds—of wheeled cars, rovers, ATVs, and utility trucks. They arrowed straight toward the walls of Punt. Mixed in with them were skimmers and sleds and grav cargo lifters and every species of airborne vehicle that the Arduans had forbidden from the very first days of their occupation.

Again, the Baldy defensive fire lagged for a moment or three before engaging—and devastating—this motley armada of vehicles. Easily targeted, each one was smashed or knocked down by Baldy missiles. They crashed, rolled, tumbled, and in so doing came apart spectacularly—and with suspicious ease, littering and making irregular the once-smooth field of the secure zone. As each battered hulk rolled to a stop, no humans emerged from the chassis—which invariably began to smoke in an unusual fashion, emitting a miniature cumulus cloud of dense, white vapor.

McGee smiled. That smoke—an IR-refractive compound that rendered almost all thermal imaging useless—was swiftly obscuring the wreck-strewn ground that hemmed in Punt like a semicircular junkyard. The twisted frames of the slain vehicles also burned surprisingly well, sending greasy black plumes through the white billows: each chassis had been inundated with motor oil, which, once aflame, burned long and low. Those fires not only played further havoc with the enemy's targeting sensors, but also sent up an acrid pall that hung over the Baldies' security zone—which had, only ten minutes before, been as clear and flat and easily viewed as a billiard table.

Perfect, thought McGee. "Jon," he called out, "have you identified the remaining Baldy PDF systems here on the northern extents?"

"Every one, Tank."

"And you've plotted the limits of their arcs of fire?"

"You bet."

"Okay, then, Marines: helmets on and seal up. You outriders will need to hunker down for a minute or two—just like the main attack forces are doing right now."

"Why?" asked Ben Ramirez.

"Because, Ben, if my guess is right, the real Baldy response is going to be arriving just about now—"

As the word "now" left McGee's mouth, they heard—high above—the first, faint rumble of a sonic boom. And then another.

"Enemy air! Inbound!" McGee yelled, and then ducked down in his watchpost.

"Overseer Iakkut?"

"Yes?"

"We will be in effective range of our target in ten minutes."

"The other strike force?"

"The second formation will come to effective range of the *griarfeksh* island base approximately four minutes after we reach our target here."

"And our readiness?"

"Excellent, *Destoshaz'at*. All PDF systems are online and showing full function. Suppressive munitions are slaved to target designation systems: they will interdict any Resistance air defenses. Our forward air-control links for target identification and confirmation have been tested and are in constant communication with the exoatmospheric attack craft."

"And the nuclear munitions?"

"Awaiting your release order for activation."

Iakkut let his mounting wave of (triumph, pride) fill the command vehicle and willed it outward through the general *selnarm* link to the rest of the attack forces. "In the name of the Martyrs—and especially in memory of my discarnate friend, Torhok—I instruct you to arm the warheads."

✧ ✧ ✧

Heide inspected his portable battle-comp's display: the *faux*-3-D representation in its flat screen rotated slowly to show the approaching two-lobed swarm of Baldy craft. The first group had come from Punt and was approaching at low altitude. Grav attack platforms, no doubt: they would attempt to suppress his defenses and designate targets for the second force. That latter cell of enemy craft—which had come down from orbit—was probably carrying the hammer with which the Arduans intended to flatten the main Resistance base.

Heide considered his defensive grid. It would probably be most prudent to engage the lead flight with his conventional systems—thereby inviting them to believe that the Resistance had fairly limited AA capabilities. "Sites Victor One through Twelve, prepare to engage the first enemy wave on my mark."

Montaño's breathless voice cut into his command channel. "Sir, the facility is not yet evacuated. And if the Baldies should launch nuclear weapons while the evacuees are still in the smugglers' tunnel . . ."

"Understood, Ensign." Heide could envision the blast effects clearly: before the old subterranean river tunnel collapsed, the ground-bursting wave of superheated plasma would rush into and through the tube, making it a mile-long blast furnace that would vaporize anyone and anything still inside. He toggled the open circuit. "It seems we must hold these attackers a little longer. Sites Victor One through Victor Twelve, you will have to engage the lead targets before they reach optimal range. We need to convince the Baldies to stand off and duel with us, clear us out before they risk bringing in their decisive ordnance. This means that, before we can use our HVMs, we will take more casualties, and they will take fewer than they might—far fewer. Is that understood?"

The conventional launch sites began signaling their affirmatives. And as Heide watched the green lights collect on his status board, he thought: *Strange. Now that death is certain—either from nuclear or conventional ordnance, it hardly matters—my fear is gone.* Now, in its place, Heide had just one grim, driving impulse: he had to get as many of his people to safety as possible. But there was one particular life that it was imperative to preserve, that of a small child who should never have been in a hidden military base at all. Unfortunately, the petty machinations of one Julian Heide had put that little life in what was now mortal and immediate danger.

No, Heide swore to whatever power marked the oaths of doomed warriors, *that little boy is going to live... even if it's the last thing I ever do.*

Which, he conceded, *it might very well be.*

McGee waved to Kapinski, senior among the "outriders": members of the assault team for whom there were no seats left in either mount. "Juan, get your people down. A suborbital strike could get pretty nasty if our AA weapons experts don't get their timing just right." The Marines under Juan's nominal command did not wait for his orders, though. At McGee's warning, they threw themselves flat in the narrow space between the two overburdened house-trailers.

The sonic booms overhead became more numerous. Thirty, forty, maybe fifty: Baldy fast movers, descending to smite whatever motley collection of humans had the unmitigated and apparently insane gall to attack Punt....

McGee counted the seconds; too many seemed to go by. He looked toward the taller buildings back beyond the periphery of the littered no-man's-land and felt his heart begin to race. If those fast movers got a chance to launch their ordnance...

From several dozen buildings 100 to 150 meters behind the zone's rim of demolished structures, blinding white-hot rays stabbed skyward. High overhead, each ended in a brilliant ball of distant destruction.

But McGee and the other thousands of Resistance fighters who were sheltering desperately close to the ground never heard the tardy thunder of those explosions, because they were deafened instead by dozens of small cyclones. The vicious mid-air maelstroms had been spawned by each HVM, which, in a single instant, reached and annihilated the inbound Baldy attack craft, multiple sonic booms chasing up behind it into the light blue morning sky. The consequent vortices howled at, and jostled against, each other, spawning split-second tornadoes here and there. Lightning arced sideways between them and across a sky alight with burning columns of spontaneously combusting air that marked where the HVMs had passed but an instant before.

Poking her head up through the open hatch of the A mount, and looking out a window of one of the half-houses, Jen gaped. "What the hell were *those*?" she breathed.

"Hyper-velocity missiles," supplied McGee as he swept his binoculars across the smoke-filled no-man's-land. "They use a tiny pseudo-velocity drive generator that lasts only a fraction of a second. That's why they look like a big laser beam. Your eye doesn't work fast enough to see an object traveling thirty thousand kilometers per second. And even the Baldy defense systems can't react fast enough to shoot them down. If our operators hit their marks, they just engaged the first wave of Baldy fast movers at an altitude of twenty-five kilometers, give or take. That means there was a little less than a 0.001 second delay between each HVM's launch and its target intercept."

"So what will the Arduans do now?"

As McGee started answering, another rumble of multiple sonic booms began sounding overhead. "If they're stupid—or didn't get good sensor data—they'll try a second wave, which it sounds like they're about to do. And they'll get pretty much the same results."

"And what then?"

"Well, they'll figure out that they have to hit this whole area with something that stops our HVMs. They might try a massive EMP strike, which won't work, because HVMs are battle-hardened. Of course, if they choose to make that EMP strike the old-fashioned way—with air-bursted nukes fired from orbit—then we're done for."

"Because they'll be killing our HVMs before they can launch."

"That—and because they'll be killing all the rest of us, too. And that's pretty much all the time we've got for explanations."

"Uh—how much time *do* we have?"

"Not enough to stand around wondering about it, that's for sure."

McGee motioned for Jen to drop down through the hatch. As she did, he left his observation post—just inside the side window of the half-house—and then slid down the ladder into A mount right after her. "Let's go," he shouted and grabbed a handhold with all the magnified force his armor could generate.

As more HVMs slashed skyward, and more cyclones whipped around their wakes, two Marine grav APCs came ripping out of the ends of the two house halves. As if ferociously glad to be finally liberated from their concealment inside those flimsy structures, the wedge-shaped vehicles sprayed plywood and siding outward in a broad arc. The outriders—six Marines who were unable to fit inside the troop compartments—clung to the special netting on the sharply sloped rears of their respective craft with one hand, held their lashing lines tightly with the other.

As the two armored vehicles sped low and fast for the northern extents of Punt's walls, another barrage of 78 mm vertical-tube missiles arced over toward the Baldy city. The alien PDF systems knocked them down, creating a momentary tempest of flame and smoke high over the no-man's-land. A second later, the northernmost of the Baldy defense emplacements discovered that, while engaged with the missiles, they had failed to immediately detect the two grav APCs that were now screaming closer in nap-of-the-earth flight mode, only four meters off the ground.

At that moment, under the dense roof of rippling flame and smoke that hung over the secure zone, the main assault force—eight battalions of Marine-cadred Resistance fighters who had advanced to the edge of the dense white and black billows that ran along the ground—charged in response to a collective shrilling of athletic whistles. The Baldy weapon emplacements were not slow to respond, and the ubiquitous autonomous defense blisters rose up by the dozens to pepper away at the advancing fireteams.

But the wreckage of the automated vehicles now

provided cover and concealment to the leapfrogging combat groups. From vantage points beyond the edge of the secure zone, human heavy weapons spoke: for every two Resistance fighters that sprawled in the smoke and were still, a Baldy or one of their blisters fell permanently silent.

The general attack made the fastest progress on the north extents—largely because the Baldy PDF systems in that salient had already combined their firepower with the anti-vehicle missiles that were racing toward the two grav APCs. The Resistance foot soldiers took swift advantage of the overtaxed Baldy defenses: shoulder-fired missiles of staggering power found and silenced more alien weapon emplacements. Cluster-rocket launchers saturated the intercept sensors of the enemy PDF computers, forcing them to choose between an imminent threat to their own survival or the onrushing grav vehicles. With the Baldies thus overloaded in the north end of their line, the lighter human infantry there was able to advance under only half the amount of defensive fire that the assault was encountering elsewhere.

Inside A Mount, from the squad compartment, Jennifer watched their now-careening approach through the narrow plasteel vision slits that served as the vehicle's cockpit. Overhead, the APC's remote-turreted PDF mount whined through its nonstop sequence of target acquisitions, each quick buzz-saw pulse of its hopper-fed, high-speed coil gun preceding a corresponding missile detonation along the intended path of the grav vehicle. They had been airborne for maybe nine seconds; in that time, they had blasted down at least forty inbound missiles.

"ETA?" yelled Tank.

"Thirty seconds," the driver shouted over the stuttering roar of dozens of nearby detonations.

Two missiles loomed in front of them. Overhead, the coil gun screeched, and one of the missiles became an orange fireball. The other—seen straight on—grew from the size of a pinhead to a penny as the remote turret whined, tracking, the coil gun shrieking again—

The sound of the blast was simultaneous with a fierce sideways wrench. Alert tones started sounding from the control panel; smoke was coming into the passenger compartment; firefighting canisters spewed their contents in a single, reactive spasm; the vehicle seemed to list for a second before righting itself.

Tank turned urgently to Jon Wismer, who was watching out the rear-vision port. "Kapinski? The other outriders?"

Wismer turned back to look at Tank and shook his head.

Jen thought she was going to throw up. *It all happens so fast. So terribly fast. Young, vibrant Juan Kapinski: ever the optimist with his head in the clouds and his heart on his sleeve. Dead. One second he was part of the team, just like always; the next he's gone and we have to move on. As though it didn't matter. As though he'd never existed. Because it all happens so terribly, terribly fast.*

"Tank's APC—is it still . . . ?"

Chong nodded sharply, eyes fixed to his binoculars. "Yes, Cap. A mount is still airborne, back on course. Close, though. The blast scraped all the outriders off."

Cap stared through the smoke. "How far do you make the walls, Roon?"

Kelakos—who knew from Chong's report that Juan was dead—spoke through gritted teeth. "Two hundred meters, sir."

"Pass the word: ready on the line. Smoke grenades, just like we practiced. The first set is hand-tossed to fifty meters. The second set is by launcher to one hundred fifty meters. Chong, you and I had better split up. It wouldn't do losing both of us during the final approach."

Chong was still for a moment. "Cap, isn't it a little early to start the advance? You're gambling that Tank's APCs are going to make it and that their breaching charges are going to work against that city wall."

Cap's face was livid, but Roon knew it was anger at the circumstances, not Chong. The old soldier had turned back upon his executive officer, and his eyes were bright and unblinking. "William, if those APCs don't make it, we're all dead anyway. But if they do, they'll need us in behind them ASAP. So we're going. Now."

And Chong smiled. "Aye, aye, Cap. Lead the way."

Cap smiled back, blew his whistle three times, then lifted his rifle over his head. Whistles shrilled back.

"Marines!" he roared in a voice that somehow was audible above the explosions and gunfire.

"Oo-rah!" came the loud, grim chorus along the line.

"Follow me!" Cap Peters jumped up, waving them on with his free hand—

—just as a single hypervelocity 15 mm Baldy shell ripped through the center of his cuirass and exited the backplate in a blast of blood, bones, and lung.

Chong stared at Captain Tibor Peters's upward staring eyes for a full half second and then vaulted over the charred truck chassis behind which they'd been hiding. He charged toward the walls of Punt city, screaming, howling, crying like the wounded human animal that he was.

Within a moment, nearly a thousand throats took up that cry, and like a seething, rageful horde, the human

Resistance fighters of Bellerophon began racing through their detonating smoke grenades toward the walls that sheltered their oppressors.

The driver turned toward Tank. "El-Tee, we're in. We're under their missile arcs. I think we—"

That was when McGee saw the faint ionizing sparkle of a Baldy PDF laser only one hundred meters to the right. Metal squealed and the vehicle pitched sharply down to that side.

"Primary lifter out, Tank. I can't hold it. Gonna be a rough landing."

Shit. "How much longer can we stay up?"

"Ten seconds. Maybe."

Jen looked at McGee. "Will we coast in?"

The driver must have thought she was speaking to him. "Ma'am, this bucket has the glide characteristics of a brick. We're going in—hard. And right now."

Tank reached up, launched the breaching charge—which beat them to the wall by two seconds, blowing an immense divot out of its surface. Danilenko, ever-watchful in B mount, had evidently launched a split second later: his charge burrowed in behind the first.

It was hard to tell which mad bouncings were a product of the crash, and which wild gyrations were the result of being caught on the outer edges of the second charge's detonation. Tank's APC nosed in hard, then bounced up, shuddered, seemed ready to turn turtle, but ultimately crashed down on its belly.

Tank clawed his way over to the vision ports and saw that they had indeed plowed through Punt's wall. The bow of their vehicle was in some kind of courtyard—across which at least two dozen armed Baldies were leaping in that long, gliding run of theirs. "Hostiles," he shouted. "Engaging: danger close." He slammed his palm down on the forward suppressive munitions relays.

Four cluster-bomblet tubes embedded in the vehicle's glacis plate coughed in unison. The bombs, which would normally launch to a preset distance of seventy-five meters, could not finish out those trajectories: instead they exploded against, or first caromed off of, Punt's interior walls, overhead arches, buttresses. In a moment, the courtyard was filled with explosions and viciously whining, needle-sized bits of shrapnel. The Baldies closest to the APC went down as if savaged by an invisible phalanx of chain saws. A few at the rear may have crawled away; McGee couldn't be sure.

"Jon, get me a headcount of our people. Matto, reconfigure the PDF turret for automatic counterfire with operator override. Slave it to the driver's console. And ripple fire the prismatic anti-laser dischargers until they're dry. Jon?"

"Except for our outriders, the whole assault section reports a-okay and ready to go, Tank."

"Jen, you okay?"

"I'm fine, Sandro. Let's get out of this death trap."

"Sounds good to me. Haika, crack the ramp."

She did, lowering it just a few centimeters.

"Do you see B mount?"

"One meter behind us. If that. They look full function, Tank. Igor's giving me a thumbs-up."

"Okay, here's the drill. The remote turrets cover us until we're in. Then they're on semiautonomous counterfire until our foot sloggers get here. At that point, the turrets and whatever is left in the CBM dispensers will provide a base of fire for the approaching infantry to get in under the cover of the walls." He turned to the driver. "If you're secure at that point, set up B mount as our forward HQ, and this one as a covered aid station. Now"—he turned to the rest of the Marines in his APC—"let's do the job we came to do. Ramp down. Haika, lead us out."

"*Marines lead the way!*" she howled and dropped the ramp as the rest of the squad echoed her battle cry in a pre-charge chorus.

And out they went.

Lentsul stopped, stunned by the urgency and fierce brevity of Mretlak's send. The Resistance attack to the south had been a feint; the real attack had hit the north and had breached the wall of Punt itself. It was presumed that human troops were therefore entering the city even now. This thrust, and damage from the human bombardment, had cut off the approach Lentsul had planned on making to Safety Point Three.

Lentsul acknowledged Mretlak's send and turned to consider the forces at his disposal. He had almost a hundred Enforcers and Intelligence operatives, as well as thirty semiautonomous weapons blisters and heavier defense drones. It would have to do.

Beckoning to them with a savage *selnarmic* command of his own, Lentsul entered the subsurface access corridors at a quick trot.

"Ankaht."

"Yes, Mretlak?"

"Lentsul is on his way to you, but he will be delayed."

"Why?"

"There are humans inside the city walls."

"Down in West Shore?"

"No. In Punt proper."

"You mean here, in the north?"

"Yes. You were right."

"I was not right about anything, Mretlak, except that the first human assaults seemed . . . wrong, somehow."

"Well, that assessment was correct. The first attacks were feints. Is the rest of the Council with you?"

"Those who are currently planetside, yes."

"Good. May I ask you extend them the protection of your personal guards?"

"Temret has already stationed his Guardians in defensive positions. But they lack sufficient weapons. They only have machine-pistols. And they are not wearing any armor."

Mretlak's pause seemed very long. "Do you have a vocoder with you?"

"Yes."

"I suggest you turn it on. You might wish to refresh the other Councilors in its operation."

"They are reviewing its principles now, Mretlak. But if the humans have discerned that we—as represented by Iakkut and his renegades—are about to attack both their Resistance bases, they may not be inclined to talk."

Mretlak's pause was even longer. "You, Elder, have a distressing talent for understatement."

Ankaht summoned (drollery) with some effort. "You, Mretlak, are not the first to tell me so."

But, she thought as the link closed, *you may very well be the last.*

McGee burned off a whole cassette of 10 mm magnum discarding sabot rounds at the rude barricade of Baldy freight containers: the 5 mm superdense penetrator rods stitched a tight pattern of holes across the improvised defensive wall. McGee's thermal-imaging goggles showed what transpired on the other side: even the Baldies that had been hunkered down out of sight had been blown not merely backward, but asunder.

"Clear," McGee shouted, and the second assault team raced past him. One member of the first assault team was being patched up by Haika. Jon Wismer was checking the team's other casualty—Matthew Maotulu. Jon turned, and even before he shook his helmeted head, McGee knew the verdict from the brief slump of his shoulders. Matto was dead.

Sloppy. I was sloppy, thought McGee as he savagely threw away the empty cassette and snapped another into place. *If I had double-checked that barricade when we first saw it—*

He felt a hand on his arm, heard the protecting vantbrass creak under the strain of a superhuman grip. It was Jen, forgetting her soothing hand was encased in a powered gauntlet. "Hey, hey. Easy there, Jen. You're going to crack my armor open." The pressure eased—a little. "Jen—what is it?"

"She's here. I can feel it."

"Who's here? What do you mea—?"

"Ankaht. She's here. And she's close."

McGee looped two fingers in mid-air: all but the point- and rear-guards were to huddle up and listen. "You've detected Ankaht? Where? Which direction do we head now?" The Marines were already in a tight ring around them: at last, a target lock.

Jen shrugged. "It doesn't work like that, Tank. It's not so—so quantifiable. But generally, she's in that direction." She waved vaguely to the east. "And a little down, I think."

"You heard the lady," McGee shouted. "We've got a bearing on the target. Igor, time to distribute the suppressives." Danilenko started passing out more grenades, along with pistol-sized, one-shot flamers: a three-second flamethrower that expedited fast movement through halls or tunnels. Tank gave orders as the Marines checked and stowed the new weapons: "Fast leapfrog advance. Second Team, you have our six. And keep up—we're moving at the double time. Starting now!"

Ankaht had just convinced Tefnut ha sheri to shelter himself behind the tipped-over conference table when she felt a push at her *selnarm*, like a Youngling's earliest efforts to make its feelings felt by others. And beside its weak, tentative projection, there was something else unusual about the contact—as if it wasn't really a focused send, but rather an almost omnidirectional transmission. Which was strange to encounter at this particular moment, because the only time Ankaht could remember experiencing such a peculiar *selnarmic* contact was when she had been working with—

"Jennifer?" Ankaht snapped upright so quickly that several of her fellow Councilors started back. "Jennifer? Jennifer? Is that you? Are you there?"

But the faint pulse of contact—whether real or imagined—was gone.

"*Destoshaz'at* Iakkut, a distress call from Melantho."

"From Melantho? Relay its contents to me." Iakkut waited through the hasty overview of the ongoing human attack, the interdiction of the orbital support craft, the appearance of unprecedented and unexpected weapons of obvious military origin, the uncertain outlook for all of Punt, and the desperate plea for immediate assistance. He physically smiled; to a human, it would have looked like a rictus. "Excellent."

"Excellent? What are we to do, *Destoshaz'at*?"

"Do? Why, we do absolutely nothing. The human attack is fortuitous. Consider. The great majority of the truly race-loyal inhabitants of Punt are here with us, and we are in possession of almost all the mobile military assets of the city. So what is the loss if the city falls and the Council is destroyed along with it? And conceive of the elegance of such an outcome. It will be the humans, now, who destroy the greatest of our race-traitors—the Council and Ankaht. And so the exchange of atrocities will have been initiated by the *griarfeksh*, not us. And with our esteemed Council, and senior elder, and high priest all dead at their hands, the rest of the Children of Illudor will not fail to join us in our sad—but very necessary—resolve to exterminate the perfidious *griarfeksh*. And now tell me—how are we faring against the human SAM sites?"

"Fairly well, Overseer, but we have lost over a dozen of our sleds."

"They have held their military weapons back for such an eventuality. Impressive restraint for such an impetuous species. But their defenses are almost eliminated now, are they not?"

"The last of their missile batteries has just been silenced, *Destoshaz'at*."

"Excellent. Signal the strike craft. They may commence their attack runs now."

✧ ✧ ✧

Heide watched as the last of the icons denoting his conventional SAM sites went from green to red to gone. At almost the same instant, the transatmospheric attack craft—which had slowed their rate of descent when Heide's conventional defenses had showed their teeth—began dropping quickly, building speed as they dove in.

And they were diving in as one massive wedge.

Perfect. "Omega batteries: control?"

"Omega control here, sir."

"Do you have telemetry on the inbound transatmospheric attack craft?"

"Yes, sir. We've had plenty of time for optical and passive tracking. Give the word and I can illuminate them with our active sensors. We'll have lock in one, maybe two seconds."

"Do so, and launch your HVMs in three waves."

"As per preprogrammed protocol seven. Yes, sir."

Heide's communications specialist gulped. "But Captain Heide, what about the Baldy Security sleds?"

"Ignore them. The meteorological effects of the HVMs will get most of them."

"But what about the rest of them, sir? At this range, they'll chop us to pieces."

Heide turned to look at the young man. "Yes, or—even if we don't lift a finger to strike back—we'll still be vaporized by a nuclear blast. Do you have a strong preference between the two experiences, corporal?"

The young man went so pale that he almost looked blue.

"So carry out your orders. Then get to your shelter." *Because,* Heide thought with a grim smile, *if you* don't *hurry, you may get to experience both forms of annihilation before this minute is over.*

✧ ✧ ✧

Iakkut blinked at the changes beneath him. One moment, the landscape a kilometer below seemed quiescent, beaten: a dozen thin tendrils of smoke stretched into the sky, marking the sites of now-destroyed defensive missile sites. The rest of the terrain—dotted here and there by small communities—appeared senseless, like a stunned opponent laid out to be slain by the final *skeerba* strike that was even now descending through the clouds.

And then, in one apocalyptic instant, everything changed: blue-white beams seemed to leap up from the surface of the planet itself. His lead sleds' PDF systems had registered a flicker of something going past them—and then those vehicles were tumbling through the air, buffeted by the cyclonic side-winds and ferocious vortices left in the wake of whatever had ripped past them.

"Operations, report. What was—what are they?"

"Overseer, I am not sure. The sensors seemed to show readings consistent with a pseudo-velocity drive field. But it only lasted an insta—"

Iakkut knew. The humans had HVMs. He had read about them in the *griarfeksh* military manuals—once he was permitted to study them, that is. HVMs had seen extremely infrequent use since the Bug War because they were so widely destructive: their meteorological aftereffects threatened friend and foe alike. But the humans *couldn't* have had a stockpile of HVMs all this time, because the *griarfeksh* would surely have used them before now—

"Destoshaz'at!"

The urgency of his operations prime told Iakkut what the incoming message was before it was relayed. "They have struck our transatmospheric attack craft, of course."

"Yes, sir. Half are—are gone, sir!"

Faint shockwaves from overhead—the exploding craft of the strike group—replaced the diminished buffeting of dying cyclones. "Ops: all sleds counterfire at all known or suspected HVM launch sites. Comms, send this to the remaining transatmospheric attack craft: new launch protocol, for immediate execution. One half of nuclear ordnance is to blanket map grids T 7 through X 42 with airbursting warheads at seventy meters mean altitude. Second half of nuclear ordnance to be directed against our pre-ranged target coordinates: do not wait for our laser designation. Ops, can we recalibrate our PDF's to—?"

That was when the second wave of HVMs—just as numerous as the first—jutted skyward. One of the near-relativistic missiles, racing aloft to impale its nuke-carrying target, passed within fifty meters of Iakkut's command delta. The powerful suction generated by the vacuum of its 30,000-kilometer-per-second passage pulled in Iakkut's vehicle, tearing pieces off it—a split second before the sudden reconstriction of spontaneously combusting air pincered it, breaching the Security sled's light hull.

The superheated and burning air rushed into the interior of the craft, discarnating Iakkut so quickly he had no time to revisit the momentary misgiving he had mentally permitted himself while walking to join his waiting forces on Punt's predawn airfield, Emz'hem's blood still dripping from his skeerba:

Who knows? Perhaps today I shall not simply fight for the Martyrs, but become one myself.

As the skies continued to flash violently overhead and the winds tore at the roof of Heide's topside HQ/OP, he watched the last of the Baldy sleds spew out a torrent of smaller rockets, a good number of which were angling toward him. At the same moment, high above, the few surviving fast movers glittered fitfully: the multiple ignitions of mass missile launches. Then the plumes of the inbound weapons billowed out behind them, ballooning in size as the salvo raced toward the ground.

Heide cleared his throat. "Ensign Montaño?"

"Yes?" came the young voice, tinny through the hardwired commo lines.

"Send this signal in the clear: 'Well done, all—and Godspeed.' Set for continuous loop—and then get into your shelter, Ensign."

If Montaño replied, Heide did not hear it. With a perfect presence of mind, and a strange inner peace, he watched the burgeoning missiles descend toward him.

Eighteen kilometers away, Marina Cheung waited as the last of the evacuees emerged from the bird-infested smuggler's tunnel, waving them down into a rocky defile that had overhead blast cover, thanks to a sheltering bluff. She had already heard Heide's simple farewell message play three times, and, as she snugged Zander's uncommonly sturdy toddler body close against her own fairly small torso and began racing down to join the others, she heard the announcement start a fourth time—

An intense light abruptly outlined the craggy, sheltering bluff into a sharp black silhouette. Marina heard Heide's announcement end, cut off by a sharp, rising squeal that was in turn almost drowned out by the sound of a dozen fry pans full of crackling bacon. Then, for the slimmest of instants—silence: the line was dead, the birds were still. But then she heard the roar rising and felt the first tremor shoot through the ground beneath her feet.

As she felt the inexplicable urge of Lot's wife rise within her, she yelled aloud—as much to herself as the others: "Don't look back—no matter what!"

McGee had to grab Jen's shoulder and pull her back. His fiancée turned around with a wave up the corridor and a vigorous nod. "She's here, just down this hall. I know it. I can feel it."

McGee looked at her carefully and then matched her nod with one of his own. "Okay, then, here we go. Igor, you provide our base of fire. Jon, you keep team five back here and hold off any Baldies who come after us. Haika, you and I lead the charge. Jen"—who was ready to protest—"you stay with Harry and he stays with you. Either of you disobey that and I'll shoot you myself." He tried to make it sound like a joke: it didn't help that he was more than half-serious. And now he had to take the single action that, like passing a point of no return, put every last iota of the attack plan on the line: he switched on his radio, triggered a fast, preprogrammed set of squelches, and waited two seconds before sending: "Bullet to Breech, Bullet to Breech: come in Breech."

"Bullet, this is Breech." And because the answering voice was Chong's, McGee didn't have to ask: he knew. Cap was dead. "Bullet, we are triangulating on your signal now. I estimate we are only four minutes from your current position, over."

"Breech, we are approximately fifty meters north by northeast of our objective. I say again: fifty meters north by northeast of our terminal objective. Do you copy?"

"I copy, Bullet. We are at company strength now and following your UV-dye trail with black-light and goggles. We estimate—" And then the signal went dead.

McGee looked around at his assault team. "The Baldies have jammed our signal. The main attack wave is maybe five minutes behind us. Are you ready to take it the rest of the way?" Faceless, the remaining sixteen pitted and scarred battle-suits arrayed around him all made a stiff helmet-nodding motion. "Then let's get going. Igor, start the music."

Danilenko nodded and leaned out into the corridor: a fusillade of 5 mm bullets immediately spattered off his breastplate. He fired back, his coil gun screaming out fifty 4 mm needles per second. From farther down the hall, it sounded like he had shredded a garbage can filled with wrenches.

Harry smirked. "Scratch one blister. Let's do this."

McGee nodded solemnly—and led them around the corner at a run.

Ankaht ignored Temret's repeated exhortations that she should retreat behind the table with the rest of the Councilors. She ignored it because she felt something growing, something familiar.

(Eager, desperate, pleading), she sent: "Jennifer?"

Then bullets—heavy, murderous projectiles—started showering through the doorway: the far wall was quickly pocked and then began disintegrating. Her Guardians returned fire, taking what cover they could behind the sole autonomous blister that Mretlak's technical specialists had approved for her secure use. The blister fired a spread of missiles up the hall—and was then riddled by a sleetstorm of smaller, faster projectiles. It shuddered backward, hammered by the relentless torrent of fire, and then corkscrewed off to the side and into a corner, shedding parts as it tumbled away. The Guardian next to Temret jumped up to return fire—and the top half of his body seemed to explode into a bloody spray.

"Elder! You must get under cover!"

Still oblivious, Ankaht repeated her *selnarm* pulse—but as a terrified scream: "*Jennifer*!"

Lentsul had heard the firing from up ahead and charged the last two hundred meters.

Or rather, he had meant to. Rounding a corner halfway to Safety Point Three, the advance wedge of his Enforcers went down under a hail of high-power gunfire. One of the survivors—her left cluster blown off in a gruesome amputation—sent an image through her pain, before she lost consciousness and then discarnated: the other end of the hall was guarded by huge, crouching anthropomorphic shapes. Like humanoid robots. But no, this was the combat armor that Torhok and Urkhot and the rest of the self-satisfied *Destoshaz* radicals had confidently asserted the humans could not have on Bellerophon. After all, they had smugly reasoned, the *griarfeksh* lacked the self control to defer the use of such powerful weapons. Lentsul could have spit in disdain: *A pity you are not around to see—and experience—your error firsthand, you* Destoshaz *dolts.*

But, as usual, it fell to an orderly *Ixturshaz* to clean up the mess made by just such idiots. "Blisters to the front," Lentsul ordered.

"How many, Commander?"

"All but five."

"All but five? But sir, if we encounter further Resistance—"

"*Bilbuxhat*-witted oaf, if we do not push this human rear guard aside immediately, they will reach our

Councilors—if they have not already. I say again, all but five blisters: salvo all missiles at any targets. Three seconds after they begin, we charge in behind them. Fire at anything. Do not stop to check if the enemy are dead: press on to Safety Point Three. Are you with me?"

Stunned, the Arduans ringing the *Ixturshaz*—the smallest one there—sent (accord, resolve, ferocity).

"Then release the blisters: all attack!"

The first of the shining, floating cylinders swept around the corner and into the hallway—where it was promptly torn to pieces by a weapon that fired smaller projectiles, but more rapidly, than the guns which the humans had used first.

Then three blisters went around the corner together, and some survived long enough to launch their missiles.

Lentsul clutched his machine-pistol and thought: *To save the Councilors—that is a little thing. But to avenge you, Heshfet—to achieve that, I will kill all of them.*

All *of them.*

Too many things happened for Ankaht to control them all. The humans, largely impervious to the Arduan weapons in their immense armor, charged into the room, killing all the Guardians but Temret—who went down, but Ankaht could tell he was only wounded, momentarily feigning death.

Four of the suited humans advanced deeper into the room: one was very large, the other three were somewhat small.

And in that smaller trio, somewhere, was Jennifer. Ankaht knew it.

But even in that instant, the smaller trio broke apart,

two heading toward Ankaht, another one going over to check the bodies of her Guardians.

At the same moment that the one checking the bodies leaned over Temret, one of the two approaching Ankaht undid her helmet—and a lock of Jennifer's long, light-colored hair tumbled out.

"Jennifer!" Ankaht croaked aloud.

The sound startled them all—and that was the moment of distraction that Temret had been waiting for. His arm whipped his machine-pistol up, slammed it against the faceplate of the small armored human standing over him, and his lesser tentacles squeezed the trigger. At that range, and using armor-penetrating ammunition, even the machine-pistol was able to pierce the visor: it shattered under the high-speed hammering of the bullets. The small human fell backward, limp, landing with a crash against the futile barricades that Temret's Guardians had erected.

Jen's mouth was open in the human expression of shock. The other small human spun, and stood rigid as if stunned—but Ankaht could also read a sudden spike of murderous rage. The large human trained his weapon on Temret, just as five other human warriors charged into the room, aiming their weapons in the same direction.

Ankaht sent an (URGENT) command to Temret: "Drop your weapon immediately."

"Honored Elder, I—"

"Immediately." And then she croaked out, "Mistake. Killing stops now. Please."

The humans all seemed to freeze in place—because the vocoder had translated her words perfectly. Ankaht looked behind her. Old Tefnut ha sheri stood there, cradling the translation machine carefully, its pickup aimed directly at her.

"It seemed a prudent moment to activate the device," he sent.

Jennifer walked forward, extending a hand toward Ankaht. She felt ambivalence in the Arduan. "I am here to stop this war," Jennifer sent, worrying that she was so out of practice that she might not have transmitted the concepts clearly enough.

But Ankaht's eyes registered understanding—even as they looked at the armor Jennifer was wearing and the two carbines she was carrying as part of her load. "You come oddly equipped to speak of peace, Jennifer Peitchkov."

"I had little choice, Ankaht. We didn't exactly get an invitation to come and chat. But if it makes any difference, these two weapons are not mine. I refused to kill any Arduans when I agreed to join this mission."

"Whether the weapons are yours or one of your soldiers, what is the difference? They were brought to kill us. Perhaps—to kill me, Jennifer Peitchkov?"

Jennifer felt her heart sink at Ankaht's apparent belief that she would agree to carry out such an intent. "Ankaht! Surely you must know better than this."

"I do now, for your feelings just told me so—and quite clearly. But then, Jennifer—since it is obvious you were not killed trying to escape from Punt—why did you not contact me? Why did you not reach out? Why have you let all the bloodletting rise to a flood between our peoples?"

"Ankaht, look into me, into all my thoughts, and know this: I will keep nothing from you. But just as you struggled against reluctance and ignorance from your own people—and threats, as well—so have I. My life—and my child's—have been threatened both for the sake of my loyalty to you and for the work we did together."

Ankaht was still for a long moment. "I see and feel this clearly, Jennifer. Although we lived worlds apart on the same planet, we have nonetheless suffered many of the same worries, the same threats."

Tank loomed behind her and murmured, "Is this her? Is this Ankaht?"

"Yes."

"How's it going?"

"Pretty well. Why?"

"Because we don't have a lot of time. And because it will be good to be able to tell Harry that Haika died for something worthwhile."

Ankaht looked around: Harry Li was kneeling—almost like a penitent—alongside the small suit of armor with the shattered faceplate.

Ankaht obviously had felt Jennifer's heart plummet at the sight. Her three eyes closed slowly, reverently. "Dear Jennifer Peitchkov, we must stop this."

"That's what I came for, Ankaht."

"And how do you propose we begin?"

"I must begin by taking you—and all the Council—hostage."

Ankaht could hardly send through the shock. "You came all this way, suffered all these losses—just to take the Council captive? Jennifer, the Children of Illudor do not hold our lives to be so precious. Indeed, there are many among the *Destoshaz* caste who would be ecstatic to learn that you are removing us. Such a strategy will fulfill their chief goals. It will silence all of the moderate leadership, precipitate the slaughter of your Resistance, and ensure the demise of the only two of us who have ever been able to really, genuinely communicate. Jennifer, you of all humans must know this." She stopped and considered the grave, unruffled certainty of Jennifer's mind. "Indeed, you *do* know this."

Jennifer nodded. "I know it. All of it. And more. I know that the majority of your people understand that if you—if this Council—were to be destroyed, it would also destroy the last hope of ending this war. Of avoiding the extermination of one or both of our species. It would weaken your people at a time when they can least afford it."

The biggest human received a message from a newly arrived—and much battered—armored figure, who gasped out something fast and desperate. The large human turned to Jennifer. "Honey, we don't have a lot of time left. The Baldi—the Arduans will be here in less than a minute. They've overrun Jon Wismer's rear guard. He's dead, Jennifer."

Ankaht felt Jennifer slip away, as though someone had struck deep into her body with a long, cold weapon. This—Jon—had been someone for whom she had felt a great, gentle fondness, much as a sister would for a brother. "Jennifer, yes, you are right in all this. But to stop this killing—to make Jon's death the last: how does taking us hostage help achieve that?"

"Because"—and Jennifer turned her suddenly sunken eyes back upon Ankaht, who saw for the first time just how quickly a changed emotional state could make a human look haggard and unhealthy—"because, Ankaht, now that we've taken you hostage, we are surrendering to you." Jennifer nodded. The big human stepped back from his covered position at the doorway. He called his twelve remaining soldiers from their posts, gathering them to him. Standing before Ankaht, they all cast their weapons to the ground.

Behind Ankaht, Tefnut ha sheri actually cried out in surprise. It was a strangled sound, and Jennifer looked concerned for a moment, but Ankaht calmed her as she asked, "You came here—fought through all our defenses, died by the hundreds—just to take us hostage, and then surrender to us?"

Jennifer nodded again. "What else would make you—all of you—believe how strongly we want to talk to you, to make peace? Here we stand, at last able to cripple your people at their darkest, weakest hour—and you are powerless to prevent it."

Ankaht imitated—stiffly—Jennifer's nod. "And at that same moment, you choose instead to capitulate. You hold us in your hands, able to do us great injury, but instead you let us go—and more, you put your fates in our 'hands.'" Ankaht felt tears of wonder and hope streaming down her face and did not care: she was proud to wear them. She turned and opened her *selnarm* so all could receive her statement—and challenge. "Can any of you doubt the power and truth of this gesture? Can any of you harbor any suspicion that humans are not persons, are not furnished with souls as great as those within the Children of Illudor? Can even *you* still doubt it?" she finished, aiming the question at Lentsul, who, at the head of a dozen Enforcers and several blisters, rushed into the room, weapons leveled at the humans.

Lentsul, who had sensed some of the exchange, wondered if the Eldest Sleeper had, in fact, been permanently addled by her many centuries in cryogenic sleep. "Elder," he sent quickly, "this could be a trap, a ruse. These are clever creatures—"

"Good Lentsul, I do not recognize your *narmata* at this moment. It is changed—flooded with fury, with hurt. You are not thinking clearly."

"No, Elder. It is you who is not thinking clearly. Even if these dozen humans mean to surrender, the rest of their forces are still fighting. Hundreds are headed this way. To this very chamber. Do you think *they* will surrender?"

The human subject Peitchkov had evidently understood much of what he had sent. "Surrender. They. Will. At. Signal. From. Us."

Lentsul ignored her. "That signal is probably a way for this advance team to confirm that their attack's primary target—the Council—is all here. I suspect they will fire one of their HVMs at these coordinates as soon as she is allowed to transmit the sig—"

"Lentsul—"

He was resolved not to succumb to Ankaht's masterful philosophizing and speculation; not now. So he countered with logic. "This human female has come to surrender? Very well, what are her terms?"

"Lentsul, she has imposed no terms—"

The human subject Peitchkov sent as well as said, "One requirement only. That we talk. If we surrender to you. You must talk with us."

Lentsul quickly concurred. "That is acceptable. Now, order all your approaching forces to lay down their arms."

Ankaht was pleased, amazed. "And will you, too, agree to this, Lentsul?"

Lentsul waved his weapon in impatience. "Of course,

of course." There wasn't much time left. In forty seconds, the lead elements of the main human force would arrive. That left just about enough time to make sure that the main attack force got the surrender signal and could be disarmed by his own forces. Then, when they were defenseless, Lentsul could arrange for the safe and efficient euthanization of each and every one of the savage—

"Lentsul." He heard his name spoken, and heard it—flat and featureless—through the *selnarm* link furnished by the vocoder. Tefnut ha sheri had brought it over to Jennifer, who was looking straight at him.

Suspicious, he aimed his gun directly at her unarmored head. "Signal your forces to disarm. Now."

"I will signal them to wait for two minutes, if you lift your jamming." She nodded to the largest human. Lentsul calculated the probability that this was part of an elaborate ruse, decided it was unlikely, and sent the override command to the electronic-warfare control center. The large human next to subject Peitchkov immediately sent a quick signal; Lentsul pulsed the jamming to reassert. The human looked up in annoyance.

But subject Peitchkov was unperturbed. Instead, she folded her hands—immense armored gauntlets—calmly.

"Lentsul, I do not know you. But I feel—through Ankaht, and others—that you are a protector of your people. That you protect them with your wits, more than your strength."

Lentsul kept his weapon aimed directly at the human's head.

"So I know you are too smart to miss the opportunity this puts before you. You would be foolish not to realize that once we lay down our weapons, you could quite easily turn the tables on us. You could disarm and slaughter us all, thereby eliminating the Resistance and saving the Council. No doubt you would be a hero."

Lentsul wondered if he should shoot subject Peitchkov now: she had guessed too much of his intent. But he felt Ankaht's razor-edged attention on his every move.

The human continued her jabbering. "But before you think too well of such a plan, think through all of its consequences. If it turns out that we do indeed relent—that all our forces lay down their arms—then no Arduan can deny that we acted in good faith. All of the Children of Illudor would be compelled to admit that we spent our lives—the only ones we live before being swallowed up by *xenzhet-narmat'ai*—to make clear a single point: how badly we, and this war, could hurt you. And yet, having proven and brought that threat to your very doorstep, and with our *skeerba* at your throat, we nonetheless stayed our hands. And why? To prove that we want to speak with you, not kill you. And now you have given your word to do no less.

"If, however, it turns out that you have lied and intend to slaughter us all as soon as we lay down our arms, then I ask you to contemplate the aftermath of such a betrayal, even if you believe us animals. In short, I ask you to think on this:

"When the sun sets on this day, will you—and the millions of Arduans who shall inherit the consequences of your actions—truly be able to go to your mirrors, and with all three eyes seeking truth—"

Ill'sblood! Where did she learn that saying?

"—will you be able to tell your reflection: 'I am the sentient one, the good one, the righteous one. But the creatures who refrained from destroying our leaders—and who relented because we promised them fair parley under a flag of truce—they are but animals.' For if, at the end of such a day, you can still see yourselves as just and sentient, and us as evil and bestial, then there probably never could be peace between us.

"So if this is the plan to which you are committed—to betray us, and your own honor as well—then enjoy the dubious gains of that treachery for the short time you have left. For when the rest of humanity comes—and as sure as the sun rises each day, they will come—you will wish you had simply remained to die when Sekahmant went nova. For the fury of that destruction will seem mild compared to the vengeance our brothers and sisters will bring down upon you. And it will not be fierce and unremitting because you killed us, but because you *betrayed* us."

Lentsul answered; the vocoder produced his sneer with distressing faithfulness. "That is a rather warlike note upon which to end your appeal for peace, Jennifer Peitchkov."

She shook her head. "But I am not done. Do not be afraid." She wedged open her suit's right greave and turned a recessed dial. Then she reached up under and behind her left armpit and pressed a small control stud. With a hiss and a set of rapid clacks, the immense protective suit seemed to sag on her. She reached across her body, undid a side hinge—and both her breastplate and faulds fell away, carrying the rest of the upper armor with them.

With only the immense greaves and boots on, her body looked almost tragically thin and weak. But she shuffled forward until she was within a meter of Lentsul. At which point, she got down on her knees. "In our species, this is the posture we adopt when asking something from a master, from a person before whom we may show no pride. I am, however, a proud woman of a proud people, so bear that in mind when I tell you why I kneel: not for myself, or our warriors, or yours—but for all our children, all our young. And for all those who will never be born if their parents are consumed by this war-day, and the bloody months and years that would surely follow. In the name of those unborn children, and for their lives, I beg—abjectly beg—that you *genuinely* consider our humble request to parley. Lentsul, Ankaht, all who hear my plea, believe this if you believe nothing else: as a mother, my love for those unborn innocents is greater than my pride. If you, too, are sentient creatures, can you feel any less? Can you, in good conscience, ignore such an appeal?"

Lentsul analyzed Jennifer's words for obvious falsehoods or contradictions. They did not contain any, but their veracity could not be conclusively verified, either—and the future of his species might very well depend upon what he did next. Dispassionate analysis of the situation indicated that there was no justifiable reason to take any risks.

"Lentsul," sent Ankaht. "Put down your weapon."

"No, Eldest. We need assurances."

The big human pulled off his helmet—revealing the face of Peitchkov's mate. Hardly a surprise.

The vocoder reproduced the tone of the human's voice as being strangely calm, even casual. "Look. I'm a soldier, not a diplomat. So let me break this down for you. This deal is as good as it gets. For either of us. If you don't meet us halfway, what happens? You kill us all. But before we all die, we kill lots of you, including your most important leaders. And then what? Internal power struggles? Political problems in your fleet when it's got its back against the wall? Yes, we know your Fleet is in trouble, because even our naked-eye telescopes tell us you're getting this system ready for a siege. And think about this: do you think we used *all* our HVMs today? Do you think we deployed and risked *all* our best trained individuals? *All* our milspec gear? C'mon, think about it. If we got in here once . . ."

The implication hung in the air like a poised blade, like the razor's edge of uncertainty upon which each one of them was now poised.

The subject Peitchkov reached out one slender hand for the gun Lentsul had aimed at her forehead. "Lentsul, please, let's stop the killing."

He looked down and saw her pleading eyes. In the same instant, he saw Heshfet's haughty, wonderful profile towering above him. He heard subject Peitchkov's words echoing in his conscience. He felt his hate for Heshfet's murderers fill his *selnarm*. The war between the two emotions intensified, tremored down through the rigid cluster in which he clutched his machine-pistol, and shuddered out into the already-quivering tentacle that was wrapped tightly about the weapon's trigger.

Which, if squeezed, would surely be the death of them all. But that was not of primary importance now. The lives in this room did not matter. Only the future of his race—the coming generations who would inherit the consequences of his next act—had any significance. And he, an *Ixturshaz*, had no choice but to act in accordance with his training, his caste. He made the calculations and discovered which course of action optimized the chances that Illudor's Children would survive.

"What I do," he sent clearly, gun steady, "I must do for the unborn Children of Illudor."

His tentacles flexed restively, unwillingly, and then opened.

Lentsul's gun fell to the floor.

TRNS Li Han, *Allied Fleet, BR-02 Warp Nexus*

Ian Trevayne stood motionless, hands wrapped in a tight knot behind his back. "I don't trust them."

"Neither do I," Mags agreed hollowly.

The day had begun with twenty-two Baldy relay drones cycling through the warp point from Madras. Each one of them had been dutifully blasted to subatomic particles on the assumption that any Baldy attempt at communication must, perforce, simply be a new trick.

But when they sent nine through all at once, and a fragment of a message got transmitted, it was clear that there was a genuine intent to communicate.

But what should have ostensibly been a cause for some guarded optimism turned grim soon enough. The message had been: "must communicate about regrettable deeds." "Regrettable deeds?" Trevayne had hardly known what to think. In a war where millions had died, infants had been executed, and whole towns annihilated, what new species of apocalypse or atrocity could constitute special mention as a particularly "regrettable deed"?

Mags had evidently been thinking the same thought. "I just hope they didn't use biologicals on Bellerophon."

Trevayne nodded tightly. That had been his fear, too. The one thing that might compel the Baldies to meet under a white flag was a runaway doomsday bug that they didn't know how to turn off, or treat, due to their rudimentary understanding of human biology. Of course, they might need the same kind of help if they were trying to contend with the aftereffects of fallout, had the "regrettable deeds" been nuclear in nature.

The Baldy ship which had eventually come through from Madras was not a warship at all, but a humble pinnace, ominously silent. It had docked with a special "liaison vessel" Trevayne had prepared: an expendable craft that had carried an all-volunteer crew of cleaners and sweepers, who had in due course declared the ship and its occupants clean.

Those occupants were now on board Trevayne's flagship and due in the triple-guarded conference room at any moment. Mags was uncharacteristically still. "It could be a good sign that one of the two envoys is human," Trevayne observed.

"Could be," she answered. "Or it could mean they've learned how to make one of us a complete puppet."

"Mags, if you'd rather not be here for—"

"No, Ian, no. I want to see the creatures that killed my mother. I want to—"

The door chimed. "Come in," invited Trevayne. The guards did not change posture, but their hands were tighter around the grips of their guns.

The two beings that entered together made as strange a pair as any Trevayne had ever seen: a tall, spare woman in her early thirties, and a short, dark Arduan.

Trevayne drew himself up. "Since you did not elect to transmit your names or titles, I hardly know how to politely begin."

The human woman smiled—but it was the Baldy who spoke. "I am. Ankaht. Councilor, Eldest Sleeper.

Special envoy. To humans. I am also. Your prisoner. And. If necessary. A sacrifice."

"I beg your pardon—a *sacrifice*?"

The human hastened to explain. "Admiral, my name is Jennifer Peitchkov. I am Ankaht's—well, her translator. Ankaht is still trying to learn our language, and she insisted on constructing her introduction without my help. What she means by 'sacrifice' is that, if necessary, she voluntarily submits to execution in partial recompense for the 'regrettable deeds' of her people."

Trevayne glared, aghast. "Damn it, Miss Peitchkov, I know what a sacrifice is. But have you bothered to inform this Ankaht that we are not such barbarians as she obviously presumes? With an introduction such as that, I have to wonder: Why has she come here? To commit ritual suicide?"

"No, Admiral," said the Baldy named Ankaht. "I come. To make. Peace."

39

A Final Twist of the Thread

Twist ye, twine ye! even so
Mingle shades of joy and woe,
Hope and fear, and peace and strife,
In the thread of human life
—Scott

Heliobarbus District, Melantho, Bellerophon

Alessandro McGee stepped out of the government transport, waved it on, scanned the bayside promenade that all the locals called the DropWalk, and spied what he was looking for: a lithe woman with long, sandy-blond hair hovering close to a formidable toddler who was obviously learning the finer points of how to run.

One part of McGee urged him to race over to them, to waste not one second of this precious existence apart from them—but the other part of him won out and slowed him to a stroll. This way, he could watch them together, because sometimes the deepest cherishing of others was attained more completely through observation than interaction.

So, when he finally sauntered up to the pair two minutes later, he had watched Zander progress from assaying a few unsteady strides to a sustained, if precarious, trot. But when the little fellow looked up—all the way up—and saw that the person who had come to join them was his father, his eyes disappeared behind chubby, smiling cheeks and he ran—truly ran—forward with a gleeful "Dada!"

Zander actually completed five long strides before—a smile still on his face—he started headfirst down toward the paving stones. But two great hands intervened, caught him up, and tossed him high into the air. Zander screamed in delight, the sound of his happy abandon mixing with the cries of the Terran seagulls that had long ago been transplanted to this world.

"Like his father," commented Jennifer, mischief in her tone.

"How so?"

"Always getting ahead of himself." She poked McGee in his immense ribcage and held her hands out for Zander. "It's that time."

"Hey, I can change his diapers."

"I know. I taught you. No, it's the other time."

"Oh," said McGee. He handed Zander off to his mom, who offered him a bottle—which he refused. Jen went to a bench, settled down, and settled the toddler on her breast: probably because of all the tumult in his young life, Zander seemed in no hurry to be weaned. Jennifer stared, gray-eyed, out over the wind-sparked whitecaps rolling across Salamisene Bay. "So, is it done?"

"Done and done," affirmed McGee. "Truce signed, relocation schedule finalized, hands and clusters shaken. The war is officially over as of"—he checked his watch—"eighty-four minutes ago."

"And not a moment too soon." Jennifer's sigh was a sound of relief and mourning: too many friends had died for there to be any joy in it. "Any last-minute wrinkles?"

"Other than your absence?"

Jen cut a sideways look at him. "This was just the formal dance, Tank. I was there for all the real choreography."

"And well done, too. Ankaht was a star."

"She always is."

"You like her, don't you?"

"Yes, I do. I really do. And we are all very lucky that she is who she is. Not everyone could have endured, survived, and excelled during such an insane chain of events."

McGee nodded. "Which was, for some, the sticking point."

"What? Ankaht?"

"No. Coming to a 'correct version' of the chain of events that set us on the path to one disaster after another."

"But the Arduans agreed to take responsibility for the war and be identified as both the aggressors and the losers."

"Yes, but that was too much for most of the *Destoshaz* radicals, and not enough for some of our new Baldicide Brotherhood, as they're calling themselves."

"Ugh. Those troglodytes."

"Which ones are you referring to—ours or theirs?"

Jen smiled. "Touché. And all too true."

"At any rate, the extremists on both sides had their respective hissy fits. Ours were louder—'the only good Baldy is a dead Baldy' chanters—but theirs are more . . . worrisome."

"How do you mean?"

"Jen, the *Destoshaz* extemists are apparently trying to find ways to join this Arduan Admiral Amunsit and her fleet in the Zarzuela system."

"What? They want to join the other Dispersate that landed near Orion space?"

"They consider doing so to be their true racial duty. No theatrics—just hard, cold, genocidal resolve."

"Well, isn't it just grand how peace is breaking out all over."

"What's tricky is how to handle them. Are they under our jurisdiction or the Arduan Council's? If the *Destoshaz* radicals agitate—or attempt to sabotage the peace process—here on Bellerophon, it's unclear who should or would stop them. Just as it's unclear who has the final authority to declare their actions a violation of the peace treaty."

"Well, I suspect the politicos will be wrestling over that one for a few months."

"At least. Fortunately, all the other agreements fell into place pretty easily, thanks to all the pre-Treaty work—and linguistic choreography by you and Ankaht."

"So the Arduan relocation to Megarea is ironed out?"

"Yup. It will be gradual, of course. They'll stay in charge here, defenses intact, until half their noncombatants have relocated to Megarea. Then they'll complete their departure from the Bellerophon system."

"And the other worlds?"

McGee nodded. "They'll be out of all our other systems within the month. Except for their reconstruction teams. The Council actually welcomed that as the primary form of war reparations. They feel it will increase interspecies contact and will help change the image of Arduans from destroyers to builders and helpers."

"It just might," agreed Jennifer. "But they're going to have to settle the war brewing around the Second Dispersate in Zarzuela before the old image is put to rest."

"Which means the diplomatic mission to the PSU is just that much more crucial." McGee thought about saying more but decided not to.

Jen smiled. "You're learning, Tank. Thanks for not pushing me to join the mission. Yes, I've had second thoughts about turning down the role of chief interpreter—but they'll find someone else. In fact, until I said 'no,' neither side was committed enough to put together a search process to find others like me—humans who can make a quasi-*selnarmic* connection with the Arduans. So the way I see it, I'm doing them a favor. Besides"—and her voice got lower, and a bit grim—"I suspect Ankaht will be back here soon enough."

"Oh? Why do you think that?"

"Because this is where the real image problems are, Tank. This war was far, far away from Old Terra and the rest of the Heart Worlds; even for the Republic, this was a foreign war. But for us Rimfolk—and strangely, for the Arduans as well—this was a fight on home soil. And besides, this is where almost all the real technical and cultural exchange is going to be for the first ten years or so. Megarea may become their new home, but it's at the ass-end of nowhere. Conversely, Bellerophon is a new hub for several important interstellar polities, particularly with the new Borden warp point connecting the far Rim to the Republic. Hey, why the sly smile, Sandro?"

"I was just thinking of Megarea, and all the Hotspur warp points the Arduans have been given permission to explore."

"Yes, what about them?"

"Seems Narrok has half convinced the Council that that should not be their primary route of expansion."

"Oh no? What does he have in mind—Tangri space?"

"As a matter of fact, yes."

"You're joking."

"Nope. And there's some logic to Narrok's perspective. He's got a fleet full of revved-up *Destoshaz* who, if told they have to conceive of themselves as completely *defeated*, could be new recruits for the radicals. Following Narrok's plan, he would simply tell his troops that peace has been reached with the humans because it was found that our differences were reconcilable. Consequently, the Children of Illudor can now prosecute war to its fullest extent upon the savage and irremediable Tangri overlords."

Jen snorted out a bitter laugh. "Making peace so you can make war somewhere else. Which in turn helps to keep the peace you just made. What a brave new world we live in."

McGee shrugged. "Yep, it's screwed up—but Narrok is right about this: if he keeps all those fence-sitting *Destoshaz* together, under his tutelage, and fighting a truly despicable foe, he stands a better than even chance of bringing them around to more uniformly moderate political attitudes. The alternative is—"

"—is a fleet that might rebel and turn on us. No, I see the wisdom of Narrok's plan, and I don't blame him for promoting it, but that doesn't change the howling irony of it all."

"No," agreed McGee, slipping an arm around her shoulder, "it doesn't. Not in the least."

Jen looked down at their son, who had nodded

off, lips bubbling out milk remainders in rhythm to the respirations of his sleep. "And this is all of deep and abiding interest to you, isn't it, Alexander Peters Peitchkov-McGee?" She looked out to sea again, her eyes suddenly liquid bright. "I miss Cap Peters," she said hoarsely, "and Jon and all the others. I wish we could have named him for all of them." She paused. "Even Heide. He deserves some remembrance, at least."

"Yes," McGee sighed. "At the last, he was bigger than his fears. That's why I've proposed that when we rebuild Van Felsen Base on the site of the old Acrocotinth, we make sure it is serviced by runways and pads that are called Heide Airfield."

Jen let the tears run down her face, now that she was able to smile through them. "He'd have liked that."

"Well," observed McGee, "I figure a planet chock-full of names from ancient heroes certainly must have room for a few modern ones as well."

Jennifer leaned against him. "Yes, I expect it can bear up under the strain. After all, *we* did. And now, finally, we're safe." She turned to McGee and placed a very tender kiss on his cheek as she hugged Zander close. "At last. We're safe. We're all safe."

TRNS Li Han, *Allied Fleet, Bellerophon*

Rank hath its privileges. The admiral's quarters aboard *Li Han* boasted a wide-curving outside viewscreen.

The Trevaynes stood before it, gazing at the blue-and-white-and tan curve of Bellerophon as viewed from low orbit. In the distance, the shuttle carrying Cyrus Waldeck receded toward his flagship.

"I hope Cyrus doesn't find RFNS *Zephrain* too

cramped now," said Mags with a mischievous twinkle. "After all, she's only a supermonitor."

"He *did* seem a bit overwhelmed by this ship, didn't he?" chuckled Ian Trevayne.

"He might even acquire a case of... uh, flagship envy."

"Hardly likely. Too bloody many rebels in this one," Trevayne deadpanned, earning an elbow in the ribs.

It had been almost anticlimactic. After the finalization of the treaty, Waldeck had brought Second Fleet into the Bellerophon system from Astria, peacefully transiting the warp point they had tried so often and so bloodily to fight their way through. A cynical person (which Trevayne of course was not) might have reflected that the presence in Bellerophon's skies of Second Fleet in addition to his own forces—a combined array of naval power without precedent in history—provided a doubtless unnecessary assurance that the terms of the treaty would be adhered to.

"At any rate," he continued, grasping his wife by the arms to forestall any additional jabs, "I think Cyrus is more interested in heading out for Tangri space to assume his new command without unnecessary delay. And he hasn't asked for any DTs or SDTs, which would be unnecessary at this stage of that campaign."

They had been conferring with Waldeck on the developing collapse of the Tangri Confederation. As long as the liberation of Bellerophon had been the first priority, Trevayne had left the campaign at that end to subordinates. Their progress hadn't been entirely satisfactory. True, the Tangri fleets—decimated, scattered, and without reliable bases—were no longer a serious threat. But the organization of the freed systems was proving a problem.

"I'm surprised Cyrus even wanted that command

when you offered it to him," said Mags, suddenly serious. "Of course, his role as the commander of Second Fleet is no longer relevant. But by now the problem on the Tangri front has become less one of fighting than of military administration."

"Nation-building, as it was once called." Trevayne nodded. "It's not just a matter of telling the *zemlixi* and the subjugated non-Tangri races that they're free and then moving on." He took on a brooding look. "Remember I once said that the Tangri had, for reasons connected to their environment and biology, taken an abnormal historical path, as though Genghis Khan's Mongols had conquered all of Old Terra? You have to imagine not just a conquest but a wholesale leveling and blighting of the higher cultures—the Mongols really did do that in the Islamic heartlands and in Kievan Russia, with some very unfortunate long-term historical consequences in both cases. So the *zemlixi* have nothing to fall back on. Any highly developed political societies they may ever have had have been forgotten for centuries. Fortunately, I think Cyrus understands this."

"That may not be the hardest thing he has to adjust to," said Mags with renewed mischievousness.

"That's right! If anything comes of this idea of the Baldies taking part in the Tangri campaign—"

"The Arduans," Mags corrected him primly.

"Yes, we have to call them that now, don't we? Well, at least Cyrus isn't without experience in dealing with diverse allies. In Second Fleet he's had Orions—even though he's miserably allergic to their fur—and Ophiuchi and Gorm and—"

"And even rebels," Mags finished for him dryly. "A situation we can identify with, can't we?"

"Oh?" Trevayne sat down on the bed—a double one, specially installed—and reclined back on his elbows to listen.

"Well, considering the physiologically youthful body concealing your evil middle-aged mind, and the fact that I've had access to the full anagathic regimen from youth, we probably have a long future to look forward to—"

"Yes," he interrupted her with a sigh. "And neither you nor anyone else can imagine what it's like for me to be able to savor the sensation of having a future."

"But consider the complications!" She perched beside him on the bed. "You're a citizen of the Terran Federation—which, strictly speaking, no longer exists as an independent political entity—"

"Actually, I think that makes me automatically a citizen of the Pan-Sentient Union. Although I suppose you'd have to call me a very well-established naturalized citizen of the Rim Federation, whose citizens have a kind of ill-defined dual citizenship in the PSU. To tell you the truth, I've never puzzled out just exactly *what* my current citizenship status is."

"Well, you *must* be a citizen of the Rim Federation, considering that you're its military commander-in-chief! I, on the other hand, am a citizen of the Terran Republic, a senior officer in its navy, and the daughter of rebels against the Federation."

"And your point would be?"

"Don't be deliberately obtuse! You must admit it's not exactly a recipe for a conventional marriage!"

Trevayne's eyes took on a look with which she'd become familiar. "Conventionality is the last refuge of the small-minded," he intoned.

She glared at him. "As with at least two-thirds of

your quotes, I can't identify the source. Who came up with *that* one?"

"I did," he admitted blandly.

This time it was her fist that went into his rib cage. There followed a wrestling match whose most conspicuous feature was the eagerness of each party to lose. It concluded with her on top, finalizing her victory with an extended kiss.

"Actually," he said when he'd caught his breath, "there's a very simple solution to the problems you've raised."

"Oh?"

"Yes. I can resign my commission with the Rim Federation—some would say it's about time—and become a citizen of the Terran Republic."

She rolled limply off him and stared, her almond eyes as round as nature permitted them to get.

"Well, well, well!" He smiled. "I've finally succeeded in flooring you. Figuratively, that is, as opposed to literally."

For once she didn't rise to the bait. "If I didn't know better, I'd swear you were serious."

"But I am." And all at once she could see he *was* serious. "You see, I'm one of the few people left alive who remember what the Fringe Revolution was really like. And even those other few—your godparents, Miriam Ortega, Cyrus—don't have the fresh recollection I do. What I was really fighting for was the ideal of human unity, which I identified with the Terran Federation to which I had given my oath. This, even though I was—as nobody seems to remember these days—sympathetic to the Fringers. Bloody hell, my first wife was from Novaya Rodina! And my children . . ." All at once, he couldn't go on.

"Yes, Ian, I know," she said softly. "Your wife and daughter, killed by the revolutionaries. And your son—"

"Whom I killed," he finished for her unflinchingly. "Well, for once what 'everyone knows' is true. I did that, in the name of my ideal of unity. I couldn't permit myself to realize that the Terran Federation had forfeited the right to be the standard-bearer of that unity. And I didn't understand—as so many haven't understood throughout history—that unity doesn't have to involve a unitary state. I think we've proved that now, even if it took the Baldies—sorry, the Arduans—to help us."

"But Ian," she protested, wanting with all her soul to believe this but needing to be certain that *he* wanted it, too, "considering your historical role in the founding of the Rim Federation—"

He laughed. "I do love the Rim in many ways. But—and I've never told anyone this—it will be a relief to get away from there, where they insist on putting me on a pedestal. Bloody hell, they even put me *literally* on a pedestal, outside Government House! And with that outrageously inaccurate quote on the pedestal!"

"'Terra expects that every man will do his duty,'" she quoted before he could. "The admiral doth protest too much, methinks! Genji Yoshinaka was right about that bogus quote. You just *love* it!"

With a theatrical growl on Trevayne's part, the wrestling match on the bed resumed. Just before it came to its inevitable and mutually desired conclusion, he paused to whisper into her ear, "At any rate, it doesn't matter. It's the future that matters, not the past."

EPILOGUE

The young man and the strangely spry and ageless old man emerged from the ballroom foyer into the East Shore Plaza's atrium skyway. It was a long glass tube that led from the hotel's Conference and Banquet Center to its prestigious Executive Service Suites: a miniarcology of luxurious—and supremely secure—apartments normally assigned to visiting dignitaries and celebrities.

The old man, whose telescoping cane remained folded in his hand like an old Imperator's baton, bumped a shoulder into his younger—and not facially dissimilar—companion. "So, have you decided to forgive me for getting you sent out here?"

"To be honest, Uncle Kevin, when I agreed, I thought I was doing you a favor. Now I realize that it was you who was doing me a favor—for which I am very grateful."

"Grateful? Because I almost got you killed?"

"No. For guiding me to a time and place where I was really needed—and made a real difference."

Antediluvian Kevin Sanders shrugged. "Seemed like a waste, you knocking about in the Heart Worlds, Ossian. Not much to do there—not much that matters, anyhow. But now, after this, whatever you choose to do you'll do with more insight, more appreciation, and more reverence."

Wethermere started at the last word, a word he would never have expected to hear from his fey and ever-waggish relative. "'Reverence?'"

"Sure. You've seen real life and real death—and have had a hand in measuring out both."

"I wish I hadn't."

Sanders nodded. "No good man wants to. It's a bad fit, after all, the power of life and death entrusted to us frail, fallible humans. But that's the nature of our existence, and now you've done more than just hear the pieties and axioms about the burdens of command. You've lived it. And that, my boy, will change you."

"It already has."

Sanders clucked his tongue, and the voice that emerged from his finely lined lips was pure Tidewater drawl. "You evah were a fast learner, nephew."

Wethermere smiled. "You mean, like the way I figured out that we're heading to the *real* interspeciate summit just now?"

Kevin smiled back. "Like I said, a fast learner. What tipped you off?"

"Well, first, the timing of your arrival. Once the Astria warp point was reopened, you could have come through any time in the last three weeks, but instead you chose yesterday to get here. Just in time for the formal signing of the truce—but also just in time for this little informal chat with Ankaht. So small, and so informal, that it's just the three of us. Which makes me wonder: why me? Why not Ian Trevayne?"

"Ian Trevayne? Son, he wanted you here—in his stead."

"What?"

"Ossian, Ian is a statesman only when he must be. He is a soldier by inclination and profession. But you—well, he saw your file, and, as he put it, you had been 'washed by many waters.' Meaning that while you have acquitted yourself quite well on the field of battle, it's only one of your many gifts. Ian is a genius, make no mistake. But he knows he's not a polymath—and when it comes to statecraft with a race as alien as the Arduans, that's the kind of mind we need."

"You mean, one like yours."

"And yours, too, nephew. Runs in the family, I 'spect."

Wethermere kept his profound doubts about the inheritability of such a trait to himself. "So, what's our objective, Uncle?"

As they entered the elevator that would bring them to Ankaht's suite—and which would electronically assess and scan every fiber of their apparel and bodies—Kevin stared at his shoes, as if searching for the correct phrase. "Our objective is to talk about the real future, about all the things that the diplomats either don't want to mention or don't have the imagination to foresee. And, of course, to get you established as the PSU's covert operative inside the interspeciate Military Liaison Mission."

Ossian goggled. "You want me to be a spy?"

"Tut, tut, boy. You use such pejorative terms. Let's say instead that you will surreptitiously observe and report how things are progressing between our two species."

"So you're asking me to lie, on a daily basis, to all the people—both humans and Arduans—that I'll be working with."

"Oh, I didn't say anything about lying, Ossian. In

fact, one of the most important reasons for our meeting Ankaht is so that she can get a look at who she's going to be working with."

"Does Ankaht know that my actual assignment out here was always through Naval Intelligence?"

"Most assuredly so, Nephew."

"And does she know that my new job is to be a sp—a 'covert operative,' tasked with watching her race?"

"Well, of course she does. Good grief, boy, we'd have to be low-grade morons to think we can keep secrets from the Arduans. It will be a while before we learn what they can and can't do with their telempathy. But that's all besides the point. It was *her* idea to set up an additional, *confidential* liaison between our upper echelons and theirs. The Military Liaison Mission serves a fine purpose on its own—but it's also an excellent cover for whoever becomes the secure conduit between our intelligence community and the reliable Arduan leaders."

"And I'm that conduit."

"And so you are."

"What a nice way to repay all my new friends in both the Republic and Federation, and establish myself as the very soul of honesty to the Arduans. My ostensible job of ensuring peace and cooperation between our races is all just a cover for me to work as Terra's confidential agent on-site."

"Yes, but your job involves a great deal more than that. You are also our eyes and ears upon the evolving relationships between all three of those groups, and so you'll also be a tripwire if the relations between them become—well, strained."

"So you can dictate policy to them?"

"So that we might be able to intercede in time,

before misunderstandings escalate into war. And in so doing, save thousands, maybe millions, of lives."

Well, Wethermere reflected, put that way, his new job didn't sound quite so bad. Which was also, obviously, his sly old uncle's intent. But it just might be the truth, as well.

The elevator came to a smooth stop. The doors opened. Ankaht was already waiting in the receiving room before them, a massive and very complex vocoder on the table beside her. "Welcome," announced her voice from the vocoder as she rose and—stiffly—offered her right cluster: its ten tentacles were paired into five dyads that resembled extended fingers.

Wethermere and Sanders advanced and shook "hands" with her, Sanders adding, "Your acquisition of our traditional greeting does us great honor, ma'am."

Ankaht made a recognizably dismissive gesture with her other cluster: the vocoder announced, "The honor is mine, esteeme—" The machine voice went abruptly silent: the small dark Arduan gave a sudden start, all three eyes opening very wide as they moved from one human to the other. "You are—related." She said it as a statement, not a question.

"Yes, ma'am," confirmed Wethermere.

"Most people say you can see the resemblance in our eyes," added Sanders.

"No. No, I cannot detect that. Familial similarities are far too subtle for us Arduans to discern."

"Then how did you know we are related?"

She looked at Wethermere carefully. "It is as if you both—but you particularly—sleep atop a mountain of intertwined *shaxzhutok'ix*, unknowing of all the lives that reside within you from the past."

Wethermere remembered Krishmahnta and smiled. "You mean like an Old Soul?"

"Yes—the Hindu concept." Ankaht's attention was now not merely focused on Wethermere; it was riveted upon him. She changed color a bit, and Wethermere had the fleeting sense that she was concentrating—or exerting some other mental focus—so intently that she grew pale. He stepped slightly closer to her, feeling his uncle's keen eyes measuring every nuance of this unexpected scene. "Are you well, Elder?"

"I am—quite well. This is a fascinating sensation, and I will reflect upon it later. But now, where are my manners? Please be seated. May I offer you refreshments?"

Sanders shook his head. "No, thank you, Councilor—or do you prefer Ambassador, now?"

Although she did not smile, the voice that emerged from the vocoder seemed rich with wry amusement and self-effacing wit. "I should think Ankaht will be quite sufficient. And before we go any further, I must thank you, Mr. Sanders, for ensuring that the final version of the truce included an explanation of how and why my people had such profound initial difficulties in understanding your people."

Kevin answered with a slow, gracious nod. "But of course, ma'am. The cascading misinterpretations that led to our tragic first contact were truths that had to be included. As did mention of Admiral Narrok's exemplary actions in both repelling the Tangri and providing aid and assistance to the human worlds savaged by that now-mutual enemy. I dare say those deeds went a long way to silencing some of the less congenial members of my species' delegation."

"Very true, Mr. Sanders. But I could not help but

notice that your senior delegates kindly *omitted* one key fact that sheds a less favorable light on the war between our races in general, and our conduct of it, specifically."

"I presume you are referring to the caste-specific xenophobia some Arduans displayed toward human communities?"

"Your diplomatic generosity is outdone only by your tact, Mr. Sanders—but let us speak plainly. The most aggressive of the *Destoshaz*, who ultimately became part of the Martyrs' Movement, would still gladly exterminate your species in its entirety. This is a unique cultural aberration in our long history, and—as my delegation promised yours today—we are resolved not to allow it to occur again. However, I must share with you my personal reservations regarding our ability to make good on that promise."

"Oh? Why so, Ambassador?"

"Regrettably, it seems likely that the radical *Destoshaz* represent a devolved version of their caste. Which presents my race with a problem that may persist for quite some time."

Sanders cocked his head. "Perhaps not, ma'am. Our sociologists have pretty conclusively shown that, once freed from the constant trauma of a crisis, both individual and social evolutionary structures begin to return to their pre-crisis norms."

Ankaht's eyes were lidded. "I fear it may prove otherwise with Arduans. Our advances in evolution—both physiological and social—are directly tied to increases in our memories of past lives and in our *selnarm*. Unfortunately, these increases have never been uniformly distributed among Arduans. For *shaxzhu* such as myself, and the *Selnarshaz* caste as well, our personal identity largely arises from our memories of the totality of our species and therefore cuts across the boundaries of caste and gender and even epoch. Conversely, while the *Destoshaz* have always derived their identities mostly from personal experience, their post-Dispersal predominance has been paralleled by dramatic changes in behavior. They are more reactionary, less nuanced, more susceptible to charismatic leaders, and deeply suspicious of anything that they consider abstract or intangible. This means they are not only supremely dismissive of *shaxzhutok* but even spurn participation in the communal meditations that are the very core of our race's *narmata*. So, they who need the leavening effects of our mental community the most are the most closed and resistant to it."

Kevin stroked his prominent chin. "So you fear that you won't be able to control the regressed *Destoshaz* enough to ensure compliance with the terms of the truce."

"The problem is ultimately more serious than that—because it now seems certain that our entire species is undergoing regression."

"Even you *shaxzhu*?"

"Yes, although our regression is not detected as changes in individual qualities, but rather in generational quantities."

Sanders frowned. "What do you mean?"

"The *shaxzhu* that are born today are personally no different than those I remember on Ardu. But the *numbers* of us born now have declined to historical lows. And since the *shaxzhu* trait is random and inborn, rather than caste-conferred, we are powerless to change this demographic trend—which is ominous. Our historical studies show a very marked correlation between the growth of the *shaxzhu* population and proportionate increases in our social and individual evolution. We are now trapped in an inverse process of decline."

Wethermere understood. "And since you have no way to create more *shaxzhu*, you can't alter the rate at which your race can return from its regressed state."

"You see it with all three eyes, Ossian Wethermere."

Sanders nodded, following the logic. "And this also means that your society is poised on the brink of bitter class warfare—a resentful *Destoshaz* majority ready to slap down the *shaxzhu* elite who enjoy their social status by genetic accident."

"Yes, Kevin Sanders. Amongst the radicals, this attitude already exists."

Wethermere nodded. "And so you need our help to reverse these trends."

Ankaht's eyelids cycled slowly. "So you see it then."

"Yes," answered Wethermere, who felt the pieces falling together even as he articulated them. "You need our general expertise in genetics—which we've necessarily pursued more assiduously than you. You're hoping that we can identify whatever genetic code—or complex of codes—creates a *shaxzhu*. Because if we can, then you could selectively breed a higher proportion of *shaxzhu* and accelerate your recovery from regression."

"Just so. But the mere act of doing so could generate a civil war."

"Only if the process were conducted openly," Sanders observed mildly.

Ankaht closed all three of her eyes. "It does not please us to work in secret from the others of our race, but the alternative—an increasing dominance of the *Destoshaz* radicals—could lead to further conflicts with humans. Ultimately, you might be justly compelled to exterminate us in order to save yourselves. Assuming, of course, a deeper social schism does not consume the Children of Illudor first."

Wethermere frowned. "What kind of schism are you referring to?"

Ankaht spread wide the tentacles of both clusters: it was like an open-armed appeal from a pair of immense sea anemones. "My apologies. I shall explicate. Contact with humans has challenged our view of the universe. Simply put, if we are not the only intelligent beings in existence, then what of our status as the only and chosen Children of Illudor and the monotheistic cosmology we have built upon it? A sustained analysis of this quandary portends a catastrophic theological dispute." And Ankaht visibly shuddered.

And for a reason, and by a process, he could not identify, Wethermere knew what distressed her so profoundly. "You are having your first crisis of faith—and most of your race doesn't even know it yet."

"Exactly. But that is, as your saying has it, only the tip of the iceberg. If Illudor is not the One Deity, then we are not the elect of creation. If we are not the elect of creation, then our *narmata*—our link with each other—is not a divine gift. Perhaps, therefore, even our concept of Illudor is but a confection."

Sanders frowned. "But then where would your memories of past lives come from?"

"Perhaps rather than being a deity, what we call Illudor is our label for a collective entity made up of all our consciousnesses, yet greater than the sum of its parts. In that event, it may use us as the repository of its collective memories. And so we must therefore ask this terrifying question: Do we Arduans truly have immortal, reborn souls—or are we constructs summoned into brief existence by some macroentity which uses us as both its body and its living memory archive? This is our own version of what your late-Industrial-era philosophers and novelists labeled an existential crisis."

Sanders nodded sagely, even as he changed the topic. "Ambassador, I can see that these issues warrant a long—and involved—discussion, so I am going to suggest that you continue them with my nephew here. He will be your confidential strategic liaison, and in that role will have reason to coordinate with you on all cultural and political affairs as we jointly formulate plans for dealing with other Dispersates. And it is to that latter issue that I would like to address my final questions."

"Of course, Mr. Sanders."

"What might the Arduans of later Dispersates know of this war? And of our technology?"

Ankaht's tentacles rose and drooped. "Probably very little, if anything—but it is difficult to speculate on this with any precision. Firstly, although *selnarm* is superluminal, clear transmission of specific thoughts is only possible within the same heliosphere."

"Why?"

Ankaht's tentacles reprised their earlier motions, which Wethermere read as a dismayed shrug. "We do not know why the precision of our messages decreases when they are sent across interstellar space. Before we left Ardu, we had no awareness of this phenomenon. And once we had left, it was too late to conduct any effective research into it."

"So, if you are unable to communicate precise information across such distances, what is the nature of your exchange?"

"We *shaxzhu*, and those of the *Selnarshaz* caste, can feel a great wave of death or suffering at almost any range. But that is, of course, a collective transmission of shock or emotion. Individual relay of data is far more restricted—perhaps because the signal of a single sender is so much weaker. Consequently, individual sendings take the form of invocations of collectively held memories." Ankaht either sensed, or saw, their puzzled expressions. "We *shaxzhu* concentrate upon and send the memory of a particular evocative moment in our shared history. The message is, by implication, related to a broadly accepted race lesson associated with that event. That lesson is the message. Obviously such sendings are very imprecise and subject to all sorts of misinterpretation."

Sanders tapped his telescoped cane against his knee. "So it is unlikely that other Dispersates, even if they somehow learned of this war, would have any reason to change their intended destinations."

"Not as a result of our signals. But they could have had other reasons to do so, such as improved long-range sensing that shows which systems in this region of space have planets with biospheres and which do not. And given the advances in drive technology that followed our departure, they would have had the ability to act upon that information."

Wethermere leaned forward. "So, by logical extrapolation, later Dispersates are not only able to change the destinations of their journeys but are also able to change the duration of their journeys as well—which is why the Second Dispersate invaded the Zarzuela system only a few months after you landed on Bellerophon."

"This is correct."

"So, given that many of the stars in our warp-point network lie just a few degrees off the same course followed by your Dispersate, it seems that if they wanted to, the subsequent Dispersates could conceivably coordinate themselves to arrive in any of a dozen of our systems, and to do so at roughly the same time."

Ankaht's eyes turned toward Ossian slowly, half-lidded. "This is my single greatest fear—particularly if the trend toward racial regression is as prevalent in these later Dispersates as it has been in our first two."

Sanders shifted uneasily. "Ankaht, this raises my final question—one which my government specifically tasked me to ask."

"Please proceed."

"What of the later Dispersates' communications with your own fleet? Can you not infer some of their intents from the shared race memories they must have sent out during the course of their travels?"

"I'm sure we could, Mr. Sanders—except that, long before we reached the halfway point of our own journey, all the other Dispersates fell silent within a span of five decades."

"But—why?"

"We do not know, and at that time, the crew of the First Dispersate did not task their *shaxzhu* to ask."

Wethermere leaned farther forward. "But *you've* been asking, haven't you, Ankaht?"

She turned back slowly in his direction. "You do indeed see with all three eyes, Ossian Wethermere. Yes, even before your Resistance reclaimed Jennifer

Peitchkov from our custody, I had decided that the silence of the other Dispersates had to be explored. I gathered several of our most powerful and experienced *shaxzhu*, and together we attempted to reach out to the other Star Wanderers, to learn what had caused their silence, to determine where they were destined, and especially to inquire why the many earlier generations of their journeys had left no new memories for us, and why none of the souls that had lived and died in their fleets had ever become carnate in ours."

Wethermere nodded and spoke as a fact what he had originally conceived as a question. "And there was no answer."

Ankaht's eyes met his. "There was no answer. Despite our daily attempts, which we continue even now."

Wethermere looked out the window at the self-climbing cranes and grav-platforms which denoted Melantho's energetic self-resurrection. "I think the coming years may be busy ones for us, Ambassador."

Ankaht's eyes closed wearily. "I think so, too, Ossian Wethermere. I think so, too."

APPENDIX

Arduan Terms and Concepts

Terms rendered in the Arduan tongue throughout the novel are shown here (and in the body of the text) ***in italics***. The transliterated forms of the terms are presented here **without italics**.

'ai: the way (or path or calling or discipline or spiritual domain) of something; used solely as a modifying suffix.

almgr'sh: an Arduan scavenger that was capable of both self-fertilization and fertilization by a wide number of related species. It gave forth litters of ten to twelve young, amongst which there was often arresting genetic and physical variation. Its unusual combination of pronounced concupiscence and plentiful, chaotically diverse offspring made it a natural object of ridicule and contempt for Arduans (who despise both disorder and sexual indiscriminacy). The term, applied as an epithet, has a meaning roughly equivalent to "skank-whore."

Anaht'doh Kainat: Star Wanderers.

assed'ai: zen balance/yin-yang ("the way of balance").

Asth: a continent on Ardu; later, a new star system.

'at: senior, prime, or first.

at'holodahk: insult to enlightenment.

befthel: a "triple-blink," or instant of reflexive and complete eye-closing. It can be a sign of impending, possibly debilitating, shock.

bilbuxhat: a kine-like draft animal of Ardu.

crivan: a color in the ultraviolet range invisible to humans.

dest'ah: conflict (arising from the root concept of discarnation, or *dest*).

dest: to be discarnated; the death of a person.

desta'tuni: literally, "Death-Vowed." A ritualized, sanctified "suicide mission" for the good of the Race.

Destolfi montu shilkiene: a philosophical statement—"death is but a tiny thing."

Destoshaz: warrior caste. Literally, "the caste that traffics in (or is habituated to) discarnation" (of self, others, or both).

Destoshaz'ai: the way (or path or calling or discipline) of the warrior.

Destoshaz'ai-as-sulhaji: literally, "the way of the warrior as (the path to and attainment of) true enlightenment." Originally, the caste's delineation of behaviors and values that made their warrior ethos the acme of racial perfection and service to Illudor. By the time the First Dispersate had arrived at Bellerophon/New Ardu, it had become both the creed and name for a militant supremacist movement (rather than genuine "philosophy") among the *Destoshaz*. In this movement, the traditional desiderata of the caste became secondary to a blend of authoritarianism, hero-worship, pre-Enlightenment ritual and values, a distrust of *shaxzhutok*, a presumption of both speciate superiority and speciate exclusivity of personhood, and aggressive militarism.

discarnate: what a sentient does when it expires.

erzhu: nimble, dextrous.

Erzhushaz: the artificer caste, in which the presumed challenge of such artifacture would be associated with manual dexterity: e.g.; pottery, smithing, glassblowing. Ultimately, "makers."

flixit: a small, songbird-like creature that superficially resembles a cross between a bird and a lizard.

griarfeksh: a bald, semi-aquatic scavenger with nasty habits.

herrm: a color humans cannot perceive.

holodah: a *satori*-like state of enlightenment.

holodah'kri'at: senior high priest.

holodah'kri: high priest.

holodah-ra-nekt: honor carriers/bearers (honor surrogates); the term is used exclusively by the *Destoshaz*, since in the formulation, the concept of *holodah* ("enlightenment") is conflated with the principle of "honor."

Hre'selna: a category of simple biots—most akin to Terran jellyfish—that radiate a weak form of protoselnarm. These creatures employ the protoselnarm as their only sense and cannot swarm for mating season without it. Early in their electronic age, the Arduans recognized that the ability of these creatures to detect and react to changes in *selnarm* could be exploited so as to provide instantaneous-relay command circuitry. In the *Urret-fah'ah* minesweeper, *Hre'selna* biots were used to obviate the need for the weapons to wait upon post-transit reorientation of their electronics. Instead, the moment each specially-bred *Hre'selna* biot completed warp transit, it sought the correct electronic signal. Failing to find it—since the electronics were not functional yet—it sent a *selnarm* pulse to other *Hre'selna*, which, upon receiving that pulse, actuated piezoelectric launcher-initiators. The result: the ship's missiles were deployed almost 1.5 seconds before its command electronics had sufficiently recovered from warp-point transit to perform the same task.

hwa: a prefix denoting junior, lesser, apprentice, aspirant. It never carries a negative connotation; it simply indicates one who is still being mentored to assume the title modified by the *hwa*. So *hwa'kri* is "aspirant priest," or, in conventional English usage, an acolyte. It tends to be a formal term, used for traditional roles. It would be idiomatically perverse to apply it to something like a technical competency: one would not call a gunnery trainee a "*hwa*'gunner" because there is no alteration of social status or role intrinsic to one's skill in gunnery.

Ill'sblood: equivalent to the early Modern English "god's blood" or "s'blood" (now simply "bloody"). A profound profanity.

Illudor: the name of God.

incarnate: can be used either as a noun or as a verb. As a verb, it means to have one's soul returned to physical existence. As such, it is distinct—both as a concept and a term—from the purely physical phenomenon and context of "birth" and is, in Arduan metaphysics, presumed to precede the physical processes of returning to material form. Thus, Arduans believe that only after their souls are selected and sent forth for incarnation, are they then conceived, gestated, and born.

'ix: a collection of incidents or objects (however, it cannot be used to designate a "class" of objects, only their multiplicity). Cannot be used as a referent for persons.

ixt: numbers.

ixt'un: to calculate, mathematics.

Ixturshaz: the calculators, a caste that is held to be slightly less important than either *Selnarshazi or shaxzhu*. This is because their skills are considered more trainable than the first two (which are, respectively, largely or wholly innate) and so less individually crucial to the function of the community.

Ixturshaz: a thinker, one who calculates, uses logic/deduction.

'kai: a sanctified quest or holy way or path or calling. It can signify divine favor, inspiration, or character—without referring to or partaking of godhead itself. The divine tenor of this word is never vernacularized into a purely mundane usage: it always invokes the presumed presence, consecration, or will of Illudor. So a *'kaiKri* would be the closest Arduan synonym for a saint: a divinely touched, favored, and/or selected priest.

kreevix: an insect like a mayfly.

kri: priest.

maatkah: a form of Arduan hand-to-hand combat.

maatkahshak: training in a particular school or style of *maatkah*.

matsokah: training of the soul.

murn: a color invisible to humans on the infrared end of the spectrum.

Myrtak: the Arduan Einstein.

narmata: group harmony or harmonious action.

***nerjet*-motleyed**: the *nerjet* was a common, small lizard on Ardu that was reviled and renowned for its horribly clashing colors. For the Arduans, whose sense of smell is very restricted (being registered through the mouth), the concept of "stink" is not particularly significant. However, their powerful visual dependency and acuity renders certain color- or pattern-combinations as almost nauseating. The *nerjet* was Ardu's visual equivalent of a skunk. The epithet "*nerjet*-motleyed" essentially translates, into human terms and senses, as "shit-reeking." It is a common, crude, but nonprofane, curse. By comparison, "Ill'sblood" is quite profane and strongly frowned upon.

ranarmata: chaos, disharmony in action; willful disarray.

Sekahmant: a blue giant star 1.973 parsecs from the Arduan sun.

seln: to sense with great precision, almost at "connoisseur."

selnarm: the empathetic sense.

Selnarshaz: sensitives, those who have profound *selnarmic* talents. This is often, but not preponderantly, associated with superior intellect. They are communication facilitators, many are teachers, psychologists.

shaxzhu: one who has many, detailed past-life memories.

shaxzhutok: the state of having past-life memories.

shotan: sense/taste.

skeerba: a three-bladed knife that sits on the tentacle like a set of brass knuckles.

soka: life force; the tangible/lived soul (as against the potential soul when discarnate).

sokhata: soul building.

ssers: flexible, pliant.

Ssershaz: the versatility caste, or "those who may do many things." Now the "free safeties" of Arduan society, they have diminished almost as greatly as the *shaxzhu*. They were originally the Arduans who possessed no particular casted skills of any other area; they were a default set, and comprised the menial or mass labor of pre-industrial Ardu.

ssersxhu: versatility.

sulhaji: true vision.

threem: nautilus shell, reddish, of Ardu.

tun: promise, vow, or oath.

tuni: promised, dedicated to, or reserved for.

urm: the seven senses; particularly the sense of touch, tactile quality.

vrel: a color invisible to humans.

xen-narmatum: forever outside order.

xenzhet-narmat'ai: literally, "the place of eternal death beyond order or hope." (Where "place" is taken to mean a nonphysical domain that preternaturally and ultimately exemplifies the principle which is vested/sited there. Hence the suffix, "ai.")

yihrt: a large murn- and black-colored predator on Ardu.

zhed'bid: "terminal drone"; an automated transponder, jettisoned from an Arduan ship when destruction is imminent.

zhet: to die; what a nonsentient does when it expires.

zheteksh: that category of being which may truly (i.e. permanently) die. Consequently, this word also meant "nonsentients." Since Arduans traditionally linked personhood to the possession of *selnarm*, not to thought, they had a tendency to lump all non-*selnarmic* creatures together.

zhetteh: to kill; specifically, to cause to permanently die, as distinct from causing to become discarnate (i.e., *dest*).

zifrik: a colony-complex of ant-bees of Ardu. They created sophisticated structures but were not intelligent (either by human or Arduan standards).

The following is an excerpt from:

WAR MAID'S CHOICE

DAVID WEBER

Available from Baen Books
July 2012
hardcover

Chapter One

"I always love watching this part," Brandark Brandarkson, of the Bloody Sword hradani, murmured from behind his hand.

He and Bahzell Bahnakson stood in an enormous lantern-lit tunnel, surrounded by what anyone would have had to call "an unlikely crowd." He and Bahzell were its only hradani members, and Bahzell was a Horse Stealer of Clan Iron Axe, which had been the Bloody Swords' fiercest rival for generations. In fact, he wasn't just "a" Horse Stealer; he was the youngest son of Prince Bahnak Karathson, ruler of the Northern Confederation of Hradani . . . who'd *conquered* the Bloody Sword little more than six years ago. As if that pairing weren't bad enough, there were the dozen or so dwarves, a matching number of humans, and the huge roan stallion behind Bahzell. Up until a very few years ago, the possibility of that eclectic blend being gathered in one place without swordplay, bloodshed, and mayhem would have been ridiculous. And the fact that all of the humans in question were Sothōii, the bitter traditional enemies of *all* hradani, Horse Stealers and Bloody Swords alike, would only have made it even more unlikely.

Of course, Brandark was a pretty unlikely sight all by himself. Very few Norfressans would have been prepared to behold a six-foot, two-inch hradani dressed in the very height of foppish fashion, from his embroidered silken doublet to his brilliantly shined riding boots—black, with tasteful silver tassels—and the long feather adorning the soft cloth cap adjusted to the perfect rakish angle on his head. The balalaika slung across his back would only have completed their stupefaction.

His towering companion, who was well over a foot and a half taller than he, was an almost equally unlikely sight, although in a very different way. Bahzell wore finely wrought chain mail and a polished steel breastplate, and instead of a balalaika, he carried a two-handed sword with a five-foot blade across *his* back. Aside from his size (which was enormous, even for a Horse Stealer) and the high quality of his gear, his martial appearance would have suited the stereotype of a hradani far better than Brandark's sartorial splendor . . . if not for his green surcoat, badged with the crossed mace and sword of Tomanāk Orfressa. The notion of a hradani champion of Tomanāk wasn't something the average Norfressan could be expected to wrap his mind around easily, and the roan courser watching alertly over his shoulder made it even worse. After all, if there was one being in all of Norfressa who could be counted upon to hate hradani even more than two-legged Sothōii did, it had to be a Sothōii *courser*.

"*Shhhhh!*" one of the dwarves scolded, turning to glare at Brandark. "If you distract her now, I'm going to have Walsharno step on you!"

"You don't scare me," Brandark retorted (albeit in an even softer tone), grinning down at him. Sermandahknarthas zoi'Harkanath was three times Brandark's age and the senior engineer on what had been dubbed the Gullet Tunnel, but he was also barely two thirds as tall as the Bloody Sword and his head barely topped Bahzell's belt buckle. "Walsharno *likes* me. He won't step on me without a lot better reason than your petty irritation!"

The colossal stallion—he stood over eight feet tall at the shoulder—tilted his head, ears cocked thoughtfully. Then he reached out and shoved Brandark between the shoulder blades with his nose. Despite his dandified appearance, the hradani was a solid, thick-boned plug of muscle and gristle, with shoulders so broad he looked almost squat, in spite of his height. He easily weighed two hundred and fifty pounds, none of it fat, and no one would have called him an easily brushed aside lightweight. But the stallion weighed over two tons, and Brandark staggered forward under the "gentle" push. He turned to look over his shoulder, his expression betrayed, and Bahzell laughed.

"Walsharno says as how he'll *always* have a 'better reason' when it comes to stepping on such as you, little man," he rumbled in an earthquake bass. "Mind, I think he's after exaggerating a *wee* bit... but not so much as all that."

"Will the both of you *please* be quiet?" Serman demanded. "This is a very ticklish moment and—"

"Yes, it is," a female voice agreed tartly. "And I would be grateful if all *three* of you could manage to keep your mouths shut for fifteen seconds at a time! Unless you'd like the next section of this tunnel to go straight down... and begin directly underneath you!"

Serman closed his mouth with an almost audible click, and Bahzell chuckled softly. It was a *very* soft chuckle, however. He didn't really think Chanharsadahknarthi zoihan'Harkanath would suddenly open a yawning pit under his feet, but he was in no tearing hurry to test the theory. Besides, she had a point.

Brandark contented himself with one last glower at Walsharno—who only curled his lips to show his teeth and shook his head in very horselike, mane-flipping amusement—then crossed his arms and concentrated on looking martyred. It wasn't a very convincing performance, especially given his obvious interest in what was about to happen, and Bahzell smiled and patted

Walsharno's shoulder as he watched his friend's long nose almost quiver in fascination.

Quiet fell. It wasn't really a silence, for the shouts and sounds of construction gangs came up the steadily climbing tunnel from behind them, but those noises were distant. In a way, they only made the quiet even more profound, and Chanharsa closed her eyes once more. Her hands were outstretched, palms pressed flat against the smooth, vertical wall at the end of the tunnel, and she leaned forward, resting her forehead between them. She stood that way for several minutes, her posture relaxed, yet the others could literally feel the concentration pouring off of her.

It wasn't the first time Bahzell had watched this same scene, but the dwarvish art of sarthnaiskarmanthar was seldom seen outside the dwarves' subterranean cities, and like Brandark, he found it endlessly fascinating. Sarthnaiskarmanthar was the talent which truly set dwarves off from the other Races of Man and allowed them to undertake their monumental engineering projects, and they guarded their sarthnaisks (the word translated roughly as "stone herds" or "stone shepherds") like the priceless treasures they were.

There'd been occasions, especially during the dark and dreadful days of the Fall of Kontovar, when enslaved sarthnaisks had been valued by their captors above almost all other prisoners . . . and all too often driven until their talent consumed them. The dwarves had sworn that would never happen again, and any sarthnaisk was always accompanied by his personal armsman on any trip beyond the safe caverns of his—or, in this case, *her*—home city. Chanharsa, on the other hand, was accompanied by *eight* armsmen, and another sixteen waited at the tunnel's entrance for her return. It was an impressive display of security, but Chanharsadahknarthi zoihan'Harkanath wasn't just "any" sarthnaisk. According to Serman, the tunnel's chief engineer, she was the strongest sarthnaisk Dwarvenhame had seen in at least two generations (which Bahzell, having seen her work, readily believed), not to mention a blood kinswoman of Kilthandahknarthas dihna'Harkanath, the head of Clan Harkanath. It would be . . . unfortunate if anything were to happen to Lady Chanharsa.

At the moment, the diminutive sarthnaisk (she was well under four feet in height) didn't really look all that impressive. In fact, she didn't *look* as if she was doing anything more than simply leaning against the rock, but Bahzell knew how hard she was actually concentrating as she extended her senses, using her talent to run immaterial fingers through the solid stone in front of her. She was feeling fault lines, sampling quartz and rock, tasting the elusive flavor of minerals, metal ores, and water. He also understood exactly why sarthnaiskarmanthar fascinated the keenly inquiring scholar who lived inside Brandark, but unlike his Bloody Sword friend, Bahzell *understood* what Chanharsa was doing, just as he understood why she could never truly explain it to Brandark or anyone who didn't possess the same talent. Or one very like it, at any rate.

As it happened, Bahzell did possess a similar talent. He had no ability to taste or shape stone, but he was a champion of Tomanāk, and the war god gifted his champions with the ability to heal. Yet not all of them were equally skilled as healers, for it was an ability which depended on the clarity with which the individual champion could open his mind to an injury or illness and truly believe he could do anything about it. It depended upon his ability to *understand* that damage, to accept it in all its often ghastly reality, and then to not only overlay his mental "map" of that damage with a vision of health but actually impose that vision upon the injury. To open himself as a channel or conduit between his deity and the mortal world and use that conduit—or allow *it* to use *him*, perhaps—to make that internal, personal image of restored well-being and vitality the reality. It all sounded simple enough, yet words could describe only the what, not the how of accomplishing it, and it was extraordinarily difficult to actually do.

Sarthnaiskarmanthar functioned in a similar fashion, although according to Wencit of Rūm (who certainly ought to know) a sarthnaisk's work was at least a little simpler because living creatures were in a constant state of change as blood pumped through their veins and oxygen flowed in and out of their lungs. Stone was in a constant state of change, as well, but it was a far slower and more gradual change, a process of ages and eons, not minute-to-minute or even second-to-second transformations. It didn't clamor and try to distract the way living bone and tissue did as the sarthnaisk formed the detailed mental image of what he intended to impose upon the stone's reality. Of course, stone was also more resistant *to* change, but that was where his training came in. Like a skilled mishuk martial artist, the sarthnaisk used balance and precision and focus against the monolithic resistance of stone and earth. He found the points within the existing matrix where a tiny push, a slight shift, began the process of change and put all the weight of the stone itself behind it, like deep mountain snow sliding down to drive boulders and shattered trees before it.

The trick was to stay in control, to *shape* the avalanche, to fit that instant of total plasticity to the sarthnaisk's vision, and steering an avalanche was always a . . . challenging proposition.

He smiled at the thought, and then his eyes narrowed and his foxlike ears folded back slightly as Chanharsa drew a deep, deep breath. Her shoulders rose as she filled her lungs, and then the stone *changed*.

Bahzell had seen her do this over a dozen times now, yet he still couldn't quite force what he saw to make sense. It wasn't that it happened too quickly for the eye to see, although that was what he'd thought the first time he'd watched it. No, the problem was that the eye wasn't *intended* to see it. Or perhaps that the mind hadn't been designed to understand it...or accept it. The smooth, flat wall of stone flowed like smoke under Chanharsa's palms, yet it was a *solid* smoke, a surface which continued to support her weight as she leaned even harder against it. A glow streamed out from her hands, spreading across the entire face of stone in a bright web of light, pulsing in time with her heartbeat, and that glow—that web—flowed away from her, sinking deeper and deeper into the smoky rock. In some way Bahzell would never be able to explain, he could *see* the glow stretching away from them, probing out through hundreds of cubic yards of stone and earth. He couldn't estimate how far into the rock he could "see," but the glow grew dimmer as it moved farther and farther away from him.

A minute slipped past. Then another. Three of them. And then—

Chanharsadahknarthi zoihan'Harkanath staggered ever so slightly as the stone under her hands vanished, and an abrupt, cool fist of breeze flowed over them from behind as air rushed up the tunnel to fill the suddenly created cavity before her. Her shoulders sagged, and one of her armsmen stepped forward quickly, taking her elbow and supporting her until she could regain her balance. She leaned against him for a moment, then inhaled again and shook her head, pushing herself back upright, and Bahzell heard a mutter of awe from the spectators . . . most of whom had seen her do exactly the same thing at least as often as he had.

On the other hand, it wasn't something a man got used to seeing.

The tunnel had suddenly grown at least sixty yards longer. The tunnel roof was thirty feet above its floor, and the tunnel walls were sixty-five feet apart, wide enough for three heavy freight wagons to pass abreast. Its sloped floor was ballroom smooth yet textured to give feet or hooves solid traction, and two square-cut channels—six feet deep and two feet wide—ran the tunnel's full length, fifteen feet out from each wall. Every angle and surface was perfectly, precisely cut and shaped . . . and glossy smooth, gleaming as if they'd been hand polished, without a single tool mark anywhere. The new tunnel section had freed a sizable spring on its southern wall and water foamed and rushed from it like a fountain, but Chanharsa had allowed for that. Another, shorter channel had been cut across the tunnel floor, crossing the first two at right angles, this one deep enough that none of the newborn stream's water escaped into the first two as it flooded into its new bed and sent a wave front flowing across the tunnel to plunge gurgling and rushing into an opening in the northern wall. Two broad, gently arched bridges crossed the sudden musical chuckle of water—not built, but simply *formed*, as strong and immovably solid as the rock around them—and sunlight probed down from above through the air shaft piercing the tunnel roof. That shaft was two feet in diameter and over eighty feet deep, and patterns of reflected sunlight from the stream danced across the smooth stone walls.

"Well, I see I managed to get it mostly right despite all

that distracting chatter going on behind me," Chanharsa observed, turning to give the hradani her best glare.

It was, Bahzell admitted, quite a good glare, considering that it was coming from someone less than half his own height. It wasn't remotely as potent as the one Kilthan could have produced, but she was twenty-five years younger than Serman, which made her less than half Kilthan's age. In another fifty years or so, possibly even as little as thirty or forty, he was sure she'd be able to match the panache Kilthan could put into the same expression.

"And it's not surprised I am, at all," he assured her with a broad smile. "For such a wee, tiny thing you've quite a way with rock."

"Which means I ought to have 'quite a way' with hradani *brains*, doesn't it?" she observed affably, and his smile turned into a laugh.

"You've a way to go still before you match old Kilthan, but I see you've the talent for it," he said. "I'm thinking it needs a bit more curl to the upper lip and the eyes a mite narrower, though, wouldn't you say, Brandark?"

"No, I most definitely *wouldn't* say," the Bloody Sword said promptly. "I'm in enough trouble with her already."

Several people laughed, though at least one of Chanharsa's armsmen looked less than amused by the hradani's levity. Chanharsa only grinned. Despite the many differences between them, hradani and dwarves were much alike in at least one respect. Their womenfolk enjoyed a far higher degree of freedom and equality—license, some might have called it—than those of the other Races of Man. Besides, Bahzell and Brandark were friends of the family.

"Uncle Kilthan always said you were smarter than you looked, Brandark," she said now. "Of course, being smarter than *you* look isn't that much of an accomplishment, is it?" She smiled sweetly.

"Why is it that *he's* the one who insulted your ability to glare properly and *I'm* the one who's getting whacked?" The Bloody Sword's tone was aggrieved and he did his level best to look hurt.

"Because the world is full of injustice," she told him.

The sarthnaisk gave her armsman's shoulder a pat, then walked to the edge of the bridged channel and gazed down into the rushing water. Despite the tartness of her exchange with the two hradani, a curiously serene sense of joy seemed to fill the air about her, and Bahzell stepped up beside her. He understood that serenity; he felt something very like it every time he was privileged to heal, and he let one enormous hand rest very gently on her shoulder as he inhaled the damp, fresh breath of moisture rising from the boistrous stream.

"It's a fine piece of work you've done," he told her. "And it's grateful I am for your help. And for Kilthan's, of course."

"I suppose it's a bit undutiful of me to point out that Uncle Kilthan—and the rest of Silver Cavern—is going to be minting money when this little project is completed," she replied dryly, but her hand rose to touch his gently as she spoke.

"Aye," he acknowledged. "And so are my folk and Tellian's. Which isn't to say as how I'm any less grateful for it."

"Well, I imagine you've accomplished the odd little job or two to deserve it. That's what Uncle Kilthan said when he proposed this whole notion to the clan elders, anyway. Along with pointing out the fact that the clan was going to make fairly obscene amounts of profit, even by our standards, in the long haul, of course." She shook her head. "It's amazing how successful that second argument usually is with our folk."

She looked up at him, and the topaz eyes she shared with her uncle gleamed wickedly in the sunlight pouring through the air shaft. Of course, Kilthan wasn't *actually* her uncle, Bahzell reminded himself. Only a dwarf could possibly keep all of the intricacies of their family structures and clan relationships straight. Serman really was Kilthan's nephew, the son of his younger sister, but the exact nature of Chanharsa's relationship with Clan Harkanath's head was rather more complicated than that. In fact, Bahzell didn't have a clue what it truly was, although the fact that she was "*dah*knarthi" rather than "*al*knarthi" indicated that it was a blood relationship, rather than solely one by marriage, as did those eyes. And dwarves understood that *proper* explanations of consanguinity, collateral family lines, and connections by marriage quickly caused the eyes of the other Races of Man to glaze over, which made "uncle" or "aunt"—or the even more splendidly ambiguous "kinsman"—perfectly acceptable (if scandalously imprecise) substitutes.

"Aye, and money's not so bad an argument where my folk are concerned, come to that," he acknowledged. "Not that there's not those amongst us as would still prefer to be *plundering* those trade caravans like good, honest hradani! Still and all, I'm thinking my Da's in a fair way to convincing them to change their ways."

"True," Brandark said, stepping up on Chanharsa's other side. "I find it sad, somehow, to see so many good, unwashed barbarian Horse Stealers succumbing to the sweet sound of kormaks falling into their purses." He heaved a huge sigh. "Such decadence. Why, the next thing I know, they're all going to be taking *baths*!"

"Just you be keeping it up, little man," Bahzell rumbled. "I've no need to ask Walsharno to be stepping on you, and I'm thinking as how you'd be getting a bath of your own—aye, and making a fine dam—if I was after shoving your head into that drain hole yonder."

"Speaking of drains," the Bloody Sword said brightly, pointedly not glancing at Bahzell as he looked down at Chanharsa, "where does that one come out?"

"Into the Gullet, like the others." She shrugged. "By the time we're done, we'll probably have a river, or at least a fairly substantial stream, flowing back down it again. Year-round, I mean, not just whenever the snow melts up on the Wind Plain."

Brandark nodded, but his expression was thoughtful. They'd gotten farther and farther away from the narrow chasm which twisted down the towering height of the Escarpment from Glanharrow to the hradani city state of Hurgrum. The Balthar River had once flowed through that channel, before a massive earthquake had diverted it, long, long ago. That diversion had created The Bogs, as the vast, swampy area along the West Riding's border with the South Riding were called, when it pushed the diminished Balthar to the north and cut it off from the tributary which had drained them into the Hangnysti, below the Escarpment. The Gullet remained, however, still snaking its own broken-back way to the Hangnysti, which made it a natural place to dispose of any water that turned up in the course of boring the tunnel through the Escarpment. By now, though, the head of the tunnel was the better part of a mile from the Gullet, and he rubbed the tip of his truncated left ear as he cocked an eyebrow at her.

"I thought you could only do this sort of thing"—he waved at the newly created length of tunnel—"a few dozen yards at a time," he observed.

"*Most* sarthnaisks could only do 'this sort of thing' a few dozen *feet* at a time," she corrected him tartly. She gave him a sharp look for good measure, then shrugged. "Still,

I take your point. But cutting a drainage channel is a lot simpler and more straightforward than cutting the tunnel itself. Each section of the tunnel is new and unique, and that requires a lot of concentration and focus, but I've made scores—probably even hundreds—of simple culverts and drainage systems. By now, it's almost more reflex than thought to throw one in whenever I need it, and it's even simpler than usual in this case. It's mostly just a matter of visualizing a straight line with the proper downslope, and I just . . . tell it which direction to go and what to do when it gets there." She shrugged again. "I'm sorry, Brandark. I know you're still trying to figure out how I do it, and I wish I could explain it better, but there it is."

"Unsatisfied curiosity is my lot in life," he told her with a smile. "Well, that and following Bahzell around from one scrape to another." He shook his head. "It's a dirty job, but someone has to do it. Hirahim only knows what would happen to him if I weren't there to pull him out again!"

"A *fine* dam, I'm thinking," Bahzell murmured, and Chanharsa laughed.

"You two deserve each other," she declared. "*I*, on the other hand, deserve a glass of good wine and a hot bath for my labors."

"And so you do," Bahzell agreed as Walsharno came over to join them.

Coursers, by and large, were only mildly curious about how the Races of Man, with the clever hands they themselves had been denied, accomplished all the things they seemed to find with which to occupy themselves. Those of them who bonded with human—or, in one highly unusual case, with hradani—riders tended to be more curious than others, but even Walsharno was more interested in results than processes. He looked down into the flowing water for a moment, then turned his head to Bahzell. The Horse Stealer looked back at him, listening to a voice only he could hear, then nodded.

"Walsharno's a suggestion," he told Chanharsa.

"He does?"

"Aye," Bahzell said simply, and then he picked her up like an infant and set her neatly on Walsharno's saddle.

The sarthnaisk gave a little squeak of astonishment and clutched at the saddle horn as she suddenly found herself perched more than twice her own height above the tunnel floor. A saddle sized for someone of Bahzell's dimensions was a very substantial seat for someone *her* size, however. In fact, it was almost large enough to serve her as a sofa as she sat sidesaddle on the courser's back.

The armsman who'd frowned at her exchange with the hradani took a quick step towards them, then stopped as Chanharsa relaxed and her face blossomed into a huge smile. However happy she might have been, *he* obviously wasn't at all pleased about having his charge on the back of such a monstrously tall mount. Even a small horse was huge for a dwarf, and a courser was anything but small. On the other hand, very few people were foolish enough to *argue* with a courser . . . and the coursers honored even fewer people by agreeing to bear them.

"I'd not be fretting about it too much," Bahzell told the armsman with a sympathetic smile. "Walsharno's not one for letting folk fall off his back. Why, look at what he's put up with from me! And your lady's the right of it; she *is* after deserving that hot bath of hers, so what say we be getting her to it?"

—end excerpt—